Seven
Blades in Black

Seven
Blades in Black

THE GRAVE OF EMPIRES
BOOK ONE

Sam Sykes

GOLLANCZ

LONDON

First published in Great Britain in 2019 by Gollancz
an imprint of the Orion Publishing Group Ltd
Carmelite House, 50 Victoria Embankment
London EC4Y 0DZ

An Hachette UK Company

1 3 5 7 9 10 8 6 4 2

A CIP catalogue record for this book is
available from the British Library.

ISBN (Trade paperback) 978 1 473 21823 9
ISBN (eBook) 978 1 473 21825 3

Printed in Great Britain by Clays Ltd, Elcograf, S.p.A

For the readers who wouldn't stay down

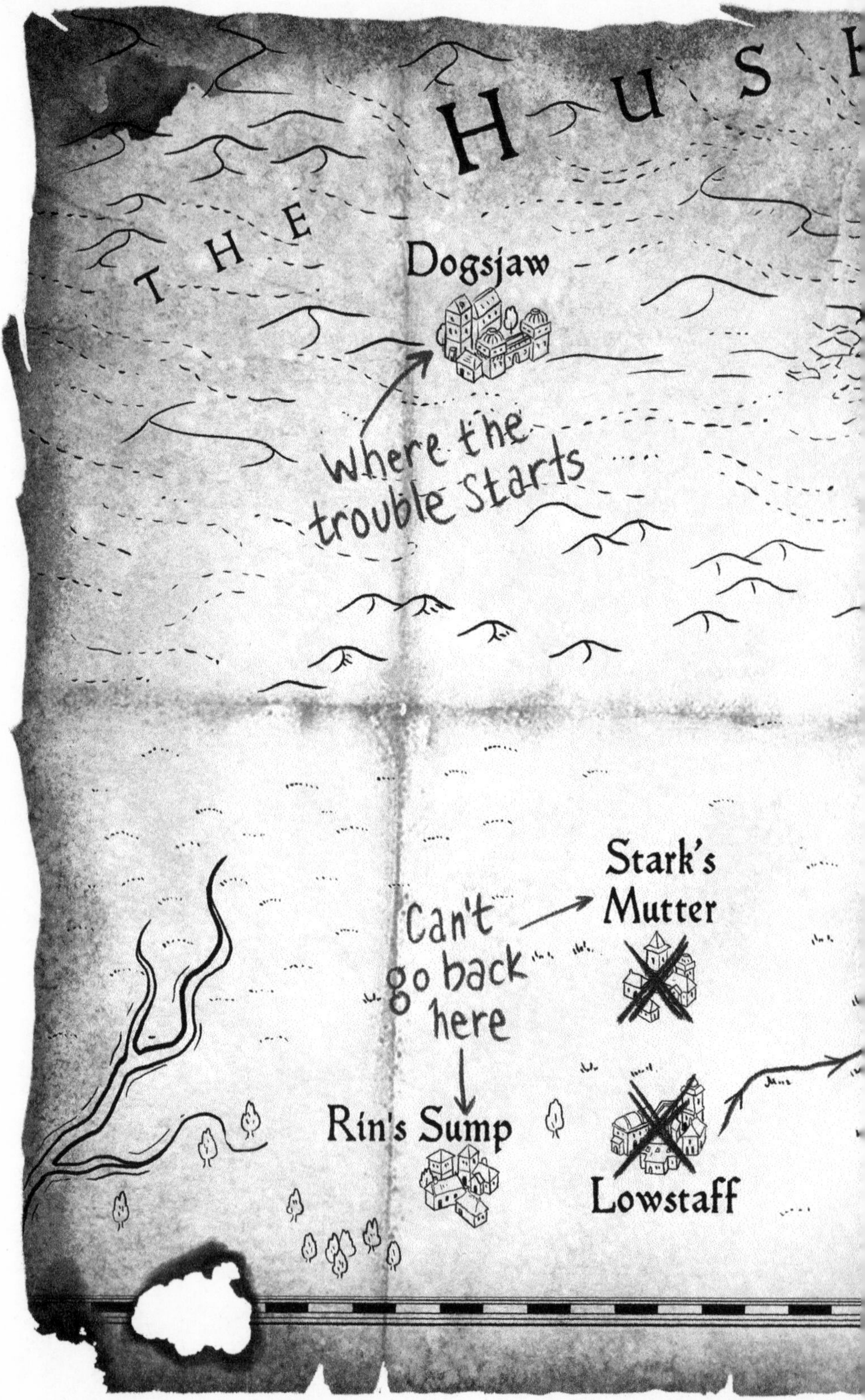

THE HUSH
Dogsjaw
where the trouble starts
Stark's Mutter
Can't go back here
Rin's Sump
Lowstaff

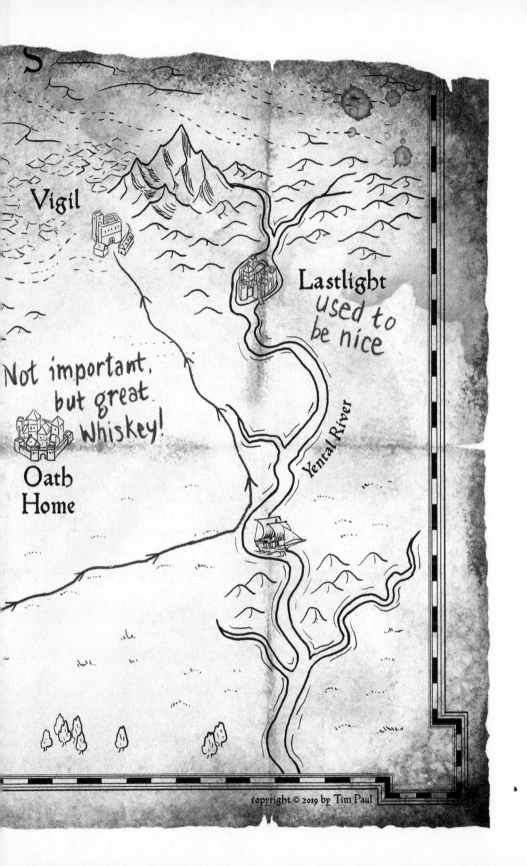

S

Vigil

Lastlight
used to
be nice

Not important,
but great
Whiskey!

Oath
Home

Yental River

ONE

HIGHTOWER

Everyone loved a good execution.

From the walls of Imperial Cathama to the farthest reach of the Revolution, there was no citizen of the Scar who could think of a finer way to spend an afternoon than watching the walls get painted with bits of dissidents. And behind the walls of Revolutionary Hightower that day, there was an electricity in the air felt by every citizen.

Crowds gathered to watch the dirt, still damp from yesterday's execution, be swept away from the stake. The firing squad sat nearby, polishing their gunpikes and placing bets on who would hit the heart of the poor asshole who got tied up today. Merchants barked nearby, selling everything from refreshments to souvenirs so people could remember this day where everyone got off work for a few short hours to see another enemy of the Revolution be strung up and gunned down.

Not like there was a hell of a lot else to do in Hightower lately.

For her part, Governor-Militant Tretta Stern did her best to ignore all of it: the crowds gathering beneath her window outside the prison, their voices crowing for blood, the wailing children and the laughing men. She kept her focus on the image in the mirror as she straightened her uniform's blue coat. Civilians could be excused such craven bloodlust. Officers of the Revolution answered a higher call.

Her black hair, severely short-cropped and oiled against her head, was befitting an officer. Jacket cinched tight, trousers pressed and belted, saber at her hip, all without a trace of dust, lint, or rust. And most crucially, the face that had sent a hundred foes to the grave with a word stared back at her, unflinching.

One might wonder what the point in getting dressed up for an execution was; after all, it wasn't like the criminal scum who would be buried in a shallow grave in six hours would give a shit. But being an officer of the Revolution meant upholding certain standards. And Tretta hadn't earned her post by being slack.

She took a moment to adjust the medals on her lapel before leaving her quarters. Two guards fired off crisp salutes before straightening their gunpikes and marching exactly three rigid paces behind her. Morning sunlight poured in through the windows as they marched down the stairs to Cadre Command. Guards and officers alike called to attention at her passing, raising arms as they saluted. She offered a cursory nod in response, bidding them at ease as she made her way to the farthest door of the room.

The guard stationed there glanced up. "Governor-Militant," he acknowledged, saluting.

"Sergeant," Tretta replied. "How have you found the prisoner?"

"Recalcitrant and disrespectful," he said. "The prisoner began the morning by hurling the assigned porridge at the guard detail, spewing several obscenities, and making forceful suggestions as to the professional and personal conduct of the guard's mother." He sniffed, lip curling. "In summation, more or less what we'd expect from a Vagrant."

Tretta spared an impressed look. Considering the situation, she had expected much worse.

She made a gesture. The guard complied, unlocking the massive iron door and pushing it open. She and her escorts descended into the darkness of Hightower's prison, and the silence of empty cells greeted her.

Like all Revolutionary outposts, Hightower had been built to accommodate prisoners: Imperium aggressors, counterrevolutionaries, bandit outlaws, and even the occasional Vagrant. Unlike most Revolutionary outposts, Hightower was far away from any battleground in the Scar and didn't see much use for its cells. Any captive outlaw tended to be executed in fairly short order for crimes against the Revolution, as the civilians tended to become restless without the entertainment.

In all her time stationed at Hightower, Tretta had visited the prison exactly twice, including today. The first time had been to offer an Imperium spy posing as a bandit clemency in exchange for information. Thirty minutes later, she put him in front of the firing squad. Up until then, he'd been the longest-serving captive in Hightower.

Thus far, her current prisoner had broken the record by two days.

The interrogation room lay at the very end of the row of cells, another iron door flanked by two guards. Both fired off a salute as they pulled open the door, its hinges groaning.

Twenty feet by twenty feet, possessed of nothing more than a table with two chairs and a narrow slit of a window by which to catch a beam of light, the interrogation room was little more than a slightly larger cell with a slightly nicer door. The window, set high up near the ceiling, afforded no ventilation and the room was stifling hot.

Not that you'd know it from looking at the prisoner.

A woman—perhaps in her late twenties, Tretta suspected—sat at one end of the table. Dressed in dirty trousers and boots to match, the sleeves and hem of her white shirt cut to bare the tattoos racing down her forearms and most of the great scar that wended its way from her collarbone down to her belly; it was the sort of garish garb you'd expect to find on a Vagrant. Her hair, Imperial white, was shorn roughly on the sides and tied back in an unruly tail. And despite the suffocating heat, she was calm, serene, and pale as ice.

There was nothing about this woman that Tretta didn't despise.

She didn't look up as the Governor-Militant entered, paid no heed to the pair of armed men trailing behind her. Her hands, manacled

together, rested patiently atop the table. Even when Tretta took a
seat across from her, she hardly seemed to notice. The prisoner's eyes,
pale and as blue as shallow water, seemed to be looking somewhere
else. Her face, thin and sharp and marred by a long scar over her
right eye, seemed unperturbed by her imminent gruesome death.

That galled Tretta more than she would have liked to admit.

The Governor-Militant leaned forward, steepling her fingers in
front of her, giving the woman a chance to realize what a world of
shit she was in. But after a minute of silence, she merely held out one
hand. A sheaf of papers appeared there a moment later, thrust forward by one of her guards. She laid it out before her and idly flipped
through it.

"I won't tell you that you can save yourself," she said after a time.
"An officer of the Revolution speaks only truths." She glanced up at
the woman, who did not react. "Within six hours, you'll be executed
for crimes against the Glorious Revolution of the Fist and Flame.
Nothing you can say will change this fact. You deserve to die for
your crimes." She narrowed her eyes. "And you will."

The woman, at last, reacted. Her manacles rattled a little as she
reached up and scratched at the scars on her face.

Tretta sneered and continued. "What you can change," she said,
"is how quickly it goes. The Revolution is not beyond mercy." She
flipped to a page, held it up before her. "In exchange for information
regarding the events of the week of Masens eleventh through twen-
tieth, up to and including the massacre of the township of Stark's
Mutter, the destruction of the freehold of Lowstaff, and the disap-
pearance of Revolutionary Low Sergeant Cavric Proud, I am willing
to guarantee, on behalf of the Cadre, a swift and humane death."

She set the paper aside, leaned forward. The woman stared just to
the left of Tretta's gaze.

"A lot of people are dead because of you," Tretta said. "One of our
soldiers is missing because of you. Before these six hours are up and
you're dead and buried, two things are going to happen: I'm going to
find out precisely what happened and you're going to decide whether

you go by a single bullet or a hundred blades." She laid her hands flat on the table. "What you say next will determine how much blood we see today. Think very carefully before you speak."

At this, the woman finally looked into Tretta's eyes. No fear there, she looked calm and placid as ever. And when she spoke, it was weakly.

"May I," she said, "have a drink?"

Tretta blinked. "A drink."

The woman smiled softly at her manacled hands. "It's hot."

Tretta narrowed her eyes but made a gesture all the same. One of her guards slipped out the door, returning a moment later with a jug and a glass. He filled it, slid it over to the prisoner. She took it up and sipped at it, smacked her lips, then looked down at the glass.

"The fuck is this?" she asked.

Tretta furrowed her brow. "Water. What else would it be?"

"I was figuring gin or something," she said.

"You asked for water."

"I asked for a *drink*," the woman shot back. "With all the fuss you're making about how you're going to kill me, I thought you'd at least send me out with something decent. Don't I get a final request?"

Tretta's face screwed up in offense. "*No.*"

The woman made a pouting face. "I would in Cathama."

"You're not *in* Cathama," Tretta snarled. "You're not anywhere near the Imperium and the only imperialist scum within a thousand miles are all buried in graves beside the one I intend to put *you* in."

"Yeah, you've been pretty clear on that," the woman replied, making a flippant gesture. "Crimes against the Revolution and so on. Not that I'd ever call you a liar, madam, but are you sure you've got the right girl? There's plenty of scum in the Scar who must have offended you worse than me."

"I am *certain*." Tretta seized the papers, flipped to a page toward the front. "Prisoner number fifteen-fifteen-five, alias"—she glared over the paper at the woman—"Sal the Cacophony."

Sal's lip curled into a crooked grin. She made as elegant a bow as one could when manacled and sitting in a chair.

"Madam."

"Real identity unknown, place of birth unknown, hometown unknown," Tretta continued, reading from the paper. "Professed occupation: bounty hunter."

"I prefer 'manhunter.' Sounds more dramatic."

"Convicted—recently—of murder in twelve townships, arson in three freeholds, unlawful possession of Revolutionary Relics, heresy against Haven, petty larceny—"

"There was nothing petty about that larceny." She reached forward. "Let me see that sheet."

"—blasphemy, illegal use of magic, kidnapping, extortion, and so on and so on and so on." Tretta slammed the paper down against the table. "In short, everything I would expect from a common Vagrant. And like a common Vagrant, I expect not a damn soul in the Scar is going to shed a tear over what puts you in the ground. But what makes you different is that you've got the chance to do something vaguely good before you die, which is a sight more than what your fellow scum get before the birds pick their corpses clean."

She clenched her jaw, spat her next words. "So, if you've got any decency left to your name, however fake it might be, you'll tell me what happened. In Stark's Mutter, in Lowstaff, and to my soldier, Cavric Proud."

Sal pursed her lips, regarded Tretta through an ice-water stare. She stiffened in her chair and Tretta matched her pose. The two women stared each other down for a moment, as though either of them expected the other to tear out a blade and start swinging.

As it was, Tretta nearly did just that when Sal finally broke the silence.

"Have you seen many Vagrants dead, madam?" she asked, voice soft.

"Many," Tretta replied, terse.

"When they died, what did they say?"

Tretta narrowed her eyes. "Cursing, mostly. Cursing the Imperium they served, cursing the luck that sent them to me, cursing me for sending them back to the hell that spawned them."

"I guess no one ever knows what their last words will be." Sal traced a finger across the scar over her eye, her eyes fixed on some distant spot beyond the walls of her cell. "But I know mine won't be cursing." She clicked her tongue. "I'll tell you what you want to know, madam, about Lowstaff, about Cavric, everything. I'll give you everything you want and you can put a bullet in my head or cut it off or have me torn apart by birds. I won't protest. All I ask is one thing."

Tretta tensed and reached for her saber as Sal leaned across the table. And a grin as long and sharp as a blade etched itself across her face.

"Remember my last words."

Tretta didn't achieve her rank by indulging prisoners, let alone ones as vile as a Vagrant. She achieved it through the support and respect of the men and women who saluted her every morning. And she didn't get that by letting their fates go unknown.

And so, for the sake of them and the Revolution she served, she nodded. And the Vagrant leaned back in her chair and closed her eyes.

"It started," she said softly, "with the last rain."

TWO

RIN'S SUMP

You ever want to know what a man is made of, you do three things.

First, you see what he does when the weather turns nasty.

When it rains in Cathama, the pampered Imperials crowd beneath the awnings in their cafés and wait for their mages to change the skies. When it snows in Haven, they file right into church and thank their Lord for it. And when it gets hot in Weiless, as you know, they ascribe the sun to an Imperial plot and vow to redouble their Revolutionary efforts.

But in the Scar? When it pours rain and thunders so hard that you swim through the streets and can't hear yourself drown? Well, they just pull their cloaks tighter and keep going.

And that's just what I was doing that night when I got into this whole mess.

Rin's Sump, as you can guess by the name, was the sort of town where rain didn't bother people much. Even when lightning flashed so bright you'd swear it was day, life in the Scar was hard enough that a little apocalyptic weather wouldn't hinder anyone. And as the streets turned to mud under their feet and the roofs shook beneath the weight of the downpour, the people of the township just tucked their chins into their coats, pulled their hats down low, and kept going about their business.

Just like I was doing. One more shapeless, sexless figure in the streets, hidden beneath a cloak and a scarf pulled around her head. No one raised a brow at my white hair, looked at me like they were guessing what I had under my cloak, or even so much as glanced at me. They had their own shit to deal with that night.

Which was fine by me. So did I. And the kind of shit I got into, I could always use a few less eyes on me.

Every other house in Rin's Sump was dark as night, but the tavern—a dingy little two-story shack at the center of town—was lit up. Light shone bright enough to illuminate the dirt on the windows, the stripped paint on the front, and the ugly sign swinging on squeaky hinges: RALP'S LAST RESORT.

Apt name.

And it proved even more apt when I pushed the door open and took a glance inside.

Standing there, sopping wet, water dripping off me to form a small ocean around my boots, I imagined I looked a little like a dead cat hauled out of an outhouse. And I *still* looked a damn sight better than the inside of that bar.

A fine layer of dust tried nobly to obscure a much-less-fine layer of splinters over the ill-tended-to chairs and tables lining the common hall. A stage that probably once had hosted a variety of bad acts now stood dark; a single voccaphone stood in their place, playing a tune that was popular back when the guy who wrote it was still alive. Rooms upstairs had probably once held a few prostitutes, if there ever were prostitutes luckless enough to work a township like this. I'd have called the place a mausoleum if it weren't for the people, but they looked like they might have found a crypt a little cozier.

There were a few kids—two boys, a girl—in the back, sipping on whatever bottle of swill they could afford and staring at the table. Laborers, I wagered—some young punks the locals used for cheap jobs with cheap pay to buy cheap liquor. And behind the bar was a large man in dirty clothes, idly rubbing the only clean glass in the place with a cloth.

He set that glass down as I approached. The cloth he had been polishing it with was likely used to polish something else, if the grime around the glass was any evidence.

No matter. I wouldn't need to be here long.

Ralp—I assumed—didn't bother asking me what I wanted. In the Scar, you're lucky if they give you a choice of two drinks. And if you had any luck at all, you didn't wind up in a place called Rin's Sump.

He reached for a cask behind the bar but stopped as I cleared my throat and shot him a warning glare. With a nod, he held up a bottle of whiskey—Avonin & Sons, by the look of the black label—and looked at me for approval. I nodded, tossed a silver knuckle on the counter. He didn't start pouring until he picked it up, made sure it was real, and pocketed it.

"Passing through?" he asked, with the kind of tone that suggested habit more than interest.

"Does anyone ever stay?" I asked back, taking a sip of bitter brown.

"Only if they make enough mistakes." Ralp shot a pointed glance to the youths drinking in the corner. "Your first was stopping in here instead of moving on. Roads are going to be mud for days after this. No one's getting out without a bird."

"I've got a mount," I said, grinning over my glass. "And here I thought you'd be happy for a little extra money."

"Won't turn down metal," Ralp said. He eyed me over, raising a brow as it seemed to suddenly dawn on him that I was a woman under that wet, stinking cloak. "But if you really want to make me happy—"

"I'll tell you what." I held up a finger. "Finishing that thought might make you happy in the short term, but keeping it to yourself will make you not get punched in the mouth in the long term." I smiled as sweetly as a woman with my kinds of scars could. "A simple pleasure, sir, but a lasting one."

Ralp glanced me over again, rubbed his mouth thoughtfully, and bobbed his head. "Yeah, I'd say you're right about that."

"But I do have something just as good." I tossed another three knuckles onto the bar. As he reached for them, I slammed something else in front of him. "That is, assuming you can make *me* happy."

I unfolded the paper, slid it over. Scrawled in ink across its yellow surface was a leering mask of an opera actor upon a head full of wild hair, tastefully framed in a black box with a very large sum written beneath it and the words *DEATH WARRANT* above it.

"Son of a bitch!" Ralp's eyebrows rose, along with his voice. "You're looking for *that* son of a bitch?"

I held a finger to my lips, glanced out the corner of my eye. The youths hadn't seemed to notice that particular outburst, their eyes still on their bottle.

"He has a name," I said. "Daiga the Phantom. What do you know about him?"

When you're in my line of work, you start to read faces pretty well. You can tell who the liars are just by looking at them. And I could tell by the wrinkles around Ralp's eyes and mouth that he was used to smiling big and wide. Which meant he had to have told a few lies in his day, probably most of them to himself.

That didn't make him good at it.

"Nothing," he said. "I've heard the name, but nothing else."

"*Nothing* else?"

"I know whatever they're offering for his death can't be worth what he can do." Ralp looked at me pointedly.

I looked back. And I, just as pointedly, pulled my cloak aside to reveal the hilt of the sword at my hip.

"He has something I want," I replied.

"Hope you find someone else who can find it." He searched for something to busy his hands, eventually settling on one of the many dirty glasses and began to polish it. "I don't know anything of mages, let alone Vagrants like that... *man*. They're funny stories you tell around the bar. I haven't had enough customers for that in a long time." He sniffed. "Truth is, madam, I don't know that I'd even notice if someone like that showed up around here."

"Birdshit." I leaned in even closer, hissing through my teeth, "I've been here three days and the most exciting thing I've seen was an old man accusing his wine bottle of lechery."

"He has a condition—"

"And before I came in here, I glanced around back and saw your shipment." I narrowed my eyes. "Lot of crates of wine for a man with no customers. Where are you sending them?"

Ralp stared at the bar. "I don't know. But if you don't get out, I'll call the peacekeepers and—"

"Ralp," I said, frowning. "I'm going to be sad if you make me hurt you over lies this pathetic."

"I said I *don't know*," he muttered. "Someone else picks them up."

"Who? What's Daiga using them for?"

"I don't know any of that, either. I try to know as little as fucking possible about that freak or any other freak like him." All pretenses gone, there was real fear in his eyes. "I don't make it my business to know anything about no mage, Vagrant or otherwise. It's not healthy."

"But you'll take his metal all the same, I see."

"I took your metal, too. The rest of the Scar might be flush with gold, but Rin's Sump is dry as six-day-old birdshit. If a Vagrant gives me money for not asking questions, I'm all too fucking happy to do it."

"Yeah?"

I pulled the other side of my cloak back, revealing another hilt of a very different weapon. Carved wood, black and shiny as sin, not so much as a splinter out of place. Brass glimmered like it just wanted me to take it out and show it off.

At my hip, I could feel the gun burning, begging to be unleashed.

"As it turns out, asking questions makes me unhappy, too, Ralp. What do you suppose we do about that?"

Sweat appeared on Ralp's brow. He licked his lips, looked wild-eyed at my piece before he looked right back into the ugliest grin I could manage.

Don't get me wrong, I didn't feel *particularly* great about doing something as pedestrian as flashing a gun. It feels so terribly dramatic, and not in the good way. But you must believe me: I was expecting this to go smoothly. I hadn't prepared anything cleverer at the time. And, if I'm honest, this particular gun makes one hell of a statement.

I certainly wasn't going to feel bad about this.

Behind me, I could hear a hammer click. Cold metal pressed against the back of my neck.

"I got some ideas," someone grunted.

Now *this* I might feel bad about.

Ralp backed away from the bar—though not before he scooped up the knuckles I left there, the shit—and scampered away to a back room. I let my hands lie flat on the table, my body still as a statue as I stood there.

"The Phantom doesn't like people asking about him." Male voice. Young. I could tell that even without him prodding me with the weapon like it was something else. "Thinks it's terrible rude. I happen to agree with him."

"As do I," I replied, keeping my voice soft. "I must seem even more rude right now, keeping my back to you." I spoke slowly, calmly. "I'm going to turn around and face you."

"N-no!" His voice cracked a little. "Don't do that."

I was already doing it, though. I kept my eyes open, my lips pursed, my face the very picture of serenity as I pushed the scarf back over my head.

Not that I *felt* serene, mind you. My heart was hammering my ribs at that moment—you never get too used to having a gun jammed in your face, no matter how many times it happens. But it had happened enough times that I had learned a few things: I could tell a shaky hand by the feel of a barrel against my head; I could tell how far back a hammer was pulled by the sound.

And I knew that, if someone was intent on killing you, you damn well better make them look you in the eye while they do it.

When I turned around, I recognized the youth from the table—

some soft-faced, wide-eyed punk with a mess of hair and a cluster of acne on his cheeks. He had a hand cannon leveled at my face. The other boy and the girl stood behind him, holding a pair of autobows and pretending to know how to use them.

Good weapons—too good for this hole masquerading as a township. It was unheard of to even see a weapon using severium this far away from a major city. But good weapons didn't make good fighters. I saw their eyes darting nervously around, their hands quivering, too small to hold steel that heavy.

"You're young," I observed.

"Yeah? What of it?" the kid asked.

"Too soft to be working for a Vagrant," I said. "Daiga must be desperate."

"The Phantom's not desperate!" He tried to sound convincing, but the crack in his voice was anything but. "He's just on the run. He's going to get out of this shithole soon enough and take us with him when he does."

"Yeah," the girl growled from behind him. "He's going to show us magic, teach us how to be mages like him. We already hit an Imperial caravan with him! Scored a haul like—"

"I'm sure he was very impressed." I kept my eyes locked firmly on those of the kid in front of me, pointedly looking past the barrel. "Why else would he have given you the very important task of picking up his wine?"

"Shut up!" the kid all but screeched. "Shut your fucking mouth! The Phantom—"

"Daiga," I corrected.

"The Phantom said to kill anyone who came asking after him, any Imperial or . . . or . . . Revolutionary or . . ."

"Child," I said. "I'm no Imperial, no Revolutionary. Daiga's no hero who can get you out of here." I stared into his eyes, forced myself not to blink. "And you're no killer."

His hands shook a little. Arm was getting tired. He held the hand cannon up higher to compensate.

"You've got a shit deal here," I said. "I know. But pulling that trigger isn't going to make it better." I took a breath. "Put it down."

Second thing you do to see what a man is made of, you put a weapon in his hands.

If he's got any sense, he'll put it right back down. If you're fresh out of luck, he'll hold it as tenderly as he would hold his wife. But as much as I don't believe in luck, I believe in sensible people even less, so most of the time you get people like this kid: scared, powerless, thinking a piece of metal that makes loud noises will make anything different.

So when he realized it wouldn't, when his arm dipped just a little, I knew I had this.

I grabbed him by the wrist, pushed the cannon away, and twisted his arm behind his back in one swift movement. He screamed as I pulled him close against me, circled my other arm around his neck, and looked over his shoulder at his friends. They hadn't even raised their autobows before they realized what I had done.

"Listen up," I snarled. "You want to put holes in your friend, you pull the triggers right now. You want everyone to come out of this alive, you put those things down and tell me where Daiga's hiding out."

I watched them intently, waiting for them to realize the shit they were in, waiting for them to drop their gazes, then their weapons.

Only, they didn't.

They looked nervously at each other, saw the fear in each other's eyes, fed off it. They raised their weapons, pointed them at me, fingers on the triggers. They took aim like they thought they wouldn't hit their friend.

And that's when I knew this whole thing had just gone to shit.

I shoved the kid out of the way just as I heard the air go alive with the screaming of autobows. Tiny motors whirred as they cried out, bolts flying from thrumming strings. Their shots went wide, missing both of us. I leapt behind the bar, ducked beneath it.

I heard wood splinter as they fired, bolt after bolt, into the wood, like they hoped the bar would just disintegrate if they poured enough metal into it. Sooner or later, they'd run out of ammunition, but I couldn't wait for that.

Especially not once I heard the hand cannon go off.

A colossal flash of fire lit up the room. The ancient reek of severium smoke filled the air. And a gaping hole was now where half a bar had once been.

I pulled my scarf low against a shower of smoking splinters raining over me. He held a primate's weapon—those things were just as likely to explode as fire—but it made a lot of noise and did a lot of damage, so I imagined he didn't give a shit.

Besides, as I heard him reloading, I came to the same realization that he no doubt had.

He only needed to hit once. And I only had half a bar left to hide behind.

I pulled my gun free from its holster and it greeted me, all bright and shiny and eager to please. It burned warm, a seething joy coursing through my glove and into my palm. His bright brass barrel, carved like a dragon's mouth, grinned at me as if to ask what fun thing we were about to do.

I hate to disappoint him.

Another hand went into the bag at my hip. The shells met my fingers. Across each of their cases, engraved in the silver, I could feel the writing. I ran my hands over each one, mouthing the letters as I did.

Hellfire—too deadly. Hoarfrost—too slow. Discordance—there's my girl.

I pulled it out, flipped the gun's chamber open, slid the Discordance shell in. I drew the hammer back, counted to three, then rose up behind the bar.

And, for the briefest of moments, I saw the look on the kid's face. I've seen it a thousand times before and it never gets old. Eyes go wide, mouth goes slack as they stare down the barrel of my gun and, with numb lips, whisper the same word.

They knew his name.

I didn't aim; with Discordance, you don't have to. I pulled the trigger, laid the shot right beneath their feet. The bullet streaked out. An instant later, it hit the wood. And an instant after that?

Well, I guess I ruined Ralp's bar.

The spell kicked in as soon as metal hit wood. There was a flash of bright light. Then the air swelled and tore itself apart as a noise so loud it took on a rippling, shimmering shape exploded out into a sphere.

The kids were hurled aside. They flew like they had wings, tumbling through the air along with the shattered floorboards and chairs. Their screams would be drowned out by the spell if they had any breath left to make them. The girl struck the railing to the stairs and tumbled down them bonelessly. The boy skidded across the tables before coming to a halt against the wall.

When I hopped over the bar, I surveyed the wreckage. Tables were shattered, chairs were splintered, and where the bullet had struck, the floorboards had been torn up and the earth had been carved into a perfectly smooth bowl.

Discordance is a hell of a spell: not lethal, but hurts enough that you might wish it were. Imperials used to use it to suppress riots in the colonies before the riots became revolutions and nonlethal spells weren't cutting it.

I found the kid lying next to the door, breathing shallowly. I glanced at his friends long enough to make sure they were, too. Might have been stupid to leave them like that, but I won't have it said that I was so stupid I couldn't think of a way to stop a bunch of punks without killing them.

Of course, they didn't need to know that, did they?

I grabbed the kid by the lapel of his coat, slammed him against the wall, put my big, grinning gun in his face.

"Daiga tell you what this is?" I pressed the barrel up under his chin. "Daiga tell you about me?"

The kid, wide-eyed and slack-jawed, nodded feverishly back at me.

"You know what I've done with this, then," I snarled. "You know I'm not going to ask you again. Where is he?"

"T-the old ruins," he stammered. "Four hours east of here, at the foot of the mountain. I ... I can show you if you—"

"I don't." I threw him to the ground. "I'm going to let you live, child. But you're going to do something for me."

"Y-yeah! Anything!"

"First, you're going to tell me what you do for a living."

"I'm an apprentice!" he said. "Scribe's apprentice!"

"You need both hands for that?"

He looked at me weird. "Uh, no?"

And then he screamed as I brought the heel of my boot down on his hand and heard each finger break under it.

I suppose it would have been more poetic to make him swear to give up his life of crime. In truth, I'd tried that before in my more callow days. Enough scars and mistakes later, I learned that experience teaches best.

I didn't kill kids, sure, but I also didn't let them put weapons in my face and walk away unscathed, either.

"Second," I said, leaning down. "You're going to tell me what you're going to tell your peacekeepers when they ask you who did this."

Last thing you do if you want to know what a man is made of, you look him dead in the eye and listen when he says your name.

And the kid fumbled around it for a while, trying to find his way around the fear in his eyes and the pain in his hand, before he said to me:

"Sal the Cacophony."

He sounded like he was going to piss himself.

I put my weapon away, pulled my scarf back up over my head, and made my way back out into the storm. There were going to be a lot of people here before too long with a lot of questions. I didn't have time for that.

I had a mage to kill, after all.

THREE

THE SCAR

The rain cleared up fifteen minutes after I left Ralp's, leaving me with the stink of damp earth and sodden grass.

Four hours later, just before dawn cringed and realized it had to look at the Scar one more day, I found the ruins.

And two minutes after that, I realized today wasn't going to be a good day.

It had once been a fortress, I imagined—one of those collections of palisades, barracks, and towers that had once been crucial during the wars. Forts like these changed hands between the Imperium and the Revolution so frequently that no one could remember which side first built them. And after a few years of drenched autumns, freezing winters, and blazing summers had taken their toll, neither side wanted to claim the embarrassment of owning one.

Forts like these, you didn't go to unless you had need for a ruinous, dangerous death trap of a hideout.

Daiga the Phantom, like any Vagrant, had plenty of need.

At the foot of the mountain, just like the kid said, there it was. Two big stone towers, their windows long dark and their stairs long crumbled, flanked a high stone wall, a great gash dividing it where cannon or magic had torn through it ages ago.

We came walking up to it slowly, my ears open and listening for any sound of ambush. When it didn't come, I hopped off and took a good, long look over the ruined wreck of a fort.

"I figure he's deep." I pointed toward the towers. "He's a Grasp-mage, so he'll hide with things he can levitate. I bet he could pull those towers down on any mob that came looking for him. That's the sort of effort he's probably not willing to spend on one person, though." I glanced back at her. "That makes sense, right?"

My mount glanced back at me. If she saw a flaw in my theory, she didn't say anything.

Which made sense.

What with her being a giant fucking bird and all.

Four feet of legs ending in wicked talons, two feet of long, naked neck with big, angry eyes and a sharp, ugly beak, all connected by a fat sphere of coarse black feathers. Congeniality looked as mean, as dumb, and as angry as you would want a Badlander breed to look. The Scar isn't a place for pretty birds.

At my continued stare, she let out a low gurgling sound.

"Glad we agree."

I reached into her saddlebags, rooted around until I felt the famil-iar chill of three thick shells at the bottom of the bag. Thick as a rich man's finger, made of pure silver, each one engraved with elegant bloodred script of a dead language.

Hellfire.

Hoarfrost.

Discordance.

Tried and true, with hundreds of corpses to testify. These were what you brought to fight a Vagrant. I pulled my gun free and flipped the cylinder out. I loaded all three chambers, fitting each one with a bullet, before I snapped him shut. I didn't bother checking the sights or the hammer.

That sort of thing, the gun took care of for me.

I slipped him back into my belt, reached into the saddlebag one more time, and grabbed something limp and furry.

"Here you are, miss." I tossed the dead rabbit to Congeniality. She watched it fall for a second before her neck went taut and her hooked beak caught the thing and started swallowing. "Not so fast, darling. Make it last."

You can't trust a Badlander to do much except survive. And I didn't need this ornery girl running away, looking for food or doing anything except waiting patiently for me to kill a magical bastard. She'd take a few minutes to eat that rabbit, then at least an hour before she vomited the bones and fur back up.

Only one person would be leaving here alive today. It wouldn't take that long to find out which.

Scarf pulled up around my face, mud under my feet, sky turning a pale blue, I went off to fight a man who could kill me with a thought.

The towers loomed large over me as I picked my way through the gap in the wall and through the ruin. The rain made the old wood stink of age, made the towers groan ominously as the moisture seeped out of them.

If I had any doubts that he was here before, the thought left me as I heard a faint sound weaving its way through the fort. A woman's voice, deep and resonant, climbing to a high pitch as she sang a long and sad song, accompanied by the sound of violins sighing softly.

Opera. *The Lady's Lament*, if I remembered correctly.

That told me three things.

Daiga had very old taste in music.

Daiga knew I was here.

Daiga didn't give a shit.

I couldn't blame him. Most of the barracks and storehouses had been burned away and looted over the years, leaving only a few piles of rubble and timber amid the skeletons of their old buildings. No place to ambush from. No way to sneak around. Any way I was coming, it would have to be direct.

And so that's how I came.

And that's how I found Daiga the Phantom.

Tall, slender, wrapped in elegant—if soiled—clothes of black and red, he sat in a pristine chair, reclining so the length of his body sprawled out over a rug on the damp earth. A necklace of trinkets—rings, folded-up letters, even a spoon—hung around his thin throat. His face was obscured by an opera mask in the shape of a leering demon, eyes black and hollow, mouth curled up in a toothy smile. He looked exactly like he did in his wanted poster.

Stacks of weapons—swords, spears, shields, bows—surrounded him like the hoard of some great beast. He had enough crates of sundries to feed the army that died here. But for all that, his attention was on the tiny table sitting in front of him, and the voccaphone playing on it, the dulcet opera music rising out of its horn.

He didn't seem to notice me at all. Instead, he swayed to the music, his gloved fingers conducting an orchestra in his head.

"I've no particular use for the machinations of those barbarians in their Revolutionary farce." Without looking at me, Daiga spoke in a voice so mellifluously cultured it probably wore a silk dress. "Weapons of war that strain to do what magic can do so effortlessly. Even this contraption is nothing compared to the real Cathama stage." He sighed as the opera struck a high note. "But, stranded as one is outside the Empress's good graces, it's a blessing to still have a few reminders of civility, no?"

I stepped out into the courtyard—no sense in hiding. I stood as close as I dared, looking at the voccaphone while it blared its music. I shrugged.

"The machine cracks every time she hits a high note," I said. "They can make a bow that fires ten bolts in three seconds, but they can never fix that fucking crack."

"Language." Daiga continued to conduct his imaginary orchestra. "You've been out here too long, I fear. No appreciation for a marvel such as this. Even the dim culture of this land is preferable to no culture at all, hmm?"

He waved a hand. His eyes glowed a faint purple behind his mask. From the table, a teacup rose of its own volition and into his hand.

He took a long sip behind the mask, then made a chiding click of his tongue.

"Your pardon, madam."

Another wave of a hand beckoned another cup from the table. It hovered toward me, hung in the air. I took it, nodding a polite gratitude, and tasted old jasmine. And for a very long time, we simply sat there, sharing a cup before we got to the business of killing each other.

"I did not expect to be found," he said, voice solemn, like he spoke in the presence of the dead. "Not least by you."

I stared at him for a moment. "You know me, then."

"I have heard the stories."

"Which ones?"

"I am only interested in one." He stared back through the empty eyes of the opera mask. "Were you truly at Vigil?"

I nodded. "I was."

"I see. And did you truly do what they say you did?"

I hesitated. "I did."

"And now you are here for me." His eyes turned away. "Did the Empress send you?"

He sounded almost hopeful, speaking through a voice ragged with disappointments. I shook my head, set the cup on a nearby crate.

"I came for another reason," I said.

His head sank low, a sigh escaping the demon's mouth. "I gave everything to the Imperium—my years, my body, and all the wisdom and violence that came with them. And now I am hunted, one more stray dog beset upon by hounds."

"No one ever gets the death they want," I replied. "Just the one they deserve." I glanced at the glistening hoards of weapons across the courtyard. "Were you hoping for an army?"

"Every good lord requires vassals," he muttered in response.

"Vagrants don't get to be lords. And they usually get better vassals than children."

The song lasted one last note, soft and fading. The voccaphone ran out, leaving nothing behind but that soft, crackling sound. Daiga's hand hung in the air, paused on that last note.

"Did you kill them?" he asked, gentle.

"They won't be coming to help you."

He nodded, solemn. "They had hopes of purpose. I had hopes of giving it to them." He gripped the armrests of his chair. "I had so many hopes."

He rose out of his chair. I took a step back, reaching for my gun. Not smart to pull it on him yet, though. You can't act twitchy around a mage, let alone one like Daiga.

"I shall commend them, once we are done. And you, too." He stood his full height, his necklace of trinkets jangling as he rose. Through the hollow eyes of his mask, he stared at me. "I have heard a story that says you honor the old ways."

That one wasn't always true. But this time, it was. I nodded, pushed my cloak back, and exposed the hilt of my gun.

And in response, he spread his long limbs out wide, made a low bow, his empty eyes locked on me.

"Shall we?"

You didn't often see people like Daiga anymore. Not in the Scar, anyway. Most people out here, let alone men in his circumstances, don't do things the old way anymore. It's all just ambushes, tricks, and murder these days. Only the Vagrants keep to the code, even when it's not always smart to do so.

We grant each other that respect. No one else will.

"Ready when you are," I said.

"Then may the Lady Merchant reward the worthy."

He reached up, long fingers trailing across his necklace before they settled on a comb. A worn and well-used thing, missing a few teeth and engraved with the initials D.K.Y. It looked old.

That's when I began to suspect I was fucked.

"Ocumani oth rethar."

And that's when I knew it.

The words boomed out of his mask like a clap of thunder. In the distance, I heard a faint sound like a ringing bell carried on the breeze. With terrifying swiftness, it rose in volume and became a sound that swept through my cloak, past my skin, and echoed in my very heart. The comb in his fingers disappeared in a flash of purple light, leaving behind only faint dust.

In less than two seconds, he had made his Barter.

And in less than three, I pointed my gun right between his eyes and squeezed the trigger.

But that second was all a Graspmage needed.

There was the crack of gunfire, a bright spark of fire exploding, the echoing sound of fiery laughter smothered by metal as something swallowed the fire.

Something like the iron shield hovering in front of him, blackened by flame.

He lowered his hand, guiding the shield away from his face. A faint glow ebbed from its surface as the wards inside it murmured to life. It hovered there, just over his chest, as his demon's face leered over the rim at me. His other hand rose, and in response, the weapons crates stirred. Swords, spears, gunpikes, all of them rose into the air, pulled by nothing, and formed a halo of steel around his head. His mask grinned as I saw my own fear reflected back to me in a dozen blades.

And now you know why they call him the Phantom.

And why I was running for my life.

I heard the thrum of bows behind me. I felt the bolts whizz past my face. I saw the wet earth shudder before me as a long spear came hurtling over my head, narrowly missing it to impale itself in front of me.

I whirled, my blade leaping to my hand just in time to strike away the sword that came flying toward me. I sent it spinning with a spray of sparks just in time for the next one to come whistling at me. One after another, I parried blows from phantom blades, spitting curses over the sound of steel clanging. One swung low, angling toward my belly. I leapt backward, my heel catching on a fragment of shattered timber.

I fell backward over a pile of rubble, tumbling into a roll and then scrambling to slam up against it. It would have been shitty cover against any fool with a gun, let alone a Graspmage. But I didn't have a lot of options available to me.

And I was about to use another one.

My gun was in my hand, metal blood pumping warm through brass skin. He rose, just as I raised him, and pointed him at the Phantom. I could tell where he was aiming—he always went right for the heart. It was only with a bit of pull that I aimed him lower and squeezed the trigger.

Daiga's shield went up. But that wasn't my target. The shell streaked low, struck the earth beneath him. A bright flash of blue swallowed the night. The earth turned white. A thick patch of frost blossomed in half a second. And in one more, four-foot-long spears of ice burst forth in a frigid white briar.

Hoarfrost. Takes a moment. But it's worth it.

Daiga narrowly caught it. He leapt into the air to avoid the reaching spikes, hovered there, swung around to affix his empty eyes upon me.

"That weapon," he hissed, all pretenses of formality gone from his voice. "*You.*"

"Me," I said. I flipped the chamber open, loaded another shell, and raised him back up. "And this."

He didn't give me a chance to fire. He waved a hand. Arrows followed, singing from six bows and forcing me back behind the barricade. I peered around, saw him reaching for his throat.

He tore another trinket from his necklace—the spoon, this time. He tossed it into the air. There was the wailing sound once more, the flash of purple light, the blast of dust.

And the six weapons hanging in the air were joined by twenty more from the crates.

More bows rose up, a halo of arrows rising with them. But there was something off about them. Across their wooden bellies, veins of blue light began to burst. Their strings pulled back, drawing arrows that crackled to life with electric light.

Wait. The thought came unbidden. The girl back at the bar. She'd said they'd hit an Imperial caravan, didn't she? Imperial caravans carry magic. My eyes dawned with realization.

Fuck me, he's got thunderbows.

And I was running.

The song of lightning followed me, an angry, screeching verse torn from twenty ragged throats. Arrows struck the earth in my wake, vibrating with electricity and bursting into bright flashes of sound and light, mud and earth torn screaming and tossed into the sky.

Another verse, of angry steel and wailing metal, followed. The air shrieked with the sounds of metal as swords came flying out, whirling in great sweeping arcs, trying to hack me to pieces as I ducked low and darted to the side. Spears fell in a great rain, in front of me, behind me, a few inches from my leg. Graspmages weren't renowned for accuracy, but they didn't have to be when they had power like Daiga.

That spoon must have been special to him.

With every flick of his hand, he pulled more weapons from their crate, sent more of them shooting, slicing, flying at me. I had to dart and dodge more and more. Eventually, I'd get tired, or I'd trip, or he'd pull the whole fucking fort down on me. I couldn't do this much longer.

But I didn't need much longer.

I skidded to a halt, brought up my gun.

Just in time to see a thunderbow, bristling with light and aimed right at me.

The howl of thunder. A scream struck from my lungs. I felt the arrow hit me right in the flank, striking my cloak and sending me flying with the explosion. I skidded across the earth, smoke rising from my body in plumes. The weapons hung in the air, expectant, as Daiga watched me, his mask's smile drinking in the sight of his latest foe dead.

Wish I could have seen his face when I staggered to my feet.

Pain shot through me. I gasped to find the breath that had been struck out of me. I was hurt to hell, but I was still alive. My cloak shimmered, a long line of letters glowing brightly down its length before they sputtered out and faded into darkness, their magic going dead.

Fucking magic.

"A luckwritten cloak," Daiga chuckled. "You are full of surprises, aren't you?"

He didn't sound impressed. Why would he? He knew that luckwrites were aptly named—good for avoiding maybe one blow before the magic in them needed to recharge. And he had *many* blows left.

His phantom panoply hovered around him, an angel with barbed wings and a halo of arrows. But my eyes weren't on his weapons. They were on him, hovering in the air a good ten inches off the ground. And right behind him, the Hoarfrost still glistened eagerly, spikes out and reaching.

I raised my gun. He pulled his grinning barrel toward the Phantom. I squeezed the trigger. The bullet flew and exploded in a bright red light. Hellfire erupted in a miniature explosion, knocking the shields back. Daiga let out a scream as the fire seeped past his shields, licked at his clothes. He fell from the air, dropping back to the ground to escape the crackle of flame.

I aimed once more. Shot once more. My gun let out a thunderous laugh as the last bullet flew.

Daiga saw it, flicked his arm up. One more shield rose to block the bullet.

Good.

A bright red light. A wall of sound and force. Discordance hit the shield like a fucking battering ram and erupted. The wall of metal kept the sound from damaging him directly, simply knocking him back. But that was fine. Discordance didn't need to kill.

That was Hoarfrost's job.

Daiga flew backward from the force of the impact, letting out a shout that lasted for just a second. After that, all I could hear was the juicy popping sound of flesh being skewered.

The weapons hung in the air for just a second longer. Then they trembled, drooped, and fell to the ground with a clatter. They formed a ring upon the earth. And at their center hung Daiga.

Impaled.

His arms were splayed out to his sides. His legs hung limp beneath him. His body twitched. And all the while, his demon mask remained grinning as he looked down at the massive icicle jutting from his chest, staining the metal trinkets of his necklace red.

He hung there for just a moment longer before his weight made the ice snap. He slumped to the earth, falling to his knees. And there he sat, hollow eyes turned to the ground as he gasped for air, groping at the icicle in his chest.

I drew my blade as I approached, slowly. No sense in taking chances with any mage, let alone one who could tear that icicle out of his chest and fling it at me. But as I came up beside him, I could see, for the first time, the eyes behind his mask.

They were wide. And terrified.

"Last…" he gasped, pausing to cough a spatter of red through his mask's mouth. "Last…words…"

I grimaced. So this was it, then. No last curses, no desperate attempts, not even a plea. Daiga the Phantom was a gentleman to the very end.

I nodded to him. I reached down and gently pulled the opera mask from his face.

I'm not sure why I imagined him younger. I'm not sure why it felt weird to look on his face—a face that could have been my grandfather's, if both of us had made better choices in life—and see his rheumy eyes shining bright with the last traces of life. Even the skeletal hands tattooed across his throat couldn't make him look any less gentle.

I'm not sure why I let him stare up at the sky and speak through a mouthful of blood.

"Lady...find me worthy..." He paused to cough. *"Ocumani... oth rethar."*

I pressed my blade against his throat. He closed his eyes. I closed mine.

"Eres va atali," I whispered in reply.

Before he turned rebel and became a Vagrant, Daigalothenes ki Yanturi was one of the greatest Graspmages in the Imperium. He was a lecturer, a scholar, a decorated war hero against the Revolution back in his younger days. His telekinesis was so strong as to have a hundred Graspmages in his bloodline.

But when I drew my sword across his throat, you know what came out?

The same wet red that comes out of everyone.

FOUR

HIGHTOWER

"Y ou knew each other, then?"

Tretta leaned over the table, her eyes in a hard glare upon her prisoner. The white-haired woman merely shrugged, leaning back in her chair and propping dusty boots up on the table.

"In the same way I knew him," Sal replied. "He'd heard my name, knew what I'd done. Among Vagrants, that's all that really matters."

"Even among Vagrants who hunt other Vagrants?" Tretta asked, sneering.

"It pays." Sal shrugged. "But most of our little family tends to find the money easier in becoming warlords or robbing caravans."

"As Daiga no doubt desired," Tretta muttered. "And he knew of your weapon, too."

"Well, obviously." Sal's grin was so wide it made her scars deepen. "Find me a man in the Scar who *hasn't* heard of the Cacophony."

Tretta was not a woman who tolerated that kind of flippant talk from her own soldiers, let alone a prisoner. Her eyes narrowed into angry slits, her frown a scar on her face. Without looking away, she raised a hand to a subordinate.

"Bring it."

"Governor-Militant!" a soldier barked back, firing off a salute.

He hurried out of the room, gone for barely a few moments before he returned with a metal box secured with a dense iron lock. He set it upon the table, saluted once more, and returned to his position at the door.

Tretta fished a key from her pocket, unlocked the box, pushed the lid off. She gazed upon its contents and paused.

The Imperials, in all their vile sorceries and superstitions, were the ones who believed in depraved magic and put their stock in the impossible. Men and women of the Revolution were made of more sensible stuff. They believed in hard things: hard metals, hard answers, hard truths.

It shamed Tretta that she should feel so hesitant to reach into the box and produce the weapon.

The Cacophony was a large gun, it had to be said, even among the gaudy and impractical weaponry of Vagrants. Though its color was that of an ancient brass organ, it was far lighter in her hands than it ought to be. Its grip was polished and black, its cylinder oversized, its barrel carved into the visage of a dragon. She studied its face—its horned brow, its grinning, toothy maw—until she met its empty gaze.

And wondered, in a fleeting and shameful thought, if it was staring back at her.

"A ridiculous weapon," she scoffed. "Ostentatious, even by Imperial standards." She tested its heft. "I'm not sure how anyone could even aim this thing." She flicked the cylinder out, frowned. "And three chambers? This thing is barely a weapon. Ridiculous."

She suddenly realized how soft her voice had gotten. Somewhere, she had stopped talking to her prisoner and started talking to herself.

"Lighter than he looks, isn't he?"

Sal leaned over the table, something mischievous and a little cruel in her smile.

"Tell me honestly, Governor-Militant...did you try to fire him?"

Tretta shot her a puzzled and slightly offended look. "*Him*? It's just a gun."

"The Cacophony's got a name," Sal replied. "Makes sense, doesn't it?"

"Perhaps. But why do you call it a man?"

Sal humored her with a half-grin. "What else would he be?"

"Our engineers studied it." Tretta placed the Cacophony back in the box. "We could not find any ammunition that fits its chambers. Whatever name you call it by, this is just another Vagrant abomination: impractical, ridiculous, and grotesque."

"Wouldn't fire for you, would he?" Sal chuckled. "No need to pretend to me, darling. The Cacophony is a fickle thing. He has to be inspired."

"But you command it, do you not?"

"You don't date much, do you, Governor-Militant?"

Tretta's left eye twitched as she wondered if it might not spare her a lot of grief to simply shoot the Vagrant in the head right now.

"Commands are fine for an army." Sal grinned. "But a relationship is built on cooperation." She gestured to the weapon. "I choose the spells that go into the bullets. I choose the bullets that go in the chamber. I choose where to point him. But it's his job, and a point of personal pride, to shape the magic."

"That's insane."

"That's the Cacophony."

"The Cacophony." Tretta removed another weapon from the box—an old, if well-tended-to, blade wrapped in worn leather. She slid it halfway out, inspected it. "What manner of odious title does this weapon possess, then?"

Sal shrugged. "I don't know. Jeff?"

"What?"

"It's just a sword." Sal leaned back in her chair. "Not even my best one."

"An *Imperial* sword," she noted, studying the blade. The steel was forged well enough to be honed, despite clearly having been sharpened far too rarely. A slight blue tint accompanied the edge, causing her brow to furrow. "An officer's weapon."

"You recognize it, then?" Sal sounded impressed.

"The Cadre is very familiar with the Imperium's perverse hierarchies. Their service to their depraved Empress is rewarded with hued blades like this." She held the weapon up for inspection. "From lowest to highest, each officer is granted a blade. Copper, bronze, silver, gold, blue, red, and the very highest in her service being granted a black blade."

"I always did appreciate a woman who knows her blades," Sal said, grinning. "Granted, the allure is diminished with you about to kill me and all."

"But why do you need a sword, when you have something like the Cacophony?"

"Two reasons." Sal held up a finger, pointed it at the Cacophony. "One, that thing doesn't really do 'nuance.' Not exactly good for everyday shooting." She held up a second finger. "Two, it shoots fireballs and giant fucking walls of sound. Ammo isn't fucking cheap."

Tretta's voice went low and threatening as she leaned over the table. "Is that how Cavric met his end, Vagrant? Will we be picking pieces of him out of the dirt?"

"Oh, don't be so dramatic." Sal waved a flippant hand as she leaned back again. "The Cacophony is for hunting Vagrants, bringing down big beasts, or on rare occasion, impressing someone with a nice set on them. But, like, *really* nice, you know? Like, kill-a-man nice, not just regular—"

"You are trying my patience."

"Anyway, the Cacophony's too proud to be used for killing your average Revolutionary goon. I've got Jeff for that." She yawned—a gesture Tretta found even more infuriating. "And in the case of your soldier Cavric, I used neither."

"And you expect me to believe that?" Tretta snarled.

"Why wouldn't you?"

"Because nothing in your story makes sense!" Tretta threw up her hands. "You expect me to believe you approached Daiga the Phantom casually, had a pleasant conversation with him, and *then* fought him? Why wouldn't you just put a bullet in his head from a hundred feet?"

Sal's mirth seeped away.

"Because that's not the code."

"Again with this 'code.'" Tretta rolled her eyes, sneering. "Has anyone else heard of it when they speak of Vagrants? Because I've only heard the sobbing pleas of the people you've robbed and the wailing screams of the people you've hunted and the tired sighs of the people burying the ones you killed. This 'code,' to me, seems like something you use to pretend you're not animals. Why would I ever believe a bunch of common outlaw scum would abide by even that?"

"Now, I just told you a story about a gun that shoots icicles and a man who moves things with his mind. What the fuck about that suggests we're common?" Sal shook her head. "The code is by Vagrants for Vagrants. A holdover from before the Dogsjaw Rebellion sent them fleeing into the Scar." She shrugged. "Some traditions die hard."

"And that's where that ridiculous language comes from, is it? That...what'd you call it? *Ocu...occa...*"

"*Ocumani oth rethar*," Sal finished.

"What is that? Some magical incantation?"

"The magic comes from the Barter, not the word." Sal leaned forward, cradling her chin in one hand as she grinned lazily. "You don't see a lot of opera in the Revolution, do you?"

"The Renowned Weiless Speakers of Indisputable Truth are some of the finest performers in all the Revolution," Tretta replied defensively.

"No, no. Not the bullshit propaganda and sermons you nuls pretend is opera. I mean *real* opera. Stories about love, about loss, about a single human being raising their hand to the sky and cursing the heavens."

Tretta sneered. "Flippant wastes of time for decadent Imperial fops."

"Now, if you had seen real opera, you'd know those words. '*Ocumani oth rethar*' is Old Imperial, what they spoke back when the first Emperor was crowned. It's the line spoken at the beginning and the ending of every opera in Cathama, by tradition and by law."

Tretta sneered. "And what does it mean?"

Sal met her with a smile. "Roughly, it means 'look upon me and tremble.' Like 'Here I am.' It's a proclamation of presence, to let everyone know you're arrived. And it's how you get her attention."

Tretta leaned forward on her hands, scowling daggers at the woman. "Whose attention?"

"Same person every Vagrant wants the attention of," Sal said. "The Lady Mer——"

There was a sudden knock at the door to the cell. Tretta whirled upon it, eyes narrowed; she had left specific instructions not to be disturbed during the interrogation.

"Enter," she said through clenched teeth.

The door creaked open. A meek, mustachioed face beneath a thinning top of black hair peeked around the corner. A soft, almost whimpering voice spoke from behind.

"Governor-Militant?" he asked. "Is this a bad time?"

"Clerk Inspire," Tretta replied. "This is a very bad time."

"Oh."

Heedless of the harshness in her voice, he came shuffling out from behind the door. Fit only to sit behind a desk, Inspire looked even less imposing standing up. His uniform hung off his skinny body. His glasses slid down his long nose.

"It's just that I have a request to return the weapon." He glanced emphatically to the box holding the Cacophony. "Cadre Command is keen to hear it's in safekeeping."

"There are no hands safer than mine, Clerk," Tretta snapped. "We will return the weapon when we're done here."

"Yes. Of course, Governor-Militant." Inspire turned to leave, but hesitated. He turned around again. "It's just that they're very insistent. It's my revolutionary duty to make sure that——"

"Any inquiries the Cadre has about it, you may direct to me, Clerk. And should one of them arrive to deliver said inquiries, only then may you disturb me again. Am I understood?"

His head bobbed in meek nodding. "Y-yes, Governor-Militant.

Sorry, Governor-Militant." He slipped behind the door and whispered, pulling it shut. "Just...you know...let me know when I should return it."

He closed the door. There was the clicking of a lock behind it. Sal watched him disappear, eyes lingering on the door as it pressed shut. She yawned, turning her attentions back to Tretta.

"Clerk Inspire, huh?" she asked. "Do you get to choose your own names in the Revolution? I always wondered."

"Enough." Her words were punctuated by her fists slamming on the table, sending the box shaking. Tretta leaned forward, all but spitting as she barked at her prisoner. "I have *had* it with your delays!" she snarled. "You will tell us what became of Cavric right this minute or I swear I will be *extremely* happy to help you see just how many inches of red-hot steel can fit in a human."

Sal blinked. She opened her mouth, as if to inquire how one came about that knowledge. But, in the first intelligent move she had made all day, she opted to say something else.

"As it happens," Sal said, "I was just getting to that part..."

FIVE

THE SCAR

I wasn't sure when I had dozed off, but when I heard his voice, I knew I was dreaming.

"And what are you laughing at?"

His eyes smiled when the rest of him didn't. His face was composed of angles, each one as sharpened and perfected as the blade he polished in his lap, his body as straight and as hard. And even though he tried to look stern when he looked at me, he couldn't hide the laughter in his eyes.

I didn't bother trying to hide mine. My laugh was long and loud back then and the only scar on my face was my smile.

"Just answer me this," I said. "Why a sword? What do you expect it to do that magic can't?"

He held up the weapon in both hands, studying it, considering it, as though—like all answers—this one also lay somewhere along its killing edge.

"There is an honesty in a sword that there isn't in magic," he replied. "Magic requires a Barter. It asks you to give up something of yourself to use it and you never know what it is you've given up until it's gone. A sword, though? That's a partnership."

"*That's* weird."

"Like this."

He was behind me. The sword was in my hand; his fingers were wrapped around mine. One arm slid around my waist, pulling me closer. With the other, he guided my hand through cuts, parries, thrusts, killing imaginary foes.

"See? It asks that you use it. And in exchange, it does what it must." His lips drifted close to my neck, his hot breath on my ear. "Just like us."

"Like us," I whispered, closing my eyes.

"You and I," he said. "I am your blade. Use me and I will do what I must."

Something wet and hot blossomed on my belly.

"Now, then," he whispered.

My blood seeped out between his fingers.

"Would you forsake me for magic?"

Hot breath in my face. A voice in my ears. A long, wet beak brushing against my cheek.

I cracked one eye open. Congeniality stared back at me, made an irritable squawk. Behind her, a bolus of fur and bones from her meal lay in a glistening pool of saliva.

"Already?" I asked, yawning. I pushed her away, leaned up against the tree I had fallen asleep beneath. "A lady would wait for supper."

Congeniality, with a ruffle of feathers and an ugly hissing sound, indicated she would not. I sighed, got to my feet, and plucked up my cloak that I had been using as a pillow. I gave it a flick and it instantly contracted to a scarf I tied around my neck. Not the most impressive enchantment, but it saves on storage.

I found another carcass in Congeniality's saddlebags. I tossed it toward her and left her to the business of devouring it as I walked past the man I had just killed and went about the ugly business of rifling through his shit.

In Cathama, the scholars call it art. In Weiless, the propagandists call it oppression. In Haven, the zealots call it witchcraft.

But out here in the Scar, it takes a Vagrant to understand what magic really is: a trade.

And like any trade, the power lies in your Barter.

It'd be too noble to call it a "sacrifice." Vagrants aren't so selfless a people. And the Lady Merchant, for as much reverence as we speak her name with, isn't that kind of patron. You want the power; she asks a price. You give her the Barter; you get what you pay for.

Daiga knew this.

I held up his necklace of trinkets, sifting through them. If you didn't know what you were looking at, you might think it junk. A lock of golden hair, a tattered red ribbon, a bent spoon; these were the treasures of a beggar, not a mage.

But strung through the necklace were a number of folded-up papers. I plucked one off at random, flipped it open. A family stared back at me: a somber child, a woman with a sad smile, and the man I had just killed. He was younger in the picture, with a head of fuller, darker hair, and his long nose and chin not quite so marred with wrinkles.

I'd have been in real trouble if he had decided to Barter this. Perhaps it meant too much to him to part with.

Memories are what the Lady Merchant asks for in exchange for the power of Graspmages. Mementos, specifically—treasured trinkets, little odds and ends that mean something to the mage. It makes sense, if you think about it: to have the ability to grasp, you need to be able to let things go. And the greater their meaning, the greater their power.

Daiga knew that, too.

But Daiga didn't know me.

And that's why his carcass was cooling in the morning sun.

Not that there was much to go through. Daiga had seen fit to leave me with a whole lot of crap I couldn't carry back. The weapons were of good stock, but I'd only ever be able to carry two at a time and it'd take days to reach a freehold big enough to buy them at a good price. Good luck to whatever bandit found them, I suppose, and better luck to whatever poor souls he decided to use them against.

And so that left me, Sal the Cacophony, Scourge of a Hundred Vagrants, rifling through an old man's underthings in his tent.

They were nice underthings, at least; Daiga had class. Daiga also had a lot of useless stuff I had to go through to find the thing I was looking for. I sighed, slammed his trunk shut, and turned toward the shelf he had beside a rather impractically plush bed. I flipped idly through the books he had collected in his time out here: mostly operas, a romance novel or two, a few military treatises. A red leather-bound copy caught my eye.

"Eduarme's Third Study of the Natural Laws and Counter-Complexities of the Scar."

Just saying it aloud made me want to blow my brains out to relieve the boredom. So, naturally, I took it and slid it into my satchel. Working as I do, I'd learned a few rules about the Scar and one of them was that there was always some rich asshole who would pay by the title length for something as thick as this.

I sighed, glanced out the tent at Daiga's corpse. It had been two hours since I cut him open and laid him out upon his robes. Congeniality was digesting by the ruined wall of the fort. The morning sun would be an afternoon sun in another two hours.

It wouldn't be long now.

I pried up the mattress of the bed, found a stack of papers, and pulled them up. But it was what lay beneath them, the glint of amber, that made me grin. From the little space he had carved in the bed frame, I pulled out a bottle of whiskey—the good stuff, Avonin before he became Avonin & Sons; the old man must have been saving it for a special occasion. Dying seemed as special as any.

I leaned back on the bed, took a swig, and unfolded the first paper.

For the regarded eyes of Professor ki Yanturi,

Consider this our final offer of clemency. It is only through the infinite wisdom of Empress Athura, Fourteenth of Her Name, and the considerable mercies of her son, Impending Emperor Althoun, Third of His Name, that we are even extending an invitation to a Vagrant such as yourself.

Your concerns regarding Althoun's magical capabilities have been noted, but his bloodline remains pure and his claim legitimate. We urge you to reconsider your treasonous acts and return to the capital.

Keep in mind that nothing like this has been offered to other Vagrants. And even among others of your deplorable calling, your crimes of sedition, extortion, misuse of Imperial knowledge and more, have been especially heinous. Yet the Empress still recalls the counsel you provided and the wisdom you offered and is willing to offer you this final chance to redeem yourself, denounce the actions of the Dogsjaw Rebellion, take the Oath, and return to Imperial service.

I hope, for your sake, that you consider this and return to Cathama.

Not what I had come to find.

It was signed by a suitably lengthy and pompous title and branded with the Imperial seal. I had pulled a dozen or more of these letters from the bodies of Vagrants I had killed. It's true that Vagrants aren't loved in the Scar and that no one has a hatred for her former subjects like the Imperium does. But it's also true that they hate nuls more than they hate traitors, so there were always letters like this tossed out to Vagrants in the hopes of tempting them back to fight the Revolution.

I crumpled it up, tossed it, flipped open the next one.

Darling,

> *How shall I compare you,*
> *Eyes wide and pure and so cruelly given,*
> *To witness a world unfit,*
> *Mouth so pure and voice so soft,*
> *To speak the unkindness of...*
> *...fuck.*

I've spent hours trying to figure out the next verse. But it all sounds so... banal, so wretched. You loved poetry. It was how we met, remember? Together, in Professor ki Malchai's class. Do you still love it, I wonder? Or does it just make you sick, like everything else you used to love about me?

I'm not going to beg your forgiveness. I am an oathbreaker. I've done terrible things out here in this barbarous realm. But I shall beg you, for the sake of Mathenica, take the money I've sent. My name has brought you undeserved shame, I know. But she's so frail and the Imperium isn't helping so

Not that one, either.

I crumpled the page up and threw it away, too. With much more urgency than the first.

I had pulled a few letters like that from Vagrants, too. Much fewer and most of them weren't that well written. But reading them always made a cold, sick feeling rise up in my gut. I didn't like knowing these sorts of things about them, their families, their troubles.

Made it harder to kill them.

I took another swig of whiskey—much deeper—and unfurled the last letter.

And that cold, sick feeling went away.

And a feeling much colder, much sicker, much more painful replaced it.

I had found what I was looking for.

Daiga—

Last chance. Meet us.

—Jindu

Jindu.

I couldn't hear my heart, my breath, the sounds of starving birds in the dead trees or the cold wind through ruins. I could hear nothing but that name, carving itself inside my head.

I forced my eyes away, down the page. The letter went on in a series of numbers and letters and symbols that made me sick just to look at. A code, obviously. I didn't want to read it. I didn't even want to touch it.

So you might have thought it was crazy to fold it neatly up and slide it back into my satchel. I wouldn't have blamed you.

But I wouldn't have told you why, either.

Not until I had drunk the rest of this whiskey. And maybe one or two more bottles for good measure.

And I was on my way to doing just that when I heard it. Coming from far away, a faint sound like a whistle dying on a breeze that didn't exist. It grew in my ears and led me out of the tent. I heard it like a child hears music for the first time, strange and weird and wonderful. I heard it like the moment I finally understood all those sappy, romantic operas I used to hate. I heard it like the moment my mother first said my name.

Everyone has their own way of describing how the Lady Merchant's song sounds.

It had already begun by the time I emerged. Daiga's corpse was stiff as a blade and hovering a good three feet over the robes I had laid him out on. He hung there for a moment before his eyes snapped wide open. His mouth gaped in a soundless scream. All that came out was a great bright flash of purple. It poured out of his mouth, out of his eyes, lighting up the daylight with an eerie glow.

And then his skin curled and withered away just like that burned paper. Slowly, his limbs and his torso and his head all seemed to bend and wrinkle up until he simply disintegrated. He fell, unceremoniously, upon the robes, a mess of purple powder. All that remained of him when she took him.

The price for magic is steep. And in the end, when you're finally called back, she takes everything.

And all that's left behind is the Dust.

There are theories on where the mages go when she takes them back, what she does with them. I don't read them. Whatever use she has for them is hers. But the Dust she leaves behind? Well, there are plenty of uses for that. Bleakbrews, luckweaves, any number of things dirty people would pay clean money for.

I pulled a jar, carefully wrapped in burlap, from my satchel. And, slowly, carefully, folding the edges of the robe to make a funnel, I emptied the Dust into it. In the end, the jar was *just* big enough for what Daiga's body left behind. A poor funeral, I know, to end up in a jar instead of a family tomb, but tombs were ostentatious wastes of spaces. Out here in the Scar, everything's in demand and there's no such thing as a senseless death.

I wrapped the jar back in the burlap, careful to make sure it was layered enough not to crack on the way back. And when it was done, I rifled through his clothes until I found it. My fingers grazed upon something sharp and came back bleeding. I reached back in and found a hilt.

For everything else Vagrants cast off when they turned traitor— their old names, their old loyalties, their old friendships—this is the one thing from their service to the Imperium that they keep. The Imperial Dagger, the first thing they were given when they enlisted and all they really leave behind when the Lady Merchant takes them.

So, yeah, if you thought I'd be an asshole for planning to hock this for a lot of money, I wouldn't hold it against you.

SIX

LOWSTAFF

No one's really sure what the Imperial blades are made of. It's a secret that their wrights take to the grave. Some say they're made out of Dust, layered and hammered together. Others say they're the carved and fire-hardened bones of mages, the few that the Lady Merchant leaves behind. Some, still, think it's a raw form of severium.

Whatever they're made of, they make a very unique sound when you drop them. And even though they're roughly half the size of a man's palm, they sound like a two-ton weight when they fall to the ground. It's a sound that immediately commands attention.

The kind of attention that Staff Sergeant Revo Courageous paid me when I burst into the offices of his Cadre Command, brushed off his Revolutionary guards, and impaled the Dagger right on his desk.

Then he looked up at me and lofted a hairy, irritated brow.

"I specifically recalled instructing the recruits to empty the trash today. Yet, here it seems to have walked right back in."

The Cadre's offices were sparsely furnished, poorly lit, and sweltering from windows too small to let in light and doors too thick to let breeze in. And Sergeant Courageous was the sort of man who thrived in those conditions. Brawny, thick in ways that his blue officer's coat had trouble containing, and possessed of a mustache that was more insect than facial hair, Courageous had given the best years of his life fighting Imperials and Vagrants across the Scar and had been amply rewarded by the Revolution with an uncomfortable chair and a nice sea of menial paperwork to slowly suffocate under.

I made it a point not to stop in freeholds too often, let alone freeholds on the ass end of civilization like Lowstaff. But there were certain things you could only get done in a city like this, which meant you occasionally ran into people like Courageous.

As I had.

Several times.

And if you've been paying attention to what I've been telling you, that should explain why he was looking at me like he was mentally fitting me for a noose.

"Yeah, well." I reached into my cloak. "I was in the neighborhood."

Courageous stiffened. The two guards flanking his desk—a tall fellow with short-cropped hair and a nice face and a short woman with a scowl—readied their gunpikes. I held up my free hand for peace as I withdrew a folded-up slip of paper and slid it across the desk.

"And I know how you love surprises," I said with a grin.

"I hate surprises," Courageous muttered, but he took the paper anyway. He unfurled it, ran his eyes over the big letters reading *DEATH WARRANT* at the top, and snorted. "So. The Phantom is dead."

"You make it sound so mundane, Courageous." I leaned forward on his desk with one hand, painted a headline across the air with the other. "Daiga the Phantom, Vagrant and Murderer, Bandit and Outlaw, Foe of the Revolution, the Imperium and Haven alike, took his seat at the black table after being heroically hunted down in a vicious battle with local heroine and incredibly brilliant and attractive manhunter, Sal the Cacophony." I shot him a grin fit for eating shit. "Now, doesn't that sound more dramatic?"

"Ostentatious. And you used 'hunted' and 'manhunter' in the same sentence. Repetitive."

Courageous read a lot of books. That's probably why he was so angry all the time.

"A more appropriate headline would be: 'Local miscreant is annoying, decides to interrupt important Revolutionary business, gets paid, and then leaves and hopefully gets run over by a passing carriage and/or drinks herself to death somewhere where I don't have to deal with the corpse.'"

"Hmm." I scratched my chin, considering. "It doesn't mention how pretty I am, but it's got the important part covered."

"Did you notice the way I gave you a variety of ways to die? I thought that was a nice touch."

"Yeah, you've always been straightforward, Courageous." I plucked the Dagger off the desk, flipped it across my knuckles like a coin. "Which is why I know that Daiga wasn't just some common outlaw you could have sent a patrol after." I leaned forward, held it up in front of him. "Even if he hadn't killed dozens of your soldiers and robbed your stores, he was still an Imperial. One of their very best, in fact. Even if he did go Vagrant, his very existence in your domain was an insult, a stain on your record you just couldn't scrub clean."

Courageous was the kind of man who had a face great for killing and bad for playing cards. His mouth twisted into a scar beneath his mustache. His brows furrowed at my every word. And this little vein on his forehead that seemed to show up whenever I was around looked like it was about to pop.

"Fortunately, you've got a nice lady like me to go take care of all that for you." I flipped the Dagger up, caught it by its hilt. "So why don't you just pay me what I'm owed for doing your dirty work and you can go tell Weiless whatever the hell you want about how he got killed in your big official report."

I know all about the Revolution's precious ethics. They've got a thousand rules handed down from their Great General on what to plant, what to eat, how to fuck, whatever. And right up at the top, just below "kill all counterrevolutionaries" is "do not consort with Vagrants," like me. But you don't get to live through as many battles as Courageous had without being a practical man.

And a practical man doesn't have ethics; he has jobs. And somehow, they've got to get done.

And so it was that he took a deep breath. His mouth straightened out. His brows relaxed. An icy professionalism settled over his face. That vein in his head stayed just as big, though, which is how I knew I still had the upper hand here.

"For the elimination of an enemy of the Glorious Revolution of the Fist and Flame"—he forced the words out like they took a tooth with each syllable—"hereby witnessed and sanctioned by an officer of the Cadre, I am authorized to offer the sum of twenty thousand notes."

"Notes?" Given that I was surrounded by men and women who all had more steel than I did and fewer compunctions about turning it on me, I probably shouldn't have laughed *quite* as loud as I did. "As kind as you are to offer me your Revolution's paper money, I'm afraid I have no particular need to wipe my ass at the moment. Hence"—I clicked my tongue—"I'm going to have to insist on metal."

Courageous's mustache twitched. "How much?"

"Ten knuckles. And a femur. Minimum."

"*TEN?*" That icy composure didn't so much melt as explode into a thousand shards. His eyes bulged out and he almost choked on his mustache. "You killed a Vagrant, not raised the damned dead! To demand that much weight in metal is...is..."

"Sir?"

One of his guards—the tall man with the nice face—leaned forward, trying to whisper. But he had a voice unused to meekness and I heard him clearly.

"The Phantom *was* a considerable hindrance to our efforts here in the region. There was criticism from High Command regarding our handling of him. And he might have even been associated with Stark's—"

Courageous turned his scowl toward the guard, who immediately cleared his throat and fell back into line, looking straight ahead.

"If the price is too steep"—I hummed thoughtfully—"I can always go see how much the Imperium will pay for it. There's an agent to the Empress right here in town, in fact."

Men with jobs, likewise, have people they answer to. And those people tend to have neither ethics, nor jobs, but an awful lot of pride that tends to get wounded by, say, losing a prize to their hated enemies due to thriftiness.

Hence why, after one minute, Courageous was looking at me like he would skip the noose and strangle me outright and why, after five, I walked out of his Cadre with a pocketful of metal.

There's a hundred ways in which the Scar lives up to its name, but my favorite is this one.

The Imperium on the East and the Revolution on the West are the fingers that squeeze it until it bursts wide open. And the blood that comes gushing out is the freeholds.

Cities ostensibly named for the fact that they pledge loyalty to no factional power, they first started out as hideouts for bandits, murderers, and other scum who saw the Scar as a place to run away or a place to plunder. Eventually, that scum found trade and investment to be more profitable than robbery and slavery and wound up establishing some semblance of order. The laws vary from freehold to freehold, of course, depending on which baron is running the place, but the universal law between them is that they hold the Imperium and the Revolution in equal contempt.

Not that this deters business with either of them, of course. Freeholds still allow Cadre Commands and Imperial agencies to operate inside their walls, as a gesture of goodwill with a very expensive price tag. Sometimes, that's not enough and one power or another will send in a small army to take it over. In most freeholds, the citizens divide their time between work, sleep, and worrying themselves stupid over which power is going to come kill them in the night.

Most freeholds, though, aren't Lowstaff.

The first thing that hit me when I walked out into the city streets—other than a blast of hot air courtesy of the afternoon sun—was a face full of dust from a passing carriage. The draft bird hauling the load squawked angrily at me, the driver adding a colorful insult in agreement, as they rumbled up the road. The dusty citizens of Lowstaff—the laborers, the draftsmen, the peacekeepers, the mothers, and the children they couldn't be bothered to keep an eye on—got out of the way more by instinct than by attentiveness. Each of them was involved in their own personal world of shit, not the slightest regard or thought for their fellow human beings. Not a one of them even looked up, let alone looked at the people walking around them. To live in Lowstaff was to spare only enough attention for your fellow man to hate him for a few precious seconds before you got back to ignoring him.

In short, my kind of town.

I pulled my scarf a little tighter around my face and set off down the dusty streets.

Lowstaff was just wealthy enough to be attractive to bandits and so was just wealthy enough for high walls to keep them out. Things like paved streets, stone buildings, or cleaning up the loafs of bird shit left lying around, they had too little money and too few fucks to remedy. The nicest building in town was the Cadre Command's cold, stone bunker ringed with barbed wire and patrolled by stone-faced guards.

The money in my pocket wouldn't be enough to draw the attention of people in a nicer city. But in Lowstaff, I had an urge to get on with my business before anyone started thinking the kind of problems they could solve with this metal outweighed the kind of problems they'd get by fucking with me.

"Madam! *Madam!*"

But it seemed I was too damn slow for that.

"Miss! Hey! Wait up!"

Footsteps followed as someone hurried to catch up to me. He ran past me, put himself in my way. And before I knew it, I was looking up at the guard from Courageous's office—the tall one—standing in front of me.

In the dim light of the command room, he had looked like just another zealous goon in a nice coat. But in the cold light of day, he looked like a zealous goon in a rather shabby coat.

Not that he wasn't handsome, in his own way; he had a strong jaw, graceful arches to his eyebrows, and his eyes weren't too close together. The scar on his cheek and the way his crooked grin matched his crooked nose couldn't hide his youthful looks. But it was his weapons that caught my eye—the short sword at his belt, the gunpike over his shoulder. They sat awkwardly on him, weight his body twitched with anticipation of shedding.

I can't say exactly why that put me ill at ease.

"Madam Cacophony," he began.

"My friends call me Sal." I squinted at him for a moment. "I suppose you can, too."

"Sal." He shot me a grin too nice for a soldier. "I just wanted to extend my thanks to you for managing the Phantom for us. We used to have a medal for Exemplary Outside Duty, but—"

I pointedly jingled my pouch. "I prefer this metal, thanks."

"No, I mean, *really* thank you," he said, his voice growing uncomfortably genuine. "I know a lot of Vagrants are vile—" He caught himself. "I mean, no offense."

I smiled at him in that polite "I'm screaming inside" way.

"But the Phantom was a problem for us. He slew at least ten of my comrades. Good men and women who gave their lives for the Revolution. Not to mention all the civilians he robbed and defiled. I just..." An exasperated joy spread across his face. "Thanks. Thank you for doing that."

And just like that, I knew what I didn't like about him.

They called themselves by different names. They called themselves a force to oppose the decadence of the Imperium and to bring freedom and glory to those poor nuls the Empress had crushed beneath her heel. But the Revolution was still just one more army filled with men like this one standing before me.

With their bright smiles and their eyes that lit up in such a way that made you think they actually believed in what they were doing, that they actually believed that the world could be made a better place.

And if you looked too long into the eyes of men like these, you might start believing it, too.

I knew a man like that, once.

"Sure." I pulled my scarf down to avoid his eyes. "I'm always happy when killing benefits someone."

"Cavric." He fumbled with his hands, unsure as to whether to offer to shake mine or salute. Eventually, he settled on the former, thrusting it out. "Cavric Proud, madam. Low Sergeant of the Glorious Revolution of the Fist and Flame."

"Cavric." I took his hand. It was strong, warm. "A pleasure."

"The pleasure is all mine, madam."

I think if he knew what kind of hell his life was going to be after meeting me, he probably wouldn't have said that.

"I should get back. Staff Sergeant doesn't like Vagrants, let alone us talking to them." He grinned, fired off a quick salute. "Keep up the good work!"

I watched him run back to command and I couldn't help but grin. It was just like a man like that to use the words *Vagrant* and *good work* in the same thought. Vagrants didn't do good work. We robbed, we cheated, we looted, and we murdered. And sometimes, we did that to each other instead of some poor, undeserving civilian. Occasionally, the world was better off for one of us killing another, but no one intelligent was ever happy to see a Vagrant.

I've heard the superstitions about us. A Vagrant looks at a pregnant woman and her baby dies at the age of two. Chickens lay black poisonous eggs if a Vagrant visits the farm. The blood of Vagrants will water a tree that will grow screaming heads.

That one's my favorite.

There are others, but the end result is that most Vagrants showing up where you live will ruin your day.

Not me, of course.

A girl like me tends to ruin your whole week.

SEVEN

LOWSTAFF

You're probably wondering why anyone would choose to live in a freehold, let alone try to make a life for themselves here. The Scar's a harsh place—harsher still if you're not afforded the protection of the Imperium or the Revolution. In fact, usually one or both of them is looking to either burn your home down or plant their flag on it. And that's to say nothing of the beasts, bandits, clansmen, and of course, Vagrants.

So why set up shop in a place like the Scar?

Same reason anyone does anything stupid: sex or money.

Of course, sex isn't any better in the Scar than somewhere more civilized, but there were a number of economic advantages to setting up shop in a freehold. Taxes were cheap, for one; there were no Revolutionaries to confiscate and redistribute your profits in the name of equality, nor Imperials to fine you for looking at a mage in a way he didn't like. Like everything in the Scar, if you could make it, you could keep it.

Assuming someone like me didn't come and take it anyway.

Which is why I found myself, in a darkened little corner of Lowstaff, standing beneath a sign with an elegant flower twisted around the words BLACK LILY APOTHECARY: TINCTURES, RESTORATIVES & ELIXIRS, pounding on a door no one was answering.

"Come on, come on!" I shouted. "I know you're fucking in there."

Really, I didn't mean to sound as mad as I did. Frankly, if I knew I was on the other side of the door, I probably wouldn't open up, either.

But I had business that day.

I glanced around the little corner and, satisfied that no one was coming out to see what all the noise was about, I took ten steps away from the door and aimed myself at the window. I took a running leap at it, my fingers catching the sill, my feet braced against the wall. Fiddling with the lock would be pointless—I knew who had made it—so I whispered an apology before smashing a window with the hilt of my sword. A quick reach later, I had it open and was pulling myself inside.

I didn't feel good about that. Or about putting my dirty boots down on a nice velvet rug. Or about the whole forced entry thing. But I knew the proprietor—she wouldn't hold it against me.

After all, this wasn't the worst thing I'd ever done to her.

The floor and walls inside the shop looked to be made of the same high-polish red wood, though it was hard to tell. Every inch of floor was covered with plush carpeting. Every inch of wall was dominated by shelves. And upon them were all the neatly organized amenities you'd expect an apothecary to have: vials of elixirs, pots of balm, jars of dried herbs, all rigidly labeled by price and ingredient and jars polished to a shine. It was the sort of interior expertly maintained to make the very forceful suggestion that people who looked—and smelled—like me ought to stay out.

But by now, you should know how good I am with following suggestions.

The door was locked and barred with two latches, in case I needed any more idea that I shouldn't be there. The counter was rife with scales, powders, and other such amenities, but no one was standing behind it. I made my way around, careful not to disturb anything.

On the other side of the counter, I shoved a heavy chair out of the way before peeling up the rug and casting it aside. A wooden floor, completely unremarkable, greeted me. And I would have sworn I was looking at just a floor if I didn't know the person who had built it.

She always did love her secrets.

I ran my hands along the wood until I found it, almost by accident. My fingernail caught the barest edge of a latch so hidden and small I could only fit two fingers under it. I groaned with the effort of prying it up, but the trapdoor itself was silent as the grave. A fitting match for the staircase underneath, dark as night as it slithered its way into a hollow beneath the shop.

I double-checked my satchel—still heavy, nothing broken, nothing leaking—and took in a deep breath before descending. My nerves were dancing like they should have when I faced Daiga. What awaited me down here, I knew was worse.

The darkness smothered me, so thick I tripped when the stairs gave out after about ten feet and turned into a straight tunnel. I felt for the left wall, pressed myself against it, and began to scoot myself down the tunnel.

I suppose if you could have seen, my face pressed against cold stone, scooting inch by inch down the corridor, you might have thought I looked pretty stupid. But you weren't in my head, trying to remember how high that trip wire that triggered a deadfall was, hoping the trapdoor wasn't any wider than the last time I was here, wondering if the last pressure plate trap at the end shot fire, spiders, or both.

Also, it was dark as hell, so you couldn't have seen me in the first place, so fuck off.

After twenty feet of picking, pressing, and praying, I saw the faintest glow at the end of the tunnel. A black square illuminated by a border of yellow light. I found a handle in the darkness, satisfied that I had put every trap behind me.

I gave a quick pull.

I heard a loud *click!*

And that's when I remembered the saw.

A flash of silver whispered through the darkness. The shriek of metal hit my ears. And not that I was *thrilled* about falling back on my ass, but I damn sure preferred it to being bisected by the spinning blade that came screaming out of the edge of the wall. I ducked low, letting it swing over me for what felt like an eternity, before it skulked back into the wall with a squeaky mutter, disappointed that it hadn't done its one job.

I crawled back to my feet. I pushed the door open. And by the dim glow of an alchemical light, I saw what was so worth protecting.

The air was stifling and thick with fumes. Beakers and vials boiled over blue-flamed burners, noxious mixtures distilling and churning out vapor of purple and green. Workbenches lined the walls; whatever wasn't laden with alchemical apparatus instead held various pieces of machinery—not dissimilar to the one that had just tried to kill me.

Racks of weapons fit in every spot not dominated by tools or beakers. Gunpikes, pistols, blades—some of which had purposes I couldn't tell, aside from killing people messily—stood on racks, in crates, wrapped in bundles. And every inch of metal, wood, or stone exposed was covered in faintly glowing script in a language no one had spoken for centuries. Illuminated by the blue light of an alchemical candle that hadn't sputtered out in six years, the room was a workshop, an armory, and an explosion waiting to happen, all in one.

You could be forgiven for not noticing the girl standing at the center of it all. Hell, I didn't.

Not until the hand cannon was in my face anyway.

I stared down its snub-nosed barrel, down to the pair of pale hands holding it. Over the sights, a pair of dark brown eyes rendered into a huge, wary stare behind a pair of gigantic glasses looked back at me. Locks of black hair fell out of a messy bun, quillpens stuck in it, to frame a pretty face locked in a tight-lipped grimace. Her face contorted at the sight of me, hands shaking along with her scowl as she aimed the gun at my heart.

Waiting for a reason.

I stared into those eyes—without blinking, without speaking—as I took a step forward. Through the fabric of my shirt, I could feel the metal of the barrel against my chest.

I raised a hand and slowly rested it upon hers. Her fingers warm and shaking under mine, I pulled one of them away from the trigger and set it alongside the barrel.

"Like this," I said. "You don't pull the trigger with both fingers."

She blinked, perplexity plain across her face and growing as I straightened out her arms.

"Arms straight. And feet planted." My hands slid down to her waist and tugged down, planting her feet on the floor. "Shoulder width. Make a foundation to fire from." I clicked my tongue and pushed her hips back slightly. "And bend at the waist, for fuck's sake. Stick your ass out a little."

Perplexity turned to offense as she opened her mouth to protest. I, however, spoke first.

"And crucially, don't point at anything you don't intend to shoot. And don't shoot anything you don't intend to kill." I met her stare again. "Do you intend to shoot?"

And she met mine. Her eyes rent large as they were behind her glasses, I could see resentment battle reluctance behind her stare, with anger sitting on the sidelines to fight whichever won. A long moment passed and I wondered if she'd actually do it.

I wouldn't have blamed her.

But eventually, she lowered the weapon. Her body shrank from an already petite frame to downright tiny as she set it back on the table. And over her shoulder, she shot me a scowl.

"You'd just leave a huge mess to clean up," she replied through a quill-sharp voice. "You always do."

You might have thought it odd that the prospect of cleaning up a mess was all that spared my life.

But then, you probably didn't know that many Freemakers.

"If you want a clean shot, you need to work on your stance," I replied as she stalked back to her workbench. "I've told you a thousand times to stick your ass out."

"And I have clarified on as many occasions that my posterior is not a concern of yours at this particular moment in time." She took a seat on a stool and plucked up a quill, returning to her work of inscribing a short dagger with the same script that dotted everything else in her workshop. "Given that yours is in my workshop, though, I must request that you remove it, posthaste. Otherwise, I will have to ask that you wait for me to change into boots that I might introduce it to."

You might have wondered why I was grinning at that statement. That is, if you knew her like I knew her.

Of course, you probably *did* know her. Or know of her anyway.

You probably heard about the time the Magnificently Impenetrable Vaults of Weiless were melted open with the aid of a potent acid. That was hers. Maybe you heard when the freehold Riverwild held off an Imperial squadron with arrows that exploded with the force of cannons. That was hers, too. And I know you haven't heard of the freehold Chatterwise, on account of it disintegrating to nothingness in the span of half an hour one fine spring morning, but that was her work as well.

The Revolutionary, the Imperial, and the common dope alike have all heard of the Freemaker whose concoctions have caused so much disaster across the Scar. She had many names. You probably knew her professional one.

They called her Twenty-Two Dead Roses in a Chipped Porcelain Vase.

Fancy, right? All the Freemakers have names like that. But when I first met her, she gave me a different one.

"Liette." I still liked the sound of it better. "I missed you, too."

I shot her a wink. And, by the look on her face, she would have preferred I shot her with a gun. She turned her glowering attentions to the work on her bench.

"If that were true, you would have had the decency to walk into more than one of my traps on your way down here," she grumbled.

"I doubt that," I replied.

"And when have I ever been dishonest?"

"Frequently."

"I meant dishonest with *you*."

"*Frequently.*" She glared at me over the rims of her glasses. "I have no doubts that you missed my expertise, Sal. Whether you missed my company, I have concerns."

"Can't it be both?" I dared to lay a hand on her bench, my fingers brushing hers. "No one can do for me what you can."

They were permitted to linger there, under a wistful stare, for just a moment before she pulled them away.

"Any Freemaker can tend to the needs of your firearm, no matter how exotic you consider it to be."

"Well, sure, but no one *cares* as much as you do." I leaned an elbow on the workbench. She pointedly pushed my elbow *off* the workbench. I put my bag on it instead and ignored the death glare she gave me. "The Cacophony likes you. He always aims better after you take care of him."

At that, she flashed me a look. Not a smile. Liette didn't have a lot of smiles to spare in the first place, and she had wasted many of them on me a long time ago. But there was the barest tremble of her lips, the ghost of a grin I had once known very well before I killed it.

"Weapons don't have emotions," she said.

"They do when you're done with them."

"And *I* don't have time to spare. What do you want, Sal?"

"I need some help with something."

"Many people do. Such as the people who meet you. Though, typically, that help consists of medical aid or compensation for property damage." She continued scribing that peculiar script along the dagger, narrowing her eyes. "As I have no intent of indulging either, I must insist you depart before——"

"Third law."

That got her attention. She shot bolt upright, fingers clenching around her quill so tightly it snapped, and the angry look she shot me was the sort of thing you usually save for men talented enough to urinate across the gravestones of your mother, grandmother, and great-grandmother all at the same time.

She always hated when I invoked the Laws of the Freemakers.

While they were strictly independent, managing a collective of the most brilliant and least inhibited creators in the Scar did require *some* order. And while their beloved Laws were labyrinthine and indecipherable enough to be created by a group of renegade alchemists, machinists, and wrights, the first seven were easy enough to remember.

Like my personal favorite, the third.

"All debts between a Freemaker and anyone providing assistance to the Cause must be honored by the Freemaker," I said, leaning forward with a smile even I would punch off my face. "I'm sure I've done enough for you to warrant that. Remember when I obtained that forbidden tome of Imperial script for you?"

"Stole," she corrected. "You stole it. And that was repaid by me providing you with enough ammunition for your weapon to decimate a small township. Which you did."

"What about the time I killed those bandits who burned down your last workshop?"

"Repaid by me healing your heat-induced injuries after you burned down *their* hideout, along with my research they stole."

"What about that one baron's carcass you wanted?"

She looked wounded. "You said that was a gift."

"Well," I sighed. "I suppose it's a good thing I brought you something, then, isn't it?"

"Not an apology, I would wager."

I would have been insulted. But, in fairness, I *was* an asshole.

"Something better," I said.

I peeled back the leather flap of the satchel. She glanced up as soon as she saw the glint of glass. I grinned, took my time in revealing it.

I couldn't resist a dramatic reveal. Still, once I pulled out that thick glass jar brimming with fine purple powder, I knew by the look on her face that it had been worth it.

See, there's only two things in this world that a Freemaker loves more than secrecy: something she doesn't understand and something that can be turned into an explosive. And there's only *one* thing in the world that can give her both, and Liette, slack-jawed, wide-eyed, and fumbling for words she had long forgotten, was looking at a whole jar of it.

There's good money in finding ingredients for Freemakers. But most scavengers are too smart or too scared to kill Vagrants. The amount of Dust I set in front of Liette could easily bring in twenty femurs, minimum, from any other Freemaker. After all we'd been through, she'd throw a fit if I asked for that much.

Of course, when she found out what I was after, she'd throw something worse. Probably at my head.

But that was a problem for later. Right now, I was watching her little hands pick up the jar, the need for delicacy fighting the need for discovery. Right now, I was watching her awe magnified behind her glasses as she looked over the jar, mentally weighing how much Dust was in there, how many wondrous things she could make with it. Right now, she was the timid little thing that I had met so long ago, the girl with the coy smile who had asked me for the most expensive drink in the tavern after I had tracked mud on her skirts.

I couldn't help but smile.

And once she saw that, she couldn't help but frown. She plucked up the jar of Dust and carried it over to a nearby footlocker. It looked almost too big for her. She had always been slight, but her clothes—her oil-stained trousers and high-necked, long-sleeved shirt—hung a little looser off her than I remembered. She hadn't been eating enough. Or sleeping enough. Or both.

I probably had something to do with one of those.

But if I asked which, there'd be trouble. So I kept my mouth shut as she set the jar inside her locker and produced a small leather case, rattling with the telltale ring of metal as she set it down in front of me. I lifted the flap, smiled at the three dozen silver slugs that smiled back at me. Across their casings, I could see the spells written: Hoarfrost, Hellfire, Sunflare, Shockgrasp, all my favorites.

"Three dozen," I said, glancing up at her. "You like me, don't you?"

"I was going to keep some in reserve for the next time you decided to trouble me," she said. "But I consider that adequate payment for what you've just given me." She sat herself back down at the workbench, cast me a final glance, returned to her work. "If that's all, you can go. Try to stumble into one of the traps on your way out."

"Oh, that's not all." I held up a finger. "I said I had something for you, didn't I?"

"But you just—"

"That was for business," I said, sliding the bullets into my satchel and pulling something else out instead. "This is for you."

Now, it's certainly not true for *every* woman, but the ones I have had the good fortune to know in my life have all followed this rule.

If you need a favor, you bring her flowers.

If you need her forgiveness, you bring her jewelry.

And if you need both, you bring her a book.

And if that sounds stupid to you, then you've never seen someone's face light up as Liette's did when I pulled out *Eduarme's Third Study of the Natural Laws and Counter-Complexities of the Scar* and laid it before her. Her eyes went big, but her mouth went small. When I showed her the Dust, she had been alive with wonder and intrigue. But when I gave her the book?

She was hungry.

"That's..." She paused, visibly resisted the urge to lick her lips. "That's a very rare text." She looked up at me, scorn gone and replaced with that hungry stare. "Where did you get it?"

"Found it," I said.

A lie, and she knew it. But not the biggest lie I had ever told her. Not even the biggest lie I would tell her today, and she knew *that*, too. But she also knew that if I had brought her a book, it meant I had a big problem. And so she took it, held it tightly to her chest, and asked me once more, with a weary sigh that had broken my heart the first time I had heard it.

"What do you want, Sal?"

And I smiled. And I leaned over the workbench. And I tried not to think about what an asshole I was.

And I told her.

EIGHT

LOWSTAFF

I haven't had a place to call my own in many years. There's a lot I miss from it—my own bed, a door I could close, baths—but what I miss most was having walls to decorate.

That might sound odd, I guess, but there's something satisfyingly...apparent about hanging yourself on a wall. Be it a trophy taken from war, a great beast, or just a really nice picture, what you put on your walls is your declaration to the world, the words you speak to whoever can hear you.

In Liette's case, those words were probably something like: *If it were possible to make love to books, I would.*

Downstairs, Liette's shop was neatly organized and pleasingly sparse. Upstairs, Liette's parlor was a madwoman's design.

Every wall was lined with shelves and every shelf was positively bursting with books. Some of them were crammed to the breaking point, some of them sagged in the middle from the weight of heavy tomes, some of them just gave the fuck up. Books grew in piles and columns across the carpeted floor, a forest of paper and leather that seemed to blossom out of the floor. Books, opened and pages marked, lay in a haphazard spread across the table in the middle of the room and upon the armrests of the sofa facing it.

There was probably some order to it—there always was, with

Freemakers—but I couldn't even begin to fathom it. Absently, I reached down to the nearest precarious tower of books and plucked off the top volume and flipped it open to a random word on a random page.

"What the fuck is a"—I squinted, trying to sound it out—"duo... duode..."

"Duodenum," a voice spoke from the next room. "It's the first part of the intestines in most creatures, immediately after the stomach. Prone to ulcers, it's where the principal digestive process begins." I could feel her smirk through the walls. "Are you reading *Agarne's Intermediate Anatomy*?"

"Why do you ask?"

"I know what arrests your attention," she replied. "And that one has naked people on the cover."

"Maybe I wanted to brush up on my..." I glanced at the cover. A man in the midst of dissection stared back at me. "Dead... guys." I cringed. "Are you going to be much longer in there?"

"You requested a drink."

"I thought you'd have finally gotten around to putting a liquor cabinet in here," I said. "It'd be nicer for guests anyway. You could make it fit if you took out one of these bookshelves."

A deathly silence rose from the other room.

"If I preferred people to books, I suppose I could," Liette replied, voice cold as a knife in the back.

The Freemakers assembled out of a desire to collect and share knowledge away from the prying eyes of factions who might use it for primitive means. As it was, they tended to value privacy and knowledge above most else.

Liette, as you might have guessed from a woman who keeps a killsaw in her basement, tended to value them above all else. She always preferred paper to people. People were noisome, demanding, judgmental. Books gave everything and asked nothing more than to be taken care of.

I found her priorities charming.

"But, as I am not completely fucking insane, I'll keep the shelves, thank you."

Others did not.

It probably would have been smarter to find another Freemaker. I knew a few—a few cheaper, a few less hostile, a few who might even be trusted not to betray me. But I wasn't going to find anyone better.

Not for what I needed.

But it would have been smarter. Wiser. Kinder. This wasn't the first time I had come to her, gift in my hand and smile on my lips. And it wouldn't be the last time I left her, tears in her eyes and empty words in my mouth. People like us, we weren't made for happy endings. Not with the sort of things we did.

It's not too late, I told myself.

I ran through it in my head: don't say another word, grab my belt, walk out the door, never look back. She wouldn't take offense. Hell, she'd be grateful that I spared her the trouble of throwing me out. She wouldn't curse my name; she wouldn't mind me leaving without a word; she wouldn't...

She wouldn't go looking for me.

Not again.

It would be smarter to go. It would be wiser to find someone else to help me. It would be kinder to pretend this never happened.

And if you've ever met someone who makes you ignore the wise thing, the smart thing, and the kind thing to do, you'd know why I came to her.

"Pardon the wait."

I turned. And I barely recognized the woman standing in the doorway.

It was Liette, of course. Same dark hair, same dark eyes, same pale skin, and same flat features. But the oil-stained clothes were replaced by an elegant, high-necked dress with skirt cut just above the tops of her black boots. The big glasses were gone, a pair of daintier spectacles resting on the bridge of her small nose. And the work gloves had been discarded, revealing the careful, delicate hands I tried hard not to look at.

She looked like a lady.

And I guess that sounds dumb when I say it, but fuck me, I sometimes forget she was one.

"I had to dig this one out of my dresser." She approached with a pair of glasses in her hand, passed me one. "I don't typically have cause to drink."

"Then you don't typically have cause to *live*," I replied, taking the glass. I took a sip. My cheeks bulged with the taste of sweet tang as I looked down at the dark liquid within. I swallowed. "What kind of whiskey is *this*?"

She stared at me, blinked. "It's wine."

"Wine." I paused, swirled my glass, sniffed. "So, do I just look like I've given up on life or was that an educated guess on your part?"

"It won't kill you to experience a little culture." She stared at me from over the edge of her glass as she sipped. "Given the swill you drink, I'd be astonished if anything could kill you."

"If everyone thought like you, my life would be easier."

"If everyone thought like *me*, the world would smell nicer, run better, and have significantly fewer morons in it." She reached out for the glass. "If you don't like it, though..."

I pulled it away, sipped it with greedy spite. It might be wine, but I'd not have it said that Sal the Cacophony ever refused a drink.

Liette rolled her eyes. "I take it, then," she said, "your appearance here is related to someone believing they can and should kill you. Daiga the Phantom, was it?"

I furrowed my brow. "How could you tell?"

"I hear things."

I didn't bother asking. I didn't have to. All I had to do was wait, take a long sip of wine, and...

"Specifically, the clerk at Cadre Command is under my employ via a system of blackmail and carefully orchestrated incentive-based guidance."

There it was.

"Of course, he suspected he could threaten *me* into coercion first," she continued. "I insisted on rectifying the error in his thought and suspected it would be a better use of both of our time if he did so through providing me with information on the Revolution's movements."

I hid my smile behind my wineglass. Some people, I supposed, would find this sort of boasting distasteful. Personally, I had a certain professional admiration for anyone possessed of the kind of planning that could make the unbreakable Revolution bend to her will.

Also, when she brags, her voice gets all high-pitched and excited and it's adorable.

"Well, shit," I said, "look at you and your fancy little spies."

"I could have used spies," she replied, her voice sliding back to its usual careful flatness. "Or I could have just listened to literally any-one talking about the woman with the tattoos and scars who came in carrying a giant gun."

And here I thought this was the kind of town that didn't gossip.

"When you brought the Dust, that sealed it." She folded her arms, swirled her glass as she looked me over. "You found something among Daiga's possessions that you can't drink, smoke, break, or sell, but not something you want to leave behind; hence you brought it to me."

You might think, to listen to her, that Liette is exceptionally clever. And that's true, but it's also true that she happens to know me particularly well and also that she's kind of an asshole. I wasn't going to hold any of that against her now, though.

I drained the rest of my wine, set the glass aside as I pulled my scarf away and reached for my belt. I tugged a folded scrap of paper free, held it up between two fingers.

"He was carrying a message," I said. "Coded. I can't read a word of it."

"That's usually the purpose of a code, yes," Liette replied in an I've-never-been-punched-in-the-face tone of voice. "If it were a Revolutionary or Imperial letter, I assume you'd be busy extorting them right now."

"Right, but since I'm hoping to extort *you*, it's Vagrant business," I replied. "If it were any normal code, I'd have gone to any normal thug. But it's magic." I extended the paper to her. "And I need a wright."

Her mouth pursed into a thin line, eyes widening at the word I had just uttered. Being a Freemaker had earned her the ire of every faction, but being a Spellwright marked her for death. The art was blasphemous to Haven, profane to the Revolution, and high treason to the Imperium. A Freemaker in town, one might simply ignore as a harmless eccentric. Someone who practiced wrighting was a criminal.

And yet...

She stared at the paper for a good long moment, unable to take her eyes away from it. Anyone else would have seen it as just cause for throwing me out. But she didn't. She couldn't. She had sworn an oath to collect all the knowledge in the world she could.

And I always knew she couldn't resist a challenge.

She took the paper, held it between her hands, and eyed it with hungry intent. Her hands shook; then the rest of her followed as she let out a sigh that pulled her stare down.

"Sal..."

She spoke my name. Not cursed it, not screamed it, just... said it. And I almost didn't hear what she said next.

"I...I don't know."

I would have asked why. I would have begged or pleaded or tried to trick her. I'm pretty good at some of those things.

"We know how this starts," she whispered, looking away from me. "And I know how it ends. It's never just Vagrant business or any kind of business, favor or not. I just don't..." She shook her head. "I'm sorry."

But I couldn't trick someone as smart as her. I couldn't beg or plead with someone who would give me what I wanted if I did. And I couldn't have asked why. Because she just might have told me the answer.

And so I just nodded. And I slid the paper back into my belt and adjusted my scarf around my neck. And I looked toward the stairs and thought about how many steps I would have to force myself to walk without looking back before I could pretend I hadn't ever thought this would have been a good idea.

And that's when she grabbed my wrist.

I looked back, but she wasn't looking at me. Not at my face, anyway. Her eyes went lower, past my shirt and vest and down to my midsection. And they went wide.

"What the hell happened?" she demanded.

"With what?" I glanced down toward the expanse of bare and scarred skin. "My shirt? I guess it's a little tacky, but it's fucking hot out there."

"Not that, you dumbshit."

She pulled my scarf away, exposing my side and the purple-black bruise blossoming across it like a dead flower. She thrust an accusing finger at it.

"That."

"Oh. That."

I meant to say something more clever, but the truth is I hadn't even noticed. Luckwritten material can keep an arrow—even one shot from a thunderbow—from going through your lungs, but it still hurts like hell when it hits you. It's not the first time I've been bruised by a blow that would have otherwise killed me. Hell, I walk out of the Scar with worse than that almost every day.

Which was why I thought it slightly odd when Liette looked up at me with absolute fury in her eyes.

"If that shot had hit you, you'd be dead," she growled in a voice patently unused to growling.

"Most shots do that, yeah. But it was only an arrow. The scarf's magic held out and—"

"I didn't fucking give that scarf to you so you could go treating it like a fucking suit of armor, you shit." She thrust a hand toward me. "Hand it over."

My eyebrows shot up. There were only two things I could ever do to make Liette curse and one of them was mistreating her work. All the same, I slipped it off and handed it over.

She held it up, looked it over with a gaze that was less scrutinizing and more obsessed. She flipped it over in her hands, searching every thread for weakness.

"It's perfect," she muttered. "Nothing out of place, no holes, no rips. It shouldn't leave a mark like that."

"I mean, it kept me from dying. That's something."

"It's supposed to keep you from getting *hurt*, dumbass." She whirled on me with a snarl that turned to a wince as she looked down at my midriff and beheld the full extent of the bruise. "Fuck me, that's bad."

"It's fine," I said.

"Who's the fucking doctor here?"

I blinked. "Neither of us?"

"Well, if I was a little dumber, I would be one, so hold the fuck still."

True, I sometimes forgot she was a lady. But in fairness, she rarely bothered to remind anyone. But she was also a Freemaker—any perceived flaw with one of her creations was an insult deeper than the human language had words for. How I'd forgotten that, I'll never know. But she was quick to remind me as she knelt down before me and placed her hands on my skin.

I bit back the shudder that ran through me. I've been shot, stabbed, strangled, and one time, beaten with a fish. I wouldn't let it be said that Sal the Cacophony trembled when a girl touched her.

"Look at this fucking mess," she muttered, delicately running hands around my bruise, inspecting it. In another moment, though, I didn't tremble at all. My body remembered these hands, these delicate fingers sliding across my skin. And for the first time in a long time, I felt my muscles relax, felt the tension slide off me like a weight.

I felt safe.

"How do you manage to do that, Sal?" Her voice trailed softer as her hand trailed lower. She found a scar at my hip, a great gash that had healed badly, traced its edge with careful fingers. "How the hell..."

She looked up at me. I looked down at her.

And what I saw was empty of anger or spite or all the things she had been pretending not to feel. What I saw was the girl with the coy smile she never showed anyone else and the big eyes that no one ever had the nerve to look into.

And she was looking at me.

And smiling softer than anyone I'd ever seen.

"How does someone as clever as you manage to hurt yourself this much?"

I didn't have an answer for that. I didn't have any words for her then. I'm sure they were there somewhere, hidden away in some rehearsed place I had planned to bring them out of when I met her, but I just... couldn't remember them. I couldn't remember how to do much of anything except slide my hands down to meet hers.

I took her fingers in mine, pulled her gently to her feet. Her eyes met mine, staring up at me just as much as she needed to as one of her hands slipped away, slid down my side, and found the scars painted there. They didn't hurt, not when she touched them. Not even when her other hand slid up to my cheek, traced fingers across the jagged line crossing my eye and...

If you're lucky, you meet a lot of people you like enough to touch them. If you're really lucky, you meet a few who you like enough to let them touch you back. But if you're very lucky, you meet that one person who touches you in a way that makes you feel like you're standing up a little straighter, like you're breathing a little clearer, like you were walking hunched over your whole life and you didn't even know it.

And if you're smart, you'll hold on to that for as long as you can.

But if you're me, you know that's not very long at all.

Just like I knew it had been a mistake when she drew away from me and smiled. Just like I knew that I'd do it again, just like I always would, for as long as I could. Just like I knew I was going to regret this.

She buried that smile in my shoulder, pulled close to me, whispered in my ear.

"You smell terrible."

NINE

LOWSTAFF

Now, it's true that the Freemakers have invented the world's deadliest weapons of destruction that have, in turn, been directly responsible for the *millions* of gallons of blood that have watered this cold land and the carpet of corpses it wears like a cloak.

But it's also true that one of them invented the shower, so it kind of evens out, right?

Don't get me wrong, killing is bad and all. But fuck, there's just something about the shiver of nerves as the bronze pipes rattle and the first drops come out to wash off all the dust and the blood and the grime that I've worn like a second and then a third skin.

Once I get the water on my scars and my fingers in my hair, I stop feeling like a Vagrant for just a few minutes and I get to feel like a person again.

But nothing good lasts, does it? Whiskey runs out. Blood runs dry. Lovers fall asleep before you do. And, sure as birds eat rabbits, water turns cold.

I've walked through rainstorms and sleet and not felt a thing, but fuck me if the first cold drops after the hot water's run out don't send me leaping. I damn near broke my neck as I fumbled around for the bronze chain that turns the thing off. The pipes stopped rattling. The hiss of steam fell silent.

Liette didn't have to let me use her facilities—though I suspect she would rather have me do that than hang around whatever smells I had picked up. The tiny, tiled room had a bronze spigot and a bronze chain up top, separated by a wooden wall on one side and a vanity and toilet on the other. There were freehold barons with money to burn who didn't have rooms like this in their homes. While the invention of toilets had been shared—mostly out of concern for public hygiene—the Freemakers still hoarded the showers for themselves.

And their friends, of course.

My feet slapped across the wet tile as I went to the vanity. I looked myself over long enough to press my hair into place with my palms and make sure I wasn't bleeding from anywhere I hadn't noticed. But I didn't see any blood in my reflection. I didn't see anything except long stretches of skin, the tattoos of birds and clouds and thunder racing up my arms and shoulders.

And my scars.

I tried not to look at them, but it didn't matter. Even without looking, I could feel them: knotted flesh mapping my sides, clawing their way down my legs, and the biggest one slithering from my collarbone down to my belly. No matter how I tried to hide them beneath my tattoos, they were always there. They were like living things; sometimes they felt like they were crawling across my body.

I watched my body in the mirror, the scars moving with each breath. They were harder to look at when I was clean. Under a layer of dirt and blood, they felt like just more grime from the road. Clean as they were now, they felt new, freshly carved.

My eyes settled on one crawling across my side. And if I stared at it long enough, I could almost see the blade bursting through my body again.

My hand shot out without me realizing it, sending the vanity spinning as I stalked away from it and back to my pile of clothes.

I was almost reluctant to put them back on, my shirt and trousers and vest still reeking of grime. But as nice as this was, I had a lot to do that day.

And as soon as I knew exactly *what* it was I needed to do, I intended to get right to it.

I eased the bath door open. Far and away from either the organized carnage of her workshop or the haphazard knowledge of her parlor, Liette's bedroom was a quiet, modest affair. Just a reclining sofa, a few treasured pieces of art hanging on the wall, a few nice clothes in a nice dresser, and a large, silk-sheeted bed that I tried to avoid looking at.

Even here, though, there were books.

I did my time in Cathama, so I'm literate, of course. But like most sane people, I only read sane things: operas, gazettes, trashy action novels, and so forth. Liette, though, saved her best books for her bedroom. The thickest, most polished ones lay neatly organized on tables, on sofas, and on the dresser was one particularly hefty one bound in black leather.

The Emperor's Last Whisper, I recognized.

Because I had given it to her.

Just one more thing to avoid looking at, I supposed. Seemed her home was full of them.

I fell silent as I approached the parlor, stopping in the doorway as I saw her standing there. In the middle of the chaos of pages and leather, she stood, unaware of me watching. Unaware of what she was looking at.

In her hands, she held my scarf, staring at its threads. She raised it hesitantly, like it was made of harsh edges instead of cotton. Slowly, she wrapped it around her shoulders, drew in a deep breath, and smiled.

I remembered the first time she did that. I remember she had asked me what kind of woman I was that I would need such protection. I remember I told her I was an honest woman who ran into a bit of trouble now and again.

The very first lie I told her.

Not the last.

And, if there was going to be any solace about what happened next today, I told myself that at least it wouldn't be the worst lie I had ever told her.

I eased the door shut, then cleared my throat loudly, gave her plenty of time to know I was coming. And when I opened the door again and strode into her parlor, my scarf was draped over the chair across from her and her eyes were on a book laid out upon the table.

And next to it, a simple scrap of paper I had plucked out of a dead man's belongings.

"It's too much to hope that you didn't use all my hot water, I take it?" Liette asked without looking up.

"There's a lot of ways I could disappoint you," I said as I plucked up my scarf and took a seat. "And since I'm not dragging dead men to your door or using your house for a shootout, I'd say using your hot water is doing pretty good."

"Mmm." She regarded me over the rim of her spectacles. "You always were considerate like that."

"Well, I'm pretty, too, but let's not get distracted." I leaned forward, glancing at the paper on the table. "Have you figured it out?"

Her answer was a thoughtful hum. Daiga's missive, the one signed by Jindu, sprawled out as a list of indecipherable gibberish surrounded by a small circle of inkwells, pouches, and quills. One of Liette's dainty fingers traveled down it, sigil by sigil, tapping at the end of it.

"It's by a Freemaker. Another wright," she said. "The sigils belong to A Frustrated Author Burns His House at Midnight."

I raised my brows, impressed. "That's a long name. He must be pretty important."

"I can't tell if you're sarcastic or ignorant."

"Me neither." I gestured to the inkwells. "Those are his, too, then?"

"No," Liette replied. "These were a gift."

I stiffened up in the chair without realizing it. "From *who*?"

She glanced at me. That ghost of a smile tugged at her lips. "Not important," she said, knowing damn well it *was*. "You were right, though. It's not a code. It's magic, only readable by those it's meant for." She plucked out a handful of dust from one of her pouches, scattered it over the letters. "Or by those smarter than the wright who made it."

One by one, the letters winked to life, alight with a dim glow. The paper twitched, as if alive, as a faint humming noise drifted out of it. She tapped one sigil with a finger and it let out a single, dulcet tone that sang out a word.

"Come..."

"Singing script," I muttered. "I thought that was a lost art."

"It is," Liette replied. "To everyone outside the Imperium, that is. And me, of course. And whoever wrote this. And possibly one or two other spellwrights I don't know about but, beyond that, it is absolutely a lost art."

She rapped her fingers across the other sigils. In a melodic song, they rang out a quiet tune.

"Come to us. We will be at Stark's Mutter, Sixth Harvest. You were spurned from the Imperium, hunted by the dogs of the false Emperor. We grant you the opportunity to take it all back. Your art. Your life. Your Imperium. Come to us. We shall be waiting."

"Curious," Liette hummed. "Stark's Mutter is only ten miles from here. And Sixth Harvest was two days ago. I hadn't heard of anything coming out of there, but..."

Her voice drifted off as she realized I wasn't listening. My eyes were locked on the paper. My ears were full of the letter's voice. A voice I hadn't thought I'd hear ever again.

Until I put a blade through the mouth that spoke it.

Two days ago. I had missed him by just two days. If I had been a little faster in tracking down Daiga, if I had broken a few more skulls, burned a few more houses. Fuck what they'd say about me.

But I had missed the date. And there was no changing that. I tried telling myself that, tried to remain calm. It didn't work.

"Does it say for what?" I asked.

"No," she said. "Just the date, the location, and the—"

She didn't fall silent. Normal people fall silent; they go quiet when they're scared of what they'll say next. Liette's not a normal person.

When she goes silent, she puts both boots down and doesn't fucking move.

"And what?"

Unless someone moves her.

"And what, Liette?"

"Sal..." Her voice was soft as petals falling from a dead flower. "Why did you come to me?"

"To find out what was in the letter and—"

"No, why did you come to *me*?"

I paused, stared at her. "Because you're the best."

"I am not just the best." She stared at her dainty little hands on the table. "I am brilliant. Brilliant enough to know that nothing else in this letter will make you happy. Let me tell you to take your gun and your bullets and send you on your way. Go on shooting, killing, drinking, gambling. Come back when you're out of money, out of whiskey, out of luck, whatever. I'll give you more bullets and we can go on pretending that's all we do to each other."

She had a way with words, Liette. You'd expect as much from a woman with a name as long as hers. And she was as smart as you'd expect from a woman with as many books as she had. And I knew that, if I were even half as smart as she was, I'd have taken her advice, taken my bullets, and gone on my merry way.

But I was a practical woman.

Practical women make practical decisions.

And mine was to sit there and stare at her, in the way I always did when I wanted something. Soldiers, outlaws, and Vagrants have looked into my eyes and pissed themselves, pulled out guns or known they were going to die. But when Liette looked into my eyes, the eyes I showed her like I showed her all that time ago, I knew what she saw.

Because I had only ever shown it to two people.

And I was ready to kill one of them.

"What's in the letter?" I asked.

She met my eyes. "Names."

I nodded slowly. I reached into my vest, into the hidden pocket. And there, right next to my heart, I found an ancient scrap of paper folded into a tight square. Delicately, so as not to shred the old and frayed edges, I unfolded it and laid it out on my lap.

"Tell me," I said.

"Sal, please—"

"Tell me."

In the silence before she spoke, I could feel something between us break. Something tender and fragile that I'd never taken very good care of.

But she held the letter up. She ran a finger across the sigils. And his voice sang out.

"Galta the Thorn."

I looked at the paper in my lap. And there was her name.

"Riccu the Knock."

His, too, two names beneath the first one.

"Zanze the Beast."

Him.

"Taltho the Scourge."

And him.

"Kresh the Tempest."

And him.

"Vraki the Gate."

And him.

She paused, spoke the last name like all curses should be spoken.

Slowly, with great hesitation and the knowledge that someone would die.

"Jindu the Blade."

And there. Right at the very top. In red ink. The very first one I had thought of when I started this list.

Seven names. Seven out of thirty-three. It might have seemed small, maybe. But there was another name on my list that had taken a lot of bullets, a lot of blood, and a lot of bodies so that I could finally cross it out. I would have killed for one name.

For seven?

I'd burn the world to cinders.

I folded the paper back up, replaced it in my vest. I went to the coat rack by her door. I strapped my belts around my waist, strapped my holster to my thigh. The Cacophony all but leapt into my hands. I could feel him warm in my palm.

He had heard every name, too.

"Sal," Liette called after me. "Wait."

I didn't say anything as I pulled my scarf around me and slung my satchel over my shoulder. I couldn't afford to listen. We had done this dance so many times our feet bled whenever the music came on. I said not a word as I stalked away.

"Wait!"

But she did.

"Sal," she said, rising from her chair. "I can't let you go."

"Would you *kindly* spare me?" I sneered over my shoulder. "Is this the part where you make some heartfelt plea about the emptiness of vengeance? Or is it some speech about the cycle of violence? Either way, if you've got any respect for me, spare me this cheap, back-alley opera shit and—"

"I can't let you go," Liette interrupted, clearly and forcefully, "because you're bleeding all over my floor."

My feet shifted. The rug made a grotesque squishing noise beneath me. I looked down and saw the dark puddle at my feet, a perfect match for the wound dribbling blood down my side.

It hurt, don't get me wrong.

But she was never going to shut up about this.

TEN

HIGHTOWER

In her illustrious career in service to the Revolution, Tretta Stern had kept meticulous record of how many executions she had been a part of.

As a field corporal, she had personally gunned down six soldiers for cowardice, two for theft, and one for rape. When she had been promoted to lieutenant, she had recommended execution for twenty-three for desertion, eleven for counterrevolutionary thought, and six for collusion with Imperial forces. And once she had achieved the lofty station of Governor-Militant, she had personally looked into the eyes and ordered the guns that killed every man and woman she had ever had executed in the city walls.

Execution was a grim order, but this was a grim war in a grim land, and she would not be the one to fail the Revolution by shirking her duties. After so many bodies, it was rare she ever faltered when the time came to hand down the orders to the firing squad.

But this?

This was the first time she had ever had so many reasons to execute a person and found herself at a loss to decide which one was most pertinent.

Sal the Cacophony, across the table, took a long sip of water. She looked up over the rim of her cup to Tretta's baffled expression and quirked a white eyebrow.

"What?" she asked.

"Those names..." Tretta whispered.

"Which one? Liette's?" She smiled, wistful. "It's beautiful, isn't it?"

"No, you fool!" Tretta slammed her hands down on the table, its width and weight all that kept her from leaping across and throttling the woman. "Galta the Thorn! Riccu the Knock! Zanze the Beast!"

"And Taltho and Kresh and Vraki." Sal yawned as she poured herself another glass from the pitcher. "I know, they're all kind of pretentious, aren't they? See, the thing about the Cacophony is that it's long and interesting, but it doesn't necessarily imply malice, so it doesn't sound like I'm trying too hard to be intimidating and—"

"We know those names," Tretta said icily. "The first time I ever saw them was three years ago, in big red print at the top of a debriefing carried by a messenger who rode all night to reach me. And since then, I've seen them plastered on every propaganda poster and newspaper in Weiless."

"Really?" Sal smirked. "They'd be delighted to know they were that famous."

She reached for her cup. Tretta's fists came down on the table again, sending it tumbling to the floor. Sal watched it shatter with a wince.

"Well, that was rude." She began to look up. "What am I going to drink—"

She was cut off as a pair of gloved hands seized her by her collar. Tretta hauled her from her chair, held her up by her shirt, thrust her scowling, snarling face into Sal's.

"I was content to think of you as just one more thug," she growled. "One more Vagrant wandering the desert that happened to stumble into circumstances larger than herself. I was content to let your confession be easy and your death painless. But that was before you spoke those names."

Sal, for her part, did not flinch at Tretta's hands around her collar, nor at her hot breath blasting her in the face with each word. She simply stared back, flatly.

"Does that mean we aren't going to be friends?" she asked.

Tretta hurled her back in the chair, its legs groaning as it slid along the floor and struck the wall with a cracking sound. Sal's head struck the stone but barely made a noise. She brought her manacled hands up to the back of her skull, drew away fingers with a smear of blood on them. She betrayed not a hint of pain nor fear as she looked at Tretta, who stared at her down the length of a finger thrust in Sal's face.

"Until you uttered those names, you were going to receive a clean death. But I can guarantee you that I will ship an interrogator here all the way from the Great General's office to beat every last *syllable* out of your mouth if you don't tell me what you know about them." She twisted her finger up, holding it in front of Sal's face. "One chance," she said. "Do not test me."

Like any Revolutionary guardswoman, Tretta Stern had a career that was measured in blood, not length. She had stared into the eyes of Imperial swine, Vagrant scum, and counterrevolutionary deserters alike and had seen all the hatred, malice, and fear that a dying man spat into the world before he bled his last on the dust. But in the dim light of that cell, in the cold blue of her prisoner's eyes, Tretta found something she had never before encountered for the second time that day.

Sal stared back at her, into the face of the woman who could have her tortured, dismembered, or fed to dogs, and showed absolutely nothing but an empty expression and a tired sigh.

"Fine," she said. She leaned back in her chair. "I take it if you know those names, you know the Crown Conspiracy."

Tretta grunted an acknowledgment.

Nul spies in the capital had been reporting back to Weiless a steady stream of growing discontentment among the mages of the Empire. Once it was revealed the young, yet-to-be-crowned Emperor

Althoun possessed no magical talent whatsoever, the mages had rebelled.

It was proof, the Revolutionary philosophers had said, of the Imperium's sheer arrogance. To them, nuls were barely worthy of humanity, let alone leadership. Faced with ten thousand years of loyalty to the empire they had built against ten thousand years of lording over their lessers, the mages made their choice.

And they chose war.

Some went loudly, rioting and turning on their former comrades. Others disappeared quietly into the Scar to become Vagrants and make their own fortunes.

But a few of them were not content with either of those.

The specifics of the conspiracy were hazy. The plot they had conspired to overthrow the Imperial family and install a proper mage upon the throne either had never been fully unearthed or fully leaked from the palace. All that was known was that thirty-four of the Empress's brightest, closest, and most talented mages had launched a quiet revolt to kill her, her son, and her court and had failed to do so.

Even though the court had failed to capture them after their botched operation, the loss of such talent did not go unnoticed by the Revolutionary leaders in Weiless. The Revolution had made significant gains—some of them led by Tretta herself—in the confusing aftermath.

Those had been good times.

Until, of course, those thirty-four had resurfaced in the Scar and Weiless found itself dealing with some of the most powerful Vagrants they had ever known.

"I'll skip the overview," Sal said. "An educated woman like you no doubt knows what happened with the Conspiracy itself." A grin scarred itself across her face. "And an educated woman like *me* knows your Glorious General has been hunting for the conspirators ever since they escaped into the Scar."

"The Revolution is dedicated to bringing all Imperial swine to justice," Tretta growled in reply. "The Crown Conspirators, the Vagrants…" She spat the next word. "The hated criminal, Red Cloud…"

"Red Cloud?" Sal grinned. "Well, shit, if I could give you her, we wouldn't be having this conversation, would we? It'd be hard to do that with you kissing me out of gratitude and all."

Tretta narrowed her eyes upon that haughty scar. Perhaps she should have hit the woman harder.

"What'd you say your surname was?" Sal said. "Stern?"

Tretta blinked, surprised. "I don't recall telling you, but yes. It is Stern."

"Stern, Stern…" Sal's manacles clinked as she tapped her chin thoughtfully. "Above a Proud but beneath a Courageous and *well* beneath a Merciful. Your family must have arrived late to the Revolution, no?" She smirked. "That's why the General gave your father the name of Stern."

"You're familiar with Revolutionary history," Tretta observed.

"The Revolution is still young, at least compared to the Imperium. There's not much to know. But I do know that your General has offered a number of rewards for anyone who can bring him information on the conspirators." She clicked her tongue. "What'd he offer you, Governor-Militant Stern? A new post? A new rank?" She quirked a brow. "Or a new name?"

The emptiness was gone from Sal's eyes. And Tretta decided she liked the predatory slyness that replaced it much less.

"A promotion is nice, sure, but it ends after you die, doesn't it? But a new name?" Sal grinned, crossed her arms, leaned back. "Well, that's a new rank for your entire family, isn't it? Governor-Militant Stern is high up, but Governor-Militant Merciful or Ferocious would be through the fucking clouds, wouldn't she? More rations for your spouse, better doctors for your ailing father, nicer schools for your son."

"I don't have any children," Tretta said.

"Whatever, I—"

"And my father is in excellent health."

"All right, don't go overthinking it," Sal said. "Point being, your General would bump you up to a Courageous, minimum, to know that even one of them was dead for sure. And, honey, you've got a girl who can tell you what happened to seven of them."

"You're saying seven of them are dead."

"I didn't say that."

"Then they're alive?"

"Didn't say that, either."

"I don't have time for your word games," Tretta growled.

Sal's laughter was an expensive wineglass shattering on a cold stone floor. "Fine, fine. But I'll tell you this for certain. Kill me now, you'll never know what happened to them. Or Lowstaff. Or Cavric."

"There will be someone who does." Tretta tried to smirk, though, so unused to the gesture, it looked more like an uncomfortable sneer. "You just admitted to consorting with the wanted criminal Twenty-Two Dead Roses in a Chipped Porcelain Vase, as well as gave us her location. We can find her."

"You can *look* for her, certainly. But a woman who thinks two sentences constitutes a word game isn't going to find her. Whatever you find in that smoldering crater that was her workshop in Lowstaff, too, you're welcome to. You're more likely to kill yourself than find any trace of her whereabouts."

"Then we'll search for her by her true name. Liette."

"You won't find *her*, either."

Tretta growled. "And why not?"

Sal's grin softened into something distant and tired. She looked down at her hands and whispered, "Because that was a name," she said, "she gave only to me."

"I should have you killed just on principle," Tretta snapped. "No creature as irritating as you should be alive."

"Fine by me. But I don't think your Great General will react well once he learns you had a chance to find out what happened to seven conspirators and ruined it by killing me."

"Don't pretend to know how we operate," Tretta said, sneering. "And *don't* pretend to think the General would ever spare a thought for one more dead Vagrant."

"Well, I'd never presume to grasp the intricacies of your gloriously reverent Revolution or whatever the fuck adjectives you use for it. But whatever I don't know, I hear. And I've heard that in the last year alone, your benevolent General has carried out three different purges of his ranks." Sal offered a lazy grin. "A man paranoid enough to kill his best friend three times over is paranoid enough to find out anything, eventually. Or did you honestly think that your soldiers report to you and you alone?"

And for the final time that day, something else had happened to Tretta that had never happened before.

Her blood ran cold.

Something dark and doubtful wriggled its way into the back of her skull, snaked down her spine, and coiled around her ribs. She shook it off, told herself it was just a Vagrant trick—they all knew magic and none knew morals. This, too, was just some moment of buffoonery. And she moved forward to tell Sal just that.

With the back of her hand.

But at that moment, the door creaked. She looked over her shoulder, saw the narrow gap of light where the door was opened. And the dark eye peering out from between it.

"Clerk Inspire," she said, spitting the name. "How long have you been there?"

"I didn't mean to interrupt, madam." The cell door groaned open as the clerk shuffled in, hands folded in a show of obeisance. "You seemed absorbed with your task and I was loath to interrupt and—"

"And you interrupted all the same." Tretta rubbed her eyes. "Speak, then, and stop wasting my time."

"Oh, that's just it, madam. There's no time left to waste." He glanced up toward the window, where the orange light of the setting sun seeped through. "It's time, madam. The firing squad is ready. The crowds have gathered." Beneath his mustache, an ugly smile bloomed. "The execution is at hand."

"The execution happens when I say it does," Tretta replied.

"It does, madam, of course, but..." He cast a nervous glance toward Sal, who stared impassively back. "But you *did* say that it would take place at this time. We let the populace know and they are ready for a firing. It would be a"—he paused to lick his mustache—"*shame* to let them down."

The emphasis did not go unnoticed by Tretta, nor the implication unheeded. It would not so much be a shame as it would be an issue of citywide importance. Scarfolk beneath Revolutionary protection should expect two things: orderly promptness and severe punishment for those who disrupt it. To push the execution back would do both, emboldening those few counterrevolutionaries she had not yet stamped out.

Besides, she reasoned, this was a Vagrant. The differences between them only went as deep as whatever garish, stupid costumes they chose to wear. At their hearts, every one of them was an Imperial; thus, every one of them was a filthy, arrogant liar. This one, whatever else she might claim to be, was no different.

Better to kill her now.

And yet that dark, wriggling doubt continued to worm its way through her belly. And that promise of a new name, of a new life for her and her family, continued to shine brightly on some distant horizon. But beyond any of that, it was one crystalline, clear image that filled her mind.

Her signature on the bottom of the letter she would have to send to the Proud family to inform them that she had failed to bring their son Cavric home.

She sighed, glanced at Inspire.

"Tell the squad to remain at the ready," she said. "The execution is delayed by two hours."

"Two hours?" The clerk's eyes went wide. "But everyone will be at dinner by then! The crowds, they—"

"They will go eat if they want. They will stay if they want. They will cause trouble if they want and then they will join the prisoner on the execution line." She pointed a finger at Inspire. "Make *that* much clear. Inform the Staff Sergeant to double the guards."

"But...but..."

"Another word, Inspire, and it'll be insubordination. The Revolution tells this city when to move, not the clock." She gestured to the cell door. "Go."

Inspire spared a worried glance at Sal before scurrying back to the door. He paused, glancing over his shoulder.

"Forgive me, madam, but...about the weapon..."

"If I have to tell the Staff Sergeant myself, Inspire, I'll be telling him to find a cell for you as well."

The door clanged shut. The air held still. Tretta walked back to her chair, pulled it to the table, and sat, hands lying flat upon the wood. She stared evenly at Sal across the length.

"Whatever else you tell me," she said, "I cannot guarantee your life."

"I'm aware of that."

"It is a matter of duty. Those who violate the laws of the Revolution must pay."

"Uh-huh."

"For the glory and safety of our continuous march, we must—"

"Shit, woman, delaying my execution will be pointless if you make me strangle myself to avoid hearing this." She scooted her chair back to the table. "I knew I was going to die the moment they brought me here. Life isn't what concerns me anymore. I've done what I was put here to do."

"Then what—"

"My story," she said. "What I tell you, you write down. Down to the fucking letter, you write it. You tell it. You remember it. You let it be known what Sal the Cacophony did before she went cackling to hell and left this dark earth to all you dumb motherfuckers."

Tretta narrowed her eyes. "Why?"

Sal smiled. "*Ocumani oth rethar.*"

"Of course," she said, rolling her eyes. "More Imperial garbage. Try to keep that to a minimum, would you?"

"You're going to like this next part, then," Sal said. "It involves everyone *but* Imperials…"

ELEVEN

LOWSTAFF

There's a line from one of my favorite operas that goes something like this.

"A thousand people may you find like a thousand flowers, a thousand scents upon the wind—here, savored, and gone."

I really liked that line. Or I did before I came to the Scar, anyway. Since then, I've come to believe it gives people a little too much credit. In my experience, they're not really like flowers, so much as they are like wounds, hundreds of little cuts you collect over the years.

Some of them you barely notice, healing up and leaving nary a mark behind. Some of them you feel deep and stitch up bad and you carry the scar of them for the rest of your days. And then some of them...

"OW!"

...you keep picking at.

"Would you fucking be careful?"

No matter how much you know you shouldn't.

Liette looked up from her seat beside the bed, a decided lack of amusement playing across her face as she did. She held up a quill and daubed it in a glowing inkwell. She then proceeded to hold my arm down as she scrawled a faint script around my wound, pointedly ignoring my wince.

"Hold still," she muttered, scribbling. "You've been riding with this thing all day. It's a wonder it hasn't gotten infected yet."

"Yeah, a fucking miracle," I replied, wincing again.

"Oh, don't be such a baby," she said. "I've seen you take worse hits than this."

She glared up at me over her glasses, strands of hair falling down a sweat-plastered brow and making her look like some kind of especially annoyed animal in an especially nice-smelling thicket. She'd been at this for the better part of four hours—the first two spent pushing me into bed. But if she hadn't aggravated my wound in doing so, I'd already be on the road to Stark's Mutter.

The thunderbow had hit me harder than I thought. The scarf had kept it from punching through my insides, but it had hit hard enough to give me the makings of a wound. Then with the ride here, the breaking in, the traps, the shower, everything... it just decided now was the perfect time to show up and start bleeding everywhere.

She was right, of course. I had taken worse hits. Some of them on her behalf. I didn't mind the pain. Not nearly as much as the delay.

Galta the Thorn. Kresh the Tempest. Riccu the Knock.

I could hear their names, over and over, in my head. Weighty words, carved out of iron and sharpened on a crude whetstone and stabbed directly into my back.

Taltho the Scourge. Zanze the Beast.

I could see faces whenever I blinked. Leering grins and laughter from a place without air or light that disappeared as soon as I opened my eyes.

Vraki the Gate.

I could hear his voice.

Jindu the Blade.

Whispering to me from that dark place.

"I'm sorry."

And I felt a pain harsher than any wound could give.

He was out there. They all were. Every name on my list. And now that I had the worst of them cornered in some shitty little piece of the Scar, I was doing something other than chasing them down and putting the Cacophony through their teeth. I was lying here, like some mewling kitten, while some arrogant, know-it-all, piece of—

"*FUCK!*" I shrieked as a stinging sensation shot up my side.

"It's worse than it looks," Liette replied. "But you'll be all right."

"I'm not in pain. I'm just pissed."

"Because it hurts."

"Because you had whiskey all this time and didn't tell me."

She clicked her tongue as her quill continued to dart across my side, painting precise sigils around my wound, chiding me to keep still. Spellwrighting is an art, and like any art, it has its pupils and its masters. The art of convincing a sword it can explode into flame is trivial. The art of wrighting flesh so that a wound can be persuaded to heal faster demanded precision.

Precision that was not helped by the canvas—that is, me—twitching, screaming, or otherwise cursing. I could hardly help it, though—the sensation of my flesh closing itself wasn't the worst agony I'd felt even in these last few days, but it still fucking hurt.

"You drink too much anyway," she muttered.

"I disagree. If I'd had whiskey instead of wine, I wouldn't have this urge to slap you right now."

"*And* you fight too much," she replied, a note of ire creeping into her voice.

"Again, I refer you back to your previously mentioned unslapped face as evidence of—"

"*And you fucking complain too much,*" she snapped at me suddenly, throwing down the quill and reaching out to seize me by the neck and force me to look down at my side. "Or do you not fucking see the wound?"

I did. A large gash had opened up around the bruise where the arrow had struck. Ringed as it was by her sigils, I could see how nasty it was.

"You always do this." Her voice came out as an angry hiss as she shoved me away. "You *always* go off with a sword and that...that fucking *weapon* and you think you're invincible and then you get bloodied and beaten and you come back to me and expect me to act like just because you don't give a shit what happens to you, neither should I and..."

Her hands hung in the air in front of her, fingers extended and shaking as though she could just tear an answer out of thin air with them. Or like she could strangle me until she felt better. But, failing both of those, she curled them into fists and dropped them in her lap. She looked down at them, those hands that could make a piece of silk as strong as steel, and seemed to wonder why they couldn't do what she wanted them to.

"Why can't I make you stop?" she whispered.

To me. To herself. It didn't matter.

I still felt her words. Not like iron jammed in my back. But like glass, cutting something soft and important inside me.

I reached for her hand. And when she pulled away, I fully knew why.

"Do you remember the last time we saw each other?" she asked.

I let my hand drop. It fell on the sheets, leaden and limp. I remembered. I had heard a name muttered in a tavern when I went to buy a bottle of wine for her—I wanted something harder, but I wanted to do something nice for her. I had gotten it; we had shared it; I hadn't said a word all night. The next day, I had stepped out just to go ask after that name.

Four months later, I had found Daiga.

And I had killed him.

And here I was.

"When you walked out my door, I swore it would be the last time I saw you," she said, painfully soft. "Not because I didn't want to see you again, but because I knew this might be the time you don't come back and one day I'll hear a tale about how Sal the Cacophony was rotting in a hole in the ground somewhere in the Scar I'd never find."

"I came back."

I wanted to sound plaintive. But even the words tasted sour on my tongue, insincere.

"You did," she said. "And I knew you would because you always do. It's always something that brings you here and something that makes you stay and I keep thinking that this time you'll be here forever, but..." She closed her eyes. "I told myself this time I wouldn't let you in. But you went and broke my fucking window, didn't you?"

I don't know why I reached out for her. Maybe I thought I'd make it better, like I could find the words I needed to say if I could just touch her, just hold her hand. But when I found her fingers in mine, I didn't find any words.

I just found her hand. The hand that found me in the night when I couldn't sleep. The hand that pulled me up over a ledge as a lot of people with a lot of swords chased after me. The hand that I let touch my scars, let linger on them, let make me feel like they weren't part of a broken woman...

The hand that would be patching up my wounds instead of making things if I kept doing this.

This time, it was me who pulled away. I pushed myself up, my side screaming as I did. She lodged some kind of protest that I tried not to listen to as I headed for the door. She was right. It was me who kept coming back, me who kept bringing blood to her door. The right thing to do was leave. What curses she hurled at me, that was the price to pay. I could ignore words.

Her standing in the doorway, though, I couldn't.

"What the fuck do you think you're doing?" she demanded, throwing her arms out as if either of them could stop me.

"Going," I replied. I sighed. "You're right, I need to—"

"You need to stop and *think* for once," she snapped, neatly severing my words at the neck. "What in the fuck did I say that you interpreted as 'let me just run out the door with a massive wound and go get another to go with it?'"

"But you just said I—"

"You didn't hear anything I said because you don't *listen* to me," she growled. "You never fucking do. You always assume you know what the answer is and leave before I can even finish a sentence. So let me be perfectly clear when I tell you this."

Her eyes turned deadly serious behind her glasses. Fuck me, had they always been that big?

"I know the names on that list," she said. "I know what they've done. I know what'll happen to you if you go after them."

Liette was a Freemaker, a seeker of truth. She didn't know how to lie. She didn't know what would happen. Because if she did, she would know why I couldn't stay.

"Birdshit," I hissed. "If you really knew what they'd done, you'd know why them being summoned together by that letter is such a bad thing. You'd know how many people will die by their hands if I don't stop them." I narrowed my eyes. "You don't know what they've done. You don't know what they can do."

"I…" She started to protest, but her voice, along with her gaze, fell silent. "Fine. I don't know. But I know you ran off and got hurt trying to get their names. I know you touched your scars when you heard them. I know you whisper a name in your sleep sometimes." She stared up at me over the rims of her glasses. "And it isn't mine."

People are wounds. They cut and they hurt and they bleed. Some hurt for a little while and go away. Some don't stop hurting until you make them.

Liette was always out to make it stop. She couldn't conceive of a world in which she couldn't fix everything. It was what made me ask her name. It was what made me find out her true name. And it was what made her stand in front of me like this, her arms held out wide.

Like she could stop me.

I tried to push past her. She pushed back.

"Get out of the way," I growled.

"No," she replied.

"What, you think you can stop me?"

"Yes."

"How?"

"I'm Twenty-Two Dead Roses in a Chipped Porcelain Vase," she replied, puffing up as much as she could. "I breathe life into the inanimate and answer the riddles of reality over tea. I can stop you."

"Yeah?" I put a hand on the side of her head and rudely shoved her aside. "You're also short."

She staggered away as I stalked through the door. I hadn't even cleared the threshold when I heard her snarl and felt her hand. She had reached for my arm, but her fingers found my wound instead, sending a lance of pain shooting up through my flank. I let out a scream and fell to my knees, clutching my side.

"*SAL!*" She fell beside me, arms on my shoulders. "I'm...I'm sorry! I just wanted to stop you! I thought...I didn't mean..."

"Get off me," I growled, pulling myself back onto my feet using the door. "I'm fine. I'm..."

"You're hurt."

"*Because you fucking grabbed my wound, you prick!*" I shrugged her off, tried to stalk back through the door. "Just let me..."

She didn't. She was in my way again, trying to shove me back. I had half a foot and twenty pounds on her, but as it turns out, getting hit where you're already bleeding makes it hard to fight back.

I reached out to shove her away again. She caught my wrist, shoved hard. I bit back a cry as I felt the wall against my back. I scowled down at her. She looked up at me.

And I saw her.

She wasn't a fighter, but she was fighting me. She wasn't a healer, but she was trying to help me. I could have shoved her away, kicked her in the shins, punched her, beaten her, broken her if I wanted to. And she knew all that. She'd seen me do it to people.

But she was still fighting me. She was still holding on to me.

And I don't know what she saw when she looked back at me. I don't know if she saw an ingrate or a Vagrant or just another wound that wouldn't close. But she saw me.

And she leaned up.

And the silk of her dress pressed against my belly.

And her lips found mine.

I don't know how long it lasted. It didn't make anything stop hurting. But I didn't pull away. And when it was over, I looked at her.

"What kind of two-coin opera shit..." I whispered. "Did you expect that to stop me?"

I don't know if she did. All I knew is she turned away. And I couldn't let her do that.

I grabbed her by her shoulders, whirled her around, and pressed her against the wall. I leaned down, pulled her into me. I found her taste, her scent, all of her in one breath that I drew in and couldn't let go.

The blood left my legs. The wind left my lungs. The wound, maybe. Or maybe something else. I couldn't think of what and I didn't care. I collapsed, finding my way to the bed only by luck and her hands. We fell there, her atop me, and we saw each other.

And we knew how this ended. We knew it wouldn't be happy. Not for people like us. But maybe...

Maybe this was as close as we would get.

She leaned down, placed her lips upon the scar on my cheek. She went lower, kissed the one on my neck. She slid lower, her lips brushing the scar on my ribs, her breath hot on the scar on my belly, her teeth lightly grazing the scar on my hip as she pulled my belt free, pulled my leggings low, and found me with her tongue.

I closed my eyes. I felt her. And she felt me.

And, for a little while, we could pretend this was all we needed.

TWELVE

ELSEWHERE

I remember the first time I met him. Back then, it had seemed like a dream as well.

Like it did now.

I was small. And wanting to be smaller, I huddled in a corner and curled myself tight, pulling tiny knees up to my chest and cradling them in tiny hands. When I still wasn't small enough, I buried my head and shut my eyes. Somehow, I thought, if I became small enough, no one would notice me. They'd look at me and think I was some misplaced thing that had no real reason to be here, in this great hall.

And then they'd let me go home.

So I shut my eyes. And I willed myself to be smaller. And I waited until what felt like an eternity had passed. And I opened my eyes.

And I was still there. In that big, empty hall full of empty beds that weren't mine and brimming with people I didn't know. They called it a barracks. I didn't know what that word meant, but it wasn't home. And no one was coming to take me there. And I started to cry.

I don't know how small I was. I couldn't remember the last time I cried. Nor do I know how long or how loud I cried. I didn't know anything until I felt someone's hands around my shoulders.

I don't remember the man, though I'd seen him in my dreams.

I don't remember whether he was tall or short or fat or thin. But I remember his eyes. They were wide and white and full of fear. And his mouth fumbled with words I could barely understand.

"Don't cry," he hissed. "Don't cry, don't cry. You can't cry. If you cry, they'll think it's my fault. They'll think it's—"

To be honest, I don't remember the rest of what he said. I don't remember much else.

Except the boy.

"Get your hands off of her!"

He appeared beside the man, a foot shorter and a hundred pounds smaller. He appeared out of the darkness of that room and, with a tiny hand, struck the man across the cheek.

The man, much bigger than him, cringed away. He held up his arms before him, as though he expected worse from the boy, as though those skinny little arms could cleave through him. He backed away, whining apologies, until he slid into the darkness.

"Did he hurt you?" the boy asked me. His voice was softer back then.

I shook my head. He sighed.

"You can't let the nuls touch you like that. It's not what they're supposed to do. Not to us." I didn't look up, but I knew he was smiling at me. "Don't worry, I didn't hurt him. We protect them, the nuls, the whole Imperium, really. And in exchange, they serve us. That's how it's always been. Mages protect. They must have sent you here because they knew you could protect people."

I looked up enough to see his feet. A blade, way too big for someone so small, dragged on the floor behind him. He adjusted it, pulling his belt up around a tiny waist.

"They say I'll grow into it," he said. "But that it's important to start training with it now. I guess it looks kind of silly right now, doesn't it?"

I didn't look up. I stared at my knees and kept crying. He shuffled his feet, adjusted his sword again.

"They don't send you home. No matter how hard you cry. I've tried."

I didn't believe him. He hadn't cried hard enough. I could.

"Do you…want to go get something to eat? The kitchens are closed, but they have to open up for mages."

I shook my head.

"Aren't you hungry?"

I nodded.

"Why don't you want to go?"

"What if my mother and father come by when I'm gone? I have to wait here for them," I said through tears.

"But they're not…" He paused, drew in a breath. "Can I…wait here with you, then? Just so you're not alone?"

I paused. I nodded. He sat down beside me. And together, we waited.

After he had sat down, but before I realized no one was coming to get me, I looked up at him. His face was soft. His eyes were bright. His smile, like his sword, was too big for him.

"What's your name?" he asked me.

I told him. And I asked him what his was.

And he reached out for my hand. And I took it. And I couldn't remember when his fingers had turned to seven blackened blades or when they had punched through my skin or how so much blood was coming out of me. But when I looked back at him, his mouth was full of knives and his eyes were black pits and he spoke on a red river pouring down his chin.

"My name is Jindu."

⤛ ⋯⋙✠⋘⋯ ⤜

I woke up screaming. But I didn't know that yet.

I couldn't feel the sheets around my body, slick with my own sweat. And I couldn't see the pale moonlight filtering in through the windows. And I didn't know whose voice it was tearing out of my throat.

My head was still full of him. And when I woke up, I still saw those black pits where eyes should be. I still felt the seven blades embedded in my skin. I still smelled my own blood pouring out of me.

My scream became a roar as my hand became a fist. I lashed out, swinging at the shadows where he should have been. But everywhere I struck, he was still there. Still smiling with a mouth full of blood.

I swung again. A hand caught my wrist. Then the other. In the darkness, something caught a flash of light. And through my screaming, I heard a voice.

"SAL!"

I kept punching, but she didn't flinch away. I kept screaming, but she didn't stop crying out my name. It wasn't until I felt a warmth other than my own fever-hot body that I finally slowed down.

She was atop me, holding my hands, her hair trailing down her face in messy strands. Her eyes still looked so big without her glasses, big enough that I could make them out in the darkness. She took my hands, trembling and shaking with every breath I took, and pressed them against her naked skin.

"Sal, it's me," Liette said. "It's me. It's me."

She said that until her voice became a whisper and her body grew too heavy to stay up. She slowly slumped back down onto the bed beside me, one hand reaching around to pull me close, the other reaching up to stroke my hair.

She didn't ask me what I had seen, nor tell me it wasn't real. She did not speak anything but those two words, over and over, until my breath slowed down and the shadows stopped moving. She held me there and kissed my shoulder and pressed her brow against my body, until her breath took on a slow, slumbering rhythm.

I shut my eyes and tried to follow her. But across the room, I could feel another pair of eyes on me. Through the leather of his sheath, I could feel his brass burning, his heated scowl upon me. And though he had no tongue, I heard a voice in the darkness.

And he was laughing.

I shut that voice out best I could, along with the one that had followed me out of my head. I focused on her breathing, on the feel of her body next to mine, on that warmth that didn't burn that radiated out of her. I held on to it as long as I could, as the night rolled on into eternity.

Day would come and bring with it ugly business. Tomorrow, I would leave her. If I was kind and she was lucky, I wouldn't come back. If I was lucky and she was kind, she wouldn't ask why. I had made a promise to that thing in the leather sheath, to that list with the names on it, and tomorrow I would see it fulfilled and them dead. She would live well without me.

Happy endings weren't for people like us, her and me.

But as she pulled me closer and pressed her face into the hollow of my neck and I felt her breath on my skin...

Well, it was nice to pretend anyway.

Mercifully, I awoke to an empty bed. When the morning light filtered through the shutters of her window, there was only an empty tangle of sheets beside me. I don't know if it was luck or some discreet deity looking over me and I couldn't take the time to give thanks to either.

She hadn't gone off to make breakfast, waiting for me to come out to the scent of cooking potatoes and eggs. We weren't that kind of people. She had excused herself to some part of the house to give me an opportunity to leave without her being tempted to ask me a question, without me giving her a lie in response.

She had done me a kindness. I wouldn't waste it.

I dressed quietly, tugging on my trousers and boots, pulling my shirt over my head and my vest around my torso. I belted my sword and satchel and snapped out my scarf until it was long enough to be a cloak and pulled it around me. For a moment, I almost pretended that I could leave without him.

But I felt him burning long before I reached the door.

I lingered there, staring at him as if I could just leave. Leave him and all the carnage we had wrought, that we still would wreak, behind. But I couldn't do that to her. And I couldn't break my promise.

We made a deal, he and I.

My hand trembled over his sheath, his heat bright even from here. Yet he cooled when I wrapped my fingers around his hilt and drew him free. The Cacophony stared at me through those brass eyes, his grin broad and his laughter silent. And without a word, he seemed to ask me.

Shall we?

I slid him back into his sheath. I strapped him to my waist. And together, we walked out the door to set about our black business.

❖

I didn't know whether it had been luck or some discreet deity that had been looking over me when I had awoken. But I was certain neither of them was around when I walked out that door and regarded the woman standing in the street before me, a dark light against the pale dawn.

Liette regarded me without a word as I shut the door to her shop. She was dressed for travel, clad in a tight vest over a long shirt, a skirt draped across leggings and boots. A belt, heavy with scrollcases and inkwells, hung from her hips. Her hair had been pulled back in a severe bun, writing quills thrust in it and giving the illusion of a feathery halo behind her head. Gloved hands held the reins of a surly Congeniality, the bird letting out a low chirrup of displeasure at having been awoken before she could get her beauty sleep.

I didn't look at her as I approached, stroked Congeniality's neck, and fished out a dead rabbit from her saddlebags for her. Yet that didn't stop Liette from looking at me.

"I awoke an hour ago," she said. "I spent most of that time thinking about what I would say to convince you to stay, that chasing those names was insane."

I grunted. "What'd you come up with?"

"Nothing that I had any reason to believe would work," she replied.

"After that, I briefly considered drugging you, rendering you comatose until a time when you could see reason."

I nodded. "And?"

"And I doubted there would be such a time as you would ever see reason. Like a specialized predator, you have evolved to a point where you are immune to all forms of logic." She pushed her glasses up the bridge of her nose. "Also, given the rate and quality of your consumption, I had doubts that I had any alchemics powerful enough to subdue you."

"Fair," I said. "So how'd you arrive at trying to come along?"

"Sixth law," she replied flatly.

Fuck, I thought. *Is that the one where Freemakers are sworn to defend those who help them or the one where they're sworn to kill those who wrong them?*

"A contact of mine is in Stark's Mutter," she said. "I have to see to her safety. If that means keeping you alive while I do it, then it seems advantageous. And you will require a wright and you have no other options."

"Not true," I said. "I can find another wright—a wright I don't mind getting hurt—and shoot or break them until they do what I want."

"True," she replied. "But not easily. And not quickly enough that those names wouldn't get even farther away from you. You're already two days behind them. You can't afford to take the time to find an extra wright." She looked at me carefully. "Nor the time it would take to fight me to the point where I couldn't follow."

I squinted at her, sizing her up. "I'm bigger than you."

"You're also wounded."

"And I'm meaner."

"I'm smarter."

"I have a *very* large gun."

"And if you'd like to end this right now, feel free to turn it on me."

I stared at her for a very long time. And had I slept a little more or had at least a finger of whiskey, I'm sure I could have come up with a good retort to that. Or, at least, a better one than what I offered.

"Fucking *fine*," I grumbled. I hauled myself up onto the saddle. Congeniality squawked at the sudden weight as I took the reins. "But you stay back when I tell you to stay back and when I tell you to go, you go."

She nodded. "I will endeavor to—"

"You will," I said. "Or you'll stay the fuck here."

She swallowed hard. "I will."

I'd come up with a plan to get her far away from this mess and back to safety, I told myself. Once I had a moment to think, I could figure out how to convince her to go back to this nice town and let me ruin things without her. But I had only this moment right now, and for that moment, I had to admit she was right. I did need her. And I was running out of time.

Time that was running even slimmer as I held out my hand and she didn't take it.

"What's the problem?" I asked.

"Can you"—she cringed, gesturing to the gun—"put it away?"

"I'm going to need him before long," I said.

"I know, it's just..." She winced, looking away. "It always feels like it's looking at me."

I rolled my eyes. I didn't have time for this. I plucked the Cacophony off my belt and slid him inside a saddlebag. He didn't go quietly. My hand was still stinging when I released him and I could feel his heat even through the saddlebags as I hauled Liette up behind me and felt her wrap her arms around my waist.

It felt slightly unfair, really.

If he knew how much blood we'd spill that day at Stark's Mutter, he probably wouldn't have cared how he got there.

THIRTEEN

STARK'S MUTTER

When I arrived at the township of Stark's Mutter atop the back of my bird, the skies were blue and clear as a dream and the early afternoon sun was beaming like a light that shined only for me.

And that was the first sign I had that things were fucked.

Have you ever seen a battle? Not the little squabbles between the various factions of the Scar, but a *real* battle? I haven't. And I hope, if they're anything like the aftermath I stumbled upon, I never do.

They called it Lethic's Horn, an old-as-balls tower perpetually teetering over a collection of run-down barracks. Just a collection of crappy buildings on a hard rock in the ass-end of the desert that no one would ever give a shit about, normally. But because it happened to overlook a road that ran between two of the biggest freeholds in the Scar, people suddenly thought it was worth dying for.

Twenty squadrons of Revolutionary conscripts charged an Imperial garrison manned by thirteen mages and a few nul regulars, I'm told. I don't know what happened—I've never had a head for strategies deeper than "shoot the hell out of it"—but I saw what was left when the fighting was over.

The birds were so thick in the sky that it looked like night. And on the ground, the scavengers ate so much dead flesh they fell to the ground, bloated, and were eaten by the other scavengers. It was like the land was alive, a teeming mass of feathers and blood and shriek-ing. I couldn't even get close without a heap of them diving down on me. Nul or mage, they didn't give a shit until it came bursting out their backsides.

In Weiless, the pigeons carry messages from fort to fort. In Cathama, the peacocks sing pretty songs for pretty girls in pretty houses. But in the Scar, no one's quite so helpful nor quite so charm-ing. Out here, birds do what everyone else does: survive at someone else's expense.

I guess you might have thought that a sky clear of birds would be a good omen.

But there's three things no one from the Scar believes in: good omens, charity, and justice.

I came up to the edge of the township and the chill set in. In the shadow of the houses—tall hardwood homes on stone foundations, typical out here where the Scar's winters hit hard—the warmth of the sun shied away, like it had already seen what had happened in there and decided it didn't want to look.

It wasn't the only one.

"We're here," I said, which was harder than it seemed with some-one's arms clamped so hard around my ribs that I almost felt them crack.

Liette looked up at me through eyes that hadn't blinked since we took off. I heard her knuckles popping as she forcibly unclenched them from around my middle and slid off. She plucked a grimy feather out of her hair, then stared at it, then at me. I shrugged.

"You wanted to come."

"That thing—" she began.

"That *lady*," I corrected.

"It's too fast and it's too rough and . . . did it . . . did it *poop* while we were running?"

"She had a hearty breakfast." I patted Congeniality's neck. "Didn't you, madam? Yes, you did. You ate *so good* and—"

She cut me short with a loud squawk, bucking backward and

sending me jostling in the saddle. Either she was in an especially bad mood today or something was wrong. Both were likely, neither were answered. When I tried to pull the reins, she snapped forward and hurled me off.

I hit the ground with a grunt as she fought to pull away from me. She jerked wildly at the reins, her squawks turning to shrieks as she stamped and kicked while I tried to pull her back. Either she was going to break her neck, open my belly with her claws, or attract the attention of something that could kill both of us. What choice did I have?

I let the reins go, watched her tear off.

"*What?*" I called after her. "*Did you think that was a crack about your weight?*" I muttered, rubbed the sore spot where I had landed. "Useless fucking bird."

"Are you all right?" Liette rushed to my side, reaching for my still-healing wound.

"I'm fine." I waved her off, pulled my scarf around my face. "We've got bigger shit to deal with than that."

I've lost Congeniality before. She's tossed me off a few times. I once bet her on a losing hand of Triumphs, and I once chased her mostly naked through a township on fire before she vanished into the smoke. We've always found each other again. I wasn't worried about that.

Worry might be a plentiful thing, but it was still a finite amount. And all mine at that moment was reserved for whatever was beyond the walls of Stark's Mutter.

My eyes lingered on those walls. I glanced to Liette. She forced down a grimace to give me as resolute a nod as she could. I tugged my scarf up around my face. I felt the weight of Jeff at my hip, heard the jingle of shells in my pocket, and the Cacophony...

He let me know he was ready.

The gates hung wide open—another bad omen. No one who isn't dead or soon to be dead leaves a door open in the Scar. I paused at the edge, holding up a hand to halt Liette, peering around. Unpaved streets, long shadows, and a cold breeze greeted me. No one shot or spat a curse at me, so I took a few steps in.

I didn't die.

But that didn't count as a good sign. That's just luck.

I walked slowly down the streets. I'd forgive you for calling me stupid for not seeking cover. But these weren't a bunch of punks with guns I was facing this time. Fuck, these weren't even common mages. These people—the most powerful mages to have ever turned Vagrant—had thought they could challenge the Imperium and win.

Cover will help you against bullets. But against a man who can make a hurricane with a thought?

Well, he's probably not going to seek cover, either.

"It's quiet," Liette whispered, six paces behind me.

"It was," I muttered in response.

"That can't be a good sign, can it?" she said. "The world goes quiet before a Vagrant attacks."

"Says who?"

"I read it in a book."

"Uh-huh. Did the book feature prominent use of the word *throbbing*?"

Her mouth dropped open in indignant anger. I could feel her lips trembling, trying to formulate a voice for her outrage. I held up a hand for silence, not knowing if she heeded it or not. In another second, I couldn't hear her over the sound filling my ears.

A distant wailing with no earthly source. An echo of the Lady Merchant's song. A lot of magic had been expended very recently, traces of it could still be around. Not knowing what to expect would have been bad. But I knew the names on that list. I knew what to expect.

And that was worse.

Galta the Thorn.

Mendmage. My eyes drifted over the streets, onto the walls, up onto overhangs, anywhere that a nigh-invincible killer might lurk.

Zanze the Beast.

Maskmage. I tried to feel the still in the air that preceded a great panther pouncing, a great hawk swooping, a great serpent striking—he could be any of those.

Riccu the Knock.

Doormage. My ears were open for the sound—that faint ripping that would tell me a portal was opening behind me, above me, anywhere I wouldn't expect.

Taltho the Scourge.

Nightmage. I glanced at the shadows, peering close to see which ones were darker than the others, which ones could blossom into a forest of nightmares around me.

Jindu the Blade.

Him...

Well, there was no preparing for Jindu.

But the steps dragged out, mine and Liette's feet crunching on sand, until close to half an hour had passed without either of us being flung around, blown apart, or eviscerated. Which I was thankful for, don't get me wrong, but it was unexpected.

I knew the names on that list and those names knew mine. I had expected to be either murdered or well into murdering by now.

But aside from that distant echo of the Lady's song and the cold breeze and the weight of the Cacophony hanging from my hip? I was without foes.

Or so I thought.

Movement at the corner of my right eye. Every thinking part of me shut down; my body knew how to do what my head couldn't. My hand went down to my belt. The Cacophony leapt up, I could feel his hot eagerness in my hand. I swept him up, turned him toward the right. My eyes found the sight just as my thumb found the hammer and my finger the trigger. My breath fell into the comfortable rhythm of someone ready to kill.

It was a magnificent display.

I'm sure the fat black chicken that came clucking out the door was duly impressed.

The little fat bird came strutting out from the open door like he owned the fucking place, taking umbrage at my unwelcome intrusion into his domain.

"Outstanding," Liette muttered behind me. "He shall speak of this day and every poultry within six leagues shall know not to cross Sal the Cacophony."

"Oh, fuck off," I muttered.

I would have had worse words for her had a shock of pain not lanced up my arm. Bright red pain flashed behind my eyes, every inch of muscle lanced by needles. I winced, bit back a scream, not letting it out. That scream would be the difference between my arm feeling like it was on fire and it actually being on fire.

"*Sal!*" Liette rushed up to me.

"It's fine," I whispered through clenched teeth. It wasn't. But it would pass.

I had pulled out the Cacophony for a chicken. Not a Vagrant, not even a bandit; a fucking chicken. He was understandably pissed at the waste of his skills.

If I had actually shot the damn thing, he might have taken my arm off.

"It's the weapon, isn't it?" Liette ran her hand along mine, her skin cold to the touch. "Why do you even have it? What good is a weapon that hurts *you*?"

I couldn't answer that. First, because if I impugned his usefulness, the Cacophony would protest further. Second, because there was no such thing as a weapon that didn't hurt its wielder eventually.

The pain subsided and I returned him to his holster. But a sharp tingling sensation lingered in my arm. His warning. The next time I drew him, the ensuing carnage had better be *incredible*.

Jeff, though? Jeff didn't care what he got to stab.

He's easygoing like that.

I pulled out my blade and stalked toward the bird. I came to a halt as Liette seized my arm. I glared at her, largely prepared for her to ask if I was really going to swordfight a chicken over annoying me and fully prepared to assure her I was. But her eyes were on something other than me. She pointed. I followed.

And I saw the corpse.

We crept in past the door into a musty room. A township like Stark's Mutter wouldn't have a proper tavern. This dank little room full of empty tables and chairs and dusty bottles barely qualified as one. The tiny bar was too small to conceal the corpse and a long, slender arm sprawled out from behind it.

I kept Jeff upright, held my breath. Two minutes passed and nothing shot, stabbed, or exploded me. If anyone had heard the shot, they weren't coming. Soothed for the moment, I inched closer to the bar, peered around it.

The dead woman stared back at me with white eyes. I don't mean they were big, I mean they were *white*. No pupil. No iris. Her skin was wrinkled, her body shriveled. If I didn't know better, I'd have said she died an old woman. And if fate was kind, I wouldn't have known better.

But what'd I say about charity?

"Scions."

I glanced at Liette behind me. "Your contact?"

She didn't answer as she pushed past me, leaving me to watch the door while she knelt by the dead woman. She ran a pair of fingers over skin sagging from bones, as though the meat inside the woman had simply been eaten away and left her a hollowed-out bag of skin.

"Selective consumption," Liette hummed, apparently unperturbed by the horror in front of her. "Something devoured crucial aspects of her—organs, marrow, muscle—but left behind others. Like..." She furrowed her brow. "Have you ever seen a cloak without anyone in it?"

I didn't answer that. She was talking more to herself anyway. "Magic, obviously. But I've never seen a spell that could do this."

I had. Once.

Didn't like it.

Fuck me, I couldn't help but wonder what had gone through her head when it hit her. Had she thought she was safe when she hunkered down behind the bar? What did she think when she felt her muscle wasting away and the life seep out of her? Whose name did she cry out when she...

Fuck.

You get the idea.

Unfortunately, the idea I didn't want was the only one I had. Whatever had happened here, whatever they had planned, I had been too late to stop. I had known that going in. I had been prepared for seeing whatever horror they had been concocting. But I still didn't know what horror it had been, save that it had been painful.

I heard a creak from upstairs.

I heard the distant whisper of the Lady's song.

I heard the Cacophony thrum in his holster.

Magic. Close.

"What is it?"

Liette's voice came as a whisper. Wrights might have been talented, but they weren't mages. She hadn't heard the song, couldn't hear it. But she noticed I had. I made a gesture for her to remain where she was.

I shifted Jeff to my left hand, kept my right on the Cacophony. I pressed myself to the wall as I made my way upstairs, eyes on the landing above where the doors to the rooms for rent began. No shadows leapt out at me. No spells assailed my senses. By the time I reached the top, nothing greeted me but a door slightly ajar at the end of the hall.

Good enough.

I made my way down, pushed it gently open, peered inside. A humble room greeted me: a pair of beds, a writing desk, a table in the middle with an unopened bottle upon it. A pair of heavy traveler's coats hung off pegs on the wall. It was a cozy little room, perfectly the sort of thing you'd expect to find in a place like this.

Really, the corpse with the crushed throat lying in the center of the room only barely marred its charm.

"Another one," Liette observed grimly, having apparently grown impatient and followed me up. I didn't bother stopping her as she pushed past me and knelt beside the dead man, studying him. I wasn't worried until she cringed. She never cringed. "Scions," she whispered. "Look at his throat." She gestured to the twisted red husk of meat masquerading as a neck. "It's like someone crushed him."

"Probably the other agent," I replied.

"What other agent?" She looked up at me.

"He's a Revolutionary," I replied.

"That's ridiculous. He's not wearing a uniform."

"Well, he'd be a shitty spy if he was, wouldn't he?" I gestured to the beds, both immaculately made with their boots placed perfectly side by side. "A soldier can shed his uniform, but not his habits. And look." I gestured to the bottle of wine, unopened on the table. "Revolutionaries don't drink."

"That's not the most *compelling* evidence."

"True. It's more of a hunch." I plucked one of the coats off its peg, tested it for weight. I jammed Jeff's blade into its side and cut it open, reaching in to pluck out a sheaf of carefully folded papers. "*This* is evidence."

I'd forgive you for saying that it seemed a little weird that I knew where to find them. After all, the whole point of a secret pocket is usually that someone *doesn't* know where they are. And I imagined the vast majority of people would have seen these heavy coats and thought nothing of them. But for the illustrious minority of people in the Scar who have met, crossed, and been the target of Revolutionary agents before—of which I happened to be a part—we knew what to look for.

I shuffled through the papers. A mess of gibberish greeted me. Another fucking code. Not even one that could be solved as swiftly as magic. This was Revolutionary birdshit. I had read a little bit—in my line of work, you cross these assholes more than once—but my grasp was shaky at best and I could pick out only a few words.

"Two of them were dispatched here," I muttered, looking through the papers. "They were on an observation mission. They were looking for a person of interest. A Vagrant." I scanned the paper, squinting through the gibberish as if an answer might lie within. Seeing nothing, I threw the papers away. "It doesn't say which."

"Could it be...one of them? The names on your list?"

I shook my head, turned away. "Who the fuck knows?"

Liette looked down at the corpse. "He might."

A cold pang hit me as I caught the implication in her voice. "You're not serious."

"My seriousness is not the issue," Liette replied. "Yours is. And if you are intent on finding the names on your list. If..." She hesitated, then sighed. "If that will make you feel better...then there is a way." She looked meaningfully down at the body. "He's still fresh enough."

Like I said, wrighting is the act of imbuing inanimate matter with a new identity. Steel can be soft as silk; silk can burn like fire. The results differ based on the skill of the wright, the application of the sigils, and the nature of the material, but theoretically, anything could be persuaded to be something else.

Even a corpse.

I didn't like it. There were very few things I could rely on in this miserable world, but one that I had grown quite accustomed to was the fact that dead people stay dead. Or they ought to anyway. That could change, if one knew the proper wright and had reason enough to risk it. Among wrights, there were none better than Liette. And I had seven reasons.

All of them worth the risk.

I nodded reluctantly at her. Liette plucked a quill from her hair and an inkwell from her belt. She began to scrawl a few sigils across the dead man's face, each line careful and deliberate. She knew what could happen if she fucked it up.

But she was the best. And no sooner had she finished than the man's eyes snapped open. Blackened from blood that had pooled and rotted within, he stared at nothing. His lips trembled, speaking through a breathless voice that sounded like it came from a thousand miles away.

"Relentless," he gasped. "Is that you?"

I didn't know what that meant, but I wasn't about to ask. Not like he could hear me anyway. Corpsewrighting could only reliably make a sufficiently fresh body relive its last few moments. Anything more complicated than that tended to end...messily.

"Brother," he whispered. "What's wrong with your face? I heard noise in the town square. What happened? The people were taken there. Did you see the target? Did you see Vraki?"

Only one thing could make my blood run colder than a talking corpse. And it was that name. That name took me back to a light-less place, a place of cold stone and soft whispers and blood dripping onto a frozen floor. That name made me want to go running from the room.

I bit it back. I kept listening.

"Relentless? You're not...Wait, get back. GET BACK! BROTHER, IT'S...IT'S...IT'S..."

Liette hastily wiped the sigils away from his brow. He fell back to the floor, truly dead once more.

"That's it?" I asked.

"He started to repeat himself at the end there," she said. "That's as far back as his corpse can recall."

"Birdshit," I muttered. "I've seen you do more with a body than that."

"You have." She looked at me flatly. "Do you recall how that ended?" She shook her head. "If that's insufficient, Sal, then it should be proof that this was folly. They're not here. And they didn't want to be followed so badly that they did *this*"—she gestured at the man's collapsed throat—"to someone. What more do you need?"

I stared at the body, running his last words through my head. She looked at me, expectant, waiting for me to concede, to say this had all been a fool's errand, to see reason.

This wouldn't be the first time I disappointed her.

Hell, it wouldn't even be the worst I disappointed her today.

"What was that he said," I asked, "about the town square?"

FOURTEEN

STARK'S MUTTER

Magic used to be mysterious.

When humanity first discovered it, the earliest mages were burned alive by terrified nuls. Eventually, they started burning the nuls back and you know how the rest of it turned out. Magic became a science: it could be measured, reproduced, predicted. Mages figured out exactly what they'd have to give to get what they wanted, and from time to time, we all convinced ourselves that we were in control of magic.

And then, from time to time, you see something that makes you realize we're not.

And then sometimes you see what I saw on the day I walked into the town square of Stark's Mutter. And you realize you don't know shit. About magic. About humans. About what either of them are capable of.

I didn't want to think about what the town square had been before the seven conspirators had come here. I didn't want to think about the wives who had gossiped and laughed by the well. I didn't want to think about the kids who might have played here. I didn't want to think about the old men who grumbled about how hard life was beneath the eaves of the store.

But when I looked upon their bodies, I didn't have a choice.

Trees. They looked like pale trees. Their emaciated arms were withered branches. Their flabby legs were gnarled trunks in blackened earth. Their torsos were bent and cracked into unnatural angles.

The air itself was effused with wrongness. The sunlight shone dimmer here in the square. The wood of houses was warped and splintered. A nearby tree, along with the bird that had been sitting upon it, was split into a perfect, bloodless symmetry. There was a reek more profound than rot, like the odor of a thousand corpses in a sealed tomb turning to dust all at once as the door was opened.

And all of it—every trace of vileness, every whiff of foulness—emanated from the circle at the center.

It was carved into the earth with such impossibly even alien perfection that no human could have done it. The circle stretched to engulf the entire town square, blasting the earth a lightless black and polishing it to glossless obsidian. Inside it, the trees that had once been people were frozen, their feet sunken into the black earth, their bodies twisted as they struggled and failed to escape, even as their faces were locked onto the center, unable to look away.

Their bodies were withered. The meat of their flesh had been rotted away. They had died slowly. In pain. In fear. Leaving behind nothing but a hellscape bereft of light, bereft of sound.

Except the retching, anyway.

I glanced over my shoulder and saw Liette leaning against the nearby house, her body shuddering with each ragged breath as she vomited upon the road.

"How are we doing back there?" I asked.

"Just a..." She held up a hand without looking up. "I'll be..." Unless the end of that sentence was "puking my last six meals up," she was a liar. "What...what *happened*?"

"Summoning," I replied. "Not a good one."

Not that any of them were. Tearing open a wound between worlds was an inexact art at best. It was a visceral magic; even the ones that went well left a lingering injury in creation—an injury that made most decent people, including Liette, react as she did.

I didn't mind, though. It had smelled much worse the first time anyway.

"A what?" Liette came staggering up beside me, wiping her mouth with a handkerchief. "They can do that?"

"One of them can," I muttered, my eyes scanning the horror frozen in time. "He's not called Vraki the Gate because he holds the door open for women."

"And . . . what did he summon?"

I didn't want to tell her. In the right hands, summoning could be a fairly benign act—or at least, as benign as tearing otherworldly creatures of destruction into ours can be. Sometimes it's a dragonfly with stained glass wings, sometimes a cat with six legs and human eyes, sometimes a man-shaped thing that explodes.

But that wasn't what had come out. Because Vraki's hands weren't the right ones.

If you knew anything about the Crown Conspiracy, you knew his name. And once you knew his name, you knew the stories.

He's a prodigy, they say, born beloved by the Lady Merchant, never has to pay a Barter to get his power. They say he engineered the Crown Conspiracy by drawing black spirits into our world. They say he gutted his favorite consort when she didn't cheer loud enough for him at a friendly duel. They say he . . .

Well, they said a lot of things about him that I didn't believe.

Of course, if you knew him, you knew those were just stories.

You also knew the truth was worse.

"Whatever it was," Liette said, pointing off into the distance, "it had to have been big."

Across the square stood a pleasant little house that would have been decidedly more pleasant without the giant fucking hole torn in its side. Past the hole, I could see a devastated kitchen where something had charged through. And past *that*, I could see another hole in another house behind this one. And another, and another, leading to a hole in the township's walls that it had punched through during its escape.

It wasn't the devastation that made my blood run cold. A jagged tear and shattered timbers, I could have chalked up to anything. But these holes were warped, fluid, as though the wood and stone itself had bent impossibly of their own volition to get out of the creature's way, appalled at what they had seen.

Only one creature could have done that.

Fuck me. I knew the Crown Conspiracy was reckless. I knew Vraki was desperate.

I didn't ever fucking think he'd try to summon a Scrath.

If you'd have asked me to explain what one was, or why knowing one was out there in the Scar made me want to turn around and run as far as I could in the opposite direction, I wouldn't have answered.

I'd have simply gestured to its handiwork—to the people made into trees, to the terrifying perfection of its devastation, to the way creation tried to escape its approach—and if you had any sense, you'd not ask again.

"This can't be real."

As it turned out, though, sense was a rare commodity out here. Liette, over her nausea and her terror alike, now crept warily toward the site of the summoning. Keeping a distance from any of the corpses—and pointedly avoiding their gazes—she studied the ruin.

"This is unlike any magic I've read about," she whispered. "What was it intended to accomplish?"

"It didn't," I replied. "Something went wrong."

"Like what?"

I couldn't answer that. I couldn't tell her that the fact that the Scrath escaped meant the summoning had gone wrong and Vraki had lost control of it. I couldn't tell her any of that because when I thought about her asking how I knew that, I couldn't think of an answer that I could ever tell her and still have her look me in the eye.

"Too much collateral damage," I settled on saying. "A summoning done right is clean. Relatively, anyway." I walked among the corpses, glancing around the blackened, polished earth. "But a summoning for something this big takes an immense amount of magic. Magic that even Vraki wouldn't have."

"Perhaps he used a focusing object," Liette offered.

"Why do you say that?"

"Because I just found one."

She held in her hands what had once been an obelisk. Or something like one. It was broken into three pieces and useless now, but it had once been a focus, a rare object that could occasionally amplify a spell. But you didn't see these in respectable places like the Imperium. You only ever saw them in places where magic hadn't been refined, among shamans and hedge wizards and...

"Haven," I whispered. I pointed at writing that had been chiseled into the stone's surface. "This came from Haven. This is one of their insane religious ramblings."

"Let's keep an open mind, shall we?" Liette scoffed. "Just because something is religious does not necessarily make it insane." She studied the writing and hummed. "Though *this* particular something is decidedly fucking nuts. Haven doesn't part with its treasures willingly. Or at all, even."

"Then they'll be looking for them." I took the fragments from her, slid them into my satchel. "Which is a good reason for us to get going before they..."

She wasn't listening to me. Or looking at me. What she *was* doing was making me miss the times when she was doubled over, vomiting.

Liette approached one of the people, a tall tree-corpse planted in the earth, and removed an inkwell from her belt and a quill from her hair. She daubed the quill as she studied the corpse's face, looking for an appropriate surface upon which to scrawl.

"*No*," I said, realizing what she was doing. "Corpsewrighting is bad enough when the corpses *aren't* ravaged by unspeakable, unknown magic."

"The fact that they are is reason enough to find out," Liette replied, settling on a spot on the corpse's cheek. "We've never seen this kind of magic before. We have to know how it worked. Only the dead can tell us."

"Woman, *I* can tell you." I spread my arms out, gesturing to the devastation. "Someone cast a spell, summoned something horrific, and then *this* shit happened. It's not a scientific inquiry to figure out that—"

"Second law."

My brow furrowed at her curt words. Because I knew she wouldn't be dissuaded. Curiosity I could curtail, but she loved her oaths more than she loved me.

The Laws of the Freemakers, myriad as they are, are no more rigid than they are in their second law: the law that commands them to defy empires, to aggravate revolutions, and to pursue their quest for knowledge no matter the cost.

"That which is forbidden..." she began.

"Is mandatory," I finished. I looked around—the township was clear, and if it would give me an edge to finding Vraki, I could stomach a little forbidden art. "Just hurry it up."

"Wrighting is a delicate art," she replied, snootier than a woman about to scribble on a corpse should sound. She reached out with her quill. "If progress could be rushed as you wish it to be, then we'd all be—"

That's when the corpse grabbed her.

Its blackened fingers wrapped around her wrist, seizing her. She was screaming, but I only knew that because of her open mouth and the fear on her face. I couldn't hear anything over the sound of the corpse's own wail.

"WHERE ARE THEY?" it screamed. "PLEASE, SAVE THEM!"

"*SAL!*" she shrieked, fighting to get free.

I rushed up behind the corpse—if it even was one—and jammed my sword through its ribs. It came out the other side of blackened flesh, but the thing didn't so much as drop an octave.

"THEY TOOK THEM! THEY TOOK THE CHILDREN!" it screamed, dragging Liette closer to it. "HE SAID THE SUMMONING NEEDED A VESSEL! HE TOOK THE CHILDREN!"

Liette fought as hard as she could, just as I fought to dislodge my sword, but the corpse was oblivious to either of us. But it didn't bite her or claw her or anything you'd expect a corpse to do. It took her by the shoulders, forced her to look at it. And in the light reflected off its pallid eyes, I knew this was no corpse.

This thing was still alive.

"SAVE THEM!" he screamed. "Savethemsavethemsavethemsave themsavethem..."

My sword came free. Blood, blackened and thickened to a burnt stew, followed. The corpse—now truly one—slumped over as its life ebbed away and its voice with it. But its words still lingered in my head.

Children. Vessels. Tribute.

Vraki had done worse than what I had thought he was capable of. He took more than just lives.

I looked to Liette, but her eyes were still on the corpse. Her mouth hung open, at a loss for either words or breath, as her body trembled upon shaking legs, arms wrapped around her where the corpse had touched her.

"Liette," I said, reaching for her.

Her eyes turned to me, and in her glasses, I could see the horror in her eyes magnified. She looked at me, me with my dripping blade and the black life staining my skin, and shook so hard I thought she might fall to pieces. My hand fell, my voice with it. I froze. I had been looked at this way before.

But never by her.

She turned. She ran. She disappeared behind a house.

I didn't call after her. I couldn't find the words to do so. Despite all that we'd seen together, I sometimes forgot she wasn't like me. She hadn't seen what I'd seen. And she'd never seen *anything* like that. I couldn't blame her for running.

"Do you hear that, Brothers?"

Until I heard the sound of approaching footsteps. Then I could certainly blame her.

I crept to the edge of the public house, peered around its corner at the main street that led back to the town gate. I caught sight of naked flesh, black tattoos, red cloth, and crucially, a brand of a great, crimson eye.

And, to my credit, I managed not to shit myself.

I turned and sped back, quick as I dared and quiet as I could, to the town square. Liette was gone. And I didn't have time to search for her.

Not with Haveners coming toward me.

I remembered seeing a building there, one of those frontier-style deals with the big-ass doors designed to keep outlaws out. I found it, pushed myself in, pressed the considerably-big-ass-but-not-nearly-big-ass-enough-to-keep-those-maniacs-out door shut and barred it. I slipped down to the window, pressed myself against it, pulled the Cacophony out, and checked to make sure I had a shell chambered.

I suppose, if anyone was watching, they might have thought this looked a little much.

But if anyone thought that, they probably didn't know the kind of men I had just seen. That was understandable. You never understood the hounds of Haven until you saw them work. And then, usually, you were dead.

Liette understood. And I hoped to whatever would listen that she knew to stay out of sight.

Through a hole punched in the window's glass, I heard them coming: feet dragging across the dirt, the crackling of flame, a racking cough. And then the ragged, lunatic voice.

"Ah, behold," a shrill and distinctly feminine voice cackled, "the perversion is discovered."

Three men came striding into the town square, naked but for their trousers and boots and the thick red bandanas tied around their eyes. Every inch of bare skin was covered in bloodied wounds, broad sigils of an eye weeping blood etched into their chests. They held burning torches, even though it was a clear, sunny day.

Men like these didn't use fire for its light.

At their center was a woman, bent and ragged beneath her red robes, even though her skin was fair and youthful. It wasn't age that made her need to lean on a staff. And it sure as fuck wasn't age that had gouged out her eyes and left two gaping red holes behind, either.

The process of becoming one of the few and revered Sightless Sisters, Haven's bloodhounds, was a mystery, but no one ever came out of it looking prettier.

With her empty sockets, she looked over the black circle at the center of town and smiled, her grin full of sharpened teeth.

"We are blessed in filth, Brothers," she hissed. "A ripe *trove* of decay to be purged. The Seeing God is pleased with our service."

I've never begrudged anyone a belief in a god. Personally, I've known too many people to believe that anyone out there is looking out for them, but the Scar's a tough place. People who can't get by with whiskey get by with gods. There used to be a hundred or so little cults to one deity or another promising salvation from the beasts and outlaws of the world. That was before Haven threw up its walls and went from a quaint collection of hamlets to an army of witch hunters eager to incinerate anyone not of their faith.

"What is it, Honored Sister?" one of the men asked. "I cannot see."

"No?" the woman replied. "Permit me to illuminate."

There was a faint hissing sound. And in those black pits that used to be eyes, fiery lights kindled. Like lanterns, they cast a red glow as she swept her gaze across the square.

"The air is quiet. The sun is cold. Even the birds think the place too foul." She rapped her staff against the hard black earth. "But this magic could not be wrought by mortal hands, no matter how unclean. Can you not feel it, Brothers? A fiend was summoned here by seven souls." She paused, searching the air through those fiery sockets. "It left. Two followed in pursuit. A third lurked nearby and left. The remaining four took lost lambs from this humble place of living. And they used the Seeing God's treasure to do it..."

Whatever rituals turned Haven's gentle temple maidens into the cackling, maimed Sightless Sisters were a mystery to all but them. All that was known was that it left them completely unhinged and with a peculiar gift for sniffing out anything magical, be it mage, Dust, or even a relic.

Like the one I was carrying.

Fuck.

"A great power was beckoned here," the Sister muttered. "A great heresy was created."

"All magic is heresy," another man grunted. "'The foe that hides must see the light. The beast that creeps must fear the day. The man who speaks unclean must be burned clean of lies.'"

"The scripture is clear, Brother," the woman muttered. "But there is heresy and there is blight. One follows the other, as birds follow carrion. A great evil has been unleashed here"—she slowly craned her lights about—"and it has not left."

For one single, breathless second, she looked directly at me. My eyes met her red sockets and the fiery lights fixed upon me. I ducked down.

Fuck.

Like I said, no one knows much about the Seeing God. But what we do know is that he gave his followers something. Something old and powerful. Something that the brightest scholars in the Imperium couldn't explain. And something that I very much could do without trying to murder me at that moment.

Now what, exactly, the powers did seemed to vary from follower to follower. But one constant is that they could sniff out magic sure as a bird finds corpses. But she couldn't have sensed the Cacophony, could she?

The gun grew warmer in my palm, as if in answer. Wouldn't have surprised me if the fucking thing was calling to them. That'd be just like him.

I drew his hammer back. I held my breath. I waited for the sound of footsteps approaching, of glass breaking, of doors shattering.

What I heard, instead, was a racking, wheezing cough.

"Sister?" one of them said. "What is it?"

"Too much foulness in the air," she snarled. The lights sputtered out and her sockets went dark again. "I cannot find the source of the taint." She swept a ragged hand out over the village. "Seek, Brothers. Find the perversion that offends our Lord's sensibilities. And should it elude you"—she hissed through rancid teeth—"burn it out."

Footsteps. Grunting. Movement. I poked my head up and saw them wandering off, spreading out in search. What does and doesn't offend a Havener is fairly vague, but while their mysteries are long, their attention spans are short. They have a thousand questions, but only one answer, and I knew I didn't have long before they found someone that wasn't me.

I had to find Liette.

When I was sure they were gone, I eased the door open and scampered out, hurrying back to the main street. I didn't hear anyone following me, no shouts of alarm or holy scriptures recited or whatever makes them all hot. The public house was the tallest building in the township. I could get to the top of it and make for the roofs, find Liette from above. We'd make our way out from there.

Great plan.

Sure would be a shame if, oh, say, a bunch of Revolutionaries happened to arrive just then.

The groan of metal wheels. The shrieking of iron. The roar of an engine. The cloud of black smoke heralded the beast's arrival as a great monster of metal and smog came barreling over the horizon, heading straight toward me. An iron carriage mounted on great wheels that chewed up the earth beneath it, belching flame and smoke from vents on its side, roaring as it came forward.

I knew what it was before I saw it. But the damn thing moved so fast that, in another second, I could see the sigil branded across its front. A cog with two crossed sabers.

A Revolutionary Iron Boar.

So, I said I didn't believe in a god and I mostly meant it. I don't think there's a benevolent being out there to keep us from doing wrong and protect us from harm. But then, not all gods are benevolent, are they?

And if you had told me, right then and there, that there was a divine being of immeasurable power and he used every ounce of it to exclusively fuck with me?

Now *that* I'd believe.

FIFTEEN

STARK'S MUTTER

The first Iron Boar was unleashed a mere ten years ago. Mounted on wheels that chewed up the earth, a great iron monstrosity belching flame smashed through the gates of an Imperium garrison and flooded it with enough Revolutionary soldiers to kill half of the conscripts within and capture the rest. It was a surprise to the Imperium, who until that point thought that the Revolution's mechanists had reached the limits of their ingenuity.

Of course, we later learned that, to make the damn thing, the Great General had forced two thousand laborers to work themselves to death to mine the iron. Sixty skilled workers were killed forging it. The three machinists who had designed it were later branded counterrevolutionaries and hanged themselves. All told, the Revolution had killed over two thousand of its own to kill just over a hundred of the enemy.

But that was a fact. Facts don't matter in war. Legends do. And two legends were born that day. One was the Iron Boar itself, an engine of such speed and terrible destruction that every Imperium garrison in the Scar ordered itself fortified. And the other?

The Great General's legendary ability to give less of a shit about his people than the enemy gave about theirs.

My own legend was a little meager by comparison, but by the end of the day, I hoped it would say: "Stared down a sixteen-ton iron monstrosity and did *not* curl into a ball and wait to die."

I turned and bolted back for the public house, slamming the door behind me. I didn't bother barring it; I had no time. Instead, I ran up the stairs to the end of the hall on the second floor. I wasn't thinking of anything except getting as far away as I could.

The Iron Boar groaned to a halt. Its wheels screeched, its metal sides shuddering as the engine's doors slammed open. Gunpikes flashed, blue coats fluttered as a squadron of men and women leapt out of the engine's belly and rushed toward the town gates.

They dashed for cover, making certain that the main street was clear before carefully filing in and assembling in a neat little square, six of them in all, gunpikes neatly shouldered, badges bright and shiny.

Say one thing for Revolutionaries: all that propaganda and brainwashing makes for one *very* nice formation.

"Main street clear, Sergeant!" one of them, a young lady in an old coat, cried out. "Awaiting orders!"

A familiar shape came trotting in through the gates a moment later: a tall fellow in a dirty blue coat, his gunpike weathered and worn, his hair and skin dark and grimy. In the shadowed light of Lowstaff, I had thought he looked handsome in a weird way. I had to admit, he looked a little better in the cold day of Stark's Mutter: strong jaw, bright eyes, scars in the places honest men got them.

What was his name again?

"No hostiles detected, Sergeant Proud!" the woman barked.

"None?" Cavric asked as he made his way to the front of the square.

"None, sir," the lady replied.

Cavric cast a frown down the empty street. "No hostiles, no civilians, no anything," he muttered. "We made enough noise to wake the dead. Someone should have come out to investigate by now." Cavric shook his head. "If Relentless and Vindictive are still here, they're either hiding or…"

"Is that fear I detect in you, Low Sergeant?"

A rumbling voice emerged from the Boar, followed by a rumbling man to match. A great hulk of a man, his frame straining against his coat and his face looking like it had been carved out of rock by another rock, set foot upon the earth. Taller and vaster than any other soldier assembled, he had the physique of someone who could tear a man in half and the demeanor of someone who wouldn't rule out eating the remains.

And somehow, that *still* wasn't the scariest thing about him.

That honor was reserved for the weapon in his hands.

If you could even recognize it as a weapon, that is. He held it in both hands, long and heavy like a firearm, but there wasn't a scrap of metal on it. Rather, it looked like it had been taken from the stone—not carved, but woven, as though someone had reached into the heart of a very old rock and simply shaped it until it looked like a weapon. At the end of what would have been its barrel, a polished crystal glistened in lieu of a gun's maw.

I've had the misfortune of seeing a handful of them up close and I still don't know how to describe the Revolutionary Relics. To this day, no one outside the Revolution knew where they came from or how they worked—only that they were enough to allow a ragtag bunch of former slaves to hold off the magical onslaught from the Imperium.

So yeah, I wasn't feeling great to see one here.

"Fear is the staple crop in the counterrevolutionary's plowshare," the man muttered, eyes on Cavric. "Do you bring such thoughts to your table, Low Sergeant?"

The soldiers snapped to attention, more rigidly and with considerably more terror than they had for Cavric. The Low Sergeant merely inclined his head, refusing to break the man's gaze.

"Relic Guard Onerous," he said. "I was merely laying out all possibilities ahead of us."

"Agents Relentless and Vindictive were sent to monitor this township by the Great General himself," Onerous replied. "And I"—he patted the bizarre weapon—"along with the Harmonious Fist of Inevitable Truth, was sent to retrieve them. Do you doubt the Great General would have chosen either of us if the possibility of failure crossed his mind?"

Cavric looked pointedly away. "I do not believe so, Relic Guard."

"See, then, that you lead by example." Onerous swept a gaze over the streets. "The Vagrants were last seen here. We do not leave until they are dead or Relentless and Vindictive are found." He glanced back to Cavric. "Do you find this amenable, Low Sergeant?"

Cavric said nothing. Relic Guards were handpicked by the Great General to use his weapons. They acted as his authority and there was only ever one correct answer to any question they asked.

Well, technically two, if you consider whatever screams you make as you're torn apart by weapons that should not exist to be an answer.

"The Great General's wishes are clear," Onerous said, leading the way. "Anyone not sworn to the Revolution dies here."

"Savage. Diligent," Cavric spoke up. Two soldiers at the back of the square snapped to attention. "Take the gate here. Raise the alarm if you see anyone in or out." He pointed to two more soldiers. "Brilliant. Contemplative. Sweep the alleys, check the flanks, search wherever he may have been stashed." He nodded at the remaining two soldiers. "Able and Generous, you're with me. We rally at the main square in fifteen minutes and plan from there. Stay sharp. Stay alert. Stay safe. Ten thousand years."

"*Ten thousand years!*" the soldiers barked in perfect unison as they split off to carry out their orders.

I grimaced, hearing their gunpikes rattle as they locked them into firing position. It was a primate's weapon—inaccurate, inelegant, and little more than a fancy spear that could fire a single bullet.

But when that bullet was a severium charge, you didn't need to be accurate or elegant. You didn't see severium outside the Revolution that often for a reason—it could tear through armor, shields, and if they weren't careful, whoever was firing it.

So, yeah, things didn't get *less* complicated with that shit around.

"And by the General's graces, keep each other in view," Cavric called after them. "Raise the alarm if you lose someone. Relentless would never forgive me if I let anyone get killed searching for him."

I watched them file away and I had to admit, I was a little impressed. Most Revolutionaries I knew were either brainwashed fanatics or corrupt bureaucrats. I didn't think I had ever seen one give even half a shit about his soldiers.

Handsome, honest, *and* kind. Low Sergeant Cavric Proud was proving to be quite the impressive man.

It'd be a real shame if I had to kill him here.

If he was as smart as I hoped he was or as dumb as he looked, though, it wouldn't come to that. I could make it out of here alive, if I was careful.

All I had to do was find Liette...

And avoid the five Revolutionaries...

And their high-powered gunpikes...

And their death-spewing weapon...

And the insane cult of witch hunters prowling around...

And...

Well, at that point, I supposed I had better get on with it before I started realizing how bad this sounded.

I moved to pull Jeff out, but something burned against my leg. I could feel the Cacophony in his sheath, the metal almost groaning in its desire to be out. I didn't plan on wasting *any* bullets here, let alone magical ones, but if the heat searing through my trousers was any indication, he was feeling insistent.

Sometimes, I just had to spoil him.

He all but leapt into my hand, no longer quite so heavy as his eagerness burned into my palm. I slipped another slug—Discordance—into the chamber, racked it. The plan was still to get out without anyone noticing me, but I'd never had that kind of luck before. And if I was going to make a mess out of this...

Well, shit, I might as well make it glorious, right?

I waited until the Revolutionaries vanished from view down below. I made my way down the stairs, crept through the public house, and out the door—too risky to go back up on the roofs with this many eyes in the township. I glanced up and down the street—the sentries kept their backs to me, while the rest of them were long gone. Creeping quickly as I dared, I slipped out the door and into a nearby alley.

I tried to picture Stark's Mutter in my head. It was a big enough town that there must be more than one entrance, probably a rear gate opposite the first one. Liette would figure it out, too, and make for that entrance. I could make it through the alleys, get to that gate before they could post more sentries there, then flee.

And I was keen on doing just that, weaving my way through the cramped spaces between the houses, when I heard a breathless voice whisper.

"Mother of fuck..."

I crept around to the corner of the alley and saw that it emptied out into the town square, with all its twisted corpses and hard black earth.

Cavric and his two soldiers stood there, the discipline and fervor having left them as they gazed upon the horror of Vraki's handiwork. Their gunpikes hung at their sides, their eyes were wide in uncomprehending horror, and their mouths...

"Fuck...*FUCK*."

...were at a decided loss for words.

"Sergeant," one soldier whispered. "Could one of these be..."

"None of them look like Relentless." Cavric shook his head. "But...damn. This is what he was sent to find. We're too late..." His breath left him on a cold, hopeless sigh. "Too fucking late."

"Imperial animals, sir," the other soldier growled. "Vagrant or no, every mage is a damned psychopath. We should return with a full battalion, burn every house to the ground, and—"

"We have our orders," Cavric interrupted. "We won't find our agents with fire. And it..." He took one last look over the sacrificial site before turning away. "It won't help these people. Keep your eyes open and your triggers clear. If there are any survivors left from... *this*... I want them found and I want them safe."

"But, sir, the Relic Guard gave us no orders to save civilians."

"He shouldn't have to."

Like I said, it'd be a real shame if I had to kill Cavric Proud here.

But I'm a practical girl. I don't waste food, I don't waste liquor, and I don't waste shots.

Cavric was standing out in the open. His gaze was somewhere far away from where I was hiding. His head was in the Cacophony's sights as I drew the gun's hammer back and aimed.

It was a good call, I knew, a smart one. The chain of command that held the Revolution together was made of glass: stiff and inflexible, but fragile. Years of propaganda had done nothing to teach them how to think for themselves. If I killed Cavric now, the rest of them would go running, paralyzed without someone to give them orders. I could easily find Liette and escape in the chaos.

Hell, I told myself, I wouldn't even need to hit his head. A Discordance slug aimed right at his body would knock his lungs clear out of his rib cage. Just one shot and I could just fucking *stroll* out...

My hand trembled. My eye twitched. My finger tightened around the Cacophony's trigger.

Lady only knows why I didn't pull it.

Maybe there were just too few honest people left in the Scar. Maybe I had killed far too many. Or maybe I really was just that fucking stupid.

Either way, I lowered the Cacophony. I bit back the pain as he burned in my hand, incensed at being denied a kill. But it was a slow, weak burn; clearly, he hadn't thought Cavric to be all that worth killing to begin with.

Maybe we're both just romantics at heart.

I kept him close, all the same, as I slipped back into the alley and made my way between the houses. The fifth alley emptied onto a road, and once I peered out, I found a grin growing on my face. There it was, just about a hundred feet away: the rear gate, a wooden affair with its doors wide open and waiting for me to just stroll through.

But my grin died as soon as I saw the fragile shadow of a girl standing between it and me, arms wrapped around her body and staring down at the ground.

"Liette!" I cried out, rushing toward her. She didn't look up. Not until I laid a hand on her shoulder. She jerked away, her nails flailing out and striking me across the cheek. I seized her by the shoulders. "*Easy*," I hissed. "Easy."

It took another moment of labored breathing and three more of trembling before she steadied long enough to look at me and see me. And still, the fear didn't ebb from her stare. Not as she pulled free of me. Not as she turned away.

"You're not hurt," I observed, searching her for blood and seeing none. "I'm not, either, in case you were wondering." I fingered the spot where she'd hit me. "Not that I'm not flattered that you remembered what I taught you about going for the eyes, but aim a little higher next time."

She didn't say a word. She didn't move. And I didn't have time for her to sort this out.

"Listen," I said, approaching her again, "I know what you saw was fucked-up, but we can't stay and—"

"Did Vraki do that?"

Her voice sounded so soft, so uncertain, I almost didn't believe it was her.

"Did his magic do that to those people?" She turned and faced me. Her silence was easier to deal with than the tears in her eyes. "Is he going to do that to you?"

I had a thousand retorts for that. A thousand threats, a thousand boasts, a thousand assurances that I wasn't afraid of dying at his hands. But she wouldn't have believed any of them.

She knew what I dreamed of.

"Is that what you're leaving for?" she asked. "To go and chase down people who can do...*that*?"

"You saw what they did," I replied. "I can't let them do that to anyone else."

"That's not why you're doing it. That's not why you're chasing them. That's not..." She gritted her teeth, clutched her head, trying to claw an answer out of her skull. "How can you be so determined to go after *that*? How can you just...just..."

I've heard the pleas of men about to die by my hand. I've seen the hate on their lips as they curse my name. I've watched people draw blades and form armies to try to bring me down. Never did I know how much damage I could do until she looked at me, tears in her eyes, and spoke.

"What am I doing wrong that you'd choose *this* over me?"

Maybe there were words that could have explained it, why I had to find those names and stop them—words about what had happened here, words about finding the missing children, words that didn't taste like birdshit on my tongue when I spoke them. But I didn't have time to find them.

"Come on," I muttered. "We can't stay here. The town's crawling with enemies we can't afford to face."

The Cacophony sizzled in my hand, sullen, but he didn't do anything worse as I headed for the gate, Liette behind me. Don't get me wrong; on my list of things I hate, disappointing my magical Hellfire-spewing gun was pretty high on the list. But just above that was dying horribly to witch hunters or gun-toting fanatics.

And at the very top?

"You there! HALT!"

Coincidence.

Motherfucker, but I *hate* coincidence.

I whirled, pushing Liette behind me, my eyes staring down the Cacophony's sights at the young girl standing fifteen feet away from me. A shot from here wouldn't leave anything but a stain.

Fuck me, I should have pulled the trigger.

The age of conscription in the Revolution is fifteen. Propaganda training begins as soon as they can talk. Kids get two brief years to be young before Weiless starts turning them into soldiers. The minute they turn three, they know that one day they'll meet a grisly, violent end. Just like this girl knew that.

But I looked into those too-wide eyes and that mouth hanging just a little open and I knew that if I pulled that trigger, all that would be said of my legend was that Sal the Cacophony killed a scared little girl who didn't know any better.

I wasn't ready to add that chapter to my life.

"In... in the name of the... in the name of the R-Revo—" the girl tried to stammer out. Her gunpike was shaking; this was the first time she had pointed it at anything other than a target.

"Kid," I said. "You aim that at me for five more seconds, the Revolution isn't going to remember your name." I drew the hammer back with an emphatic *click*. "I'm going to blow it off the face of the Scar, along with the rest of you."

I could feel Liette's eyes boring into the back of my head, but I couldn't stop. It was working. I could see the doubt blossom in her eyes, the fear take hold. The blood thundering in her heart was making her arms tired, her legs weak. Another second and she'd drop the weapon and I'd be off.

"Hold it right there!"

As it turned out, though, a second was all her friends needed to ruin *that* plan. I heard hammers clicking, felt that cold dread that comes from knowing a barrel's pointed at you. I turned and saw them. Two more soldiers in the alley I had just come from. Footsteps at my back told me another pair were upon me, cutting off our escape.

The luckwrighting in my scarf could take the shot. If I kept myself between them and Liette, she'd be okay. With a little luck, we'd both survive. Still, I took some small comfort in knowing it could be worse.

"Hold your fire! Hold your fire, damn you!"

But I guess even small comforts aren't for women like me, eh?

Cavric came up from the alley. He took the situation in with a few seconds and a quick glance. And while the look on his face suggested he was certainly confused to see me here, he seemed to quickly deduce the general situation of me pointing a big-ass gun at one of his soldiers.

The smallest comfort I could manage was that Onerous and his big fucking Relic wasn't with them.

"Everyone, let's just stay calm," he said in that soothing tone of voice that suggested he didn't have a lot of experience getting people to put down their weapons. Sure enough, his soldiers didn't seem to hear him; I could feel their fingers itching their triggers. "Sal," he said, turning toward me, "what are you doing here?"

"Oh, you know..." I sniffed. "Stuff."

"That's an awfully big gun for doing stuff."

"I've got a very long to-do list, Sergeant Proud," I replied, never taking my eyes off the soldier. "Your children put their toys down, I'll go back to doing it and I won't add 'blowing a bunch of dumb assholes' brains out' to it."

"She knows something, Sergeant," one of the soldiers said. "I know it. She knows something about Relentless. Why else would a Vagrant be skulking around?"

Cavric held a breath. "Sal, if you'd calm down and come with us, we'd—"

"Touch me and you'll bury your boys here, Sergeant," I replied.

He glanced over my shoulder at Liette, concern in his eyes. "Your companion, she's—"

Liette huddled behind me. I held my arm out in front of her, snarled.

"Touch *her* and I won't leave enough to bury."

He didn't know me well. But the look in his eyes told me he knew enough to know I wasn't lying. "There's no need for this to escalate." He glanced toward his soldiers. "If we all just lower our weapons..."

The intricacies of the Revolution's chain of command were lost on me, but presumably the gentle way he made a suggestion to his troops instead of, you know, actually commanding them was probably why Cavric was a *low* sergeant.

I heard a hammer click behind me.

"Soldiers," Cavric said, warning. "This won't help us find Relentless. Lower your weapons."

Too late now. What little discipline they had was overwhelmed by fear.

I heard someone take two steps closer from behind.

"By the General's graces," Cavric said, "don't *do* this!"

They weren't listening. I wasn't listening. We were all running it through in our heads, a hundred different ways this could end, all of them badly. My body tensed, my finger twitched. I got ready to pull the trigger and run.

I heard a gunshot go off behind me.

I heard a scream.

And I heard a body hit the ground.

I whirled, saw the smoke from the barrel of the soldier's gunpike as he toppled to the ground. I saw the blood leaking out from the gaping wound in his chest. I saw the red glistening off the machete of the tattooed, half-clad Havener standing over him with a manic grin on his face.

"My, my..." The Sightless Sister croaked out as she shambled forward, her remaining two henchmen running up to reinforce their brother. "Such treasures the Seeing God has sent us today. A single heretic, a slew of atheists, and a..."

Her eyeless sockets turned toward me. Her wrinkled lips curled into a snarl. Her mouth opened in a shriek and...

Well, you know when you meet someone new and you don't know their name but they know yours and it's really awkward?

"Slaughter the heretics!"

And they also want to kill you?

"Bring me that weapon! Bring me the Cacophony!"

Yeah.

That.

SIXTEEN

STARK'S MUTTER

Now, it's true that among the kidnappings, the burning of people at the stake, the destruction of entire towns and whatnot, not a lot of Scarfolk have many nice things to say about the good people of Haven. But spend a little time around them, you start to learn that they have a lot of good qualities.

"BLEED, HERETIC!"

Like their enthusiasm.

The Havener, the big fellow with the bloody blade, came leaping over the twitching body of the soldier. Red painted the air as he swung his sword madly, dashing toward me with a shriek on his lips and blood on his mouth. He charged past the Revolutionaries, completely heedless of them.

Right up until they fired, anyway.

Gunpikes cracked. Clouds of smoke blossomed in the street. I heard a bullet go past my ear just before I heard it punch through a human skull. Five little red flowers bloomed on the Havener's skin, the biggest and brightest right in the middle of his forehead.

I glanced behind me. Cavric was still staring down the sights of his gunpike, eyes trained on the Havener.

That turned out to be a good idea. Because, as I learned once I felt hands wrap around my throat, he actually wasn't quite dead.

"*Bleed... bleed... bleed...*" the Havener growled, and I wasn't sure if he was talking about me or himself. He had dropped his weapons to grab my neck, tactics forgotten in the urge to kill me with what strength hadn't leaked out of him yet. But blood was streaming from the holes punched through his body and his grip was weak.

Weak enough that he felt it when Liette rushed up and jammed her quill right into a vein in his wrists. He screamed. I whipped the Cacophony up, smashed his grip against the Havener's skull. Bone crunched, and the bastard finally took the hint, falling to the ground, unmoving. And in my hand, I could feel the gun growing pleasantly warm to the touch.

He liked this.

And he was going to like this next part a lot more.

"Fire! Fire at will! Bring them down!"

Cavric was screaming more for his benefit than his soldiers. Their weapons were already reloaded and blazing, firing round after round at the Haveners. It was the reckless, eyes-closed, first-day-on-the-job terrified shooting, no one bothering to aim or even to look.

Which made it a fucking pain to get out of the way.

I went low, grabbing Liette by the hand and hurrying to the other side of the street and ducking into another alley, which, as it turned out, had the town's wall at the other end, making it about the best place to get pinned down I could have chosen.

"*Stay,*" I snarled as I shoved her into the alley.

She didn't question me, offering me only the briefest of nods. Despite knowing exactly which muscle to stab a man to get him to let go, she wasn't a fighter. But neither was I.

Me and the gun in my hand? We were killers.

As I turned and peered out into the street, the Cacophony was humming in my hand, waiting to be unleashed. In the fracas of screaming fanatics and cracking fire, I imagined he could cause a lot of chaos. But chaos is only useful if it's pointed away from you. And at that moment, the street was *alive* with flying bullets.

"Death to heretics!"

Not that this seemed to bother the Haveners.

In the middle of the street, the closest Revolutionary was back-pedaling in a desperate attempt to get back to his comrades, squeezing off a shot. It whizzed past the Havener rushing toward him, bit through a bleeding arm. It didn't seem to slow the Havener down one bit as he took a flying leap and landed on the soldier, bearing him to the ground.

Metal wailed, blood flew as the Havener's blade pumped mechanically, carving through the feeble, flailing defense the soldier put up as he screamed for someone to help him.

I hoped his comrades heard him. Because *I* sure wasn't feeling like getting murdered.

Blood sprayed as another bullet took the Havener in the ribs. It should have killed him. I have no idea how it didn't. Neither did the soldier who fired it. The poor Revolutionary dope merely stared, slack-jawed, as the Havener picked up his ever-burning torch and hurled it, spinning, through the air to take the soldier right in the face.

He went down screaming, clawing at his seared flesh. His comrade leaned down to help him. Admirable, but not smart. Neither of them saw it when the Havener leapt upon them and tore into them with his blade.

The air was alive with terror, with blood, with bullets. The two Revolutionaries went down screaming, punching and flailing with their gunpikes. Their comrades thrust their weapons into the Havener's flanks. He just howled with anger, heedless of anything but the blood on his blade and the bodies under him.

The reek of fear and fluid mingled with the acrid tang of gunsmoke, neither of which were enough to smother the sounds of the dying.

I bolted out of the alley, hoping that, what with the wanton murder and shooting, no one would miss me when I ran for the gates. Of course, that plan had been better before I remembered there were *three* Haveners.

I pulled to a halt just in time to narrowly avoid the swinging blade.

The Havener roared, stepping into his next swing as he lunged at me again. I couldn't tell the difference between the fanatics most of the time, but I recognized this one. Or rather, I recognized his facial wounds. I had just nearly caved this fucker's head in a moment ago.

So how the hell was he still up?

He leapt toward me. Jeff was out and in my hand, rising up to meet his thick blade. I caught him at the crossguard, drove my knee up into his groin. And when that didn't do it, I brought the Cacophony up there instead.

Brass smashed between his legs, sent him reeling to the ground. And even with the kick to the jaw I gave him, he wouldn't take the hint. He was already scrabbling to get back to his feet.

I glanced around. There was Havener blood on the ground, but no Havener corpses to go with it. They continued to fight, through bullet wounds and lacerations the Revolutionaries had given them, showing no signs of even being tired, let alone dying.

Amid the blood and steel flashing through the air, I could just barely make out the glow of a pair of hellish lights in eyeless sockets. The Sister stood nearby, leaning on her staff, sharpened teeth twisted in a smile as her eyes burned with unearthly light.

Her. Whatever fucked-up magic she had was keeping her brothers alive and fighting. Take her out, I knew, and I had a chance at ending this. I dropped to one knee, flipped the Cacophony's chamber open, and jammed my sword into the earth. I heard the jingle of metal shells, the screaming of the dying…

"The Great General is with us, brothers."

And, cutting cleanly through it, the sound of things getting much worse.

At the other end of the alley, Relic Guard Onerous appeared. Unfazed by the carnage, he stepped over the corpses of his fallen brethren. He stood tall, raising the Relic, that alien weapon, in his hands and leveling it down the alley. In his hands, the strange stone weapon began to stir—not fired. Something like a Relic doesn't do a thing so rudimentary as "fire."

No.

That weapon woke up.

And screamed.

I've been unlucky enough to be on the receiving end of a Relic once before. And though I was lucky enough to live, I'll never forget the sound it made. The sound of earth groaning under your feet. The sound of stone screaming as it tore itself out of the ground. The sound that sent me pressing myself, belly-down, into the dirt and covering my head.

For all the good it would do.

The crystal on the end of the Relic glowed with a painfully bright light. And from it, a hail of projectiles launched. Thin and needle-like, yet brighter than a sun, it was as though hardened bolts of light spat from the Relic's maw. They flew on rasping whistles, leaving the reek of smoking air in their wake as they punched clean, perfectly shaped holes through wood, through dirt...

Through flesh.

The Haveners' mouths gaped open, in screams or in curses, I didn't know. The sound of their agony was lost beneath that groaning noise, those rasping whispers, as the light punched through them. They fell, one after the other. The first in two pieces, the second in six, the third with one tremendous hole through his chest.

Or so I thought. I couldn't count them accurately from down here. I couldn't hear them over the groaning weapon. And I didn't dare look up. Not until the sound died in my ears and the smell of burning blood hung in a still, quiet air.

No smoke. No fires. No more blood than had been there when the weapon started firing. Relics were not weapons of carnage. They were weapons of cleansing. They were not employed to kill, but to wipe clean.

The Haveners lay where they had fallen, their wounds bloodless, as though someone had simply reached out and plucked skin and bone and organ out of them and left behind husks. The Revolutionaries, those who had remained, lay not far away. And the ones who had been granted the grisly deaths at the hands of the Haveners almost looked luckier than the ones who had been rent apart by their comrade.

Relics were of no origin that anyone but the Great General knew. They could snipe a bird's eye from a hundred yards and leave not a drop of blood. But they were only as good as their wielder. And if he didn't happen to care where he hit...

A familiar sight caught my eye. In a pool of blood, against the wall of a building, Cavric lay facedown in the dust. His hands still curled feebly around the gunpike, as though he weren't ready to quit, even now. I couldn't tell if he had died by the Relic or by the Haveners.

"Ah, fuck..."

I wasn't sure why I said that. I wasn't sure why it bothered me. Whatever they said about protecting the common people of the Scar, the Revolutionaries were as savage, brutish, and vicious as the people they fought against. A few more dead ones shouldn't have bothered me.

But, fuck, he had just seemed so *nice*, you know?

I made to inch toward him, as if to see if he had somehow been spared. Or maybe just to close his eyes. I didn't know. And it didn't matter.

"Do not weep for them."

I had another problem.

I twisted onto my back, bringing my blade up as a shadow fell upon me. A heavy boot followed, its heel catching me at the elbow and bringing it back down to the earth. I screamed as pain lanced through the joint, my arm pinned beneath a heavy foot and my blade with it.

"A Revolutionary's greatest goal is to give his life in pursuit of the Mandate." Onerous stood over me, the weapon still twitching, alive in his grasp. "They would have been proud to have seen the Great General's will done. And they would have been insulted to see their lives mourned by a Vagrant such as yourself."

He aimed the Relic at me. And I know this sounds crazy, but I somehow thought the damn thing was smiling at me.

"Sal the Cacophony."

"You've heard of me," I replied, wincing in pain.

"Among the Revolution, your name is known, your vile deeds are written, and your treachery is legendary."

"You're exaggerating."

There was the sound of boots on the ground nearby. Onerous and I both looked up to see Liette emerging from the alley, a bloodied quill intended for him in her hand. He narrowed his eyes, unsure what to make of this frail woman's sudden appearance.

I, however, was very sure of what to make of it.

I pivoted, swinging my legs up even as I swung my head away from the Relic's maw. Onerous glanced down just in time to see both my legs wrap around his left and use the weight of my lower body to pull him off his feet. He screamed, struggling to aim the weapon toward me. I brought my scarf up with my free hand, wrapping it around his wrist and pulling the weapon away. With my other hand, I brought up my sword and jammed it up through his armpit.

The weapon fell from his grasp. His scream tore through the air. He lay, bleeding, upon the earth.

"If my treachery were *truly* legendary," I said, "you would have expected something like that."

I glanced toward Liette, who stared back in alarm. But before I could say a word to her, another voice spoke.

"Dear me, dear me . . ."

The Sightless Sister came shambling up, unfazed by the carnage and untouched by the Relic's fire. Leaning heavily on her staff, her glowing sockets rested upon the least damaged of her kin.

"I confess, to my eternal shame, that the rumors of your capacity for violence would be so inadequate," she said through a sharp-toothed smile. "Cacophony. Our scriptures are rife with tales of your malevolence."

Funny how, in all of this knowledge about me, not one of them ever mentioned how pretty I was.

"Had I known, I would have invoked him sooner."

She pressed the tip of her staff to the brow of the dead Havener.

And, though I like to think I was a well-traveled woman, I almost vomited to see him stir back to life.

"*Sister*..." the Havener gasped, reaching up with one trembling hand to find her withered fingers. "*I... I have failed him. I have failed the God...*"

"You have, brother," she replied. She shook her head and lay her hand upon his brow. "But you shall be with him soon. Your immortal soul shall answer to him. But your flesh..."

She smiled broadly. Her staff glowed.

"He has a use for your vessel."

A red light consumed her body. It flowed from her flesh into his. The Havener's body stiffened upright. I saw the fist that was his heart glow crimson, the light racing through his veins. Her grin was black against the light.

I started backing away, uncertain of what I was dealing with, but damn certain I didn't want to stay to see it finished. Yet before I had taken three steps, I heard something behind me. Groaning stone, a weapon stirring to life, a rasping curse from a dying man's lips.

"Ten thousand years," Onerous snarled.

I whirled. He held the weapon in the hand that still worked. The Relic sighed itself alive and fired. A bolt of light cut through the sky. I leapt to the side and tumbled away as the bolt sped past me. The Sightless Sister fell, a hole punched through her throat, a grin still etched on her face.

One heartbeat. That was all it took to kill her. So fast.

And too fucking late.

Even as the Sister's body fell, smiling and lifeless, the Havener was rising. His body stiffened, his shattered spine suddenly ramrod straight. His heart continued to beat, the glow racing through his veins brightening with every audible thump. He bent over, let out a guttural, raw-throated howl. He clutched his belly as though he were about to be sick.

As I was about to find out, he was going to be much worse.

Magic, *true* magic, comes from the Lady Merchant. You make the

Barter, you get the power. It's the way the Imperium was built, the way the Emperors held power for sixty generations.

But there are other ways.

It isn't an art what the priests of Haven do. The power granted to them by their Seeing God isn't like that of the Lady Merchant's. The scholars of the Imperium call it pagan magic, regard it with the same amused disdain one might look at a child draped in adult clothes in an attempt to look grown up. The Seeing God's power is unreliable; its effects are uncontrollable; its costs are unpredictable.

But the results are hard to argue with.

With every labored breath, the Havener's skin bubbled. A bright red line of light appeared at the top of his brow, bisected him down the center. His body rose, but his skin didn't, flesh sloughing off to pool on the floor like discarded clothing. A towering mass of naked sinew, steam peeling off red flesh and veins alight with a hellish glow stared down at me through a blackened skull for a face.

The Havener was gone.

And what was left was a monster I had only heard about in drunken tales.

"*Liette!*" I screamed, not taking my eyes from the monster. "*RUN!*"

He turned, peering out of deep sockets. Huge. Fleshless. Bristling with throbbing muscle and bits of bone jutting from his sinew. In the face of such horror, Revolutionary, Imperial, and Scarfolk alike had crumpled into a numb, shrieking heap.

Onerous, however, started shooting.

The Relic wailed to life. A bolt of light tore through the monstrosity's shoulder. It snarled—not in pain, but in rage. It leapt. It sailed through the air, over my head, and landed.

On Onerous.

The Relic flew from his hands, just as his blood flew from his mouth, as his spine snapped under the creature's weight, folding him in half. I scrambled to my feet, trying to get away from it as it turned a baleful pair of sockets toward me.

I backpedaled over corpses and bloodstained dirt. He came lumbering forward, loping on overlong arms like some kind of primate. He reached a hand toward me. My blade flashed, caught two of his oversized fingers. But a Relic's fire had only just bothered him. A blade didn't even seem to tickle him, breaking out a tiny pinprick of blood across his hand.

And he smiled like he had been waiting for that.

I turned. I bolted. Legs like tree trunks tensed and sent him leaping into the air, his roar echoing. I rushed to get out of the way as he came crashing down, but it didn't matter. He struck the earth like a boulder, sending the ground quaking and knocking me off my feet and onto my ass. My blade flew from my hand.

I scrambled to face him, one hand fumbling for a handful of shells in my satchel and hastily jamming two of them into the Cacophony's chamber. He whirled on me, his mandibular grin lined up with the Cacophony's sights. What the fuck had I put in the chamber? Hoarfrost? Hellfire? Steel Python? No time to question—all I could do was pull and hope I liked the answer.

I got it in the explosion of flames as a slug burst across his chest and erupted into a bright, fiery blossom. He howled as Hellfire spread across his skin, gnawing at his sinew and blackening his bone spurs. He became a wailing, writhing pyre, flailing his burning arms and roaring to be heard above the crackling of flames.

But he wasn't dying.

Why the *fuck* wasn't he dying?

I leapt to my feet, took off running, one hand flipping open the Cacophony's chamber; one hand rummaging around in my pouch. I could see I had slammed Hoarfrost in the chamber, unspent. I pulled out another shell.

"Hoarfrost?" I screamed at whatever god oversees disorganized ammo pouches. "What the fuck am I going to do with *two*?"

No time to wait for a divine reply. I jammed it into the chamber, reached for another.

Something shot out before I could, crushed the wind from me as it wrapped around my waist. The Cacophony fell from my hand as I was hoisted up into the air. I felt my body crushed between five great fingers, the air squeezed out of my lungs as I was brought before the monstrosity's hollow eyes. Smoke poured from a smile that spread across a face blackened by flame in a smug, self-satisfied manner. Or a hungry, perverse manner. Or just a lunatic manner.

The thing had a skull for a face—I couldn't fucking tell what it was thinking.

Nor did it matter. He tightened his fingers. I felt bones about to break. I felt a scream die in my throat, no air left to voice it. I felt the blood rush into my ears, deafening me to everything.

Almost everything.

I heard the rush of tiny feet, the scrawl of quill and ink. Liette appeared by its ankle, hastily scribbling something onto the brute's calf. I wanted to scream at her for not running, but again, I was being choked. Instead, I saw her dreadful work take shape.

Like I said, wrighting flesh is a master's art. It requires a still canvas and a careful application. If the patient is moving—or, say, choking the life out of someone—as the script is applied, like Liette was doing, things can go awry.

Like how the brute's calf muscle exploded in a bright flash of light.

He screamed, falling to a knee and lashing out with a hand. Liette narrowly darted away from the blow, stumbling and falling to her face. Stupid of her to try that. She wasn't a fighter. The brute hadn't let me go and now he raised a great hand to crush her where she lay.

The crack of gunfire rang out. A bright red dot burst across the monster's brow. He paused, like he had just been bitten by a mosquito, turned toward his left. Another shot. Another bright red dot. This one much bigger as the bullet took him right in the eye.

Apparently, the thing *could* feel pain. Or at least anger so great that it was indistinguishable from pain. He dropped me. I fell to the ground, gasping for air, the blood fighting to return itself to my veins. Darkness crept away from my eyes and I could see my untimely savior, tiny and blue and dark-haired against the monster advancing toward him.

I *knew* there was a reason I liked Cavric.

He stood there, his comrades' gunpikes assembled in a crude panoply at his feet, not even shaken by the two-ton naked slab of flesh lumbering toward him. He aimed, he fired; another bright red burst slowed the monster. He tossed the spent gunpike aside to join two other empty ones. He picked up another, aimed, fired. He was choosing his shots, firing off carefully, hoping to bring the thing down before he had to make a futile run for it. Here, a kneecap exploded. There, a bullet punched through teeth. With every shot, the beast slowed.

But didn't stop.

I found the Cacophony, felt his warmth calling to me. I plucked him up, pulled the first slug I could find out of my pouch, and slammed it into the final chamber. Discordance. I hoped he liked it as much as I did.

The monster swung a massive arm just as Cavric leapt out of the way. Not quick enough. The thing's hand grazed his side. But even a graze was enough to send him rolling across the ground and smashing against a wall. The thing roared, bringing both arms up to crush him into paste.

The clack of a chamber.

The click of a trigger.

The sound of the Cacophony's shot rang out, louder than any gunpike. The first shell burst across the beast's back. Hoarfrost spread over his blackened sinew, a virulent disease of blue and white. It shimmered and cracked and bit past the scorched skin and sank into the muscles with freezing fingers.

The monster turned toward me, his skin cracking and breaking as he did. The spell was doing its job; in another four seconds, he'd be damn near unable to move. And in another two, he'd have crushed my skull.

I pulled, fired the second shell. Another burst of Hoarfrost spread across him, covering his flesh in a layer of ice. He reached out with a stiffening arm, the sound of ice popping and cracking as he did. His fingers were two inches from my face when they froze solid.

His body went rigid. His mouth was frozen in gaping, silent fury. His empty eyes darted about madly in a head that wouldn't move, trying to figure out just what the fuck had happened and how the hell he was going to get out.

And I sure wasn't going to give him time for that.

I aimed the Cacophony straight for his mouth. I shut my eyes tightly. I whispered to no one.

"Eres va atali."

I pulled the trigger, fired Discordance right into his skull.

Like I said, I don't buy into religion. And so I didn't expect anyone to answer when I offered two prayers: that this was going to kill him and that none of the ensuing mess would get in my mouth.

I still don't believe in gods.

Because only one of those prayers got answered.

SEVENTEEN

STARK'S MUTTER

Shells and good whiskey were two commodities hard to come by in the Scar. But since I had just squandered three of the former in one day, I figured I could be forgiven a few fingers of the latter, too.

I tossed the flask back. I took a deep sip of the burning liquid. I swirled it around in my mouth and spat it out onto the ground. I smacked my lips. I blanched.

No good. I could still taste that fucker's brains.

Or what I assumed was brains, anyway. Really, it had all come out in one big mess of thick red chunks. The monster's body lay nearby, still rigid with frost, steam coiling out of the fragmented red stump where his skull had been. It had been an impressive kill, I had to admit; the Cacophony was almost vibrating in his sheath with lingering excitement.

But my eyes were on the shriveled-up corpse that lay twenty feet away from him. It might sound cold that, of all the people who died in Stark's Mutter that day, I should feel bad for the loss of one person, specifically. But if it did, I'd tell you to shut your ears, because what I said next would have made me sound like a real asshole.

"Should have left you alive." I wandered over to the corpse, squatted down on my haunches, and stared right into the Sightless Sister's empty sockets. "I bet you'd be real useful right about now."

Her lips were still twisted into a grin; she knew that was a lie as well as I did. What torture I could have done to make her talk would have seemed like a gentle tickle compared to whatever Haven had done to make her into this gnarled thing that lay before me.

But I would have given it my best shot at least. It was the only lead I had left.

Haven's magic was a mystery to everyone but the Seeing God and his followers. No one knew where their magic came from or what it did. So if anyone was going to understand how to effectively use a magic that the Imperium *didn't* understand how to use, it would be them.

And when it came to summoning, the Imperium knew not much.

Vraki had gotten his hands on one of Haven's mysterious trinkets that amplified magic, let him do things he shouldn't be able to.

And the Haveners had followed its scent to Stark's Mutter. But how had he gotten it? Years of the Imperium sending its best Maskmages and the Revolution ordering its most cunning spies into Haven had turned up nothing but a shit-ton of corpses impaled on their walls. Vraki was a Prodigy, one of the best, but even he and the rest of the seven didn't have what it took to pilfer a relic out of Haven.

But... that didn't mean it couldn't be done.

It probably wouldn't surprise you to know that the Scar had its share of rogues. But the Scar is a hard place; it chews up the amateurs and shits out the best, most cold-blooded scum to ever skulk in the shadows. Instead of bandits, we have Vagrants. Instead of drug peddlers, we have Freemakers. And instead of thieves...

We have the Ashmouths.

Not a coin is lifted from a pocket that they don't know about. Not a secret is whispered that they don't listen in on. And not a deal goes down that they don't get a cut of. They'd been a pain in the sides of the Imperium, the Revolution, and more: saboteurs, assassins, and smugglers who had cost the world's powers almost as much as their wars had.

If they hadn't sold it to Vraki themselves, they knew where he got it. And where all those other names that were with him went— the Sightless Sister had confirmed they'd all been here. But getting ahold of them wasn't precisely easy. After all, they had managed to operate in the Scar without getting caught by the two greatest militaries in the world for years now.

But those were just armies.

I was Sal the Cacophony.

I had my ways.

"I think he might be dead."

And one of them was busy attending to the other.

Liette crouched over the limp figure of Cavric, unmoving in the bloodied dust. She had scrawled a few healing sigils over his wounds, but she was apparently unconvinced of their effectiveness.

"Is he breathing?" I asked.

She tapped her quill against his temple. "Technically, yes."

I squinted. "No one *technically* breathes. He either is or he isn't."

"One *technically* breathes in the same way that one *technically* can drink enough to suddenly be able to fellate oneself," she replied, rising up and dusting her skirt off. "That is, the process itself is doable and the result is charming if one happens to give a shit." She pushed her glasses up her nose. "As my particular defecations are considerably more precious than most, I hope you'll understand that I don't see much point in sparing them on another Revolutionary lackwit."

I rubbed my eyes, my frustration twofold. One because I had asked her not to bring that up again and two because I needed this guy alive.

"Can you wright him back to life or not?" I asked.

"Obviously," she replied. Her eyes drifted to the mess of bone and blood that had been the mutated Havener. "I'd consider it a far more valuable use of my time to study this anomaly, though. This might be the first physical evidence of Haven's magic left behind."

"Yeah, and you'd be evidence of how easily he can turn a woman into a fine paste if it weren't for me," I growled. "You'd be dead if it weren't for me. Third law." I pointed at Cavric. "Bring him back."

"What for? Do you like him?" She surveyed his body suspiciously. "Is he...funny or something?"

"I'll make you a deal," I said. "If he dies, then I'll drop it and you can go splashing in that thing's guts. But until then, you keep working."

Liette regarded me carefully in that way she did whenever she wanted to accuse me of something. She'd never come out and say it, of course—it wasn't that she didn't like men, despite not having much use for them outside a professional setting. It was more that...

Intellect like hers is a curse. The more you understand of the world, the less of it you trust. She's always been too aware of how quickly people can die, can break, can leave.

But intellect doesn't make it hurt less when they do.

"My head..."

A nearby groan spared me that conversation.

I spared a look for Liette as I made my way over to Cavric, now roused from his momentary brush with death. He got to his hands and knees, groaning. He held his head like he was checking to make sure it was still there. I didn't blame him; not many take a hit like that and make it out.

"Easy. Don't move too quick."

I knelt down, helped him off his knees and onto his ass. I propped him against the side of the house he had struck. He looked up at the splintered crater in the wood his body had left and blinked dumbly.

"Did *I* do that?"

"Technically, *he* did." I jerked a thumb back toward the headless beast behind us. "But credit where it's due: you made a lovely dent." I looked him over. No signs of heavy bleeding. "So...how are you?"

"Been better," he grunted. He spat onto the earth and I saw the phlegm was clear—no internal bleeding.

"Anything broken?"

He shook his head. "Not that I can feel. Though, admittedly, I'm still figuring out if I *can* feel. I should have taken a hit like that and been—" He paused as he noticed the sigils scrawled across his hand, then looked up at me with eyes wide with terror. "This is wrighting. *Magic.*"

"You're welcome," Liette muttered behind me.

"You took a heavy hit," I replied, ignoring her addendum. "I know the Revolution frowns on magic, but there was no other way to keep you stable and okay you aren't even listening, are you."

Panic fueled his fingers as he tried to scratch the sigils off his flesh. The Revolution was steeped in distrust of magic—being the down-trodden slaves of mages for ten thousand years will do that—but this was something I didn't need.

"Hey, *hey.*" I seized his wrists. "Calm down. It's not going to kill you."

"It could," Liette offered. "Applied incorrectly, at least." She adjusted her glasses. "If I was capable of doing anything incorrectly, that might be a concern."

"It goes against every line of every book of *every* teaching the Great General graced us with!" Cavric fought against my grip, feebly. "It's an abomination! It's unnatural! It's—"

"Keeping you alive," I finished for him. "Once we're sure that's not going to change, you can wipe it off. Your Great General doesn't have to know."

"My soldiers," he whispered.

"Huh?" I blinked. "Oh, yeah, them." I glanced at the dark red patches on the earth and I supposed he was wondering why there weren't corpses to go with them. "Yeah, no, I don't think they'll be talking to anyone, either. I loaded them up on your iron death machine. Figured you'd want to take them back to Lowstaff for a burial."

"Cremation," he corrected. "Burial is land that could be used for industry." He grunted as he tried to rise, failed, fell back to the earth. "Or so the Great General says."

"At the rate you nuls die, I can kind of see his logic." I sniffed. "Doesn't your Glorious General teach you how to fight Haveners?"

"We weren't expecting to *find* Haveners," he replied. "Or anyone, really. This was intended to be a simple extraction mission. We were looking for our spies, Agents Relentless and Vindictive. They were posted here observing some fugitives."

Cavric was a rare fellow, no doubt. Not often you meet anyone who'll just tell you what they were up to, let alone a Revolutionary. Though, I noted he didn't mention that Relentless had been looking for Vagrants. Or perhaps no one had bothered telling him.

"You can have another look around if you want," I replied, shrugging. "But I didn't find anyone here who wasn't already dead."

One horror was replaced with another upon his face as I saw the realization come creeping in. He had seen the town square. He knew what had happened to the townspeople.

"That's... that's right. They're..."

Revolutionaries typically don't find themselves at a loss for words—years of propaganda training sees to that. Revolutionaries also don't typically look like they're about to shed tears over a bunch of dead townsfolk. Cavric, I gathered, was not your typical Revolutionary.

Probably why he was just a low sergeant.

"And..." He glanced from me toward Liette. "And what were you two doing here?"

"Stopping by," I replied.

"Whilst pursuing stupidity," Liette muttered.

"What'd she say about pursuing?" Cavric asked.

"Knowledge. Pursuing knowledge. You know how scholars are."

"It sounded like she said stupidity—"

"Stark's Mutter was on our way to the next freehold," I hastily interrupted. "Wandered in, found this mess, then..." I gestured toward the blood. "Well, you know."

"And you just decided to stick around?"

"Don't tell me you're going to act surprised that a woman who shoots people for money went looking for trouble."

Lies didn't always come so easy for me. I was raised with the same values as all good little girls: don't lie, sit pretty, don't shoot people. But this was the Scar—not like a bird is going to stop from clawing your guts out to comment on how well-mannered you are.

Still, the suspicion melted from Cavric's face, replaced by a weary sigh. He trusted easily, this man. He hadn't been lied to enough to tell the difference between an honest person and someone like me. And part of me felt just a little worse for having lent him the impression I was someone he could trust.

Sometimes I think I did that a little too easily.

"Yeah, fair enough," he said. He sighed. "If Relentless were here and alive, he'd have come out by now. And if he's here and dead, I'll need more people to move him." He tried to rise again, this time with more success and a little help from me. "I'll have to let Cadre Command know about this, anyway. I'll come back with more soldiers and we'll give this place a proper look-through."

"Proper, huh?" I steadied him on his feet as he swayed.

"You sound skeptical."

"For Revolutionaries, 'proper' typically means a firing squad and vigorous mortar fire," Liette said, voice souring.

"I...That's not..." He sighed, shook his head, gave up. "We're not all that...zealous. And yeah, this township will probably be burnt to the ground for mercy's sake. But the people here deserve to be put to rest after what they were put through. I promise that they'll have that at least."

"Ah, Revolutionary mercy," Liette muttered. "Can we expect the full Revolutionary blessing and have you urinate on the ashes?"

I shot her a glare, looked over to him. "Can you walk?"

"I think so." He began with a stagger, but his pace soon steadied and we made our way back toward the town gates. "You could come with me, you know. Both of you. Sergeant Courageous would reward you for—"

"Courageous would find a reason to suspect my complicity and have me tortured for information he knew I didn't have."

"He wouldn't..." Cavric's face fell. "Yeah...he would."

We walked the remaining length in silence until we came to the gates. The Iron Boar stood, idle and silent in the afternoon sun. Without its engines belching smoke and fire, it looked like just another hunk of metal.

"What will you do now?" Cavric asked me as he made his way toward the machine's door.

"Get out of here before your comrades show up and burn the place down," Liette said, glancing over at the township. "Whatever could be learned here will be smothered beneath small-minded terror."

"Not that I don't appreciate the assistance"—Cavric glanced over the sigils on his hand, wiped them on his coat as he glared at Liette—"but there's no need for snideness. The Revolution is here to help." He glanced toward me, nodded. "Like you."

I bit back a cringe when he said that. The smile he shot me was uncomfortably honest.

I gestured toward the Iron Boar with my chin. "You can drive this thing?"

"I've been trained, yeah." He patted the engine's iron hide, smiled at the resonant sound. "She'll bring my soldiers home for the rest they deserve." He looked over his shoulder at me with a smile he should have saved for a better person than I was. "And it's all thanks to you, Sal. Whatever Courageous might write down in the official report, I'm going to make it known that you did the right thing. If the Revolution can ever make it up to you for..."

His voice died as he slid the door open and beheld a hold empty of his comrades' corpses.

Like I said, Cavric had a nice smile. All honest men have that smile. It's a rare thing in any part of the world, let alone the Scar. Rare and worth protecting.

Damn near broke my heart when I saw it melt off his face as he turned around and stared down the barrel of the Cacophony.

"As a matter of fact," I said as I pulled the hammer back, "there *is* a little favor I've been meaning to ask."

EIGHTEEN

HIGHTOWER

H e's dead, then?"

Tretta spat the question, her hands following, fists slamming down on the table as she all but lunged over the table toward her prisoner. The water cup, freshly refilled, went flying from the impact, dousing Sal as it did.

"So, two things," Sal said as she calmly wiped water from her face. "First of all, I didn't say he was dead. Second, can we perhaps work on the whole 'screaming and throwing things whenever I hear something I don't like' thing you do?"

"*And* Haven is involved with this entire mess?" Tretta snarled, though Sal didn't seem to notice.

"Maybe we could do a substitution method. Like the next time you feel like slamming your hands down and making a mess, just reach for a nice apple instead. That way, you'll get a positive outcome and a healthy snack for—"

"Do *not* toy with me, woman," Tretta growled as she leaned over the table, narrowing her eyes. "It's *you* who's charged for the atrocities at Stark's Mutter, not rogue Vagrants. Why should I believe anything that comes out of your mouth?"

"First of all, 'rogue Vagrant' is an unnecessary qualifier, since all Vagrants are rogues by way of having broken their oaths to the

Imperium. Secondly"—Sal shrugged—"why would I lie? You're already going to kill me."

"And if you don't tell me what *really* happened, I'll—"

"You'll what? Kill me even *deader*?" Sal yawned as she reclined in her chair. "You're already going to execute me, honey."

Tretta had the thought, not for the first time, that she would be well within her rights to reach for the hand cannon at her belt and shoot her dead right there, on principle, at least. Cadre Command would forgive her, she knew. They might even overlook the loss of a Revolutionary soldier if it meant disposing of a hated Vagrant, especially one this aggravating.

Without quite realizing it, her hand had slid down to her belt. And, without quite realizing why, she took a deep breath, pulled her hand away from the grip of the gun, and sat back down.

Cadre Command probably *would* overlook the loss of a soldier. It had been speeches, birthright, and favors that had gotten them their place. And it had been soldiers who had gotten her hers. Soldiers who had sworn to follow her and who she had sworn to protect. Soldiers like Cavric.

And whether it was him, his body, or just his fate that was uncovered by listening to this annoying—*profoundly* annoying—woman, then that was an agony she could suffer.

For now.

"There we are," Sal said, her smile wedging itself into a small, angry space between Tretta's brows. "Now, just keep breathing deeply and listen to the soothing sound of my voice."

No breath could come deep enough for Tretta to accomplish that. She growled at Sal to keep herself from strangling that soothing voice out of her prisoner's mouth.

"So Cavric is not dead," she said.

"I didn't say that, either."

"Does this sort of thing come naturally to you or do you actually sit down and think of reasons for people to shoot you in the face?"

"Well, talent can only get you so far." With infuriating comfort,

Sal stretched her manacled hands high above her head and yawned. The scar across her chest stretched with the effort. "But, at that point, Cavric was alive and well. He did, after all, help me out against the Haveners. It'd have been a touch rude to kill him then, wouldn't it?"

"Haven's complicity in this complicates things," Tretta muttered. "The presence of Vagrant criminals was a foregone conclusion and I would have laid odds that Imperial swine were also involved, but we are not officially at war with the Seeing God."

"Last month, I heard an entire squadron of Revolution spies turned up burning on their Kindling Wall. Or had you just sent them out to deliver a fruit basket?"

She narrowed her eyes. "The methods of the fanatics are a subject of persistent interest to the Great General. This object you spoke of, the focusing crystal—"

"What makes you think it was a crystal?"

Tretta blinked, unsure. "I ... merely assumed ... the facets would be more conducive to ..."

Sal waved a hand. "You can just say you think crystals sound more magicky. Everyone does." She chuckled. "Haven's magic is unstable, at best. They don't follow the laws of the Lady Merchant, so their trinkets pick up the slack. Sometimes they're idols, symbols, but they all serve the same purpose."

"And if summoning is as dangerous as you say, it would behoove Vraki the Gate to have one on hand."

"Careful," Sal said, winking. "You're starting to sound a little rational, miss. Why, what would your comrades say if they heard—"

"Where is it?" Tretta snapped, pointedly biting the head off the rest of that quip. "What happened to it?"

"If I knew where it was still, I'd have it," Sal replied. "And if I had it, I'd have sold it. And if I'd sold it, I'd be neck-deep in a throng of whiskey-soaked naked bodies." She glanced over Tretta, hummed. "Since neither of us appears to be in a hurry to take our clothes off, it's safe to assume I don't know where it is."

"If it amplifies magic, why would Vraki leave it behind?"

"Why not?" Sal shrugged. "So long as he held it, Haven would have been able to track him. And it's not like he needed it. He *is* a Prodigy, you know."

She hadn't said the word with any particular malice, nor even with any of her infuriating smugness. Yet, all the same, it sank into Tretta's ear, traveled down her spine to bore into the base of her neck, and sent a hot flash of anger through her limbs that made her want to shoot someone.

That word.

"Prodigy," she would have spat the word, had it seemed sufficient. As it stood, it would have seemed more fitting to cut her hand open and bleed the word out onto the table.

Sal, to her credit, seemed to notice the change. The smile dissipated from her face, replaced by a cool, even stare and a soft, gentle whisper.

"You know of them," she said.

"Every son and daughter of the Revolution knows of the hated Prodigies," Tretta muttered. "Every honest Scarfolk, cowering bandit, and insect crawling across a pile of birdshit baking in the sun knows the Prodigies. Your Imperium, in its infinite decadence, already profanes the natural order with its magic. And despite your ability to wreak havoc with a thought, the Prodigies are yet insistent on further depravity.

"They cast magic without cost," Tretta snarled, her fingers struggling to carve furrows into the table. "As the rest of the Imperium defies mortal limitations, the Prodigies defy even those flimsy laws. They are without limits, without conscience, and what does the Imperium do with these abominations?

"*THEY PROMOTE THEM!*" She slammed a fist onto the table. "They give them armies! They give them riches! They heap honor upon these mass murderers and hail them as heroes, coddling them even as they kill without discrimination, slaughtering soldier and civilian alike. To call them murderers would be to say they have thought. To call them animals would be to say they act on instinct. They are abominations. Monsters. *Demons*."

She didn't notice that she had started breathing heavily. Nor did she notice the heat burning behind her face. She only barely noticed her prisoner when she looked up and saw Sal staring, wide-eyed, across the table at her.

"Uh, all right…" Sal blinked. "You, uh, feel better now that you've got all that out?"

Tretta didn't dignify that with a shout or a slap or a shot. She curled her lip in a disgusted sneer at the woman.

"Do you deny it? Any of it?"

Sal stared at her and said nothing.

"The annals of the Revolution are rife with the crimes of the Imperium," she continued. "The Great General led us to unite to liberate ourselves from your Imperialist yoke. And rather than leave us to our newfound freedom, they sent the Prodigies. They sent Vraki; they sent Torle of the Void; they sent the Ashbreather's Three, they sent *Red Cloud*."

Only after the name was spoken did she feel the breath returning to her. Only after it hung between them, a profanity etched into the air, did she feel the heat begin to seep out of her face. But it wasn't the cleansing breath of a burden lifted that filled her lungs, nor was the heat replaced by something cool and comforting.

Speaking the name was like opening a wound.

She hadn't been there the day it happened. The day Red Cloud had appeared over the skies of a Revolutionary garrison and set them ablaze with a thought. She hadn't been given the honor of dying with her comrades. But she had been there when it was over. She had been given the opportunity to see the aftermath.

The people—the soldiers, the merchants, the civilians—all entangled in a mass of molten flesh. The luckiest of them nothing but blackened skeletons that turned to dust in a strong breeze, any memory of them lost on the wind. But the lucky had been few. Everyone else had been half-charred, flesh seared from sinew, sinew melted from bone, but never wholly, never completely, never enough to give them merciful deaths.

In their last moments, they had reached for the gates or the doors of the barracks, trying to escape. They had fallen to their knees and prayed to gods they had forsaken, begged for mercy from masters they had walked away from. They had clung together, hoping to shield each other from the worst of it and being spared nothing.

Tretta remembered their eyes, still seeping smoke where the stares accusing her of failing them should have been.

Red Cloud didn't even give her the chance to feel ashamed.

The Revolution had failed those people. As she had failed the Revolution. As she had failed everyone. She, who had been sworn to protect them—the merchants, the soldiers, the *families*—hadn't even been there to fire a single, impotent shot.

There had been more battles. More sightings. More of Red Cloud, the murderer, the monster, the Prodigy. Tretta had never been there to fight, though, to die with her comrades. Always, Red Cloud had appeared like a bad dream and disappeared just as suddenly, leaving ash and molten skin in her wake.

To think about it did not fill Tretta with fury. Somehow, it always seemed so inadequate, so inconsequential. Rather, when she thought of Red Cloud, as she did then, her body shook not with anger, but with the force of holding back her tears, with the effort of trying to block out the memories.

She always succeeded at one of those.

"I don't."

Tretta turned toward Sal, careful not to let the prisoner see the moisture in her eyes.

"I don't deny any of it," Sal said. "It's been a long time since I was with the Imperium, but I knew the Prodigies enough to know what they were capable of. When Vraki went Vagrant, only then did the Imperium learn what they had in their ranks." She sighed, looked down at her manacles. "Didn't do much good, though, did it? It's never the people outside your house you should worry about. They can only kill you. It's the people inside that can hurt you."

"And is that," Tretta whispered, "what Cavric felt when you betrayed him?"

Sal looked up. That slow grin returned to her, the dimmest white light in the shadow that had fallen across her face. Tretta hated to see it, hated more that looking at it made blocking out the memories a little easier.

"I was just getting to that," Sal said, reaching for another cup of water. "If you're done interrupting, that is..."

Tretta's hand shot out, seized Sal by her manacled wrist. It brought her the smallest, most spiteful smile to hear the prisoner gasp in alarm when she did. Firmly, she took the cup in one hand and raised Sal's wrists in the other. Her eyes raced across the woman's tattoos, taking in the lengths of winged birds, thundering clouds, and twisting dragons running up the length of her arms to terminate upon the skin of her neck.

They twisted in a pattern known only to their bearer, yet even there, Tretta could see the scars. Knots of pale flesh broke the whites and blues that her inked skin nobly tried to hide.

"The Imperium wouldn't have let you wear these, I assume," Tretta hummed. Her eyes drifted down to the expanse of scarred skin left bare by the woman's garish outfit. "Am I to assume you went Vagrant because you found their uniforms too stifling?"

"I went Vagrant for the same reasons as anyone," Sal replied. "I liked bleeding for my own name better than bleeding for someone else's." Her face screwed up in puzzlement. "Or... was that you flirting with me? It's hard to tell with you."

Tretta sneered, shoved her backward in her seat. "I merely wanted to know what I should write down when I turn in my report of your execution. The eccentricities of Vagrants are impossible to keep up with. Ridiculous costumery, bizarre tattoos, and that weird thing you keep saying... what is it? *Eres... aris...*"

Sal held up a hand, as though offended she would even try to pronounce it. "*Eres va atali*. It's a beautiful phrase, I'll thank you not to butcher it."

"What does it mean?"

"It means"—Sal paused, smiled softly—"'I used to fly.'"

"Another silly opera saying?"

"Sort of." She turned her smile up toward Tretta. "It's only ever been uttered once, though, after a great tragedy."

Tretta was ashamed to realize the softness of that smile caught her off guard. She was further shamed to hear that her own voice had grown gentle in response.

"What tragedy?"

And, at that, Sal's smile went from soft to extremely punchable.

"So you *are* trying to flirt with me. Governor-Militant, I don't usually go for military types, but if you did your hair a little nicer—"

Tretta held up a hand. "You can continue with this line of commentary or you can tell me what happened to Cavric." She narrowed her eyes. "Only one of those ends with your arms not being broken, though."

NINETEEN

THE SCAR

I've ridden in an Iron Boar twice before—once when I was trying to steal one and once when I was trying to blow one up. It's an unpleasant affair. The thing is designed to plow through the Scar's untamed badlands, so it's always bumpy and uncomfortable. The seats are hard and unpadded. The air is stifling inside. The engine makes so much noise that you can hardly hear yourself think.

And let me tell you, the experience is *not* enhanced by having to point a gun at the back of someone's head the whole time.

I only occasionally glanced at Cavric, seated at the front of the machine, alternately glancing out its front visors and periscope. I had stopped keeping an eye on him after the first thirty minutes of our trip. Mostly, I just stared out the thin slits masquerading as windows, watching the endless dry plains of the steppe slowly transition into a lusher, greener grassland.

The Yental River would be close now. And on it, I'd find the people who had sold Vraki the obelisk he used to draw enough power to do what he did in Stark's Mutter. Not knowing where he'd gone after he'd summoned the Scrath, that was my sole lead.

I'd tried to explain that to Cavric, of course, but he just kept going *on* about the whole "me abducting him at gunpoint" thing.

I suppose it would have been wiser to watch him, of course, but then again, wisdom seemed like it was for people who *didn't* have guns that exploded peoples' heads with pure sound. The Cacophony, lying in my lap, would tell me if anything was amiss.

Not that I'd really be able to tell what was amiss. Or what was going on, really. I sure as fuck didn't know how this thing worked.

The wheels and shell of the vehicle were mortal metal forged by honest toil, but the engine—that beating heart that made it move—was all Relic. A sphere of that same woven stone, pulsating with a hidden light as it groaned to life, hovered at the front of the vehicle, floating a few inches off a metal console. Through a complex series of cranks, levers, and muttered curses, Cavric willed it to move in a way I couldn't comprehend, let alone tell if he was messing with me.

I was doubly impressed..

Once for the fact that he was able to get it to move at all and twice for the fact that he was able to do it all with Liette peering over his shoulder like a particularly inquisitive parrot.

"Astonishing." Her previous distaste for the man was no match for her imminent curiosity and she forgot how eager she had been to see him die as she pushed down on him, leaning over him to stare, agog, at the Relic engine. "I have never once, in all my years, been able to see one of these devices up close."

I rolled my eyes. I would have pointed out that she was only twenty-eight, but she did so love saying dramatic crap like "in all my years." It made her sound smarter, she liked to think.

"I've heard rumors, of course, and I've obtained from Revolutionary defectors through bribery, blackmail, and this one time, a jar of spiders, but *still*." She adjusted her glasses, her eyes too small to take everything in. "The Revolution guards this information closer than it does their children. They always recover these things from battlefields and crashes before we can even get close to them. I might be the first Freemaker in *history* to see one operational and up close."

Don't get me wrong, it probably would have been more polite to remind her we were technically in the middle of kidnapping this guy.

But she just looked so *happy*.

Cavric, to his immense credit, didn't complain. He didn't even look back at me. Possibly because the complex series of levers and wheels that were needed to steer the Iron Boar demanded close attention. Possibly because he thought I'd shoot him if he did.

"You can stop pointing that at me," he muttered from the seat. "If you shoot it inside here, you'll kill us both."

Or possibly because he couldn't stand to be reminded that he had once looked at me like I wasn't a killer.

Take your pick, they're all fine reasons.

"That's a possibility, sure," I replied, letting the Cacophony dangle lazily from my fingers. "But at least this way, you can tell your cadre you were forced to steal this thing and didn't betray your precious Revolutionary playdate willingly."

"Revolutionary *Mandate*," he spat, along with a curse I didn't bother listening to. Revolutionaries didn't know any good ones, anyway.

That's not to say I felt particularly *good* about what I was doing, but I'm a practical woman. Your average bird—like Congeniality—can cover forty miles per day, if you don't want to kill it or piss it off so much it kills you. An Iron Boar can take a whole squadron of Revolutionary soldiers nearly quadruple that in a few hours. And where I was going was even farther than that.

What I had seen at Stark's Mutter continued to gnaw at me. The peoples' faces, twisted in the last moments of horror, their mouths agape with the pleas for mercy they never got to speak. Just a bunch of dumb hicks who moved out in the middle of nowhere, completely unaware that men like Vraki even existed, let alone that he would come for them one day, that he would herd them like cattle, steal their children, fill their last waking moments with incomprehensible agony, all to summon something whose name they didn't even know.

But that was what men like Vraki did. They didn't care.

And men like Jindu... they cared. But they did it, anyway.

Men like Jindu were worse.

I realized it was probably Jindu who had retrieved the Havener's focus. Cruel men, like Vraki, could never get past what they want to get what they need. Men like Vraki had wants. Men like Jindu had ways.

Just like I had my ways.

Only my ways involved his ways getting splattered over the wall in a gory mess, along with the rest of him.

Just as soon as I found him. And the rest of them.

There weren't many ways to get in contact with the Ashmouths. Like all good criminals, they're usually the ones who find *you*. But there were a few options. *Very* few. And they relied on getting to a very specific place in a very short amount of time.

I'm sure if I had bothered to explain all this to Cavric, he would have understood. Or, at the very least, he wouldn't have glowered over his shoulder at me with such hatred in his eyes.

"I think I've figured it out." Liette, oblivious to this conversation and my brooding, reached out and pointed to the Relic. "It powers the innards of the machine, that much is clear, but it does so by speaking to the vehicle, correct? This sound it makes, like…" She squinted as the engine continued to groan. "It's almost like… language."

"The Relics are the great equalizers," Cavric responded, just like he had no doubt been trained by *multitudes* of propaganda to do. "They were discovered by the Great General and handed down to common men and women to respond to the perversion of the mages. It is by his will they operate and by his will they deliver us victory." His eyes widened as Liette reached out to touch the engine. "And they are not for—*Hey! HEY!*"

The engine let out an agonized sound as her fingers grazed its surface. The entire vehicle shook. Liette let out a cry as she fell backward, to be caught by me. I glared at Cavric as he fought to control the metal monstrosity.

"Eyes on the road, if you don't mind," I said, setting Liette back on her feet.

"Yeah," he muttered. "Wouldn't want to accidentally run into all the fucking *nothing* out here, would I?" He snorted, scowled back out the visor. "This route leads into the middle of nowhere. If you wanted to kill me, you could have just done it back at Stark's Mutter."

"If I wanted to kill you, I would have spared myself all this whining."

"I'm not *whining*," Cavric said.

"Fine. You're putting up a very valiant defiance. When I recount this story, I'll be sure to tell everyone how fiercely you resisted me every step of the way." I sniffed. "But when I do, I'm going to give you a girl's voice."

"What? Why a—" He paused, shook his head, not *quite* ready to follow that line of thought. "Fuck it. Where the hell do you even want to go?"

"I told you. Yental River. Couple hundred miles due east. You'll know it when you see it, what with it being a giant fucking lot of water." I peered out the visor, saw the sun sinking low. "Only step on it, would you?"

"Step on what?"

"The... the thing that makes this thing go. That's how it works, right?"

"I *just* said it had a language, didn't I?" Liette, undeterred, returned to Cavric's side as she shot me a glare. "It's like you don't even listen to me."

"I listen to you when you're *not* saying insane shit," I shot back, pointing accusingly at her. "The rarity of that occasion is entirely on *you*."

"You wear ignorance like a crown as you feast upon a thickheaded fantasy of lies," she replied—and I was pretty sure I should be insulted, even if I couldn't quite make out what she was accusing me of. "If you bothered to listen to me more, your quality of life would improve immeasurably."

"Well, why don't we ever get to talk about what *I* want to talk about?" I demanded.

"Because we have already covered the conversational breadth of guns, tits, and whiskey."

I sniffed, a little more petulant than I would have liked to appear. "I like other stuff."

"*IT'S SEVERIUM!*" Cavric suddenly let out an exasperated shout. "The Iron Boar runs on severium, same as the ammunition we use for our gunpikes." He pointed to the Relic. "*This* Relic dictates how much is burned, which is, in turn, commanded by *this* crank, and it goes where I want it to by me pulling *this* lever, so now that we all know, can we *please* either stop talking or just shoot me in the head right now?"

I stared at the back of his head. "You got a girlfriend, Cavric?"

He cast a confused look at me. "What? No."

"Imagine that." I sighed. "Listen, I promise, get me where I need to go, you can take this piece of shit wherever you want. Go back to Lowstaff, make your reports, tell them the big bad Vagrant lady made you do it, whatever. Your comrades' bodies are all in the public house at Stark's Mutter; they'll be safe from scavengers. Once I get to the Yental, you and I are done." I held up my hand. "I promise."

"How many other people have you made a promise like that with?" he asked.

I hadn't expected that question. Nor had I expected to look to Liette. Nor had I expected her gaze to linger on me for a moment before she turned away.

"Two," I said.

"And how many times have you kept it?"

I scratched at a scar on my face. "Once."

"Yeah. Sure," he grumbled as we rolled on. After a long moment, he took in a deep breath. "Just one more question, then." He looked over his shoulder and over my head. "Why did you bring *that* thing along?"

I followed his gaze upward. Congeniality looked down at me with her big, yellow scowl. From the back of the vehicle, she let out an irritated squawk. It had taken some coaxing, some cursing, and a *lot* of threatening, but once we had managed to get her into the Iron Boar, she settled down well enough. Or, at least, she had only vomited angrily once, which was pretty good for her.

"Well, I wasn't going to leave her *behind*," I said. "She's the best company I've had in all my years out here."

Liette coughed pointedly. I sighed, rubbed my head.

"Uh-huh." Cavric pulled a lever. The engines roared. "You got a boyfriend, Sal?"

"No," I said.

"Imagine that," he muttered as we rumbled off into the distance.

TWENTY

THE SCAR

I don't sleep well.

Another perk of living out in the Scar, I guess, along with old wounds, frayed nerves, and one too many nights where I woke up to a blade at my throat. Liquor helps. So does company. Most nights, though, I don't get more than a few hours.

But when I do...

I dream of a red sky.

I knew the one I was staring at. I had seen it a hundred times in a hundred dreams before. Stretching out crimson and veined with black smoke, the sky stretched just as endlessly as it always had.

A perfect match for the sea of fire below.

Waves of orange flame lapped, reaching enviously toward a sky that yawned forever beyond its grasp. Within the roiling fire beneath, the shapes of humans—running and screaming, weeping and dying—were visible as man-shaped shadows that rose black against the flames and vanished beneath a fiery breeze. A city of homes and shops and walls crumbled to ash inside the inferno.

I had seen this before, too.

I'd have called it hell, except I felt no pain, no fear, no sorrow staring down at them. I was too high up, standing atop a spire that loomed over the city, untouched by the flame. From here, they looked like just more wisps of smoke, birthed out of the inferno and lost on a fiery breeze. And though their mouths were gaping open in fear and pain, I could hear no sound from them. I never could.

This was how it always went, every time I closed my eyes. The red sky. The fire. The people and their screams I couldn't hear.

"Do you feel bad?"

And him.

Jindu sat, thin as the bloodied blade in his lap, beside me. His legs dangled off the ledge of the battlement, kicking idly as smoke coiled up from below. He watched the blaze, almost bored.

I shook my head. "No."

"Liar," he shot back.

He always knew, back then. I hadn't been as good at lying. I had no reason to be.

"I suppose I'm just confused," I said, looking back to those tiny black shapes. "They weren't all soldiers. They didn't even fight back. They didn't deserve what the Empress ordered."

"It has nothing to do with deserve." Jindu pointed to the shapes, rising and reaching out of the inferno. "They are nuls. Whatever grand titles their Revolution gives them, they were born nuls. We weren't. The Lady Merchant gave us our gifts. Did we deserve them?"

"She gave them to us for a reason," I whispered into the smoke.

"Which reason?" he asked. "We paid our Barters. We swore our oaths. We gave up our humanity, our freedom, our corpses to carve out the Imperium they thrived under. Did they deserve our protection?"

"We had the power to do so," I said. "If we didn't protect them, who would?"

"And after years of us sacrificing everything so they could prosper under us, they call us monsters. Oppressors. Abominations. They take up arms against us. Do we deserve that?"

I didn't have an answer for that. I used to, once. The traitorous Revolutionaries sought to overthrow the Imperium that had been built upon the sacrifice of mages, their Great General striving to undo all that we had worked and bled to achieve. The Empress said they were ruthless, murderous, ungrateful. The Empress said they had to be stopped. Jindu said so. Vraki said so. They all did.

So did I. It had made sense, once.

A lot of things had made sense before I watched this city burn.

"They didn't fight back," I whispered.

"They did," Jindu said. "They might not have had weapons, but they spat on our sacrifice; they laughed at our protection; they forsook us."

"They're burning…"

"As they would burn us, and everything we bled for, to the very ground, if we didn't stop them."

I swallowed hot air and smoke. My lungs burned. Sweat fell down my brow to stain my red coat. In my ears, over the roar of flames and the cracking of smoldering wood, I could hear something.

"They're screaming."

"Sal…"

His hand was on my wrist. His fingers punched through my skin. I looked down and saw blades where digits should be, my blood oozing out between his knuckles. I looked back at him and saw red bubbling out his mouth.

"We had no choice."

I screamed.

I leapt.

I remembered this part. I flew from the battlements, arms spread out wide, wings of smoke rising beneath me to carry me. I closed my eyes, expecting the sky to embrace me and carry me away.

Only, this time it didn't.

This time, I fell.

I screamed. I landed hard on blackened ground, surrounded by wreaths of flame. And from within, they emerged.

Women. Children. Men. Old. Young. Limping. Running. Sobbing. And screaming. Every last one of them.

They were twisted and blackened, shambling out of the fire with their clothes grafted to bubbling skin. Their eyes had been seared out of their skulls and their faces burned away. Not a shred of color remained on their blackened bodies, except the hellish orange glow from their mouths as their lips parted.

As their screams filled my ears.

As their blackened limbs reached out for me.

And pulled me into the fire.

———⊷⊷⊶———

I woke up.

Being flung out of a seat will do that to you.

I scrambled in a half-terrified fog, groping around the floor through hazy vision and the sound of a bird's alarmed shrieks as I searched for my gun. Old instinct. Like I said, I don't sleep well.

I found it, my fingers wrapping around a grip that was warmer than metal had a right to be. I lifted the Cacophony, pulled the hammer back, and pointed it in the direction I thought Cavric was, certain that he had finally found his spine and was ready to kill me.

My breathing slowed. My vision cleared. Liette lay groaning on the floor before me. Congeniality's squawking quieted. And once I had the chance to see what I was aiming at, I could see that Cavric wasn't looking at me. And I could see that we were no longer moving.

He pressed the control lever forward. The engines roared. I heard earth being chewed up and spat out by the wheels underneath. But the Iron Boar didn't move an inch. Cavric muttered a curse, tried it again, to a similar result.

"What's the matter?" Liette asked, pulling herself up from the floor.

"We've stopped," he growled in reply.

"I can see that. I'm not stupid."

"Then why'd you ask?" He shot a glare at me and then turned his gaze back down to the control panel. "We must have hit something."

"Like a rock?" I muttered.

"Yes, like a rock. Or a fallen tree. Or something else that's big and heavy and might also stop a several-ton slab of iron powered by a Relic."

I sniffed, clicked my tongue. "You know, you are *very* cranky when you've been abducted."

"I don't know what the hell it is." He let out an exasperated sigh, rose to his feet. "I can't see a damn thing out there. I'll have to get out and—"

I placed my hand on his shoulder, pointedly letting the other hand guide the Cacophony back into his sheath, where my fingers lingered on his grip. I offered Cavric as warm a smile as a woman who had threatened to blow his brains out could.

"*I'll* get out and have a look," I said. "You stay here." I glanced at Liette. "And *you* with him."

"You don't know how the machine works," Liette said. "You could—"

"Pretty sure the point of a Relic is that *no one* knows how it works. If I need you, I'll call for you." I released Cavric, pulled the door open. Cold air blew in.

"What if there's trouble?" he called after me.

"Golly, what if? I hope I have a nice big fuck-off gun to deal with it." I paused, glanced back at him. "Speaking of...if this is a trick and you try to drive off and leave me..."

"Yeah, yeah." I can't lie; I was a little offended at how he rolled his eyes. "You'll shoot me."

"If you're lucky," I said. "If you're not, you'll have to deal with *her* on your own."

I gestured with my chin. Cavric followed and locked eyes with the beady orange scowl of Congeniality. The bird's feathers ruffled as she let out a low rasping sound. Whatever defiance had been lurking in Cavric's eyes died, though when he looked back to me, I could see he was still full of regular old pissed off.

That was fine, though. I had plenty of people pissed off at me. Some of them could spit fire. And until Cavric could either spit something worse or shoot fire from somewhere more impressive, I didn't see a need to dwell on it.

I took a step toward the door. Five small fingers clamped around my wrist. I glanced down, saw Liette looking intently at me.

"Be careful," she said.

"I always am."

She eyed the scars across my skin. "Your body is positively littered with evidence to the contrary."

"Yes." I pried her fingers off. "They're scars from how careful I am."

"That doesn't even make sense," she began to protest.

But I was already out the door.

The night air greeted me cold and damp. The moon hung high, just a few hours before midnight. I had slept longer than I thought, which bothered me. Felt like wasting time somehow.

The broken badlands that had surrounded Stark's Mutter were gone here, as was the crisp, dry air. The closer you got to the Yental, the more verdant the land became. Dry earth became damp grasslands and the air grew thick with moisture.

Which made it a damn mystery how we could have hit anything out here. There weren't any trees or rocks in sight. And a vehicle that can plow through a trenched field and bash down gates shouldn't have trouble with this soft earth at all.

This is why I hated machines. The Revolution loved them, of course, touting their fucking engines and wheels as the future beyond birds. But birds, at least, were easy to understand. You give them food, they go. If they don't go, you give them a smack. How do you make an engine do that?

Give it a smack and it just explodes.

I wandered around the exterior of the Iron Boar, looking for anything I might have missed. The thing's metal hide glistened in the moonlight, showing me no scar or dent, not so much as a scratch that might have slowed it down. I scratched my head, reached for my gun. Admittedly, I had no real reason to think that shooting it would improve the situation any, but it was how I solved most of my problems, so...

But I stopped once I saw it. It was impossible to make out the details in the dark, but I could see a shadowy mess of something lodged in the thing's front wheel. Mud, maybe. Or maybe we had driven through a bird pile somewhere. It'd be pretty fitting if I was stopped by a bunch of shit.

I squatted down next to it, reached in. Something wet and sticky greeted me, which was about what I was expecting. I didn't really start worrying until I noticed how warm it felt. That's right about the time I felt fingers reach for me, too.

I jerked my hand back with a shout. Something limp and wet tumbled out from the wheel and flopped down in front of me like a dead fish. I fell back, reaching for my gun again, but held off. It wasn't moving.

Severed arms tended not to.

I squinted. I could see the rest of him now. Or what I assumed was a him. A shattered jaw, a twisted arm, a single eyeball wide open in horror and the other pulped into a ground-up mess, all of him jammed up in the wheel. That'd do it, I supposed.

There's no real rule that says "When you find a dead body, go the opposite direction," but it's just good sense. Given that you've known me this long, though, I don't need to tell you why I ignored it. And you wouldn't need to know why I regretted looking up and over the field as the clouds broke and the moon shone down.

Corpses.

Somehow, everything I do ends up with corpses.

Twenty? Thirty? It was hard to tell in the dark. But if I squinted hard enough, I could just make out a few key details. A fine red coat here, emblazed with the sigil of the royal flame and chalice. A thick blue coat there, its plait bearing pins of two sabers crossed over a cog. Black scars across the land from magic. Freshly spent shells and fallen gunpikes.

Imperials.

Revolutionaries.

And a hell of a lot of scavenger birds.

Something about this stretch of grass, I guessed, they had thought was worth killing each other over. And they had done so with gusto, if the body count was any estimation. But the battle was long over. The steam had long cleared. Carrion fliers flitted down to peck at the corpses, only to fly away when the striding Badlanders came sauntering up to pluck out the good pieces.

The first time you see something like this, you vomit and spend the next three days wide awake. The second time, you scream and you weep. By the third time, and every other time, you just get a few words.

"Ah, shit."

Like those.

When you see the aftermath of a battle, you want to imagine something dramatic. You want to see corpses strewn about, tossed from where the massive explosions ripped apart the land. You want to see the lone carcass on the hill, his cold hands still wrapped around the banner he died trying to plant in the soil. You want to see some kind of *meaning* to it.

But you only ever get that in opera.

Here, all I could see were poor bastards. There was a poor bastard who died clutching his gun to his chest like it would protect him. There was a red streak where a poor bastard had pulled his bleeding self away before dying. And right in front of me was a poor bastard who died with a look of surprise on his face like he tried to figure out what he was supposed to be killing for right at the end.

In opera, you get drama. Here, the corpses just fell wherever they did. No reason. No meaning. Just coins that had once been humans: dropped idly and forgotten.

"FUCK."

His scream echoed across the field. Smaller birds scattered. The Badlanders didn't even look up. I glanced over my shoulder, saw Cavric slumped against the frame of the door. His eyes glistened in the moonlight, wide and full of horror.

"I thought I told you to wait," I said.

He wasn't listening to me. I do believe he couldn't hear anything at that point. He staggered out of the door, legs numb, and missed the first step, toppling onto the earth. He clambered back up, walked past me, and stared out over the carnage.

"Fuck..." he whispered again. "*Fuck.*"

"Yes, very dramatic." I glanced around, wary. "Keep your voice down, would you?"

Not that I expected an ambush—the birds certainly weren't about to look up from their feast at his outburst—but it always pays to be quiet if you don't know who might be listening.

"I just...What the...How..." Cavric's mouth hung open, searching for the right word to convey the right outrage and found the one that never stopped working. "Fuck..."

"Something like that," I said. Not that I intended to sound callous, but...well, you saw back at Stark's Mutter. This wasn't even the goriest thing I had done *today*.

Cavric, however, stared out over the corpses, searching them like he expected them to get back up at any moment and tell him what had happened. His eyes were wide, his mouth open, his hands helpless and empty.

"Curious," Liette said as she stepped out of the Boar and adjusted her glasses. "We're miles from any designated combat area. What were they fighting over?"

"*Nothing,*" Cavric snapped. "There's nothing here. There's nothing within *miles* of here. No forts, no locations, no...*nothing*. Nothing to fight over." He shook a little, unsteady. "Why would they do this?"

"I don't know." I slicked my hair back. "This close to the Yental, they could have been two scouting regiments looking for cargo drops and found each other instead." I shrugged. "Or maybe they just didn't like each other very much. Who knows?"

He looked at me, mouth agog, like what I had just said was worse than when I had put my gun in his face.

"How could you?" he almost whimpered.

"This can't be the first time you've seen a dead body."

"It isn't," he said. "It's...I just haven't seen anything like this." He stared back out over them and swallowed. "Not like this."

He was a Low Sergeant, a commander of soldiers. There was no reason he *shouldn't* have seen something like this. But then, the Revolution throws around ranks based on loyalty to the General, not experience.

Hell of a thing, I guessed, to see something like this, to look at what you've been fighting for, what you've been killing for, without the glorious operas and the marching songs and the tapestries. Hell of a thing to look at it and just see the blood and the bodies.

I remember the first time I ever did.

Somehow, back then, I thought that was the worst thing I'd ever do in my life.

And somehow, right now, looking at Cavric and knowing he'd one day stop seeing people and start seeing just blood and bone... that felt worse.

At least, until he clambered to his feet and stormed back into the Boar. I reached for my gun, ready to fire in case he tried to flee. I wasn't ready, however, when he emerged with a canister in his arms.

"What's that?" I asked.

"Oil," he said.

"For the Boar's wheels?" Liette asked.

"For them," he replied.

He waved away a pair of birds, who squawked in indignation as he began to pour a thick liquid over the corpse they had been feasting on. The realization hit me in one second. The anger in the next.

"Oh, fuck no," I growled. "We have to reach the Yental River by dawn. We don't have time for theatrics like this."

"They're not theatrics," he said, moving to the next body and dousing it with oil. "They're people."

"They're *corpses*," I spat. "And if you don't want to be one, too, you'll..."

I had a number of good ways to finish that threat. I'd made a lot of them during my time in the Scar, after all. Of course, they weren't very effective when the subject wasn't listening. Cavric simply moved from corpse to corpse, Imperial and Revolutionary, dousing them with oil, heedless of the very angry woman in a hurry and her big, fuck-off gun.

"Come on," I muttered to my side. "You're driving."

Liette looked at me quizzically, as though I had just uttered a riddle and not a command. I growled, gestured back toward the Boar with my chin.

"I know you've already figured out how to make that thing work," I said. "You probably knew the minute you touched it." I glanced back toward Cavric. "If he wants to stay, let him. We have business."

She opened her mouth as if to say something, but only a sigh came out. She pulled a paper from her scroll case, a quill from her hair, daubed the latter in ink, and scrawled on the former. The paper lit up into a quiet flame a moment later and she followed in Cavric's wake, toward the nearest corpse.

"What the fuck are you doing?" I all but screamed. The Cacophony grew cold in my grip, decidedly displeased by this display of sentimentality.

"Helping," Liette said.

"Oh, for fuck's sake, they're just *bodies*."

"They're people." She looked over her shoulder at me. "So are we."

"This isn't the fucking *time*." I reached out, snatched her by the arm. I forced my words through clenched teeth. "Do you not fucking get it? Every minute we waste, they get farther away. If we delay much longer, they'll—"

"They'll draw breath for a few moments longer," Liette said, her voice a cold contrast to the fire in her hand. "You'll still kill them, won't you?"

There was a snide tone to her voice that made my jaw clench and fever burn behind my eyes.

"They have to *die*."

"Do they have to die?" she asked softly. "Or do you have to kill them?"

Liette wasn't talented with words. She didn't watch opera—said it was pointless and manipulative. She didn't read poetry—not when she could read a nice, meaty treatise or manual. Her skill was with machines, ink, sigils, not language.

I had no idea why what she said hit me like a fist in the belly.

I dropped her arm. I pulled my scarf tight around my face. I stalked away. Behind me, fires began to blossom as she set the corpses ablaze. I kept walking through the cold night until my feet found stone instead of dirt and trees thinned out, giving way to ruined pillars and destroyed walls.

You found these ruins now and again in isolated places. We weren't the first people in the Scar and only a few Freemakers had bothered investigating who'd lived here before. I, for one, wasn't looking for any historical enlightenment, just a dark place I could hide until I stopped hearing her voice and my scars stopped aching. I didn't think much of the ruined roof I stepped beneath or the desolate pillars rising around me.

Not until I saw the corpses.

They weren't like the others. I wouldn't have stopped dead in my tracks for a body killed by bullet or blade or spell. But there was a quiet tranquility about the corpses of slain Revolutionaries and Imperials that lay about the ruins—there were no signs of battle, no great pools of blood; it was as though they had simply grown tired and stopped.

I edged my way toward one of the bodies, lying facedown in the dirt, one arm draped over his head, as though he were trying to take a nap. I leaned down, nudged him onto his back, hoping to see what had killed him painted on his face.

Only, he didn't have one.

A smooth plain of skin, polished to featurelessness, stood where a nose, eyes, mouth, and ears should be. I dropped the corpse and recoiled, reaching for my weapon instinctively. But as I looked around, I saw he wasn't the only one.

Smooth stumps where limbs should be, empty expanses of skin where eyes should be, clean holes from which organs had been taken out—it was like someone had simply plucked out parts of the soldiers to add to their own.

And I found the cause of it at the center of the morbid scene.

Another corpse, but not quite human. To glance at it, you'd have called it a very large hairless dog, and if you were lucky at all, you'd never do more than glance at it. It lay on its side, unmoving, four limbs splayed out from an emaciated body wrapped in withered flesh. Its hind legs were bestial, but its forelegs ended in a pair of human hands. One of its ears was long and pointed like a hound's, but the other was a rounded human ear. And its face...

I stared at it. And the terrified face of the human the beast had stolen it from stared back at me.

There are only two ways humans ever encounter nith hounds: the way I did—with it dead and bled out from a hundred wounds—and the way these poor bastards had.

Scholars call it a hound only because they have no other way to describe these flesh-taking atrocities. They hunger for flesh, but not in the good old honest way of other beasts. Nith hounds take pieces of people—hands, feet, hearts, faces—and graft them onto themselves. Perhaps out of hunger. Or anxiety. Or whatever the fuck drives a beast to do that—no one knows because nith hounds, like Scraths, come from somewhere else, somewhere not of this world.

Somewhere dark and far away that only a few people know the name of and fewer still know how to call from. And one of those people was at the top of my list.

Vraki had been here. That was what had drawn the Imperials here, I wagered. Which, in turn, had attracted the Revolutionaries and the two had fought for the privilege of dying to this fucking monstrosity sprawled out before me.

These things were Vraki's specialty. Even though the Imperium had disapproved, he'd always had a talent for calling nith hounds. He must have summoned it to cover for him. But what was he doing while it was?

I found the answer against the ruined wall.

A faint scorch mark was smeared across the ruined stone, and surrounding it were blackened sigils that had once glowed brightly. Anchoring sigils, I realized, the work of a wright who knew how to stabilize a portal. Riccu the Knock had been with him. He had opened the portal. The sigils had kept it open, but where did it lead? And who had gone through it?

The answer crept into my head on cold, skittering legs. I remembered Stark's Mutter, the corpse that had screamed, the message he had given me.

The children who had vanished.

Vraki had taken them through a portal, somewhere far away. The realization made my scars ache, made my eyes burn.

We'd taken too fucking long. Too much time wasted on Liette, on Cavric, on her fucking touches and his fucking whining. They'd gotten away. They'd taken the children. *They'd taken everything from me and—*

Something whispered in my head. Something burned softly at my hip. The Cacophony seethed quietly, bade me breathe deep. I did so, smelled the cold air and the tang of blood. I let go of the thought and held on to the hilt of the gun.

It burned in me, chased away the cold thoughts, gave me room to think.

Portals were magic, but magic had limits. To haul that many people through, it couldn't have extended too far. The nith hound hadn't yet dissipated into nothingness as its corpse was called back to whatever hole it had been yanked out of. We weren't too far behind. Vraki was still heading somewhere.

And I knew how to find out where.

I let go of the Cacophony, whispered a word of thanks. He was looking out for me, when no one else was. We made a deal, he and I. He still remembered it.

I headed back down the hill, away from the corpses. I was ready to tell Liette and Cavric what I had found, ready to show them proof that we couldn't waste more time here. I wasn't ready for the sight of them standing side by side, watching a dozen man-sized pyres burn across the grassland.

I can't say why I didn't call out to them. Or why I walked a little slower and more silently as I approached them. Maybe I didn't want to interrupt this, knowing how much it meant to them. Or maybe I just wasn't done hurting from what she had said.

"Thanks." Cavric's voice rose on the darkness. "For the fire." He rubbed the back of his head. "I guess it was stupid, though. She was right. They are just bodies."

Liette didn't reply. She didn't say a word as they stared over the burning bodies. Cavric's sigh came so heavy, I thought he'd collapse under its weight.

"I just wanted them to have peace. Guess I was too late for that, though." He shook his head. "Waste of life. Waste of time. She was right. She was right about—"

"She wasn't." Liette's voice came curt and cold as a knife. "Neither are you." She gestured to the bodies. "She saw empty corpses. You saw people you failed."

"What did you see?" he asked.

She hesitated a moment. "Sinew. Skin. Three hundred twenty pairs of muscles. Two hundred six bones. Endless amounts of nerves and blood and everything else that makes up a person, alive or dead."

"You act like they're machines."

"They are," Liette said. "That's only a bad thing if you don't appreciate what a machine can do. Neither of us know what these people did when they were alive, whose lives they improved, what they managed to fix. They simply... did it. And now we did this. And in doing so, we fixed one more thing."

"Huh," Cavric said. "Didn't expect you to be the type to understand this."

"I understand things that need fixing," she said. "I understand broken things." She closed her eyes. "I understand her."

I felt something cold twisting inside me, hearing that. A close and tender ache, closer than even my scars.

Maybe it wasn't that Liette didn't understand words. Maybe it was that she understood them too well. Maybe she could see that behind whatever legends there were about me, whatever threats and curses they made when they spoke of me, whatever weight my name carried, it was all just words.

Words that just hid me. Just one more broken thing.

And maybe that's why I didn't say anything as I watched the fires burn, as I watched the smoke rise into the sky, as I watched the bodies blacken.

TWENTY-ONE

THE SCAR

Don't get me wrong, I'm a sensitive sort. And not just in that way you say you are when you want to impress someone pretty. I can appreciate the value of mourning as much as anyone.

But come the fuck *on*, we still had a schedule to keep.

Reasonable, right? I had thought so when I made my case to Cavric as to why we needed to keep moving. He had disagreed, of course, citing numerous reasons—respect for the dead, reflecting on the horror, and so on—that I might have found compelling in other circumstances.

But, well, I was the one with the weapons, so...

My attentions were on my sword, quietly cleaning it as the Iron Boar's growling engines carried the rattling heap of iron across the plains toward a distant destination. Congeniality, curled up beside me, let out quiet chirping noises now and again as Liette stood nearby, thumbing through a Revolutionary engineering manual she had found and pausing to occasionally chuckle at its contents, but that was as close to talking as we got in that Boar.

It was nice.

Good morning.

Mind you, it was decidedly less so once I heard the voice in my head.

Halt your vehicle and silence your engines, if you'd be so kind.

"What was that?"

Cavric's voice was hoarse with worry as he looked around, terrified. I couldn't quite answer him yet. While I knew those thoughts weren't coming out of my head—or his—I didn't quite know where they were coming from.

I'd really rather hate to resort to killing you.

But I was getting a good idea.

"Who is that?" Cavric whispered. "What's happening?"

"Quiet." I slid Jeff back into its sheath as I got to my feet and looked around. "It's just telepathy."

"*Just* telepathy?" he all but screamed.

"Be calm," Liette cautioned. "Its power is limited so long as you don't think too loudly."

"What does that even *mean*?"

Ah, good, I'm dealing with someone with passing knowledge of the arts. The voice in my head was lyrical in tone, pointed in its eloquence. *To whom am I speaking?*

"This..." Cavric, finally catching on, struggled to find the proper tone to communicate with a guy speaking inside his skull. "This is Low Sergeant Cavric Proud of the Glorious—"

"A gentleman always introduces himself first," I brusquely cut him off. "Or are we *not* dealing with an officer of the Imperium?"

Ah, where are my manners. A laugh echoed inside my head—that sort of airy, fake laughter that told me I was dealing with a dickhead. *You have the pleasure of conversing with Imperial Judge Karthrien yun Acalpos.*

"What's a judge doing all the way out here?"

My cavalry has been dispatched at the request of Her Imperial Majesty, Empress Athura the Fourteenth, in response to a skirmish with some nul scum. I beg your forgiveness in assuming the worst of you, but seeing a Revolutionary mechanical abomination fleeing the scene causes me some concern.

"We didn't do anything!" Cavric protested to the thin air. "We just saw it! We were…we…" His face screwed up as he looked at me. "How do I, like…Should I just *think* about it and they see it or what?"

"Not like that, idiot," I snapped.

Oh, well done, madam. But you might have told him earlier. I can already see the scene in his head. My, my, what a mess. He chuckled inside my skull. *Shall we do this politely? You lot pull over and let us conduct a civil investigation over what you know?*

"We've got a schedule to keep," I replied, "so if you wouldn't mind fucking off out of our head now…"

There's hardly a need for rudeness. I'd hate to bring my birds down upon you.

"You said cavalry, right?" I asked. "There's not a bird alive that can move faster than this thing." I rapped the metal of the Boar's interior. "And you know that, so you wouldn't tell us to stop unless you knew you could catch us, am I right?" I peered out the slitted windows of the Boar, searching the fields. "Am I, Karthrien?"

Oh, clever. I do, indeed, have my ways. I'd simply hate to waste them on what could be a civil discussion. Now, kindly offer us your response. Will this surrender be peaceable?

As impressive as the ability to read minds sounds, telepathy isn't considered a high art. To truly glimpse into the bundle of anxieties, fears, and hatreds that make up another human's mind is to spend the next few days crying into a bucket. Hence, its only true use is to convey and read surface thinking: the immediate and deliberate thoughts that pop up in a human's mind.

Like the thought I was having at that moment as I immediately and deliberately envisioned Karthrien, or what I imagined him to look like, picking up a sloshing chamber pot, lifting it to his lips, and—

Oh, you are depraved. His thoughts resonated angrily in my skull. *What scum am I communicating with?*

"No one," I replied. "Just a traveler."

Really? That's not what your friend is thinking. If I just peer into his head, I can see…

There was a long pause.

By the Empress. You're…

I sighed. No use hiding it anymore, thanks to Cavric's wandering thoughts.

"Sal the Cacophony," I said. "Yeah."

There was a longer pause.

The Vagrant?

I knew he couldn't see it, but I couldn't help but grin. "So, you've heard of me, huh?" I asked. "Nice things?"

There was a much longer pause.

And then, I got an answer.

There was the distant whistle of air torn apart, a faint sound of electricity crackling, a quiet whisper of something flying. And then, a second later, everything got way too fucking loud.

Cavric screamed. Congeniality leapt to her feet, shrieking. Liette clung to a bench to stay upright. The engines roared and metal groaned. The Boar went rocking on its treads as something hit its side like a boulder. A great rent scarred itself across the vehicle's armor, arcs of blue electricity dancing across the wound.

I peered out the great gaping hole in the Boar's side and saw a shadow swooping across the earth. The outline of a slender body and huge wings slid across the ground, pulled up alongside the Boar, and slowed down. I heard the crackle of electricity again.

"Get fucking *down*!" I screamed.

More for my own benefit than anyone else's. No one else, human or bird, knew what was happening as a bolt of lightning fell out of a clear sky and struck the Boar again, rocking it on its wheels.

There was an angry roar of metal and fire, followed by a decidedly less impressive hiss of steam. I heard a clunking sound as something came unhinged underneath the Boar and I felt us begin to slow.

"*What was that?*" Cavric demanded.

"Thunderbow," Liette muttered, adjusting her glasses.

"What?"

"A bow that shoots thunder—how much clearer does it have to be?" I growled.

"Thunder isn't something you can shoot!" Cavric protested.

"I didn't fucking name the thing," I snapped back.

"Whatever it is, it grazed the engine," Cavric said, tugging madly on the controls. "I can keep her going, but not for much longer."

"I suspect that was the point," Liette observed, staring at the rent in the hull.

"What makes you say that?"

I stared out the hole in the Boar's side. Over a hill, I saw distant figures come loping on great, avian legs. Their beaks and feathers, tinted with Imperial violet, came starkly into view. And by the time they were close enough for me to make out their weapons, I could see the crests upon the breastplates of the Imperial cavalry.

"Cavaliers," I muttered. I rushed to the Boar's door, started pulling it open. "Can you fix this thing? Either of you?"

"I can fix it or I can pilot it, but I can't do both," Cavric said.

"A Relic engine's nature remains a mystery to everyone," Liette replied. "I doubt even their masters know how it truly works. Regardless, the reliant machinery it powers is a buffoon's work, easily fixed and—"

"Yes or no," I growled.

She narrowed her eyes, plucked a quill from her hair. "Of course I fucking can."

"Great. Do what you can," I said. "I'll take care of the rest."

"What?" Alarm crossed her face. "What 'rest'? What are you planning?"

I couldn't hear him over the roar of wind as I pulled the door open. I drew the Cacophony, heard his brass giggle as I flipped his chamber open and loaded three shells. I glanced at Cavric over my shoulder.

"Man, if I had a plan, I probably wouldn't be doing shit like this."

I let out a sharp whistle. Congeniality came lurching toward the door. She glanced, curious, out at the plains roaring beneath the Boar's treads. Then, she crouched, readying herself and leapt out.

And I followed.

She didn't so much as break a stride as I landed in the saddle and took hold of her reins. So many hours riding in a noisy metal box had left her legs aching. And while I couldn't quite tell the emotion behind the squawking sound she loosed, I liked to think it was bloodthirsty and ready for a fight.

Goodness knows she was about to have one.

As the Boar pulled ahead, I saw them. Their feathers were pristine ivory tipped with amethyst. Their slender legs moved in perfect harmony, long beaks thrust forward like lances. Their riders, in polished armor and crested helmets, rolled with their gait with expertise, a chorus of weapons alight with flamewritten sigils held high overhead in anticipatory triumph.

Imperium Cavaliers. A dozen of the prettiest people you'd ever have the pleasure to be murdered by. Whatever you might have thought about their shining armor and graceful steeds, every man and woman was a trained killer equipped with magical weaponry and each bird beneath them was a fearless fighter bristling with razor beaks and claws.

If we had driven through the night, we would have passed them. But *someone* had to go and have compassion for the dead.

I held the Cacophony high as I pulled on my bird's reins, sending her closer to the pack of cavalry. They spotted me immediately, shifted seamlessly from pursuit to battle formation. Those armed with bows fell behind as six birds strode to the front, their riders wielding brass-colored polearms. A shout went up from the lead rider, and in response, the heads of their weapons erupted into fire.

Flameglaives. Fucking perfect.

I aimed the Cacophony at them as they veered, tongues of fire forming roaring lances as they spurred their mounts toward me. I narrowed my eyes, aimed a little lower, right in their path, and I pulled the trigger.

Hoarfrost shot out, struck the earth. Two birds managed to cross over it. And then...

"HOLY SHIT!"

The lead rider's shout was all I heard before the groan of ice. Crystalline spikes erupted, petals on a great blue flower. Birds shrieked— the lucky ones slipped and went tumbling as ice blossomed beneath them, the unlucky letting out barely a squawk before a spike of ice punched through their frail bodies. Credit to the survivors, though—they barely even stopped, pulling themselves free from the frigid fracas and spurring on toward me.

Fewer than before. But still far too many.

Their formation broke, those still alive scattering out to avoid being hit all at once like that again. I slipped the Cacophony back into his sheath and pulled Jeff free. You might have called it foolish, pulling regular steel to fight a pack of mages. But they knew how to fight magic and how to avoid it—I'd just be throwing away shells trying to pick them off. And whatever else you might have heard, a mage wasn't invincible just by birth. They were flesh and blood, just like you and me...

Only they had bows that shot lightning.

Like the one that was drawn on me when I looked back up.

I saw the soldier's stern face illuminated by azure light as her arrow burst to electric life. It hummed as she drew her massive, polished bow back and let it loose. I only had the presence of mind to duck out of sheer instinct. And even then, I could feel barbs of electricity pluck at my skin, pain digging into my body on tiny crackling claws, as it sailed overhead and struck the earth behind us, erupting into a blue globe of thunder and sparks.

Congeniality let out a shriek and started fighting me for control. As though the sight of an explosion of thunder and shrieking sparks that swallowed the day and bathed the world in a hellish, destructive blue light were something to be afraid of.

The big baby.

The Revolution has fancy guns that make the earth shake, but they don't have Dust. The smiths of Cathama can take a dead mage's remains and fold it into weapons of such unnatural power that they'd match the Revolution's biggest cannon for sheer force. Thunderbows, frostbrands, flameglaives—against such weaponry, you'd think your average blade would be about as effective as a toy.

And in the hands of anyone else, it might be.

But they hadn't decided to get in the way of anyone else, had they?

I saw the soldier drawing another arrow from her quiver and I saw my chance with it. I jerked Congeniality's reins hard, sending her charging toward the cavalier. There was a flash of panic on the rider's face as she realized I wasn't running away from her. She choked— the arrow went wide, sailing past me and pricking at my flesh. Congeniality slammed against the rider's bird, knocking her off balance as she drew another arrow. I leaned over, jammed my sword into her ribs, and tore it free in a burst of red. She toppled lifelessly from her saddle, her arrow flying high into the air.

My grin lasted just as long as it took to look up and see the arrow burst into sparks as it reached the height of its arc and then fall down.

Right into my path.

I pulled Congeniality back as it struck the earth in front of her and exploded in a shower of light and soil. She reared, shrieking and trying desperately to backpedal, which, when you're a gigantic murderbird, isn't particularly graceful. Or conducive to keeping a rider on.

She tossed me from the saddle and I landed hard on the earth, the wind kicked out of me. Over the sound of me trying to gulp down air, I could hear the rumble of talons on the earth. Eyes still rolling in my head, I could make out the blurry shapes of three riders thundering across the plains. Not letting a little thing like a potential concussion stop me, I scrambled to my feet, blade held high as the birds drew close.

The cavaliers wheeled right, arrows drawn as they took off in pursuit of a trail of black smoke winding across the sky. Perhaps they didn't notice me. Or perhaps they didn't think me a threat. I'd have been offended if I didn't realize what they were going for.

The Boar.

Fuck.

I sheathed Jeff and glanced around for Congeniality, found her not twenty feet away, the panic of the flash of thunder now subsumed by the intense desire to sniff her own asshole. That was plenty of distance to think of a suitable swear word for her by the time I got to her. But before I could even get moving, I heard the whisper of flame behind me.

I leapt away as a gout of flame raked the earth where I had stood, leaving behind a patch of black earth scarred by howling fires. Through sheets of red, I could see the rider, a smirk across his face painted in shadow by the smoldering head of his flameglaive.

"Fuck."

I know I said I'd think of another swear, but I was a little preoccupied running from the flaming wall of death pursuing me. I ran as hard as I could, rushing toward Congeniality as the rider spurred after me, his flameglaive spewing gouts of red laughter in my wake, the earth belching smoke as it ate the land behind me.

Congeniality let out a disgruntled squawk as I leapt atop her and kicked her flanks.

"Go, bitch, go!"

That wasn't how one addressed a lady. But if the urgency in my voice didn't make her go, the fire certainly did. As flames lapped at her heels, she took off running.

I tried to find enough breath through the smoke to think. I had to get clear of the rider, far from the flames, far enough to take a shot. I spurred Congeniality forward, reached for the Cacophony at my hip.

But his bird was smaller, more agile. And, as it turned out, a hell of a lot faster.

I caught him out of the corner of my eye, pulling his bird up alongside me and leveling his flameglaive. I could see the sawed teeth of its head grinning beneath a veil of flame as it burst into bright red, eager to consume me.

In an inescapable situation like this, the only two possible reactions are stupidity or panic.

I'll give you a guess which one I chose.

I jerked Congeniality to the right, sent her slamming against the other bird. I reached out, seized the flameglaive beneath its head, and forced it upward, a plume of flame erupting into the sky. He had range and speed on me—if we tried to run, I'd be incinerated. The only way out now was staying close enough to keep it pointed away.

Neither his nor my own snarling could be heard over the roar of flame as we struggled with the glaive, me trying to keep him from pointing it at me, him quite insistent that I'd look better as a pile of cinders. But he was bigger and stronger, and I was winded. Even with both hands, I could feel my grip weakening, the tip pointing toward me.

I growled, kicking Congeniality, but she couldn't move faster than the bird at her flank. From the corner of my eye, I saw that bird peer toward her and lash out with its razor-thin beak, carving a red line across Congeniality's breast.

That *certainly* wasn't how one addressed a lady.

Congeniality turned an indignant yellow-eyed scowl toward the bird. Her broad beak snapped down, clamping onto the bird's neck. It was smaller, lighter, more maneuverable. But she was a Badlander—bigger, stronger, and so, *so* much meaner.

The bird shrieked in alarm as Congeniality jerked its neck in her beak. The snap of its neck was louder even than the roar of flame. The rider let out a shriek to match as his bird disappeared from under him, the glaive slipping from his hands and into mine as he went tumbling to the earth to be trampled beneath talons.

"Damn, girl." I watched his bloodied body roll across the plains as we put him behind us. "You couldn't do that earlier?"

Congeniality didn't know any words beyond *food* and *don't shit there*, but she let out a warning squawk all the same. I was content to leave it lie as I spurred her forward.

The Boar drove into view, veering wildly left and right as it weaved between electric explosions, the remaining riders trying to pull up beside it and finish it off. I had to admit, I was impressed by Cavric's driving. I didn't know that a thing as clunky as the Boar could move like that. Neither did the Imperium, for that matter. Their eyes were focused on their aim and not, say, on the woman with the big fiery weapon riding up behind them.

I raised the glaive, pulled up behind them. They'd slowed down to improve their aim. Mistake. I leveled the weapon at them, clutched it tight. Flames washed out and over, sending one rider down in a screaming, blackened heap. The other glanced over his shoulder just in time to catch a tongue of fire to the face.

I spurred Congeniality on, toward the Boar. We got close to the door and I gave her reins a tug. Clever girl that she was, she leapt in, body shuddering with the effort. I clung to the top of the door frame, pulled myself up top to the roof. There had been a dozen riders and I had killed only four. I clambered to my feet, ready to pick them off from above.

But as I looked up, I saw the remaining riders falling back. I smirked. Perhaps they'd seen the tattoos and the gun and saw who I was. Perhaps they realized the stupidity of trying to pick a fight with Sal the Cacophony.

A shadow streaked across the plains. I heard a scream from above. I looked up.

Or perhaps, I thought, they just figured out they could sit back and let the giant fucking flying bird finish me off.

You wouldn't have seen it, at first, a pair of great gray wings falling out of a great gray sky. I only knew what I was looking at once I saw the black talons, the bright red beak across a giant owl's face, the great eyebrows that trailed behind it like banners in the wind.

A Grukai.

Even as gigantic murderbirds went, Grukai were exceptional for their size, ferocity, and exceptionally foul demeanors. The Imperium used these for shock missions, swooping down to seize Revolutionaries from battle lines and tear them apart in the sky, raining viscera upon their horrified comrades.

I suppose I should have been flattered that Judge Karthrien saw fit to use it just for me.

And maybe I would, after I was done shitting myself. But when Karthrien drew his long blade and spurred the bird toward me, all I could think to do was duck.

I couldn't hear the rush of the beast's wings as it sailed over me. But I felt the great breath of wind, the chill of its shadow, and more importantly, the bright blossom of pain as a single talon ripped through my back and drew a bright line across my spine.

My mouth erupted in a scream as my body erupted in agony. I was lucky to escape with just that. If I had been a little slower, if its claw had gone a little deeper, I'd have watched it sailing away with my spine in its talons. As it stood, when I bit back the pain long enough to get back to my feet, I saw my blood painted across the sky as the Grukai sailed across.

As it wheeled around.

As it came back toward me.

Its owlish eyes were trained on me. It had seen my trick, learned from it. It wouldn't miss this time and I wouldn't get more than one shot.

Pain and fear made me fumble as I unsheathed the Cacophony. He cooled as my fingers wrapped around his grip, bidding me to be calm. I drew a breath, held it. I raised the gun, felt him grow bright in my hands as I aimed him toward the onrushing bird.

I had one shot.

I pulled the trigger. The shell shrieked into the wind. The Grukai tumbled out of the way, ready to dodge before I had even fired. In a moment of fear, I knew I'd missed and my heart dropped into my belly.

And then Hellfire exploded.

Fire bloomed across the sky in a triumphant cackle. Red claws raked out in all directions, seizing the Grukai's wings in burning fingers. The beast shrieked, twisting violently through the air and leaving a trail of burning feathers in its wake. My heart leapt out of my guts and into my grin as I watched Karthrien fly from his saddle and sail through the air on a plume of smoke.

He tumbled like a fly with one wing, twisting in the wind as his bird went skidding to the earth in a spray of soil. My sole regret was that I was too far away to hear him scream. All I could hear was the roar of the engines, the screaming of the bird, and...

And the Lady's song.

"Of course," I sighed.

I saw him whip his hand out. A chorus of black tendrils burst from his glove, reaching out in the blink of an eye to sink thorny claws into the roof of the Boar. In another second, they tensed. They pulled. I glanced up from them to see him flying through the air, pulled by the tendrils toward me, his blade aloft.

And coming down.

I pulled the flameglaive up just in time to feel my arms almost snap under the weight of the blow. His sword, a long and jagged-looking edge masquerading as a civilized weapon, smashed into the haft of the glaive, bearing me down to my knees. I dropped the Cacophony, taking the weapon in both hands as I tried to hold back the strike.

He was stronger, taller, and decidedly less drinking-out-of-a-chamber-pot than I had imagined. His arms, left bare by the Imperial uniform he wore, barely tensed as he drove me back with his blade. Beneath the visor of his helmet, his eyes almost looked bored.

"I confess being impressed, Vagrant." Karthrien's voice betrayed a decided lack of effort on his part. "I saw you use magic keen as any mage, yet I heard no song. Was that the work of the weapon you wield?" He pressed a little harder, driving me a little lower. "A crime worthy of immediate and painful death, but don't let that diminish your accomplishment."

"You're too kind, asshole," I grunted in reply, fully aware that it was hard to sound intimidating on one knee and visibly struggling.

My eyes darted to the edge of the Boar's roof. The Cacophony trembled precariously across the roof, ready to tumble off. I could feel his burn from here—worried that he'd fall off, but far, far more pissed off that I had dropped him. But even through his burn, I could feel a sudden chill creeping across my skin.

Karthrien's blade was enveloped in a blue mist, ice forming across the metal and biting through the glaive's haft. A frostbrand—of fucking course he would have a frostbrand. It's not fucking enough to have a giant killer bird or a bunch of creepy-ass tendrils; he needs a magic fucking frosty-sword as well.

Fucking mages.

"I feel I should apologize, too," he said, voice still frighteningly effortless. "I admit that our information on you has been discouragingly sparse in comparison to more, shall we say, well-known Vagrants like the Hardrock or the Dervish."

"The *Dervish*?" I spat, incensed. "How do you know about *him*? He throws fucking rocks! His name doesn't even make sense!"

"Now, now, don't be bitter. Your name will be the toast of Cathama when I make my report." He seized his weapon in both hands, pressed down. "You'll be dead, of course, but I promise the talk will be tasteful."

Wood cracked. Frost whispered. The glaive split in two in my hands. I narrowly had time to roll away before his blade sank down, a jagged blade of ice biting through the metal of the roof. I rolled to my feet, aimed the head of the flameglaive at him, shut my eyes, and concentrated.

Flame erupted in a roaring sheet of laughter, washing over Karthrien. He pulled his blade out, raised it before him. The fire parted like a wave, slithering off to either side of him as his frostbrand's magic absorbed the heat, steam cloaking him in white clouds. From behind it, I saw him swing his blade. Shards of frost shot out in a fan, a jagged piece grazing my arm. Blood blossomed, the flames guttering as the glaive's head fell from my hand.

I made a lame reach for it as it tumbled off the roof. It would have been too little even if I *hadn't* felt a boot kick me in the chest. I rolled back onto the roof, grimacing as a leather heel dug into my belly. Painful as it was, it wasn't quite as bad as the frigid gasp of air as the frostbrand leveled at my throat.

"She uses magic without a song. She uses a flameglaive like she was born holding one." Karthrien flipped the visor of his helmet up to regard me through disdainful eyes. "What manner of Vagrant are..."

He paused as he took me in. Without the visor of his helm, without the rush of battle to distract him, he regarded me through eyes that grew wide with recognition. His mouth hung open as he whispered breathlessly:

"You."

"Me," I replied.

My boot shot up, caught him in the belly. He staggered away toward the edge of the roof, grunting in surprise and pain. When he regained his senses, he looked up into the grinning barrel of the Cacophony.

"And him."

I pulled the trigger.

Discordance erupted, a wall of sound and force that sent us both flying. But only one of us had seen it coming. So while I tumbled to the edge of the roof and narrowly managed to cling to it, he went flying into the air, with neither bird nor magic to save him.

I clawed my way back onto the roof. Through veils of smoke and the acrid tang of electricity and twisted metal, I watched him vanish in the wake of chewed earth left by the Boar. I drew breaths that came with stinging pain.

That hadn't gone well.

Not that I had expected it to go better—nothing is ever improved with the addition of tentacles, after all. But we had lost too much time and the Boar was rattling ominously as it rumbled across the plains. It was worrying to see the Imperium active this far away from any garrison. Almost as worrying as the look that Karthrien had given me just before I blew him away.

All told, it was a lot of mess and all I had to show for it was the sound of his scream in my ears.

But I'd say it was worth it.

TWENTY-TWO

YENTAL RIVER

There are a thousand tales about the Ashmouths.

It's said they once plundered the Mad Emperor's Tomb and evaded his everlasting curse. It's rumored they once assassinated every member of the Great General's advisory board in a single night. And some have even said that they move so silently that no Relic, spell, or sight of Haven can ever detect them.

It's impossible to say which of these are true, which are the imaginings of a public house drunk, and which are the ones the Ashmouths made up to further their own reputation as people you don't want to fuck with.

If you want someone dead who can't be killed, the Ashmouths are the only people who can kill them. If you want something stolen that can't be found, the Ashmouths are the only people who can find it. And if you want to conduct business of a nefarious nature without their approval, the Ashmouths are the only people you can't escape.

Which made the fact that my ass was currently rubbing itself all over their property particularly dangerous.

The crates had been stacked neatly beneath the eaves of a pair of bowing willows on a quiet little cove at the edge of the Yental's deepest stretch, each one marked with the sigil of a black tongue extended from twin rows of grinning teeth, a clear warning to anyone who thought they'd lucked out by finding caches of weapons, alchemics, and whatever other smuggled goods were in this thing.

Granted, I hadn't looked in any of them, let alone taken something from them, but the Ashmouths weren't likely to take kindly to me sitting on them. And they *certainly* weren't likely to take kindly to Congeniality devouring a dead rabbit next to them, spattering the crates with its entrails.

But fuck it. We were both tired. Tired enough that we hadn't joined Liette and Cavric in their foraging.

The battle on the plains had taken more time out of our schedule and more blood out of me than I cared to admit. Despite what crude treatments I could manage in the rattling Boar, my back still stung from the cut and my bones still ached. Congeniality, too, was so exhausted she barely had the energy to messily devour a dead animal.

Not that the Ashmouths would care, of course. Chances were good they'd kill one of us and force-feed our remains to the other one.

That is, if they ever showed up. For all the rumors surrounding them, there is not one legend of them being punctual.

The sun was hidden behind an endless cloak of gray overhead, making it impossible to tell what time it was. The Yental stretched lazily out before me, bereft of anything but a fog bank so dense I couldn't see the other shoreline. Not so much as a ripple of a curious fish disturbed its rambling mutter as it flowed northward.

And the Ashmouths were nowhere to be seen.

These goods were meant for them, it was certain. What wasn't certain was when they'd pick them up. There were hundreds of drop-off points like this around the Yental. If this wasn't the right one for the right time, I'd miss my chance to make contact with them entirely. That meant I'd never find out how Vraki got the obelisk that allowed him to summon his Scrath. That meant I'd never stop him. That meant I'd never kill him. Or Taltho. Or Riccu.

Or Jindu.

That thought was like a crack in my skull, and through it, all the other cold, dark little words came flowing out.

They'd escape me. With the children from Stark's Mutter. With whatever plot they were thinking up. With black laughter on their lips as they got away with it, again.

Just like they had before.

I'd never cross their names off the list.

I'd never dream and see something other than their faces.

I'd never be able to hear Liette tell me never to come back and tell myself it was worth it.

I wasn't that good a liar.

I wasn't that good a shot.

I wasn't that...

Stop. I became aware of my breath flowing out of me in short gasps, my heart hammering against my ribs. *Close your eyes.* I forced them shut, forced everything to go quiet. *Breathe.*

I did.

Or I tried, anyway.

If this wasn't the right drop-off point, I'd find it. If I couldn't find it, I'd find someone who knew and make them tell me. If I couldn't find that, I'd just start shooting until it sorted itself out. I'd make Cavric drive me all over creation if need be.

My hand wrapped around the Cacophony at my hip. He grew warm in my grasp.

I'd find Vraki.

We'll end him. All of them.

"Hello?"

I glanced up at the sound of Cavric's voice. I couldn't see him through the mist. But I heard him.

"Hello..."

And someone else.

"Are you..." There was confusion in his voice. "Are you all right, madam?"

"All right... madam... are you?"

The voice that spoke back was soft, delicate, beautifully feminine.

And I was off my ass.

I hopped off the crate, headed toward the sound of his voice as he spoke uncertainly into the fog.

"You seem distressed."

"*Dis…tress…*" The voice purred back to him. "*Seem?*"

I picked up speed, reaching for Jeff at my hip as I rushed down the sandy shore of the cove. I picked out his form through the fog, staring down into the surf of the lake. And, shortly thereafter, picked out the form staring back at him from the river.

She was beautiful: a perfect, porcelain face framed by ebon silk hair that spilled down her body. She was perfectly slender, skin completely flawless, and if you'll forgive me some coarseness, her tits and ass were the sort of thing you'd end up killing a man over if she asked you to. She was flawless, a perfectly formed woman.

Which was, after all, the point.

"I'm Cavric Proud," he said, stepping forward. "Low Sergeant of the Revolution. Is there any way I can help you, madam?"

"*Low…Sergeant…*" She spoke each word hesitantly, tasting them through a soft smile. And she raised her slender arms to him, approached him as she rose out of the water. "*Help.*"

He waded into the water toward her. I couldn't say I blamed him. If I was a little dumber, I probably would have, too. But I didn't have time to chastise him for that. I had barely gotten close enough to draw when she leapt at him.

That lilting, soft voice became a screech. Those arms grew long, fingers sprouting talons. And that beautiful, porcelain face split in half with a broad smile brimming with sharp, twisted teeth.

"*By the General!*" Cavric screamed, falling backward.

"*By, by, by,*" she cackled, lunging at him again.

Her claws caught him by the lapels of his coat, dragged him forward. Her mouth gaped wide, a black stalk of a tongue lashing out toward his face, barbs glistening out of it with a sheen of viscous saliva. She hauled him forward as he struggled against her, eyes bulging from her head with anticipation.

For the few seconds it took to carve them out, anyway.

A blade flashed. A bright line creased across her face, running from her brow through her jaw. She paused, blinking her remaining eye, unsure what to make of this. She turned toward me, saw my blade glistening.

And jamming into her throat.

She staggered backward as I tore a hole in her throat, spraying viscous scum from her flesh. She turned to flee back into the water, leaking from her wounds. I leapt, ramming my sword through her spine. She froze there for a single breath.

Then she dissipated, her body collapsing into a mess of green leaves, vines, and thorns that settled upon the river before disappearing beneath the water, leaving me calmly wiping off my blade as Cavric stared at the ripples that had almost killed him.

"What..." he gasped, turning horrified eyes to me. "What the fuck was *that*?"

"Kelpbride," I said, sheathing Jeff. "Try not to talk to them too much."

He stared at me. "*What*?"

"They remember every word they hear," a voice chimed from behind us.

Liette appeared from a nearby willow copse, a bundle of picked plants in one hand, the other adjusting her glasses. She observed the plants dissipating into the water, sinking beneath the surface.

"Quite fascinating, really. They're mimic hunters, taking pleasing shapes to lure their victims into the water where they can be dragged away and later devoured," she said. "They aren't born knowing language, though, so each new word they learn makes their disguise more effective, you know." She glanced at Cavric's terrified expression. "I mean, obviously you know *now*."

Cavric glanced from Liette to me, unblinking, mouth agape. I rolled my eyes.

"Oh, come on, that isn't even the weirdest thing you've seen this *week*." I glared at Liette. "And I thought I told you two to stay together."

"I saw some samples I needed nearby," Liette replied. "I trusted he would be fine on his own."

"Well, he wasn't. He could have been killed."

"Well, he wasn't," Liette repeated dryly. "I doubt he minds as much as—"

"SHUT UP!"

There's a moment in opera called the *raisu ath naccori*. Roughly translated from Old Imperial, it means "reason for fury." It's the moment the character snaps, when their moral thresholds have been crossed and left in tatters, when they're finally motivated to shriek into the night and set out to change the course of events. It's characterized by screaming, breaking stuff, and if it's any good, at least one angry sexual overture.

Cavric stared at me, the horror and shock drained from his face and replaced with numb emptiness.

"Fuck this," he muttered, throwing up his hands.

I had expected something more dramatic. But then, they do have shitty opera in Weiless.

"Fuck this," he repeated, clambering to his feet and crawling out of the river. "Fuck this river, fuck these plant-women, fuck this world." He paused as he stalked away to struggle with kicking a wet reed off his boot. "Fuck this plant in particular."

"Hey," I called after him as he stalked past me, raising the Cacophony for emphasis. "*Hey!* Where are you going? I need you to—"

"And *fuck you*, Sal." He whirled, leveling a finger at me. "Fuck your plan, fuck your gun, and fuck helping you." He whirled back about, started walking off into the gloom of the Scar. "I could have breathed my last gasp, rasping for air as my own blood filled my lungs and the Haveners force-fed me my own eyes and I'd still be luckier than I would be ending up alive and with you."

I blinked. I'd like to have taken the time to curse him out after that, but really, I was rather impressed by that outburst. Maybe the opera wasn't as bad as I thought. Also, I still needed him.

"Where are you going?" I said. "Congeniality's watching the Iron Boar. You aren't getting in without me and you *aren't* getting past her."

Congeniality glanced up at the sound of her name and, rather unhelpfully to my threat, didn't so much as glance at Cavric as he pushed past her. Not that it mattered, though. Cavric didn't notice her, either.

"Keep it. I don't care."

"What? That's Revolutionary property, man! Don't you care about it?"

"It's a chunk of metal." He scowled over his shoulder. "The Revolution isn't about machines or metal. It's about men. Women. *People.* It's about protecting those who can't protect themselves and doing the right thing for them. It's *not* about escorting a Vagrant and her smelly bird to commit evil fuckery with plant...women...*things!*" He threw up his hands. "Do whatever the fuck you want. I've got duties to attend to."

I watched him go. It would have been easy to shoot him in the back. But what I threw at him wasn't a bullet. What I threw at him was much worse.

"Do those duties include leaving kids to die?"

He froze with such swiftness, he almost buckled over. I might as well have kicked him in the business. And I'm not saying it wasn't a cheap shot. But I'm not saying I was wrong, either.

"What?" he asked.

"You came to Stark's Mutter to find your soldiers, right?"

"Agents Relentless and Vindictive," Cavric said. "We were given information regarding Vagrants of particular interest to Cadre Command. Our men were after them."

"And did your men know what those Vagrants were after?"

Cavric shook his head. I stared out over the Yental.

"But you did," I said. "Or you do now anyway."

"What?" he asked, breathless.

"You saw their work in the town square, in the black earth, in the corpses." I glanced sidelong at Cavric. "Did your Cadre Command ever teach you about Scraths?"

Cavric's mouth hung open. He stiffened. "Of course. They're monsters. Like all things magical."

"Not like all things magical," Liette countered softly. "Knowledge on the Scraths is...limited. Even to the Freemakers. They come from elsewhere, capable of being called only by a select few mages and only at great cost. They do not belong in this world, and thus aren't bound by its laws. But by the same token, they cannot exist outside a native host."

Cavric swallowed hard. "Meaning..."

"Meaning," I said, "a Scrath needs a body. Sometimes, it needs many bodies, in case the first one doesn't fit." Without realizing it, I ran a finger down the long scar on my chest. "Younger ones fight less, live longer." I closed my eyes. "Stretch more."

I didn't see the terror in his stare. I didn't need to. I could feel it— the same raw, unbelieving horror that every nul experienced when they realized just how vast the gulf was between what made them and what made a mage. I could feel him searching for an answer to this, mouth fumbling for the words to express whatever fear and fury battled inside his mouth.

"Why do they want a Scrath in this world?" Cavric's voice shattered the silence. "Do you know?"

I opened my eyes and saw a man desperate for an answer, for a reason why anyone would do something so heinous. I'd seen this stare before, in widows waiting for news of their husbands and grandfathers sitting at their doors awaiting the return of their children, this desperate need to believe that something good could come from something so vile.

Hardest thing in the world to lie to a stare like that.

"No," I said. "But I'm going to find out. And I'm going to stop it." I pulled my scarf up a little tighter around my face. "You can go if you want. You've taken us far enough. But if you want to help someone... well, here's your chance."

His voice fell silent as his eyes fell to his feet. I wish he had cursed at me, disbelieved me, or maybe just started screaming. Anything to break the silence. Because in the silence, I could feel Liette's stare like a blade in my neck.

She hadn't said anything, but I could see the anger burning behind her glasses. She knew I was chasing names, Vagrants, murderers. But somehow I think she thought it was just one more little whimsy of mine, like I'd go out, kill a few people, and we'd go back and sip wine and pretend we could be normal.

Maybe she hadn't known until now that I was chasing monsters. Or maybe she always had and just wanted to pretend otherwise. Maybe...

Maybe she just wanted to pretend I wasn't so broken.

I could feel the wind beginning to blow. I turned and saw black clouds rolling across the sky, lazily following the river and creeping toward us. A cloud of mist, thick and dense as a wall, came slithering across the surface of the river and I was all too happy to see it.

"Took them long enough," I muttered.

At that, Cavric started. Liette gasped, dropping her plants. And in the time it took them to do that, the mist had all but enveloped us. It swept over the river, across the bank, and over our heads in a matter of seconds. By the time he had reached for a gunpike that wasn't there—what he thought it would do against mist was anyone's guess—we were drowned in a thick gray cloud.

"What kind of profane magic is this?" he whispered.

I didn't bother answering. Revolutionaries have minds like machines. They like their operas straightforward, their food unseasoned, and their marriages arranged. All indiscretion, no imagination, and *precious* little perception, otherwise he might have noticed that the mist, thick and dense and rife with the smell of water as it was, wasn't actually leaving condensation anywhere.

I suppose I could have explained the magic that created it, if I felt so inclined. But in another few seconds, I heard the dull growl of an engine. And by that point, I figured he'd understand, assuming we weren't shot.

The boat came sliding out of the mist, a heavy thing of metal and timber with a broad, flat bow, propelled by waterwheels on either side of it. Its engine, far unlike that noisy thing in the Iron Boar, murmured quietly as it propelled the boat to the shore. Its bow slid down, forming a metal ramp. And as black shadows formed in the mist and skulked down the ramp toward us, I laid a hand on the Cacophony.

Guns won't do anything against mist, to be sure. But against the scrawny little shit that made them?

It'd do, if he didn't feel like playing nice.

I wagered there were about six of them in total, even though I could count only three; Ashmouths prefer to leave about half their numbers out of sight. I couldn't tell their genders behind the black coats that obscured their bodies and the black masks they wore, carved to resemble crows, but it wasn't like that mattered. After all, the black bows they had drawn upon me didn't give a shit whether a man or woman loosed the arrow.

Still, they hadn't shot me yet, so that was a good sign.

Unless they wanted to take me alive and torture me to reveal how I found their drop site, which was a bad sign.

Or they knew me by sight and realized I might be of use to them and could make a deal with them, which was a good sign.

Or they knew me by sight and remembered all the shit I've pulled that's ruined their myriad of operations and were busy thinking of the perfect way to force-feed me my own entrails while I was still alive, which was a bad sign.

So, you get what I mean when I say it's hard to deal with the Ashmouths.

"My, my..." a shrill, nasally voice said from the shadows of the boat. "Can you imagine my luck? Coming out to a forsaken shoreline in the middle of nowhere and finding the famous Sal the Cacophony waiting for me?"

Boots polished to a high sheen clicked on the metal ramp. Delicate fingers pulled black gloves over lily-white hands. Brass buttons on the finest black coat I had ever seen glistened in the dark. From beneath a head of coiffed black hair, a pair of eyes with dark circles under them, and a long, pointed nose, I was given a glimpse of a sneer so mean and ugly that it would make a pregnant woman miscarry just to look at.

One of the many talents of Necla the Shroud.

"I wonder which Scion I pissed off to make this happen," he said, making a face like he had just stepped in something.

"Oh, kitten," I said, making a mock pout, "if any of the Scions paid attention to you, you'd have been struck by lightning the second you crawled out the snatch."

Necla's eyes narrowed that way where you just *know* they've already decided to kill you and are just fantasizing about where they'll mount your head. But I wasn't worried. A Nightmage's power isn't as straightforward as throwing fire or shitting lightning. Theirs is an art of patience, forethought, and surprise.

Or, in Necla's case, laziness, apathy, and not-wanting-to-expend-effort-on-cleaning-up-the-mess.

"Don't let me catch any arrows flying," he said to the Ashmouths. "She'll only make this a big pain in my ass if you try to fight." He cocked a brow at me. "Unless you *came* here to get shot up, in which case—"

I made a show of easing my hand off the Cacophony. "Would you hate me if I said I didn't come here to fight?"

"No more than I already do." Necla looked over my head to Cavric, his lip curling up in distaste at the sight of his uniform. "And what about them? The Ashmouths don't care for Revolutionaries." His eyes narrowed on Liette. "Or misers."

"The Freemakers pursue knowledge for its own sake." Liette glanced at him over the top of her glasses. "And it is not for sale."

"The Ashmouths don't care for anyone who doesn't come with a lot of metal." I grunted toward Cavric. "They're both with me. I'm happy to be peaceable, but if anyone wants to make a problem out of them..."

I laid my hand on the Cacophony.

"I'm even happier to talk it over."

I won't lie, I got just the *teensiest* bit excited at the way Necla's eyes went wide.

"Put up your weapons," he whispered to the Ashmouths. "Grab the cargo and we'll be on our way."

As I predicted, three more black-clad thugs emerged from the shadows of the boat and joined their friends in moving down and hooking up ropes to the giant cargo box to drag it back up the ramp.

Necla sniffed toward me. "A pleasure seeing you again, Sal. Let's do it again when one of us is dead."

"I'll be more than happy to," I said, "if you can do a favor for me." I met the despair creasing his face with deadly seriousness. "I need to speak with the Three."

"No," he replied tersely.

"It's an emergency."

"*No.*"

"I'm tracking someone down. They'll know where to find them."

"What happened, Sal?" he asked. "Someone skip out on you before they could buy you breakfast?"

"It's more important than that." I let the insult slide off me; only reason Necla insulted my bedroom proclivities was because he had none of his own to speak of.

"Yes, I bet it is." He rolled his eyes. "Just like the last one was. And the one before that. You're always chasing someone, Sal, whether to kill them"—he pointedly glanced toward Cavric and Liette—"or to keep them. I'm never sure which is worse, and I am perfectly content to let it remain a mystery that doesn't involve me and *definitely* does not involve the Three."

Behind me, Cavric shuffled out of the way as the Ashmouths

hauled their load back up the ramp. Necla stepped aside and moved to go back onto the boat, sparing a snide glower for me.

"If you'll excuse me, Sal..."

"I most certainly will not," I replied, "Necladamius ki Samoria."

His back went straight as a blade. He turned around with painstaking slowness. And when I saw his face, it was twisted in ire.

When a mage goes Vagrant, we leave *everything* about our old lives behind. We take up new professions; we take up new names. Vagrants are always touchy being called by their old names and Nightmages are touchier than most.

See, the Lady Merchant cuts them a nice deal. Theirs is the power of illusion, able to induce hallucinations, alter the world of sight and sound to their liking—like this dense mist that surrounded us that Necla so expertly pulled out of his own head.

But in exchange for the ability to shape perception, the Lady demands a high Barter. Nightmages give up their ability to dream. And after that, whatever nightmares they're left mean that most of them choose to sleep as little as possible. Among the more prolific users, the insomnia is bad enough to induce madness.

But among mild users, like Necla here, it's just enough to make him a regular old cranky dickwipe.

Admittedly, it wasn't exactly wise to have done that, but it got his attention at least.

"You know me," I said, sounding as threatening as a woman surrounded by a Nightmage and six people with guns could. "You know I'm going to get what I want, whether you help me or not."

"I know you'll try," Necla said, "and I know you'll die doing so."

"Agreed," I replied. "But I'll make such a fucking mess of things the Three'll have your head for failing to stop me sooner." I pulled my scarf back. "Or, if you're feeling reasonable, we could work something out."

He stiffened, like he expected me to pull another gun out of my scarf and shoot him then and there. "Please," he hissed, "you couldn't possibly have anything I—"

"Redfavor."

That caught his attention. Necla's mouth hung open. Poor skinny bastard looked like he was about to topple over right there.

"What?" he asked, breathless.

I reached into my satchel and plucked out a jagged tooth from some badlands beast I had shot long ago. It had been a snakehead, I think, a real savage of a reptile that wanders the dark places. Their teeth are long, thin, and twisted as hell to rip their prey apart. But what's interesting about them is that whether they've eaten or not, their teeth are always red.

Which is all that mattered to Necla right now.

"Redfavor," I said. I held up the crimson tooth for his inspection. "Get me in to see the Three, it's yours."

Every Vagrant looks at a Redfavor like this.

It's true that we all want the things that normal people want: love, wealth, food, safety, fancy hats. But it's also true that we can usually just take those things with our magic. Every nation needs a currency and ours is Redfavor. It can be anything, big or small, so long as it's the color of blood. We trade them, Vagrant to Vagrant, and it has the only thing of value we can ever offer each other.

A favor.

No matter what it is, no matter when they ask for it, someone holds your Redfavor, you have to give it. The Vagrant who gives it, gives it freely. The Vagrant who welches on it does so knowing he's free game afterward. If you've ever heard tales of Vagrants launching themselves at a fortress they have no chance of taking or of blowing up a town for reasons no one can fathom, chances are good they did it because someone called in their Redfavor.

Personally, I didn't think Necla wanted anything quite like that. I didn't know *what* a weirdo like that *would* want. But I did know that I needed to track down Vraki. And for that, I knew I needed to do this.

Necla quietly reached out and took the tooth from my hand. He looked it over briefly and then, with reverent care, slipped it into a pocket of his coat and buttoned it. He looked back at me and nodded.

"If they decide to kill you for interrupting them," he said, "I'm not responsible."

"Understood," I said.

"And if your friends make a move they shouldn't, they're fair game."

"*WHAT?*" Cavric shrieked, though Liette merely glared.

"Right," I said, holding up a hand to cut off his protest.

"And if you even *think* about repeating what you see—"

"For fuck's sake, man," I groaned. "I *get* it. You're a very scary man who works for very scary people. Can we hurry this the fuck up already?"

Necla scowled at me, but to his credit, he at least shut up. He slinked back onto the ship. I gestured for the others to follow as I went up the ramp. The deck was modest and unfurnished, designed only for carrying its tremendous cargo. The boat's engine purred to life. I heard the hiss of spray as it drew away from the shoreline. Metal groaned and the ramp began to draw itself back up.

"This doesn't feel right," Cavric muttered to me. "We can't trust them."

"The Ashmouths' integrity is technically spotless," Liette pointed out. "Though, in fairness, that reputation is specific to their assassination contracts."

"Oh, well, good," Cavric muttered. "I would hate to impugn their honor."

"What, just because they're a bunch of thieves and murderers, you think we can't trust them?" I tugged my scarf up over my face. "Aren't we judgy."

"His wariness is not misplaced," Liette said. "Your humor, though, is."

"They're not going to kill us. The Ashmouths don't operate like that."

"What? They have some thieves' code of honor?" Cavric scoffed.

"Thieves only have honor in opera, darling." The deck slammed shut with an iron groan, and in the silence, the mist enclosed us. "In real life, they have standards."

TWENTY-THREE

THE *WEARY MOTHER*

If I could ever see myself saying anything to him that wasn't an insult, I'd say that Necla the Shroud's talents as a Nightmage were exceptional.

Even on the transport ship's deck, I could hardly see my hand in front of my face. The mist he had conjured was thicker than night, smothering me like it wanted to choke me. Knowing Necla, it just might. Normally, I'd be worried about that, but the only way out of a Redfavor is death and I knew he wouldn't toss his away so easily.

If he wanted to, though, he need only push me over.

I could barely see them, but I could hear them. And I knew they could sense me. They giggled and laughed to each other in lilting, disjointed noises. I could see the silhouettes of their slender shapes through the mist. And I could feel the Kelpbrides' hungry smiles on me.

Their giggles quieted. Water splashed as, one by one, they vanished under the river. I was left at the bow of the boat, staring into an endless gray. I had only barely begun to wonder what had scared them off when I got my answer.

Before us, the mists began to part. Looming out of the endless gray, I saw it only as a shadow.

A great fucking mountain of a shadow.

Its sides were heavy iron, yet it glided through the water like a ghost. A pair of titanic waterwheels propelled it, yet it made not a sound. It was as big as a township, yet you'd never have seen it if you weren't meant to.

You've heard about it, I bet. In the tales that get passed back and forth by drunks, there's always one story about it. Some say it's a black barge that plies through the rivers of the Scar, appearing as a black shadow at night and disappearing during the daytime. Others say it's the ship that takes the dead to the other side, stopping to collect the lost souls from the river. And just a few call it a superweapon that the Ashmouths keep in case they ever just want to extend a big old exploding middle finger to the world.

At the very least, I bet you've heard its name.

The *Weary Mother*. The floating fortress of the Ashmouths.

When every land power in the Scar wants you dead, the water is the only place you're safe. The *Mother* wanders up and down the rivers, surrounded by predators and shrouded from sight, thanks to the likes of Necla and every other Vagrant on the Ashmouths' payroll. Like wasps from a hive, their assassins flit out from the ship and return to it once their contracts are filled. No one finds it unless they're meant to find it. And no one outside the Ashmouths who goes in it ever comes out again.

So, you knew what I was about to do was a pretty stupid idea.

In the distance behind us, thunderclouds gathered ominously. I heard the rumble of the heavens, as if in agreement of the stupidity of my idea. Or maybe that was just another one of Necla's tricks.

The transport ship pulled up alongside the great black barge, affixing itself to a loading ramp built into its hull. Ashmouths leapt onto the ramp, expertly landing and rigging chains to hook the transport to the ship. A gangplank lowered, and Necla led me down one ramp and up another onto the deck of the ship, Cavric and Liette following close behind.

Cabins sealed with iron doors marched the length of the deck, a narrow walkway that wrapped around the ship. In and out of them flitted Ashmouths, clad in black from head to toe, sparing us only a wary glance behind their masks before opening doors, careful not to reveal what was inside, and disappearing. They spared us no particular respects as Necla led us around the deck, but I noticed they gave him a wide berth.

And hey, they didn't shoot us. So, you know, small victories.

"They won't attack you." Necla must have sensed my anxiousness—or maybe he was just being a dick—as he approached a long door at the end of the deck. "But if they did, you have to know there's little you could do about it."

"Yeah, I kind of figured that once I decided to hop aboard a ship full of assassins, shithead," I grunted. "You're the big man here, I get it."

"I'm not a big man." He pushed the door open. "I just happen to work for big people."

I've only ever seen three things that made me whistle in astonishment in my life. Once after witnessing a particularly difficult maneuver in a brothel called The Cat's Lament, once after the events that led to me fleeing The Cat's Lament as it exploded in the background, and once when I saw what was behind that door.

There were a shit-load of guns, to be sure: gunpikes arranged in delicate rows, pistols heaped into piles, cannons swaddled in the dark. There were glistening flameglaives and frostbrands, humming with subdued magic. There were suits of giant mobile armor, crates of bottles of substances whose purposes were best left to the imagination, and more than a few extremely old portraits of extremely ancient secrets.

From wall to wall, the *Mother*'s hold hosted a hoard that would make a dragon blush. But only monsters have hoards.

The Ashmouths have a business.

"By the General's endless wisdom!"

It was an understandable response to the sight. I was feeling much the same, though Cavric used different words than I would have. He pushed past me, rushed into the hold, and stared around, wide-eyed.

"How...What...This is..." He fumbled over his own lips, trying to find the words. "*These are our weapons!*" He pointed to the row of gunpikes. "Those are Revolutionary guns!" He pointed to the giant armor. "That's a Revolutionary Paladin! They don't even *make* those this far south!" He rushed to a nearby crate, pried its lid off, and pulled out what appeared to be a bundle of bright red sticks bound together with black bands and rigged with an impressive-looking mechanism. "*These* are Righteous Fires of Indisputable Truth!"

"You sure?" I pulled my scarf out of my eyes. "They look like... sticks."

"Bombs," Liette added, inspecting them. "Highly adhesive incendiaries, technically speaking." She attempted to illustrate with her hands. "They explode into this sticky, flammable... goop, I guess you'd call it. It burns so bright, even water can't douse it. Incredibly painful way to die, I suspect." She plucked one of the devices up and squinted. "I always wanted one to study."

She turned a glare upon me. I rolled my eyes. She was never, ever going to let me live down forgetting her birthday.

"And they're *illegal*," Cavric shouted. "The Revolution outlawed their use because they were inhumane."

"Oh, yes." Necla rolled his eyes. "As opposed to the giant cannons, repeating guns, and other *humane* ways the Revolution kills thousands of people."

"That's... that's not the same thing," Cavric said, haltingly. "Those are honorable deaths in battlegrounds. There's a difference."

"Like... what?" Liette blinked. "In how many pieces a person is in after the slaughter?"

"It's not a slaughter!" he protested.

"What else do you call killing a lot of people?" I asked. I was genuinely curious, actually.

Cavric's mouth hung open, wordless.

Necla pushed past him, waving a hand. "The Cadre's engineers discontinued them to better refine their blast radius. We managed to persuade them to part with their prototypes."

"*Persuade?*" Cavric asked, wide-eyed. "You mean stole!"

"Or bribed. Or threatened. Blackmailed. Whatever answer you like, feel free to substitute it." Necla gestured back to the crate. "Only put it down, would you? It was expensive."

"No!" Cavric held up his hands. "I can't abide this! Dealing with assassins is one thing, but allowing them access to something like this is—"

A pair of Ashmouths seized him, hauled him through the door, and disappeared by the time I had even reached for my gun.

Necla held up a hand with a sigh. "Relax," he said. "He won't be harmed."

I narrowed my eyes at him, hand on my gun. The Cacophony's brass giggle rang in my ears. And, if the fear on his face was any indication, in Necla's, too.

"You have my word," he said.

"The word of an illusionist isn't comforting," I growled.

"I'll go with him," Liette interjected as she started after Cavric. "Just to keep an eye on things."

"Oh, for fuck's sake," I said, "I don't want *one* of you in their grasp, let alone both."

"I assure you, I will be fine. The Ashmouths still respect the old treaties with the Freemakers, I assume?" At Necla's shrug, she sighed. "At the very least, I can keep Cavric from becoming *particularly* harmed."

"Fucking splendid," I sighed, and without realizing it, muttered under my breath, "And are you going to fix *him* next?"

I hadn't expected to say it, let alone for her to hear it. But she had. And she didn't so much scowl at me as sharpen her eyes into daggers and plunge them into my throat before turning around and slamming the door behind her.

"Your...friends, if that title fits, will be perfectly fine," Necla offered. "The Three are rather leery of strangers, in general, much less thralls of the Revolution. They're simply ensuring the Revolutionary doesn't see anything that might further shatter that fragile little mind his Great General has so painstakingly polished."

"Birdshit," I snarled. "You're going to hold them to make sure I don't start shit."

"Really?" Necla placed a hand to his chest, pouting as we walked to the end of the hold and another door in its wall. "Are you suggesting we might believe that Sal the Cacophony, wielder of a gun that shoots explosions, might 'start shit'?" He grinned. "Or *give* a shit about someone?" He shook his head, pulled the door open, and gestured inside. "I'm afraid I can't bear to look such an accusation in the eye, madam. After you, please."

It blistered my ass to see that smug smile on that smug face. And normally, assassins or not, I wouldn't have hesitated shooting one off the other. But that would make me a rude guest. And the Three didn't like rudeness.

"So," he said as he walked in after me, "been busy?"

But you remember what I said about hope in the Scar.

The door opened into a stairway, switchback steps leading up and lit by dim lanterns. My boots rang out on the iron as I trudged up the steps. I stomped, trying to drown out Necla's noise.

"So, tell me about your new friend?"

It didn't work.

"You do collect them, don't you?" Necla knew he could push me. His bosses had something I wanted and he had my Redfavor. While I knew he wouldn't waste the latter, I also knew that dickwipe enjoyed having it over me. "How many has it been since I last saw you, anyway? Ten? Twenty? More?"

I politely refrained from telling him what he should do as we ascended the stairs. You don't hear many operas about a hero's patience, but I fucking expected a whole verse about mine for putting up with this shit.

"But I suppose that's your business," he sighed. "Still, it's tragic, isn't it? That was rather a tense exchange, wasn't it? I assume things didn't work out with Liette."

Remember what I said about *raisu ath naccori*? My favorites were the ones with big, dramatic monologues leading into declarations of love.

Funny enough, mine wasn't that dramatic. When I get mad, things just kind of happen.

And somehow, without quite knowing how, my forearm was on Necla's throat.

And the Cacophony was in my hand.

And the barrel was shoved right between his eyes.

"You spew whatever shit you want to me." My voice was slow, easy, and cold. "But you ever say her name again, you even *think* it, I'm going to blow your head off with the Cacophony."

Funny thing. I didn't even see the fear in Necla's eyes. I didn't see his mouth hanging open as he fumbled for words. I didn't see anything I'd have otherwise taken pleasure in. I just saw the mechanical nodding of the dumb bastard whose skull I was going to blast open if he ever spoke of her again.

"What am I going to blow off, Necla?" I asked.

"You've made your fucking point," he snarled. "Now back—"

"*What*," I said, slamming his head against the wall, "am I going to blow off?"

His voice trickled out between the wall and my forearm on a thin, raspy whisper. "My head."

"And what am I going to do it with, Necla?"

"With . . . with your gun."

"With the Cacophony."

"With the Cacophony."

As if the ability to induce hallucinations wasn't enough, Nightmages could read the surface thoughts of people. Better to weave their illusions, I supposed. Necla had looked into my head to see Liette's name. Now I wanted him to look into it and see exactly what I was going to do to him if he spoke it again.

I held his gaze for a good long while before I lowered my weapon and slid him back into his holster. I could feel his singe of disappointment as I did. I released Necla and stepped back. I looked him over, brushed a stray bit of grime off his coat, felt his skeleton try to leap out of his skin. Then I stepped back and made a gesture toward the stairs.

"After you," I said.

That was stupid, I knew. Necla could use my Redfavor for revenge. Or he could make sure that I never saw his bosses. Or he could have Cavric or Liette killed. Or he could forgo all that and use his magic to make me think my hands were snakes and use them to strangle myself or some freaky shit like that.

But I wasn't going to let it be said you uttered that name with anything less than respect around Sal the Cacophony.

Also he wasn't talking anymore.

Worth it.

The stairs ended at a door made of old, stained wood, far from the other iron gates on the ship. Without a word, Necla pulled it open and stepped aside. I walked past him, cast him a glance. He didn't look me in the eye.

I never said he wasn't smart.

TWENTY-FOUR

THE *WEARY MOTHER*

The door clicked shut behind me as I entered a dark hallway. The scent of cheap tobacco filled my nose. Ahead, the light of a single lamp burned and beckoned me forward, to the lair where it all happened.

No one knows who leads the Ashmouths. People have theories, of course: They receive commands from an evil god; they're ruled by an immortal mage who cheated death with profane magic; there's a single guy who gets assassinated and replaced every other week. All fine theories.

But the truth?

"Ha! That's *kang*, you old bitch!"

The truth is much worse.

"That's *kol*, at best. Try again. Less attitude. More intellect."

Two voices wafted out of the room on clouds of stale cigarette smoke. One gravelly and jagged, one stern and hard, both female and neither one I especially wanted to hear.

"You're just trying to avoid the shame of defeat, you diseased cow," the gravel voice rumbled. "That's ten fire tiles in a row. *Kang*."

"I count nine fire tiles and one earth, fool," the stern voice hammered in reply. "That's *kol* and I'm being generous to give you that."

I hesitated in the doorway for a moment, not quite sure of the protocol. Do I knock? Do I bow and scrape? Should someone announce me? I was never sure with the Three.

"Don't be shy, dear," another voice, soft and lilting and tossed my way like a handful of rose petals, said. "Come in, come in."

And, with that elegant entrance, I walked right into the heart of the Ashmouths.

It was a small room, bereft of any furnishings but the lamp hanging from the ceiling and the circular table that sat beneath its halo of orange light. Placed on top of it, amid drained whiskey glasses and stubbed-out cigarettes, was an Emperor's Wager board, stacked with tiles so high it suggested that the game had been going on for a *very* long time. And situated around it, patiently and methodically placing and removing tiles, were the three women who ran the organization with more blood on its hands than most militaries.

Gan. Pui. And Yoc.

Pui, tall and thin and leather-skinned, looked up in my direction. Under a tight braid of gray hair and through a mouthful of yellow teeth, she grinned at me in a way that made the skin of her face draw up around her cheekbones like a skull.

"Well, well," she rasped like she had rocks in her throat. "As I live and breathe." She took a long drag on her cigarette and let out a cough. "Sal the fucking Cacophony."

"Funny," Gan, short and built like a beer keg, her black hair in a tight bun and her eyes hidden behind dark glasses, muttered. "I don't *recall* ordering a pain in the ass." Her jowly face trembled with a growl as she placed a water tile on the board and took two wood tiles off. "Maybe one of you two hags did."

"Now, now." Yoc, old and white haired and sweet as a grandmother—if that grandmother also had people killed on the regular—smiled at me. "I'm sure she has a good reason for being here." She raised the hand that had signed the contracts that had killed a thousand men and women and took up her whiskey glass. "After all, I'm sure she knows how much we don't like having our game interrupted."

"I don't know about that," Gan said. "She seems stupid enough." She made a gesture toward Pui. "Your move, imbecile."

"Watch your fucking manners, you dry turd," Pui snarled. She spoke through teeth clenched around her cigarette as she added three earth tiles to the board. "'Course, if she came here, she better fucking tell us why before I get cross."

"Oh dear," Yoc sighed. "We wouldn't want anyone to get cross, would we?" She smiled at me. "You'd better speak up soon, dearie, before you start to seem rude."

That was good advice, really. And it was pretty stupid of me to have stayed silent as long as I did; one didn't waste the Three's time if one didn't want to end up with their teeth pried out.

But I couldn't help it. How often do you meet the three old ladies who have people killed for money?

"Er...right." I stepped forward. "Sorry about the intrusion, but—"

"Scarf, dear," Yoc said.

"What," I asked, then remembered who I was talking to, "madam?"

"Take off your scarf," Gan growled, organizing her tiles. "I hope your mother is dead so she doesn't have to see what a disrespectful child she raised."

"Right, sorry." I pulled my scarf back, made a bow for additional effort. "I'll be quick. I'm here because I think you sold something to a friend of mine."

"We sell a lot of things to a lot of friends," Pui said. "The Ashmouths make deals every day."

"I'm afraid she's right," Yoc added, placing four metal tiles down and taking two fire tiles. "Business has been brisk. I can't imagine taking the time to remember every old deal for anyone who walked in."

"It was no ordinary deal," I said. "And I'm not just anyone."

"Got a point," Pui grunted. "The Cacophony is special."

"Special pain in my snatch," Gan said. "Don't think I've forgotten the incident with the Freemaker Six Quarts of Aged Rum and his potion stock. We lost good money there."

"We agreed that it wasn't her fault, Gan sweetie," Yoc said.

"*You* agreed. *I* said we should kill her on principle."

"There was an incident at a township called Stark's Mutter," I interjected. "A Vagrant used forbidden magic to kill a lot of people."

"They'll do that, won't they?" Yoc sighed.

"I believe he killed them to summon a Scrath," I said. "I know there's precious few ways to do that and I know you hold all of them." I took a cautious step closer. "I want to know…" I paused, reconsidered. "I was *hoping* you would tell me where Vraki the Gate went. He bought something from you, I'm sure."

"Huh." Gan let out a chuckle—or she threw up a little; it was hard to tell. "The Cacophony was *hoping*. What a gentle soul she is."

"So pleasant." Pui's laughter devolved into a hacking cough. "And so polite. We should help a good girl out, shouldn't we?"

"It would be the polite thing to do," Yoc said. She paused, bit her knuckle. "Oh, drat. But if we went and gave her something for nothing, what would people think? What would people *say*?"

"There are protocols," Gan agreed. "A deal's not a deal if nothing's given." She snorted, took two earth tiles away. "Do we owe the Cacophony a favor?"

"Not that I can remember," Pui said, adding two fire tiles. "Does the Cacophony owe *us* a favor?"

"I don't think so." Yoc shook her head, took away three wood tiles. "Oh dear, that sounds like an impasse to me."

"Ah, well," Gan said.

"Tough break," Pui added.

"So sorry, dear," Yoc said. She added another wood tile and grinned. "Oh! Is that *kol*? Did I win?"

"*Please.*" I couldn't keep the whine out of my voice. "This is important. I know Vraki the Gate had an obelisk from Haven that he used. I know you're the only ones who can get such a thing. He *had* to have come to you."

"Well, if you're so fucking smart, why come to us?" Pui asked.

"Because I need to know where he went *next*," I said. "I need to know what he's planning. He's got prisoners... kids. He's going to use them for—"

"Oh my. Children, you say?" Yoc shook her head, made a tutting noise. "My, my, that is a shame. A dreadful shame."

"Right, so you'll—"

"And I expect I would care just a *teensy* bit more..." Yoc looked up at me and gave me a smile as sweet as sugar. "But you know how many orphans I've made, don't you, dear?"

"It loses its shock value after the first time," Gan agreed. "Becomes rather tiresome, if I'm honest."

"But that's not why you're really asking, is it, Cacophony?"

For the first time since I had entered, no one's eyes were on the game board. Gan and Yoc looked toward Pui. And Pui, her eyes bright even as the rest of her was withered and darkened, was looking right at me.

"Not that I doubt you're concerned with those poor little children," she said. "I expect, if you had met three ladies just a *touch* dumber than we, they might have bought it, too. But, sweetie"—she held out her hands to her companions—"we're the *Ashmouths*."

"We know everything," Gan said.

"We hear everything," Yoc added.

"And we know what the name Vraki the Gate means to you." Pui leaned forward, grinning. "He's not so unlike us, is he? A murderer, yes. A monster to some. But, at his heart, a businessman. He wanted to buy a coup of the Imperium, long ago."

"He wasn't alone," Gan muttered. "How many mages joined him? Galta? Riccu?"

"Jindu," Yoc added, her voice cutting through me.

"An ambitious plan. And the price for it..." Pui's grin grew a little broader, a little blacker. "Well, you know, don't you, dear?"

Theirs were the hands that signed a thousand death contracts a year. When they could be bothered to look up from their game, they decided who lived and died with a stroke of their pen. At a word, they could have me stripped, tied, tortured, and cut up into a thousand pieces to be fed to dogs.

Yet only when Pui said what she did, only when she looked at me like she did, like she knew what had happened all those years ago that made me write this list I carried...

Only then did I feel my blood go cold.

"You know, I *do* remember hearing something like that." Yoc's eyes turned predatory as they turned on me. "Yes, it's coming back to me. Something about a betrayal? A great mage dying in the dark? My, my. That would make *me* want to find Vraki, too."

My scars began to itch. In the back of my head, I could hear the sound of screaming, of a mouth whispering apologies, of a song with a verse I couldn't understand.

"Well, since she wants to know *so* badly," Gan said. "Perhaps we could be merciful this once and strike a deal?"

My mouth tasted dry and cold. I knew the answer, yet I asked anyway.

"What do you want?"

I felt their eyes drift to my hip. I felt his warm anger through the leather of the holster. I felt the hiss of their words.

"The Herald of the End Times," Gan whispered.

"The Mad Emperor's Legacy," Pui rasped.

"The Cacophony," Yoc said. "Give it to us, dear, and we'll tell you everything you could ever want to know about Vraki the Gate."

"And Taltho the Scourge," Pui added. "Kresh the Tempest, Riccu the Knock..."

"Jindu the Blade, Galta the Thorn, Zanze the Beast..." Gan hummed, stacking her tiles one atop the other. "We know about all of them, Cacophony. We know about your list. We know what they did. We know why you want to kill them. We know where they're going. We know when they sleep."

"And we'll tell you," Pui said. "We'll tell you where to find them. Their families, too, if you want. We'll tell you how to kill them. We'll tell you the six words you can whisper in their ears to ensure that they die in such fear and in such pain that their last words will be to speak your name, over and over, begging for release."

"We can do that," Yoc said, taking a sip of her drink. "We can do all of that and more. All we want"—she glanced toward my hip—"is that tiny little trinket there."

I believed them. Every word.

You might find it hard to believe, but the Three don't lie. Their assassins do. Their thieves do. But they don't. When you know everything, there's just no need; you can already get everything you want with the truth. So, I didn't doubt at all that they could find who I was looking for. I didn't doubt at all that they could give me what I wanted.

And I did want it.

I wanted it so bad that I could see it just now, without even closing my eyes. In the shadows cast by the swaying lamp, I could see the smoke twist and writhe. I could see Jindu come out of it, tall and lean and eyes so bright like I remembered them. I could see his lips whispering soundlessly, mouthing apologies to me and begging for forgiveness. And I could see my gun pressed against his temple, my finger on the trigger, and...

And my scars itched.

And the burden on my hip felt suddenly very heavy and warm, like a pound of flesh cut right out of me.

And I knew what my answer was.

"I can't," I whispered. My lips were so numb and my voice so distant, I almost didn't believe I had said it. "I...I can't."

"It is valuable, true," Pui sighed, a plume of smoke escaping her lips. "We could add rewards. We could give you metal. We could give you birds."

"Men. Women. Bigger guns," Gan hummed.

"Whatever you wished, dearie," Yoc said, nodding encouragingly. "We know how important it is. We're not going to cheat you. Simply name your price and the Three will oblige."

I could feel him burning. He was seething in the leather of his holster, his growl low and iron at my hesitation. He could sense my temptation. And he didn't like it. But he didn't burn me. He knew, as well as I did, what my next words were going to be.

"We made a deal, he and I," I said. "And Sal the Cacophony doesn't go back on deals."

"Mmm," Pui hummed, shrugging. "Oh well."

"More's the pity," Gan said, turning her attention back to the game.

"Glad you could stop by, dear," Yoc said, looking back down. "Door's back the way you came."

I opened my mouth to protest, but what could I say? I had already wasted their time and I knew the Three were being generous just letting me fuck off instead of having me killed for the effort.

But I couldn't leave. Not just like this. Not without another word. I hadn't avenged Stark's Mutter. I hadn't fulfilled my promise. I hadn't saved the kids.

I hadn't killed Jindu.

I had to do something. Anything. Even if that meant every Redfavor I had or ever would have.

And I was halfway to offering just that when I heard the groan of iron.

The boat pitched suddenly to the right. The Three immediately leapt over their game board, holding it down to keep it from sliding off, heedless of the glasses and other fineries that went shattering to the ground. I seized the door frame to keep from being swept off my feet.

"The fuck was that?" Pui asked.

Apparently they didn't know everything.

"Oh dear," Yoc said. "Is the water getting rough?"

"On the Yental? This time of year?" Gan said. "Don't be stupid, you old cow."

"It's Necla," I growled, pulling myself up as the ship righted itself. "Part of his magic. I saw the illusion he made of the storm following the ship. He's probably using something to make us think it's kicking up." At their glances, I shrugged. "He's an asshole like that, isn't he?"

The Three exchanged a brief glance before looking back at me.

And from the frowns scarred across their faces, I knew what their words were going to be before they spoke them.

"Necla can't make illusions that size," Gan growled.

My brow furrowed. I wanted to speculate.

Turns out there was no need, though.

In another second, the boat pitched again. Iron roared angrily. The Three shrieked as their game threatened to slide off. The lantern fell from the rafters, hit the ground, and shattered, its light winking out and casting us into darkness.

And between the howl and groan of metal and timber, and amid the howl of distant wind, I could hear someone call my name.

"Cacophony! Come out and die!"

TWENTY-FIVE

THE *WEARY MOTHER*

The first thing I noticed when I opened the door was the wind. My scarf lashed about my face, almost flying off my head.

The next thing was the screaming. A sound so distant and faint I could barely tell the difference between it and the wail of the wind.

I had a moment to wonder what was going on.

Of course, once I saw the body flying through the air, I figured it out.

I slammed myself against the door as he went hurtling past me— or at least, I assumed it was a he, but everyone kind of sounds like a little girl when they're thrown through the air at a hundred miles an hour.

The Ashmouth went tumbling in a jumble of limbs, the black cloth of his uniform shredded from his body as a gale carried him in a twisting shriek over the edge of the ship's railing to disappear into the river below.

I'd have helped him if I could. But as I turned toward the direction he had come flying from, I saw a bigger problem approaching.

I shrieked something profane but it was lost in the hurricane blowing toward me.

A wail of wind. A fit of frightfully excited laughter. Flash of gold and white. Straight and fast as a bolt from on high. I tried to duck back into the cabin and slam the door shut, but it was pulled from my hands and then from its hinges. Something flew past me with the force of a storm, tearing boards from the deck, glass from windows, doors from hinges. The few poor Ashmouth bastards who poked their heads out to see what was happening joined the cloud of wreckage that went screaming into the wind, cast out into the river like black feathers upon a gray sky.

The wind's howl dulled to a whisper. I heard the splash of bodies disappearing into water. I heard the groan of the ship as its metal bent and its wood splintered. And, between the sounds of things dying, I heard a long, delighted cackle.

I heard him laugh.

Everyone's got one—a glass shattering, a child crying, a door with a squeaky hinge slamming shut. Everyone's got a noise that takes them somewhere else, makes them someone else.

That laugh, that shrieking wail of a laugh, went through my scars, through my skin, seized something inside of me and strangled it.

The air suddenly felt too thin to breathe. No matter how hard I gasped, I couldn't get enough of it in my lungs.

The mists closed in around me. The boat disappeared. I blinked.

And I didn't know where I was anymore.

I felt cold stone on my back, so cold that I could feel it through my clothes. I saw a purple halo of light above me, gaping wide into a violet, toothless mouth. I saw droplets of red blood, my blood, gliding lazily through the empty air above me, like raindrops down a windowpane.

—※◆※—

I blinked again. I was back on the ship. The wind's whisper twisted, became a whistle, became a howl. I felt it turn, a great serpent of air and cold, and head toward me. And through its breathless wail, I heard his voice.

"Run," he spoke on the gale. "It's funnier when you run."

And I did.

My body remembered what my mind was still struggling to figure out. My legs knew to carry me across the deck. My hands knew to keep one on my scarf, the other on my gun as I ran. And my ears knew to close themselves to the sounds behind me.

The howling moan of the wind. The groan of boards and nails torn out of the deck and sent flying into nothingness. The shriek of metal and glass as doors were pulled off hinges and windows were shattered.

And through it all, his laugh.

Listen and die. Shut it out and live. My body knew. It kept me running toward the stern of the ship, past the great waterwheels, even as the rest of it came apart behind me.

I rounded a corner, flattened my back against the rear of the ship. The white of the *Weary Mother*'s wake sprawled before me. I glanced up and saw an Ashmouth run past me, a bow in his hands as he rounded the corner I had just come from and raised his weapon.

I shouted a warning. He couldn't hear me.

Not with his head cut off.

A burst of crimson painted the mist. The Ashmouth's limp body and severed head went flying off the deck to disappear into the gray. And, even shielded as I was, I almost followed them, the force of the wind nearly tearing me from my feet.

I saw him flying through the air. I saw him, thin as the black blade in his hand. I saw the mane of golden hair trailing behind him as he disappeared into the fog. I saw the droplets of blood drifting in the air.

And I was gone again.

I was back on the cold stone, somewhere far away and in a dark place. I saw shadows surrounding me, their eyes on me—some with revulsion, some with laughter, one with pity. I saw my blood floating in the air, drawn out of my flesh in rivulets, crimson sighs drawn from my weary body. I saw them slip up into the sky, disappear into the halo of purple light.

I blinked again. I was back. There was a hand on my shoulder.

The Cacophony was in my hand; I didn't know when I had

drawn him. I pulled his grinning barrel up to a breathless face. But
Necla, even staring down the barrel, didn't notice. The horror that
had made his eyes go wide was one my gun couldn't compare to.

"What..." he gasped, breathless, "what was that?"

I opened my mouth to reply. No words came out. Somewhere, in
a dark corner of my skull, something kicked me.

Talk, it told me. Sal the Cacophony doesn't sit there gaping. Not
in front of this fuck.

I forced iron into my eyes, a growl into my throat. "You mean
what *is* that," I said. "He hasn't left yet."

"Skymage," he said, staring out into the mist. "It had to be a Skymage. I've never seen magic like that."

I sneered, if only to keep the fear out of my voice. "A mage is still
a man. All men die."

"Shut up. *Shut up*," Necla hissed, clutching his head as if he could
wring a plan out of his brain. "Your gun. We need your gun. He's
moving too fast for me to pin down with my magic."

I didn't want to tell him he couldn't pin down a foe like this. His
illusions could only show people what they wanted. And he—that
shrieking, laughing demon on the sky—had taken everything he
wanted from the Lady Merchant.

And me?

I looked down at the Cacophony. He looked back at me.

We were going to take it all back.

"He said your name," Necla whispered. "He's here for you."

"He is," I grunted.

"You have to help."

"I don't."

"But—"

"But I came here, did my business, didn't get what I want, and
now I'm done." I fixed him with a hard-eyed glare. "You want me
to help, you're going to do one of two things. You either persuade
the Three that I'm worth the effort"—I glanced down at his pocket,

tapped it with the barrel of my gun—"or you just hand that little trinket I gave you back over to me."

No one knew much about the Three who led the Ashmouths, but there were three facts known to anyone who had heard their name: You didn't piss them off, you paid what you owed them, and you never got them to change their mind.

But I saw an opportunity for the third. Maybe we were in that deep of shit. Or maybe he had a really good favor he wanted.

But he looked into my eyes. He nodded. He whispered.

"Fix this."

I grunted, flipped open the Cacophony's chamber. "Try to keep him blind. Weave your mist as thick as you can," I said. "How do I get to the top of the ship?"

"There are ladders at the other end of the deck," he said. "But how—"

"Need room to fight him." I plucked three shells from my pouch, loaded them in. "Down here, he'll tear the place apart."

"And what makes you certain he'll follow you?"

"I don't know, champ." I flipped the chamber shut. "If you had a chance at killing me, would you take it?"

Necla looked at me, considered, then nodded.

"Good luck, Sal."

I grunted an acknowledgment and took off. I whirled around the deck as I heard the wind blowing wild behind me. Out there in the mist, he was searching for me, trying to figure out where I was. He'd lose patience soon, I knew, and start tearing the ship open to get at me.

I had to give him a target before then.

Fortunately, on the list of people he wanted to kill, I was close to the top.

Just like Kresh the Tempest was on mine.

The *Weary Mother* tilted under my feet as I stared down a deck that seemed suddenly impossibly long. But there it was, at the end just like Necla had said: an iron ladder welded to the hull leading upward. That's where I needed to be.

The wind started howling.

And I started running.

The air was thin, torn apart by his magic. It made my lungs burn, my heart thunder as I charged down the deck. I couldn't spare a thought for how much it might hurt. I couldn't take my eyes off that ladder. I couldn't keep my ears shut to the sound of the wind.

To the sound of his laughter.

I blinked. I was on the cold stone. My blood left me, swallowed by the light.

The wind's whisper became a howl.

I blinked. The shadows closed in around me. Their eyes winked out, one by one.

I felt my hair whipping about my face.

I blinked. The purple light filled a sky above me. I looked at my hand, impotent and fleshy. Above me, someone whispered two words.

"I'm sorry."

I said something back.

I couldn't hear what. Not over the sound of his laughter. Not over the sound of my scream.

Not over the sound of the wind behind me. Above me.

Right next to me.

My scarf whipped against my face. I leapt, tumbled to the deck, clasped my hands over my head. The gale struck a moment later, a great pillar of wind that slammed against the hull. The boat rocked beneath me, windows shattered above me, and broken glass rained down on my shoulders. In the distance, I heard him laugh. Out in the fog, I could see his rail-thin figure hovering there, black sword raised.

"Lucky as ever, Cacophony. I salute you." He drew his blade back. "It looks a lot like killing you, but don't be alarmed. Just hold still and..."

He swung. The wind screamed. I was on my feet and running again before the next gale hit, rocking the ship and threatening to knock me off my feet. But I kept my balance and I kept my speed, even as he hurled blast after blast after me, always just shy of smashing me against the hull.

Maybe his aim had turned to shit. Maybe he was toying with me. Maybe this was another one of his sick fucking games. Whatever it was, though, it wasn't luck. Sal the Cacophony didn't need luck.

The people on her list did.

My lungs were on fire, my skin was cut up from the broken glass, the iron burned in my hand. But I made it. I scrambled up the ladder, all the way to the top of the ship.

It sprawled out like an iron plain before me, empty but for six smokestacks that marched its length like long-dead gods wheezing their last. Gray plumes coiled out of their gaping maws, rising up to join the gray clouds roiling overhead. Thunder rumbled in the distance, and in the wake of its echo, I could hear him.

And I swore—to me and to the burning metal in my hands—it would be the last time I'd hear him laugh.

I let the Cacophony hang from my hand, his grip burning in anticipation, and I walked to the middle of the ship's roof. And as the wind picked up, cold and cruel as winter, I waited.

You can't outrun a Skymage. And you can't hide from them. They can be anywhere as quick as the wind can take them. The Lady Merchant gave them the power to look down on the rest of the world and sneer at the pitiful people who couldn't hope to reach them.

Just as well.

You run from a beast. You hide from a storm. But men like Kresh the Tempest, laughing men who paint the sky with blood, you do neither.

You stop. And you stand. And you look them straight in the eye.

And you tell them how they're going to die.

And when I looked up into that gray sky and saw his black shadow, I told him.

But way up there, he couldn't hear me.

He descended from the gray mist like some kind of distant god who wanted to see what suffering looked like up close. And when he emerged, I'd forgive you for saying he looked human.

Kresh was slender, well muscled, young. His body was bare but for a pair of black breeches that clung to him like a second skin and the black lightning bolts tattooed across his chest. His hair, long as he was tall and gold as wheat, danced above his head like angels in the breeze that kept him aloft. And his face, narrow and angular in all the right places and a perfect match for the weapon hanging lazily in his hand.

A sword. An Imperial blade. Black as pitch and sharp as his smile.

I remembered how both of them had bled me.

If you didn't know him, you'd say he looked beautiful.

And if you did, you'd say he looked like a monster.

"Hey, girl."

That smile, that jagged white scar masquerading as a grin, grew broader and he spoke in a voice that had tricked so many people into thinking he was human. It had fingers, that voice, spindly little ones I could feel digging their nails into my skin, trying to pull me into that dark place with the cold stone and that purple light.

But I wasn't going anywhere.

"Hey, Kresh." I regarded him carefully. "You're looking well."

"And you're looking"—my scars ached as they felt his eyes on them—"ragged. Is life rather hard down there, darling?"

"Could be worse," I replied. "I could be from Stark's Mutter."

There was a brief moment of confusion on his face. Then, as he remembered the name, the bodies, the dead, his smile almost split his face open. And he laughed that laugh again.

You've heard his laugh before. Everyone has.

It's the giggle of the cruel child who kicks a dog and lies to his parents' faces. It's the chuckle of the man who knows a woman isn't allowed to say no to him without losing teeth. It's the snicker of the bandit who tells a prisoner that all he wants is his money.

And it made my scars burn.

"You saw it, then." His voice was electric with excitement. "Or did you only see the mess it left behind?" He shook his head. "Grotesque, that, but you'd appreciate it more had you seen what preceded it."

He raised his arms. The muscles of his body flexed as he spun in a lazy circle, his hair a golden halo in the sky.

"Ah, Sal... Sal, Sal, Sal..." My name dribbled from his lips like blood from undercooked meat. "If only you'd have been there, if only you'd have seen it. The sky was black as pitch but for a pinprick of light that grew vast as a maw. The very earth shook in anticipation of what we did. And her song..." His eyes shut, his body shuddered. "I'll never hear it so pure again."

"And the people, Kresh?"

His lazy flight came to a slow halt. He turned quizzical eyes upon me.

"The people?" he asked.

"The people you murdered," I replied. "The people Vraki sacrificed for his scheme."

"Murdered..." He tasted the word, not quite sure what it meant. "Oh, right. To the nuls, I assume it was rather frightening. So many lights and noises. A few of them tried to run for help, tried to ruin everything. But they didn't get far. They never do."

I remembered the horror scarred across the faces of the people at Stark's Mutter. And I couldn't help but wonder how many of them had looked into the sky and seen that same smile I was looking at right now.

That same smile that I had seen when I lay on that cold stone.

That same smile that had that same black laughter.

That same smile I wholly intended to put a bullet through.

"So, Kresh," I said.

I was going to kill him. I was going to end him. But first...

"That's what Vraki's got you doing?"

First, I was going to hurt him.

His smile vanished. It wasn't the words that I spoke that did it.

Men like him, they didn't listen to words; they only heard noises. They knew sounds that excited them: frightened squeals, desperate pleas, wracking sobs.

The stifled yawn I offered him was none of those.

"Kresh the fucking Tempest," I said. "First to join the Crown Conspiracy. The mage who blew the towers of Revolutionary forts down with a breath and flew faster than their engines could spit fire, reduced to chasing down townspeople." I clicked my tongue. "So, which was the bigger challenge to run down? The children or the old women?"

"They shouldn't have run." He forced the words through clenched teeth. "Vraki's plan needed them, needed *me*. They could have made it easy on themselves if they had just—"

"Oh, come now, are you really blaming them?" I sniffed. "Such a talented Skymage like yourself? I thought you said it was glorious."

"It was!" he protested, shriller than he had sounded a second ago. "Vraki's plan, his summoning, he *needed* me to help him. It couldn't have succeeded without me."

"Yeah?"

"He entrusted all his most delicate tasks to me."

"I bet he did," I replied. "And I bet all of them kept you far away from the summoning."

Men like Kresh are used to being feared. They're used to people quaking, watching them, waiting in fear for their next move. You can fight them, shoot them, cut them and that might bother them. Hell, it might even kill them.

But to really hurt them?

All you had to do was look bored.

And if it kept him talking long enough to tell me what I needed to know…

"What would you know of it?"

Well, I wasn't going to stop him.

Kresh spat the words. "You, wallowing in the dirt with the nuls, scrabbling for their metal, doing their vile dirty work. What would *you* know of ambition? Of what Vraki has planned?"

"Same shit I always did," I replied. "Same stupid rituals, same pointless murders. You can talk about ambition, but you're still a cheap opera villain."

"He *needed* me, my power, my grace. His plan couldn't succeed without me."

I scratched an itch on my ass. "And did he tell you that before or after he said you were pretty?"

"And what do you even care, Sal? Are you a defender of the nuls now? Protector of the weak and innocent?" The anger twisting his face subsided, gave way to that cruel scar of a smile. "Why didn't you save them, then? Perhaps you could have."

He drew the next words out like a knife.

"If you could fly."

My scars burned at those words. My feet felt like stone weights, shackled to the floor, keenly aware of just how heavy I felt. And so was he.

But every boy, at one point, is fascinated by cruelty: how an ant twitches when you pull off its legs, how many stones it takes to kill a bird with an injured wing.

It brings them joy. It makes them feel strong. It makes them want to feel it again. And again and again. I wasn't going to give him that.

But I knew plenty of boys who pretended to be men. I knew how to hurt them, too.

"Well, shit, Kresh," I said. "Seems like all I'd need to stop you would be to ask Vraki to tell you to sit down."

The smile dropped. His face screwed up.

There's three things a man loses when you hurt him.

"What the *fuck* did you say to me?"

The first is language. He drops whatever fancy words he knows, starts saying what's really on his mind.

"It's been a few years, Kresh, but that's not long enough for you not to bark when Vraki tells you to go." I shot him a smile of my own. I hoped it hurt. "I mean, why are you here? Just had to see me?"

"I'm here to *kill* you," Kresh snarled. "Vraki asked me to—"

"Vraki doesn't ask. We both know that. Vraki told you to. And I bet you were just so happy to go scampering out."

"He *knew* you would try to stop him."

The second is poise. He stops standing up straight, he stops looking like he's in control, and he starts looking upset.

"And he sent you out to stop me? Or just to get you to stop humping his leg?"

"I have been with him since the coup." He narrowed his eyes. "Since we tried to restore the Imperium to the glory the Nul Emperor stole from it. He understood my value. *You* never did."

"Yeah, he trusted you once," I replied. "And his plan to overthrow the Imperium got righteously fucked, from what I recall. Think there might be a correlation there?"

"This time, it will succeed. *This* time, the Scraths are talking to *him*. He's almost got enough power to open the door. Soon, he'll return the Imperium to its glory!"

And the third thing he loses is sense. And then you've got him.

There it was.

Men like to talk and boys don't think about what they say. Get someone like Kresh who's not quite either and you just might get something useful out of him. Vraki was going to finish what he started. I could use that.

Kresh, though? I was done with him.

"Vraki wants you dead," he snarled. "And Vraki wants me to—"

"He *expects* you to. He gives you a bone to bite, but it's still one he wants bitten." I winked. "If you're good, maybe he'll give you a belly rub when you get back."

"Shut your fucking mouth, Sal."

Thunder rumbled in the distance. The wind around him picked up.

"Kresh, I couldn't apologize even if I wanted to," I said. "I'm on a ship in the middle of nowhere shrouded by magic. Do you honestly think you'd have been smart enough to find me if Vraki didn't tell you where to go?"

"I SAID—"

You ever have a moment when an idea seemed funny one second and then really bad the next?

"SHUT! UP!"

I saw his eyes glow. I heard the Lady Merchant's song. And then I felt the wind.

First a mutter, then a howl, then a song unto itself. A melody of notes that made no sense: mist and froth from the river, leaves and grit from the shore, shattered planks and iron bars from the ships. They swirled around him in a maelstrom of refuse, a howling song with his shrieking rage as the chorus.

Skymages aren't great with control. Kresh, less than most. In another minute, he wouldn't have to do anything; he'd have enough jagged debris to tear me apart just standing here.

I didn't see much harm in adding to it.

I leveled the Cacophony at him, didn't bother to aim, and pulled the trigger. The slug burst out, got caught in the whirlwind, and exploded in a blaze of blue light. Hoarfrost blossomed, scattered, became jagged shards of ice swirling about in the wind.

You'd probably have called me a moron for adding knife-long blades of ice to his debris, but if you could have seen what I saw, you'd know better.

I could barely see him through the whirlwind of debris, a singular shriek at the center of that screaming mess, but I got a glimpse of him, just a hint of pale flesh turning an even paler shade of blue.

She might offer us all separate deals, but the Lady Merchant's magic comes from the same place. All schools affect each other. Which is why a Skymage's wind, especially a tempestuous one like the kind Kresh conjured, could aggravate a spell like Hoarfrost and turn it from a collection of shards to a freezing wind.

I saw his skin turn blue. I smiled, checked the Cacophony's chamber. Discordance's gleam greeted me. All I had to do was keep clear of him long enough for his wind to freeze himself. Then I could shatter him like a cheap wineglass. All I had to do was keep clear of his debris long enough and hope nothing else happened to—

"Shoot! Shoot him now!"

I should have fucking known.

You'd think a bunch of assassins wouldn't go shouting what they were about to do before they did it. Necla stood at the edge of the roof, pointing up at the Skymage. Ashmouths appeared behind him, raising bows high and firing into Kresh's maelstrom.

"*Reinforcements, is it?*" Kresh's scream was one with the wind's, both of their howls tearing through the sky. "*I thought you kept the code, Sal. Are we not civilized?*"

The winds slowed a little.

The assassins, encouraged, fired again.

I ran.

I knew what happened next.

"*OCUMANI OTH RETHAR!*"

After a moment's stillness, he exploded. The Lady Merchant's song reached a crescendo in the background. A great gust of wind swept out from him in a massive blast. Grit, grime, jagged ice blades, iron shrapnel, shredded planks, and who the fuck knew what else exploded across the ship's roof in a hailstorm of shit.

I heard their bodies explode, bones fracturing as timber drove through them, skin splitting as shrapnel ripped them apart. I saw their blood paint the sky, red droplets exploding out of them, hovering in the air for a moment before being sucked back into the whirlwind.

I never saw the timber coming.

Not until it struck me in the back.

Not until it knocked me off the roof and into the sky, where the wind howled in my ears.

And the river came rushing up to meet me.

TWENTY-SIX
THE *WEARY MOTHER*

No one dies without regrets.

No matter what opera tells you, a death without wishing things had gone differently just means you were never really hoping for anything good in the first place. And when you die, you wish you had done what you always hoped for.

If you're lucky, you have the standard ones: you wish you had more money, more sex, more fun. If you're unlucky, you have the bad ones: you wish you hadn't left her; you wish you hadn't trusted him; you wish you were sharing your last breath with more than an empty room and an empty bottle.

And if you're me...

Please.

You're flailing beneath a river.

Please. Not like this.

Struggling to hold on to your gun as you scramble for the surface, struggling to keep air in your lungs and thoughts out of your head.

If I have to die...

Talking in your head to anyone who might be listening.

Let me take them with me.

I broke the surface with a gasp and a spray of froth as the *Weary*

Mother made its way lazily down the river, heedless of the violence erupting on its roof.

It wasn't moving fast at least. I could still reach it. I could feel the Cacophony in my hand, burning angrily at only getting to fire one shot before I had been knocked off. I didn't want to disappoint him.

And I had just started swimming toward the boat when I heard the voice.

"*Hel...lo*," a soft, singing voice came from below.

I felt fingers wrap around my ankle.

"*Dis...tress?*"

I felt something pull.

"*Help.*"

I disappeared beneath the water. I looked down and, through the darkness of the river, I saw her looking up at me.

The Kelpbride, her arms a tangle of weeds and thorns, had her fingers wrapped around my leg. Her face, beautiful and feminine, hair floating as fronds, looked up at me with a gentle smile as she pulled me under.

"*Help*," she whispered.

"*Help, help, help...*" Her voice echoed.

I saw more of them, rising up from the gloom. Each one in the shape of a beautiful young girl, their hands reaching out for me as they swam toward me. One by one, their eyes turned toward me. One by one, their hands reached for me. One by one, their mouths split open to reveal broad, thorny teeth.

"*Help*," the one holding me whispered.

Honey, you asked for it.

I kicked her square in the face, smashing that pretty porcelain under the heel of my boot. She let out a sound more confused than pained as I pulled away and started swimming. I broke the surface again, saw the *Mother* floating away nearby, and started swimming, drawing in cold gasps through the mist. She was moving quick, but I could make it. I could get aboard and—

"Help."

Arms appeared around my throat, pulling me down.

"Help."

Arms coiled around my waist, hauling me deeper.

"Help."

Three of them wrapped around me, dragging me below once again. And just before I vanished beneath the surface, I heard one more voice.

"Look out, Sal!"

I saw the arc of a bright light as it flew through the mist, plummeted into the water behind me, and disappeared along with me as I was dragged under.

And then I heard the explosion.

The light erupted in the gloomy waves, a burst of flame that roared too bright to be smothered by the water. Fire swept out through the waves, spitting out steam as it reached out with sticky, tarry fingers to grasp at the Kelpbrides. Their screams rivaled its cackling flames as the fires lapped at their flesh, unwilling to go out even beneath the water. In a twisting, flaming shriek, they released me and tore off beneath the waves, desperately trying to put out the fires that wouldn't die.

I kicked my way back to the surface, broke it with a gasp of ragged air. I heard a splash from my right. A few scraps of wood bound together bobbed in the water. A long rope led from the bundle, across the water, to the deck of the *Weary Mother*. At the railing, I saw them, a flash of blue coat and dark hair in the gray mist. Together, they grunted, hauling me toward the ship.

And it wasn't the first time I wondered if Cavric and Liette would have been so eager to save me if they knew the pain I'd cause them.

I grabbed on to the wood, kicked my way forward as they pulled me to the edge of the ship and hauled me out of the water. Cavric held me down as Liette used the edge of a knife to scrape fiery tar from my shoulders and toss it back into the water.

The Righteous Fires of Indisputable Whatever. That fucking bomb she was going on about. If I hadn't been wearing my scarf, it would have eaten me, too, like it did the Kelpbrides.

If there isn't a word for people you're glad to see and also kind of want to punch in the genitals, *Cavric* or *Liette* is a good place to start.

I pulled sopping hair from my eyes. I looked up at him, his nose that wasn't quite straight and his eyes that didn't belong on a soldier. And she stared down at me, every ounce of ire and anger ebbed away and replaced by fear. Together, they helped me to my feet.

They hadn't left.

"The fuck have you two been?"

I suppose, considering all that, I might have sounded a tad ungrateful. Liette didn't seem particularly bothered, though, as she inspected me for damage.

"Interrogations were suddenly concluded by the presence of an unknown disturbance." Liette glanced skyward, toward the sound of ruckus. "Then unknown, at any rate. I anticipated that the Ashmouths would not begrudge me the acquisition of these." She patted a satchel at her hip, the bombs jutting out from inside. "Dare I ask what's been going on?"

The answer came as another Ashmouth plummeted down to crash into the water. And, like his terrified scream, it was a confusing answer that didn't tell her much.

"You want the long version or the short version?" I asked.

"I want whichever version that sees us getting off this ship alive," Cavric replied.

"Then let's just not talk."

I hurried to the end of the lower deck, found a ladder heading upward. Above, I could see torrents of wind flinging debris, shredded metal, and the occasional carcass overboard. Kresh's golden mane whipped about as he flew circles around the ship's roof, arrows flying in pursuit of him.

Ashmouths, it was said, were so canny and clever they could blend in with any culture, speak any language, disappear into any society. It was not said, however, that they were smart enough to figure out that shooting at a guy who moves quick as the wind was a stupid idea. They were used to clean shots from afar, knives in the dark, poison in wineglasses; this kind of fight was beyond them, beyond anyone, really.

Except me.

But even I couldn't handle it by myself.

It wouldn't occur to me until much later, after many drinks and many more regrets, that I hadn't even hesitated to jump on the ladder and let Cavric follow me. I had him at my back without even thinking that he might put a bullet in it. Maybe I was getting lazy. Maybe I was getting desperate.

"A nul with a fancy mask is still just a nul!"

Or maybe I really, *really* wanted to kill this guy.

I glanced up, saw Kresh's form flash across the sky, his blade a black blur as he flew past a smokestack. The metal groaned as he cut clean through, sending a ton of steel and gasping smoke clattering down over the edge, barreling toward me.

Something snatched my boot, jerked me down. I let out a cry that was lost as the smokestack crashed against the side of the hull where I had just been, rebounded off, and vanished into the water.

I glanced down. Cavric looked up, his hand around my boot, and grunted.

"Careful."

"No shit." I shot him a smile for a reason I didn't know, tapped my boot. "May I?"

He released my foot and I started climbing again. There'd be time for gratitude later. Assuming we were still alive, anyway.

I clambered onto the roof and found the carnage that greeted me. The metal of the roof had been shredded into twisted patches. One smokestack had been severed, another caved in. And amid these all, scattered like black flowers on thorny vines, lay the Ashmouths: impaled on twisted spikes of iron, smashed through the walls of smokestacks, or just bent and crushed and left upon the roof like withered petals.

And over the macabre garden, Kresh flew, cackling. His breath was rasping and heavy, but it didn't stop his laughter. His eyes were wild and wide with delight. He was happy amid the carnage and destruction, his breath coming short with his laughter.

He was using too much magic.

This was it. I could see him weakening, his flight getting sloppier. I saw my opportunity.

And he saw me.

"CACOPHONY!"

He twisted in the air, eyes settling on me, the white-haired woman standing on the roof. He took his blade up, a cry on his lips as he flew straight at me. I fumbled for my gun, tried to point up toward him, to squeeze off a shot as he came barreling toward me. But my hands were too unsteady, my grip too unsure.

And he was just too fast.

His sword punched through my chest. My eyes went wide. I stood, frozen on his blade for a long moment, before a trail of blood wept down my mouth. My stare stuck open, my body shuddered as I coughed, a torrent of red falling from my mouth.

Kresh's eyes were aflame with delight. His smile was so broad it nearly split his skull apart. He laughed, almost in disbelief of his own fortune, as he jerked his sword free.

And I slumped to the roof, unmoving and breathless.

TWENTY-SEVEN

THE *WEARY MOTHER*

My blood pooled beneath my corpse. My body lay motionless on the roof, one more carcass among many. Red poured out of my body through a great, twisted gash in the center of my chest as Kresh cackled and capered above my body.

It was a real bad way to die. Painful. Slow.

Made me glad it hadn't happened to me.

"You see now, Cacophony?" he shrieked, drawing back a foot to kick my corpse. "You see what happens when you challenge Vraki?"

He anticipated a hard rattle of bone against his foot. What he got, however, was nearly swept onto his ass as his boot passed clean through my corpse. He blinked, tried again, found only empty air where there should have been flesh. Squinting, he put his foot down in the puddle of blood.

And when he drew it back, it came clean.

He looked up toward the smokestacks, saw Necla crouched behind it, his eyes glowing faintly purple, the Lady's song a whisper on the air. He looked down toward my corpse as the illusion vanished in a puff of mist. Then he looked to the edge of the boat, where I stood.

His eyes locked on me with a look of . . . of . . .

You ever act like you're going to throw a ball for a dog but you don't actually throw it?

Like that, except more murderous.

"CHEAT!"

His voice came breathless. The winds picked up, carrying him off his feet, pulling him into the air, the eye of a storm unto himself.

"YOU...FUCKING..."

Skymages are sometimes called the Lady's favorites. They're given the power of flight, of swiftness, of the wind itself to carry them laughing over creation. And the price?

"I'LL...KILL..."

Their breath.

With every spell, it comes harder. With every flight, there's less of it. The most careful Skymages can make it through life with only a few breathing problems.

"YOU!"

But Kresh was not careful.

He threw his head back in a scream. His eyes erupted with purple light. Over the wail of the wind, the Lady's song filled the sky.

The wind rose around him in a sheer wall, pulling him higher into the sky. The debris, the twisted metal, droplets of blood flew into the air with him, surrounding him in a maelstrom of iron and agony.

He swept a hand out. A great gale followed his lead, crashing across the roof of the ship and striking Necla like a fist. His cry was lost in the wail of wind as he went skidding over the edge.

I'd have helped, but I had my own problems.

Kresh's eyes were on me. His smile was tremendous. Though I could barely hear him over the wind, there was something that came inside from that tornado, something that sounded very much like his laughter.

But I didn't go to that place this time. I didn't think of the purple light and my blood in the air and the voice whispering "I'm sorry" in the dark, cold place.

I just thought of the gun in my hand and the murmur of the wind and the words on my lips.

"Eres va atali."

He spun in the air. He leveled his blood-slick blade at me. The wind shrieked as it carried him and his maelstrom toward me, fast as the swiftest bird.

I didn't move out of the way. I raised the Cacophony. And I aimed.

And I fired.

It streaked out as a piffling little bolt of light that ascended into the sky on an arc of luminescent smoke that quickly guttered out. I held my breath for a second, turned my eyes away.

And then the world exploded into shadows and light.

A great golden glow was birthed in a screaming, soundless life. Yellow shafts of light punched through the mist, punched through the gloom, punched through the night itself. Even with my eyes shielded as they were, I had to squint to avoid being blinded. The few unlucky Ashmouths who hadn't quite died shrieked as the spell took their sight. But I could barely hear them.

Not over the sound of Kresh.

The light took him square in the face. He screamed as his eyes were taken and the wind screamed right along with him. He went spinning through the air, control over flight, over the wind, over everything lost.

He charged, blindly, and twisted. For a brief moment, he was every bit the wailing hurricane that had killed a hundred men before he had been stopped.

And then he hit the smokestack.

His body caromed off the metal and crumpled, motionless, onto the roof. The winds died from a wail to a moan, a lament for the man who had ridden them. Softly, they ebbed around his body, as if pleading with him to get up.

I'd have called it poetic.

If I could think about anything else but finishing it.

The sound of the wind vanished into a funerary silence. The maelstrom of debris came to a slow, awkward halt, the lethal timbers and twisted metal clattering to the ground in motionless chunks.

And in the quiet that followed, I heard a proud voice let out a soft moan.

I unsheathed Jeff. Behind me, I thought I heard Cavric saying something, telling me to be careful. Or maybe that was Liette. I didn't know.

I couldn't hear him over the lonely sound of my boots clattering across the metal roof, over the sound of the gun's hammer drawn back, over the rasping breath of Kresh as he tried to struggle to his feet.

When people looked to the sky to see Kresh the Tempest, they saw a black bolt from heaven, a laughing god who grew drunk off their fear. On the ground, though, he was just a skinny kid with too-long hair and too-tight pants. His body shook and shivered as he clambered to his feet. His voice was mirthless and soft as he wheezed:

"Not . . . not like this . . ." He held up a hand. "I can't . . . die . . . like this . . ."

No "please," no "spare me." Men like Kresh didn't beg. Men like Kresh didn't ask. They took. And when they couldn't take anymore, they did what everyone does when they're called to the black table.

"I can . . . tell you . . ."

They bargained.

"Vraki . . . Galta . . . Taltho . . ." Names he had once sworn oaths to came tumbling out of his breathless mouth, lay limp on the floor. "I can tell you . . . where . . . how . . ." He waved his hand. "Let me . . . find a better death. You . . . you win . . ."

"Sounds like a surrender to me," Cavric said, stepping forward. "Those names have a lot of blood on them. He could be a big help." He looked at me so intently I could feel his eyes through my scars. "Take him in, Sal."

Take him in.

Like he was just a criminal. Like he hadn't laughed that laugh. Like he hadn't been there on that dark night.

"Sal . . ." Kresh whispered. "Please. I can tell you . . . everything."

"You can save a lot of lives, Sal," Cavric said.

It was true. I could.

Those names were steeped in blood, it was true. They had killed many, would kill many more, it was true. I could save them.

"Sal."

The wind had quieted and her voice came just as gentle. I turned and saw her there, Liette staring at me, like she had when she pulled me out of the water. No anger in her eyes. Just fear. But that had been a fear that I'd been hurt, that I'd almost died, that she might have lost me.

In her eyes now, I saw the fear that she already had.

I looked back down at him, that gasping, wheezing boy as he reached up a hand, as his black blade lay limp and useless. My eyes lingered on its edge, remembering how it had felt, how it had looked with my blood glistening on it.

Each one of the names on my list had a blade just as black.

I could find out where all those names were, if I just let this one go. I could follow those names, cross them off, if I only agreed to let this one stand. I could tell Kresh that I agreed, that I was going to let him live.

But...

"Sal, what are you doing?"

I wasn't going to have it said Sal the Cacophony was a liar.

"*Wait!*" Cavric shouted.

I heard him.

As I raised my sword.

As I brought it down.

As I rammed it through Kresh's throat.

TWENTY-EIGHT

HIGHTOWER

At the end of the hour, Tretta suddenly became aware of a severe ache in her forehead.

Her brows, she realized, had been steadily furrowing themselves for the past hour. And as soon as she felt the pain of them unclenching, she became aware of the tension under which her entire body had been held: her knuckles sore from clutching her hand, her leg tired from nervously bouncing her knee, her jaw aching from having clenched it tighter and tighter with every word.

Yet, for all the pain that came from this, all of it was forgotten and replaced by a much more familiar ache as she looked across the table.

"What?" she demanded of the woman staring incredulously at her.

"Not a thing." Sal's smile was easy as she held up her hands in surrender. "This is just the first time you haven't interrupted me with an outburst or by slamming the table." A look of mild umbrage crossed her features. "Or was I simply not interesting enough to warrant it this time? Should I be offended?"

"And how," Tretta snarled through gritted teeth, "am I supposed to react?"

"Well, I just described gunning down a man who flew through the sky. A little shock might be nice. Maybe you could grasp the table and utter something dramatic like 'This world has gone mad' or—"

"Shut up."

"No, that's a little too common," Sal replied, scratching her chin. "Maybe like 'Who could have known even gods could fall' or—"

Tretta didn't bother interrupting this time. Not with words at least. She placed both hands on the table and pointedly shoved as she rose, thrusting the end of it into Sal's midriff and sending her doubling over, grunting.

Her stiff body complained, but Tretta rolled out those aches as she began to pace the length of the chamber.

"If you can be trusted..." She caught herself. "If your *words* can be trusted, you're telling me that not only did you abduct a soldier of the Revolution, steal our closely guarded engine, and deliver *both* to a gang of assassins we've been trying to clear out, but also that we have traitors within the Revolution who would sell our technology to ruthless murderers?"

"Oh, come *on*." Sal rubbed where the table had struck her belly, looking wounded. "I tell you a grand tale of adventure, replete with romance and a gunfight, and all you heard was the part about the engine?"

"And further, you say that the *Weary Mother* actually exists," Tretta growled. "The Ashmouths' ship was said to be a myth."

"Who do you think said it was a myth? The Ashmouths prefer to be thought of as such." Sal shrugged. "I suppose they'll be pissed I told you, but hey, you're going to have me executed, so what are they going to do?"

Tretta only barely heard the Vagrant. Her words did not so much gnaw at Tretta as bite her by the neck and shake her violently back and forth. And, as if to break that grip free, she shook her head.

"No," she announced loud enough that she might believe it. "You're lying."

"About which part?" Sal leaned back. "I admit, I might have embellished a few of my lines, but I can't say something clever *every* time."

"About the Righteous Fires."

Sal paused. "Why would I lie about that?"

"Oh, I have no doubt the Ashmouths are in possession of our technology. By some murder or theft, it's possible." Tretta rubbed an ache out of her knuckles. "But by treason... impossible."

"Oh yeah?" Sal grinned. "You think they infiltrated Weiless, the capital of the Revolution, snuck past its teeming armies and giant engines of destruction, penetrated its vault under guard by a hundred thousand men, and pilfered the bombs themselves?"

"As you said, they prefer to be thought of as mythical."

"If we all were what we thought we should be, you'd be telling me I smelled nice." Sal took a sip from her water cup. "Why would they go to all that trouble just to steal an engine? Why not steal state secrets to blackmail your General with? Why do *either* of those when they could just pay someone to give it to them?"

"Because the Revolution is incorruptible!" Tretta shouted without realizing it. "It burned itself free of the Imperium's decadence and the taint of its magic, a verdant tree rising from the sick swamp of its society. And with the Great General's guidance, we've made this world safe for the pure and uncorrupted who will never again be slaves to mages! Our nation is forged in truth, our vows in fire, our machines and our bonds in iron! Unbreakable! Immutable! Cavric knew this."

She looked imperiously down her nose at Sal.

"Which is why he tried to stop you."

Her prisoner simply stared back at Tretta. It was with some morbid pride that, even though it lasted but a moment, she noted indignation painting itself across Sal's features. And her next words came slow and venomous.

"That's a real nice speech," Sal said. "How many times did your commanding officer beat you before you could recite it by verse?"

"Your envy reeks." Tretta resisted giving her prisoner the satisfaction of slapping her. "A Vagrant from the Imperium, you saw firsthand the corruption that made the Revolution necessary and forsook even those frail loyalties to pursue greed and violence for no other reason than your own."

"That and the fashion." Sal pulled back the sleeves of her shirt, exposing the dancing storm clouds and birds tattooed across her arms. "But, at the very least, when someone's out to kill me, I see it coming."

Tretta narrowed her eyes. "The Revolution protects its—"

"Yeah, it's nice and all." Sal waved a hand, yawning. "You nuls put together a fine nation and it serves everyone well. But with or without magic, we're all still human. A man can't get his dick wet from patriotism. National pride won't keep any girl warm at night."

"But it *can't* happen," Tretta said, all too aware of the quaver in her voice. "Not to us. It happens to *other* nations, other people."

"Yeah..."

Sal's eyes grew empty as they drifted down to her hands. She ran a finger down to her tattoos.

"That's how it's supposed to go, isn't it?"

The woman's silence did not go unnoticed by Tretta—if only because this was the first time since their meeting that Tretta could recall feeling something other than infuriated annoyance. Rather, it was a stoked curiosity that drove her to pull her chair up and sit back down at the table.

"He knew you," Tretta said. "The Skymage."

"I said as much, didn't I?" Sal asked without looking up.

"That would imply a degree of honesty, which would imply that there is somewhere inside you that is not filled with shit where honesty could lie. What you did was *hint* that he knew you." Tretta leaned forward, hands clasped together in thought. "One assumes you knew the Crown Conspirators based on your having a list of their names, some reason to pursue them. But that could be anything: an insult, an unpaid debt, whatever petty reason Vagrants kill each other over."

"Take your pick. They were a fruit basket of assholes." Sal paused, considered. "An ass basket, if you will."

The Vagrant leaned back in her chair, yawning again as she kicked her feet onto the table and slid her shackled hands behind her head. Her face settled into bored disinterest, easy as she might slip on a cloak. But Tretta had interrogated many prisoners. She had seen enough such cloaks to recognize where their stitches frayed.

And she saw it in Sal's face. The woman's jaw was tight. Her posture was too awkward, too rigid to be naturally bored. And her eyes, though they played at disinterest beneath heavy lids, watched Tretta a little too intently, as though studying to see if she bought it.

Tretta pursed her lips.

"What is your favorite opera?" she asked.

To Tretta's satisfaction, surprise scarred itself across Sal's face. "Huh?"

"Before I learned better, mine was *A Young Man's Two Fancies*," Tretta continued. "An Imperial opera, technically illegal in Weiless, but all officer candidates are required to study it to understand the Imperium's treacherous mind. It's a military story, you know; the General believes it provides insight into how the enemy thinks."

"Then your General has shit ideas, as well as shit tastes. *Two Fancies* is a child's opera."

"I will agree with one of those sentences and beat you within an inch of your life if you repeat the other." Tretta leaned back and folded her arms over her chest. "Yes, *Two Fancies* is what a child thinks war is. I learned that once I read all the verses about the eyes. There were quite a few lines about the horror of men's eyes as they marched off to battle and met their fates. They just went on and on."

"They do love their poetry in Cathama."

"Exactly. Those lines were made to affirm the beliefs of decadent hedonists in the Imperium, to confirm that war was simply one vast drama, so they need never stay up at night wondering what hell they were sending their soldiers to." Tretta idly pulled her glove tighter. "My first battle, I don't remember what anyone's eyes looked like. We all wore the same glassy-eyed stare, like lenses in spectacles."

She clenched her hand into a fist. The stitches of her glove creaked tighter under the strain.

"What I remember," she said, "were the smiles."

There. Tretta wouldn't have noticed it if she hadn't been looking for it. While Sal's face settled back into boredom, her jaw clenched tightly on the right side. The side with her scar.

"I remember those. The men and women who waded through the mud and corpses. Their eyes were as empty as ours, but their mouths were wide and smiling, even as people screamed around them and choked in the melting snow. Like they were born to be there, like they were made for violence." She regarded Sal through cold eyes. "Like Kresh the Tempest."

Sal didn't bother to hide the contempt creeping onto her face. Or maybe she simply wasn't capable of it. When she turned her face away, Tretta leaned forward again.

"You knew that smile too well," she said. "You knew what he had done because you had seen it firsthand. And if you knew him, I wager you knew the other ones." She narrowed her eyes. "You were part of them, weren't you? You were involved in the Crown Conspiracy. You *know* more than you're telling and—"

"*The Veils of My Lady*," Sal suddenly said.

Tretta did not so much flinch as reel, as though struck. "What?"

"That's my favorite opera," Sal replied. "*The Veils of My Lady*. The original version, not that reimagining they did."

"Don't try to change the subject."

"I'm not. You asked. I answered. And your General seems to think you can tell a lot about a person by their favorite opera."

Tretta furrowed her brow. "*The Veils* is . . . irrelevant. Convoluted and pointless."

"Oh? Don't you remember the opening verse?" Sal closed her eyes, whispered, " 'Where war and spell cannot separate two, how can two stand so close and yet ne'er see each other's eyes?' "

"It's a ridiculous verse and a more ridiculous question."

"That's the beauty of it. It's the question of how two people can be so in love that they cannot be separated by war, yet lack something so profound that they cannot find their feelings for each other."

"It's just a silly love story."

In their brief time together, Tretta had become keenly aware of the panoply of her prisoner's smiles—the petty smirks, the haughty grins—but the smile spreading across her face, soft and restrained by the scars it stretched against, she hadn't seen yet.

"I like love stories."

She didn't like it.

"That's still of no use to—" Tretta grunted.

"And the reason it's my favorite," Sal interrupted, "is that the answer to the question is in the first act. You remember, right? They go through war, pain, suffering, all the while adhering to traditions that make them unable to confront their love for one another. You keep wondering why they can't just come out and say it, but if they *did*, then it wouldn't be *their* love; it would just be another courtship."

Sal ran a finger along the rim of her water cup. From beneath half-lidded eyes, she looked over at Tretta.

"You have to hear the end of the story."

Tretta felt the curiosity ebb from her face. Slowly, she lowered her hands and placed them on the table. It was, she decided, the only reliable way she could keep from leaping across and strangling her insufferable captive.

Even that, though, proved insufficient. She rose from her chair, its legs screeching across the floor, and stalked to the door. And though her coat was half an inch thick and could ward off the chill of Weiless winters, she could still feel Sal's crooked grin jammed into her back like a blade.

"Listen, if you're going out," Sal called after her, "could you bring back some wine? You don't want it said the Revolution executes people after just giving them water, do you?"

Tretta could live with them saying that.

Tretta could live with them saying, "The Revolution executes exceptionally annoying people by force-feeding them wine, bottle and all." But bureaucracy being what it was, she opted to leave so she was not further tempted to do that.

After all, the garrison had only one bottle of wine and she was saving that for something special.

She slammed the door shut behind her. The sound of its metal groan and crack of wood as it splintered the door frame echoed through the office. She would have *thought* this would be ample warning to everyone within earshot that she was not in the mood to entertain stupidity.

And yet, somehow, Clerk Inspire was standing in front of her again.

"*Oh!*" As if it were somehow possible for him to become tinier, he almost folded over himself with the force of his cringe. "Oh, my apologies, Governor-Militant. It's just that—"

"Not now," Tretta growled, pushing past him.

Or attempting to, at any rate. He showed surprising boldness by moving back in front of her.

"I don't mean to be a problem, madam, truly," he said, obviously either lying or stupid. "But it's just, the time for the execution, previously delayed, has come upon us."

Had it? Tretta glanced to the window. The sun had set completely. The hazy orange dots of streetlamps speckled the glass. By their light, she could see the crowds continue to gather, roiling angrily. Flashes of Revolutionary uniforms broke up crowds with swinging sticks.

They had warned her about this, the officers of Cadre Command. Executions must be ruthless, efficient, and above all, prompt. If the Revolution cannot do something so simple as kill a person on time, people will begin to wonder how it can run a government, how it can protect a people, how it can oppose the Imperium.

They'll begin to wonder what *they* can get away with . . .

If word got out about her laxity in enforcing the execution—no, *when* it got out (there were always snitches looking for an opportunity to curry favor with the Cadre's lust for law)—it would end poorly for her, possibly even with a new, lesser name.

And yet . . . she was close. To what, she didn't know, but there was something to this prisoner, buried beneath shit so thick it came out of her mouth. Sal *knew* something about the Crown Conspiracy. And if Tretta could know that, too, then she could also learn where to find the remaining conspirators. To capture and slay the traitors who had stymied the Imperium—and, of course, to protect the people they threatened—would give the Revolution a victory so great they'd write propaganda about it for years. They'd have to invent a new name just to give it to her.

Her eyes drifted from the window to the door and the young guard standing beside it.

Or, she thought, maybe she could just get drunk and fuck someone and worry about it tomorrow.

He had been transferred here just a month ago, couldn't be more than twenty-six—old enough to know what he was doing, not so old that he was just scars and spite like the rest of them...like *her*. They had exchanged idle pleasantries—as much flirting as the Revolution allowed, though a woman of her station would have certain needs and certain privileges to have those needs met, if he agreed to it.

It was tempting. More than it had ever been during the wars and stresses of command, it was tempting to forget everything. The blood-hungry crowd outside, the betrayals lurking in her Revolution, the insufferable woman who had brought them to light. Just get drunk, she told herself, fuck that guard, then shoot Sal in the head and call it a day. Simple. Efficient.

Who could blame her?

Cavric's mother, a little voice spoke up. *Cavric's father. Your mother. Your father. The Revolution. Everyone who believed in you enough to put you in the position where you could find a lost soldier. They'd blame you. You'd blame yourself.*

And Cavric would still be missing.

She had hoped that voice in the back of her head had died somewhere out in the battlefields. It tended to pop up in the most aggravating places. She rolled her eyes, sighed, made her decision.

"Soldier," she called out.

The guard perked to attentiveness, like he had been waiting for her to acknowledge him—she knew what else he had been waiting for. He rushed over, stopped a touch closer than was protocol, fired off a crisp salute.

"Madam?" he asked.

"The execution has been delayed until tomorrow morning," she said. "Inform the guards to disperse the crowds. Lethal force is authorized if they are noncompliant."

"*What?*" Clerk Inspire squealed. "Governor-Militant, you can't defy protocol like this! The Vagrant, she is dangerous. She is savage. Her weapon is—"

"And see Clerk Inspire to his desk while you're at it."

"Yes, madam." The guard seized the clerk by his shoulders, escorting him bodily toward his desk at the back of the room.

"After that, please inform the cook that we'll need food." Tretta spat the command, loathing that she had to do that. "If the prisoner isn't going to be killed, she'll have to be fed another day." She returned the guard's nod as he set Clerk Inspire forcibly into his seat, then paused. "And, soldier?"

"Madam?" he asked.

"In my chambers, there is a bottle of wine." The pause dragged out, a blade in a cold body. "Retrieve it for me. And two glasses."

TWENTY-NINE

THE SCAR

To the Cacophony,

Dearest sweetling,

Pain in our asses,

We'd like to extend our gratitude on behalf of salvaging our ship. Simultaneously, we'd like to extend one or several digits in explicit gesture, as it was because of you that the Weary Mother *was put in danger in the first place.*

That ship works hard, you dumb bitch.

Still, the damage was considered mostly superficial, as you, nobly, went out to do battle with the offending Skymage. Sadly, you did not die in the process, but we do hope you sustained enough wounds to be painful.

Ah, well. Maybe next time.

Fortunately, it appears he still held his Imperial blade—goodness knows where, wearing as little as that boy does—and the bounty

*of Kresh the Tempest will pay handsomely. We've already begun the
bidding at sixteen pounds of metal.*

Turns out you're good for something other than being shit.

*Given your selfless act, the bounty, the Dust we'll harvest from his
carcass and the fact that you made us a shit-ton of money, the Ashmouths, in their immense virtue, have opted not to have you murdered, maimed, or tortured.*

Congratulations.

*In addition, we see fit to reward you with the information you were
seeking. It is true, we bartered with Vraki the Gate for a focal obelisk we liberated from Haven's vaults. And it is true that we know
what he intends to use it for. By now, you probably do, too. Or
do you?*

*Regardless, as you no doubt know, he requires an immense amount
of magic to do so. Such a device can merely call to a Scrath, put out
the welcome mat, so to speak. To let it in, a host is required in the
form of a sacrifice. Or several.*

But you knew that already, didn't you, dear?

*But to do what Vraki is intending, the sacrifice will need to be much
bigger and the stage will need to be much more . . . special. A Scrath
can be beckoned with magic. But what Vraki wants to do with it
will require an entire nation.*

*Now, we can't tell you exactly where he's gone, of course. If it got out
that the Ashmouths betrayed clients, who would deal with us again?
Not to mention, ridding us of the Tempest only goes so far. We have
standards.*

Also, we hate you.

You understand.

But we can point you in the right direction. From Stark's Mutter, Vraki, seeking a great amount of latent magic to tap into, went north. You remember what happened in the north, don't you, dear?

Well, we've said too much. Destroy this letter after you read it, naturally, or we'll find you.

Best wishes,
Yoc

Die well,
Pui

Go fuck yourself,
Gan

The Husks.

The thought came so suddenly I didn't even know if it was my own. But it hung there, two words that I couldn't think of without feeling a pain in my chest and an ache in my scar. They rang in my head, a cracked bell in a cold tower, and each time they did, my breath grew shorter.

The Husks.

The three had been enigmatic—just enough to be professional—but they didn't have to be anything else. They knew that their letter, along with what Kresh had said, would leave me only one conclusion.

Vraki had his plan. He had his Scrath. He had his vessels. He simply needed magic to make it all work. An immense amount of it, so much that it would suffuse the air and water and soil. And he couldn't get it here.

He'd gone back to the Husks.

And now I would, too.

I looked over the Yental. Necla's shroud of mist was already far down the river, the *Weary Mother*, and all its massive glory, was vanishing farther into the fog. The storm that had heralded Kresh's arrival had turned to a distant sigh of thunder and a muttering drizzle.

The damp wasn't enough to threaten the fire I had built at least. And I wasted no time in crumpling up the note and tossing it into the flames—professional courtesy for the Three.

Then I reached into my pocket, pulled out a square of weathered parchment, and looked at the long list of names in faded ink. I leaned over it to protect it from the rain as I produced a pen and drew a bold black line through three words.

~~Kresh the Tempest.~~

I stared at it, that little line, ink wet like a wound, alongside two other older, faded lines. They reminded me of scars, like my own, black lines that told a black tale. Thirty other names stared back at me, contemplatively, as if asking me if I was still thinking about them.

I closed my eyes. I let out a deep sigh. I folded the paper back up and slid it into my coat pocket. My hand brushed against the grip of the Cacophony, his heat having died down to a warmth that was pleasant against the chill of the rain. The fight had left him satisfied.

At least one of us was.

I had no regrets. Kresh had to die for a lot of reasons. And it wasn't that I felt hollow, either—anyone who tells you that revenge is empty is someone who doesn't try hard enough at it.

It's just that I felt . . . powerless.

It hadn't been more than a few hours ago, but I could barely remember his face. I couldn't recall the fear in his eyes, the sputter of his lips as he pleaded with me. Even after I had put a blade through his throat, I could still see his grin. I could still hear his laughter. I could still remember the dark place it took me to.

It was like he wasn't even dead. Or not dead enough.

I wondered if he ever would be. If any of them would be.

If Jindu would be.

Now *that* question made me feel empty. But only because I knew the answer.

The raindrops grew fatter above my head. The fire began to sputter at my feet. I left it to die and made my way back up the riverbank, where the Iron Boar stood cold and quiet as a tomb. Without its engines belching flame, it reminded me of some shell of a long-dead beetle, an ugly metal blight on the plains.

Funny thing about weapons, when you've got no one at hand to kill, you kind of start noticing how ugly they are.

I rolled up to the door, rapped on it twice. No answer. The rain began to seep past my scarf and down my shirt. I muttered a curse under my breath and pounded on the door again. It opened, but only after I was almost soaked through.

"Fuck's sake," I growled, "were you doing your hair?"

An apology would have been nice. Sarcasm would have been acceptable. A curse right back would have been expected.

What I got from Cavric, though, was nothing. He simply stood there, staring down at me, empty-eyed. Then he quietly slunk away, back to the pilot's chair.

I grumbled, but made no further grievance as I entered and slid the door shut behind me. I peeled off my scarf, draped it across the bench to dry. I fingered the hem of my shirt, tempted to add it to the pile to dry out. It wasn't modesty that kept it on my back—rather, it was the ache on my arms and back. The damp had never been good for my scars. Neither had heat. Neither had other peoples' prying eyes.

Eyes like Liette. Unlike Cavric, who turned his back to me, I couldn't escape her stare. She watched every move I made, as though I were suddenly some new person, some creature, who had crawled out of the rain. Maybe she thought I was.

And part of me—a spiteful, bitter part that hadn't left me since that dark night—wanted to ask her if this new thing was still broken, still in need of fixing.

"Shit's coming down out there," I said instead. "Strong as this engine is, I don't think it can chew through mud. We'll wait until morning to get going. Congeniality should be finished hunting by then and wander back, too."

Cavric said nothing that would make me remind him who had the bigger gun here, so I assumed he was all right with the plan. I glanced up, saw him staring out the visor, watching the rain fall as it drummed out a metal rhythm on the Boar's hull.

"Now, I know I said I'd turn you loose after I spoke with the Ashmouths," I said, "but it turns out I'll need your services for one more task. I need to get north in a hurry, toward..."

The words were choked out of my mouth as the images came flooding into my mind. Visions of flame and fire, of bodies blackening and skies without stars and winds that spoke on hateful, screaming voices. Visions that I thought I'd only ever see in dreams. And, bad as they were, I hoped I'd never go back to see them in person.

"Toward the Husks," I finally said, and the words tasted foul in my mouth.

He didn't look back at me. Funny, I had certainly expected some pushback at *that*. But he simply sat there and stared out the window. I got a little bolder.

"I know it's dangerous. But don't worry, I won't ask you to go in any deeper than I need you to." I paused, grinned. "I mean, if *you* want to go deeper, I won't stop you. But I might need a little wine first and—"

"You killed him."

He spoke so softly I could hardly hear him over the rainfall. Funny, though, it was that softness that caught my ear. A voice like that belonged on someone innocent. You didn't find those in the Scar.

"Huh?"

"You killed him," he repeated. Slowly, he turned around in his seat, looked at me with those empty eyes. "He begged for his life... and you killed him."

Ah. So that's what had him upset.

Now, I already told you I thought Cavric was handsome. Better than handsome, he looked gentle. Even empty as his eyes were now, they still looked soft, kinder than anything I'd seen in this place. I wasn't keen on taking that away from him.

But there was some shit I just wasn't prepared to eat, no matter how fragrant.

"Yes." My voice came out clipped, short. "I did."

"Like an animal," Cavric said. "You gutted him."

I thought of something clever to say. I couldn't. What came out of my mouth, I didn't even think about.

"He *was* an animal."

"He was a man."

"You've seen me kill plenty of men."

"Not ones who were on their knees," Liette whispered from behind me.

"He only looked like a man," I growled. "The most vicious animals always do." I snorted. "What, should I have left him alive?"

"Yes!" Cavric flinched. "No... I mean, I don't know. He was a killer and a Vagrant, I know that. But he was surrendering; he was offering information. You shouldn't have just... just..."

"Yes," I said. "I should have. I didn't kill a man. I killed Kresh the Tempest."

"He was still—"

"He was Kresh the *fucking* Tempest," I snarled. "And before that, he was Kreshtharan ki Nazjuna, the most unhinged Skymage in a school of magic famous for being unhinged. He spun winds so fierce they flayed Revolutionaries alive and scattered their blood for twenty miles. He ran down Havener pilgrims, chasing them until piss ran down their legs and spit went dry in their mouths before he tore the breath from their lungs. *All* this, he did for the Imperium...

"And once he went Vagrant," I said, "he stopped being merciful.

After all he did, you expect me to believe that he deserved better than I gave him just because he was on his knees and blubbering a few words you liked? Do you believe me?" I whirled on Liette. "Do *you*?"

I kept my eyes flitting between them, even as their eyes flinched away. I slammed my fist against the Boar's walls, shook the metal.

"Do you believe me?"

"I . . . I do."

It wasn't when she screamed or cursed or spat that Liette's voice stung me. It's when it was halting, hesitant—like it was when she spoke then—that I worried. She says it so often that you start not to believe it, but she really is brilliant. Everything she does is deliberate and meticulous and so painstakingly chosen that it hurts.

So when she couldn't find words, I knew something was wrong.

"I believe you had to kill him," she whispered, "I just . . . I don't . . ."

She met my gaze for a long, terrible moment. A moment in which I remembered every time I felt her fingers on my scar and every time she pressed her lips to my neck. A moment in which I saw all of those fading away and leaving me only with the long, slow look on her face she wore now.

"I don't know if he had to die."

I swallowed that look. Swallowed all the anger and pain that came with it. I stood tall, imperious, forced everything I was feeling out of my eyes and into my heart.

"He did," I replied. "Vagrants are dangerous. All of us. And out of all of us, none are more dangerous than me."

"I know that," Cavric grumbled.

"You don't," I snapped, whirling on him. "If you did, you'd know what a dumb motherfucker you were being by pretending I didn't know what I was doing."

"I know you did."

"Then why the fuck are you—"

"Because shit like this isn't supposed to happen!"

His shout shot him to his feet. His eyes weren't empty anymore.

They looked at me, full of fire and anger and the kind of hate I've seen in every face I never wanted to see it in. His hands were curled into fists, trembling at his sides. He leaned forward, like he wanted to use them. I wasn't ashamed to say I took a step back; at that moment, he started looking like a man who knew how to kill.

"The Revolution was born in the fires of justice!" he shouted at me. "When we left the Imperium, they laughed. They called us nuls, upstarts, *animals*! We proved them wrong. We had codes; we had laws; we had a *better way*." His hands tightened into angry fists. "We don't kill the Imperials because they deserve to die; we kill them to protect that way. We don't rape, we don't torture, and we sure as shit don't put swords through people begging for their lives!"

You don't see fire in someone's eyes like I saw in Cavric's that moment. Not anymore, anyway. Fire like that is dangerous; it inspires people, tricks them into throwing their lives away for a lot of dumb, pretty words.

I didn't feel bad for pouring water over that.

"I'm not a Revolutionary," I said. "But justice is what I brought."

"Stabbing a man isn't justice," Cavric snarled.

"The fuck it isn't," I snapped back. "If you believe any of the shit you just spewed about your Revolution, then you don't know what justice is. The whole fucking Scar doesn't. They'll turn a murderer loose if he's got money, send a rapist on his way if he comes from the right family, break a poor man's hands if they want him to sign a confession and all the while the rich men in the nice coats and shiny badges trade whiskey and cigars and congratulate themselves on the laws they wrote so they'll never have to face them."

It wasn't until I saw the fear creep back into his face that I felt the anger that had flooded mine. And right there, hot as the blood behind my eyes, the Cacophony was burning at my hip.

"Because justice isn't for the victim, is it? It's not for the girl crying every night or the boy burying his father. It's for the killer, it's for the judge, it's for the shits like you who want to feel like you're above it all, like forgiving a killer makes up for not being able to protect his victims." I spat on the floor. "A man kills and you fawn over him and wonder what went wrong. A man dies and you shrug and step over the corpse."

"That's not true," Cavric said. Or rather, Cavric tried to say. His wasn't the voice of a sure man; he didn't mean it wasn't true—he meant it *shouldn't* be true.

"It is," I growled. "Justice isn't warm and comforting like you think it is. It's cold and it's quick. And if you knew Kresh—not the little kid crying on the ground, but Kresh the fucking Tempest—if you knew what he'd done, you wouldn't be pissing me off like this."

And then he looked at me. No fire. No emptiness. No softness. He looked at me with eyes that I wasn't used to being looked at with. And when he spoke, his voice just hurt to hear.

"What did he do to you?"

And that's when I realized why I didn't like him looking at me. Why I didn't like Liette looking at me. Why I didn't want them asking, thinking, *knowing* why I walked around like there was a knife in my chest.

And I gave them both the same answer: a cold silence I didn't know I had in me until I was asked a question like that. It was better than the real answer. We have all these operas that talk about the truth in great, elegant terms: wings that liberate us from lies, light that we shine into darkness. But that's just opera. That's not the truth. Truth is clumsy, angry, sputtered through tears and apologies and accusations.

The real answer was that I didn't want to answer.

The real answer was that I didn't want to remember that dark place, that light, that voice whispering "I'm sorry."

The real answer was that I wanted to remember Kresh's smile not as a white knife looming over me but as an empty mouth in a dead man's head on the roof of the *Weary Mother*.

The real answer was that I didn't want to say the words that would remind me of just how heavy these scars on me weighed and how much they hurt when the nights got cold.

"Don't worry about me," I said, soft like I meant it. "Don't worry about what he's done, what any of them did. Worry about what they're *going* to do. Worry about what you saw back in Stark's Mutter, worry that you'll see that happen to a hundred more, a thousand more, women, children, and men, if I don't stop them."

Now that...that sounded good. That sounded not clumsy at all. Pure elegance. Lies usually do. The truth is a nasty thing planted in fertile soil and it grows uncontrollably.

But lies? Lies are crafted. Lies are mined from a dark place, hammered into shape and sharpened to a fine point. Lies are fantastic. People love lies.

That's why we love opera so much.

That's the thing about lies. You can forge them hard as you can, polish them to a high shine, make them so sharp they could cut rock, but it's still your hand that throws them. And every time you do, you risk missing.

And me? I'm a good shot.

But not that good.

THIRTY

THE HUSKS

B efore it was the Imperium, it was the Empire.
Before they were the Revolution, they were a bunch of servant nuls.

And before it was the Husks, the blasted hellscape of bombed-out cities, blackened plains, and incinerated townships was one of the most beautiful places in the Scar.

You know the history, of course. A little over a generation ago, the Mad Emperor became convinced there lay a land beyond the ocean, and just before he was deposed by his daughter, he was proven right when the Empire discovered the Scar and it was decided that the Imperium was a loftier title.

He sent his nul servitors over to colonize the land. The nuls discovered severium and the Relics. Severium made their weapons and machines. And when the Imperium landed on the shores of the Scar with its mages, it wasn't a legion of vassals that awaited them. It was the Revolution.

You've heard of all the stories that followed. The battles, the wars, the blood shed over the land.

But none of them ever talk about how pretty it was.

Back then, they called it *Edania Alcari*—or *A Blue Promise* in old Imperial.

Among the badlands and shadowy forests of the Scar, it was a pristine heaven. Rolling grasslands across which gigantic beasts and flocks of long-legged birds roamed. Great, rushing rivers that carved blue scars out through the stony mountains. Deep caves that provided endless ore and verdant forests that offered feasts of timber and game.

The few nuls and Imperials who got to work on that land and raise their cities were blessed, they said.

Of course, you know what happened next.

The grasslands got chewed up by Revolutionary tanks and turned to ash by Imperial magic. The beasts were converted to war and the birds were turned to food. Imperial magic froze the rivers to try to starve the Revolutionaries out. The caves and mines were bombed to rubble by Revolutionaries trying to deny Imperials their resources. The forests were scorched to black skeletons, the plains were turned to dust, and the cities they built on them—those wondrous marvels of technology and magic...

Well, they became the Husks.

The skeletons of the old world. The corpse of the peace that had existed for those few fleeting moments when the nuls knew their place and the Imperials thought no one could challenge them. The great monument to the war that gave the Scar its name.

Some look upon the Husks and are struck with awe, a forlorn wonder for what the world had been in that brief moment it knew harmony. Some look upon the Husks and feel an immense sorrow, burdened by an intense despair that mankind's monuments could be so easily and thoroughly annihilated.

And me?

I was in conversation with the metal in my hands.

Congeniality had returned early the next morning by the time the rain had cleared and the mud was firm enough to drive over. We had spent most of the day plowing ahead, following the Yental until it forked off and then heading farther north into the Husks. Which, as it turned out, was plenty of time to feel intimidation, awe, sorrow, and finally whatever this feeling was that currently coursed through my veins.

The hours spent rattling around in the Boar had turned every emotion to some nebulous, trembling churn of dread and sorrow that flowed through me. With every trembling breath, they pumped from my throat, into my heart, and down into my hands. And there he fed upon them. The Cacophony's brass seemed to rattle with a life all its own, taking every drop of that dread and drinking it through a grin that steadily grew broader.

That was insane, of course. He was just a gun.

Well, not *just* a gun, but certainly not capable of life.

But that was outside the Husks. Inside its whirling storms, "life" did not adhere to its standard definitions.

I forced myself to look away from the gun—if only to try to ignore the feeling that he was looking back at me—but the Boar offered little reprieve. Congeniality was curled up, weary from her wandering; Cavric was piloting; and Liette…

Liette was still silent. Still soft. Still not looking at me.

Not when I looked at her anyway. I could feel her eyes lingering on me when I looked away. I could feel her mouth struggling for words, for questions, for the right thing she could say to fix me.

And whenever I did, I would just look down at my hands, at my tattoos, at my scars. And I'd wonder which made me angrier—that she thought I needed to be fixed or that, even if I agreed, I had no fucking idea how to do that.

And every time I did, I felt the gun burn a little brighter, a pulse of warmth coursing through him, once, twice, again. Like the beating of a heart.

"How far?" I growled to the back of Cavric's head, to keep the sound out of my ears.

"The Husks cover three hundred miles. We've burned through most of our fuel reserves and have maybe enough to take us another fifty and still be able to return to friendly territory." He glanced over his shoulder. "So, if you have a destination in mind more specific than 'north,' now's the time."

The Ashmouths hadn't told me exactly where in the Husks that Vraki had gone. But then, they hadn't needed to. I knew Vraki well enough to know that he was a lot of things: a murderous lunatic and brilliant, as murderous lunatics so often were. But he wasn't creative.

Summoning was a rare enough art that its practitioners were a handful, and even those couldn't summon Scraths. Vraki's plot required immense amounts of magic, such as the kind that could only be found in a land so scarred by its use that it was positively suffused with it. But toying with that much power was dangerous enough that he'd want to minimize the risks, and to do that, he'd go to a place he felt familiar.

Among the Husks, with their corpses and charred ruins, there were plenty of places that Vraki would feel right at home. But now that I knew he needed more power than he had, there was only one he would head to.

Because there was only one he was responsible for.

I didn't tell Cavric that. Mostly because I wasn't planning on Cavric being around for it. Once we got close enough, I was intending on clonking him on the head, disappearing with Congeniality, and letting him wake up and make his way back to wherever he needed to.

He was a nice guy. But a nice guy in an organization that still had significant reason to try to kill me. Plus he had just been a *real* good sport about the whole "being kidnapped" thing. He had taken me far enough and I'd be happy to see him leave.

"At the very least," he muttered, "tell me where to pull over so I can air this thing out."

Whether he left without his eyes being pecked out, though, wasn't up to me.

Congeniality, curled up in the corner, craned her neck and loosed an indignant squawk. She probably knew he was talking about her—she had always been clever like that, the little dickens. She had also been eating something particularly foul, too, so maybe Cavric had a point.

Liette, too, looked up. And again, opened her mouth, and again I felt my scars ache. So I started to move.

I clambered to my feet and hauled the Boar's door open. A blast of dust and grit met me as I leaned out, one hand on the door frame, the other pulling my scarf up as a blast of hot wind and grit struck my face.

Nothing but ash stretched out as far as I could see—plains of scorched earth mingled with stone and trees that had been blasted to powder ages ago. In the distance, great whirlwinds of dust and char choked the sky and blotted out any sign of day. Ash and dust, ash and...

"Wait," I whispered.

There. Silhouetted against the grit painting the sky, I could see the remnants of buildings, hollowed-out skeletons of towers and barracks, gates torn apart and walls split open like fruit smashed on pavement. Even destroyed, though, they stood firm, if not tall, opting to be sundered rather than simply decay into nothingness. The dust storm thick enough to choke out the sky couldn't obscure its foreboding ruin, nor diminish the marvel of its workmanship. And through the whirling grit, I could see a lonely spire rising, crowned with the tattered remnants of a banner that the winds could not yet tear apart.

I knew that tower. I knew this fort.

And, as I felt the Cacophony burn in my hands, I knew I wasn't the only one.

"There!" I cried out to be heard over the moan of wind. "Another mile ahead! Pull over there!"

"What?" Cavric shouted back. "Are you sure?"

I was. Scions help me, but I was dead sure.

The Boar's engines let out a roar, rumbling forward. The silhouette grew bolder as we drew closer. I could see the shattered windows and the smashed smokestacks of forges. I could see towers struggling to stay upright and gates still clinging to their rotted hinges. It stood at the foot of a mountain rising like the crown upon the ruined brow of an old and beaten king.

Once, this fort had been as proud as that mountain. Once, it had held a thousand soldiers and five thousand happy people: craftsmen and women, wives and husbands, families. Once, it had been the greatest ring on the hand of the Revolution.

Until the day Vraki the Gate walked through its doors.

Dust crunched beneath wheels. Engines went from a roar to a growl. The Iron Boar fell silent. In its wake, the wind spoke. Not like how it spoke for Kresh; it didn't howl or scream or anything like that. It muttered, it moaned, it made the sounds of mothers who buried their children and fathers who woke up nightly and saw empty spaces beside them in bed.

One of the Husk's many quirks. And one of the few that wouldn't kill you.

I hopped out of the Boar. Something brittle snapped beneath my boot. I didn't look down; I knew I'd see something looking back at me.

I heard a louder snap as Congeniality came out behind me. She landed with a troubled squawk and a wary look around, but nothing more. Beasts avoid the Husks for the same reason people should. Still, for a girl who was once neck-deep in a week-old dead man's guts, it seemed a little unreasonable to me that she'd be this skittish. At least she put on a braver face than...

"*General's graces!*" Cavric poked his head out of the Boar, clinging to the edge of its door. "That's not natural, is it?" He winced as the wind kicked up and let out a moan. "Why's it making that *sound*?"

I tried to ignore it. "I don't hear anything." I was about to say that I could certainly *smell* him shitting himself, but I figured I'd already threatened to shoot him a bunch of times—why be mean? "Listen, if you don't want to go..."

Cavric cut me off with a shake of his head. He looked warily at the earth before leaping down. His boots sank to the ankle in ash and grit. He chased the cringe from his face with a weary smile.

"Like you said," he told me, "it's not about me. It's about what they're going to do."

Fuck me, he believed it. Every fucking word I gave him. Even after all he'd seen, I hadn't killed that part of him that still believed people were fundamentally good. Most people who come to the Scar silence that little voice quick. A few unlucky ones live long enough to see it die. And some...

"The land is wounded."

Some never had it to begin with.

"Constant exposure to magic has altered the landscape." Liette held up an arm to ward off the blowing dust—though it did nothing to ward off the voices. "Long-term exposure to the Husks tends to result in madness. We shouldn't linger." I could feel her eyes on the back of my head. "We shouldn't be here at all."

My scars ached. The Cacophony burned. The wind howled. I chose to focus on only one of those, pulling my scarf up around my face.

I took Congeniality by her reins, gave her a tug. She moved easy enough. With a gesture of my chin, I led my party into the dust, toward that looming shadow.

"Wait a minute," Cavric said as he hurried to catch up. "I should have a weapon."

"Nah," I replied.

"I wouldn't stab you in the back. You have my word."

"Oh, I don't doubt it."

"Then why not?"

"Because she only trusts weapons in her own hands," Liette muttered.

"*Or*," I snapped over my shoulder, "it's because if you run into any creature out here, the only thing a weapon will be good for is turning it on yourself before it has a chance to eat you." I sniffed.

"And if it ate you, it'd eat the weapon, too, and then how would I kill *my*self?"

That answer didn't satisfy anyone. But no one was talking anymore. So hey.

The sound of crunching beneath our feet was drowned out by the wind. I could hear Cavric jump every time it spoke, every time it whispered in his ear. I could see Liette pull her arms around her, put her head low, trying to ignore them. I kept my calm, though. But only because I was listening to something different.

Ask a nul what the difference was between himself and a mage and he'll tell you it's power: mages lord their magic over the nuls, look down on them because they can't move shit with their mind or whatever. Ask a mage, though, and he'll say it's that nuls have no sense of music.

They can't hear the Lady Merchant.

And neither could Cavric. He only heard the wind carrying all the agonies and pains it had seen. Liette, too, would only have heard a hysteria of empty noises—wrighting was an art, but not a true art.

But me? I heard music. Weaving between the moans and whispers, I could hear her song. Sometimes far away, like an echo without a source. Sometimes close, like she was walking right beside me. Her voice wandered the wastes of the Husks, carried on the wind in search of a Barter she had forgotten to collect. It was horrifying. It made a cold snake coil around my spine. And I hoped it would never end.

"SHIT!"

Cavric's voice? I could have done without.

I whirled at the sound of his cry, Cacophony leaping to my hand and pointing at where his terrified eyes stared. And immediately, I saw it.

You could say it looked human. It walked on two legs, had two arms, a torso, and a head all loosely clinging together. But it didn't have a body—not the kind you're thinking of. Rather, it was formed from the dust and the grit and the wind, all of it whipped into coils that vaguely resembled limbs. It staggered across the wastes with an awkward gait, its body trembling as it tried to stay together. It reminded me unpleasantly of a toddler learning how to walk.

And like a toddler, it had one hell of a scream.

The cloud of dust that had been a vague face swirled, formed a vague mouth out of rocks and grime. That mouth craned open and it loosed a great, keening wail that carried farther and louder than any wind could hope to.

"What the fuck?" I became aware of Cavric huddled defensively behind Congeniality. "What the fuck *is* that?"

"Echo," I replied, holstering the Cacophony.

"What?"

"An Echo." Liette stepped precariously close to the thing, as though she were simply studying a peculiar insect and not, say, a walking collection of screams. "Also known as windwraiths. They're common to this area of the Husks. Harmless."

"Harmless?" Cavric looked at her, almost offended. "*Harmless?* You look on some kind of... of *ghost* and you think it's harmless? *Harmless?*"

"An Echo isn't a ghost," Liette scoffed. "Don't be ridiculous. It's simply the remains of a coagulated, formless memory born from intense pain or fear and given shape and noise by latent magical essence lingering in the environment. Simple."

Cavric blinked. "Oh. But..."

"*SIMPLE,*" she snapped.

The Echo turned toward us, began staggering forward. I didn't look at it, didn't acknowledge it, and most importantly, didn't think about it. Cavric, on the other hand, was staring at it, wide-eyed and slack-jawed.

And soon enough, the Echo was staring back at him.

The dust that made up its face began to take shape, the wind whipping a nose, a mouth, a pair of eyes and ears out of the shapeless grime. The body followed, turning from coils of dust into a shapely woman's figure swaddled by a heavy military coat. Her hair was close-shorn, her body tall and rigid, her features fair. She would have been fairly attractive, had her eyes not been alive with anguish and her mouth not gaping open in a scream.

"*HOLY SHIT!*" Cavric's shout came out of him so loud it knocked him on his ass. He scrambled away on hands and feet. "*HOLY SHIT, HOLY SHIT, HOLY SHIT!*"

"Recognize someone?" I asked.

"That's... that's Sabritha," Cavric found the breath to gasp. "My cousin. She... she took the officer's exam—*tried* to take the officer's exam. She... she didn't... The physical, it killed..." He stared at me. "*How?*"

"Cavric, please." Liette sighed. "It's drawn to your memories, psychically feeding off whatever trauma you're projecting or have buried inside you and taking its shape from those. How much easier can I make this?"

"But why's it getting *closer?*"

I drew Jeff, stepped forward, and brought it up through the Echo's gritty neck. A spray of gravel and dust burst out, a crude facsimile of blood, and the rest of it followed, collapsing into a heap of debris. Cavric watched it, eyes agape.

"How... how did you..."

I shrugged. "It died because you remembered that blades should kill people."

He stared at me with eyes vacant of everything but fear. But at least he got to his feet. And so I simply sighed and looked out over the wastelands.

"Look," I sighed. "You know the Husks didn't always look like this, right?"

"Of course," he said, finally finding his words. "The first military history lessons in the officer's academy regards the horrors the Imperium inflicted on this region and the brave sacrifices of the Revolutionaries who fought to defend it."

"Not the *best* of defenses they did, was it?" Liette asked, staring out over the wastes.

I shook my head. "Yeah, Revolutionaries died out here. But so did mages. At the peak of the fighting, it was thousands who fell here. They littered the land, more corpses than anyone could collect. Their bodies shriveled and dissipated. Their Dust was cast onto the wind, seeped into the earth, drained into the streams."

I gestured about to the swirling tempests, the scorched earth.

"Magic did this, sure. Some of it, anyway. Skymages tore the winds apart. Fire and frost turned the earth to dust." I cleared my throat. "Regular dust, not capital *d* Dust. Usually, magic like that lasts only as long as the mage who cast it. But so much magic combined with so much Dust meant you've got..."

"The perfect place," Cavric muttered. "I see. This is why the Vagrants came here. For what Vraki's planning, he needs a lot of magic."

"And it's in the very fucking air here," I replied. "You're probably breathing some dead bastard now."

I heard the rustle of cloth as he pulled his collar up around his nose and mouth. I'd have taken longer to smile at that, but I didn't have time. I heard the Lady's song grow in my ears. The wind kicked up; the dust grew heavy. Congeniality pulled at her reins, squawking.

And suddenly, they were all around me. Forming out of the winds, rising out of the dirt, building first as legs and then torsos, sprouting arms and forming skulls out of nothingness. The dirt gave them eyes that couldn't blink, mouths that couldn't close. But the voices, they had those.

And they were screaming.

The howls of the Echoes filled the skies, louder than the wind or even the Lady's song. They shambled forward on legs that dissipated beneath them, reaching out with arms that twisted and turned to dust in the wind. Their eyes of dust were turned upon me. Their mouths gaped open and they spoke a language only I knew.

Whispers. Accusations. But above all else, pleas. Pleas for mercy. Pleas for life. Pleas for loved ones to be spared.

My heart dropped. My blood went cold. I heard every word they spoke.

And I ran.

"Come on!" I snapped, tugging on Congeniality's reins and hurrying toward the distant fort. "Keep moving! Don't look back! Don't listen to them!"

"What's happening?" Cavric asked, hurrying to catch up. "I didn't remember any of this! Is it one of you they're remembering?"

"Latent memories, maybe," Liette shouted as she followed. "The Husks are a mystery."

"But you said they were harmless!" Cavric shouted as their screams filled the sky.

"I said *one* was harmless!" she screamed back as she pushed past him and we fled into the maelstrom.

The Echoes didn't pursue us. They were fleeting things, insubstantial as the wind and dust that made them, incapable of focusing on much. When we neared the fort, they dissipated and were lost on the wind, their screams with them.

Their voices still rang in my ears, though. Their whispers, their screams, their *pleas*—I could hear them over my ragged breath, a breath I couldn't control anymore. They clung to me, as close as my scars, until I gritted my teeth and shut my eyes and shut them out.

And the silence set in, leaving me only the sound of my own breath, echoing.

I couldn't stop it. I'd stared killers in the eye and seen townships so rife with suffering that they'd be kinder as graveyards and not blinked. Yet I couldn't find the strength to close my mouth, to stop my heart from thundering and gulping down grimy air.

Not after they loomed before me.

I saw the gates first. The walls, seared with flame and pockmarked by impacts, held proudly enough, but it was the gates that put up the greatest effort. Their hinges torn and bars slashed, they still tried to cling mightily upright and defend their charge. Good, thick wood, banded with iron, rotted and rusted but still standing after all these years, thick enough to repel cannon fire.

Yet... they hadn't done anything against what brought them down.

"Are you all right?"

I looked down. Liette's fingers were on my arm. "Fine," I lied, pushing her away.

"You don't look fine," she said, watching me as I stalked away to catch up to Cavric ahead.

"This place," Cavric whispered, almost reverently. "I've seen these gates before."

He had. In a painting or a treatise. These gates were well known. Impenetrable, some had once called them. There were legends of the waves of soldiers they had repelled, of the cannon fire they had shrugged off. I had heard them all by the time I first laid eyes on them.

And when they were torn apart in an instant, I forgot them all. Same as everyone else did.

Even for all the gashes and holes rent in them, the walls kept most of the wind out. Sturdy design, built to last forever. Thick brown clouds of dust swirled overhead, loosing petulant moans and muttered complaints at being denied entry.

I wouldn't have come to this place unless I needed to. Unlike Vraki, this place held no good memories for me.

The buildings were right where I remembered them. The barracks were at the north end, close to the gates. Houses for the families of soldiers and workers laid out in the east, parallel to the tracks that led into the mine carved into the mountain. Furnaces and forges were set in the low valley near the southern wall, overseen by a lonely spire with a lonely banner.

That had once been the Cadre Command. That had once been a tower from which the Revolutionary guard had once looked over a land that was once called something other than the Husks. A land they had once believed would be their new paradise, free from masters, from mages.

One evening, that had all changed.

On the evening they saw a small Imperial regiment approaching, they didn't say shit. No siren. No warning. No evacuation orders for the miners and the steelworkers and their families. They didn't do anything more than muster a Revolutionary detachment with a few gunpikes to go out and rout them.

Why wouldn't they? It had just been a few Imperials, after all: a tall, skinny boy with a sword; a handsome man in a nice coat; and just a handful of Imperial troopers with them, including a young girl with white hair.

Business proceeded as usual that night. No one thought it odd that the Revolutionaries sent out to fight were taking long in returning. The miners were concerned with food rations and new uniforms for the winter, not with Imperial posturing. Amid the smoke being belched out by the furnaces, no one even noticed the flames at first.

Not until the gates were blown wide open.

"Vigil."

My scars burned at the name. The Cacophony rattled, like he was amused—or the wind, I didn't know. I glanced over and saw Cavric, gawping up at the tower. The wind and dust had cleared just enough that the sigil atop that tattered banner was just visible enough to make out the crossed pickax and hammer. A worn and ragged symbol, but to see the light in Cavric's eyes, you would have thought he was looking upon the Seeing God himself.

"I knew it," he whispered. "I *knew* it! We covered this in the academy! This was Vigil!" He looked to me, smiling broadly. "The ring on the finger of the Revolution's reach! The forge of the vanguard! The birthplace of the Boar, the Rattler, the Dragoon!"

"Never heard of it," I muttered in a voice too weak from a mouth too dry for that lie to be believed.

"A collection of houses near a merely impressive mountain," Liette said. "That warrants importance to the Revolution, one supposes."

"Important?" He let out an incredulous laugh. "This was one of the earliest fortresses of the Revolution, established right after we freed ourselves from the Imperium!" He gestured to the mountain as though he were introducing me to a large, stony girlfriend. "This mine alone put thousands of people to work and produced more weapons for the army than we had ever known! The farmlands surrounding this place fed entire cities! It withheld against *countless* Imperial attacks!"

"Oh? What happened to it?" I almost choked on the words.

Cavric's face didn't just fall. The guy looked at the ground like he was searching for a gun to put in his mouth. His voice got real low and his hands hung limp at his sides.

"It fell..." he said. He shook his head, found his composure. "Obviously, it fell. Imperial attack. Treachery."

He stared somewhere far away, some distant memory of what Vigil used to be, some story of what it used to mean. There had been stories about how it had gone from the Revolution's shining city to its biggest graveyard. Some of them even got a lot of details right. But...

It hadn't been treachery that night.

There hadn't been any sneaking or subterfuge. The Imperials had strolled up to the smoldering gates like they were arriving for a dinner party, in their nicest suits and brightest colors. They walked right up to the Revolutionaries sent to stop them. They walked right through them.

No one opened the gates for them; they simply knocked very hard. The guards who came rushing up to defend it met with the skinny boy with the sword and then they died. And then people came out to see what was happening. Fathers picked up their pickaxes from work. Mothers tried to hide the excited children who ran out to see what the noise was about. Children pushed past them, ran out anyway. They all looked out to see the tall man in the fancy suit who looked back at them and smiled gently and said a few quiet words and he heard a very quiet song.

Then everyone had looked to the sky. And they had seen it go red.

And, three hours later when their bodies lay twisted into coils of ash, Vraki the Gate had his name.

"The records never said what happened here," Cavric said. I didn't like the excitement in his voice. It didn't belong in a place like this. "Or what we left behind."

I reached out as he started to hurry off, but he was too quick. "Wait!"

"This was the pride of the Revolution once!" he cried back as he hurried off into the ruins. "There might be something here that we can use to stop those people!"

"Damn it, Cavric!" Anger leapt into my voice, unbidden. "Isn't it fucking obvious? There's nothing here!"

The wind howled, drowning the screams I hurled after him. He just kept hurrying, disappearing behind a blackened skeleton of a building.

"Are you listening?" Anger turned to fear, panic making my voice hoarse. "There's nothing here! Come back!" I started after him. *"COME BACK!"*

My foot struck something. There was the sound of breaking, like a burned-out tree crumbling to ash. The reek of something old and seared filled my nostrils.

Don't look down.

I told myself this. In my head, over and over.

Don't look down.

I tried to hammer it into my skull, make it a spike that would stiffen my spine, make it impossible to look.

Don't look down.

But that thought became a lead weight settling behind my brow, dragging my eyes toward the earth. The wind shifted the sand under my boot. Fragments of ashen bone were revealed, a black stain on the earth, as a skull peered out from beneath the earth. And with its mouth gaping wide open, the wind seemed to whisper in my ear.

"I don't want to die."

I don't remember when my breath left me. I don't remember when my blood followed. I don't know how I fell to my hands and knees, breathing hard and gasping for air, my limbs numb. Except for my fingers. My fingers could feel the earth beneath me, coarse and gritty.

My fingers could feel just how many other black bones were under that sand.

"SAL!"

Liette's hands were on me, but I couldn't feel them. I couldn't feel the wind blowing against my skin or her breath hot on my neck as she tried to pull me to my feet. I could only feel my scar, pulsating like it had a heart of its own, from my collarbone to my belly, fresh as the day I got it.

"I knew it," she whispered. "I fucking knew something was wrong." She pulled on me again, too damn small to move me but too damn stubborn to realize it. "Why didn't you say anything?"

I had something to say to that. Didn't I? I couldn't think. It was like all the thoughts had left me, swept right out of my head on the wind. What was left behind was a blackness, vast and resonant, into which a voice that I didn't recognize as mine echoed.

"How can you be surprised? You already knew I was broken."

It took me a minute to realize I had said that, that those words had leaked out of my mouth on my stale breath. But I had. And she had heard. And she looked at me like I had just put my sword through her.

Maybe it would have hurt less if I had.

"What?" she asked, breathless.

"That's why you're here, isn't it?" I staggered to bloodless feet, swaying in the wind. "No contacts to save, no laws to enforce, no reason to be out here except for me." I stared at her through eyes I couldn't blink anymore. "To try to fix me again."

My mind felt painfully full. Full of the screaming wind. Full of the pleading voices in it. Full of the bones beneath my feet. So full I couldn't stop the words coming out of my mouth. So full it hurt, and my scars hurt and my body hurt and it all hurt so bad I just... I don't know.

Maybe I wanted someone else to hurt like that.

"Am I wrong?" I asked.

Silence. Wind. Pain.

"AM I?"

She stared at me, her mouth hanging open, at a loss for words. Her hair whipped about her face in messy strands, torn free from her perfect bun. Her tiny fists curled up, trembling, aching for something to break, something to strike me with, something to hold on to.

"You are." Her voice was hard and small, a scalpel blade on my skin. "I don't want to fix you. Not anymore." Her eyes trembled, water filling them. "Because I don't fucking know how."

Her lips quivered, searching for the words. Her eyes swept over the wastes, looking for an answer. Something that would make me understand, something that would make this hurt less.

"Do you *know* how brilliant I am, Sal?" She snapped her fingers. "It's that easy for me. To make anything. I can craft alchemics that can take away pain. I can craft a weapon that would sell for enough metal to make us live in comfort for twenty lifetimes. I can be anywhere, make anything, do anything, *give you* anything. Anything you wanted."

She threw her hands out, gesturing to the devastation around us: the charred homes, the blackened bricks, the shifting sands from which skeletal fingers reached out toward a sky masked by wailing wind.

"And you chose this. Look at it." Her voice rose to a scream over the wind. "*LOOK.* You chose *this* over me. You chose *this* over everything I can do for you. You chose a pile of rubble, a list of names, that... that fucking *gun* over me." She gritted her teeth, as though she could force the tears back into her face. "And I don't know what I'm doing wrong that you would do that."

"It's not about you," I snarled back. My words felt strange on my mouth, distant in my own head. "It's about them. If I don't stop them—"

"Don't say 'if.' You'll stop them. Because you want to stop them. And you never let anything get in the way of what you want. I don't worry that you won't. I worry that you will." She wrapped her arms around her, head lowered. "You'll kill those seven names. You'll kill every last name on your list. And it still won't be enough. You'll keep hunting, keep fighting, keep *leaving* and I'll...I'll..."

She let those words drop. She let her eyes drop. And for a long moment, it seemed like every other part of her might drop and become just one more corpse on this dark earth.

But she didn't. She looked back up at me. And I've had wounds that hurt less than the stare she shot me.

"You make me feel like a fucking idiot, you know?" she asked. "Knowing all of this, I'd still stay. I'd still be with you. If you just told me that someday this would stop."

She stared at me. I said nothing.

"Sal," she whispered.

The winds howled.

"Please," she rasped.

My ears were filled with voices not my own. My head was empty of thoughts, things I could say to make this right. I could have found them, if I really tried. I could have told her something sweet, that she was all I ever wanted, that I wanted nothing more than to stop this.

But I couldn't lie to her. Not about this.

And I couldn't tell her that I knew when this day would stop.

She didn't say anything, either. She turned away from me. The winds kicked up, howling in my ears, burying the sounds of her footsteps. The sands became sheets of grit, painting her as a shadow against the wastes, steadily growing smaller.

I watched her, silent.

As she walked away.

As she disappeared.

And, even as the wind howled, I could hear something else. Coming from the distant mountain, cutting through the winds and earth alike, seeping into my skin and my skull. I heard a single, beautiful note of a song in a language meant only for me.

The Lady Merchant's song rang out, answering a mage's call.

And I followed it.

THIRTY-ONE

VIGIL

In the darkness of the mountain, I knew only sound.

My own breathing, ragged and full of dirt through my scarf. My heart pounding steadily beneath my scar. The Lady Merchant's song, unbearably distant and painfully close.

And through it all: him.

The sizzle of his brass, burning through the leather of his sheath. The rattle of his metal as I walked through the tunnels. The faint, rasping sound of his burning, seething in such a way that, if I didn't know better, I would have sworn was his laughter.

The Cacophony was pleased.

Pleased to be following the sound of the Lady's song. Pleased to know that, at the end of it, we would find Vraki. Pleased to be rid of distractions, of Cavric, of Liette...

Liette.

I could hear the thoughts, too. The ones in the back of my head that told me I shouldn't have left her, that I should go back for her, that I'd never find anything in the dark that would ever be as good as her. But those thoughts were muffled, smothered beneath the dark and buried beneath the sound.

Breath, ragged. Heart, beating. The Cacophony, laughing.

I was too close now to turn back. For Liette. For Cavric. For anything. Everything I needed was down here. In the stone under my feet. In the walls closing in. In the light dying behind me and the song of magic beckoning me forward.

By the last traces of light that doggedly followed me in, I could make out withered support beams, rusted-out tracks, discarded picks and hammers. Vigil's mountain had been a mine once. Back when there had been people instead of corpses.

Another sound hit me. Wind wailing. Earth moving. A scream. A plea for mercy. A voice meant solely for me.

Sound took shape before me in a pillar of wind and dust, pulling itself out of the shadows and dust of the tunnel. Loose rocks and grit whipped themselves about into columns, pulled themselves together into a body, smoothed themselves into a body and a face to go with them.

An Echo.

Damn thing followed me in. It took shape in an instant, its body growing more distinct with every staggering step it took toward me. From a shapeless cloud of dust and grime, it became a person, wrapped in a thick coat, a military saber at its hip and an expression of horror painted across its dusty face.

A Revolutionary. Or…was it? The uniform fit, but the face didn't. Its visage was twisted into a mask of panic. Its cheeks sunken to the bone and its lips peeled back to the gum. Its eyes were empty of anything but fear, a corpse learned to walk. And instead of a scream, its mouth gaped open in a raspy, dust-choked moan.

"Help me."

It shambled toward me. I drew Jeff.

"I can't find my family."

It raised its arms. I could see its pupils carved out of sand.

"What's happening to us? My skin is—"

I thrust. Sand exploded out the back of its head. It collapsed into a heap of dust and rocks. Its scream rattled in the confines of the tunnel, seeped into my ears.

I shut my eyes tightly, trying to force out the pain in my ears.

Eventually, the ringing abated. My head cleared just a little. I opened my eyes.

I shouldn't have.

There were more. Pulling themselves out of the dust, pulling bodies out of the stone and the stagnant air, polishing sand into limbs and gravel into faces. Women. Men. Children. Soldiers. Merchants. Mothers. Elders. All of them with sunken faces, fear in their eyes, limbs withered and twisted.

And all of them shambling toward me.

And even though my ears were ringing, I could still hear them.

"What are they doing? We're civilians! We've done nothing!"

No. I could feel them.

"They're coming! Get the children to the bunkers! Get them out!"

In my ears. In my head. In my skin.

"What's happening to me? I'm...I'm falling apart! My hands... Look at my hands!"

Crawling over me, through me, whispers on spider legs.

"Why are they doing this? What did we do wrong? We surrender! WE SURRENDER!"

Their voices became one long, loud screaming sound of crunching dust and grinding stone. They became a wall of dust and horrified faces, of withered limbs and rotted hands, reaching for me.

Had to run. Had to get free. The voice at the back of my head was howling, pounding at the walls of my skull, trying to be heard over the endless drone of their agony.

I started backing up. I held my blade out defensively. I took another step backward.

And I fell.

I expected to hit the stone and feel the bite of rock tearing through my clothes, my skin. But I didn't. I felt the great yawn of nothingness beneath me as I plummeted through darkness, a cold wind whipping about me as I fell faster and faster toward a bottom that didn't exist.

A pinprick of light blossomed in the distance. In another second, it exploded into a blinding burst. The darkness was swallowed up by an endless white light I had to shield my eyes against. I blinked my eyes and, when the blindness cleared...

I was surrounded by eternal blue.

A sky. Wide and clear and as azure as an ocean, it opened up around me. No earth rushing up to greet me. No water rising up around me. Nothing but an endless expanse of blue sky and cold, clear air.

I breathed it in. It hurt my lungs like I used to love. Clouds crawled lazily around me in beautiful patterns and shapes I recognized from long ago. Birds soared through the sky, paying me no mind. I was just like them, after all.

I belonged up here.

I couldn't hear the ringing in my ears or the screams of the dead or anything but the rush of wind. I couldn't feel my scars ache as a smile pulled itself onto my face. I couldn't feel the chill as tears came, unbidden, to my eyes. I could barely feel my lips move as the words came to me, without me even thinking them.

"Eres va atali..."

Then, the world changed.

The sky became purple, then orange, as though some massive hands somewhere started strangling it, trying to choke the air from the sky itself. And then, as though those same hands had grown impatient and decided simply to cut the sky's throat and be done with it, everything turned red. It bled into the sky, crimson stains blossoming across the expanse. The birds became black, ashen shadows. The cold air became choked with the scent of smoke and flame. And the clouds...

All the clouds were red.   ·

I hit the earth, felt the sand explode beneath me. It didn't kill me. But it should have.

I clambered to my feet. Before I saw anything else, I saw the red sky, licked by tongues of flame rising from the houses, choked with smoke and cinders swirling in columns like swarms of insects. I saw the walls of Vigil, the holes punched in them still smoking. I saw the people.

And they were dying.

Children sobbed, mothers dragging them along by their hands as they dropped toys in their wake. Soldiers dropped their gunpikes and ran, screaming before their bodies blackened and twisted and became like dead trees. Officers bellowed orders before bright silver flashed across their throats and sent their heads tumbling from their shoulders.

I saw Vraki, standing at the center of it, his black coat whipping about him, his hair long and wild and his face alight with delighted awe at his own strength. He wove his hands and portals opened. Great hands clawed out of nothingness. Baying nith hounds leapt into existence to pursue those too stupid to know there was no escape.

I saw Jindu, rushing about, sword in hand, darting between bullets and spears thrust at him. His face was empty, emotionless, barely registering the bodies falling around him or the blood spattering his cheeks.

But it wasn't them that the people ran from. Their eyes were skyward, locked on the red shadow looming over them, a bloodstain upon the soot-kissed sky. It extended its hands. It made a noise that sounded like a song. And from its fingers, flame poured out in great, roaring gouts.

In the moments before their voices were snuffed out beneath the laughter of fire, they spoke its name.

"Red Cloud."

Its fire swept over the mothers and their children. It swept over the soldiers and their officers. It swept over the elders and the sick and the weeping and the begging and the bleeding. And when I opened my mouth to scream, I couldn't hear it, because the fire swept over me, too.

An instant of bright red heat.

And then darkness.

And cold, stagnant air. And stone under my knees and above my head and all around me.

Back in the tunnels, I told myself. *I'm back in the tunnels.*

And I tried to slow my breathing, but it didn't work. And through my gasping, I could hear footsteps.

I looked up. I saw her come to me. She emerged from the darkness, radiant and pale and pristine in her nice clothes and her eyes bright and keen behind her big spectacles. Her smile was softer now, and sad. She stood before me and knelt beside me and reached up a finger to dry a tear from my eye.

"I was...gone, Liette," I whispered to her, my voice too weak to carry its own weight. "I was back in Vigil, under the red sky. I saw everyone dying and I...and I..."

"And you did nothing." Liette lay a hand on my shoulder. "I know, Sal."

"You don't," I said. "I made sure you didn't."

"But I always did," she said. "When you cried out in your sleep, when you stared off as I was talking to you, when you whispered curses you thought I couldn't hear...I knew. I know you were there when they died. I know you couldn't stop it."

My head felt like someone had driven a dozen iron spikes into it, like it was too heavy for my neck. I turned my gaze to the ground, to my hands groping at the dirt under me. I spoke through the foul, sour taste in my mouth.

"How?" I asked. "How can you even look at me?"

"The same way I always have."

She reached down and she took my hand. I looked up into her smile, her bright eyes behind those spectacles. She helped me to my feet and she smoothed a lock of my hair over my ear.

"I forgive you, Sal."

The word hit me like a fist.

"I forgive you," she said. "For everything."

And the tears stopped coming. And my heart slowed down. And my head didn't feel so heavy. And my scars ached as I closed my eyes.

"Yeah?" I asked.

"Yes," she said. She turned and she began walking. "Now, come. It's only a little farther. Once we're—"

I didn't hear her.

Not over the sound of metal on leather as I pulled Jeff from his sheath. Not over the whisper of steel as I swung. Not over the sound of flesh parting and blood pattering on the ground.

I won't tell you what it felt like.

But I'll tell you what happened once she hit the ground.

She started curling at the edges, at her fingers and toes. Her boots shriveled up. Her gloves withered away. Her skin turned black as coal, then became dust, blowing away in a cloud of dried ink. It spread across her body, up her limbs and over her torso and over the mess where her eyes had been until she became a black cloud that hissed into the air. Just a few more flecks of dust, swallowed up by the wind.

And then she was gone.

She wasn't a body anymore. She wasn't real. She never had been, no matter how badly I wished she was. She was just a dream torn out of my head and made real. Those last words had confirmed it to me.

I could believe in a lot of crazy shit. I could believe in dead people made out of dirt. I could believe an eternal, endless sky. I could believe in red shadows flying overhead and fire falling from a red cloud and I could believe in thousands dying in pain and fear.

But I could never believe that she would ever forgive me.

The sound of her hissing into dust filled the stale air of the tunnel, the last gasp of sound before the tunnel plunged into a cold, quiet dark, silent but for my breath.

And my voice.

"That was pretty good," I said to the darkness. "You almost got me."

I looked out into the gloom. The void stretched out endlessly before me, so thick that it swallowed my words just as soon as I threw them out into it.

"You read my mind for that one, didn't you?" I shook my head.

"Serves me right, I suppose, for thinking you wouldn't use her against me." I slid Jeff into his sheath. "That bit with the sky was new, though. How long did you spend thinking that up?"

I suppose, to you, I would have looked crazy, talking into the darkness like that. I suppose I would have looked even crazier as I drew the Cacophony and checked his chamber to make sure I had something painful loaded. But you weren't there.

You couldn't feel the darkness looking back at me.

I clicked the chamber shut, stared out into the gloom.

"You going to come out?" I asked. "Or am I going to have to light this place up?"

You wouldn't have seen it, at a glance. Hell, I barely did, even knowing what to look for. I stared into the dark for a long while, and to me, it just looked like an endless void. But I let my eyes relax, my mind clear, and soon enough, I saw it. There, in the gloom, was a patch of darkness that was just a shade darker than the rest.

And it began to move.

Its steps came slow and with the sound of feet dragging across stone. It shambled closer, an ungainly and teetering limp that made it more distinct with every step. Soon, I could make out a shape that had once been tall but now stood hunched over. I could make out long legs bent awkwardly; I could make out long arms hanging low from stooped shoulders and ending in hands, the only part of him that was bare, that were tattooed with dead trees. I could make out a pair of bloodshot eyes.

Staring right at me.

"Sal," he groaned, voice like he had just swallowed glass.

I nodded toward him. "Taltho."

You probably never even heard the name of Taltho the Scourge. But if you'd spent any time at all in the Scar, I guarantee you knew his work.

You probably heard about the regiment of Revolutionaries who all suddenly turned their gunpikes on each other and fired. Or maybe the one about the wealthy heiress in Beggar's Fists who started screaming about spiders in the middle of a crowded ball and started clawing her own face off. Or the tavern in Redriver where twenty men walked into the main room, ordered a stiff drink, then quietly put their own knives through their throats.

Vagrants love fame, it's true, and Nightmages are no different. But whereas most want our names remembered, Nightmages want to be known only by the bodies they leave in their wake. And even among Nightmages, Taltho was something different.

Not that you'd know it to look at him.

The creature that stepped out into view barely looked like he could stand, let alone put me through the hell I had just seen. He was bent, trembling, and every inch of his lanky body was wrapped in dirty white bandages, as though he suffered from some disease that didn't even have a name yet. All that was visible were a pair of eyes, unblinking and bloodshot, and two rows of teeth, bereft of lips.

"Unwelcome," he said.

"Should have used something other than your birdshit tricks to try to kill me, then," I said. "It might have worked."

"Liar."

I grinned. More for my own sake than for his; after what I had just seen, I felt like I had to do it.

"Yeah, you always did see right through me, Talthonanac." I glanced at his face. "Probably because you never blink. I would have come to kill you sooner or later."

"Unlikely."

I regarded him coldly. "You've been awake too long, Taltho. Your memory's going." I raised the Cacophony. "You must not remember what you fucks did back in Cathama, or you'd never stop thinking about me."

I took a step forward.

"You'd never stop wondering when I was going to come for you. All of you."

I aimed the Cacophony at him.

"And your very last thought would be my name."

I took another step.

"Sal the Caco—"

Another step behind me. I whirled around, Jeff in hand, and plunged his blade into soft flesh. He sank to the hilt in someone's chest. In the darkness, I could only see the reflected lights of a pair of dark eyes as they looked down, bemused, at the sword jutting out of their sternum.

Those eyes flashed purple. The Lady's song filled my ears. One hand tore the blade free from flesh, left not even a scar behind. The other hand?

It flashed out of the darkness to crack against my temple and send me collapsing to the ground.

I had one last moment to see Taltho, staring at me with those unblinking eyes, before I hit the ground. I couldn't feel the stone beneath me, couldn't feel anything but numb cold where working arms and legs had been just a moment ago. Fortunately, I could still use my eyes.

"*Ha!* What'd I tell you? I *told* you she'd fall for it!"

Unfortunately, I could also still use my ears.

"How long were you thinking up that line, Sal?" a voice, feminine and as pleasant as a rusty nail being hammered into my ear. "Fuck, I bet you thought you sounded like such a badass. 'And your very last thought would be my name.' Ha!" She cackled in delight at her own crude imitation of my voice. "Sounds a little less dramatic if you shit yourself and go rigid while you're saying it, don't it?"

I hadn't shit myself at least. But that was probably the only thing about this situation that I could smile at. I knew who was coming even before her black boots came to a stop in front of me. And even before she knelt down so I could look right into those dark little eyes set in a face like a hatchet's edge, I knew I was in trouble.

"Sal," Galta the Thorn said through a smile as broad and jagged as a knife wound, "how long's it been?"

THIRTY-TWO

HIGHTOWER

Vigil.

Tretta swirled her glass of wine, staring into its darkness. She knew the name of the fortress, of course. Along with Dutiful's Wall, Long Watch, Greenriver, Bentnail, and of course, Stern's Last Word. "The Unbreakable Six" was the third song any child in Weiless learned, right after the Revolutionary Anthem and "Praise Unto the General."

She leaned against the wall, closed her eyes. How did it go, again?

"Walls, eternal and wide,
Break the Imperial tide,
Revolutionary hammer crafts Revolutionary spirit!
Unbreakable as the Six and eternal as the sky!"

Somehow, muttering it to herself in a dark hall didn't sound the same as when a thousand military cadets were singing it in unison with an accompanying hundred-strong military band.

But then, maybe it was fitting, given that the Unbreakable Six had been broken ages ago.

She felt a pang of anger at herself for the counterrevolutionary thought. The Great General said that the fortresses were not broken, that someday they would once again form the bulwark against the Imperium and become the shining wall to safeguard the Scar for the children of the Revolution.

The Great General was always right. Even when she had no idea how he could be.

The Unbreakable Six had been the first defenses built when the Revolutionaries—back then, simply called "the nuls" by their oppressors—had thrown off their Imperial masters under his leadership. When the decadent oppressors had returned, it was his Unbreakable Six that kept safe the Revolution.

At first.

The counterattack stretched into a campaign. Dutiful's Wall had been sunk beneath the earth by magic. Long Watch had exploded when the garrison chose to detonate its severium reserves rather than surrender. Greenriver had been taken by the Imperium. Bentnail was a freehold overrun by outlaws. And Stern's Last Word, her family's namesake, had been lost in the Husks.

There were songs about how they were lost. The operas of Weiless had dedicated countless plays to how they would be reclaimed and the Imperial swine would be cast out. Each of the Unbreakable Six had its own opera.

Except Vigil.

No one sang of Vigil. No one spoke of its once-verdant fields or thriving mines or happy families. No one wanted to remember that those shattered ruins and blackened skulls had once been home to so many. Of Vigil, there were only whispers, only tears, only names.

Vraki. Jindu.

Red Cloud.

They knew nothing else. Only that three Imperial mages had arrived and an hour later, Vigil had been a graveyard. The handful of soldiers who had accompanied them had never been known, had never even been spoken of, mere footnotes in a long treatise on Imperial villainy. Tretta herself had barely even remembered there were other Imperials besides the three present.

And now one of them was her prisoner.

It was rare that Tretta did not regret delaying an execution, but she was feeling more and more justified in her decision. Whatever issues Cadre Command would take with her sparing the Vagrant would be minuscule if it meant she could deliver them the fate of Vigil. They might even promote her again. They might even bring her to meet the General.

She had never laid eyes on him outside the portraits. No one in her class had. But when she thought of the moment when she met him, it was not his face that she saw. It was her own. Polished and bright and smiling at the commanders and captains and officers who nodded and smiled and saluted as she walked down the halls of Weiless headquarters. And at the end of those long halls? It was Cavric, the Low Sergeant, she saw. The life she had saved. The Revolutionary she hadn't left behind.

That would be a fine reward, she thought. That would be a fitting victory.

If she didn't die of old age before she saw it, anyway.

"Are you almost done?" Tretta's bellow was accompanied by her fist pounding on a wooden door. "It's been nearly half an hour."

"I *was* almost done," a voice called back. "Then you went and interrupted me."

"It's a toilet, not a library," Tretta growled, rubbing her eyes.

"I can't help it. Wine goes right through me. Can you hear me?"

"I'm talking to you, aren't I?"

"No, not, like, hear my voice. But can you hear me…*going*?"

Tretta blinked, recoiling. "Does it matter?"

"Well, I can't go if you're listening! Can you play some music or something?"

"For fuck's sake, what *difference* does it make?" Tretta slammed her fist against the door. "I already *know* what you're doing in there!"

"Is this what passes for etiquette in the Revolution? You people truly are savages."

"I'm under no obligation to accommodate your vanity."

"And *I'm* under no obligation *not* to piss all over your nice floors. I just thought we'd all be happier this way."

"Five seconds." Tretta kicked the door for emphasis. "Then you're either out here or I'm in there. And in one of those situations, I'm armed."

"All right, all right! Take it easy, for fuck's sake."

There was a grunting sound, which Tretta dutifully strained to ignore, followed by the sound of water disappearing down the drain. A sigh that was almost *too* relieved later, the door creaked open and a pair of blue eyes peered out.

"It would have been quicker," Sal said, holding up her manacled wrists, "without these. Not to mention more humane."

"It's not a matter of humanity," Tretta replied tersely. "It's a matter of security."

"Security." Sal lofted a single white eyebrow. "What exactly did you think I was going to do in the toilet?"

Tretta had heard the sounds of a hundred men dying at once without flinching. It annoyed her, to some extent, that Sal's particular choice of words should cause a rush of warmth to flush her cheeks.

But, to a greater extent, it just pissed her off.

"Out of a necessity for information, I have been accommodating," she said through clenched teeth. "Out of a necessity to maintain a standard, I might not be."

"Of course. I meant no offense. I was simply curious if Weiless's academies taught you how everything worked down there." Before Tretta could reply—or strike her—Sal proffered an arm to her, as if inviting her out for a stroll. "Shall we?"

Tretta eyed her arm and considered striking her anyway, just on general principle. But that was time that would be better spent finding out the fate of Cavric. She settled for roughly seizing Sal's arm and leading her down the hall.

"You were at Vigil, then," Tretta muttered, "the night it was destroyed. You were a soldier for the Imperium, there to support Vraki." She narrowed her eyes, spat the name. "And Red Cloud."

"I was," Sal said. "I saw it...I saw everything."

"Then you see how necessary the Revolution is," Tretta said.

"You've witnessed the barbarity of the Imperium and their hated Prodigies firsthand. You know what it is we stand against."

"I do," Sal replied. "But I doubt you do." She quirked a brow at the woman. "Does it surprise you to know I was in the Imperial army?"

"A Vagrant is defined by treason," Tretta said. "You wouldn't be one if you hadn't betrayed someone."

"I thought you'd approve of me abandoning the Imperium."

"That is between you and your abominable goddess." Tretta guided Sal down the stairs and back to the Cadre's office. "My concern is for what happened to my soldier." She shot a glare at Sal. "You *did* see Cavric again?"

"If I hadn't, you'd never find out what happened to him," Sal replied. "And then you'd go and shoot me and get my brains all over the floors I so courteously didn't piss on."

"I don't know if it's that you're a Vagrant, an Imperial, or worse that makes you think you can threaten me with urination—"

"I think it's your nice coat," Sal replied. "You seem like the type that'd be bothered by stains."

"—but it's pointless. I know you're trying to distract me." She jerked hard on Sal's arm, forcing her to a halt. She sharpened her scowl to a fine point and thrust it right between her prisoner's eyes. "But no matter what oaths you swore to whom and which you've broken, I will exact justice from you. By choice or by blade."

Sal met her stare. And there was no more mirth, no joke waiting to be unleashed, no snide comment waiting to pounce. The eyes that met Tretta's were clear and blue as the sky after a storm, eyes fit for the scar that ran down the right one, eyes that belonged on dead men and the men who killed them.

And her voice was soft as night.

"Well," she said, "I hope it's sharp."

Tretta was a hard woman. A hard woman who felt the urge to remind this Vagrant that she had seen hundreds go to their deaths before this one and would again. A hard woman who wouldn't flinch at words like that.

"Soldier!" she barked.

That said, there was nothing that said a hard woman couldn't delegate.

"Governor-Militant!"

A pair of soldiers—apparently neither one sure which she had called—came rushing up, skidding to a halt and firing off crisp salutes. They looked just a touch confused when she shoved Sal toward them, but took the woman by either arm regardless.

"Take the prisoner back to the interrogation room," she said. "Leave her there until I return and lock the door behind you." She fixed a wary look upon Sal. "And do *not* talk to her. Am I understood?"

"Yes, madam!"

Another salute, a jerk on Sal's arms, and they were off. And just for a moment, Sal's eyes, still so blue and so empty, lingered on Tretta before they, and the scarred woman they were fixed in, disappeared down the hall.

It was easy to forget she was a killer, Tretta thought. She had a way of talking, between the flashy descriptions and the eloquent verse, making it seem like they all deserved it, like she wouldn't have killed them if they weren't guilty. But if Vagrants were defined first by treason, there was one hell of a knife fight for second place between violence, lying, and the sheer effortlessness with which they did either.

Tretta narrowed her eyes, scowling at the hall down which her prisoner had just disappeared. She'd had a gnawing at the back of her neck since she'd first laid eyes on Sal, an irritating pain that grew more aggravated with every word she spoke. But only now did she recognize it for what it was: the creeping suspicion that she was being made a fool of.

"Governor-Militant," a shrill voice piped up, "a word?"

Then again, she thought resentfully, given the many, *many* pains in her neck around here, perhaps she was having trouble telling one from the other.

"Clerk Inspire." She spoke his name before turning around with such icy contempt that she hoped he would take the hint and not be there when she did. Alas. "I don't have time for this."

"But I didn't say anything yet!" Inspire protested, cringing as she turned on him. "You can't possibly assume you don't have time for what I haven't said."

"Were that true, Inspire, I wouldn't have this latent desire to punch you in the face." She waved a hand. "Make it quick."

"O-of course." Inspire's head nearly fell off with the force at which he nodded. "I merely meant to bring up the subject of the Vagrant's confession. You know"—he cast a conspiratorial look about before leaning in and whispering—"about Vigil."

The urge to punch Inspire in the face vanished and was, in about a second, replaced with a white-hot urge to shoot him in the head. Given that Tretta instead settled for seizing him by the throat, shoving him into a nearby alcove, and slamming him against the wall, she thought she had struck a good compromise.

"Clerk," she whispered, her voice jagged and harsh, "you are going to do three things, in order. You are going to tell me what you know of what the Vagrant said, you are going to tell me *how* you know it, and you are never going to speak a word of either inside or outside this command ever again. Or else you will be doing one thing and doing it very quickly once I draw my hand cannon. Do you understand?"

"Y-yes, madam! Of course, madam!" Inspire squealed, holding up his hands like they would stop her from doing anything. "I...I merely overheard! I...I...I was coming to the door and I heard her whisper the name and then I...I couldn't...I had to..."

"Breathe, Inspire, while it's still only mildly difficult."

He inhaled sharply. His gaze steadied, just enough to make an effort to meet her eyes. "Madam," he said, voice low, "I believe she's telling the truth. Part of it, anyway."

"Part of it," Tretta repeated.

"I've been over the maps of the area," Inspire said. "Paperwork, when I served in Central Bookkeeping. She described the layout of the fortress perfectly. I do believe she's been there before."

"Get to the lie."

"But she's not telling us all she knows," Inspire whispered. "She claims to have been a simple soldier, yes? But why would a simple soldier be present with Prodigies like Vraki the Gate and Red Cloud?"

Tretta narrowed her eyes. "Bodyguard, perhaps. Prodigies are not invincible."

"But they are valuable to the Imperium," Inspire retorted. "So much so that they wouldn't send just anyone with them."

"What are you angling at, Inspire?"

Inspire, for the first time since she had known him, stood up straight and looked her dead in the eye.

"There is another Cadre Command in Tranquility, a day's ride by Iron Boar. Currently visiting there on routine inspection is one Regarn Gentle." Something of a cringe crossed his face. "I've sent the paperwork to your desk before. I trust you know the name."

Tretta did. Even if Inspire *hadn't* sent her the notification, she knew the name of Regarn Gentle, along with every person in her graduating class. Even the common foot soldiers of the farthest outpost in the Scar knew the name of the Great General's personal interrogator.

"High Torturer" had been the original name for his office, before the Great General had it abolished—the title, that is, not the practice. Extreme interrogation techniques were still necessary; after all, the Revolution had as many enemies as injustice did. And no one knew more about the subject than Regarn Gentle. His efforts had uncovered more Imperial plots, bandit hideouts, and counterrevolutionary insurgents than teeth pulled out of his victims' heads.

Or so the Great General had said.

"He can be here quickly," Inspire said. "Or she can be there even quicker. He could find out what she knows about Red Cloud. And the General could find out it was you—and your cadre—that did it."

The thought was tempting.

More than tempting, if Tretta was honest. The images of those comfortable halls, their walls laden with the portraits of great Revolutionary heroes and applauding officers in pristine suits drifted back to her mind. Those great offices of great people who had done great things, all welcoming her as though she belonged there.

They would hail her for finding more about Red Cloud, to take the first step on the road to avenging all those Revolutionaries slain like dogs by the Prodigy's murderous wrath at Vigil and beyond. Justice, at last, would come to the one creature that deserved it most.

The thought was more than tempting. The thought was exhilarating.

And then, unbidden, her mind drifted elsewhere, to a cold room in a cold house in the coldest city in the Scar. To Sal, stretched out on a metal table, bleeding and bruised and shackled. And to those blue eyes of hers, cold and empty even as Regarn Gentle's steady hands carved new scars on her body.

She shut her eyes tightly.

She released Inspire, let him slump back against the wall.

"No," she said. "Not yet. I will continue the interrogation. If my efforts prove fruitless—"

"Then we have no time," Inspire interjected with more of a spine than she thought he had. "Gentle is due north by tomorrow evening. He will be moving farther out of our grasp!"

"Then we'll let him go," she said. "We'll think of something else."

"But...but..." he sputtered in irritation. "What *need* is there to think of something else when we have the solution right—"

"Because, Inspire," Tretta replied, "it is not a question of need, but of duty. Mine is to get to the bottom of this, as I see fit. Yours is to trust in the wisdom the General has shown in assigning me this command." She affixed a careful glare on him. "If you find dispute with his decision, though, I fully welcome all criticism in the form of a written letter, signed and dated by you. Which I will gladly have sent by my swiftest bird to Tranquility for Regarn Gentle's perusal."

Some men, when scared, had the blood drain from their faces. Men like Inspire, who had been born scared, seemed to have their entire skeletal system ooze out the soles of their feet, courteously stopping just short of soiling himself.

Sal was right about one thing—they were nice floors.

"Clerk," she said, offering a nod.

"G-Governor-Militant." Inspire met it with a trembling salute.

She walked away from him, through the office, down the hall, and toward the interrogation room.

Inspire was a coward, but not a fool. Sal knew more than she was letting on. It would have been wiser, in the long view, to have Regarn take a look at her, for many reasons.

And Inspire knew that, too. He no doubt entertained his own fantasies of luxurious halls and powerful people greeting him. If she took too long with this prisoner, he wouldn't do her the luxury of informing her before reaching out to someone like Regarn Gentle. By this time tomorrow, Revolutionary inquisitors would be at her door.

It wasn't out of concern for Sal that Tretta had refused the idea.

She was loyal enough to the Revolution to have fought their wars and she had fought enough wars to know the realities of men like Gentle. Hundreds of innocents had been tortured to find Imperial spies, his accusations seeing as many good soldiers put to death as bad. His results had gotten him his station. The fate of a nation was on his shoulders.

The fate of a common soldier like Cavric was on hers.

THIRTY-THREE

VIGIL

When you wake up and find yourself tied up and blindfolded, you've either had a really bad night or you're about to have a really good one.

And if you've been paying attention, you know by now that I don't have good nights.

There's an animal panic that comes, a desire to thrash and snarl and spit as though any of that could break you free. And that panic shook me awake, my heart hammering against my ribs and my breath coming swift and ragged. But—not to brag—I'd done this enough to know that panic only robs you of the strength and wit you need to escape. I managed to fight it down.

Turns out it's a lot easier when you can't move.

Feeling returned to me slowly. Warmth crawled back into my muscles, fresh aches and pains greeting me. And none were keener than the bite of hemp securing my wrists behind my back and the choke of cloth wrapped around my eyes. But the gravel rubbing against my side as I tried to move was definitely trying its damnedest.

Still in the tunnel, I thought, drawing in a lungful of cold, still air. As feeling returned to my legs, I managed to find my way to my knees. *I'm still in the tunnel.*

Everything else that happened was a blur oozing out of my brain that felt like it had been baking in an oven for the past hour. I remembered red: red skies, red clouds, red light. I remembered collapsing, unable to move. I remembered eyes staring down at me, a broad grin and...

"Alive."

I froze. As if Taltho's voice were ice water poured into my veins. And once I did, I could feel him, even if I couldn't see him. I could feel his just-too-dark presence and his bloodshot eyes on me. His voice crawled across my scars.

"Lucky."

"A Mendmage doesn't need *luck*. This was *skill*, you creepy fuck."

Galta's voice was a slight relief to hear, if only because her voice made me want to cut my ears off rather than pour acid into them like Taltho's did. I heard her approach, her boots heavy and clicking on the stone floor, her voice echoing off the walls.

"Skill and stupidity, anyway. For a minute there, I thought she wasn't going to fall for it. But then she did and *pow!*" Her laugh was a brick hurled through a window. "You saw that, right? Tell me you saw it."

"Impressive."

"Yeah, I thought so." I felt her grin twist on her face like it was a knife in my flesh. "I never thought I'd see you again, Sal, after that night, let alone see you like this." I felt the hard toe of her boot nudge me in the side. "I read stories about you, you know. Sal the fucking Cacophony, killing Vagrants and wrecking shit, just like the old days."

She let out a low and ugly hum that turned into a lower and uglier laugh.

"Funny, though. They all talked about how much of a hard-ass you were. Not a damn one ever mentioned you on your knees." I heard the click of her finger tapping on her chin, obnoxiously deliberate. "To see you like this, it's enough to render me speechless."

I'd tell you that I'd been in a situation like this before and that'd be true. Hell, I'd tell you I'd been in even worse situations than this, and that'd be true, too. I could also tell you that I'd learned the only way out was to keep a calm head, a still tongue, and not say anything to make it worse.

"Well, shit, Galta. If I knew seeing me like this would make you shut up, I'd have chopped off my fucking legs."

Of course, that'd be a lie.

I felt a lot of things in the next second: her grin twisting to a snarl, the growl tearing out of her throat. Mostly, though, I just felt her boot slamming into my belly.

"It's *because*"—she kicked me in the side, driving me back to the ground—"only I, Galta the *fucking* Thorn"—she added another kick to my ribs as I tried to crawl away—"could bring your pompous fucking ass to her fucking *knees*"—she paused to let me scream as she drove her foot into my side—"you *shit*."

"Asses...don't...have knees," I said, though I imagined that line would have been cleverer if I wasn't about to spit up blood.

She kicked harder than I remembered.

I shouldn't have done that, I knew. Galta would be a vicious little fiend even if she *weren't* a Mendmage.

It's not considered a high art, but the Imperium appreciates the work of the Mendmages. As the name implies, their power is to heal. Their magic means that so long as they're conscious enough to use it, they can come back from almost any blow, be it a gunpike blast, poison, or specifically, my sword through their fucking chests.

They're the savages on the front lines, the unkillable terrors who wade through enemy soldiers without bleeding or dying. Soldiers under their command do not die and no weapon harms them for long.

"You piece of shit..."

I felt her fingers at my side, drifting across my skin before she pushed just a little harder. I let out a shriek as a talon pierced my middle, sinking up to her first knuckle and drawing a gout of blood that wept down my skin.

"How mighty are you now, Cacophony?" Her hand shot out,

wrapped around my throat. I felt something hard and sharp graze my neck as she started to squeeze. "How fucking mighty are you now, you—"

"Patience."

As bad as she hurt me, the sound of Taltho's voice hurt worse. Galta let out an aggravated sigh as her hand disappeared from my throat and wrapped around my arm, hauling me to shaking feet.

"Yeah, yeah," she muttered. "Let's get this done."

Someone with a stiffer spine might have resisted, might have struggled or at least cursed at them. Hell, a minute ago, I might have, too. But getting the shit kicked out of you changes your perspective. I knew Galta. I knew she needed only the barest reason to hurt me, to kill me.

And Taltho? I knew he needed even less of an excuse.

So I walked on shaky legs, trying to catch my breath, as she dragged me blindly along the stone floor. We walked until she jerked me to a halt, shoving me up against a wall of the tunnel.

I could feel her eyes on me—eyes like hers, I could have felt all the way across the Scar. And by the ache in my scars, I knew what she was looking for. That ache belonged to her, as much as me, and she sought it out. Her fingers traced the scar across my eye. My lip curled up in a sneer.

"I remember when you got this one."

Her whisper was soft, almost reverent. Her hand slid lower, pulled back the collar of my shirt and saw the ink of the tattoos scrawled on my collarbone. Her fingers ran along the length of my arm, found another scar beneath the inked birds and clouds, and rubbed it with an unnerving affection. .

"These are new," she almost purred. "How long has it been, Sal? How is it one of us isn't dead?"

"I was getting to it," I replied, a little shakier than I would have liked.

"Yeah…" Galta's voice dropped low in her throat. "I fucking bet you were."

A pair of fingers hooked the blindfold, tore it off. I blinked, let my eyes adjust—it was dark, darker than evening could have possibly been, but not dark enough to mask the briar of a woman standing before me.

Galtathamora ki Zhandi, I'm convinced, was not so much born as she was hammered out of a bunch of broken swords and ax heads by a real dick of a blacksmith. She was a scrawny, five-foot-nothing mess of sharp angles, a thin face with thin eyes and a thin little scar of a smile, sporting tattoos of twisted masses of briars running down her temples.

Frankly, she would have looked unnerving enough even without the spikes jutting out of her.

Out of her knuckles, out of her fingers, out of her skin, her namesake blossomed: tiny black thorns spreading in chaotic, chitinous rashes. A broad plate had grown across her chin, a jagged horn burst out of her brow, giving her the impression of a perpetual scowl. Even her hair was oiled up into little spikes to match.

A Mendmage's power is immense. But so is the Barter. The Lady Merchant gives them incredible healing capabilities, but she takes their blood. And her thirst for it is endless.

To keep their hearts beating and lungs breathing, they quaff alchemics whose names I can't even pronounce. It keeps them alive, but alchemics were never meant to replenish that much of a human body. It alters them, changes their body makeup, until they're less human and more...

"Holy shit, Galta," I said, wincing. "Have you been using your magic a lot or did you just fuck a rosebush?"

I thought that was clever. She didn't. She rewarded me with another talon dug into my side. I screamed, buckled, slumped against the wall of the tunnel. Her sneer was sharper than her thorns, drinking in my pain.

"There's so much I want to take from you, Sal," she said. "But shit isn't one of them." She gestured to her clothes, chuckling. "Thought I'd start with this, though."

It took me a moment to see through the pain. She wore something fancy around her waist. Her black blade, the one she'd taken from the Imperium, hung there. Along with my satchel. Along with my sword. And around her neck was a scarf…

My scarf.

My eyes widened. My heart raced. The pain was forgotten as I looked toward its hidden pocket.

The list, I thought, everything forgotten except that word. *She's got the fucking list.*

She didn't know what she had, I was sure of that, or how bad I needed it back. But she knew I was angry. And, if the big, jagged grin on her face was any indication, she was drinking it up.

"What do you think?" Galta ran her fingers along the scarf's cloth. She saw my scowl fester on my face, reached out and took me by the cheeks as if I were a child. "Aw, don't be mad. It looks better on me, anyway."

She pulled the scarf's tail aside. And if my heart hammered at the sight of her with my list, it dropped into the pit of my belly and turned to stone at the sight of what was draped across her hips.

"Not as good as *this*, though."

Of all the angers I felt, I could feel his the keenest. Even as he hung in his holster across her hips, I could feel his heat. It'd sound crazy to say it, but I knew at that moment, the Cacophony was staring right at me and whispering the dirtiest word he could think of.

"You always had the neatest stuff, Sal," Galta purred, sipping my anger like it were a fine brand of whiskey and she was planning on getting fucked. "Makes me glad we were the ones picked to come out here. Isn't that right, Taltho?"

My gaze drifted over her shoulder. In the darkness beyond, his bloodshot eyes stared at me. His yellowed teeth glistened, no lips to show whether he was smiling or frowning.

"Fortunate."

Her words didn't hit me so much as sink into me, knives up to the hilt.

"Vraki sent you," I muttered. "He knew I'd come looking for him and he sent you to ambush me."

"Maybe he did." Galta sneered at me. "He *is* cunning like that."

"He's a piece of shit that sprouted legs and learned how to walk," I snapped. "And he knew I'd come looking for him where he took his first steps." I narrowed my eyes, searched her face. "No. He sent you here for another reason."

"Yeah?" Galta's sneer twisted into a smile. "And what's it say about you that we caught you by chance, Sal? Sal the fucking Cacophony captured while we were running errands?"

Errands.

I ignored the shrill mockery of her voice—with considerable effort—and focused on that word. Galta was paranoid, but paranoid doesn't mean careful. They hadn't come out here to find me. Not *just* to find me, anyway.

"Yeah, Vraki knew. We all knew, Sal." Her eyes narrowed to razor-thin slits. "We'd be fucking idiots not to know after that day." Her thorns clicked together as her face contorted in a sneer. "That day you fucked up everything and made us all Vagrants."

I felt myself slipping back. Back to that dark place. I felt the cold stone on my back, saw my blood dancing in the air, heard that voice whispering that apology.

But I didn't fall. Not like I did back on the river. I held on. I tightened my hands so hard into fists that I thought the ropes might just snap them off. I swallowed that fear, buried it under anger, stared at Galta the Thorn until I just saw a thick neck waiting for me to strangle.

"I remember," I replied. "I remember all the words Vraki used to say he could fix the Imperium. I remember you all believing them." I forced the smallest, cruelest smile I could manage onto my lips. "I remember your face when you finally figured out he was lying."

I expected a slap for that, at the minimum. I expected cursing, spitting, maybe a stabbing—two, if she was really feeling up to it. But what I got, after she gave me that long, cold stare of hers, was worse.

I held my breath as her hand reached out and took a step backward and found only stone behind me. I stood, stock-still, as her hand—those thorns jutting from her fingers, her knuckles—trailed across my shoulder, toward my throat, and rested there contemplatively for a moment before sliding carefully down my chest. They drummed thoughtfully on my stomach for a moment before slithering over to my arm. And there, beneath the cloth of my sleeve, upon the muscle of my bicep, she lay a single, thorny digit.

And then came the blood.

She pressed it in slowly. I could feel flesh part, sinew open, blood flow beneath the talon as her claw found its way into my flesh. I could feel my body shake with the scream I refused to give her. I could feel the chill of her eyes, of her voice, as she looked on me and whispered:

"How does it feel, Sal?"

She twisted her talon. I nearly bit my tongue off to keep from screaming. You'd have thought, maybe, that I'd be mad for preferring to drown in my own blood than give her a single note of a shriek. But if you did, you didn't know Galta the Thorn.

"I still get new ones, you know." She spoke calmly, not so much as raising an eyebrow as the blood seeped out onto her finger. "I just wake up and my face isn't what it looked like when I went to sleep; my fingers don't look right; my body isn't the way I remember it."

I wanted to retort. I wanted to say something clever. And, if I wasn't a good twist of a knuckle away from shitting myself, I might have. But if I opened my mouth, the only thing that was going to come out was a lot of crying—not the pretty kind.

"Years of chugging potions, just to keep my body functioning so it could make more power, more magic for the Imperium." She shook her head. "I still did it. We all did it. Me, Taltho, Vraki." She narrowed her eyes. "Jindu."

Hearing that name didn't hurt as much as the talon. But it came close. And when she pulled her claw free and left that weeping hole in my arm, that name was still wedged inside my skin like a blade.

"We served the Imperium, faithfully, loyally, and without hesitation." She held up that bloodied digit. "And in exchange, we asked only one thing."

"*Understanding*," Taltho rasped from the darkness.

"The old emperors, they understood," Galta said. "They knew what the Lady Merchant asked of us. They knew the price we paid to build the Imperium, to keep it safe. Even if they weren't fighting the wars, they knew what we were giving up to do so."

A look of shock crossed her face, as though she could barely believe it even as she spoke it.

"But a nul? A nul *emperor*?" she asked. "What would he know of sacrifice? What would he know of Barter? He'd sit on his little throne that we won for him and never know what we gave up so he could warm his ass with our blood." Her face contorted in rage as she looked at her finger, red with my blood. "I never know who I'm looking at in the mirror anymore. I can never touch anyone without hurting them. I *paid* the Lady, I *paid* the Imperium, and what was *my* reward?"

"Power," I grunted through the pain. "More than most people have, or ever will."

"What would you know of it, either?" she sneered at me. "You knew nothing of sacrifice, what we went through. But Vraki did. That's why he was going to give us a new emperor, a *true* emperor."

"A Scrath," I said. "A monster in a fancy fucking coat." I looked at her through eyes hot with fever pain. "And he's going to do it again. He's going to kill children to do it."

She didn't deny it. She didn't even flinch when I said it.

"He's going to look out for us," she said. "No one else will."

"No one else *needs* to," I spat out. "You fucking *can't die*. You *have* your power. What more do you need? A kiss on the forehead?"

"Don't fucking talk to me like you're a saint," she snarled, thorns clicking as her brows furrowed. "I know what you've done to earn your name. I know who you've killed. I know how many are dead. What the fuck makes you different than us save that we've got a vision and you've got however much metal they give you?"

I straightened up. I looked her dead in the eyes. And if she was going to kill me, then I hoped she was ready to be staring at these eyes every time she closed her own.

"Because they tell stories about me," I said. "And they'll tell the story, one day, of when I put a blade in you, in Taltho, in every last one of you. They'll say Sal the Cacophony watched Galta the Thorn's corpse hit the dirt. They'll say she turned around and never spoke your name again."

Galta, like I said, was paranoid. She lives her life in pain and it made her cautious. But paranoia isn't careful, the same way panic isn't self-preservation. If all you think about is pain, all you see is the ways the world can hurt you, and all you want to do is hurt it first.

Just like Galta wanted to do when she reached down to my belt she wore around her waist, tore the Cacophony from his holster, and put it up against my head.

And I had to hide my grin. She knew the name of the gun, I'd wager, but she didn't know the gun himself. But I did. I could feel his heat as the barrel pressed against my brow. I could feel the smile in his metal. And I knew what he was going to do once she tried to pull that trigger.

But she didn't.

A hand wrapped in bandages appeared on Galta's shoulder. Taltho stepped out of the shadows, looming over her. He turned his bloodshot eyes upon her and rasped.

"Remember."

And Galta looked at him. And I could see her finger twitch and her face tremble as she swallowed back the urge to do it. And I had to fight down the urge to scream when she lowered the Cacophony.

"We weren't here for you, you're right," Galta said. "But he knew you were going to come. And he told us we should kill you." She looked at me, scrutinizing. "Vraki said to make it slow. Painful."

I waited for the second part of that thought, whether it was going to be a word or a knife in my gut.

"But Jindu asked us not to."

It was words. But I wish it had been the knife.

That name cut me just as deep. And what came flowing out...

Jindu's voice, laughing and smiling. His eyes, bright and curious and with no room for war. And his face, just as sharp as it ever was. After all this time, I could still recall it, trace it in my head like it was just one more scar on my body. And I wondered if he remembered my face. And if he did, if he remembered what it looked like when he saw me last.

"I said you didn't deserve it."

Galta wrapped a thorned hand around my arm, pulled me deeper into the mine. My legs, shaking and bloodless, could hardly resist as she hauled me into the darkness.

"I said you'd kill us all one day," she said, "like you said you would." She paused, bitterness creeping into her next words. "Like you killed Kresh."

"You know about that, huh?" I asked.

"I know Vraki sent Kresh after you. I know you're here and Kresh isn't." The anger crept back into her voice. "So yeah, I know he's dead."

"Then you know the rest of you are, too," I replied coldly.

"Maybe," she said. "Or maybe you take your own advice. Maybe you look at the people you killed and decided you had enough. Maybe you take this chance Jindu asked us to give you and do something with it." She glanced my way. "I know what Taltho made you see. I know who you thought you were shooting."

"*Disturbing*," Taltho rasped, following us.

My brow furrowed. My jaw clenched. It wasn't Liette, I told myself. It was a shadow, a trick, a bunch of dust and lies. It wasn't Liette.

I hadn't killed Liette.

I wasn't that woman. Not yet.

"If you think you're going to lecture me on killing," I muttered, "just fucking kill me now and spare me."

We came to a sudden stop. Galta dragged me to stand before her.

"Jindu asked us not to. We agreed."

She gave me a sharp shove. I staggered two steps forward. The third hit nothing but darkness and empty air.

"Don't make us liars now, Sal."

There was so much I still wanted to tell her. I wanted to tell her Vraki could be the smartest man in the world, Jindu the quickest, Galta and Taltho and all the other names on my list the greatest mages who ever lived and it wouldn't matter.

They were all still going to be dead.

I tried to find my balance, but my arms were tied behind me. I tried to curse her, but all that came out of my mouth was a scream.

Then I saw the steam rising off the hand clutching the Cacophony. I felt the heat radiating from him.

Took him fucking long enough.

Galta shrieked, dropped the gun. She lashed out, driving me backward. I fell. The Cacophony bounced off the rock and followed me as we both tumbled back into a great, yawning darkness.

And together, we disappeared.

THIRTY-FOUR

SOMEWHERE DARK

M y dream starts beautifully. And that's how I know it's a
nightmare.

I open my eyes and he's standing there. He stood that way he
does, effortlessly tall—his back straight as the sword at his hip, his
eyes locked on a horizon so far away I can't see it, but it all looks so
easy for him.

I guess for Jindu everything came easy.

He raised a perfect hand to a perfect brow and he looked down
over a valley I'd never seen before. The wind stirred the grasses,
made a tapestry of green that shuddered and sighed like a living
thing. Clouds, so white they barely held back the sun, drifted lazily
overhead. And the breeze fell silent when he spoke.

"Where's it going to be?"

His voice was deep, and so solid you could lean on it.

I stood beside him. I stared down into the valley, to the little river
winding its way from the hills into the lake, a single blue thread in
my green tapestry. I pointed to a flat stretch of land right beside it.

"Right there." I had to speak loud to be heard over the wind.
"Two stories."

"Two?"

"What? Don't I deserve two?"

"You deserve twenty," he laughed. "But the land isn't level enough for that."

"I'd bring in a couple of mages, move some earth, sand it down until you could balance a glass of wine on it."

"All right, all right. Two stories. What else?"

"An art gallery in the back. A nice, deep cellar for wine, naturally. A bed big enough that I'll have to file a permit for it." I scratched my cheek and I couldn't feel a single scar. "Two kitchens. Two dining rooms. One guest room."

"Why only one?"

"Three guest rooms tells people I'm ready for them at any time. It encourages them to drop in anytime they please. I don't need that. I could be doing anything in there."

"Like what?" At my glare, he grinned, held his hands up. "All right, all right. Why not two, then?"

"Two guest rooms is no good, either. A lady with two guest rooms is a lady who enjoys people's company. It says, 'Come on by, I have some friends I want you to meet.' Who's got time for that shit?"

"Reasonable. What does one say?"

"One guest room says I'll put your ass up for a *little* bit, but don't get comfortable and don't come without a bottle of something expensive."

"You've thought about this."

"Since the day I joined." I pointed to a spot to the left. "Over there, a livery and corral for riding birds." I pointed to the right. "There, a garden." I pointed to the river. "There, a little dock with a little boat to row down to the lake."

Jindu nodded slowly, taking it all in. And with those big eyes of his, that could see anything, anywhere, I knew he was seeing it. A smile tugged at his lips, turned into a laugh.

"Birdshit," he said.

"What?"

I hated how petulant I sounded.

"No, it's beautiful, but... it's not you, is it?" He looked at me and smiled. "Okay, the bird corral is and the wine cellar, sure. But you'd never use the kitchens, you would never have enough company to justify *one* dining room, let alone two, and the boat? Really?"

"I like boats."

"You like *big* boats. The kind we ride on missions. On that river, you'd have some kind of gondola like they have in Cathama's canals." He held up his hands, grinning. "Don't get me wrong. It's a Cathama noblelady's wet dream."

He held his hand out to me.

"But it's not you."

I studied his hand. His palms were creased, calloused where they should be from years of holding a blade, letting a hilt dance across his hand like a living thing. But the tips of his fingers were still soft, the kind that could pluck a harp, the kind that wouldn't feel coarse when they slid down your skin.

Not a killer's hand. An expert's hand. So pale and clean that I couldn't ever imagine it sullied.

I took it.

I always did.

"You asked what I wanted once the war was over," I replied. "I mean, if we're going nuts, I'll take the Empress's crown jewels, the sages' secret manuscripts, the biggest, loudest gun the Revolutionaries can make, and you, atop a carriage full of metal pulled by two big white birds." I winked. "But I thought I'd keep it realistic."

"And realistic to you is…a house?"

"A *nice* house."

"You could have more."

"You didn't ask what I could have. You asked what I wanted."

"I did." He laid his hand on top of mine. It felt warm. "And you want me?"

"I want everything." I looked long to the sky overhead. The sun began to set. The clouds became orange with its dying light. "And you."

His smile was the opposite of the rest of him. Its softness, its tenderness, looked so out of place on a man who carried his blade so close. But when his smile vanished, the empty place where it had been was a frown, sharp and cruel and a perfect fit for him.

I was afraid to ask. I always was. He could never just be angry, just show me what he was thinking with his face. He always let that frown creep in. He always made me guess.

"What's wrong?" I asked.

"It's a nice dream," he said, soft as a dagger leaving its sheath. "But the war won't end. Not while the Imperium is still corrupted."

"Not again," I sighed. "Can we talk about something else for once?"

"Something else?" That sheath-soft voice became a blade, drawn and naked and screeching. "*Something else* besides the Imperium we served, that our friends fought and died for, being twisted by a . . . a *nul?*"

"He's the Emperor."

"He shouldn't be. That shouldn't happen. Vraki told me—" I looked away. But I still felt that sharp frown. "What?"

"I don't want to hear about Vraki. Not here. Not ever."

"He has a plan to—"

"*Ever*," I snarled. "We came here to talk about the future. Not the Imperium and not whatever that fucking freak thinks is wrong with it."

"I *am* thinking about the future. I'm thinking about a future we mages built, a future we mages *protected*, a future where the Imperium is safe and you're safe within it."

I felt something prick on my finger. I looked down. A droplet of blood blossomed upon my fingertip where he had touched me.

"And for that. For you."

He drew his fingers down across my wrist. Bright red furrows appeared in my flesh, carved by the barest touch. I felt the panic before I felt the pain and tried to pull my hand away. He held me so gently, his fingers just barely pinching around my wrist. I could see my blood leak down those soft tips, pool in that creased palm.

"I would give..."

I grabbed my hand. I dug my feet into the earth to pull away. The ground turned to black mud beneath me, choked with grime and the dead. The clouds swirled overhead, gorging themselves on the dying sunlight, becoming as bright and red as the blood staining my hand.

"Everything."

His voice was a thousand miles away, to that faraway place only he could see. He grabbed me by the shoulder. His fingers sliced through my coat, my fabric, my skin. I felt blood burst beneath his touch. I felt the skin part away like cloth beneath scissors. I looked at him as he leaned forward, his mouth full of knives and every toothsome blade perfectly polished.

He pressed his lips against mine.

I screamed.

And I choked on my own blood.

THIRTY-FIVE

VIGIL

Breath comes first. My lips parted. I sucked in a cold lungful of stale air and dust. It filled me like a living thing, flooding my lungs, making sure that I was alive enough for the next part.

Pain comes second.

My body woke up before I did, the aches and agonies crawling through me on spider legs. The landing had been hard, but the fall had been brief; no bones felt broken, at first impression.

But it was hard to tell, what with my arms being twisted behind my back.

To my credit, I managed only to cry out a little as I worked my wrists free of the ropes. I could hear my bones pop back into place, rubbed the agony of my arms and wrists as I pulled them back in front of me.

Tight knots, they had rubbed my wrists raw. But they hadn't been good ones. Galta never could do anything right that wasn't killing people.

Turns out, she was even shit at that.

I slowed my breathing, let the pain work its way out of me, settle down to a dull hangover of an ache.

After that, the world came back to me in pieces, a broken window I put back together. I struggled to my hands and knees, felt the cold stone under my fingers. I breathed deep of stale cavern air. And, as I got to my feet, I could feel the darkness closing in around me. It was alive down here, a writhing, curious thing that slithered around me, coiled up close to me, whispered in my ear.

And it was his voice I heard.

I wish I could have told you it was Taltho, some lingering nightmare from his magic. That's not how it works, though. Nightmages can see what's in your head, but not your heart. They can toy with your fears but they can only guess at what really hurts you. The real pain, the ones hidden under all the scars and bad dreams...

The only person who can hurt you that way is you.

I could see him all around me, fading in and out of the nightmare he had followed me out of. He was a shattered mirror of a man. I could see him only in fragments: his eyes bright and cheerful, his hands expert and powerful, his lips always moving, always whispering, always trying to tell me something. And if I listened, I could have figured out what.

But, at that moment, something else called to me. And he spoke louder.

I felt a flash of pain, older and closer than any of my scars. It began small at first—an itch in my palm I couldn't scratch. But every breath I took, it stoked itself, a fire spreading through my fingers, my wrists, up my arm. With each step I took, it got worse, an inferno that ate all my lesser pains for fuel. By the time I fell to my knees, it was burning inside me.

And I reached into the darkness. And I felt my fingers wrap around a wooden grip. The burning dissipated in an instant. And in the wake of that terrible pain, I could feel the Cacophony's smile, as if to say...

"What kept you?"

I didn't smile back as I picked him up. I didn't need to. We'd done this before, he and I. Separated, be it by darkness or miles or worlds, we always found each other the same way. And we'd keep on finding each other until every last name was crossed off my list.

So I figured we'd better get to it.

I walked forward, hand outstretched until I found the rough stone of a wall and began to follow it out. The Cacophony's call burned away the lesser pains: the bumps and aches and bloodied scratches Galta had left me. Not that it felt *good*, mind you, but at least I could think about something other than how beat up I felt.

Something like Vraki.

But even thinking about him made me hurt.

I was so close. Everything had made sense. Summoning a Scrath is a complex thing: it needs a ritual, a host, and a lot of fucking power. Vraki had everything but that last bit. He was going to find it in the Husks, surely. He was going to revisit the site of his greatest victory, the day he walked beneath a sky full of red clouds and bloodied the Revolution's nose with a single wave of his hand.

It all sounded so intelligent when I thought it out. How the fuck did it go awry?

Vraki wasn't there. What's more, he knew I was coming. He knew where I was. He had sent Kresh to kill me, after all. How did he know where I was? How did he know I was tracking him?

And where had he fled?

Had to get back to the surface. Had to find the others. Had to find Congeniality, Cavric, Liette…

Liette.

Liette, with those shy eyes behind those big spectacles. Liette, with that too-rare smile I had fought to see so many times. Liette…

Cold and on the ground with a hole in her throat.

Stop that. I shook my head. I gritted my teeth. *That was Taltho. Not her. Not you. Not real. You didn't kill her.*

And, again, that little thought that I wished to hell I could say wasn't mine, whispered to me.

Yet.

I wanted to tell myself that wasn't true, that I'd never hurt her. But then I thought back to how she looked at me when she turned around and disappeared without saying a word. How broken I must have been in her eyes, how jagged and sharp I must have been for her to cut herself on me.

I wanted to tell myself that I had a list. I wanted to tell myself that only the names on the list were the ones who were going to get hurt. But I'd been doing this long enough to know that was a lie.

So did she.

And my thoughts broke like a dam with too many leaks.

"What am I doing wrong?"

Liette.

"What did he do to you?"

Cavric.

"For you, I would give everything."

Jindu.

And I felt like I was choking on my own blood again. I felt like I was drowning on dry land. I felt like I wanted to tear my throat out so I could breathe again. I felt like I wanted to take out my gun and start shooting until things made sense. Failing all that, I did the only other thing I could think of.

"WILL EVERYONE SHUT THE FUCK UP?"

I screamed.

"...will everyone..."

And something screamed back.

"...shut up fuck shut up the shut..."

Every part of me froze. My blood went cold in my veins. My muscles went rigid. My eyes refused to blink. Even my heart fell quiet, too afraid to beat lest something out there hear it.

In the vast and empty darkness before me, I could hear something. Talking. Whining. Whimpering.

"...everyoneeveryoneEVERYONEeveryoneeveryone..."

Taltho's magic, maybe, something he left behind when he messed with my head. Maybe an errant thought that finally leaked out of a hole in my head. Maybe just my imagination, the pain making me hear things.

Or maybe I wasn't alone down here.

Given the fact that I held the Cacophony a little tighter, I'll let you decide which one I was leaning toward.

I picked my steps carefully as I made my way along the rough wall. I held my breath, made my footfalls as silent as I could. In the long dark, I couldn't hear anything else but the empty air and the old rocks. And neither of them said a word.

A light blossomed in the distance, pale and cold. I held myself steady as I moved toward it, kept my breathing shallow and my finger ready. It grew with every step until I emerged from the darkness.

Into what, I didn't know.

A vast cavern sprawled out before me. High overhead, silvery rays of moonlight pierced through gaps in a rocky cavern ceiling. They reached into the gloom, and from the stones, something reached back.

Violet. Pale and beautiful and veined with white, like the color of lilacs holding their breath just before winter kills them. They mapped the cavern walls, stretched across the stones in delicate spiderwebbing patterns, veins of ore that glowed with a faint, crystalline light. It almost looked alive, straining to escape the rocks that held it prisoner, sighing ethereal light when it realized it couldn't.

Severium.

The ore that turned the Revolution from an unruly pack of nuls to a war machine; it webbed the cavern's floor in untapped veins, its glow pulsating like the beating of a metal heart.

It illuminated a great pit below, ridden with the remains of what had been left behind: half-collapsed scaffoldings, abandoned tools and carts, the occasional body left cold in the dark. But hidden in the stones, I could see more lights, colder and crueler and far more familiar.

Relics. I saw their woven stone shapes, impossibly wrought from a material older and darker than the stone they were embedded in. Engines, weapons, great suits of armor and things I'd never seen before in Revolutionary hands—at least a dozen of the glowing things jutted out, trapped in the stone and so close to freedom, like reaching hands.

This, then, was why the Imperium had sent their best to Vigil.

Did the people above know? I wondered. Did they know that this was all beneath their feet? Did they know they had been given a death sentence?

I tried not to think about it. I tried to keep my eyes on the path ahead of me.

But even with all the light, I could see the shadows: the stalagmites and stalactites jutting from the rocks like teeth in the maw of a great beast, the lurching shapes of buried Relics, the long black cloaks cast by the pale light. And, in any one of them, something could be waiting to kill me.

Not that that stopped me—I wouldn't get a lot done if I hesitated every time someone meant to murder me.

From the tunnel where I had emerged, the floor gave out into a long, stone slope. I took a step onto it, trying to pick out footholds in the dim light. I realized what a bad idea that was right about the time I slipped and fell on my ass. I bit back a cry as I slid, uncontrollably, down the slope and landed hard on the cavern floor below.

I rolled to my knees, held the Cacophony up in both hands, pointed out into the dark.

No movement. No voices. Nothing.

Maybe it had been magic. Or maybe I was just going insane. Either would have been preferable.

I lowered my gun as I rose to my feet. I squinted into the dark, peering among the rocks. Weaving its way in a jagged, haphazard path was an old miners' trail with no obvious route or end.

Still, it wasn't like I could go back the way I came. With no other choice and my gun held close, I started to pick my way along the trails.

I winced every time my boots hit the stone. In the silence of the cavern, even the softest fall of my feet sounded deafening. The darkness swallowed sound here—no murmur of wind or grumble of errant stones. You would think I'd have found that comforting.

But my body was held so tense it felt I'd squeeze my skeleton out of my mouth. Between each step, I was listening. For the sound of something following behind me, of something stalking the stones above me, of something muttering in the dark—I didn't know.

Do this sort of thing long enough, a lot of things stop scaring you. Magic, weapons, even the beasts of the Scar—the big man-eating sons of bitches that can rip a body in two pieces and swallow one before the other hits the ground—don't scare you if you know how they work.

Forgive the cliché, but if I'm afraid of anything, it's the unknown.

Not the grand, cosmic "Where do we go when we die?" unknown— I know where I'm headed. No, it's the cold-knife-in-the-belly unknown I fear. The feeling that wrenches your guts when you know something's wrong, but your head and your heart conspire to trick you into thinking that everything's all right. That unknown, the knowledge that something bad is going to happen, you just don't know what it is…

Or who's going to do it.

That I fear.

I fought it the best I could. I kept a steady heart and a clear head. And both of them told me what my gut already knew: I couldn't keep picking down this trail and hope I'd find a way out before something else found me. I had to take a chance.

And I found it the minute I looked up.

Beneath a shaft of soft silver light, at the center of a clearing in the cavern, a rock loomed tall above the rest of his gray, silent brothers. Center of the cavern, good visibility, with a command of the surroundings—it would be a great vantage to get an idea of where I was.

Or a great point to be spotted by whatever was lurking down here, then stalked, killed, and summarily dismembered, disemboweled, and/or devoured, depending on your point of view.

But hey, you know me. I'm an optimistic woman.

I slunk to the rock, found it pocked enough for me to climb. I scrambled up the face of the rock, uncomfortably aware of how clear a target I was beneath this light. But when I reached the top, it was hard to say that it wasn't worth it.

From up here, I could see the cavern entwined. The metal glittered beneath the light, reaching out invitingly to the shadows with silver, delicate fingers. And the shadows, shy and unassuming, reached back to wrap black hands around those sparkling lights in a tender embrace.

Even with the threat of death looming over me, I admitted it was beautiful.

But not half as beautiful as the sight I saw at the far edge of the cavern.

I wouldn't have noticed it if not for this little dance between the light and the dark. There, against the wall of the cavern, was a deeper sort of shadow than the ones painting the cavern floor. And as I squinted, I could see that it wasn't just a shadow, but a hole carved into the rock.

A way out. Or a way to nowhere. But it was a way. And the only way I had left to me.

I bit back my glee as I slid down the rock, but I couldn't help feeling at least a little excited. I was almost out of here. And from there, it wouldn't be hard to track down Galta, put a bullet in her head, get my list back, and cross one name off.

Things were starting to look up.

Which would explain why, as I hit the bottom of the rock, I saw a shadow emerging into the clearing.

Tall and thin and twisted like a withered tree, it staggered forward on unsteady legs. It turned a pendulous head toward the shaft of light and, with a voice that tore itself from a pair of rasping lips, croaked:

"Hello…"

THIRTY-SIX

MINES OF VIGIL

I want to tell you it was a man.

It was about the right height, about the right build, stood on two legs. I want to tell you it was something normal, just another guy with a grudge I would have to take down. I could handle a man.

I've gotten quite good at killing them.

Men didn't make my blood go cold when I looked at them.

I don't know how else to describe it. It stood at the perimeter of the light, just a withered and frail shadow. But even without seeing it, I could feel ice freeze in my veins. That cold knife in my belly twisted, sent that frigid chill coursing through my bowels, my muscles, every part of me until I couldn't move.

It would see me if I moved.

It swung its head back and forth and the movement was... wrong. It twitched and bobbed in an unnatural way, like a teakettle on a stick. Was it looking for something? Was that just how it moved? Or was it simply trying to make up its mind on how best to kill me?

"HeeeelllloooOOOOO..."

If my blood ran cold at the sight of it, my heart damn near stopped at the sound of it. Its voice came out all wrong, like a bleating sheep trying to figure out how to speak. I couldn't tell if it was asking a question, making a greeting, or just screaming.

It swiveled again, turned its back to me. I took another chance.

I found the last shred of warmth inside me, forced it to carry me behind the rock. I held the Cacophony close to my chest, like a child holding her doll. I could feel him burning in my hand; I'd be scared of that sensation again someday. But not now.

Now, I needed him.

I shut my eyes. I couldn't bear to look at that dead-tree shape again, couldn't bear the thought of it. But when I heard that shuffling step, like big feet dragged across the stones, I couldn't think of anything else. I heard it walking. I heard its voice.

"GLORY."

It shrieked a single word out of that bleating, croaking mouth. But the sound didn't echo. The entire cavern stood quiet, afraid to contradict the thing.

"...glory...glory to...glorygloryglory GLORYglorygloryglory...to the Rev...Revo...glory to the..."

Was it speaking? Screaming? Muttering? I couldn't tell. The words came out hesitant, like it was trying to figure out what they meant, tasting them for significance.

"...tenth morning...emergency. EMERGENCY. Scourge. Scourgescourgescourge...identity. Glory to...tell wife...wife...wifewifewifewife...tell wife...Long life. Wifelifelonglifewife."

I couldn't tell you how I understood what it was saying. I couldn't tell you how I picked out the words from that mad, bleating gibber coming out of its mouth. But I knew the words it spoke.

And I recognized them.

"...glory...to...the...Revolution..."

Where my blood had been cold before, it now burned hot. I could feel that rush of panic, that old animal fear we never left behind when we built our cities, surging through my veins, begging me to run, to scream, to fall down and cry.

Fuck me, I knew what that thing was.

Maybe it was instinct that made me dare to peer out around the corner, the desire to see my foe. Maybe it was that fear, telling me to know where it was so I could flee it. But I think, in my heart, it was a morbid curiosity.

I had never seen a Scrath up close.

It stood at the center of the clearing, beneath the silver light. And it was a man.

Or it had been, once. It was tall and dark of skin, naked but for a tattered blue jacket hanging around its torso. It had a head, two arms, two legs. But that was all of its humanity that remained.

Its limbs were withered and twisted, bent at wrong angles and possessing extra joints. Its body trembled and shuddered as it staggered from foot to foot, as though it couldn't quite get the hang of standing up. Its head was... backward, like someone had grabbed its jaw in one hand and its nose in the other and pulled them in opposite directions. Its mouth hung open as a barely discernible mass of broken teeth and writhing tongue. Its eyes bulged out of its sockets and rotated around, unblinking.

The thing looked like it had simply taken a man, put him on as a suit, and found it couldn't quite figure out how he was supposed to fit.

"Tell my... my wife... wifewifewife... Long Life... to the General... tenth morning."

It spoke without moving its lips. It forced the words out of its throat, its tongue lolling as it did. And I winced.

Nothing about summoning a Scrath is easy, but pulling it into our world is as close as it gets. Once it's out, it has a good chance of simply exploding, killing everything within a mile. If it doesn't do that, it sometimes goes haywire and starts killing, shrieking, eating everything it can get its hands on. But if, by some miracle, it doesn't do either of those things, it can't survive in our world.

It needs a host.

A host like Agent Relentless.

The man Cavric had come to Stark's Mutter to find. The man

who had the bad fucking luck to run into Vraki the Gate. The man who wasn't a man. Not anymore. Now he was just a sack of misshapen meat that the Scrath rode around in.

I'd feel sorry for the poor bastard if I wasn't sure the damn thing would kill me in an instant.

To look at it, you'd be unnerved, maybe even disgusted, but you wouldn't know what it could do. Though it might look frail, a Scrath wasn't of this world. Things like bullets or blades didn't bother it. It could leap higher and run faster than any human and tear boulders apart and trees from the earth without blinking...

"Glory... glory to... glory to... General... my wife?"

Its face twitched. It couldn't remember the words. And, frustrated, it threw its head back.

Oh, also, they can scream.

"aaaaaaaaAAAAAAAAAAAAAAAAAHHHHH—"

Really fucking loud.

I put my hands to ears that felt like they were going to explode in bright sprays of blood. I shut my eyes to keep them from rattling out of their sockets. The cavern shook, screaming right along with that damn thing, sending rocks falling in waves and dust falling in sheets. Everything in me screamed to run. It was only because my muscles still felt frozen that I didn't.

After a time, its voice abated. Silence fell over the cavern again. Through the ringing in my ears, I could hear it shuffle this way and that as it looked around.

"... hello..."

I could hear it walking on shaking, trembling limbs as it wandered off into the darkness.

"... helllloooOOoooo..."

I could hear it fading, disappearing.

"... hellohelloHELLOhellohellohello..."

Until it was gone.

And only then, I felt brave enough to speak.

"Fuck."

Or squeak, at least. My voice came out in a hushed whisper, but it came and I couldn't stop it.

"Fuck, fuck, *fuck*."

That was what Galta and Taltho were here for. They weren't lying in wait for me. They were after *this* thing. Vraki must have fucked it up somehow and they had chased it all the way here. This thing had been the result of all that death at Stark's Mutter.

Vraki would have wanted them to retrieve it. But when they had chased it down here, they probably saw no reason to go down after something that could just as easily rip them apart.

Or me.

That shit Galta. Said she'd spare me and threw me down here with that thing.

I'd have been angrier if I didn't know what this truly meant. One Scrath was difficult to control. Two would have been impossible. Vraki hadn't been able to control this one, so he'd turned it loose.

Which meant he was ready to summon his new one.

And all those kids he had kidnapped as hosts were about to...

I shook that thought from my head. I couldn't afford to dwell on it. Or to dwell in here. I had to get the fuck out, Scrath or no.

I flipped open the Cacophony's chamber, counted the shells. *Hellfire. Hoarfrost. Discordance.* Good on their own.

Against a Scrath? Who the fuck knew? But then, if it came to the point where I had to shoot the thing, I was probably already dead.

Low to the ground, I hurried through the cavern, moving swift as I dared. Somewhere in the dark, I could hear the Scrath's bleating, croaking gibberish, the shuffling of its withered feet. It made no effort to hide where it was and you might have thought that'd have given me some comfort.

But if you did, I'd say you haven't been paying attention.

Scraths aren't a part of this world. They don't *fit*. Their sounds come out all wrong and nature just doesn't know what to do with them. They don't cause an echo, a reverberation, anything. It spoke one word and sounded like it was a thousand miles away; it spoke another and sounded like it was right next to me. The damn thing could be anywhere. Across the cavern. Looming up behind me.

Or right the fuck in front of me.

The shadows twitched. I leapt behind a nearby rock, pressed myself to it. I peered out and saw it, its dead-tree shape shambling across the trail, twisted head lolling on a too-thin neck as it emerged from behind one rock and disappeared behind another. I waited the longest minute of my life before I dared to move again.

For whatever good that would do me.

You can't predict a Scrath. You can't listen for them. You can't smell them. And if you see them coming, you're already fucking dead. The best you can do is wait for those spider legs running down your spine, that cold knife twisting that tells you something's about to go wrong, and hope that's enough to get you out in one piece.

And *that* was all assuming any of the shit I was telling myself could be trusted. Where Scraths were concerned, our knowledge came secondhand from severed fingers. Over a thousand years, the sages of the Imperium had only been able to piece together whatever fragments of knowledge they could salvage from a Scrath's victims. I had no idea if any of this was true, if any of it would help me.

I'm used to no help. I'm used to the odds being stacked against me. And I wish I could tell you either of those made me less scared.

I wish I could.

I forced my head clear; thinking would only cause that panic in me to well up, cause me to make mistakes. I didn't bother listening to its burbling, bleating voice; it couldn't be trusted, anyway. I let everything seep out of me in a stale, shuddering breath—the fear, the hate, the desire to just curl up and start sobbing—so that there was nothing left in me but a great emptiness waiting to be filled.

When that cold knife came, I was going to feel it.

"... *going* ... *going to* ... *promotion* ... *General rewards* ... *protects* ... *seeseeseeSEEseesee* ..."

I could hear its voice as the faintest of whispers, so far away it might as well be on the other side of the world, let alone the cave. I ignored it, kept my eyes on the end of the cavern.

"...*life*...*better*...*childrenchildrenchildren*...*you'll ssseeeeEEEEEeee*... *wife*...*my wife*..."

I could hear it on the other side of the cavern now, just on the other side of the boulders, voice not raising an echo even as it bellowed, bleated. I pushed my fear out of me, looked up at the dark hole in the wall growing ever bigger.

"...*last*...*last*...*PROMISE*...*we happy*...*will be*...*we*...*so happy*... *so happy*...*you and I and I and I*..."

It kept repeating itself, stuck on that word, and every time it spoke, it sounded somewhere else inside the cavern. I ignored it, all of it, kept moving, kept my head up, my eyes locked. The cavern hole was getting bigger, so close I could almost see inside it. I dared to pick up speed, let myself move faster. My heart was pounding in my chest. My blood was going cold. I felt a stab of fear inside my bowels. I felt—

I froze.

My heart fell silent. My blood stilled. My feet locked.

And I knew it was staring at me.

"...*happy*...*we'll be happy*..."

Slowly, so slowly I could hear the vertebrae in my neck popping, I turned around. And there it was. Standing right behind me in the middle of the trail. It shuddered unsteadily, its dead-tree shape swaying in some imaginary breeze. Its head lolled back and forth, forward and backward, yet it always kept one of those bulging, unblinking, quivering eyes on me.

"...*my wife*..."

Its tongue lolled. The twisted mass of teeth and gums pulled open. Its voice rose to a bleating shriek.

"*MY WIFE.*"

Its arm shot out, stretching impossibly long. I heard the bones snap, the skin stretch as its fingers extended as long as knives, reaching for me. My blood was cold, my body frozen, I couldn't move.

I couldn't.

But he could.

And whether it was me or the Cacophony that pulled up and aimed his grinning barrel at the thing, I didn't care. I pulled the trigger. There was a bright flash of gunfire. The Hellfire shell blazed, flew toward the Scrath, past its reaching fingers, right for the twisted mass of its head.

And then it vanished.

Impossibly quick, the Scrath's arm snapped back, caught the bullet out of midair. It shouldn't have been possible. But then, neither should the Scrath.

The shell exploded in its hand, torrents of flame leaking out between its clenched fingers. What should have been an eruption of red hell was just a few pitiful crimson ribbons. When it unclasped its hand and the spent shell clattered to the ground, there was no visible damage. The skin was blackened, little more than a layer of soot covering it, but it didn't look remotely fazed.

The Scrath just kept staring at its hand, like it couldn't believe what it was seeing. It wasn't hurt. But something, the last shred of the man it wore like a suit, knew that it *should* hurt. Yet it didn't. It was wrong. And it knew it. It knew it didn't fit, didn't belong.

And so…

"*aaaaaaAAAAAAAAAAAAAAAA—*"

It screamed.

The stones shook. The light darkened. The cavern seemed to scream right along with it.

And I was running.

I didn't fight the fear anymore. I let it surge up through me, up through my veins, into my heart, forcing me to move. It carried me down the trail, toward the cavern opening. I couldn't hear my heart pounding or my feet hammering the stone or my breath running short.

I couldn't hear anything over it screaming.

I looked behind me. It was chasing me. Its legs were too long, twisting and bending and cracking as it took massive strides toward me. Its tongue flapped about like a banner in the wind as the scream tore itself out of the Scrath's throat. It drew back a hand, swung it at me. In as much time as it took me to curse, its arm had grown twenty feet long. I ducked as it arced overhead, swung toward a cluster of towering stalagmites.

And went right through them.

It was nothing but a bunch of sinew and bones, but it tore stone apart like it was cotton. The rocks fell into my path; I was going too fast and tripped.

I hit the ground, scrambled to my hands and knees, twisted to land on my rear. I picked the Cacophony up in both hands, aimed him down the trail. In flashes of dying light and fleeing shadows, I saw it. Its teeth and tongue glistening with saliva. Its too-long arms and too-long legs hauling its twisted body toward me. Its quivering, teary eye locked on me.

I pulled the trigger.

Hoarfrost flew, striking it square in the chest. The frost blossomed over it, covered its skin in icy patches. Its step slowed, grew slower with every stride. And by the time its teeth were close enough to my face that I could see the black hole from which its scream died, it was frozen.

Why it worked, I don't know. Maybe it froze because it knew that's what frost did. Or maybe the Cacophony was just stronger than whatever foul magic had called it to this world. I wasn't sure. And if you had asked me if I had cared, I would have punched you in the face and left you to die.

I was running.

I hadn't even taken five steps when I heard the frost begin to crack, the scream start to tear itself out of the ice. By the time I'd taken ten, I heard the ice shards hit the ground and the thing take off running again. But I didn't care. I couldn't care.

I was there.

The cavern hole loomed up before me. I could see it and the

ancient wooden beams that held it upright. A secondary mine entrance, it must have been started by the Revolution and never finished.

Considerate of them.

I hauled myself up onto the ledge where it was, ran through the hole, into the darkness. The stone groaned around me as the light faded behind me. Blackness swallowed me whole, eating sound and sight alike, until I couldn't see my own hand in front of my face.

Let alone the Scrath's.

Fingers wrapped around my ankle. I tripped, fell. I twisted onto my back. I couldn't see it.

"...*hurts...hurts too much...need new...*"

But I could hear it.

"...*new skin...new body...new new new...*"

And I could feel it pulling me.

"*myskinmyskinmyskinMYSKINMYSKINMYSKIN—*"

One shot left. Discordance. If I hit it in the face, it might release me. But I couldn't see it. I didn't know how far back it was. I couldn't aim, I couldn't—

The Cacophony burned in my hand, whispered an angry secret that only I could understand.

And I realized I didn't need to aim.

Not at it.

I slid along the ground as the Scrath pulled me closer, back into the cavern. I tilted the Cacophony up. I aimed toward what I thought was the ceiling. I pulled the trigger.

And everything went to shit in a real big hurry.

A bright flash of gunfire. I saw the Scrath's quivering eyes and flapping tongue for just a moment. The shell hit a wooden beam holding the ceiling up. Discordance erupted in a burst of sound. The shock waves tore into the wall, sent me flying backward, caused the Scrath's grip to loosen.

It screamed.

But the mountain screamed louder.

Beams wailed, broke. Earth groaned, shifted. Boulders sobbed, fell. The ceiling came crashing down. I hauled myself to my feet, started running. Dust fell around me in sheets. I kept running. Wood splintered and fell and rocks buried it. I kept running. A cold light blossomed before me.

I didn't stop running until my legs gave out and my breath ran out and I fell to my knees in the sand and gasped for air.

When I looked behind me, there was no more tunnel, just a sheer rock face and a mess of stones at the bottom where a tunnel had once been. The mountain groaned as it settled down, and even through the great sigh of rock, I thought I could still hear the Scrath.

Screaming.

I paused, watching that pile of rocks, hearing the creature shrieking through it. My heart wouldn't start beating again, as though it expected me to turn around and see the Scrath there, waiting for me. Seconds of wordless agony passed. They turned to minutes. And soon, the sound of the Scrath passed, too.

And I was left with the wailing of the wind and the sound of my own laughter.

I didn't know why—it wasn't funny. Maybe it was a release, the sound of my nerves prying themselves apart from the twisted bundle they had become. Or maybe I just didn't know what else to do.

So I kept laughing.

I turned and I started walking away from the rubble, trudging down the slope of the mountain, my boots sinking into the sand as I did. The winds moaned around me, as though the Husks were protesting my rudeness in laughing.

And I couldn't stop.

I kept walking. But for some reason, it got harder with each step. My boots were harder to pull out of the sand. My legs shook more each time my feet came down. It felt like something in me, something important, was draining out of me, left in puddles in each footprint I left behind.

And I kept laughing. And each time I did, it hurt.

I looked down at my hands. In one, the Cacophony. In the other, my blood.

And that was all I had left. A piece of metal and pieces of me.

No magic scarf. No list. No leads. No Liette.

Liette.

I don't know why, but I wanted her right then. I wanted her near me, to touch her and feel something other than cold, other than pain. Part of me thought that I would look up and see her, waiting there for me, ready to forgive me. That part of me needed her, needed a lot of things.

But when I looked up and saw only the wastes of the Husks stretched out before me, that part of me fell silent.

And I was left with nothing.

Liette was gone. Cavric, too. Jindu was gone, a name that made my scars ache, a bad dream I couldn't get rid of. Galta was gone. Taltho was gone. Vraki was... was...

I didn't know. I didn't know where he had gone. He hadn't been where he was supposed to be, where I was supposed to kill him, where I was supposed to save his sacrifices. I didn't know where he was or how to find or how... how to...

I couldn't remember when I had fallen to my knees. I couldn't remember when the laughter had made my throat run hoarse. I couldn't remember when the hot tears started trailing down my cheeks, over my scars.

The fear left me. That rush of blood that had kept my legs moving and heart pounding in the dark tunnels, it just... ebbed out of me like blood from a wound. And with it went my hate, my sorrow, my anger. And when it was all gone, there was nothing left inside of me. Nothing to keep me going.

No reason to stand back up.

The Cacophony fell from my hand, suddenly too heavy for me to hold. My head felt like iron, craning back on my neck as my mouth pulled itself open and I let out a scream into the night. But even that felt empty, like I didn't even have enough in me to scream.

And I wondered if this was how it would feel when I crossed that last name off my list, when I put that last bullet in that last head. All this time, I had thought I'd have something after all of it was done—some home to call my own, someone to go with it. But what if this was it? I had no one to shoot, no one to hunt, no one to kill.

What if it was all just emptiness?

I felt something warm. I looked down at my side. Blood ebbed out of a gash. My wound had reopened. From the Scrath? Or the rockfall? I couldn't remember what had done it. I couldn't remember when all that blood had painted my middle red. I knew I had to treat it, to fix it, but I couldn't remember how.

I got to my feet, even though I couldn't feel them under me. I turned toward the horizon, even though I could barely see it through the darkness clouding the corners of my eyes. I started walking.

Even though I didn't see a point.

Pain has a way of dragging time out. You can lose hours, days, years of your life to it, either in fear of it or waiting for it to stop. And so I wasn't sure how long I'd been walking or where I was when the wailing began again.

"Sal…"

Distant voices on the wind called my name, echoing off walls of swirling grit and grime.

"Sal."

That's where I was heading, then. Toward the voices that called me to the black table to answer for my crimes, to face my crimes.

"Would you wait the fuck up?"

Only they were being awfully rude about it.

A flicker of movement caught my eye. A great shadow appeared in the swirling winds, approaching me. I braced myself, anticipating some ghastly specter come to take me back.

That might have smelled better.

Congeniality came stalking out of the sands and paused before me, canting her head to the side as she appraised me. Her avian eyes betrayed no emotion, but I swore she looked almost accusatory.

Which I sure as hell wasn't going to take from a bird who had left me to chase a fucking turkey.

"SAL!"

His voice was distant. His shape was shadowed. But I knew his step, that enthusiastic rush of a man who wasn't afraid to look undignified. He came out of the sheets of grit, waving his hands, concern painted on a face caked with grime and sweat.

Cavric hadn't left.

"Found...the bird..." He came to a slow, wheezing halt, gesturing at Congeniality. "Couldn't find you...or Liette. Boar gone... followed the bird. Didn't know what happened." He stared at the great gash in my side. "Fuck me. What *did* happen?"

I looked at him. I smiled.

And I pitched forward, collapsing on top of him.

THIRTY-SEVEN

THE REDWAY

I know what you're thinking.

"Gosh, she really ought to wear armor or something, given the rate at which she gets injured."

To which I have two answers.

The first being: Fuck you, I look fabulous.

The second, though?

You might notice a running theme among the people trying to kill me. Crazed Revolutionaries with high-powered weapons, men turned into gigantic monsters by a mad god, mages who can make you see ghosts, and creatures who can take magical bullets to the face and not even flinch.

A full suit of plate is of no use against things that can shoot through it, tear it off, or crush you inside it like a tin of potted meat.

You occasionally get some rich fucker who thinks he's going to play Vagrant Hunter, decking himself out in fancy armor that some shady huckster swears is anti-magic. If he's lucky, he gets shot, stabbed, or eaten before he finds out the hard way that no armor can save you from a mage. If he isn't, he gets to die in his nice metal suit before someone pries it off him and sells it for scrap.

Still, I couldn't help but wonder if a big fuck-off sheet of metal between me and whatever's trying to kill me would be useful. Especially if it could have prevented the situation I found myself in.

"You ought to wear armor or something," Cavric said as he daubed the wound at my side with a whiskey-soaked rag. "Or at least a nicer shirt."

"Everyone's got a fucking opinion," I muttered, wincing at the pain.

"Not everyone's got a bloody hole in them, though." I could feel the frown carve itself on Cavric's face as he stared at my wound. "This looks really bad, Sal. I don't even know that much medicine."

"How much *do* you know?"

"Only field medic stuff I was taught in the academy."

"Does any of it involve talking?"

He blinked. "Uh . . . no?"

"Then get on with it."

My back was turned to him as I lay on my side, but I could hear everything he was doing. I heard his weary sigh, I heard him running a needle over the campfire to sterilize it, I heard him thread it, I heard his hand lay on my side to steady me . . .

And then I heard my cry of pain as he started to sew my wound shut.

"Hold. Still," he hissed.

"Stop. Being. Shit at this," I snarled back. I took in a deep breath, bit the pain back. "Fuck. Keep my mind off this."

"How?"

"Tell me something."

"Like about me?" Pleasant surprise played in his voice. "Well, I guess I'd start with my mother. We didn't get the name Proud until she proved her valor by cutting open—"

"No, not about that." I paused. "But hold on to that story, because I do want to hear it." I winced. "Tell me what you found in Vigil."

"I already did."

"Tell me again now that I'm not about to die from blood loss."

"Oh." His voice steadied, along with his hands, as he continued the sutures. "There was no evidence of anything the Revolution might have left behind. The Imperials..." He hesitated, swallowing anger. "Red Cloud...didn't leave anything behind. Anything not broken was ash. But I found a campsite with some supplies. Probably belonged to whoever you found in the mines."

I had told him a bit about what had happened, but not everything. I told him about Galta and Taltho, but not what they had told me. I told him enough about the Scrath, but only enough to keep him focused on stopping another one from coming out. I told him about Liette...

"Sal," he said, "we should go back for her."

And apparently too fucking much.

"She left of her own volition," I muttered.

"And she took the fucking Boar," he said. "Only a Revolutionary should be able to pilot it."

Yeah, she's clever like that, I resisted telling him. No point in upsetting him.

"At least she'll be safe in the Husks in that thing," he said, "but that's Revolutionary property. We should go back. We should—"

"We should finish what we started," I replied. "We go looking for her, we miss our chance to stop Vraki and save his hostages."

"Right..." His voice was solemn. "But why did she leave in the first place? And how are we going to do this without a Boar to—"

"Tell me what else you found."

He sighed. "The supplies were all marked. With *that* sigil."

He gestured to the satchel that lay nearby—the satchel that held the dwindling medical supplies he was currently using on me. Emblazoned upon it was a brand, the kind that freeholds slap on their shit in case they get stolen by outlaws or Vagrants less nice than me. But this brand was special.

This brand glowed.

In the dark of the night, a sigil of a lantern glowed in red and white. The faintest of magics kept it alight in the dark. To look at it, you might have called it a frivolous use of a limited power. But me?

I called it a lead.

That was the sigil of Lastlight, the Scar's most renowned freehold. Renowned for its proximity to the Husks, its fabulous wealth, and the fact that it was fucking hard as hell to steal from it. For Galta and Taltho to have them, they must have come through that freehold.

And maybe they left something behind.

It was a desperate hope, I'll admit, but they don't come in any other variety out here. And I had nothing else. No Liette, no Iron Boar, and no fucking time left to sit here bleeding out.

"Okay." Cavric pulled the needle free and did some quick knotwork. But I could hear the wince in his voice. "I did the best I could."

I looked down at my flank. There hadn't been enough thread in the satchel, and what there was strained to hold the skin together. The gashes weren't closed, but they at least wouldn't rip any wider, unless I moved suddenly. Or slowly. Or blinked.

If I had the time, I could lie still and hope for the best.

But I didn't have the time and hope isn't a thing you count on in the Scar. I needed real treatment. And since there weren't any wrights way the fuck out here, that meant finding real medical supplies. Wherever I was going to find them, it wasn't going to be on my ass.

I got to my feet unsteadily—half out of pain, half out of consideration for the flimsy sutures. Cavric steadied me as I walked to a rock where my clothes lay. I had shredded my only spare shirt into makeshift bandages that I carefully wrapped around my midriff. They were already stained by drops of red by the time I tied them off.

I pulled on my other shirt and frowned at it. Stained with blood from Galta's thorn and riddled with tears from my escape from the mines, it only barely hid the bandaged wound in my side, leaving an expanse of scarred flesh bare.

But, as the saying goes, people about to die from massive blood loss can't be choosers.

"All right," I said, trying to ignore the pain I felt from just talking. "I need to go look around. Keep the fire warm while I'm gone, all right?"

"Okay," Cavric said uneasily. "But are you sure that's—"

"I wasn't talking to you."

He glanced over his shoulder. Congeniality looked up from her spot, curled across the fire. She looked at him with those big eyes and her beak craned open. For a very brief moment, my pain-addled brain thought she was about to say something.

Right up until she made a gagging sound and vomited up a ball of hair and bones from her digested rabbit, anyway.

"Don't worry." I patted Cavric's shoulder as he cringed in disgust. "That means she likes you."

I turned to leave. He grabbed my hand.

"Be careful, okay?" he asked. "We can't lose more than we already have."

I wasn't used to looks like the one he gave me—looks full of earnest concern—from people I *liked*, let alone from people I had kidnapped at gunpoint. I didn't deserve that concern. Didn't deserve even this shit job he had done on my wound.

But I had them both. And now I had to do what good I could with them.

I owed him that much.

I patted his arm, nodded, and trudged up a steep slope.

I had made camp in the shadow of a hill, a great slab of dirt and stones that punched through the rocky scrublands that bordered the Husks. It wouldn't do much to conceal me from any predators roaming the wilds, but it would at least keep me safe from prying human eyes.

And where I was, those were a bigger concern.

I got to the top of the hill. Far off in the east, the Yental River coiled sharply inland, carving its way through the earth. But closer, to my west, a different kind of river stretched out.

They hadn't called it the Redway to begin with. Originally, the long and winding road that skirted the Husks had been called the Emperor's Walk—no one knew why, since no Emperor had ever set foot in the Scar, let alone walked it. It had started as an important road system between Imperium outposts. So important that the Revolution had thrown thousands of soldiers to their deaths in an attempt to wrest it from Imperium control.

Years passed. Corpses piled up. Wars turned beautiful lands into the Husks. The road earned a more fitting name.

Nowadays, the Redway's main use was a thoroughfare for traders between freeholds. Merchants ran caravans through it, profiting off the raiders and adventurers who emerged from the Husks with Imperium and Revolutionary relics. Bandit gangs squatted on the sidelines, looking for easy marks.

I watched it crawl across the land and disappear into the hills. Wide enough for ten men to walk abreast. Endlessly long. And so, so empty.

I crouched down, rested my arms on my knees, and began to think. I didn't like it.

Not that I consider myself an idiot, of course. I'm just more used to immediate gratification. I prefer gunfire, glasses of whiskey, and pleasurable company. Things that move from moment to moment, bullet to bullet, hand to hand.

When I'm moving, it's all instinct and no thinking, my scars telling me how to act and the Cacophony telling me who needs to die. When I'm thinking, my mind gets to wandering down a long road that leads to dark places.

I don't know why I came back, why I was still alive, if that light I saw was even real or just some vision that entered me as the blood left me. But I was here and Vraki was still so far away. He had known where I was, which meant he knew where I'd be looking for him, which meant where I was looking was precisely where he *wouldn't* be. Even if he *had* been to Lastlight, where could he be now? He was too far ahead. Which meant that I wouldn't find him before he summoned his new Scrath, before he used his sacrifices, before everyone died and he won and I lost and I'd be left alone with all the corpses of the people I couldn't save and . . .

See what I mean?

I shut my eyes tight, gritted my teeth. Pain surged through my side. I focused on it, pain to pain, heartbeat to heartbeat, that steady rhythm of agony that pulled me off that long road and reminded me that I couldn't save anyone if I was dead.

The nearest freehold was miles away at a hard ride. Congeniality could make it, but I couldn't. Not with these stitches.

This close to the Husks, an herb worth any medicinal use would be near impossible to find. Traveling wasn't an option. Sitting still wasn't an option. I needed a plan, the most brilliant, determined, luckiest plan I had ever come up with.

Or, failing that, the stupidest.

My eyes were drawn down the road at the sight of orange lights dancing in the darkness. I squinted, tracking them as they swayed back and forth with a steady rhythm.

Lanterns.

And between their light and the moon, I could make out the immense shapes being hauled down the road.

Massive carts, wooden sides reinforced with iron and roofs topped with banners, came rumbling down the path. Three of them, at least, each hauled by a pair of great, hoofed rothacs. Horned beasts of burden, each one twice as big as a bird and six times as heavy, they lowed in complaint as they pulled their wheeled burdens down the Redway. And in response, they received only the crack of a whip and a bellowed curse.

Guards. Men and women—at least a dozen that I could count— rode alongside the carts atop birds, carrying lanterns on long poles. I could see a few autobows from here, and I'd wager they had more firepower I couldn't see. But that wasn't what caught my attention.

That was reserved for the banners.

They hung limp in the breezeless night, each one hanging from the top of a cart, proudly displaying a sigil. A glowing sigil.

"Lastlight," I whispered.

I don't believe in gods, so I don't believe in divine providence. I do, however, believe in luck. Regardless of whatever else the appearance of this caravan heralded, wagons bound for Lastlight would be brimming with supplies. And they would be exceedingly valuable supplies, as no bandit, soldier, or Vagrant was dumb enough to fuck with Lastlight, the only freehold to have ever repelled both Imperium and Revolutionary assaults.

Which made what I was about to do *particularly* insane.

But, I told myself as I eased up and headed back down the hill, there wasn't much choice. Lastlight didn't get rich by giving things away for free. And I didn't have anything to barter with outside of the trash in Congeniality's saddlebags.

I wasn't going to make it to Lastlight without what was in those carts. And I wasn't going to get it from a dozen armed guards without something to persuade them. Which meant what I was about to do next either had to be incredibly brilliant or incredibly stupid.

You can go ahead and guess which one it turned out to be.

THIRTY-EIGHT

THE REDWAY

I f you're ever not sure who's in charge, look for the biggest hat.

That's not a hard-and-fast rule or anything, but it's usually a good guess. And, as the Lastlight caravan came rumbling up the Redway, it proved true.

The carts themselves were stolid, imposing iron. The rothacs that pulled them were beasts of matted black fur with jagged, singular horns. The guards that flanked them were men and women coated by dust, grime, and resentment.

But the woman who led them?

She was an angel from a very expensive heaven.

Pale and slender as a vase, she sat imperiously upon the seat of the lead cart. Her dress was bright crimson silk lined with pristine white fur. Her skin was flawless, as if the dust of the road just couldn't afford to touch it, and not a strand of hair could be seen from beneath the immense red hat she wore, replete with a white feather so big it looked like it came from a bird long extinct. A red jewel in an iron crown, she surveyed the road ahead of her, disinterest battling contempt in her gaze.

And when she saw a single dirty woman with scars on her face, tattoos on her arms, and a gun in her hands, contempt finally won out.

She didn't bother to tell me to move. Likely, she reasoned I would either get out of the way or her rothacs would run me over. She wasn't wrong. The ungulates were two tons of muscle topped with jagged horns. A sensible woman would have gotten out of the way.

Sal the Cacophony, however, did not move for anyone.

I didn't bother looking at the rothacs. I didn't waste a single glance for the guards who readied their weapons and looked down the road, curious, at this lone woman in a spare, shabby cloak and hood blocking their way. My eyes were on the woman in red.

She was the one who'd give me what I wanted.

Cavric had thought this plan was crazy and I had told him only half of it. But it wasn't like we had many other options. An earnest fight would be over quickly. My only chance at getting what I needed out of this was through guile.

And a shitload of luck.

Her face was painted in icy contempt as her carts came rolling toward me. But that melted away, replaced by burning fury, as the rothacs let out a guttural lowing sound and came to a shuddering halt. The whole caravan backed up as, one by one, the rothacs stopped, letting out distressed bellows.

"What is this?"

Yet even through that, I could hear the sharp edge of her voice. She turned to the young man driving the lead cart, a handsome kid with a shaggy mop of blond hair and a dirty coat, and sneered so hard I thought her face would dislocate.

"We do *not* have time for this," she spat. "Get them moving!"

"I can't!" the kid protested, impotently cracking the reins in demonstration. "They won't move!"

"They're well trained," I said.

I didn't raise my voice or make threats. That sort of thing was for bandits or your average Vagrants.

Sal the Cacophony simply spoke. And anyone who didn't want to die listened. That's what I needed them to believe.

"Obviously not," the woman replied, her voice struggling to regain its icy composure. "As they seem to have decided to *stop* doing their job."

"Oh, I disagree." My grin was as crooked as my scars. "What else would you call a beast that knows it's rude to pass by without introducing yourself *but* well trained?"

I met the woman's eyes. To look at her, I thought her a rich girl playing at hard labor, some baron's heiress reluctantly fulfilling her duties for a fat, absent father.

But to have her look at *me*, I knew that wasn't the case. Hers was a flint-eyed scowl used to looking over every inch of a weapon to find an impurity, a scrutinizing glare that had counted every coin she had ever wrung from a purse, thin and sharp as a scalpel used to cutting open flesh to find a weakness.

I'd seen the same stare in every murderer, mercenary, and merchant who knew their business a little too well. This woman had earned every piece of finery she wore and would be all too happy to turn all her painstakingly selected hired thugs on me to protect them.

"Renita."

But, for the moment, she was content to give me her name instead of a blade.

"Renita Avonin," she said, pride suffusing every syllable.

"Avonin," I whistled. "Like Avonin and Sons? The whiskeymakers?"

"Avonin and *Family*, ever since *I* started overseeing production," she replied sharply. "You've heard of us."

I had. Everyone from Lastlight to Lowstaff had heard that name. It was, after all, branded into the flesh of over a thousand would-be cheats, frauds, and debtors who got on their bad side.

"And where's your wealthy father?" I asked.

"Entrusting business to his wealthy daughter," Renita snapped. "One who can very easily afford all these autobows pointed on you and a *very* nice coffin for you, should you try anything more stupid than you already have." She made a commanding gesture. "You've already made me late. If you'd be so kind to move, I'll be on my way and spare you no bolts to go along with the spit I intend to hurl at you."

She seemed nice.

"I've heard no stories about the generosity of the Avonins," I replied. "But I like to think it's never too late to make a positive change." I glanced from beneath my hood, over her head, to the carts lined up and down the road. "Me, for example? I think I'd like to be a little reasonable tonight. Seems you've got plenty to spare. You give me what I want, I'll be happy to move out of your way and you can fuck along to Lastlight."

The guards who heard this chuckled. It must have seemed funny, this dirty-looking girl in the middle of the road demanding favors from an Avonin. But Renita was not laughing. Renita, instead, looked like I had just asked her if she had delivered her baby out the wrong end.

"You possess an abundance of nerve, madam," she spat, frigid.

"I won't ask for much," I said, holding up a hand for calm. "A bag of metal, a couple of bottles of whiskey, a healer's kit..." I paused, considering. "Also a pen and some paper."

Renita quirked a single, incredulous brow. "What for?"

"So I can write 'Fuck you, don't ask questions.'" I eyed one of the guards, let my gaze linger on the sword in her lap. "And one of those nice blades you've got there. That seems a reasonable request of an Avonin."

"I am corrected," Renita said. "You do not possess nerve so much as a malady of the brain." Her guards' laughter grew louder. "Who, exactly, do you think you are to demand such of me?"

I smiled.

I tipped my hood up.

And I told her.

"Sal the Cacophony."

The laughter died.

The guards went wide-eyed.

And they looked me over.

They searched me for lies, something to indicate that I was some punk using someone else's name. But they saw the tattoos covering my arms. They saw the scars.

They saw the Cacophony.

Do this as long as I have, you come to savor the moments when people recognize your name. It starts with the wild eyes and the nervous shuffling. It becomes nervous glances cast toward each other, searching for support. It turns into fear spreading across faces, breath coming up short, eyes twitching as they look for a way out.

Those moments? When you get them?

"Fuck's sake, that's really her."

Better than sex.

I could see them looking at each other, leaning over on their birds, whispering to each other. Over the mutter of the rothacs, I could hear them trade the stories.

"She's killed over twenty Vagrants with that fucking gun of hers."

True.

"I heard she shot down a Revolution tank with that thing."

Lie.

"She once shot the Bleakhollow Blackguards dead to a man because they stole a chicken from her."

Half true. There was bad blood between me and the Blackguards before that. But it had been a *real* nice chicken.

"...killed twenty men in one night..."

The whispers spread.

"...that gun's fucking evil, a demon..."

Like poison in the veins.

"...she'll kill us all, just give her what she..."

And music in my ears.

"*Enough,*" Renita barked loud enough to silence them. She scowled down at the kid sitting next to her. "Spur the rothacs, Dennec. Run her down."

"I'm trying!" Dennec protested. "But, madam..." He looked at me with big, wide eyes and swallowed hard. "It's like they know."

Well, to be fair, it was much more likely they knew the scent of Congeniality's shit I had spread around the road. The reek of a predatory bird would make any beast nervous.

"Your help seems to have heard of me." I let the Cacophony dangle from my fingers. "You can ask them, but I don't think they know any stories about how patient I am. Now maybe you've got enough of them to kill me and maybe you don't. But if this gets ugly, I'll be taking a few of them to the black table with me. And I wager it'll cost more to replace them than it will to give me what I ask for."

I yawned, scratched my scars with the barrel of the Cacophony. You'd never have guessed, to look at me, that my heart was thundering so hard I thought my ribs might crack.

"So, you know . . . up to you."

Renita fixed me with a glare that transcended anger, slipped right past hate, and went into an emotion so cold and vicious I don't think I had a word for it. I could see the scales tipping in her head, weighing the number of her guards versus the obvious fear they had for me. Eventually, the rage on her face simmered away, leaving behind a bitter, resentful contempt.

Contempt I could work with.

She glanced at a guard, gestured with her chin. He pulled his bird to the back of the cart, rooted around in it for a few moments before emerging with a satchel. My wounds, hidden beneath my shirt, ached at the sight of it. I fought to keep the eagerness off my face. The fear wide on his eyes, he came forward tentatively to hand it over.

Or rather, he had *started* to do that when his mistress suddenly spoke.

"One moment."

I looked back at Renita. The contempt was gone now, replaced by something cold and analytical. She studied me carefully, as if she could suddenly see right through my cloak and onto the bloody bandages wrapped around me.

"The healer's kit," she said. "What do you need it for?"

"Road's a dangerous place," I replied, just a moment too late. "I like to be prepared."

Her eyes ran over me. That cold, appraising stare took in the red stains on the hem of my cloak, the tattered cloth, the tension of my belly.

"You're bloodied," she observed.

"I am." I forced venom into my voice. "The last guy I asked for something was slower than you are."

She didn't move. She didn't even blink. "Surely, if it's such a necessity, you'd have one already." A frigid smile tugged at the corners of her mouth. "Unless you had such need of one you'd waylay a heavily armed caravan."

I narrowed my eyes. My heart raced. And, to see the look on her face, you'd think she could hear it.

"I'll tell you what, Madam Cacophony," she said. "You can help yourself to anything in my cart"—she gestured to the kid beside her—"including Dennec, if you can climb up here on your own and get it."

I hesitated too long. I stepped forward too slow. My leg quivered just a little too much when I did.

And she saw it.

And she knew.

"Ordinarily, Madam Cacophony, I'd have you shot and be done with it," Renita said. "But, as you say, it's never too late to make a positive impact. Or an example." She glanced to Dennec. "Inform our passenger that we have need of his services."

Dennec's eyes went wide, but he nodded weakly. He turned to the nearest guard.

"Wake him up," he said.

The guard grinned, spurred his bird to the last cart. My heart pounded.

"Come on out, friend!" The guard thumped his autobow's butt against the cart's side. "Madam Avonin requests your presence."

Metal groaned. Wheels creaked. Something tremendous rose from inside the cart. My scars ached.

The rothacs let out a nervous lowing sound. The guards scattered as their birds squawked nervously. The back of the cart bowed low as something heavy walked to its edge, then sprang up as it hopped off.

The Cacophony burned in my hand. I held it up, ready to fire, but the guards only backed away instead of fleeing outright. Whatever they had in that wagon, they were more afraid of than they were of the Cacophony.

Do this as long as I have, you come to recognize a different sort of moment. It starts with the birds and beasts going quiet. It becomes a great, shadowy shape trudging forward. It turns into your wounds aching and your body quivering and the realization that everything has gone horribly wrong.

It's not better than sex.

But it does feel like you're fucked.

THIRTY-NINE

THE REDWAY

L ike all the best killers, he arrived without saying a word.
No threats, no boasts, no laughter. He walked across the sand, unpretentious. His eyes were clear and his back was straight. And though the guards fell quiet and the birds nervously edged away from him, he paid them no mind. He simply walked up to me and looked me straight in the eyes.

And the man who had come to kill me spoke my name.

"Sal," he said, voice soft and emotionless.

I returned his stare as well as I was able. He stood a head taller than me, his muscular body so lean and hard that he looked like the last masterpiece of a dying artisan. His dark skin was left generously exposed by the scanty kilt he wore around his waist and every inch of it, from his broad chest to his thick arms to his massive legs, was bereft of a single scar. All that adorned his skin was the craggy mountainous scene that was tattooed in a sleeve from his right wrist to his shoulder.

Inclining my head to such a creature seemed a touch inadequate, but I did anyway.

"Calto," I replied.

If you spent more than a month in the Scar, you'd heard of this man, even if you'd never heard his name. And you'd know why I didn't shoot and abandon all hope of not angering him.

The massacre at Fort Legacy, where a hole was punched through walls two feet thick and every last Imperium soldier was split apart? That was him. The seven-car Revolutionary train that was derailed and its stores looted? That was him. Jarva's Concern, the town that was a freehold one day and a pile of smoldering wreckage the next?

Every time the earth shakes. Every time a town collapses. Every time a lot of people die at once, everyone in the Scar with any intellect holds their breath and prays it isn't a sign that Calto the Hardrock is in town.

And if I thought any god could have helped me then, I would have prayed, too.

"Master Hardrock," Renita called down to him. "This Vagrant has insulted my caravan, my employees, and myself with her brazenness. I request that you handle her, as per the terms of our arrangement."

Calto didn't look at her. Calto barely seemed like he was looking at me. His eyes were distant—not empty, but lacking something important. I got the distinct impression that, when he looked at me, he didn't see a person so much as several layers of sinew and skin arranged over a skeleton.

A wise woman would have run. And while I didn't consider myself particularly wise, I would have done the same if not for three things.

One, I'd never outrun him on foot. Two, my stitches would burst and I'd bleed to death. And three?

Sal the Cacophony doesn't run.

I held my breath as he stood there, silently considering. Not considering whether he could kill me; there wasn't a creature on two legs or more that Calto couldn't kill. Rather, he was considering whether it was worth it, wondering what impression I'd left on him those few times we crossed paths.

"Mmm." He rolled his head from side to side, drew an audible cracking sound from his neck. "Ten knuckles."

Renita's eyes bulged and her body tensed, the very thought of parting with a piece of metal causing a very small seizure.

"Ten knuckles is no small price," she said. "And not at all what—"

"Gold."

That very small seizure became a very restrained aneurysm. "Are you *fucking* with me?" Renita growled. "We agreed to pay you for protecting us by transporting you."

"Vagrants cost extra." Calto eyed me. "The Cacophony costs gold." He waved a hand. "Or I can let your men handle it. It is of no concern."

I wanted to grin. But I didn't.

You can tell Calto the Hardrock what to do in the same sense you can tell a storm not to destroy your farm. You can go out there and threaten it, scream at it, offer it money, but in the end, the storm will do whatever it pleases. It might swoop in and destroy your life, it might pass you by with nothing more than a gentle rain, or it might simply dissipate and leave you be.

I watched him carefully. And he watched me with passing disinterest. And I thought that maybe, just maybe, there was a chance that he'd decide the trouble of killing me wasn't worth it and just walk away.

"Fine," Renita sighed. "Kill her."

But hey, fuck me for being optimistic, right?

His eyes glowed purple. He raised one foot. His fists clenched. The glow brightened. His foot came down.

I heard the Lady's song.

And then the earth screamed.

The sands exploded up in curtains. The birds reared and fell to the earth, their riders tumbling with them. The carts rattled on their iron wheels. The rothacs let out frightened lows. The earth shook so hard I could feel my teeth rattle in my skull.

And Calto had taken only one step.

The guards had just started getting to their feet when he started running. They fell once again, the earth knocked from under their feet as he charged. The rothacs wailed and pulled against their yokes. The birds screeched as their riders tried to get them under control. And none of them could be heard over the sound of the earth rumbling beneath Calto's stride.

He rushed toward me, faster than a man that big ought to be able to move. I kept my gun steady, watched for my opportunity. He didn't seem to think much of evasion, running headlong toward me. I watched until he got close enough. I watched him leap into the air. I watched him begin to come down . . .

And I realized the flaw in my plan.

I scrambled away, went running as he hit the earth like a stone. The earth groaned, shifted under my feet. I kept my footing only because I had been expecting and then, only just. I stumbled, staggered, clamped a hand over my stitches.

No blood stained my fingers. Not yet.

I turned and aimed the Cacophony at him. He was a black shadow against the cloud of dust that had risen in the wake of his fall, the dying gasp of the earth. Through the dissipating dust, I could see his face: unhurried, unconcerned, unimpressed.

Siegemages were like that.

The Lady gave them their power, made them heavier, denser, stronger. Siegemage magic could give a little girl the power to break down a fortress door with her skull and an old woman the power to hurl a man forty yards with one hand.

Or, in the case of Calto, to break my skull with the flick of his fingers. Not that he seemed all that hurried to do so.

See, in exchange for all that power, the Lady extracts a heavy toll. You get the power to be as heavy and strong as a stone, but you pay in your ability to feel. First, she takes your fear, then your happiness, then your sorrow, then your anger, then your pain, and so on. A Siegemage goes on living long enough, he eventually becomes an emotionless, empty husk, remembering nothing of laughter or tears or heartbreak or anything that isn't killing.

And Calto had lived longer than most.

It wasn't a man who walked out of that cloud of dust. It was a machine, cold-blooded and good for nothing but death and destruction. And, as he walked toward me, I knew the only way I was going to get out of this was with one of us in the ground.

"So, how've you been, Calto?"

But that didn't mean we couldn't be civil about it.

"Fine," he replied. "You?"

The code, you might call it. We might kill each other from time to time, but Vagrants liked things to be done a certain way. And I liked every advantage I could muster, including keeping him distracted.

"Been better," I replied.

He walked toward me, implacable and unblinking. "I'm sorry to hear that."

I raised the Cacophony at him. I drew the hammer back. I aimed.

"Thanks. That means a lot."

I pulled the trigger.

Hellfire burst from his grinning barrel. The shell streaked through the sky in a second, planted itself in Calto's chest. Flames erupted in an inferno, red jaws opening to swallow him whole. A pillar of fire engulfed him, swept over his flesh, and made him disappear behind a veil of flame.

Any man, bird, or beast would have been incinerated by that kind of blast. It should have been enough to render anything inside it to ash.

But if you've known me this long, you know nothing is ever that easy for me.

The flames let out a final roar before they dissipated. What was left was blackened earth, coils of rising smoke, and at the center of it, Calto the Hardrock. Unscathed by the flame, he walked out of the scorched earth having lost nothing more than his kilt.

You wouldn't think that the most unnerving part of him walking out of a pillar of flame unhurt would be that he did so naked.

But you'd be wrong.

"Ah, fuck," I muttered.

"I agree," Calto replied.

He started rushing toward me, the earth screaming at his step. I tensed but didn't run; he didn't feel pain like I did. He'd chase me down in a few short, screaming breaths. I backed up until I felt a stone against my back, nowhere to run.

He drew his fist back. His stride brought him closer. I could see his eyes.

And somehow, through the fear, I felt vaguely offended that a man about to pulp my head should look so bored.

He leapt. His fist came down. I darted, leaping to the side, falling into a tumble.

A shriek tore itself from my throat as I came to my feet. I felt warm blood weep out and stain my shirt.

My stitches had split.

But my head hadn't been reduced to a fine red mist, so, hey, relativity.

I got to my feet, clutching my side as I backed away. I saw Calto grunting, struggling to pull his hand free from the boulder it was stuck in. It was a sizable thing, at least half again as big as he was, but it still groaned and cracked as it clung to his fist.

"I'm surprised, Calto," I said, fighting to hold on to my breath. "This task seems beneath you."

"It was a happy arrangement," he replied, not looking up. "I was on the way to the Lastlight already. They offered me quite a bit of metal in exchange for killing people."

"In exchange for guard duty."

"Whatever." He sneered. "You are correct, though. I am bound for greater things. And I shall find them in Lastlight." He looked at me, his eyes empty. "And with the Gate."

"The Gate?" My eyes widened. "Vraki. So he *is* in Lastlight." Through the pain, my mind somehow managed to pull the pieces together. "Son of a bitch, you're going to join him?"

"He is in need of new people. I am told that you are the cause of that."

"Shit, Calto," I spat. "You...you can't do that."

He pulled his hand free of the stone, fragments of rock falling from his knuckles. "I can do anything, Sal."

"Vraki is a killer," I snarled, backing away. "He's a lunatic, a madman chasing an insane plan. Just listen to me. I know what he's going to do and—"

"I have heard his plan," Calto replied. "He will return a mage to the Emperor's throne. He will remake this world for mages once more."

"Since when have you cared about that?"

"I don't." Calto seized the boulder. With a sigh of dust and a groan of earth, he hoisted it high over his head. "But it's something to do."

I took off running. My wound hurt, but getting crushed by a boulder would hurt a lot worse. But even as I ran, I knew my pace was uneven, my legs wouldn't keep up. And so did Calto.

"*Ocumani oth rethar*, Sal," he bellowed.

I felt a shadow fall over me. I looked up. The boulder came crashing down. The Cacophony burned in my hand, told me what to do. Without thinking I whirled, I aimed, I shot.

Discordance flew, struck true, exploded. In a wave of sound that drowned out the explosion of rubble, it blew the stone apart. Fragments of rock fell in a heavy rain, landing unceremoniously in tiny plumes of dust.

I shielded myself from the rubble, escaped with only a few pebbles landing on me. It had been dumb luck that kept me alive; if Calto hadn't weakened the rock already, Discordance wouldn't have done much but make a lot of noise before the boulder crushed me.

As it was, it only delayed my death.

Calto walked toward me, through the falling rain of dust, leisurely as he might stroll through a park in Cathama. And why shouldn't he? He knew I was wounded. He could see my blood. He saw no reason to hurry.

Wish I could have said the same.

My body tried to hurry away from him. My mind tried to hurry to think up a plan. Neither of them had much luck. My wound was bleeding badly. My brain was on fire with fear and pain. And my gun had nothing left but Hoarfrost.

So at least I could give him awkwardly erect nipples before he killed me.

Out of desperation, I let out a sharp, angry whistle. If Congeniality was close, she'd hear me. And if she wasn't too far, too slow, or just too ornery, she'd come. And then I'd have at least a few more breaths before Calto ran me down and killed me.

Yeah, I didn't like this plan, either.

He was getting closer. I was bleeding more. I had no more options.

Except the dumbest thing I could think of for the second time that night.

I veered sharply, ignored the pain and the blood as I ran a circle around Calto, back toward the caravan. He quirked a brow, puzzled as to why I wasn't making this more fun for him, before he saw me rushing toward the carts. Then his eyes widened. Then he was no longer walking so leisurely.

He thought I was heading to kill the people paying him. His concern would be for protecting them first. Good. I needed him distracted.

Otherwise, he'd see this coming.

Renita and the caravan guards looked confused as to what I was doing, no doubt seeing that Calto's mad dash was closing in on me. I could see the bewilderment plain on their faces. I could see Renita's brow furrow suspiciously as I looked up at her.

As I grinned.

As I whirled about and aimed at the ground.

And fired.

The shell exploded, struck the earth in a blossom of ice. Hoarfrost erupted in a bunch of icy brambles, jutting up through the earth to form a frigid blue hedge in front of Calto. Naturally, he didn't give a shit. He kept charging, lowered his head, burst through the icy spikes without even hesitating.

That was fine. It wasn't the spiky part I was planning on tripping him up with.

That part came an instant later.

The frigid brambles might have been gone, but the icy patch beneath remained, and as his foot came down in just the right way, he went skidding. He had been moving too fast to control himself, his charge turning into a wild, staggering struggle to right himself. And as he went flailing across the ice, he couldn't stop himself as he went bellowing past me and rushed right for the carts.

Renita put it together quicker than anyone else did. With a scream—either for her safety or for those very nice clothes that were about to get dirty—she leapt from the cart. Dennec followed her, leaping off as Calto came barreling in.

There was the shriek of metal as his face collided with the cart. The rothacs lowed. The cart groaned as it went rising up on its wheels and, then, with delicious slowness, went collapsing over onto its side.

The guards fled, pulling their birds clear. The rothacs wailed, their hooves flailing as they were knocked onto their sides, suspended by their yokes. Of Calto, there was no sign. But I couldn't count on a man who walked out of a pillar of flame unscathed to be hindered by a little thing like running face-first into an iron cart.

Fortunately for me, help arrived with a squawk and a foul odor.

Congeniality came rushing over the hill, fashionably late. To her credit, she was at least hurried as she came running down the hillside and pulled up to a halt next to me. I spared her a stroke of her beak with one hand while I searched in the saddlebags with another.

Fucking hell, where'd I put it? I thought as my fingers groped through the contents. Dead rabbit, dead rabbit, half a dead rabbit, empty bottle—why do I keep the fucking bottles—Hoarfrost, Discordance, Hoarfrost...

The metal behind me groaned as something very big and screaming some very creative curses pulled itself free of the wreckage. My fingers wrapped around a shell, felt the spell written on the side of it.

Ah. There you are.

I pulled it out in just in time to see Congeniality squawk and run from me. In another second, I turned and saw why. I barely had time to hurl myself to the ground as two tons of flailing, bellowing, pissing rothac went sailing over my head.

I got up, looked toward the cart. Calto was already tearing the second rothac free from the yoke.

"Sal the Cacophony," he snarled. "You are annoying."

He seized the beast by its neck. It let out an animal bellow, legs wagging as it he raised it over his head.

"I did not believe you could be so much trouble as Vraki said. Alas." He narrowed his eyes. "Like all unbelievers, I am keen to repent."

As speeches went, that one wasn't bad. I felt kind of bad for only half listening. My attentions were on the sights of the Cacophony as I lined him up, as I drew the hammer back, as I whispered into the night…

"*Eres va atali*, Calto."

I pulled the trigger and fired.

And Sunflare did the rest.

The shell erupted in a bright white light, banished the night in one brilliant flash. I shielded my eyes to be spared the worst of it. Though, fortunately, not so long that I didn't see what happened next.

Siegemages go so long without feeling pain, they never know what to do when it actually hurts them. And when the light assaulted Calto's eyes, he did what anyone else would have done. He screamed, he shut them tight, and instinctively clapped his hands over them, too late.

Why the fuck do they always do that?

The rothac fell from his grasp, fell atop him, and bore him to the ground in a thrashing, lowing heap. Blinded, Calto found his ways to his knees. Unhindered, the rothac found its feet. And, in another instant, Calto also found its feet as it lashed out with a vicious kick. Its hooves sent Calto staggering forward, plowing into a nearby guard. Blinded, furious, he did what came naturally to all killers.

I don't know if you've ever seen a man's skull get hammered into his belly like a stake, but if you get the chance, I recommend looking away.

Calto wasn't used to being helpless, he wasn't used to losing, and he wasn't sure where I was. That combination made for a savage spectacle as he thrashed blindly through the caravan, swinging his massive fists, smashing the carts and the few guards stupid enough to try to stop him. He was well past caring who he killed. His temper needed to be quenched in blood; mine, theirs, he didn't care.

He never did.

The scene was chaos. The rothacs lowed, strained at their yokes, broke free, and began thrashing. The birds shrieked, bolted, and tossed the riders who weren't strong enough to hold them. The guards smart enough not to get in Calto's way struggled between avoiding him, calming their beasts, and trying to find their wayward boss.

Now would have been a good time to run.

I wouldn't blame you for calling me stupid for rushing toward it.

But I didn't have a choice. My gun was empty. My body was on fire. My side was weeping blood. And my eyes were on the satchel on the ground, in the middle of the carnage.

I darted forward, kept low, kept silent. Not that I really needed to, what with the screaming people and the howling beasts and Calto smashing the caravan apart. I drew up short, held my breath as he charged past to blindly plow into another cart. I ducked under a rothac's kick as one of the beasts stampeded past me. I brought the Cacophony up and smashed his grip against the jaw of the only guard stupid enough to try to stop me.

I picked my way to the satchel, mercifully untouched by the chaos. Its flap was open and within I could see the telltale white of a healer's kit and, nestled with it, a few bars of metal and a single bottle of whiskey.

I glowered. You might think it crazy to have taken offense at seeing a single bottle of whiskey, given the circumstances.

But I had told Renita I wanted two. After I had gone to all this fucking trouble, I wasn't walking away shorthanded.

I plucked up the satchel, cast a glance about the wreckage of the caravan until I saw a glimmer of glass. There, tumbling out of an upturned crate and nestled in straw, a few vials of liquid spilled out. Not the fine brown of whiskey, but a deep, ugly purple that danced and swirled.

My eyes lit up.

Not whiskey.

But I sure as fuck wasn't going to pass up bleakbrew when I saw it.

I snatched up a vial, carefully slid it into the satchel. I had just reached down to take more when the cart next to me groaned. It shuddered with a sudden impact as Calto struck it, teetering over.

Now it was time to run.

I bit back a scream as I hauled myself to my feet and took off running. With a crash, the cart toppled over where I had just been, burying whatever was left beneath a mess of tangled iron. My side was screaming as I tore off into the hills, but I took a moment to glance over my shoulder.

Calto stood at the center of the wreckage, the beasts and guards fled, the carts destroyed. He flailed wildly with his fists and, finding nothing but air to vent his frustrations on, let out a roar that shook the earth. The blindness would wear off before long and he'd be looking for my body in the wreckage. I planned on being far away when he realized I wasn't there.

Siegemages are a lot of things: invulnerable, implacable, and most importantly, impatient. It turns out when you spend most of your life being able to shrug off bullets like they were raindrops, you don't really bother to learn the little things like, say, tracking a fleeing woman through twisting hills.

I ran as far as I could before my side threatened to split me apart. The blood ran red and warm down my side, made my shirt stick to my skin. The pain had burned itself out in my body, leaving behind a cold numbness. I didn't have much time.

Fortunately, I didn't need it. Not anymore.

"Sal!"

Cavric came running up, steadying me as I nearly collapsed. He hurried me away from the carnage, putting it far behind us.

"*That* was your fucking plan?" he asked. "You said you were going to negotiate!"

"I did," I said. "It didn't go well."

"You can't keep doing this," he growled as we rounded a dune. "You can't keep just doing shit and hoping it works out. You *need* to—"

"I need to do something else right now," I said, pulling a hand away from my side and holding up a bloody palm. "If you don't mind."

We crouched in the shadow of a hill. I struggled to catch my breath, failed. I was drawing in ragged, gurgling rasps, my hands shaking as I reached into the satchel and found that little bottle.

It was tiny, no bigger than the palm of my hand. I could have broken it if I squeezed too hard. The liquid inside looked thick and viscous, an unhealthy purple color that resembled the sickly sheen of sunlight on oil. Yet when I held it up to my eyes, it danced, as though alive. And, despite it being a mess of sludge in a bottle, I got the distinct impression that it was looking at me.

Bleakbrew was weird like that.

"Is that..." Cavric's eyes went wide with horrified recognition. "Sal, you can't..."

I didn't have time for him to finish that thought. Or to listen to him. Or to be sickened. With one hand pressed against my wound, I pried the cork free of the bottle with my teeth. A slender coil of liquid slithered out through the bottleneck, as if peering at me. I winced, shut my eyes, opened my mouth, and tilted the bottle back.

It fought me, struggling to go back in the bottle as I poured it down my throat. I could feel it moving all the way down as it slid past my tongue with the taste of bile on fire, oozed down my gullet, and settled in a gruesome coil in the pit of my stomach. I could still feel it moving in my belly.

But not for long.

Suddenly, my body reignited with pain. A bright and angry fire exploded inside me, chasing away the numbness. I fell to my knees, doubled over, robbed of the breath I needed to get out the scream trapped in my throat. My muscles seized. My breath went quiet. My vision darkened.

But that was just how it worked. First, it tried to kill you. And if it couldn't...

Under my hand, I could feel sinew closing. I could feel blood slithering back into my body. I could feel the skin reaching out to each other with a thousand little hands, pulling itself tightly together and sealing shut.

My senses were overwhelmed with agony, my eyelids fluttered as I threatened to pass out, yet even through it all, I couldn't help but marvel at the process.

You never get used to bleakbrew.

The pain eventually passed. My breath returned, and when it did, it came slow and easy as it should. I looked down at my side. My skin, whole and hale and unbroken, greeted me. My body was still caked with dried blood, but fuck if I was going to complain about that.

I looked at the bottle in my hand, frowned. You might call it a miracle, this shit. I might have, too, if I didn't know where it came from. And when I looked up and saw Cavric's terror, I knew he wasn't so lucky, either.

"That's..." he whispered. "That's a mage you just drank, Sal. That's a *person*."

I pretended I was still struggling for breath. I pretended it hurt too much to look up. I pretended it was anything except the fact that I couldn't stand the way he was looking at me.

It's not smart to think about what happens to a mage after he turns to Dust. If they're given a noble purpose, they're made into something useful like ink for a wright. If not, they might be studied by a Freemaker. But it's an unlucky bastard who gets made into bleakbrew.

It can heal anything, it's said; disease, wounds, broken bones are all cured by a gulp of the stuff. But the process to make it is known by only a few.

And the price?

No one's sure exactly how they do it, but occasionally a Freemaker with too much knowledge and too few scruples awakens a pile of Dust. The barest hint of the mage's consciousness—fears, angers, sorrows—is stilled and forced into a cramped bottle to live in a glass tomb, knowing nothing but terror and fury, before it's eaten alive. It stays alive in there, a living creature that fixes you from the inside, absorbing toxins, cleansing decay, repairing wounds before it dissipates.

That is, if it doesn't kill you. One of you dies, of course, for how else can you restore a life than by taking one?

It's rare stuff, expensive stuff—dangerous to hold, let alone create. It explained how Renita Avonin had made her money, but I wasn't thinking about that.

I was thinking about the poor bastard I had just drunk. And, though it chilled me to do so, I couldn't help but wonder if it was someone I knew.

"I had to." I dropped the bottle to the ground. "There wasn't any other way."

I got to my feet and started to stagger away. I wanted to be far away now—far away from Cavric and his prying eyes, from the shattered bottle of the person I just drank, from everything that made me think Liette was right to think I was broken.

But he didn't let me get more than two steps.

He didn't grab me. He didn't pull me back or curse at me or demand I stop. He just put his hand on my shoulder. And somehow, that was enough to make me stop.

"I believe you," he said, painfully soft. "I believe you didn't see another way. But…" He sighed. "There is. There has to be."

"I don't recall hearing you say anything," I muttered.

"Because you *never* asked me!" he shouted. "You never *tell* me anything. Maybe I could have thought of something. Or maybe I couldn't, I don't know. But we could have tried, if you had trusted me. There has to be another way other than breaking yourself to do it."

He squeezed my shoulder. His hand felt warm.

"Because if you do," he said, "no one else can stop Vraki."

The wind blew softly, carrying with it the smell of burned earth and melting ice. I turned to stare at him. And he, who had every reason to hate me and every chance to run and leave me to die, stared back at me.

And he smiled.

"We have to trust each other," he said. "We don't have anything else left."

I don't know what made him this way. I don't know where the Revolution failed to turn him into an unthinking thrall of the Great General. I don't know how the Scar hadn't turned him into another monster.

But, for once, I didn't want to know.

I smiled back. And he picked up the satchel. And together, we started climbing the hill.

We found Congeniality at the top, peering at me curiously. Clever girl must have followed us. I smiled wearily, stroked her beak as Cavric slipped the satchel and its supplies into her saddlebags.

Almost died, I thought. But I got some metal and some whiskey out of it. Fair trade, I'd say. I sniffed. A pity I couldn't get one of those fancy blades, though.

I heard the click of a weapon behind me.

I turned around, slow, and saw him standing there. Knees shaking, hands trembling with the weight of the gun, eyes wide under the shaggy mop of sand-colored hair on his head, the boy who had been driving the cart with Renita stood at the edge of the hill.

Pointing a hand cannon at me.

"Don't do it, son," Cavric said to the young man.

I held up my hand to keep him back. I started walking toward the kid.

From the look in his eye, it was the first time he'd ever drawn that weapon on another living person.

And it's not that I didn't want his first time to be special, but I had already faced down a creature from beyond worlds, a beast the size of a boulder, and a Siegemage who could hurl that beast through the air like it was a ball.

Whatever would they say if Sal the Cacophony was suddenly scared of a little thing like that?

I walked forward, slowly, eyes locked on his eyes. He backed away, right up until he hit the edge of the hill. He looked behind him and, when he looked up, the barrel of the gun was six inches from my chest.

I glanced down at it, then looked back at him. And without blinking, I took it by the barrel and pulled it out of his hands. He fell back with a shriek, landing on his rear end. And when he looked up into the grinning mouth of the Cacophony drawn on him, he let out a much less dignified sound.

Cavric held his breath behind me, dreading what I might do.

My eyes, narrowed to thin razors, drifted to the clean white of his clothes. I made a gesture with the Cacophony.

"And give me your fucking shirt."

He didn't ask why I wanted it; he simply got right to unbuttoning.

I decided I liked this guy.

"Tell me," I said to him, "when you tell people how this all went down, what are you going to say?"

His lips trembled, trying to find the words as he handed over his shirt. "I'll...I'll say that Sal the Cacophony showed up, robbed us blind, and—"

"Honey." I drew the Cacophony's hammer back. "You can do better than that."

"I'll say that Sal the Cacophony appeared from nowhere!" he blurted out in a fitful cry. "As though from a nightmare that chased us into the waking world, she was upon us in the time it took to scream her name!" He hid behind his hands, sputtering. "I'll say that she spat fire and frost like the breath of a dragon! The winds stood still for fear of drawing her attention! The greatest Siegemage was struck blind by the brightness of her glory! And when she left, only blood and ash and silence lay in her wake!"

"Damn." I raised both eyebrows. "What's your name again?"

"Dennec, madam," he wheezed.

"You've got a real way with words, Dennec. You ever think about going into opera?"

"N-no, madam."

"Huh." I eased the Cacophony's hammer back down, sheathed him. "Well, give it some thought."

And with his—pardon, *my*—new shirt slung over my shoulder, I turned and walked back to my bird, my hand on my gun, Cavric at my side, my mind on the hardest-earned bottle of whiskey I'd ever have.

FORTY

LASTLIGHT

"Try to understand."

The guard, a fellow with better grooming and a cleaner uniform than you'd expect, clasped gloved hands together, plaintive.

"Lastlight is a freehold, yes. But it is not the typical hive of whiskey-soaked thieves masquerading as a civilization you're used to. We stand under the protection of Two Lonely Old Men, wisest of Freemakers, and like all geniuses, he demands certain standards be met."

A fine sight himself in his red and white uniform with matching pin, he gestured to the gates behind him. Carved though it might have been into a graceful arch and emblazoned with the sigil of a red and white lantern, the gate looked no less sturdy for its opulence. The stone was thick and hewn with artisanal care, its walls defiantly smooth, as if daring the wilds of the Scar to come and try to blemish them. The gaggle of snipers, long crossbows gleaming, patrolling the walls would be waiting for whatever dim-witted outlaw who chose to take up that challenge.

"Our fair home has been host to empresses, barons, generals, the greatest men and women to stride across the Scar. Dignitaries from every nation, scholars of every culture. Proud people are made humble in the wake of Lastlight. We are accustomed to a certain standard of visitor and, against even the most blistering storm, refuse to relax that standard so much as an inch."

The guard looked at me pointedly.

I, through eyes ringed by dark, sleepless circles, looked back. I brushed dirt from my tattered, bloodstained shirt and scratched an errant itch on my ass. I snorted, spat a red and green glob on the ground, and wiped my nose with the back of my hand.

"So, what are you trying to say here, pal?"

"I'm *trying* to tell you," the guard said, accompanied by a dramatic sigh fit for opera, "that the city of Lastlight is *closed* to visitors of your caliber."

"My caliber," I repeated.

"A polite way of saying a woman dressed like a thug, tattooed like a cultist, carrying a gun bigger than her head and reeking of birdshit, yes."

"All right, that's just unfair." I jerked my thumb back down the road, toward a large corral. "I stabled my bird back there, so I can't possibly *reek*. I stink, at *worst*. And secondly, how the fuck are you going to tell me the biggest freehold in the Scar isn't accepting visitors?"

"I didn't say 'visitors.'" The guard held up a finger. "I said 'visitors of your caliber.' If you'd like, I can use 'ruffian,' 'undesirable,' or 'general nuisance.'" His eyes drifted over the blood staining my shirt and the Cacophony hanging off my hip. "Though perhaps a stronger word needs to be invented for *your* particular caliber."

I restrained the urge to show him my particular caliber and instead sighed. "Listen, I'm not here to cause trouble. I just want a bathtub and a glass of something harder than water, preferably both big enough for me to disappear into." I patted the hilt of the Cacophony, ignored his seething heat. "This, you have my solemn word, never leaves the sheath."

"Your word."

"Yeah, my word."

"So, is that something people trade when they have no money or..."

I narrowed my eyes. "It's something I give when I *could* very easily blast someone's head into a pulp and make a stiff drink out of the offal, but am choosing *not* to because of how fucking *nice* I am."

"And *that* is precisely the sort of caliber we're trying to avoid here." The guard glanced around, wary. "Look, it's hardly *my* decision. Tensions are running high in the city. Two Lonely Old Men would prefer that volatile elements present be kept to a minimum until things calm down."

The sound of tromping boots drew my attention. I glanced to my side in time to see a regiment of Revolutionary soldiers, gunpikes over their shoulders, dust on their coats, march in tight formation past a pair of guards who waved them in with hardly a look.

"Well, what the fuck do you call *that*?" It would have been impolite to make the gesture I wanted to, so I settled for gesturing to the soldiers. "You don't want volatile elements but you'll gladly let in guys with guns for cocks?"

The guard rubbed his temple. "No one, even Two Lonely Old Men, can keep an army out. I, however, *can* keep one reeking"—he paused—"apologies—*stinking* outlaw out."

"Birdshit," I spat. "What have they got that I haven't?"

He blinked. "Thousands of soldiers, incredible firepower, and shirts that aren't drenched in blood."

"Is that all?"

I reached into my bag, pulled out a wad of linen. I snapped free the shirt that Dennec had so generously donated to me. And, with a little protest from the guard that turned into a *lot* of protest from all the guards, I promptly stripped off my bloodstained garment and tossed it to the ground.

Their outrage didn't last long. I was quick about my business as I pulled Dennec's shirt about me. It was frightfully large—funny, he hadn't seemed that big a kid—and I rolled up the sleeves, tied the hem off. I gestured to my new, clean, and very *not*-soaked-in-my-own-blood garment.

"How about now?"

"Now they've got thousands of soldiers, incredible firepower, and shirts that fit." He sighed, shook his head. "Kindly leave, madam. No one wants to see this turn ugly." He studied me for a moment. "Uglier, anyway."

Maybe it was the fact that I'd been riding so long without sleep I couldn't remember how long it was. Maybe it was the Cacophony burning a hole into my thigh. Or maybe it was the way the light hit this guard's face, so clean and well groomed, that made it look like it could stand a few more holes in it.

"You don't, maybe." My hand drifted to the Cacophony. He burned in anticipation. "I happen to think ugly is a good look."

Mistake.

I felt them before I even heard the strings drawing. Atop the gates, three crossbows were drawn, black bolts aimed right for me. I held my hand where it was, glanced from them to the guard before me, who shot me an insufferably smug smile.

"It'd be no uglier than the mess your corpse will leave on the pavement," he said. "But please, if not for your own squandered dignity, have some care for the poor bastard we'd make clean it up."

From any other dust-necked, shit-for-brains guard, I would have walked away long ago. From a dust-necked, shit-for-brains guard with clever insults like that, though, I had to actively fight the urge not to blow his head off and deal with the consequences.

As it was, though, I imagined he'd somehow look even more smug if I were to get shot—even with his head blown off. So I eased my hand away from the Cacophony and turned on one heel to stalk away.

My furious exit was hindered as I started limping. The Cacophony burned against my hip. If he could talk, he'd doubtlessly be demanding I turn and fight, or perhaps demanding to know why we were bothering with this city to begin with. Fortunately for me, he couldn't communicate outside of causing pain. And I found that pain easier to deal with than the futility of my situation.

Vraki hadn't been in the Husks.

The one place I was sure he'd be, he wasn't. And if he wasn't there,

I had no idea where he might be. I was out of leads. I was out of hunches. I was out of ideas, entirely, and left with only a single, desperate hope.

And it lay behind those gates.

Ah, well, I thought as I walked down the road. *At least it isn't personal.*

That thought provided the coldest of comforts as I was greeted with the sight of dozens of rejected visitors. Across the scrub grass and upon the riverbanks, they gathered in clusters: merchants tending to restless rothacs, yawning mercenaries repolishing weapons for the sixtieth time, refugees from places no one had ever heard of or would ever hear from again staring at nothing in particular with empty eyes.

It wasn't right. Or normal.

It was true that Lastlight was one of the richest freeholds in the Scar. Rich enough that it had been the desire of both Imperium and Revolutionary armies, as well as rich enough to fight those armies to a standstill and force them to come in as peaceful traders. And it was also true that Two Lonely Old Men, the Freemaker who ran it, held it under a tight fist. But it was wealthy precisely because of people like these, the people who brought trade—be it coin, blood, or news—from all around to feed into the tightly regulated machine that Two Lonely Old Men had made his city into.

For them to be barred meant Two Lonely Old Men was actively turning away money. And whatever could have occurred for him to make *that* decision, I didn't know. I only knew three things: I needed to get in, I wasn't getting in, and *someone* was being absolutely no help in achieving either.

"What was that you said back there?" I screamed at Cavric as I found him up a dune on the outskirts of the city. " 'We need to trust each other, we're all we've got, weh weh weh weh.'" *I* thought my impression of his voice was flawless, but he didn't even look over his shoulder as I approached. "Where the fuck were you?"

He didn't answer and I didn't ask again. When I saw what his eyes were locked on, neither of us had to.

I got my answer in the cloud of severium smoke hanging in the sky, in the sound of soldiers mustering for battle, in the rows of cannons marching the length of the valley below.

Three dozen gunmetal-gray gravestones, in want of bodies.

Their Relic engines hummed, sending their armor and wheels rattling against the barrels. Around them, Revolutionaries buzzed like flies, either barking out orders or heeding them. Machinists hammered on metal. Soldiers drilled with gunpikes. Commanders shot hand cannons into the air to accentuate their roars.

Everything was present for a war... except the war.

"This is... a mistake."

I wasn't the only one to notice.

"There shouldn't be this many guns here." Cavric shook his head. "There shouldn't be this many guns *anywhere* except an active battleground. This is... this..." He looked over his shoulder toward the city. "Lastlight is *neutral*. There are only a few Imperial diplomats here. Nothing that would require this kind of..." His face screwed up, as though he could chew sense out of the situation if he just gritted his teeth hard enough. "Why are they *here*?"

I looked at him. And for a moment, I thought about just shrugging and walking away. But something in me—an itch that I couldn't scratch ever since I had met him—made me speak.

"Have you gone down there and asked them?"

He looked at me with surprise. He knew as well as I did what that meant. He could go down there, tell them what had happened, be back with his people and be rid of the woman who had abducted him at gunpoint. Whatever blood or bodies or burnt wreckage I was going to leave in my wake, he could be free of it.

He could be free of me.

And that itch would hurt, turn to something sharp at the base of my skull, when he finally took off down that valley and left me and the gun to be by ourselves. But it would hurt worse if I didn't do it. I was expecting hurt.

"No."

I wasn't expecting that.

"No, that wouldn't make sense." He shook his head, pointed down to the valley below. "See the commanders? Only sergeants among them. No one down there knows anything but their orders. It'd be a waste of time." He looked over my shoulder, to the city walls. "There's no command tent in the valley, which means the higher-ups must be in the city." He nodded. "Which means we need to get in."

"Yeah," I grunted. "I tried that already. They didn't let me in."

"What? Why not?"

I shut one eye, raised one leg, let out a brief fart. "No idea."

He sighed. "We'll try another way, then."

It felt weird to be the one following him for a change—or at least, following him without pointing something stabby or shooty at his back—but I did, anyway, as he took off at a jog back to the city gates.

He just looked so *excited*, you know?

I hurried to keep up with him as he started pushing through the crowds and travelers. "What?" I said. "Are we going to charge the gates?" I drew my gun. "Like, I'm down and all, but *I* could have thought of that."

"No!" he shouted back, picking up speed. "No guns! And stay twenty feet behind me and to the right."

"What? What for?"

He shot a look over his shoulder. "Trust me."

I did. Every part of me screamed not to, to just keep running past him and start shooting and hope for the best. But I fell behind him. I held off to the right. And I watched as he burst into a sprint and came to a skidding halt in front of the gates.

"Halt!" The nice-looking guard who had stopped me earlier held up a hand, his other on his sword, though he didn't draw it. "If you please."

"Can't...can't..." Cavric's breath came dramatically short and wheezy, sweat pouring off his brow. "Trouble...in the valley. Need help."

"What help?" the guard asked, furrowing his brow. "If it's a Revolutionary matter, we can fetch your commander for you and have him here in—"

I quirked a brow, just far away enough to still hear them—Cavric had been correct, then. Regardless, he shook his head violently and pointed off to the valley.

"No time," he gasped. "Need you there *now*! A fight broke out. Some weapons went missing. They accused the Revolution. They're about to start shooting."

"What?" The guard squinted. "That's...that's a Revolutionary problem. Lastlight's peacekeepers are needed here for—"

"You fucking moron!" Cavric reached up and seized the guard by his collar. "It was Renita *Avonin* who made the accusation! The Avonins are saying the Revolution stole from them!"

It's a thing of beauty watching a lie come together.

I know that makes me sound like an asshole, but the instant I heard Cavric say it, I couldn't help but be impressed. The Revolution had guns and soldiers, but the Avonins had *money*. Lastlight wouldn't want to piss off either of them, especially with so much military build-up and with tensions as high as they theoretically were.

I watched the guard's face as he pieced this all together, the horror slowly dawning on it. He drew his blade, gestured to his fellow guards.

"You!" He pointed up to the peacekeepers on the wall. "Get word to Two Lonely Old Men. Tell him what's happened and get more men to the gates!" He grunted at the others. "The rest of you, with me!"

They took off at a run. The peacekeepers kept an eye on them. A call went out as someone summoned more bodies to the gates and travelers complained and shouted and rothacs lowed and birds squawked and absolutely no one noticed a man in a dirty coat and a woman with a scar slip past and into the streets.

And after that? We were just two more people, slipping into the crowds.

We walked for a time, disappearing down a busy avenue and vanishing into the crowd. I glanced over my shoulder and, content that we hadn't been followed, nudged Cavric with my elbow.

"You can breathe now."

He let out a sharp gasp, his eyes bulging out of their sockets as he flailed his hands. "General's graces," he said, panting, "I did *not* think that was going to work. I was sure they were going to know. I feel tingly. Do I look tingly? I feel tingly."

"Relax." I chuckled, slapping him on the back. "You did some fine fucking work."

"Praise from Sal the Cacophony, huh?" He shot me a crooked grin of his own. "I'm not sure if I should be pleased or horrified."

"A little of both is probably your safest bet."

Lastlight loomed large over us, its buildings of finely polished stone and well-hewn timbers rising into a pristine sky. And prowling atop it, peacekeepers with their fancy crossbows walked. I pulled my cloak up a little tighter around me.

"We should get out of sight soon," I muttered. "Until we're sure no one noticed your little stunt back there."

"Right," Cavric said, sighing. "I have to find where Cadre Command is and..." He held out his hands, helpless. "I don't know. Figure out what's happening and see how many people I can keep from getting hurt."

"You've got a plan?"

"No. But I can't let that stop me. They need to know we've got problems." He glanced at me sidelong. "I'd invite you to come tell them what you know about Vraki, but I don't know if I could get a Vagrant in, even to inform on another Vagrant."

"What?" I grinned. "You couldn't make up another fabulous lie?"

"That was...just a trick." He chuckled. "I couldn't think of anything else, honestly. I thought I'd try to pull what you did on the Redway and say 'Do you know who I am?' or something. But I don't think I could have done it like you did."

"Yeah, no, never ask that question unless you already know the answer," I replied. "Still, I'm impressed. Cavric Proud, lying through his fucking teeth. What *would* the Cadre say?"

"They'd understand," he said. "If it was to help prevent people getting killed, they'd understand. That's why I have to tell them about Vraki, about Stark's Mutter. The Revolution is here to help people, the downtrodden and the oppressed."

His face dropped a little and I could see his head wander back to the valley, back to the scene below. And I could see him wonder how the hell that many guns were going to keep anyone from getting hurt.

"It's supposed to be at least," he muttered.

I didn't say anything. I didn't look at him as he looked away. And despite the roar of the city—the laughter of people from café patios and the barking of merchants and the raspy crackle of voccaphones playing the latest operas—a funerary silence fell between us.

The loudest sound in the world is a man of faith beginning to doubt.

And over it, I couldn't hear anything else.

FORTY-ONE

LASTLIGHT

After a guard patrol had gotten a little too interested, Cavric and I had split up with the agreement to meet later.

Or rather, *he* had agreed to meet up later. I was still mulling it over.

We both had our own business here in the city. His might lead him back to me. And my business, the man I had come here to see...

If there was any justice, my business would lead me to Vraki.

I didn't tell him about that. And I didn't feel good about not telling him, especially after such stirring words about trust. But there are a few reasons that would make me do something like that. Revenge was one of them.

A hot bath was another.

So don't get me wrong, when I walked out onto the streets of Lastlight, the steam of the bathhouse still draped around my shoulders like a mantle, I felt bad. But I also felt clean, the chill of the air pricking the warm skin of my scars and the absence of all the blood and the dirt and the dried sweat that I had left behind to disappear down a drain. And though I knew that more blood lay ahead of me, like it always did, it was nice to pretend, for a moment, that I wasn't in the business of killing people.

For that feeling, I'd do a lot of things.

I tried to put it out of my mind when I walked out onto Lastlight's streets. And one of the richest freeholds in the Scar was all too happy to oblige.

Lastlight was everything freeholds weren't supposed to look like. The buildings were tall and elegant, built of polished stone, with windows and red tile roofs instead of barricades and thick doors. Streets cleaned of stray garbage and stray drunks alike marched one way, lining gondola-choked canals that marched the other. There were cafés instead of public houses, tailors instead of armories, places selling things like fine wines, fine plates, fine tapestries, and all the other things you would never need in the wilds.

And the lights... they were everywhere.

They hung in long, draping streams that ran from rooftop to rooftop. They drifted aimlessly across the surface of the canals, given a respectful berth by the gondolas and boats plying the waterways. Paper lanterns of crimson and ivory sleepily dotted the city and, one by one, awoke with the same soft glow as the city's sigil.

No one knew what alchemic Two Lonely Old Men had used to make them light up every day, just before sunset, without anyone lighting them. Not even other Freemakers; in fact, as far as they were concerned, such aesthetic frivolity was a waste of his considerable talents that could otherwise be dedicated to their cause.

Liette, after three glasses of wine, would rant for hours about what a dick he was. Her face would get all red and she'd scream and hop up and down and it was kind of adorable.

I missed that.

I missed a lot of things.

However fascinated I was by the lanterns, the people of Lastlight didn't share my enthusiasm.

And, for as glorious as the freehold might have been, it seemed altogether too shabby for its citizens.

No one was pushing or shoving. The air was filled with laughter, unprompted by dick jokes. There was not a single fight to be seen. Hell, these people looked like they might break if you brushed against them.

Men in coats lined with gold, their hair oiled and their beards neatly trimmed. Ladies in gowns wrapped around their bodies in shimmering skins of amethyst, emerald, colors I couldn't even tell you the name of. Even the children were dressed nicely, chasing each other on shoes that looked like they cost more than my boots, my belt, and my weapons combined.

And the clothes were the least ostentatious thing about them. Birds of a hundred different colors walked the streets—long-tailed creatures with gemstone feathers perched on the shoulders of wealthy ladies, and young men raced long-legged, ivory-feathered Imperials down the streets. The smoke of alchemic waterpipes filled the air with scents of flowers, of fruit, and—one time—of I think farts? Enchanted platters from Cathama floated in the air, serving drinks to people in cafés while unseen violinists played a tune from instruments hovering five feet in the air.

You'd think that would have been what made me feel weird.

But it felt strange to walk among them for different reasons. Me, with my scars, my tattoos, my shabby clothes, and my heavy gun at my hip. I half expected someone to call for a guard, to be charged with the crime of spoiling some rich man's view.

But they didn't look at me. They didn't talk to me. They didn't care that a killer was walking around their city, if they noticed at all.

It wasn't illegal to carry guns in Lastlight, same as any freehold. They didn't bother even glancing at me as I made my way through the evening crowds. Rather, it was me who couldn't stop staring at them.

Them laughing, them sipping wine, them walking around with the easy, languid gait of people who'd never even thought about touching a weapon, let alone using it on someone else. I watched those people walk past me.

And I don't think I could remember how to walk that way, if I ever knew in the first place.

"Step aside, citizen!"

Fortunately, the unease I felt at normalcy was suddenly replaced with the familiar tension reminding me where the fuck I was.

A voice bellowed at the top of its lungs but was drowned out by the sound of iron gears groaning and a scratchy voccaphone playing. Which, in turn, was drowned out by the sound of the earth shuddering beneath a heavy gait as a tremendous mass of iron and severium came lumbering toward me.

From afar, you might have called it a very big man. Its head, topped with a jagged horn, scraped just shy of seven and a half feet tall. Its shoulders spread far enough to take up a city street, its arms massive and its legs causing the earth to shake with every groaning step.

But in place of clothes, it wore a skin of iron, its body a mess of hard angles and hammered metal plates. In place of a face, it wore a hollow visor shrouded in a halo of steam hissing from the massive engines strapped to its back. And in place of a hand, its gigantic arm ended in a big fuck-off gun.

Up close, you'd call it a monster.

But the Revolution called it a Paladin.

"*Hail the Revolution and be at ease, citizens.*" Its voice was human, though ringing with a metallic echo as it bellowed to be heard over the voccaphone strapped to its shoulder blaring the Revolutionary anthem. "*The liberators from the Imperial filth have returned to safeguard this city.*"

The Paladins were intended to be symbols, both of might and ideal.

"They stand as bulwarks against the corrupt, crusaders against villainy, as in the legends of old," their Great General had said of them.

Only he must have thought the legends of old could have stood to have guns that could reduce a man to a bucket of steaming meat in two seconds. The Revolution slapped a Relic engine into them, strapped their biggest, heaviest weapons to them, and turned loose on the battlefield. I'd seen them mow through ranks of soldiers like they were wheat. Even knowing what I did about them, I could barely believe there was a human inside piloting that thing.

All the magic in the world could barely be as terrifying as machines sometimes.

Six Revolutionaries flanked it, marching in lockstep as they barked at citizens to clear the path, who were all too eager to do so. Yet far from the tension I felt at its passing, the citizens of Lastlight laughed and applauded in its wake. To them, it was one massive prop in a very elaborate opera.

They didn't see.

Just like they hadn't noticed me, they didn't see the soldiers. Knots of blue coats marched in formation up and down the streets, Revolutionary gunpikes bared and glistening over their shoulders as they stalked around like packs of dogs searching for fresh meat.

And they weren't the only ones.

I heard her song, first, the distant, lilting notes of the Lady Merchant. And then I spotted them. Amid the crowds, I spotted them. The glistening amethyst colors of Imperial uniforms as soldiers of Cathama strode along the promenades. The regal winged crests of the capital glistening on the breasts of officers lounging in cafés. The air felt electric with restrained magic: flameglaives eager to ignite, thunderbows crackling in anticipation.

And everywhere, *everywhere*, there was violence. In the scowls cast between patrols passing each other on the streets, in the curses hurled between officers over the canals, in the useless displays of dragging a clunky war machine like a Paladin down a crowded street.

This, I supposed, was the "volatile situation" the guard had been referring to.

Lastlight had always been a target desirable for the Imperium and the Revolution. It sat at a perfect nexus of river, road, and coast, bringing trade from all three. Either faction would be eager to have it and loath to alienate it, thus guaranteeing the most awkward truce of all time overseen by Two Lonely Old Men.

But something had changed.

There were too many soldiers on the streets. The scowls came accompanied by hands drifting toward weapons. The curses came with specific and explicit threats. These people were ready to kill.

I pulled my cloak up a little tighter around me. Whatever normalcy I might have felt was dashed now that I was aware of how many people were here who probably had a pretty good reason to kill me.

I saw the red and white colors of snipers patrolling the rooftops, their eyes on the soldiers below, their Freemaker-wrought crossbows at the ready. But they were designed to handle small problems, discreetly. I wondered if Two Lonely Old Men even knew his freehold was a powder keg, let alone how close it was to exploding.

Because his citizens didn't have a fucking clue.

Someone had to tell them, to warn them.

Someone *else*, I mean. Someone who didn't have plans already.

I shook my worries off with each hurried step I took, started making room for plans. Vraki hadn't been in Vigil, but he couldn't have gone far if he had left Galta and Taltho behind. The Crown Conspiracy had been shattered and he was a wanted man by both the Revolution and Imperium—allies weren't something he'd be tossing around easily.

He'd still be in the Husks. And if there was anyone who knew anything about where an all-powerful Prodigy about to summon an abomination from beyond the stars was, they'd be here in Lastlight.

Unfortunately, I didn't know anyone who knew anything.

Fortunately, I *did* know someone who knew everything.

*Un*fortunately, I hadn't parted with them on the best of terms.

Fortunately, as you've gathered, I don't really tend to give a shit about that sort of thing.

In my head, it sounded like a plan. But then, my head was a noisy place lately. It was full of fears: fears that I was too late, fears that I'd never save those kids, fears that Vraki was thinking six or seven steps ahead and was already gone and laughing at me.

Fears that I'd never find him. Or Jindu. Or any of them.

That they'd get away with it.

Those fears weighed on my shoulders, slowed me down as I went hurrying through the streets, pushing through the pristine crowd of pretty people, over a bridge leading to the other side of the canals, where the houses were a little shabbier and the lights a little dimmer.

And, for a brief and black moment, I wondered if those worries on my shoulders would be enough to sink me if I just jumped in.

That's when I heard it.

An avian screech cut through the sky. I felt a breeze carrying with it the scent of lilacs and embers. My muscles tensed, fearing an attack. My gun burned, ready for a fight. But my heart... my heart knew that sound.

And it sang.

I looked up and saw them. Feathers glittering the color of amethyst against the dying light of the day, long tails trailing in the breeze like kites, wings shimmering with every beat. They looked so oblivious to their majesty, like flying and painting the sky with purple was just something they did, rather than something that made my knees shake.

In perfect formation, they flew, each one guided by an Imperium rider in purple armor. The banner of Cathama, the great bird with wings outstretched, flapped overhead. They opened their beaks, each of them, and loosed a cry that cut through my skin.

Krikai.

The great birds from whom the Imperium had taken its sigil. Living omens of the Lady Merchant's favor. Beasts whose beauty and bloodthirst were awed and feared in equal measure by the Emperor's foes.

Under their shadows, children raced to keep up, the people looked up with awestruck laughter. And, at that moment, I was one of them.

I had been a girl when I had seen them last. Back then, they'd seemed impossibly majestic, a cruel joke left to remind us how ugly and earthbound we were. I remembered seeing their tails trailing as they spun elegantly in the sky. On that day, I hadn't cared about war or vengeance or metal.

On that day, I hadn't cared about anything but being like them, flying like them. And I had barely been able to hold back tears.

On this day, I couldn't.

The world suddenly seemed far too big, too full of people and too full of noises. My legs felt too small for my body; I had to lean against the bridge. Tears fell from my eyes, stinging when they seeped into my scars.

I must have looked stupid; Sal the fucking Cacophony, weeping like a little girl at the sight of a bunch of extremely fancy pigeons.

I wish I could have told you why I did.

But no one noticed. As the Krikai and their riders flew over the rooftops and disappeared, they resumed their business of being fabulous and happy. They didn't see me, still looking up at the sky, whispering.

"Eres va atali."

I wiped my eyes, pulled my cloak a little tighter. Sal the Cacophony didn't cry. Sal the Cacophony got the fuck on with things.

I needed answers. I needed a drink.

Fortunately, I knew where to find one of those.

FORTY-TWO

LASTLIGHT

If you learn any three lessons from me, they are these.
You never know a person until you see them angry. You never
know a weapon until it fails you. And you never know a city until
the sun goes down.

Most freeholds—the kind that didn't have more money than
sense—went to bed when night fell on the Scar. It doused its lights
so as to not attract predators. It shut its gates to keep bandits out. Its
people slept in short, uncomfortable spurts, ready to wake and run.

But when night fell, Lastlight opened its eyes.

Its elegant people became bawdy, trading wine for whiskey and
song for laughter. Its fancy shops became dark markets, selling
expensive alchemics and dangerous weapons instead of vases and
scarves. It didn't need the moon or the stars. It had its own.

The lanterns lit up the sky as I made way down its raucous avenues. The people who had once ignored me, now made more observant by too much drink, suddenly couldn't help but notice the
tattooed adventurer in their midst.

"My, my, madam," said one such woman, tipping forward slightly
as she approached me. "Look at you."

"Look at *you*," I shot back, grinning. She reached out a hand and

I took it, if only to keep her from tumbling headlong into the canals. "Are you well, madam?"

"Quite so," she giggled through an Imperial dialect. "One cannot say the same of you, can they, darling?" Her eyes drifted over me, eyes lighting up at every scar. "Gracious. You've been in the Scar, have you?"

"Quite so."

"And you survived?"

I smirked a little. "*Quite* so."

"How exciting!" she gasped. "We never get anything but merchants and their thugs here and *they've* never seen anything exciting but the dirt on the road. To see an adventurer is so"—her eyes drifted lower, to what I chose to believe was my gun—"dangerous."

She took my hand and ran a pair of fingers across my tattoos.

"Oh, where did you get these done? What do they mean?" Her attention span was as short as her touch as she found a scar on my wrist. "What beast did *this*?" Her hand shot out, found a scar on my side, winced. "What about *this*?"

"Cathama, for your first question." My scars tingled at her touch, sent me stepping back. Not that she wasn't still lovely, in the same way a puppy is still cute when they pee on the floor, but I only let a few people touch my scars. "The others are a longer story."

"Perhaps you'd like to tell me." Her hand splayed across my side, slid spiderlike across my belly as it eased toward the Cacophony hanging off my hip. "I trust they take all night to tell?"

My body tensed. Hairs stood up in the wake of her wandering hand. The Cacophony burned in resentment of this peasant's fingers drifting close. I laughed to hide my wince as I took her gently by the wrist and eased her hands back to her own space.

"Oh, what?" Her loveliness turned to sourness in an instant. "I thought adventurers were intended to be...adventurous."

"One, I'm not an adventurer," I replied. "Not the way you mean, anyway. Two, you're drunk and I'm not. And three, it's generally not considered a great idea to go grabbing strange women's guns." I paused. "Or to go grabbing guns when you're a strange woman."

"Pfft." She rolled her eyes. "What is it going to do? Kill me?"

I blinked. "Yes. It's a gun. That's what guns do."

"You're exaggerating."

"How?"

I glanced around. Even after dark, I could still see them. Their formations had loosened, along with their discipline, but they were still there. Revolutionary soldiers assembled in gangs, scowling at ostentatious Imperial officers glaring from their seats. They hadn't traded their weapons for wine; rather, they simply decided to have both.

"Have you just not noticed all the people waiting to shoot each other or what?" I asked the woman.

"Oh, them?" she scoffed. "What are they going to do?"

"Start shooting and kill everyone, for one."

"The first to fire a shot loses the favor of Two Lonely Old Men," the woman replied. "Which means they lose the trade contracts, their garrison, everything that wonderful Freemaker gives. What madman would try that?"

"The kind with a lot of guns."

"You've been out in the Scar too long, darling. Things are different in a freehold like Lastlight. Here, we maintain a slightly higher class of civility." She licked her lips. "So, are you going to piss on my face or am I simply wasting my time?"

I blinked.

I stared at her for a very long time.

Then I quietly pulled my cloak tighter, turned on my heel, and left.

I walked the streets, taking the right turns until the wealth thinned out and the lantern lights dimmed. The buildings became a little shabbier, the canals grew a little murkier, the scents stopped being nice and started being rank. When I rounded a corner and walked into a vast, sprawling square, the reek of whiskey and the sound of violence met me.

Lastlight was a lovely freehold, but it was still a freehold and this was still the Scar. The streets might be nicely manicured and the people might be their own version of "civilized," but dig deep enough, and you'll eventually strike a big shitty well.

And to find Beetle Square, you didn't have to dig very far at all.

The lanterns were still here, strung up in a tangled spiderweb between the cramped houses, but their wax paper was stained by smoke and their lights flickered and dimmed. The narrow canal running through it had empty bottles and fouler things bobbing in it. The stink of meat on open grills and cheap whiskey replaced the aroma of perfume and wine. The laughter here was cruder, guttural, and heralded by coarse jokes and blood loss. And the citizens here...

"One side, scarface."

They weren't here.

On any other night, I might have said something to the hulking, shirtless man who pressed past me on his way into the square. On a good night, I might have forgone with words and just gone straight to fists.

But this was not a good night, I didn't want to touch anyone as greasy-looking as him, and I was here on business.

Not that anyone else showed the same restraint. Various outlaws, bandits, smugglers, and your general variety of scum rolled around the square, alternating between drunken mobs and drunken fistfights. Holding themselves apart but still close to the violence, hooded Ashmouths lurked under shadowy eaves, observant and heedless of who might know their affiliation.

The tension I had seen on the main streets was strangely absent here. But I supposed that followed. Any Revolutionary or Imperial caught in Beetle Square would find themselves reprimanded. The most damage anyone could do here was limited to breaking bottles and throwing punches.

Not that they don't try their best, bless them, I thought as I eased past a very large woman trying to force-feed a very large man a very large fist.

The public houses here were teeming with lowlifes, any one of them brimming with secrets that might have led me to my quarry.

A few knuckles spent, a few drinks bought, and I'd know the names of everyone who had passed within twenty miles of Lastlight in the past two months.

And I'm sure if I had any desire at all to go into a house that smelled like a bird and a hog got smashed on cheap whiskey and had an evening they'd regret in the morning, I'd have all the information I needed.

But fuck that. I had *just* taken a bath.

I pushed my way through the crowds, picked my way past the fights, absently broke fingers that reached just a little too close, until I made my way to a humble little two-story building wedged between an abandoned spice shop and a boarded-up warehouse.

The smell of boiling water and fried dough reached my nose. The din of the crowd dimmed to a chattering burble within. I glanced at the sign over the door and smiled.

Grandma Athaka's Dumplings.

Same as it ever was.

I started to push open the door, then paused, remembering to take off my hood. My host was big on manners. And I could not afford to offend.

Not with the favor I was going to ask.

An old voccaphone's music greeted me as I pushed the door open, some old, grainy opera from before my time. A fitting atmosphere for the clientele.

Far removed from the sweaty brawlers, the customers here were old, white-haired men and women clad in well-worn coats and puffing on slender pipes. Most of them sat cloistered around a central table, intently observing a beetle wrestling match.

Others sat at smaller tables and counters, delicately munching on dumplings or sipping soup. Only a few bothered to furrow a suspicious white brow as I entered, but I was a much less interesting sight than the beetles battling, and I was quickly ignored.

Just as well. I was only interested in the attentions of one old person.

She sat behind a counter at the far edge of the restaurant, veiled in clouds of steam rising from pots full of boiling water. Gray hair tied up beneath a bandana, squat body wrapped up in a shirt and apron, wrinkles exacerbated by the deep-set frown in her face, she didn't even look up at me, her attentions fixed on mincing meat and vegetables and folding them into dumplings to drop in her pots.

I pulled up a chair at the counter. Her assistant, the only other person here under fifty, came trotting up.

"Welcome, weary traveler!" His exuberant smile at finally seeing someone not wrinkled was unabashed, but the patrons didn't notice. "I hope you've come with an appetite. You'll not find a better dumpling in the Scar than in Grandma Athaka's."

I smiled at him. It was nice, this kind of attention, the one when I could pretend we were just a young woman and a young man exchanging winks and smiles. I had forgotten the last time I had done this.

I had forgotten I ever did this.

"I've heard as much," I said. "And I'd like to know what's on the menu."

"Ah, you're in luck," he replied. "Tonight, we're making a special dumpling out of cabbage and peppers, a spicy treat that's—"

"If you don't mind..." I hated to interrupt but did anyway. I cast a glance toward the old woman. "I'd like to hear from the master."

The boy looked positively wounded at that. But my eyes were on the old woman as she shot me a sidelong glare, sizing me up through dark, rheumy eyes. For a moment, she looked like she was about to spit on me. Then she returned to mincing the meat.

"Spicy dumpling," she grunted. "Peppers, cabbage, pork."

"I prefer chicken," I said.

"Out of chicken," she replied.

"Beef?" I asked.

"Out of beef."

I paused, looked at her intently. "How about rothac?"

She shot me a curious look. "Rothac tastes terrible."

"But it sates any hunger."

The old woman paused chopping at that. Her sidelong glare became a full-on stare for a moment. She let out a low and ancient hum.

As she turned back to her chopping board, she accidentally knocked over a jar of spices and sent it rolling across the counter. I caught it, moved to return it to her. Her hand rested upon mine, and through thin lips, I heard her whisper, too low for anyone to hear:

"Ten minutes. Upstairs."

I nodded. She released my hand, replaced the jar.

"Going on break." She took her apron off and tossed it to her assistant, who caught it with a fumble. She gestured at me. "She gets a plate of dumplings. And some water."

"Whiskey," I corrected.

"*Water.*" She narrowed her eyes at me before turning and disappearing behind a curtain. "Be back whenever."

The assistant cast an exasperated sigh at her back before pulling some steaming dumplings from the pot and arranging them on a plate. He offered it to me, along with a cup of water and an apologetic smile.

"Sorry," he said. "I'd still give you the whiskey, but she doesn't even keep any." He awkwardly fumbled with his hands for a moment before giving me a shy look. "If you want, I could...run to one of the public houses and get a bottle?"

I smiled, waved a hand. "Don't trouble yourself. I'm sure whiskey would only ruin the taste." I plucked up a dumpling, dunked it in some sauce. "But thank you for offering."

"Anything," he replied, grinning. He coughed, looked nervous. "Uh, I mean any*time*, and if there's any*thing* I can do for you, just let me know, okay?"

"What's your name?" I asked.

"Thrish," he said, beaming. "Thrishicataca, if you're formal. My parents were, uh, from the Imperium."

I popped the dumpling in my mouth, chewed. "You serve a damn fine dumpling, Thrish."

He smiled so hard his face damn near split in half. He gave me a brief nod, turned to mincing meat and preparing more dumplings, though I could tell he was trying to hide a blush so bright you could have seen it from a mile away in the dark.

I was tempted to sit there and talk to him some more. Not that I was after anything, mind—he was cute, but too young. It just felt nice to...you know, *talk*. Not negotiate, not lie, not threaten, just talk to a nice boy who made a nice dumpling. Sometimes it was hard to remember what that was like. And every time I opened my mouth to tell another lie or curse another name, it got a little harder.

His name was Thrish. He was cute and he didn't talk to many women. And he served a damn fine dumpling.

Had I known I was about to ruin his life, I probably would have felt bad right about then.

FORTY-THREE

GRANDMA ATHAKA'S DUMPLINGS

Once, a freehold hired me to clear out a bonegrinder. Big, ugly thing, looks like a crab with a shell made out of skulls, it gets its name from the bones of its victims, which it grinds into a paste and makes into a new shell when it gets ready to breed. It lurks around carrion fields and graveyards, digging up rotten corpses to pry the bones loose. It was a hell of a fight, too much of one for what they paid me, if I'm honest.

But I digress.

The point is that, having adequate comparison, fighting something that ate and spat out corpses still did not smell as bad as this fucking attic.

Upstairs in the shop was a mess of worn pots, broken pans, and jars of preserved vegetables on rickety shelves. Normal enough for a dumpling shop to have, but amid the cooking debris were a couple of old portraits of men with important clothes, a broken vocca-phone, a trunk of old clothes, and basically every other piece of crap you'd expect an old woman to have.

I wasn't mad. It was, after all, the point.

I picked my way through the musty debris, sparing a glance for the old walls every few steps. My nostrils quivered as I did. The wood reeked of retained rain and age, but one spot, right in front of a box of single boots, smelled just slightly less weird than the rest.

I reached out, rapped my knuckles against the wall.

Behind it, someone scurried across the floor, paused to spit out a particularly nasty curse, then grunted. Old hinges groaned. A false door swung open, prompting me to step back. Warm light flooded out from behind the door, painting irritated shadows across the wrinkles of the old woman scowling at me from the doorway.

"I said ten minutes," she grumbled.

"I was eating."

"It's been *twenty*."

"Well," I said as I pushed past her, "make a shittier dumpling next time."

"Language," she hissed as she pulled the door shut behind me.

Far from the reeking corridor it hid behind, the room was a pinnacle of class. A lamp bathed it in warm orange light, painting the carpeted floors and leather furniture in a welcoming glow. Doors led off to a fancy, if small, bathroom and bedroom. The odor of wealthy things—fine tobacco, old leather, and even older liquor—filled the room.

It would be the kind of place I'd dream of owning one day, if only it had a window.

But, then, that would kind of defeat the purpose of a spy's secret lair, wouldn't it?

"This would imply I am capable of anything less than perfection." The old woman stalked into the room, her gait a little swifter, her back a little straighter. "One is not elevated to my particular position without performance unerring." She paused, cast a glower over my shoulder, her eyes suddenly keen. "Hence why you seek me out every three months."

She pointedly cast a glower at my cloak as I rolled my eyes, tossed it off. "Has it been that long?" I asked.

"You are rather like a clock in your machinations, Salazanca." The old woman shook an ache out of her withered hand. When she stopped, her fingers were thick and masculine. "At regular junctions, you can be trusted to make a tremendous racket, shoot things up, and generally make my life harder."

"That metaphor doesn't *quite* work," I replied. "Age getting to you, huh?"

She sneered at me with teeth that were no longer yellow, nor rotten. "You are well aware this is simply a disguise."

"My mistake." I grinned the sort of half-cocky, half-cringing grin that I knew she hated. "I just figured you'd been wearing it so long you actually became an old woman."

She straightened up to an imposing height she hadn't been before. Her hands, now strong and broad, clenched into fists. Her skin rippled like the waters of a disturbed lake.

And, faintly, I heard the Lady's song.

It happened so quick I could barely keep track of it, even as she changed before my eyes. Her arms grew long and elegant to match the spidery hands. Her torso stretched out, back stiffened, chest flattened to lean muscle. Her legs unbent themselves, face unwrinkled itself, bones un-olded themselves—and I'm aware that isn't a word, but really I had no idea what else to call it.

How *does* one describe the work of a Maskmage, after all?

Freaky, I suppose, would be a good start. That was what came to mind as she stood up straight, her dress and stained apron fading away as fine clothes of violet and black silk blossomed across a body that was suddenly tall, lean, and very, *very* male.

She—or rather, he—looked down at me through hawkish eyes over a long nose. And I, in exchange, cringed and looked away.

"Fuck, I'm never going to get used to that," I said. "Do you *have* to do that in front of me?"

"Language," the tall man snapped back at me, folding lithe arms over lithe chest. His voice carried with it the rasp of age, though not quite as gravelly as the woman's had been, and though his hair was no longer the dark iron gray of the old woman's, it still held an elderly man's distinguished silver.

He could assume any shape, of course, but whether he was an old woman, a young man, a child, or a dog on the street, Alothenes, Imperial spymaster, would always be a crotchety old shit underneath it all.

"And I am unconvinced that you have not seen more obscene things than a Maskmage's art." Alothenes strode toward his bedroom with the poise of a noble, paused with the pointed drama of an opera actor. "Frankly, I am unconvinced that you have not *done* things more obscene."

"Yeah? Well, I don't make you watch them, now, do I?" I called after him.

"No. You merely come to me anytime you need them cleaned up," he replied.

"Like I've never done anything for you," I shot back. "Was it or was it not your old friend who took care of those Revolutionary agents sniffing around your shop?"

"I recall a thuggish woman bedecked in tattoos and dressed like a savage handling that." He pointedly glared at me over his shoulder. "Certainly *not* the talented young woman I had the pleasure of serving the Imperium with."

"Once had," I corrected him.

"Once," he repeated, a pained note in his voice. "As it happens, I was rather happy with that arrangement. Favor for favor is a classic exchange among those of refined breeding. Yet I cannot help but cringe at the circumstances that lead you to be standing in my room."

He paused, ran an appraising eye over me.

"Speaking of which, stand up straight," he said. "Your posture is an insult."

More swiftly than I would have liked, I straightened up. "Happy?"

"Yes. Now, sit down. You're a guest." He went into his bedroom, letting my muttered insult go unchallenged as I sat down upon the sofa. "I feel stupid for asking, but may I offer you a drink?"

"You sound stupid for asking," I replied. "I'll take that drink and an explanation for what 'circumstances' you're talking about."

"Refrain from insulting my intellect, Salazanca, and I will struggle to do the same for you." I heard glass clinking from within. "Straightforward as your vision might be, you could not possibly have missed the considerable accumulation of military buildup within Lastlight."

I cleared my throat in a way I hoped wasn't suspicious. "I saw a few Revolutionary soldiers."

"A *few*? You jape, surely. Their monstrous engines arrived not a day ago bearing scores of the nul savages. They brought with them those colossal, mechanical abominations, those... those..."

"Paladins?"

"I'll thank you not to sully the noble title by associating it with them. I've been probing their presence here, hoping to divine the purpose of the sudden introduction of forces. Alas, the nuls' ignorance forever remains their greatest strength; they simply go wherever their commanders tell them."

"That's funny, because I remember specifically you screaming at me for not following your orders." I sprawled across the sofa, propped my feet on the armrest. "You turned so red, I thought you might have been shape-shifting into a tomato."

"Opting to spurn one's role in a delicate operation so that one might dally about with a civilian is not refusing to follow orders so much as outright treason." He emerged from the bedroom with two cups. He handed me one, pushed my feet off his sofa, and took a seat in a chair across me in one fluid motion. "Were you not who you were, I'd have had you executed."

"I told you I had a good excuse."

"That being?"

I smiled, swirled the liquid in my glass. "He played the harp *really* well."

Alothenes sighed so hard I thought he might twist back into that old woman. And I hated to say I smiled at it. There was a time I had lived to make him do that.

A time when we both knew the difference between friend and enemy.

I had met Alothenes ki Nadaga when he had been a little younger in flesh, if not in spirit. I offended him by belching the lyrics to his favorite opera, if I recall correctly. It might seem unusual that we should have become friends, I suppose.

Frankly, it was much more unusual that we were still talking after I went Vagrant.

The rebellion against the Nul Emperor saw the Imperium's best mages abandon them. As Maskmages went, there was no one better than Alothenes. The Lady Merchant gives them the ability to change their face, their body, their voice, everything but their heart. And, as a consummate student of opera, Alothenes could adopt and shed personalities faster than most people change clothes. His spying, subterfuge, and calculated plots had delivered the Imperium many victories and her enemies many defeats.

To this day, I have no idea why he chose to remain loyal.

The Imperium gave him wealth and prestige fitting his station, of course. But he could have more—much more—by going Vagrant. A man who could change his shape into that of a baron, a Freemaker, even an Avonin could be sitting prettily atop a pile of metal by now. Yet, even after the Nul Emperor, even after the rebellion, even after the Crown Conspiracy, he remained a servant of the Imperium.

And, inexplicably, my friend.

We'd trade favor for favor, information for information, since I'd gone Vagrant and still found the time to talk opera over wine now and again. That might seem a mercenary form of trust, but it doesn't get much better in the Scar.

And it was more than I usually got.

"I gather that, since you are not here in cause of or as the solution to Revolutionary shenanigans, you have come to me for another reason." He sighed deeply. "Which means I doubtless have the pleasure of you requiring a favor."

"A couple, actually. But first"—I held my cup up, smiled—"to friendship?"

He narrowed his eyes. "To adequate exchanges."

"I've heard of worse reasons to drink."

Our glasses clinked. I took a sip. Something cool and refreshing hit my tongue. I immediately spat it out.

"Is this water?" I asked, offended.

He shrugged. "You drink too much."

I had a vague urge to draw the Cacophony but resisted. I had, after all, come here for a favor.

"Straight to business." I pointedly emptied the water onto the floor. Before he could protest, I plucked a folded piece of paper from my pocket. "I had a run-in with Calto the Hardrock."

The ire in his face drained away so quickly I thought he might have just shifted. Alothenes, my friend, was irksome, haughty, and pretentious. Alothenes the Imperial spymaster was empty, methodical, and spoke so coldly it made my blood chill.

"Go on," he said.

"He was on his way to Lastlight," I said. "Hitched a ride with an Avonin caravan."

"Avonin," he muttered. "I trust you handled it with your usual tact."

I patted the Cacophony. "We did."

"Then I can assume they will be demanding even higher prices on their goods in the name of security."

"The Imperium can foot the bill, surely."

"The goal is to further Imperial interests, not debt." He sighed. "Still, it might be worth it if Caltothos is no longer a problem." He fixed me with a glare. "He isn't, is he?"

"Of course."

That wasn't *precisely* a lie. At any rate, Calto was no longer a problem for *me*. I could have been more specific, of course, but it was a good idea to keep a few secrets from a Maskmage. From a Maskmage who also served as Imperial spymaster, it was a necessity.

"But he wasn't coming for wine and music," I said. "He was meeting someone here. I need to know who."

He met my hard look with a certain cold softness. If I hadn't known him as I did, I would have missed the subtle shift of facial features as his magic made him appear more stoic, reserved.

"One wonders, Salazanca," he whispered, "why that is."

That would have been a good time to tell him, of course.

About the Husks. About Vraki. About everything. And I confess, looking into his eyes as I did, I almost wanted to do just that. Those words, that name, came with a sour feeling that welled up from a black place inside me and got stuck in my craw. I wanted, more than anything, to tell him, to get those names out.

But I couldn't.

Alothenes forgave me a lot. More than I deserved, really. He forgave me for being uncultured and rude around him. He forgave me for being a shitty servant to the Imperium. He forgave me, even, when I had ceased being a shitty servant and had gone Vagrant entirely.

But if I told him why I needed to find Vraki, to take the glory of killing the Imperium's greatest traitor for myself... he'd never forgive that.

It was true, he wasn't my friend. We didn't spend much time together, we didn't agree on anything, we hadn't even gotten along particularly well when we both served the Imperium. But even if he wasn't my friend, he was someone who I could turn to in the Scar, someone who I didn't have to watch my back around, someone who gave even the slightest of shits about me.

And I wasn't ready to give that up. Not yet.

"Bounty," I lied. "He's working with someone else. If I handle them both, that's more money for me."

His face betrayed neither surprise, nor offense, nor curiosity; I had a hard time deciding which one of those bothered me more.

"A bounty," he replied. "Mere metal."

"There's nothing *mere* about the stuff that keeps me alive," I muttered.

"It's the stuff that keeps you in blood, booze, and blades."

I eyed him with ire. "You got a better definition of being alive?"

"I do." His lips twitched at the edges, revealing the ghost of a smile I rarely saw even when we were on good terms. "And it's through duty."

I directed my glower away so that he couldn't see me roll my eyes. "I wish I could visit you once without hearing this fucking lecture."

"And I wish you'd go kill monsters without your midriff exposed, but it seems we're all disappointed today." His posture slumped as he leaned forward, elbows on his knees, eyes upon me. "Speak truthfully. Doesn't it wear on you?"

I saw no reason to speak truthfully to a spy, much less a man who could change into whatever shape he wanted. Yet even as I looked away from him, he persisted in both staring and speaking.

"The bloodshed, the violence, the battles," he said. "The bed you sleep in one night becomes a battleground the next. The person you kiss in the morning is at your throat when the sun sets." He sighed. "I turned down the Vagrant's life, but I know it well. There are no friends that do not become enemies and guns make for a poor family."

"And what would you know about it?" I surprised myself by snapping, surprised myself more with the heat that boiled up behind my eyes. "You talk about the Imperium like it's a noble thing, like they don't look at you and see a collection of Dust and magic they can use for their own ends. You act like we all went Vagrant out of a lust for gold and nothing more."

"I assume some nebulously clichéd definition of 'power' was also a motivator," he said. "Unless there was something else?"

"FUCKING FREEDOM, THAT'S WHAT ELSE."

The words came tearing out of my mouth, spat onto the floor to run on two newborn legs. I rose to my feet, hands clenched into fists, jaw set. The Cacophony seethed in eager approval at my hip, so hot I could feel it through the leather. But for once, I didn't care.

For once, I was burning even hotter.

"We're born with this gift, spend our lives bearing its burdens in service to others, and when we die, we don't even get to keep our corpses. I am *done* with other people taking what *I* have."

I hadn't noticed when I had tensed up so much or leaned over so far toward him. My breath came in short, angry rasps behind gritted teeth.

Maybe Galta had been right when she said I didn't understand why the Crown Conspiracy did what they did. Maybe Alothenes was right when he said I didn't understand the value of duty. Maybe there was a lot I didn't understand.

But I knew what it meant to be nothing more than what you carried. I knew what it meant when all the good you'd done, all the loves you'd had, all the jokes you told and the stories you knew and people who remembered you meant fucking less than the power that you carried.

I knew *that* well. It bothered me that he didn't. It bothered me that my jaw clenched so tight and my eyes burned so hot. And it didn't so much as bother as chafe my ass raw that Alothenes stared at me with cool dispassion and barely blinked.

His eyes traveled down the length of my body, across my tattoos and the dust on my clothes and the gun on my hip to settle onto the scar almost hidden behind my shirt. It itched under his gaze, suddenly afraid to be studied.

"And who will be with you," he whispered, "when you have nothing left?"

I hadn't noticed when I slumped back down to the sofa. I hadn't noticed when all the fire ebbed out of my voice and my demands sounded more like pleas.

I hadn't noticed when I suddenly felt so heavy. And felt like I was back in that dark place.

"Salazanca."

I looked up. His hand was extended, offered. He would never take mine without asking. He was refined like that. Maybe it was just out of habit that I reached out and took it.

But it felt good, regardless.

"Perhaps," he said softly, "it's not ideal. But then, perhaps we aren't born into ideal lives, mages. Vagrants, Imperium, whichever, we are viewed as monsters and as tools by our allies and our enemies, no matter which path we choose. For we are defined by our gift, our burden, our Barter."

He smiled at me. His lips were thinner than I remembered.

"Aren't we?"

Alothenes was more careful than most, budgeting his magic cautiously. But he still paid the same Barter as any Maskmage. The Lady Merchant gave them deception, cunning, and the ability to transform, but in exchange, she took their very identities.

I studied his face. The changes were subtle, but they were there. His eyebrows had vanished. His earlobes had disappeared. His eyelids didn't quite go all the way down anymore. The Lady Merchant was taking his face, bit by bit, and when she was done with him, this long nose and these hawkish eyes would be gone and only a smooth white slate would be left behind.

We understood each other, from time to time. We both had our scars.

"Perhaps, then," he said, squeezing my hand, "we simply don't get a normal family full of squealing brats and spouses who grow infuriated at us for things we forgot to say. Perhaps that's the real Barter we pay. But"—he looked distant for a moment—"to me, the choice was never between Vagrant and Imperium, but between dying alone and dying for something. It's not right, to have to make that choice, and it's not normal. But perhaps it's as close as we get."

He was probably right. He usually was.

But the truth was that I didn't know what normal was anymore. I thought I did once. But then I lost it, somewhere, along with everything else. And now all I had left were these scars, this gun, and a little voice that told me I would never know what normal was like again until I had crossed every name off that list.

I wanted to tell him that, of course. It would have felt nice to get it out.

Wish I could tell you why I didn't.

"Riccu the Knock was sighted here last month."

I looked up at his words. The weight shed itself from my shoulders. It wasn't a lightness I felt, but an eagerness, a desire to get up, get moving, get shooting. I was burning bright all over again.

"Riccu the Knock," I whispered.

"One of Vraki's old associates, you'll recall," Alothenes said. "I had wondered what a traitorous Vagrant"—he paused, considered me—"that *particular* traitorous Vagrant was doing in Lastlight. Calto's presence would explain it, I suppose."

It would explain more than that.

I had been agonizing over why Vraki had been so difficult to find. I hadn't considered that it would be because of a fucking Doormage. Hell, I'd have thought Riccu would be too scared to answer his summons.

Riccu, like others of his kind, could weave portals to travel hundreds of miles in the blink of an eye. That's how Vraki got between Stark's Mutter and wherever else he was going. That's how he got those kids out.

And wherever Riccu was, Vraki would be close by.

Like, sort of. You know, as close by as a portal can be. You get what the fuck I'm saying.

"He's here to pick up Calto," I said; again, not *quite* a lie, as that was probably who he was on his way to see. "Fuck me." He shot me a glare, and I smiled sheepishly. "Sorry. I mean . . . where? Where'd you see him? Where do I find him?"

"As it happens, he makes regular stops nearby to resupply," Alothenes said. "His schedule has not changed in all the time I've been observing him. By his regularity, I would assume he'd arrive exactly"—he drew out an agonizingly long hum—"tomorrow."

"*Fuck,*" I groaned.

"Language," Alothenes replied.

I didn't bother apologizing this time. He could count himself fucking lucky I didn't say worse.

This was just my fucking luck, wasn't it? To just barely miss him. Who knew if that would be time enough to save the kids, to stop Vraki, to find Jindu, to make them pay?

And yet...I didn't feel quite so heavy. Not anymore. I had a lead. I had an answer. It wasn't perfect, but it was better than I had a moment ago. Don't get me wrong, I still had questions. And none were bigger than the one that sprang to my lips.

"Well, what the shit am I supposed to do until then?"

"I had thought you might wonder," Alothenes replied. "Would it soothe you to use my facilities until then?"

It would, I couldn't lie. Alothenes didn't often loan out his room, but the temptation of a regular bath and a bed that wasn't made of dirt and birdshit was too much to pass on. What interest I showed on my face emboldened a mischievous little smirk on his face, one I had only seen twice before, and each time it had been followed by...

"And since we're catching up..." He reached into his vest, produced a thin metal pipe. The rank aroma of the dried herb packed inside it filled my nostrils. "I thought you might like to celebrate the old way."

Thesha. That old son of a bitch kept some.

"Fuck me." I held a hand up, kept my eyes on the pipe. "Sorry. But...where'd you get *thesha* all the way out here? It only grows in Cathama."

"I suppose, then, that there remain yet wiser reasons to work for Cathama beyond a bizarre definition of family, don't there?" He pulled a tindertwig from his vest, lit the pipe, and inhaled deeply. The smoke that came out was a hazy purple and filled the room. "I wouldn't waste it on the nul peasants here. They'd hardly know what to do with it. But an old..." He searched for the word, finding nothing. "For you, anyway, I suppose I can be persuaded."

I'd had smarter ideas than taking the pipe when he offered it to me. *Thesha*, when it was a raw weed growing in the wilds, had the tendency to drive any beast that so much as sniffed it berserk and drive the minds of people who touched it to madness. The average nul couldn't handle the strain it put on the mind.

But to those of us who could hear the Lady's song?

I took a deep inhale, felt the smoke fill my lungs. My body began to tingle, a thousand tiny hands pushing a thousand tiny sinews of muscle to ease. When I breathed out the cloud of purple smoke, it felt like all my worries and fears went with them.

They'd be back, of course, and I'd feel them all the keener when they visited me with a pounding headache and mouth dry as dirt. But for now, I knew where Riccu would be. For now, I knew I could find Vraki. For now, I could worry a little less.

"How does it taste, Salazanca?" he asked.

"Mmm," I replied. My eyes were already drooping. It had been ages since I had hit this stuff; my tolerance wasn't what it used to be. "Good."

"Do you feel very good, Salazanca?" he asked. His voice was flat, droning. A product of the weed, surely. "Do you feel at ease?"

"Yes." The word dribbled out of my mouth. I didn't remember saying it. I couldn't feel my lips speaking it.

"Salazanca."

Darkness ringed my vision. My breath came slow. The muscles in my body relaxed to the point they felt like jelly, like I was sinking into the sofa. The drug wasn't supposed to do this. Something was wrong. My head screamed at my heart to start pushing blood back into my limbs, but my heart had forgotten how to pound.

"Why are you really here?" Alothenes asked.

I should have shot him. I should have gotten up and left. I should have done that when I first got here. But I couldn't remember how to do any of that. I couldn't move. I couldn't think. I couldn't stop myself from speaking.

"Vraki," I muttered, the word sliding out of my mouth.

"Here?" A note of surprise in his voice, but he kept himself calm as he spoke. "Where, Salazanca?"

Don't! my head screamed to my mouth. *Don't you fucking dare. Something's wrong. He's screwed us! The drug's making us—*

"Husks," I groaned, unable to stop the word from coming out. It was as though Alothenes had pushed my brain directly to my mouth. I couldn't keep the thoughts from my lips. "Riccu…"

"He would know the way, wouldn't he?" he said. "I'm afraid he's actually here in Lastlight as we speak, in fact. Forgive me that lie, if nothing else."

Alothenes sighed, rose from his chair. I couldn't move my head to follow him. But out of the corner of my eye, I saw him change. With every step, his clothing, his skin, his hair color vanished. And by the time he reached the door, Alothenes was gone, and a young girl dressed in a simple frock and hat was standing there. He looked back at me, frowned at me through feminine lips.

"I won't ask you to thank me, Salazanca," he said. "Nor will I ask you to believe me when I say it's for the best. But your hands will be clean and a villain will be brought to justice."

He pushed the secret door open, disappeared behind it.

"Take pleasure in that, for your own sake."

I was screaming inside my head. He had drugged the drug, laced it with something. I had to fight it, had to stop him. I couldn't let him find Riccu, find Vraki, steal my revenge. I had to get to my feet.

One foot. I forced my left up. Now the other. I forced my right. Now, take one step forward.

I did.

I fell.

The floor opened up beneath me into a yawning black pit.

And I disappeared.

FORTY-FOUR

SOMEWHERE DARK

I opened my eyes and I was dead.

Or... was I soon to be dead? I couldn't quite remember.

I still drew breath, slow and steady and clean in my lungs. My limbs still worked, legs carrying me, arms swinging. My heart was quiet in a way that it hadn't been in a long time.

My body worked. But my brain was smothered, held underwater by a pair of hands with iron fingers. I couldn't remember how I got here. I couldn't remember where I came from. And I couldn't remember where *here* was.

Somewhere dark, beneath the earth and choked in the dust of a hundred dead monarchs and a thousand dead ambitions. They stared at me from the walls, their faces in the hard edges and rigid amethysts that had shaped an empire. There was the crown of Empress Litany, black iron spikes tipped with amethyst shards. There was the crown of Emperor Song the Fourth, silver coiling around a central violet gem. There was the crown of the Mad Emperor, brass and twisted, briars shaped like a grin.

This was all that was left of them. Their bodies had been taken, their Dust taken, and a few chunks of metal and rock were all that the empire they built had to remember them by. They drank the light of the lantern in my hand, going dimmer with each step I took until it disappeared completely.

I stepped into darkness.

I don't know where I came out.

"There's no need to be nervous."

Jindu was beside me. His smile was perfect and bright in the darkness. I couldn't remember when he had come. I couldn't remember why he was smiling. His smile was as bright as the sword at his hip.

"Vrakilaith has been working on a solution," he said. "He and the others have an idea how to take care of this. We're not going to serve a Nul Emperor. Not anymore."

He reached out. And he took my hand. And I couldn't remember why it hurt to have him hold it.

"We didn't enter this lightly. No matter what happens," he said. "It's worth it, right? For the Imperium?"

I closed my eyes and I spoke the worst lie I ever spoke.

I opened my eyes. And they were all there.

Kreshtharan, lingering at the corners in the darkness and laughing. Rogonoroth, arms crossed and attentive and face like a carved stone. Galtathamora, scratching at the few thorny protrusions poking out of her brow. Jindunamalar, standing beside me, smiling like he did, like everything should be okay.

I didn't know why it didn't feel like that.

All thirty-four of us were down here. They were my friends. They told me I was needed. Jindu had told me I was needed. So I had come. And for some reason, every step felt painful.

From somewhere high and far away, the barest shaft of a setting sun thrust down into the chamber. The thrones of the old council stood empty, withered and ignored from a time when we thought words could ever solve anything. At the center, the chair of the first emperor lay in collapsed rubble beneath the light of the dying sun.

And Vrakilaith stood atop it, a crown on a shattered skull.

"It can't be that simple." Zanzemalthanes looked up at Vrakilaith, scratching his featureless face. "We just . . . *make* a new emperor?"

"*Impossible*," Talthonanac rasped from the darkness.

"He's right," Galthathamora growled. "What's the use in jabbering about this shit, anyway? The army is behind the Empress. We should just go Vagrant, like the others."

"And then what?" Vrakilaith's voice, deep and resonant like a knife plunged into flesh, boomed. "After the Imperium built its palaces over our Dust, after we conquered their new world and threw down the upstart Revolution that would tear it apart, you would have us simply *leave*?"

"What other way is there?" Ricculoran muttered. "The Empress will have no more children."

"It's hardly her call to make, is it?" Kreshtharan laughed. "So she made one nul. Throw it away and try again."

"The army's thrown its lot behind her," Jindunamalar said from beside me. "It falls to us to honor the sacrifices of those who came before and those who will come after."

"The Nul Emperor will lead us to ruin," Vrakilaith said, nodding toward Jindunamalar. "He cannot hope to comprehend the power at his fingertips, let alone use it responsibly. The Empress has chosen her spawn over her nation. It falls to us to remedy this."

Rogonoroth, ever patient, spoke. "A Scrath cannot hope to be controlled, even by a Prodigy like you, Vrakilaith."

"Summoning is an art, like any other. It is a power offered, a Barter demanded."

"You speak of summoning a living, thinking creature," Moraccus protested. "What Barter could you possibly offer in exchange for that?"

"The Lady Merchant does not want us to Barter."

The mutters of the crowd quieted. Vrakilaith's eyes settled upon me. And all of theirs followed.

"She wants us to give something back."

The light vanished.

Fire.

Lightning.

Sound so fierce that it shook the walls.

I saw them in flashes, shattered fragments of a broken window. Zanzemalthanes shifting, twisting into a black serpent and rearing toward me, cast aside by a wave of my hand. Grishoktha howling, the air shaking at the wall of sound bursting from his jaws, silenced when thunder fell upon him. Galtathamora hurling her painted wards, watching them incinerate and fall to embers as flame swept over her. Jindunamalar rushing. Jindunamalar rising. Jindunamalar's blade...

Striking.

I drew in a breath.

Darkness fell upon me.

And then...light.

Not sunlight. Not lantern light. It burst in a bright halo of violet in the darkness above me. The cold stone seeped into my body. My blood hung in fragments, drifting lazily in quivering droplets across the air, weeping out of the cuts in my cheek, my belly, my legs and drifting into the sky. The light brightened. A great breath of air was drawn in. My blood vanished into the halo.

And something else came out.

It stood up on shaking legs. It opened a mouth that spanned six hands wide. It sang a song in one discordant shriek.

And the light disappeared.

I opened my eyes. I ran through the halls, blood trailing behind me. Screams burst from everywhere.

Darkness.

Light.

I crawled across the stones. I was bleeding too much. My breath was gone. I couldn't fly. I used to fly. Why couldn't I fly?

Darkness.

Light.

I couldn't go any farther. I fell down before a crown. I looked up, into brass briars. And they grinned back at me.

Darkness.

Darkness.

Darkness.

FORTY-FIVE

LASTLIGHT

Once, I took down a particularly tough bounty. I had celebrated that night with a very strong man and a much stronger whiskey. Turns out the bounty, some warlord south of the Husks, hadn't actually died and came for revenge. And also the very strong man was actually his brother. All of this happened after I had gone through two bottles of cheap brown liquor.

Anyway, words and bullets were exchanged and, the next day, I woke up alone, surrounded by dead bodies, bleeding from two holes that hadn't been in me when I passed out and suffering a hangover trying to hack its way out of my skull with an axe. That had been the most terrible way I had ever woken up.

This was worse.

My eyes snapped open as I screamed. Or tried to scream anyway. Really, what came out was more of a choked, gurgling sound. Breath and voice were likewise robbed as something stirred from inside me. I felt something moving in my belly, something that had grown sharp claws and teeth and was trying to gnaw its way out. The blood swept out of my limbs, leaving me cold and numb as everything pulled itself to my innards.

I'm not sure how I found the strength to roll onto my stomach and crawl to my hands and knees. The tears pouring from my eyes came thick and slimy as I retched, struggling to force something out from inside of me. My fingers dug into the carpet so fiercely they bled. Something came crawling out of my stomach and into my throat and it fought, with twitching, shrieking fury, to keep itself inside there.

I have never been happier to puke than I was when I finally forced the bleakbrew out of me.

It—for I had no idea what else you'd call the twitching, amorphous collection of congealed liquid other than "it"—fell out of me in a glob. It let out an angry hiss; its violet hue disappeared and was replaced with an ugly ochre shimmer as it tried to inch its way across the carpet. It left a trail of my blood and bile behind it as it twitched, shivered, and fell still, falling into a reeking pool.

I lay down next to it, drawing in ragged, gasping breaths, trying to force air into my lungs and blood into my limbs.

Bleakbrew isn't an alchemic. It's a living thing, the barest essence of a mage. How it heals isn't pleasant. Going down, it was bad. But eventually, it had to come out. And that was worse.

And that was, near as I could tell, why I was still alive.

The *thesha* had been laced with an alchemic. It made my brain go soft and the words dribble like drool out of my face. Likely, it was supposed to keep me unconscious a lot longer than it had, maybe forever. But the bleakbrew inside me had absorbed it, eaten it, and now it lay dead beside me in a pool of my own blood.

Lucky me, right?

I was just lucky that Alothenes hadn't known.

Alothenes.

It hurt to think of what had happened. Because I couldn't think of him, of those words pretending to be gentle, of that face that pretended to be caring, without rage flooding into my head and sending my skull pounding. And yet, I couldn't *stop* thinking about it.

He betrayed me. He pulled thoughts from my head and words from my lips. And now he was going to find Riccu, and from there, Vraki.

And Vraki would die as a famous criminal, the man who nearly toppled the Imperium, rotting away in a prison even as papers and books celebrated his life. And not one of them would spare a single sentence for the lives he stole, the blood he spilled.

For him to face justice, he would have to die by my hand, alone and forgotten and bleeding out on the sand. And for that to happen, I had to find Riccu before Alothenes did.

And so I let the anger fill me, send my blood boiling in my legs and push me to my feet. I staggered against the wall for support, drew in sharp, sour breaths. I could still taste the Bleakbrew on my tongue, still feel it writhing in my belly. But I ignored that, just like I ignored the pain in my skull, the agony in my limbs, the long time it took to make my way to the door.

The Cacophony burned on my hip, chiding me for falling for that trick. Alothenes had left him there with me, of course. He knew enough about the weapon to be afraid of touching him.

There was a saying about pride and how it makes a man a dumbass. But I couldn't think of it at that moment.

I pushed on the door, found it fastened shut. Maybe to keep me in, maybe to keep someone else out. I didn't care. I drew the Cacophony, aimed him at the door.

Normally, using a shell to open a door would be considered wasteful.

But I wanted to express my appreciation for that little trick of his.

And I thought I'd show it by destroying only the door.

―――◆――――

You might have thought I was mad.

Really, I understood why Alothenes did it. He was loyal to the Imperium. Vraki was the most dangerous threat to his Imperium, his Emperor, and his very way of life. He would risk anything, including our tenuous relationship, to stop him. Likewise, I knew he understood why I didn't tell him at the start. He knew what Vraki meant to me, if not exactly why.

So I wasn't mad.

I was fucking furious.

And that fury kept me moving through the streets of Lastlight, spitting curses to get people to move out of my way and shoving those who were hard of hearing. Out of the dumpling shop, out of Beetle Square, and into the fucking streets, I stormed through the alleys, struggling to figure out where, exactly, I was going.

The *thesha* didn't help.

The streets had thinned out as night became midnight, yet Lastlight was a city that didn't sleep. Merchants hawking night-wares, crowds of jubilant drinkers and knots of soldiers alike thronged the streets still. If only I could tell exactly how many there were.

The drug's lingering effects still clouded my mind, my judgment, made it hard for me to tell what was going on. Was that a crowd of three people or seven? Were those Revolutionaries scowling at me as I passed or someone else? Did I just hear my name called or did I—

You can see where this was fucking going.

As it was, I had just enough clear thought left for the grim realization that I was ten miles behind in a race I hadn't been awake to see the start of.

Riccu the Knock was my only way to Vraki and he was somewhere in a city that Alothenes knew much better than I did. Add to it, he could be any creature present on the streets—that woman laughing and sipping wine, that man vomiting in an alley, even that dog eating said vomit. He would find a suitable shape, find his quarry, and approach him before Riccu even knew he was being followed. Alothenes knew Lastlight, knew how to find people and knew how to take them.

But I knew Riccu.

Alothenes knew Ricculoran, the nervous, pensive Doormage who spent most of his time cringing from women and hiding in the Cathama libraries. He didn't know Riccu the Knock, the Vagrant who opened doors for killers and sat back and watched, the eagerness of his grin splashed with red as he watched murderers spill the blood he was too cowardly to spill himself.

But I did.

I knew the hatred that burned behind those cowering eyes. I knew that he never cringed away from a woman without scowling hatefully at her back. I knew what he craved. I knew what he feared.

And so my eyes were on the ground.

I wasn't looking for Riccu the same way an exterminator doesn't go looking for rats—they hide, they scurry, they don't come out unless no one's around. You want to get a rat, you find its nest.

Alleys were too open; anyone could get to them. But buildings would be too hard to get to in the event of an escape. Riccu would look for somewhere out of sight, yet with no locks or doors to fumble with. My eyes searched the canals for docked boats with too big cabins or shallow sections big enough for a man to walk into or . . .

There.

Beneath a bridge, I saw a doorway. I followed a stone staircase down and into the shadows below. Canal water lapped at my boots as I entered, splashing into a lightless corridor where the perfumed air quickly turned stale and the stale air quickly turned stagnant.

And when I found the red chalk square drawn on the wall of the tunnel, I smiled. It must have enraged Riccu's precious sensibilities to have to draw his portal in a sewer.

Riccu, like a lot of Doormages, is resentful. The Lady Merchant gave them an art that was already less flashy than conjuring fire or moving things with your mind. Not that teleportation wasn't useful—Doormages were crucial for the movement of the Imperium's troops—but it required a lot of setup. For anything greater than a short-range burst of movement, they needed to prepare their magic by laying out exactly where they wanted to leave and exactly where they wanted to come out; otherwise they ran the risk of appearing in, say, a wall of rock.

It was an effective art. But not a very romantic one. Riccu had always loathed that. I always wondered if that was why he used red chalk to draw his doors.

This one, a series of small runes arranged in a square on the wet stone, was big. Big enough for two people or one very large one to get through—Riccu was going to use it to bring Calto back, I wagered. And wherever "back" was, I would find Vraki there.

I had to take a breath to keep my heart from racing.

The chalk hadn't turned to ash. Riccu hadn't used the portal yet—he just wanted it ready for when he had to leave. Which meant he was still here in Lastlight. And I still had a chance to catch him.

But how?

Waiting for Riccu wasn't an option; if Alothenes didn't find him first, he'd be back with backup I was in no shape to handle.

I had to somehow figure out how to lure a guy who could step through empty space to flee to his magical portal that led to a crazed, even-more-magical mass murderer and grab him before he could open said portal and either escape to said mass murderer or bring said mass murderer through.

To my drug-addled brain, this made perfect sense.

"You there."

You ever have a moment where your stomach twists into knots, your heart beats a little faster, your breath comes a little shorter, but your head is on fire and your brain just had a very bad idea that it thinks is good?

"Wait just a fucking minute."

Yeah, that.

I instinctively crouched down behind the bridge's wall and stayed there a good ten seconds before I realized they weren't speaking to me.

If I had to hazard a guess as to who they *were* speaking to, I'd put money on the very tall naked guy standing in the middle of the road.

Calto the Hardrock did not look tired. He had to have been following me without sleep, yet he didn't have so much as a dark ring under his eye. Fatigue didn't even register on his stony face. He didn't seem particularly bothered by the burn marks on his flesh or the fact that he was nude. And he *certainly* wasn't bothered by the three red-and-white-clad peacekeepers huddled around him, glaring.

The opposite could not be said to be true.

"Just what the fuck do you think you're doing here coming into Lastlight with no fucking pants on?" One of them, a shorter fellow with a big hand cannon to compensate, thrust his weapon into Calto's face. "Did they not stop you at the gate?"

They probably tried.

Calto ignored the hand cannon, did not even look at the guard thrusting it. "I am looking for a woman," he rumbled.

"I mean, yeah," the guard replied, glancing south of his waist. "I guess you would be. And I'm sure, if you've got coin, you'll find someone to indulge you in some other fucking city. We don't let anyone in this place without pants on."

Calto stared over the man's head, looking for something across the streets. "Your laws do not concern me."

"Well, as it happens, a giant motherfucker walking with his cock flopping around definitely concerns *me*." The guard tapped the barrel of his hand cannon against Calto's massive chest. "And what concerns me, concerns Two Lonely Old Men, so unless you'd like to have the most powerful Freemaker in the Scar after you, you'll—"

That wasn't a bad threat, honestly. Few people defied Two Lonely Old Men and lived, Vagrant or otherwise. If the guard had finished it, Calto might have rethought his approach.

The guard didn't finish his threat, of course.

It was kind of hard to.

What with Calto's hand wrapped around his head.

You've probably felt it before. After a glass breaks in a crowded public house. Before two people dare each other to say something they'll regret. The space between someone saying "I love you" and someone else not saying it back. That tense moment of silence, the kind that stretches a single second into an hour, where everyone's ready to bleed and is just waiting to see who's going to do it first.

That's what I felt when Calto lifted the screaming, flailing guard off his feet.

And everyone else could feel it, too. The guards at Calto's sides aiming their autobows at him. The snipers on the rooftops drawing down on him. The Revolutionary squadron on the other side of the canal reaching for their gunpikes. The Imperial officers on a café porch leaning forward, the Lady's song in their ears.

Things were about to get properly fucked.

Which would have been a good reason to leave, honestly. The fact that Calto, an invincible murder machine masquerading as a man, was searching for me would be another good one. I could probably think of a few dozen reasons not to be there, really.

And only one reason to stay.

I needed to find Riccu.

And I bet you know which reason I listened to.

The Cacophony seethed in my hand, sensing my intent and approving with a warm grip as I raised him up and aimed him at Calto's head. My vision was still hazy, my mind foggy, as I drew on him.

Through the corners of my eyes, through the black rings circling my vision, I could see them: the laughing people, their happy homes, their sloshing wine. Through the fog inside my head, I tried to imagine what would happen to them if I pulled this trigger. Through a long, cold breath, I heard the laughter turn to screams; I smelled the wine turn to blood.

I heard them. From somewhere far away, far ahead, in a dark place filled with ash and blood, I heard them. I heard their pleas to lower the gun. I heard all the curses they'd lay on me for pulling the trigger. I heard all the weak apologies and lame justifications I'd offer after it was done. I heard the screaming, I heard the weeping, I heard the breathless whispers to gods that didn't exist.

I closed my eyes.

And I whispered my reply.

"Eres va atali."

I raised the Cacophony. I stared down the sights. I put them right between Calto's eyes. And I shouted.

"HEY, HARDROCK!"

He looked up. He saw me first, then my gun. He breathed a word.

And I pulled the trigger.

Discordance screeched toward him, took him square in the face. The wall of sound erupted in a shrieking symphony, casting the guard from Calto's hand, the other two into the water and Calto himself into the broad face of a building. He disappeared through the wall in an eruption of slate shards and shattered timber, a cloud of dust bursting from the hole he had just vanished down like the dying gasp after a great beast's last meal.

The dust hung in the air like a funeral shroud. Through the silence, I could hear voices whispering.

"Did she just say 'Hardrock'? Is that him? Is that the—"

"—she's got a gun! Is that... Oh fuck. Get the guards—"

"—Imperial trick, it must be. They're fucking—"

"—I told you letting the Revolution in would end in—"

And then I couldn't hear them. A note of perfect silence hung in the air. And through it, I could hear the Lady's song.

Stone shuddered and groaned as Calto came bursting out of the hole. People scattered and fled screaming at the sound of his roar. The earth shook beneath his feet as he saw me across the bridge and came charging toward me.

And I knew it was time to run.

The fog left me with each gasp as I went tearing off down the bridge. And by the time I could appreciate what I had just done, I couldn't stop. The earth shook under my feet with each step he took. My bones rattled as he closed the distance between us with each great stride. I could feel the horrific stillness of the street as he leapt and a great shadow grew over me.

With a cry, I lunged forward, falling into a tumble to scramble to the other side of the canal. I whirled onto my ass, gun up, and aimed, just in time to see Calto come crashing down.

And then the bridge disappeared.

The peoples' screaming was nothing compared to the great roar of stone as it broke beneath him, shattering into fragments and disappearing into the canal. Water erupted, washed over me in a spray of froth. I stared, along with dozens of other wide-eyed and breathless people, at the hole where the bridge had just been.

Believe it or not, that had actually been easier than I thought.

See, Riccu was a coward. He wouldn't compromise his safety for anyone, not even for Vraki. And there was nothing like a rampaging Siegemage to compromise safety. Amid heightened tensions, increased security, and the general feel of what-the-fuck-just-happened-ery, he'd flee to his portal and I'd catch him there. There'd be some damage, I knew, but if all I lost taking out Calto was a broken bridge and a hole in a building, I'd call that a good trade.

I honestly hadn't expected it to work as well as it did.

"Halt!"

Of course.

I looked up into the glistening blades of a dozen gunpikes aimed down at me. The Revolutionaries surrounded me, weapons drawn. At their head, a man wearing an officer's badge and carrying a hand cannon narrowed his eyes on my very distinctly Imperial white hair.

"What Imperial plot is this?" he muttered.

I opened my mouth to...do what? Warn them? Seemed a touch late for that. A touch too little, too. The gunpikes rattled as they prepared to fire.

"STOP!"

He looked tired, his uniform was filthy, and he came staggering up like a drunk three days into a weeklong bottle, but the Revolutionaries held their fire as Cavric pushed between them.

"Stop!" he rasped. He gestured to himself, breathing heavily. "Cavric Proud. Low Sergeant of the Fifty-Sixth Cadre. Out of Lowstaff."

"You're a long way from home," the officer said. "And in my way. If you'll pardon me, *Low* Sergeant Proud, I've a city to keep clean of Imperial filth."

"She's not Imperial!" Cavric threw his hands out, stepping in front of me. "Please, whatever you've been told, this city has no Imperials here! I swear!"

My face screwed up at his words. I wondered what they had been told to justify this much firepower in one area. The officer exchanged a glance with his soldiers.

"Keep your steel on them. Be wary."

He crept to the edge of the ruined bridge as Cavric moved to help me up.

"Sal," he whispered in my ear, "it's bad. I asked around. The Cadre here has been given information that the city is crawling with Imperial spies."

My heart caught in my chest. *Were they talking about Alothenes? Had he lied to me? Were there more?*

"These people are in danger, Sal," Cavric continued, gesturing to the citizens across the bridge. "We've got to get them out before—"

"No sign of the huge brute." The Revolutionary officer peered over the edge. "How does a creature that big disapp—"

There was a blur of gray. The officer swayed on his feet, like someone had just slapped him. I had just enough time to see the fist-sized stone lodged in his face before he teetered and fell over the edge of the canal.

And Calto came vaulting over.

"*VAGRANT!*" one of the Revolutionaries shrieked. "*THE FUCKING IMPERIALS ARE USING VAGRANTS! OPEN FIRE!*" He turned to one of his comrades. "*GET THE FLARE!*"

"*Wait!*" Cavric tried to scream, tried to rush toward the soldiers.

Too fucking late. Too fucking quiet.

His voice was lost in the chorus of gunfire as they turned their weapons onto Calto. Their charges sang an ugly song, sinking into his skin in bloodless, smoking holes. More missed entirely, bullets shrieking across the bridge to tear holes in citizens who fell, screaming, and did not rise again.

One of the Revolutionaries fumbled with a thick-barreled hand cannon. Cavric lunged, his hands falling well short as the soldier raised it to the sky and pulled the trigger. A blazing flare streaked into the sky and exploded in a tiny red sun.

And, over the walls, Revolutionary sirens answered.

Fuck.

I seized Cavric by the shoulder, pulled him toward me.

"Get as many people as you can out of here," I snarled as I hastily loaded the Cacophony. "And make sure you stay the hell out of my way."

"What for?" he asked. "What are you going to—"

"HARDROCK!"

I screamed. The towering Siegemage craned his head toward me. Across his impassive gaze, the barest flicker of hatred flashed.

And I started running.

The cries of the Revolutionaries became a panicked chorus, all thought given to formless screaming that ended in the crunch of bone and spatter of blood as Calto plowed through them.

I didn't dare look back.

I couldn't. I couldn't see the blood and pulped skulls beneath his feet. I couldn't afford regret, fear. I had to keep running. I had to find Riccu.

Or else this, and everything, was for nothing.

"*Out of the fucking way!*" I had the Cacophony in hand, firing off shots into the air as I ran toward a crowd of screaming people on the canal. Discordance shrieked. Hellfire blazed. "*Sal the fucking Cacophony has come to town, assholes! You want to die?*"

Some of them heard the name and ran. Some of them had seen the carnage and already started running. Most, I think, just ran from the crazed woman running down the street firing explosions into the air.

So long as they were running, I didn't fucking care.

I needed a lot of room, a lot of noise, and as few of them dead as possible. I had two of those covered. They fled screaming into alleys, ducking into shops, diving into the canals, all too happy to give me a clear path to run.

Unfortunately, that also gave the crazed, angry giant chasing me plenty of room to follow in my wake. His footsteps nearly knocked the breath from my lungs as he closed in on me, the stones shaking on the pavement. He'd close on me before too long. But that was fine. He was bigger, faster, but unwieldy. I could maneuver around him, over bridges, through alleys he couldn't follow. So long as the path remained clear and...

I heard a shriek overhead.

I heard the crackle of electricity.

And the Lady laughing a long and merry song of you-didn't-actually-think-this-was-going-to-work-did-you-you-dumb-fuck.

I caught a flash of the Krikai bird's amethyst-tinged wings just before I saw the spark of azure electricity. A thunderbow's bolt launched, a jagged streak of lightning screaming down from on high to strike the stones. I leapt backward, shielding my eyes with my arms as thunder cracked and bright blue bolts sparked in front of me.

Fuck, fuck.

I was an idiot to think the Imperium wouldn't take notice of two Vagrants fighting—they had giant birds, for fuck's sake. But there would be time for regret, and more creative curse words, later. As soon as I heard the thunderbow's crackle, I knew I had to go.

I whirled, saw Calto rampaging toward me, face empty and spattered with blood. I swallowed hard, heard the Krikai's cry louder in my ears as its rider brought it swooping down behind me. No time to plan, no time to think, no time to realize what a stupid idea this was.

I ran.

Calto's eyes widened, surprised to see me running *toward* the rampaging Siegemage who wanted to kill me, but it was short-lived. I bent low, took a sharp breath. He realized what I was going to do, swung his fists high above his head. I leapt into a slide, aiming between his legs. His fists came crashing down, splintering the stone behind me as I slid between his legs, scrambled to my hands and knees, and crawled away from him.

He turned, frowning. "This is incredibly undignified, Sal."

"You're trying to *kill* me," I gasped. "How am I supposed to act?"

"Don't turn this back on me," he said, shaking a hand free of stone shards.

"I'm just saying." I raised the Cacophony, leveled it at him.

He sighed, raised a fist. Suddenly, his face contorted in confusion and pain, along with the rest of him, as thunder rolled. His body convulsed, fingers of electricity dancing across his body. He let out a confused howl—unsure what pain was, let alone how to handle it—as he collapsed to his knees.

That had been really impressive.

Makes me wish I had been the one to do it.

The Krikai swooped upward, turning away as its rider nocked another arrow. One Vagrant down, I supposed, was as good as another—and Calto *was* a much bigger target. I guess I should have been grateful for my good luck.

And if the world wasn't burning down around me, I might have.

"TEN THOUSAND YEARS!"

From the alleys, Revolutionaries came flooding out in squadrons, a wave of blue uniforms and clattering steel. They took positions in firing squares with all the rehearsed ease of opera singers—those in front fell to their knees and raised their weapons, while those behind lay their weapons on their comrades' shoulders.

Hammers clicked. Steel shuddered. Gunfire cracks rang out. A garden of smoking flowers blossomed in the air.

I fell to the ground as the severium-charged bullets whizzed overhead. I heard them punch through flesh, heard the screams of the people, heard the blood spatter on the ground and the bodies follow. It had happened so quickly, I didn't even realize a war had broken out.

Not until the other side fought back.

Out of cafés and taverns, they came. Their robes austere and glimmering in the night, their masks empty of emotion as the Imperials launched their counterattack. The song of the Lady filled my ears. An Embermage thrust her hands out, a wave of flame crashing over the canal to wash away screaming Revolutionaries. A Frostmage reached to the sky and hauled frigid boulders from nothingness to crash down into the other side. A Graspmage wove his hands about and fallen weapons rose of their own volition to impale their former masters. And the people...

The people died.

Cut down by bullets. Incinerated by flame. Washed away beneath the canals. They fell. They screamed. They died.

Because of me.

The people, tripping over their fancy skirts and stumbling over their fancy shoes. Pulling each other into alleys, putting up tables and chairs as barriers, or simply falling to their knees and covering their heads and screaming for someone to help them. And above it all, Cavric's voice, hoarse and impotent.

"STOP! PLEASE, STOP! THEY'RE CIVILIANS!"

Civilians. Dead. Dying. Screaming. I couldn't tell who was what. Only that I had done it.

"There's one!"

I turned, saw the Revolutionary squadron rushing toward me. At their head, wearing a headband with their crest and waving a saber, a captain led the charge.

"Imperial swine! Answer for your crimes!" He skidded to a halt, pointed his saber at me. *"Fire!"*

Through the sound of violence, a single note of the Lady's song cut. Before his soldiers had even taken up positions, the ground beneath whispered breaths of hoarfrost. The sound of gunpikes cracking went unheard above the groan of cold as a wall of ice shot up behind the captain, separating him from his soldiers.

He blinked, looked down a nearby alley. A blade of ice shot out, cutting into his throat and separating him from his shoulders.

"Barbarians."

I knew the blade before I knew the voice. And when the tall man came out in a calm, confident stride, his face obscured by the metal mask of an Imperial Judge, I knew exactly how bad things had gotten.

Judge Karthrien yun Acalpos spared little more than a sneer for the headless corpse bleeding out at his feet. The frostbrand, a blade of frigid tears, crackled in his hands.

I thought I had killed him. How had he survived? I fucking hate, hate, *hate* mages.

"Leave it to a nul to make a mess of things, eh?"

Fuck, fuck, fuck.

Maybe I could have taken him. Maybe I could have even taken him and whatever reinforcements he had that were doubtlessly close by. But I didn't have time. And he hadn't noticed me. I could still get away.

I turned to run across another bridge and got exactly ten steps before I remembered things were never that easy.

Something caught my foot. When I looked down and saw the patch of shadow blossoming beneath my heel, it was too late. Tendrils of black shot out, snaked up my legs, past my waist, seizing my arms and pinning them to my sides. I snarled, the Cacophony echoed me, burning in my hand as I struggled to break free.

"Goodness." Karthrien's hum was insultingly disinterested as he approached me. "Sal the Cacophony in the same city as I am?" Behind his mask, I could feel his grin. "Such poetry befits an opera."

"An opera wouldn't be so creepy." I pulled at the tendrils again, growling. "You know this is fucking weird, right? The tentacles?"

"They're shadowgrasps, not tentacles."

"Oh, yeah, in that case, that's not weird at all." I sneered. "You dumb piece of—"

"*Silence.*" He leveled his blade at me. "From the carnage, I had expected someone a little more high profile. The Inferno, perhaps. Or the Tempest."

"The Tempest's dead, fucker," I growled. "If you'd like to see how it went, dismiss your fucking spell and fight me."

"Mmm. Typical. Starving dogs consume each other. You traitors are depressingly alike." He reached out, gingerly took me by the chin as he aimed his blade toward my belly. "So utterly predictable, despite the carnage you cause."

If I didn't have time to fight him, I sure as fuck didn't have time to indulge his posturing. My skin prickled, feeling the cold radiating off his blade as he pulled it a little closer. I held my breath, clenched my jaw, angled the Cacophony just slightly.

A little closer, you fuck, I snarled inwardly. *Just get a little closer.*

He didn't.

He got farther away.

His eyes bulged behind his mask, as a great hand appeared around his throat and hoisted him, struggling and gasping, into the air. His concentration broken, Karthrien's spell dissipated, tendrils falling away from me. I stepped back, the shock in my eyes a match for his. Calto's stare, however, was deadly calm as he squeezed his fingers a little tighter around the Judge's neck.

And something snapped.

He dropped a limp corpse to the ground, stepped over it. "This grows tiresome, Cacophony."

"Don't blame me," I said, raising the Cacophony at him. "You could have stayed in the fucking water."

He didn't even flinch away from the gun's grinning barrel. I stepped backward as he approached, giving ground to him as I drew the hammer back. He spread his massive arms wide, gesturing to the carnage raging around us.

"Gaze upon the ruin you've wrought," he said. "Your very presence wreaks destruction."

Maybe that was an accusation, or maybe it was admiration. I wanted to say I wasn't going to take that from a man who breaks things just by walking. But in every furtive glance, from the corners of my eyes, I could see flashes of gunfire, bodies sprawled in the street, piles of smoldering rubble.

And in the quiet moments between each breath, I could hear a little voice telling me he was right.

I tried to keep it down. I tried to force it beneath the pounding of my heart and the blood rushing in my ears. He was wrong. The people had escaped—I had made sure of that. I could save this. I could fix this.

"Foes of the Revolution."

But soon, I couldn't hear anything more.

"Your judgment has come."

Not over a booming voice. Not over the sound of gears whirring. Not over iron feet crushing stone.

"Gaze upon the answer to your madness."

Nor over the sound of the Revolutionary anthem blaring.

Calto's stare rose up and over my head, widening. I dared to turn around. And when I saw my own horror reflected back in the Paladin's iron carapace, I realized.

Things weren't bad.

They were much, much worse.

FORTY-SIX

LASTLIGHT

Despite the fact that they're usually trying to kill me, I admit a certain awe for the machines of the Revolution.

Nuls, of course, had no grasp of *true* art, but there is a certain aesthetic to the smooth bore of their gunpikes and the fire-spewing rumble of their engines. I mean, the sheer talent needed to make armor twice as big as a man move on its own must merit it as *some* sort of art, right?

Really, you'd have to be ignorant not to admire something like the Paladin.

"Ten thousand years."

Of course, if you were still admiring it when the guns started whirring, you probably weren't so much ignorant as stupid.

Also dead.

I liked to consider myself an intelligent person.

And when I saw it raise its arm, with the spinning barrels of the repeating gun attached to it, I did what any intelligent person would.

I turned and bolted behind the biggest thing I could find—the gigantic man currently trying to kill me.

Calto only barely seemed to notice me. His brows furrowed as he glared upon the Paladin.

"Another Revolutionary toy," he muttered. "I remain unimpressed by—"

Then the guns started firing.

It burst off shots in one continuous blazing chorus, bullets shrieking haphazardly from fiery blossoms. They ricocheted off stones, flew into nearby buildings, shots tossed off like an old lady throwing bread crumbs to birds. I lay flat behind Calto, head pressed to the ground, desperately hoping that a stray bullet didn't find me or that he didn't decide to sit down.

When the gunfire stopped and the whirring barrels quieted, I dared to look up. Calto stood over me, not moving as I cautiously got to my feet. His eyes were wide, his mouth hung open, bullet holes peppered his chest, spatters of red painting his skin. He was still alive, breathing deeply, but his face was painted with a shock he should have Bartered long ago.

For the first time in twenty years, someone had made Calto the Hardrock bleed.

Past him, on the other side of the bridge, the Paladin raised its massive arm, standing by. Smoke poured from the vents on its back as a deep voice resonated from behind its visor.

"Surrender or face consequences," it boomed.

"*Consequences?*" I shouted. "What the fuck were all those bullets supposed to be?"

"This is your last chance."

I knew whoever was driving that monstrosity had two things: an exceedingly poor grasp of how to persuade people to surrender and a shit-ton more bullets. Calto—colossal, powerful, unstoppable—was paralyzed with shock. The Paladin could probably kill me if it sneezed. Lastlight was devastated, the sounds of war and terror fighting each other to fill the sky.

The intelligent thing *would* be to surrender.

And I was an intelligent person.

To a point.

If the Paladin was perplexed by me running away, it didn't stay that way for long. I tore off down one side of the canals and hadn't gotten ten feet before I heard its engines roar to life. From the corner of my eye, across the canal, I could see the glimmer of armor and the roaring flames of engines.

I glanced to my right and saw it—all two tons of armor flying across the street on the other side of the canal, propelled by two great infernos of severium smoke roaring out of the engines on its back.

"IT CAN DO THAT?" I screamed. "NO ONE NEEDS TO DO THAT! WHY ARE YOU DOING THAT?"

It answered by raising its repeating gun. The barrels sang its shrieking song, scattering bullets across the streets. On the plus side, a gun that big was hard to aim while standing still, let alone while flying on completely unnecessary engines.

On the negative side, it was a giant fucking gun.

Sparks kicked up around me as bullets ricocheted. Corpses shuddered as haphazard gunfire tore through them. And yet, despite all that, things still somehow got worse.

A wall of ice loomed before me. It hadn't been so polite as to die when the Judge who conjured it had. No alleys to dart down, nothing to hide behind; once I hit it, the Paladin would have a shot at me that even its gun—which, I remind you, is fucking gigantic—couldn't miss.

You might have noticed by now, but there are only three ways I handle a problem. I couldn't run any farther and I didn't have any whiskey. So I picked up the Cacophony, aimed for the wall, and fired.

Discordance shrieked out, struck it with a burst of sound. The ice erupted into colossal shards. Jagged pieces punched through walls, dagger-sized icicles impaled into bodies, a massive chunk of ice went flying into the canal.

The Paladin saw my ruse, stopped firing. Its engines roared as it streaked ahead of me, rounding the bridge ahead of me to cut me off. My head and body screamed at each other to do something, but neither had any ideas.

I can't say which one of them thought it'd be smart to jump into the canal. But I did it anyway.

I hit the water, already felt the chill of ice creeping into me. I splashed madly toward the chunk of ice, scrabbled up its side as it bobbed precariously in the water. Upon the bridge, I saw the Paladin's engines die down to low roars as it craned its visor about, trying to get a look at me as the ice chunk between us slowly turned in the water.

"Do not attempt to resist your fate," it warned in its echoing voice. "Through the might of the Revolution, the sickness of Imperial aggression shall be cleansed."

That was a lot of words to say "You're fucking dead if you don't think of something." A lot of pretty accurate words, because as I fumbled with the Cacophony tucked under one arm and rooted around in my satchel with my hand, it turns out I wasn't great at thinking under pressure. Not the kind of pressure that comes from bobbing on an ice floe slowly turning toward a giant killer suit of armor anyway.

I thumbed through the shells in my satchel, searching each of them.

Hoarfrost? No, that thing's engines will melt the ice soon as it hits. Hellfire? No, no, come on, think of something better.

My fingers grazed the writing across a shell. Writing I barely remembered, I used this type of shell so rarely. It was risky.

"With your last breath, embrace your end with dignity and reflect upon the ruin you have wrought."

But it's not like anything about this situation wasn't.

Slowly, the ice floe turned. Slowly, the Paladin came into view. Slowly, its gun whirred back to life.

There was a pilot inside it, I knew. But behind its giant visor, I couldn't see them.

Pity.

I would have loved to see their face when I pulled the trigger.

The ice floe turned just enough to give me a clear shot at the bridge. I fired. The Cacophony sang a jarred, crackling tune. The shell struck the rim of the bridge and exploded in a shower of electric sparks. The air trembled around it, quivering like water. I saw the Paladin brace itself, then glance around, confused as to what that was supposed to accomplish.

Once its armor began to groan, though, I trust it figured it out.

The metal shrieked and came crashing down, electric arcs dancing across its metal hide as the Paladin was pulled to the stones of the bridge and pinned there by some unseen force. It thrashed, metal groaning, engines roaring, guns shrieking as it awkwardly struggled to get back to its feet.

I wished it all the very best luck in that.

I leapt off the ice floe, began to swim for a staircase leading out of the canal. I hadn't expected that to work. Shockgrasp—I know, but it sounded impressive at the time—was unreliable at best. It pulled anything metal toward itself, as liable to tear your own weapons out of your grasp if you weren't careful. I only ever kept three or so on me, never really expecting to use them.

But how often do you fight a giant suit of armor that moves on its own?

I pulled myself out of the canal, shaking water from my boots. The Paladin had added metallic-tinged cursing to its futile struggles, but it wouldn't be long before the spell wore off. I had to get out of here before it did.

And I would have, had I not heard the Lady's song at that moment.

Faint, hard to hear through the din of battle elsewhere in the city. But I heard it. And, as the air shimmered at the other end of the street, I saw it, too.

Or rather, him.

He was short, hunched over in the way that people think makes them harder to notice. He was wrapped in a dingy brown cloak, hard to make out amid the filth and rubble of the battlefield. You'd have a hard time noticing him, I'd assume.

What him teleporting and all.

He was at the mouth of an alley, a hooded face peering out. I could just barely make out a ratlike visage poking out of dirty cloth, an arched gate tattooed over his right eye. I blinked and he was somewhere else. There, scurrying across the bridge as a squad of Revolutionaries charged to a distant battle. I blinked. He was on the other side of the bridge. I blinked. He was on a stone staircase. I blinked. He was standing in the mouth of a tunnel I had just emerged from and looked around. And for a split second, I saw his scheming, nervous little face.

Riccu the Knock.

My plan had worked.

Or at least, the part where I flushed him out worked. The part where I caught him I was still working on. I hurried off to pursue him and had just gotten past the bridge when I heard engines roar to life.

I stopped short just in time to avoid being crushed by two tons of flame-belching metal. The Paladin flew past me, colliding into the wall of a building. It shrugged off the impact, shrugged off the grit and stone falling off its armor, as it whirled and regarded me through that empty visor.

"Imperial swine," the pilot growled from inside. "You always resort to treachery."

Coming from someone inside a giant suit of armor, that seemed a mite unfair. I was more concerned with its repeating gun humming to life, though. Nowhere to run, no cover to take, and I was out of anything that would even slow this fucker down.

Not now, my thoughts came on desperate breath. I was so close! *I WAS SO CLOSE!*

I shut my eyes tight, braced myself.

Please.

Like I said, I don't believe in gods. But I do believe that the universe is out to fuck you. And occasionally, when the universe gets just greedy enough to send two things to fuck you at once, you can turn it to your favor.

Such as when I felt the earth shuddering beneath me, heard a voice bellow behind me, saw a shadow growing above me.

I leapt away.

Calto came hammering down.

He roared, hurling himself into the Paladin. The armor's guns blazed, tearing bright blossoms of blood out of his skin. Yet he didn't care. He struck the Paladin like a boulder, the Lady's song rising, giving him strength to push against its roaring engines. He brought it to the ground, eyes alight with a violet glow.

"Well done," he growled. "Well done, indeed. I am angry. I had thought myself beyond that. Yet you have inspired me."

His fingers sank through metal like it was warm cake. The iron shrieked as he tore the visor free from its shoulders. Inside, a young Revolutionary pilot, gasping and sweating and scrambling for a tiny pistol, was torn from the cockpit. Calto hoisted him above his head, taking his neck in one hand, his ankle in the other.

"I dedicate this," Calto growled, "to you."

He pulled. Red life splattered. Two pieces of flesh and bone fell to the ground.

I would tell you more, but I was already gone. There was no way I was going to stick around for that.

Certainly not after I heard the cannons begin firing.

From very far away, I heard their sounds—as though something had simply taken the air and broken it. I felt a great rush of wind. And, high in the sky, I saw a dozen red stars born into the skies.

The cannon fire arced over the walls, great red charges descending like meteors to fall upon the city. In great gouts of flame, in bursts of rubble, in thunderous gasps of air that drank the screams of the people. One by one, they fell and tore the city apart.

And I kept running.

I rushed to the edge of the bridge, down the staircase to the tunnel's mouth. I could hear rasping breath, a body dragging itself through the darkness. Riccu had spent too much power—he was slowing down.

He was mine.

The Cacophony knew it as well as I did, burning in my hand, begging to get started. I wasn't about to deny him after all this.

"SAL!"

A voice in the dark. Two eyes on my back. I turned and looked up to the canal. The carnage raging behind him like the backdrop of a macabre opera, Cavric stood, staring at me pleadingly, hands open and impotent. His lips mouthed a word I couldn't hear over the bloodshed.

But one I knew all the same.

"Please."

And I simply stared at him.

And turned away.

And disappeared.

FORTY-SEVEN

SEWERS OF LASTLIGHT

My footsteps splashing in the water. My breath echoing off the tunnel's walls. My gun rattling in his holster.

If I closed my eyes, I could pretend that was all I heard. If I tried very hard, I could pretend I couldn't hear the battle raging on the streets above, the sounds of cannon shells falling. If I was just a little better at lying, I could pretend I didn't hear the sound of a building collapsing, of people screaming.

I was good.

But not that good.

I kept going. Through the darkness closing in, I kept going. Until I saw a bright purple light blossom in the darkness, illuminating a pale figure.

Riccu looked thinner than the last time I had seen him. He had never been a big man to begin with, but now his skin clung to his skull and he hunched over, clutching himself with withered limbs, like a dead tree curling in on itself. The portal, a bright doorway of violet light, illuminated the fear in his dark-circled eyes as he looked around the tunnel.

I pressed myself against the tunnel wall. But even if I weren't shrouded in darkness, he'd never see me. Riccu was a terrified man.

And like all terrified men, he only ever saw enemies in his head. Never the ones right in front of him.

He pulled his hood up closer around his face, slipped through his portal, and disappeared.

I stalked forward, drawing the Cacophony. The portal loomed large before me, a swirling vortex of light and soft music. I hated these things—always have, even when they were conjured up by people I didn't want to kill. The only guarantee you had that they wouldn't dump you out over a cliff or at the bottom of a river was the Doormage's word.

And Riccu's was not one I trusted.

I heard a faint scurrying, glanced down to see a fat black rat near my foot. It peered at the portal, twitching its whiskers. Curious, it slipped forward, vanishing in a flash of light.

Well, there you go, I told myself. You can't have it said that rats would go where Sal the Cacophony wouldn't. Besides...

In the distance, through the walls, I heard the sound of something exploding.

What's left here that you haven't already fucked up?

I forced that thought out of my head. Forced everything out but the truth. Whether it had been smart or whether I would die regretting it, I had done it. I'd made my choices to get to this point. And now Riccu was going to die for it.

I took in a deep breath. I closed my eyes. I stepped through.

It's a weird sensation, using a portal. No matter how often you've done it, it feels the same way each time. Once you step over the threshold, you cease to be a person and become a liquid. It feels like your skin, your hair, all parts of you turn into a thick paste and disappear down a gullet of light and sound. You want to scream, but you have no voice. You want to fight, but you have no body. You fall forever.

Until you don't.

I came out the other side gasping for breath and with the feeling of my skin on fire—I was uncomfortably aware of my organs resettling inside my body and my blood figuring out how to circulate again.

I held the Cacophony up, searching for anyone in need of a bullet to the face who might have been waiting for me. Nothing but darkness and a rat greeted me. The latter squeaked once, scurried off, and disappeared into the gloom, water splashing as it did.

Still in the sewers.

Riccu wasn't an idiot. He wouldn't make a portal leading directly to Vraki. In the event he was pursued, he'd have set up multiple doors to throw people off before heading back to rejoin whoever's boot he was licking.

He was an intelligent person. But he was scared. And everyone's only as ever smart as they are brave. Give a smart man reason to doubt, he falls to pieces.

Or, in this case, he stops covering his tracks.

The air was rank and still down here. I could hear the sound of him splashing and gasping as he made his way through the tunnels ahead of me. I crept carefully up to the corner of the tunnel and peered around.

Riccu's desperate retreat had devolved into a haggard, shambling mess. He was breathing heavily, gasping as he hobbled forward on one foot, dragging a left leg that no longer worked behind him.

Personally, I always thought Doormages got a raw deal. Their magic wasn't flashy and they were largely seen as useful tools by the Imperium they served. And in exchange for their useful-but-not-impressive powers?

The Lady Merchant took their bodies.

At first, it's not too bad: the creeping numbness that follows the use of Doormagic. Eventually, a Doormage can't teleport without limbs becoming paralyzed. And soon, if they're not careful, they become completely paralyzed. Those most dedicated to the Imperium were confined to beds, utterly helpless to move as they struggled to cast spells by blinking. Until the Lady took that, too, and left them as husks to be discarded by the Emperor they loyally served.

It wasn't hard to see why Riccu might have joined Vraki in conspiring against the Imperium. And I wouldn't have blamed him at all, if not for one thing.

He was on my list.

I followed him through the darkness as he shambled, splashed, and whispered sobbing curses under his breath. All his carefully laid plans were forgotten in the stress of battle. He was simply trying to escape now. He would lead me right to Vraki. He was slow, desperate, and terrified.

So you might be wondering how the hell I managed to lose him.

It happened quickly. One second he was there, hurrying around a corner. The next, he had vanished completely.

I whispered a curse. The fucker teleported. Stupid move—he'd only invite more paralysis into his limbs, slow himself down. But, for the moment, he was gone and I was left with nothing but silence and darkness.

Well, and a fat fucking rat.

The little rodent sat atop a pipe protruding from the wall, whiskers twitching as it canted its head at me curiously. I shot him a glare.

"And what the fuck are you looking at?" I muttered, pointing the Cacophony at him. "If I find out you had something to do with this, I'll…"

I was spared the embarrassment of wasting one of my best curses on a rodent by the sound of splashing. Faint, but I heard it. Ahead and to the right, down another corner. He was moving even slower.

I hurried to catch up, following the sound of splashing as it turned to boots on stone. Soon, the drowned tunnel of the sewer gave way to dry floor. I emerged in a vast cistern, pipes groaning as they pushed water through the walls. The faintest hint of starlight poked through a grate far overhead. And beneath it, I could see him.

He appeared as a shadow in the gloom, but I could see him standing at the center of the cistern. His back was straight. His poise was relaxed. And he was looking right at me.

"No more running?" I called out as I approached. "You always were sensible. I liked that about you."

He said nothing to me. It was a coward's tongue in that skull, rehearsing how he would plead for his life. I shouldered the Cacophony as I walked toward him.

"I won't tell you this ends with you walking away," I said. "We can do it quick, if you want. You can do the right thing and give me what you owe me. Or you can put up a fight you'll lose, make this hard for me, and die down here, just another piece of shit floating in the river."

I paused. He said nothing. He didn't move.

"If I have to," I spoke softly, "I'll make it hurt."

"I know you will."

That wasn't his voice.

"You don't lie."

That wasn't his stride as he came walking forward. That wasn't his body that stepped into the light, wasn't his long fingers resting on the pommel of a sword, wasn't his eyes regarding me.

That wasn't his perfect smile, soft and sad and tender as a knife in my back, looking at me.

"No one ever said," Jindu whispered, "that Sal the Cacophony was a liar."

FORTY-EIGHT

SEWERS OF LASTLIGHT

I've stared down beasts with the blood of my best friends glistening on their fangs. I've walked battlefields where soldiers halfway into the earth still drew breath as birds pulled out their innards. I've sat at the table of men and women who walked from one end of the Scar to the other and left a corpse in their wake for every step they took.

Never before did my blood run cold like it did when I looked into his eyes.

No malice. No spite. After all this time, all those bodies, all these scars, he looked at me without an ounce of hatred in his stare. And for a moment, I forgot how things were between us.

For a moment, I wanted to forget.

"It's good to see you, Salazanca." He took a step forward.

I had thought of this moment—dreamed of it. In my head, I had a thousand replies for them, each one sharpened over weeks to a fine tip that I would have used to push right through his heart and kill him where he stood.

But when he took that step forward, when he kept meeting my eyes, when he smiled like all that had happened had never happened…I forgot all of them. Every retort, every curse, every word I could say just drained out of me. I couldn't remember how to do anything but take a step back and hold my gun up.

My arm was shaking.

"Ah." He stopped, held his hands up as if in surrender, as if that could set me at ease. "All right." He nodded slowly. "I suppose I can't blame you for that."

For a long time we stood there. My shaking arm with the gun pointed at his face. His mouth trembling, looking for the words to say. The sound of water rushing and pipes groaning and the distant sound of people dying.

Had he always been that tall? I wondered.

In the silence between us, without words to distract me, I looked at him. He was shaped like a thin, cold knife, slender shoulders and chest tapering down to a thin waist and feet poised like he was about to come moving at me. His face was all sharp angles and hard edges, every bit like the black sword hanging at his waist.

His namesake.

Jindu the Blade.

"I've thought about it a lot, you know."

I didn't know what I expected him to say the next time I saw him. Maybe it was that. Maybe I had the perfect retort for that, somewhere in all those words I couldn't remember. As it was, I just stood there, staring down my trembling arm at him.

"That night," he said, looking away from me. "In my dreams, when I wake up in the morning, anytime I close my eyes, I keep thinking about it." He stared at the damp stones under his feet. "And in my head, it always looks like someone else who was there. Someone else who did that, someone else who walked with you, someone else who…"

He held his hands out. Empty. Like the answer was supposed to be there. Like it was just supposed to fall into his lap.

"But it was me. I know." He sighed; he closed those perfect eyes. "And no matter how much I can't take it back, I know that I…" He shook his head. "I'm sorry is what I'm trying to say. I'm sorry and I just—"

"Jindu."

That barely sounded like my voice. It had come out of my mouth without me knowing. And it barely felt like my thumb drawing the Cacophony's hammer back. But the sound of it clicking filled the room.

"Did you ever really think you'd have words that would make me not want to kill you?"

He breathed in a sharp breath. He straightened, drawn up like a blade quivering in flesh. His eyes were as soft now as they were when I first met him—but there was a hardness there, creeping in at the edges, like someone had filed off the softness and left something jagged behind.

"Salazanca."

He took a step forward.

"Don't."

My voice came out trembling. Sal the Cacophony wasn't supposed to tremble. My arm shook. Sal the Cacophony was supposed to aim true.

"Don't come any closer," I said. "Don't ever say my name again." I thrust the gun at him. "Answer me."

He stopped. I wanted him to keep coming. He frowned. I wanted him to sneer. I wanted him to give me a reason. I wanted something to make me pull the trigger. I wanted to not feel like I couldn't. I didn't know why I couldn't. I didn't know why I was wanting him to start cursing and shrieking like any other scum I've put in their graves, why I wanted him to say anything, *anything*...

"No. I never did."

But that.

"I thought I had them once," he said. "I believed if I thought long enough, spent enough time, I'd find the right ones. But...they don't exist." He shook his head. "I can't tell you anything."

"Then why are you here?" I narrowed my eyes. "Tell me. Tell me why the fuck, with all the fucking Scar for you to die in, I found you here?"

He steadied his gaze, spoke softly.

"You know why."

My arm tensed, steadied. "You're here for Riccu. To protect him. Because you're still working for Vraki."

"I don't work for anyone. I'm still dedicated to restoring the Imperium, to the cause of—"

"You work for Vraki. Knowing what he's done, what he'll do, what he did to *me*, you come and talk about words like they mean a fucking thing?"

"I know, I know, and I said I didn't have them. But it's not as simple as that. This is bigger than you or me. It's bigger than—"

"Than what?" I snarled. "That's it, then? Something's big enough and everything else doesn't matter? You and Vraki and all those fuckers want something bad enough, you don't give a shit who gets hurt to have it?"

"It was the *Imperium*," he shot back. "It was *everything* we fought for, died for. We couldn't leave it to the Nul Emperor. It *had* to be rebuilt, even if that meant sacrifice, even if—"

"IT WAS ME."

My scream echoed through the cistern, ran down a hundred tunnels, drowned in a thousand waters. If Riccu was still here, he'd have heard me, but I didn't fucking care. I didn't fucking care that I was screaming, I didn't fucking care that there were tears in my eyes, and I didn't fucking care if either of us got out of here alive anymore.

"It was *me*, Jindunamalar." My voice wracked, hurt to get out of my throat, but I didn't care about that, either. "You sacrificed *me*. You swore an oath to *me*. You looked me in the eyes and you said… you said…"

I couldn't think about it.

Not that night when he had looked at me with that perfect smile and said those three words and I had believed him. I couldn't think about it without collapsing, breaking down into a miserable heap. I wasn't that. Sal the Cacophony wasn't that.

"I know. I *know*." How the fuck did he sound like he was about to cry, too? How the *fuck* did he manage to do that? "I said it. I broke it. I did it. I know. But it was you and I against the entire Imperium. Was I supposed to let the entire world burn down?"

"*I WOULD!*" I roared back. "I didn't fucking care. The Imperium, the Revolution, who gave a shit? So long as I had you and you had me, we didn't need anything else. Not Vraki, not the Emperor, not their shitty little problems."

"They weren't little. Nothing ever was little." Jindu stared at me with hard eyes, bladed eyes. "You used to fly above it all. You never had to see what was happening on the ground. You never understood that, Salazanca."

"I told you not to say my name."

"What about your other name? Your *true* name?"

"Don't," I warned, taking a step forward.

"The name they called you, the name of the woman who I saw raining fire and thunder upon a thousand screaming souls and swore to heaven that I loved?"

"Don't."

"I spoke her name every night I went to sleep, every morning I woke up, every time I looked up into the sky and saw her there, protecting all of us and all that we had fought for."

Please.

I couldn't say it. I wanted to. I couldn't beg him. No matter how badly I never wanted to hear that name again. No matter how much it felt like blood being torn out of me when he whispered it.

"Red Cloud."

That name. His voice. My head. One of those, maybe all of them, did it.

They took me back to that place.

They took me somewhere else, to a place where I wasn't on the ground, to a place of endless blue and white. I couldn't hear the rush of water or the sound of death or anything but the sound of wind in my ears and my laugh as I tore through the sky. I couldn't feel my arm dropping or my scars aching through the breeze of the cold sky on my skin and my hair whipping about my face.

That name took me back to a place.

Where I used to fly.

"I remember those days, Salazanca."

I looked up. He was standing in front of me. How had he gotten there? How did he get in front of me without me noticing? How did he have my hand in his? Why wasn't I pulling away? Why wasn't he *dead*?

"I remember them, when we were young and it didn't matter." He spoke softly and I wanted to pretend his voice had always sounded like this, like it had never said a cruel word. "It was you and I out there, Red Cloud and the Blade, fighting against the Revolution, preserving the Imperium. Do you remember them? The days when every glass in Cathama was raised in a toast to our names?"

I wanted to tell him so many things. I wanted to tell him to die. I wanted to tell him to bleed. I wanted to tell him he was wrong.

"I remember."

I wanted to know why I said that.

"I wanted it to be that way forever." When had his voice gotten so soft? When did he draw so close to me, whispering in my ear? "I wanted it to be nothing more than us playing war. But it never was, Salazanca. Maybe you couldn't see it, flying up there, but I saw all our friends. I saw them die. I saw them torn apart by bullets, by bombs, by all the machines the Revolution churned out. I heard them. When they died with the Imperium's name on their lips. Cherotha, Makalin, Rendothones…"

"Aradunar," I whispered their names, "Sparaculus, Turindara…"

I remembered them. Sometimes I wondered what names they would have taken when they turned Vagrant. Aradunar was a Door-mage, always loved his work. Maybe he'd be Ara the Greeting or something stupid like that. He always smiled; he always looked…

How did he look?

I couldn't remember. In my head, he was just another black dot on the battlefield far below me. From those days, all I could remember was the sky, how easily I flew through it, how I couldn't anymore. I remembered the sky…

And him.

"Salazanca."

He was behind me. How did he get there? He reached up, placed his hands upon my shoulders. My skin went electric at his touch. How could he still do that to me?

"I made a mistake..." he whispered into my ear. "I wanted Vraki to be right. I wanted him to have the solution. I thought...Some part of me thought that you'd understand, what I agreed to. But I was wrong. I'm sorry."

His hands slid across my scars. They didn't hurt when he touched them. They always hurt. Why didn't they hurt now? Why were my eyes closing? Why did this feel the way it did?

"It was the dead," he said. "I couldn't stand the thought of them dying to give a throne to an emperor who didn't deserve it. I wasn't thinking. I was just listening to the wrong people and I thought... I thought..."

His hand slid down my arm, moving with a certainty his words didn't have. His fingers found mine, squeezed. And even though my brain was screaming and my heart was dying, I squeezed back and hated how good it felt to do that. How much it felt like it used to.

"But it can be that way again, Salazanca."

I couldn't keep track of his hands anymore. They were on my hand, squeezing my fingers. They were on my sides, traveling over scars that were supposed to hurt. They were around my waist, pulling me closer against him and feeling like it used to when he would hold me and feel so solid against my back, like he'd never run.

"The plan can work this time," he whispered into my ear. He smoothed my hair back. His fingers touched my cheek. "We can have a true emperor again. We can have an Imperium that will understand us again, what we've given, all we've fought for. Everything, *everything* can make sense again. We won't need to be Vagrants anymore. We can have beds, wine, all the things we used to have..."

I don't know why it felt good. I don't know why I was listening. I don't know why I didn't just pull the trigger and put a hole through his head when I had the chance. I don't know why I could only remember the feel of his hands on my skin and the sky in my face and not the cold stone on my back or the light in my eyes in the dark place.

"I won't ask you to forgive me," he said. "Or anything like that. If you want to come back to the Imperium, I'll be there at the gates of Cathama for you. If you never want to see me again, I'll go away forever. But don't let everything we've done be in vain."

He leaned closer, held me tight, whispered a blade into my ear.

"Let me make this right."

You ask the wife who stabbed her husband to death, or the father who struck his child, or the kid who wandered upstairs and came back down with a gun, they'll tell you the same thing.

It was a dark voice that made them do it.

A little, savage part of their mind that spoke dark words in a dark tongue that told them to kill, to hurt, to spill blood. Everyone's got it, they say. Everyone's got that dark voice that makes them do bad things.

But I think it's the soft voice that makes them do it.

It's a quiet whisper in the back of their minds. It's a soft, gentle sobbing through a worried smile. It tells them that things can get better, that things can feel good again, that things can be normal again.

If you just forget how bad it hurts.

Things can go back to the way they were.

I heard that voice. I heard it in every bone in my body and every breath he took as he leaned close and his lips brushed against my neck.

No.

But it wasn't my voice that said that.

Don't.

It wasn't his, either.

He is filth.

That voice wasn't soft or dark. It was hot. It was an ember growing hotter, stoking itself to a flame. It was heat in my blood. And it was warm in my hand.

He has to die.

That voice. *His* voice.

They all have to die.

I looked down at my hand. Through a cloud of steam rising between my fingers, the Cacophony's grinning barrel looked back at me. In my head, in my blood, in my *skin*, I could hear his voice, roaring louder than any voice, dark or soft, mine or his or anyone's. It howled. It screamed. It told me.

We made a deal.

My hand tightened around his grip. My heart burned in my chest. My blood boiled. My teeth set.

Revenge for ruin. Ruin for revenge.

And in my head, he howled.

ERES VO ATALI.

He was screaming. And so was I. A formless howl pulled itself out of my mouth as I whirled around, bringing him up. It tore through the cloud of black smoke that burst out of Jindu's cheek as I smashed the Cacophony against the side of his head. It filled the cistern, boiled the water, pulled the world apart.

Jindu fell back, holding a hand to his cheek. It came back with hot blood on his fingers. He looked up at me, shock and fear on his face.

And my gun in his eyes.

I pulled the trigger. Hoarfrost burst out, exploded in a spray of ice. The Lady sang. He disappeared. He showed up fifteen feet away, his bloody hand up in a plaintive cry for peace that I didn't hear.

I pulled the trigger again. Hellfire sang, erupted in a wall of fire.

He disappeared again. I saw his shadow vanish into the tunnel mouth at the other side. I saw him stare at me with those eyes once again. I saw that perfect mouth open to say the perfect word that would make all of this better.

And I pulled the trigger again.

He disappeared.

Nothing but a faint clicking sound came from the Cacophony.

The blood rushed back into my body. The breath I'd been holding exploded out of my lungs. My scars hurt so badly.

I held the Cacophony in both hands, pulling the trigger over and over, hearing nothing but that clicking sound as tears fell down my cheeks.

As I fell to my knees.

As the steam closed in around me.

As I crumpled into a heap.

FORTY-NINE

HIGHTOWER

Tretta felt cold.

She had expected to feel something else—angry and warm and full of righteous curses. She had expected to meet this moment with stern dignity, wise words, and a quote from the Great General to guide her.

But when she decided to kill Sal the Cacophony, she was cold.

As cold as the gun in her hand.

It hadn't come swiftly, the weapon. She had heard what her prisoner had said. She had taken a long moment to let the name sink into her head. And then she had risen out of her chair, drawn the hand cannon from her belt, and pressed it against her captive's forehead.

There were no speeches. No great quotations. No one had ever written the script she should follow for the moment she met the woman who had been the scourge of the Revolution for years. She had no words.

"Tell me your name."

Except those.

Sal looked back at her, down the barrel of the gun pressed against her forehead, into the unblinking eyes of her captor. Her face was empty of fear, her eyes serene and full of calm, as though she had known what was going to happen the whole time, as though there was a script for *her*, as though she had written the fucking thing.

"Governor-Militant," Sal said, "put the gun down."

"Tell me your name," Tretta repeated.

"I still have more to tell you."

"*TELL ME.*" The hammer of the weapon clicked back. Tretta's fingers shook. "*YOUR NAME.*"

Sal closed her eyes. She let out a slow sigh. And when she opened them again, there was nothing in them. No remorse. No fear. At the moment of her death, Sal the Cacophony wasn't even gracious enough to beg for her life.

"I was born in Cathama," Sal the Cacophony said. "I was a mage at birth. At age eight, I was a Prodigy. On my sixteenth birthday, I entered the Imperial army. I've killed thousands with my song, brought towers low with a breath, ended bloodlines with a thought. My name is Salazanca ki Ioril."

She stared down at her hands.

"But you know me as Red Cloud."

It should have been done with.

It shouldn't even be a word. Just three sounds. The click of the hammer. The crack of the hand cannon. The body hitting the floor.

Sal the Cacophony. Salazanca ki Ioril. Red Cloud.

They should all be dead. Vagrant. Criminal. Killer. They should all be dead by Tretta's hand. They would be, Tretta knew.

But first, they had to know.

"Roddin Dutiful," Tretta said.

Sal didn't ask who.

"Thenna Inspire," she said.

Sal didn't look confused.

"Merla Proud," Tretta said. "Keroin Proud, Herry Industrious, Calmont Furious, Anica Vengeful, Ormal Contemplative." She held a breath. "Vederic Stern."

All those names. And Sal didn't once give Tretta a reason to pull the trigger.

"My graduating class," she said. "We went through the academy together, fought together, drank together. They were assigned to Bentnail, to the Imperial front, to Vigil..." She clenched her jaw. "You killed them. All of them."

"And more," Sal said. "So many more."

It wasn't a boast. There was no arrogance or pride in her voice. It was simply a fact, fallen out of her mouth like a lump of iron and lying cold and naked and ugly on the table.

"Revolutionaries, mostly," Sal whispered. "The war was in full swing. I was sent out so many times. I had to have killed some who couldn't fight back. I don't know which." She stared at it, this ugly truth, as though it were a real thing. "From up there, they all looked the same."

"You filth," Tretta whispered. "You utter *filth*. You dare to tell me this now."

"You would have killed me otherwise."

"I'll kill you *now*."

"No, you won't." Sal looked up at Tretta. "You still don't know what happened to Cavric."

"You dare to weigh his life against the thousands you've taken?"

"It's got nothing to do with me." Sal shook her head—as best she could with a gun pressed against it. "You, Governor-Militant, won't let him disappear. You won't lose one more soldier."

How?

How did she do this?

How did she, a prisoner, act like she was in control? How did she, shackled, make Tretta feel like *she* was the prisoner? How did she, unarmed, make Tretta feel like there was a gun pressed to *her* head?

How did she make Tretta pull the weapon away?

"And why should I listen?" she asked. "Why should I listen to anything a deceiver such as yourself says?"

"I haven't deceived you at all," Sal replied. "I haven't lied. I simply haven't told you the entire story."

Tretta sat back down. She kept one hand on the hand cannon. She stared across the table.

"Tell me. All of it."

Sal closed her eyes. And she spoke.

FIFTY

LONG AGO
AND FAR AWAY

Let me tell you a story about a girl who could fly.

She was born into a good life—her house had money but not riches, her parents were respected but not adored. And when her mother held her in her arms and her eyes flashed with a purple light, her family was pleased but not enthusiastic. A mage born to them was a blessing, to be sure, but not a miracle.

That happened when she turned eight.

It's always around that age that a mage's power manifests. They hear the Lady Merchant's song, and shortly after, they demonstrate their powers. Her family was expecting it. They waited patiently to see what her art would be and what Barter the Lady would ask for it.

They expected this girl to grab a toy across the room with her mind like a Graspmage; they desperately hoped this girl would have a prestigious art like a Siegemage and break a door without trying.

But this girl flew.

One minute she was running around in her garden, chasing imaginary monsters. The next, she was over the walls. She didn't scream or cry. She simply laughed, like she could do this all along.

She flew over the roofs of her neighbors' houses; she flew around the spires of the Imperial Palace; she flew to the roosts of the Krikai, who looked at her, curious what a human was doing all the way up there.

When she got hungry, she came back home to ask her father for a snack. And she found Imperial scholars waiting for her.

They asked her questions: what did she hear when the Lady sang, how did she feel when she was flying, what price had she paid when she landed? She simply shrugged. She didn't feel any worse. She hadn't paid any price, given up anything. The power was simply there and it had been given to her.

She was a Prodigy.

And she no longer belonged to her family.

They watched her go, taken away by the carriage, smiling and waving and cheering. She cried and pounded on the window; no one told her where she was going, who these people taking her away were, why her family wasn't trying to get her back. She never remembered their names. She wondered if they would ever remember hers.

At age sixteen, she entered the Imperial army. The minders that had raised her these past years were grateful to see her go. She had been a willful child, resistant to training, responding to discipline by hurling her tutor across the room with a spell. But in the army, she found purpose.

And in the men and women she fought alongside, she found friendship. They saw her as their protector, someone who would turn the tide of the Revolutionary rebellion. And they protected her, too, and gave her a family she didn't know she wanted. They called her Salazanca, mostly. Madam ki Ioril, if they were formal. Sal, if they were close friends.

Until the day she turned twenty.

And she became Red Cloud.

She got the name from her coat, the bright red color she had insisted on. She flew over the Scar, unhindered by mountains or plains or anything. She flew where the Imperium asked her to fly and where they sent her friends marching.

And she killed.

Hundreds, thousands. With a wave of her hand, there was fire. With a breath, there was wind. With a thought, there was ruin. And she never paid a price for it. Where other mages slowed down or changed as they paid their Barters, she simply kept going, flying, killing. She never really noticed, to be honest. So long as she could still fly, she didn't think about it. So long as she came back to her friends, she didn't care.

And she had them. Quite a few, really. They loved her, but they couldn't fly. They were concerned with problems on the ground, problems they couldn't fly away from. The new emperor had been born without the light in his eyes. He was a nul. And he stood to inherit the throne. Many mages had rebelled. But not her friends. They had bigger plans.

She couldn't understand their problems. So when they asked for her help...she listened. She loved them. They loved her. That was how it was supposed to be.

And on the night they killed her, she wasn't flying.

"There's no need to be nervous."

I shot a glare toward Jindu. The light cast by the alchemical globes lining the walls of the Imperial crypts was dim, but not dim enough that I couldn't see the smirk on his face.

"I'm not nervous," I said.

"You're walking," he said. "You never walk."

I rolled my eyes. The next step I took brought me into the air, hovering off the floor. I gestured upward as my head almost struck the ceiling.

"There's no fucking room to fly in here," I growled as I came back down. "Why the hell couldn't this be done in, like, the gardens?"

"The garden," Jindu repeated flatly. "We're planning to overthrow an illegitimate tyrant, reestablish order to the Imperium, and honor the sacrifices of our comrades...and you want to do it in the garden."

"Maybe with a nice bottle of wine."

"I feel like the Empress might notice that."

"Well, if she's really illegitimate, so should her claims on the gardens, right?" I sighed, perhaps a touch too dramatically. "The ones beneath the palace have a lovely fountain and—"

"She *is* illegitimate."

Jindunamalar's growl caught me off guard. I was used to his easy laughter and his smiles. It sounded like someone else's voice in his mouth.

"And so is her son," he spoke on seething breath. "He's a nul, Salazanca. He has no idea what he's been given and he'll have no idea how to rule. The Empress refuses to renege on his claim, so we have no choice."

"*Fine.*" He was just skittish, I told myself. Soon, that smile would come back. "We'll be all sneaky, if we must." I sniffed. "Though, I don't see why now. It's been a year since the rebellion. It's taken Vrakilaith that long to come up with a plan?"

"He's careful. Vrakilaith has been working on a solution." Jindunamalar didn't look at me. His eyes were locked straight ahead, rigid as a spear. "He and the others have an idea on how to take care of this. We aren't going to serve a Nul Emperor. Not ever."

Right now, so many years and so much blood lost, it all seemed so obvious. His voice was always like a song, precise and effortless. This brusque snappishness, this growling, it wasn't him. His stride was always relaxed, as though being next to me was the easiest thing in the world. This tense, determined stutter of a walk... it wasn't his.

I didn't want to know what was going to happen. I wanted to pretend this was just a hard night for him, that it would pass. But when he took my hand, when his fingers felt cold and clammy around mine, something inside me told me that he had changed.

I wish I had listened.

"We didn't enter this lightly." He looked at me with a tense, awkward smile. "No matter what happens, it's worth it, right? For the Imperium?"

I didn't do it for the Imperium.

It was just a name, a collection of buildings, a place I was obligated to serve for reasons I didn't care to understand. Everything I did, I did for the people I knew. For the men and women who marched beneath me. For the mages who laughed and studied and drank with me.

For him.

I smiled and squeezed his hand. And I tried to ignore how cold it felt.

"For the Imperium."

The light grew faint as the voices grew loud. Our voices and our hands both fell from each other as the halls of the Imperial crypts turned into a vast circular chamber.

A bigger crypt for bigger people with bigger ideas.

Before our magic became art, before we knew what the Lady's song was, before the Imperium was even a concept, we had the Council: wise men and women who gathered here, in this chamber beneath the earth, to discuss the lofty ideals for a free world beautified by magic.

Then the first Emperor came, killed every last Council member, and that was that.

But that was all in the past. They had built the Imperial palace over the chambers of the old Council and converted them into the crypts—a place to bury the last remnants of the last Emperors, their crowns. It was a place of beautiful ideas that were never achieved and, like all those places, deliberately ignored by those in power.

The ideal place for the Crown Conspiracy, as they'd later call us, to gather: a new power plotting the death of an old power from the graveyard of an even older power.

Thirty-two bodies gathered in the chamber, around the empty thrones of the long-dead Council. Only a few faces looked up at us as we entered.

Kreshtharan spared a glance, let out that laugh of his that made my skin crawl. Galtathamora scratched the newest batch of thorns that had burst from her skin and grunted at me. Grishoktha, one hand on his gigantic cudgel, waved a massive hand at me and bellowed a greeting. But even his thunderous voice wasn't enough to distract the assembled.

Vrakilaith was holding court.

Even back then, he had looked thin. His hair was a messy red mop that hung around a face too gaunt for his young age. The Imperium had bedecked their prized Prodigy in as much finery as their tailors could make, but his clothes still hung loose and baggy around a scrawny frame.

If you looked too hard at him, you'd break him.

If you didn't look into his eyes, that is.

The Lady's song was only for her mages. But her light, the violet glow that flashed in her chosen's eyes, was for everyone else to know her mark. It came out sparsely, lighting up and fading out as a spell was born and died.

But Vrakilaith's gaze, so hard and sharp he couldn't blink for fear of cutting his eyelids, always had her light burning in them. Somewhere deeper than any of us could hope to see.

I felt those eyes, through the darkness and bodies cloistered in the gloom, when he looked up.

"It can't be that simple." Zanzemalthanes stared up at the Prodigy. Years of being a Maskmage had worn away the features of his face, but the awe in his eyes was still apparent. "We just... *make* a new Emperor?"

"It isn't that simple." Vrakilaith's voice was soft, but there was no doubt that everyone was listening. "Not in execution. But there is no other choice." He gestured up to the thin shaft of light piercing through the ceiling. "A nul has been born to the Imperial family. The Lady Merchant has forsaken them, clearly, as she'll forsake us all, if we do not act."

"But to do what you propose..." Rogonoroth, weary and rigid, let out a contemplative hum. "Summoning is already a reckless art. Even you have trouble controlling it, Prodigy. To draw a Scrath out is one thing, to make it an Emperor..."

"I am honored by your counsel," Vrakilaith replied, inclining his head. "But I am not stumbling into this blindly. Even the sages do not know as much about the art of summoning as I do. I know what its limitations are." He smiled softly. "And I know what we can do with it."

"Bad idea." Ricculoran whimpered, cowering away as he shook his head. "Bad, bad, *bad* idea."

"He's right," Dorukana growled in agreement. "The sages don't know for a reason. The art is forbidden to—"

"Attend me."

Vrakilaith never raised his voice. He never had to. When he spoke now, his voice boomed as though the Lady herself wanted us to hear him. And all fell silent.

"I am aware of the risks. I am aware of your concerns." He sighed, closed his eyes. "But I am even more aware of what we stand to lose by letting a nul inherit the throne. For the honor of our fallen comrades, those who gave their lives, we have no alternative but risk."

"How can it even work?" Grishoktha rumbled.

"A Scrath is summoned as a spirit," Vrakilaith said. "The world cannot abide the presence of something so unnatural. It will explode, destroying everything, if not introduced to a host."

"And if it is?" Shorakaia covered a haughty chuckle with the back of her hand. "It twists the host into a monster. Who would follow such a beast if you put it on the throne?"

Vrakilaith fell silent for a moment, staring at his hands. The light in his eyes danced, contemplative. And a small, cruel smile that I would one day come to loathe spread across his face.

"What if we could summon it…without a host?" he asked. "What if we could summon it in its purest form?"

"*Impossible*," Talthonanac rasped from the darkness.

"He's right. That's crazy, even for you," Galtathamora growled. "What's the use in jabbering about this shit, anyway? The army is behind the Empress. We should just go Vagrant, like the others."

"And then what?" Vrakilaith's voice, deep and resonant like a knife plunged into flesh, boomed. "After the Imperium built its palaces over our Dust, after we conquered their new world and threw down the upstart Revolution that would tear it apart, you would have us simply *leave*?"

"What other way is there?" Ricculoran muttered. "The Empress will have no more children."

"Hardly her call to make, is it?" Kreshathalar chuckled as he cleaned his nails with a knife. "So she made one nul. Throw it away and try again. She owes that much, surely."

"The army's thrown its lot behind her."

I started when I heard the voice beside me. It didn't sound like Jindunamalar. He didn't look like the person I had walked in with. He stood rigid as a spear, his face carved into a deep, angry scowl, and in his eyes flashed an uncomfortable intensity.

The same intensity I saw in Vrakilaith's.

"They all swore to her oath after the Dogsjaw Rebellion," he said. "They cowered. It falls to us to honor the sacrifices of those who came before and those who will come after."

"The Nul Emperor will lead us to ruin," Vrakilaith said, nodding. "He cannot hope to comprehend the power at his fingertips, let alone use it responsibly. The Empress has chosen her spawn over her nation. It falls to us to remedy this."

"Recklessness cannot be cured with recklessness." Rogonoroth sighed, shook his head. "Even a Prodigy cannot hope to control a Scrath."

"Summoning is an art, like any other," Vrakilaith said. "It is a power offered, a Barter demanded."

"You speak of summoning a living, thinking creature," Moraccus protested, adjusting his glasses. "A life. What Barter could you possibly offer in exchange for that?"

"Nothing." Vrakilaith held out his hands, empty. "There is nothing we can offer from ourselves for a life. But the Lady Merchant does not want us to Barter."

The mutters of the crowd quieted. Vrakilaith's eyes settled upon me. And all of theirs followed.

"She wants us to give something back."

There was scarcely any light down there. Just the barest glow offered from the shaft of light piercing down from the ceiling above. I couldn't see their faces—whether there was doubt or fear or hatred on the visages of the people I had once called my friends. All I could see were their eyes, the tiny pinpricks of light reflected in their gazes.

As they stared at me.

"What are you saying?"

My voice came out as a growl. I tensed, feeling the air stir around my feet. Something was wrong—my heart was beating faster; my scalp grew taut against my skull. It felt like there wasn't enough air down here, like there were too many bodies.

"To be a Prodigy is a gift," Vrakilaith said, softer than he had ever spoken before. "The Lady Merchant gives us power and asks for nothing in return. It is a sign of her favor. And if we return it..."

"Then we can get something else," Galtathamora said, nodding. "Like a Scrath. It's an exchange."

"A Barter," Rogonoroth muttered. "I suppose that is...logical."

"A Barter?" My voice came out as a shriek. "That's what you think I am? Something to be traded?"

"Not you," Vrakilaith said. "Not Salazanca ki Ioril. Not Red Cloud. Just the power inside you, the gift she gave you." He talked like that was supposed to soothe me. "To restore the Imperium, to return a *true* Emperor to the throne, all we require is that."

"*Possible*," Talthonanac hissed.

"An equal exchange," Moraccus whispered. "That much power returned would demand an equal amount of power back. The theory is sound."

"Sound?" I shouted, scowling into the darkness. "*Sound?* What's sound about this shit? A theory is just a fucking theory. There's no guarantee anything about it will work!"

"I have seen it."

Vrakilaith held his hands out wide, like I was just a child who needed to be calmed down. Or like he was a savior no one had asked for.

"I have opened gates to worlds beyond imagining," he said. "I have heard a song so pure that it was language in my ears. I have seen what lies on the other side. I understand your doubts, but it is all we have. A gift must be given for the Lady to show us her favor."

"Then why not *you*?" I snarled, thrusting a finger at him. "You're a Prodigy, too. Give up your own power, if you're so certain."

"He needs his power to perform the summoning," Zanzemalthanes whimpered. "No one else can do it. Try to understand, Salazanca. It's not an easy choice for any of us."

"For you, perhaps," Kreshtharan said, casually spitting on the floor. "It's not like she was using her art for anything important, anyway."

"You fuckers." I could feel the power boiling up inside me, fire on my breath and thunder in my ears. "You pieces of shit. I've fought with you, protected you, *saved* you."

"And now we're asking you to protect us once more," Vrakilaith said. "A final sacrifice for the Imperium we agreed to protect, for the people we agreed to serve. It is the only way, Salazanca."

"The only way," Rogonoroth sighed. "I suppose it is."

"Sorry, kid," Grishoktha rumbled. "If I could do it for you, I would, but…"

"Why are we even still talking?" Rinatana sighed dramatically. "Can we not just be done with it and get things back to normal?"

"Every minute we waste down here is a liability," Korthanos growled. "They'll find us if we don't act soon."

"*Imperative*," Talthonanac rasped.

I caught their faces in glimpses, in shadowed sneers and in half-hidden frowns and in cringes that disappeared when they couldn't bear to look me in the eye.

They weren't the faces I remembered laughing in the barracks when we shared a bottle of wine, the faces I remembered smiling wearily as we fought our way through savage battlefields. I didn't recognize the faces that looked at me with fear, with hatred, with envy now.

I didn't recognize any of them.

Only their black blades hanging at their hips.

"I am asking you, Salazanca." Vrakilaith clasped his hands together, plaintive. "I am pleading with you. For the Imperium, for the mages who have fought and died for you, for the duty we all swore."

Silence fell over the chamber. I saw them all looking at me, these nightmares that wore the faces of my friends, waiting for an answer. Not one of them saying there had to be another way, not one of them speaking up for me, not one of them moving to stand beside me.

Not one of them, except...

I turned and looked to Jindunamalar. He stared back at me, his perfect smile a frown now, his perfect face hidden in shadows. He stared at me, eyes alight with that awful power. Never once did he look away from me.

Not as he turned aside.

Not as he walked across the chamber.

Not as he stood with them.

And I looked over them, those half-shrouded nightmares. And my feet slowly left the floor. I drew in a deep breath, I opened my mouth, and I gave my answer.

And it was her song.

My shout burst from me in a tremendous wall of sound. It flung them from their feet, sent them flying across the room to smash against the wall and be dashed against the floor. Some of them got back to their feet quickly, some of them staggered up slowly, some of them just stayed on the floor.

Their swords came out, blades so pitch-black they were as shadows against the darkness of the chamber.

It wouldn't save them. I wouldn't forgive them.

I flew. I rose like a monolith, ancient and terrible, into the sky. I called the magic to my hands, felt the fire pour out of my fingertips in great waves. The Wardmages drew their shields as fast as they could. The Siegemages tried to weather the heat. But it burned them still, magic as pure as mine, and they screamed.

And that wouldn't save them, either.

Grishoktha roared, leapt at me with his massive club. I swung a hand and sent him, all four hundred pounds of him, smashing against the wall. Rogonoroth vanished, reappeared behind me, was swallowed in the embrace of ice that came pouring out of my hand and fell to the ground, frozen. Talthonanac wove his dark illusions around me, made the shadows stir to life and shroud around me—I let out a roar and light burst from my eyes, banishing his shadows and sending him cowering. Zanzemalthanes twisted his shape into a great black bird, his feathers sheared from his body as a bolt of lightning swept from my fingers and struck him in the chest.

They came leaping, they came casting, they came howling. And they fell to the ground frozen, burned, dashed, and maimed. Some kept getting up, some ran for cover, some sat and wailed. Not one of them apologized. Not one of them begged me to stop. Not one of them looked at me with the faces I remembered.

It shouldn't have been this easy. I should have felt some pang of guilt, some hesitation, something that would make me realize I was fighting my friends. But I couldn't see their faces in the darkness. And their voices were twisted with rage and pain. They weren't my friends.

They were just more shadows clinging to the earth.

They cut me. Lucky blows, stray grazes, some so close to piercing something vital that I could feel my heart stop for a second. Inch by inch, their black blades drew blood across my face, across my arms, across my body. But they couldn't cut clean enough, nor deep enough, nor true enough.

It didn't matter to me. Nothing mattered to me but stopping them, but punishing them, but *hurting* them. And I did. With every wave of my hand, with every word, with every scream, I made them pay. Until they all lay on the ground, groaning and gasping, except for one.

And he was staring at me with light in his eyes.

Vrakilaith threw his best at me—his lightning, his fire, his power. He was a Prodigy, too. But not like me. He couldn't match me. He couldn't best me. He couldn't *fly*.

I drew my anger, my rage, my pain into my hands. I let my fury fly out in a great, destructive burst of every magic I could think of. He met it with his own, forming a shield out of earth and dust and shadows. But as my anger bore down on him, as my scream reached its crescendo, I could see his shield cracking, I could see his concentration faltering. He took a step backward, his face contorted with pain and effort.

He screamed out a word. I didn't even hear it over the sound of my own screaming.

"JINDU!"

From the shadows, I saw him rise. He vanished, reappeared on the throne beside Vrakiliath. He vanished again, reappeared in front of me in midair. I had just enough time to see Jindunamalar's face, a long scar of a frown where his smile should have been, before he vanished again and reappeared.

Behind me.

I didn't even feel the blade until its black tip burst out my belly. I had seen him do it hundreds of times to the enemies of the Imperium. Somehow, I never thought it would feel like this.

So swift and so cold.

In. Out. And I was dead.

My rage died out in my throat. The power fell to cinders and splinters in my hands. My body went limp and I...

I fell.

He caught me in his arms, cradling me like he once did on our very first night together. How fucked up was it, I had the presence of mind to think, that I thought of that night now? He carried me, like he had carried me to bed that night. And he laid me down upon the shattered throne. I felt the cold stone on my back.

I wasn't dead. Not yet. Jindunamalar's blade was an extension of his body; it did exactly what he wanted it to. He had only intended to disable me, make me helpless to resist what happened next.

And I couldn't.

The wounded were gathered and taken out. The strong lingered behind to watch, to make sure I wouldn't fight back. It was an insult, how few of them there were. They gathered around me, my friends, and looked down at me. The light was brighter upon the broken throne. I could see their faces, finally.

And I didn't recognize any of them.

Not even his. Not as he looked down at me. Not as he whispered in that dark place.

"I'm sorry."

I could barely hear him. And in another minute, I couldn't hear anything.

Vrakilaith spoke a word. The Lady's song answered him in a clear, crystalline note that grew louder. And louder. Until it became a singular shriek, loud and painful and so terribly close.

A halo of light was birthed into life above me—a great violet bloom of luminescence, swirling like a living thing over me. It opened wide, like an eye, and for a moment, I was convinced I was staring into her face and she was looking back on me with pity.

And then . . . I felt the light pull on me.

It took my breath first. It drew the wind out of my mouth, my throat, my lungs. It took my energy next, sapping the will to move, to fight right out of me. But it reached deeper, an invisible hand that pushed through my skin and into my organs until it found something so deep within me I didn't know where and wrapped ghostly fingers around something inside me that I didn't know the name of.

Not until it pulled it out of me.

I couldn't call it pain, what I felt. I had felt pain before—pain could be measured; it had a beginning and an end. What happened to me, the agony that wracked my body, it felt . . . eternal. Like I had always been feeling it and just never noticed. Like I had never *not* felt it.

But I was screaming.

Even without breath, my voice tore itself out of my throat. Tears flowed down my cheeks, the skin trembling and quivering beneath them. I wanted to run, I wanted to move, I wanted to just lie down and die. Anything to make it stop. But I couldn't do any of that. I couldn't find the strength to do anything but scream a word.

"JINDU!"

But he didn't answer.

He didn't answer me.

I felt my flesh tear apart in bright bursts of blood. My cheek split open. A great line ripped itself across my eye. A hole tore open in my chest, from my collarbone to my belly. The light pulled my skin apart. My blood drifted out of my body and into the sky, floating lazily through the air in quivering droplets.

And then came the light.

From out of me, wispy and ephemeral, violet wept. Not like blood, but like smoke, sighing out of the wound. After my skin had been torn apart and my breath had been robbed, it was as though this was simply...leaking out of me. The light left me, like it had gotten bored of me, and drifted up into the air, past my blood, until it vanished into the halo of light.

And I was left on that broken stone. I was left bleeding out of a dozen cuts. I was left weeping, with no one to listen to me. And somehow I knew, like I knew I needed that light...

I would never fly again.

"It's done," Vrakilaith said. His eyes were on that halo above me, swirling and snaking and alive. "She accepted our gift. Now"—he drew in his breath—"we see if she will—"

He didn't finish. He didn't have to.

She would.

And she did.

That shrieking note of a song returned. The halo of light trembled, quivered. It let out an ancient sound, alive and groaning.

"*Concerning*," Talthonanac whispered.

"What's this shit?" Kreshtharan snarled. "What the fuck's she doing?"

"Vraki?" Jindu asked. "What's happening?"

Vrakilaith didn't answer. Vrakilaith *couldn't* answer. He didn't know. He simply stared at the halo, mouth agape, as he waited for the Lady Merchant's answer.

And she gave it.

It came plummeting out of the halo, falling without ceremony or grace, to land with a splatter upon the floor of the chamber. Ichor pooled around it, a great mass of flesh and shadow. It quivered and trembled like a newborn, reaching out with a shaking arm to grasp at the floor and haul itself to its feet.

A human. Maybe? It stood on two legs. It had two arms. It had a head and two eyes and a mouth. But it was . . . wrong. Its limbs were too long. It was far too tall. Its eyes were too big, saw too much, saw things we didn't want it to, things we didn't know we had. And its mouth, gaping wide and fitted with hundreds and hundreds of rows of teeth, craned open far too big and . . .

"*Oh,*" Vrakilaith gasped. "*I see.*"

It screamed.

Chaos.

Shadows flashing.

Wails in the dark, blossoms of blood, light dying out.

I don't know how I found the ability to move. I don't know how I made it out of there. I don't know how I found myself down in the halls of the crypts, my hands struggling to find enough fingers to press down on all the wounds on my body.

All I remember is falling to my knees, too terrified to go on, too pained to stand up, too weary to think of a reason not to lie down and die.

And I looked up into a crown of brass.

And it smiled back at me.

FIFTY-ONE

HIGHTOWER

There was no such thing as an Imperial citizen.

There was no such thing as an Imperial soldier.

There was no such thing as an Imperial nation, for there was no such thing as an Imperial people.

This had been the first noble truth the Great General handed down to his citizens.

The Imperium, it was known, was a collection of tools masquerading as a culture. Tools to be used at the whims of corrupt Emperors and decadent Empresses and discarded without a second thought.

You could not feel fear in the face of an Imperial soldier, nor guilt for killing an Imperial citizen, for they were not people. They were tools to be broken, and their rulers would mourn them not. To fight the Imperium was to fight an enemy without a soul.

And all that kept the humble people once derided as "nuls" from becoming more tools was the Revolution.

This was the Great General's noblest truth. It had been the first that Tretta had committed to memory, the first that she recited upon graduating from the officer's academy, the first she spoke whenever she had led her soldiers into battle. It had served her well. It had made war bearable, to think of her enemy not as flesh and blood, as sons and daughters, but as scythes and rakes used to tend a rotting garden. To be broken and cast aside.

It had been easier to think of them as tools.

Red Cloud had been one such tool—sharper than the rest, more dangerous than others, but still a tool. To think of that scourge of the Revolution, that remorseless killer, not as an unstoppable force of nature but as a simple tool had helped Tretta sharpen her fear into hatred.

She had thought of Red Cloud as just a name to be erased, just a tool to be broken, just a body to be put down. She had never thought of Red Cloud as a person, a woman with family and friends, a woman who joked and laughed...

A woman who had been betrayed.

It was with a keen resentment that she stared across the table at her prisoner. Sal had finished her story what seemed like hours ago and now sat, head bowed, eyes staring down at the hands folded in front of her, saying nothing. No explanations, no defenses, no excuses—just silence, long and agonizing as a drawn blade.

Tretta wasn't sure why it hurt, this silence. She wasn't sure why she felt that keenly wounded sensation of betrayal. And though she struggled to explain it away, it *did* feel like betrayal.

It was not enough that this woman should take her time, her dignity, with this stupid interrogation, these frivolous tales. It was not enough that she should steal away the fate of Cavric and hoard it, teasing it out in stingy increments. Sal the Cacophony, Vagrant and thief and outlaw, had taken away something much dearer.

She had stolen Tretta's hatred.

"Why would you tell me this?"

Sal didn't answer. Her body shuddered as she tried to hold something back. She bit her lower lip. She held her hands in fists and said nothing.

"What, were you hoping for mercy?" Tretta demanded. "Were you hoping that I'd let you live after hearing that... that *tripe*?"

"No. I didn't."

Sal's voice trembled. No longer smug, nor confident, nor even in control—her words came soft and shuddering on a wet breath.

"Then what? You want atonement? You think this excuses the lives you stole? You think it *explains* it?"

And Tretta's own voice sounded like cracks spreading across a thin pane of glass. Her words were breathless, almost hysterical.

"No." Sal buried her face in her hands, shook her head. "No...I don't..."

"To brag, then," Tretta snarled, rising out of her chair. "To add to your twisted fucking legend."

"*NO!*" Sal screamed.

"*THEN WHY?*" Tretta slammed her fists on the table. "Why would you tell me that story? Why would you tell me about Jindu and your friends and...and..." Her hands shook, as though she could just strangle the answer out of her prisoner. "*WHY ARE YOU TELLING ME THIS?*"

"I don't know."

Sal looked up at her captor, the serenity in her eyes melted away like snow in a spring thaw. Tears, warm and hot and ugly, came sliding freely down her cheeks to pool in her scars. Her mouth trembled, searching for the words. Her eyes darted around the chamber, as though she could find them somewhere in the stifling darkness.

"I don't know." She swallowed a damp, hot breath. "I don't know what I wanted. I just...had to say it. I had to tell someone."

She lowered her stare down to her hands upon the table. Her mouth hung open, numb. Her eyes open and empty. And yet the tears continued to fall, one by one.

"Sometimes it feels so far away, like it happened to someone else. Or it never happened to all. Like my scars just start hurting and I don't know where it came from. But then I close my eyes and I hear his voice and I just..."

No more words. Sal shut her eyes, clenched her jaw tight, pulled her hands into fists, her entire body trembling with the effort to hold on to the last part of herself that hadn't come out in tears.

And Tretta stared at her, silent.

It wasn't supposed to be like this.

Red Cloud was not supposed to cry. Red Cloud was supposed to laugh, to gloat, to look upon the ruin she had wrought and throw back her head in a shrieking cackle. Red Cloud was supposed to beg, to make excuses, to throw herself upon the Revolution's mercy. Red Cloud was supposed to be a monster, Red Cloud was supposed to be a demon, Red Cloud was supposed to be slain and everyone would rejoice at her death.

But perhaps...

Perhaps Red Cloud had died down in that chamber.

And all Tretta was left with was this woman. Not Red Cloud. Not even Sal the Cacophony. Neither a monster nor a demon. Just a quiet collection of agonies behind a thin bravado. Just this woman. Just her scars.

Just Sal.

There were no words she could offer—even if she *wanted* to comfort her, she had still slain too many, destroyed too much. Tretta could give her no atonement, no assurances, no mercy. Tretta couldn't even tell her it would be all right.

It wasn't in her to lie.

Sal didn't deserve anything, she knew. She was still a killer, still an outlaw, still a Vagrant. And Tretta had nothing she could give her. Nothing but a soft and gentle silence as she waited for Sal to finish crying.

And so she sat there. With no words.

The sole mercy she could give.

Eventually, Sal wiped her eyes with the back of her hand. She drew in a cold breath and looked back across the table at her captor. That cold serenity had returned, but there was something else, buried deep beneath the blues of her eyes. Something soft and sad and bleeding.

Perhaps it had always been there and Tretta had simply never noticed.

"Nothing has changed." The Governor-Militant spoke quietly, clearly. "You will tell me what happened to Cavric. Then you will have a glass of wine. Then I will shoot you in the head. And you will die."

Sal said nothing. She didn't even blink.

"No ceremony. No speech. One drink. One bullet. It will be clean. You won't suffer."

Sal nodded slowly.

"Okay."

And Tretta nodded back.

"Okay."

Tretta could—Tretta *should* kill her now, she knew. For the glory of the Great General. For the safety of the Revolution. For the men and women and civilians and every brave member who had died at the hands of the Imperium's greatest monster. She should simply take her hand cannon and fire a single shot.

Cavric would understand. Cavric would want it this way. Cavric would tell her not to think of him.

If he was a true soldier of the Revolution, he wouldn't mind disappearing. So long as it meant the death of Red Cloud.

But she didn't.

The gun lay where it lay. It would still be there when she found out where Cavric was. It would still fire if Sal drew a few more breaths for a few more words.

Because the Vagrant's words embedded themselves in her skull, a black shard lodged quivering in her brain.

She hadn't been given medals for lives she had taken, but for lives she had protected. Her duty was not to kill Red Cloud. Her duty was to save Cavric Proud. If she failed in that duty, if she let him become just a name in a casualty ledger, and the men and women she had sworn to protect looked her in the face...

Would they still recognize her?

"So, where was I?" Sal asked, sniffing.

And so Tretta sat. With her prisoner across from her. With her gun beside her. And Tretta listened.

"Ah, I remember now," Sal said. "Things were about to get interesting."

FIFTY-TWO

SEWERS OF LASTLIGHT

I must have killed a hundred mages in my life.

I've stared down rampaging Siegemages, the earth shaking under my feet as they charged. I've gunned down howling Skymages shrieking through a storm of their own creation. I've picked through the hallucinations of Nightmages woven from my own dreams and fears.

So you can see why it seemed a little underwhelming to find one of the most talented Doormages in the Scar just by sneaking up on him.

"Come on, come on, *come on*."

I followed the echoing sound of whimpering in the dark, a shrill voice unable to hold back trembling thoughts.

"*Jindu?*" he asked the darkness. "Is that you? Are you there?"

No one answered him but the sound of rats squeaking and the lonely dark. I would have liked to think of what that'd do to him, to whisper into the gloom and realize no one was listening, like I had. But I couldn't feel any pleasure at that.

I couldn't feel anything, at that moment.

"Shit, shit, shit," Riccu whispered from around the corner. "Come on, come on, come. Please, please, please."

I couldn't feel the tears that had dried on my face. I couldn't feel the blood that ran cold through my veins. I couldn't feel an ounce of hatred for Jindu, his touch, his smile.

All I could feel was the sound of that voice in my ears.

And the need to make it go quiet forever.

I stopped at the edge of the corner as a violet light blossomed. I peered around, saw the portal yawning to life. A great circle of purple light bloomed into being, illuminated the dank tunnel and the cowering cretin of a man before it.

"Yes! Thank you, thank you, thank you!"

My memories of Riccu the Knock were of a man alive with nerves, a man who hopped from one foot to the other, who looked around warily for the knife he always feared was waiting for him.

But the man who stood before the portal was still. He couldn't hop on a left leg that had gone numb. He couldn't wring hands with a right arm that hung limp. He couldn't look around with a neck that had gone stiff with paralysis.

I had worried I'd lost him during my encounter with Jindu. Lucky for me, Riccu was both a cruel man and a cowardly man—too eager to hurt to think clearly, too afraid to die to think quickly. He had used too much of his magic, paid too much of a price. He was slow, hobbled.

And my gun was so heavy in my hand.

I could have killed him so easily. I wouldn't even have to run. I could have just walked up, put the gun to his head, and painted the walls with him. And I admit, the thought appealed.

But then, that big portal he had just opened would close. And whoever was on the other side would go without a bullet in their brains.

And that thought did not appeal.

I watched as he slipped through the portal, hurrying as fast as his limp gait would allow. He vanished into the bright light and disappeared. I came out from behind the corner, rushing toward the portal before it closed.

But, as I did, something caught my eye, barely illuminated by the portal's light. At the edge of the circle, I could see alien letters etched into the stone and painted with red ink. Anchor sigils, commissioned by a wright to keep a portal open longer than intended.

And they looked exceedingly familiar to the sigils I had found on the letter I had plucked from Daiga's corpse. It was the same wright. Which meant...

This portal led to Vraki.

And so I had to step through it.

So I drew the Cacophony, felt him seethe reassuringly in my hand. I held the image of their faces in my head, the people who had to die. I closed my eyes. I held my breath.

I stepped through.

＋－＝◆＝－＋

No blades. No traps. No darkness.

Whatever I had been expecting, it hadn't been this.

I emerged in a room of stone bathed in a nightmare-pale light. Ancient bricks and rotting timber alike groaned, burdened by my sudden presence. They sighed clouds of splinters and dust, descending from the shattered ceiling in cloaks to settle upon the splintering floor under my feet. The entire structure—whatever it was—let out the sort of weary sound of homes that have seen a lot of blood or a lot of sorrows.

Unnerving as it was, it wasn't the most eerie sound I heard.

That honor belonged to the screaming.

Distant, loud enough to be heard through a hundred holes punched through a hundred walls. And yet so incredibly close and soft as to feel like an old woman right in my ear. Not a human noise. Nor even a mortal one. I couldn't tell you what it was. I didn't even want to guess.

"What the fuck are you doing here?"

That, though? That was a human noise. One very close and even more familiar.

I crept across the chamber, wincing at every creak of the floor beneath my feet, to the splintered door at the other edge. I glimpsed through, into a hallway of shattered floors and shredded tapestries, shafts of pale light punched through scars gouged in the walls. In silhouette, I could make them out: Riccu's shadow, quivering and hunched before Galta's thorn-blossomed figure.

"You were supposed to bring back the Hardrock," she growled. "So are you hiding him in your pants or were you stupid enough to come back alone?"

"T-there was trouble," Riccu whimpered. "A fight broke out in Lastlight. The Imperium and the Revolution started battling in the streets and—"

"And what?" She drummed her fingers on the hilt of a sword—*my* sword, still hanging around her waist, a match for *my* scarf, which she wore around her neck. "Where's Jindu? He was sent to help you, wasn't he?"

"That's what I'm trying to tell you!" Riccu whined. "The Cacophony was there!"

"Sal?" Galta asked, her voice plunging into the pit of her belly.

"S-she was," he said. "I w-wasn't followed, but I know she was—"

The thorny protrusions on her knuckles clicked as she tightened her hands into fists.

"Of course," Galta growled. "She's still alive. She should be dead, but Jindu had to be sentimental. It must be my fault, right? I'm the one who assumed we're all trying to get something done here whereas, apparently, everyone else assumed we were holding our cocks until the Cacophony came to kill us."

"But you don't have a—" Riccu began.

"Metaphor. *Metaphor*, you imbecile." She scratched at a thorny protrusion. "Can't assume Jindu killed her. He's too weak. Always was. He'll find his way back through the portal eventually."

I glanced over my shoulder. Its light was fainter, but the portal still swirled, active. I noticed the sigils etched around its circle, identical to the ones I had seen in the tunnel.

Portal magic was a chaotic thing, burning out if a Doormage didn't keep it open. But a skilled wright could stabilize it, leaving it open for anyone to use for situations like, say, bringing reinforcements out of Lastlight. It was a tricky technique, known to only clever mages.

Fortunately, two of the very cleverest—and soon to be shot to death—were right here in front of me.

I muffled the sound of the Cacophony's hammer as I cocked the gun, aimed his dragon's grin of a barrel. They stood like stark black targets against the light, their heads big and round and begging for a bullet. I couldn't miss at this range. Just two bullets and they'd both be dead. Two of the worst Vagrants in the Scar. Two names off my list.

And they'd say no one got away from Sal the Cacophony. Ever.

"You think so?" Riccu asked. "What if the Cacophony—"

"Worrying about her is what turned you into this." Galta plucked up Riccu's right arm, let it fall limp against his side. "You got scared and used too much magic, didn't you?"

"I wasn't scared," he protested. "I was *sensible*. The entire city was burning down around me!"

"It's weird that you say 'sensible' and I hear 'useless.' You come back without the Hardrock, without Jindu, without anything. We can't have fuck-ups at this point, Riccu. Vraki's already begun."

If my heart had frozen in my chest before, it all but shattered with those words.

She threw them out so casually, just an afterthought. Vraki had already begun. He was going to summon another Scrath. He was going to kill his hostages. The children might already be dead.

I'm too late.

My hands trembled as they held the gun. My finger froze—with fear, with rage, I couldn't tell. Suddenly, shooting didn't seem adequate. Suddenly, nothing I could do did.

"Fuck." Riccu's voice was breathless. "Then . . . the kids?"

Galta's only reply was a long, pregnant silence for a long, lonely moment. Then she looked down at her feet.

"Not yet."

And the blood returned to flowing to my veins. My breath came out so fast it almost sounded like sobbing.

"But soon." She hesitated for a moment. "Listen, you . . . you don't have to be there. When it happens."

"Yeah...thanks." Riccu stared down at his limp leg. "Do you think it's right, Galta? I mean...kids." He shook his head. "We used to be soldiers. We used to be the best in the Imperium."

"A lot of things used to be," Galta replied. "The Imperium used to be for mages." She turned away from him. "It will be again. We've come too far to back down, Riccu." She waved a thorn-encrusted hand. "Go. Rest. It won't be long now."

I could still do it.

I could even see it in my head.

One shell in Galta—Hoarfrost, to keep it quiet. Riccu spooks, runs, doesn't get far with his body being what it is. He falls as I pull my sword from Galta's hip. He wouldn't even feel it when I put the blade through his skull.

Or even easier: I put one shell through Galta's face. Riccu, curious and alarmed, looks up and gets another one through his face. Both dead. Two more names off my list.

I thought of a dozen scenarios: them begging for mercy, them strangled to death with my bare hands, them quietly apologizing, admitting they deserved it and bowing their heads and waiting for the click of the hammer.

And yet, in all of them, I could only think of one end.

They both died. Vraki knows I'm here, speeds up his plot, makes a mistake, and kills the children. Or they're hidden elsewhere and I never find them. Or they were locked behind a warded door that couldn't be opened without Galta. There were a dozen ways it could happen, but in all of them, I ended up with more corpses than I wanted.

I sighed. I lowered my weapon. I watched Galta stalk off, Riccu limp away; both of them disappear.

Whatever else they say, they'll say Sal the Cacophony did the right thing. Now and again, at least.

I couldn't kill them until I knew where the children were and how to get them out. And before I could figure out where they were, I had to figure out where I was.

I counted the shambling steps of Riccu until I couldn't hear them anymore. I stepped out of the chamber and into the halls.

The walls were sagging beneath their own weight, but the stone wasn't old, however cracked it might have been. The tapestries and crests that lined the walls were shredded, burned, melted beyond recognition. Through gouges in the wall, I could hear the sound of distant wailing, like what I heard in the Husks, except...

Terrified.

The wind had wailed with a sort of melancholy back in Vigil, the weary sigh of a world that had seen too much suffering and had too few ideas how to stop it. But here, the whispered moans that seeped through the walls carried a note of panic, a shrieking scream of some-one who stared at that same suffering and hadn't looked away in years.

I was back in the Husks, then. Even deeper than Vigil, where the battles had been fought the fiercest and the wounds left by years of magical warfare hadn't even begun to heal.

Why here? How much magic did Vraki *need* for his plot?

I followed the shrieking wind. I had come here prepared for some-thing bad.

But I wasn't prepared for just how bad it was.

I rounded the corner of the hall, came out atop a battlement. The wind struck me with a screaming gale, forcing me to shield my face and cling to the stone for purchase. My eyes squinted against the harshness of the light, the kind of offensive pale you only see in your nightmares. And through them, I could see the bowed shapes of towers sagging, the flayed flesh of banners whipping in a wind that wouldn't cease, the shadows of figures frozen in a death that had brought no peace.

And I knew where I was.

There was nothing that had ever made Fort Dogsjaw special. It had never been crucial for defense, never a hub for trade, it hadn't even been named for anything special—the commander just liked the sound of it. It lived its whole life a regular, boring Imperial fort on the edge of the Husks.

It only got important at the time of its death.

Over three hundred mages and a few thousand regulars had assembled here in one day—some to receive assignments, some to man the garrison, some to head back to Cathama on leave. They had been laughing, cursing, drinking when the news came that the new Emperor of Cathama was a nul, born with no magic.

And then there had been a moment of silence.

And then the Imperium, as we knew it, died.

I hadn't been there on the day it happened, but I heard the tales. It started as arguments—loyalists calling for continued devotion to the Imperium, dissidents wondering how any mage could follow a nul, let alone serve one. It had escalated to name-calling. Then a punch was thrown. Then someone had cast a spell.

And the rebellion began.

And by day's end, Fort Dogsjaw saw its halls and yards empty of life.

It didn't end there. The dissent spread across the Scar, and within the week, several hundred of the Imperium's best mages had abandoned their liege and become the first Vagrants. In the mass desertion that followed, the Imperium simply forgot Dogsjaw, the humble little fortress that became the biggest graveyard for mages in the world.

I saw its legacy in the ruin. In the towers that had been bent low and sundered by Siegemages fighting. In the jagged crystals of Frostmages' ice that hadn't melted after all these years. In the countless standing corpses of the courtyard, forever frozen in their last moments as blackened husks that had gazed upon power that should not have been unleashed all at once.

Anyone else might not have noticed the tiny figure standing at the center of the courtyard, the gaunt man with the unruly hair with his hands cast to the clouds, speaking to a bright halo of light in the darkened skies above.

Among the wreckage, Vraki the Gate looked like just another carcass who hadn't realized he was dead yet.

But I couldn't see anything else.

And I couldn't even look at him without remembering that dark place, that cold stone, that bright light. And though the wind screamed and the dead sighed, I couldn't hear anything but that voice whispering in my ear.

"I'm sorry."

Part of me wasn't ready for this. That part of me always thought of revenge as a fantasy, something I'd nurture in my darker thoughts. That part of me looked upon the person who took my flight and wanted to curl into a ball and cry.

But I wasn't listening to that part of me. Because another part of me was talking—it spoke through a mouthful of blood and bent iron, spat page-long curses in a language that burned scholars' ears off just to hear. That part of me spoke from a dark and empty place inside me, where its words echoed until they filled every last part of me. And they told me.

"End him."

A groaning sound cut through the shrieking of the wind, the sound of air unraveling before a storm hits and the sigh of dead trees before they become husks. Vraki extended his arms to the sky above like a lover reaching out for a romance he could never have. And, as if it also reached out, a great halo of light yawned a little wider.

Its light was dim, a pale purple that grew deeper each time it expanded. The winds whirled around it in a shrieking harmony, pleading for it to stop. Yet the sound of creation groaning was louder still, as if the sky itself cried out in agony for what horror was soon to be torn out of it.

The summoning had begun.

And, from the looks of the things crawling around in the courtyard, it had begun ages ago. A collection of human parts attached to underfed, four-legged bodies—nith hounds. Some walked on human hands instead of paws. Some bayed through mouths that struggled to sound, like pleas for help. Some bore human faces, locked in the last moments of terror before the hounds had taken them for their own use.

They paced, they growled, they occasionally stopped and howled. But their eyes were locked onto that great light, as though they awaited what would come from it.

But nothing had, so far as I could see. No Scraths summoned. No children to be turned into vessels for it. I still had time to save them. How much, I didn't know. But I didn't have the luxury of figuring it out.

My eyes searched the courtyard as my mind searched my thoughts. Imperial forts tended to follow a common layout and I doubted Vraki would have used somewhere else to hide his sacrifices when he had a perfectly good prison right here. I squinted at a shadowy corner at the edge of the courtyard, barely making out a barred slit of a window at the base of a tower.

There.

All I had to do was reach the other side of the courtyard without being seen by one of the homicidal mages inside here, hope that the children were actually *there*, and find some way to kill said homicidal mages, get said children out, and escape through a magical portal to a dank sewer, all before a horrific monstrosity from beyond the stars was torn out of another existence and arrived in ours with a powerful urge to kill or cause an explosion that would kill everything within six miles.

It's a good thing I didn't say that aloud; otherwise it might sound absolutely psychotic.

I crossed the battlements, keeping low. Vraki didn't look up to see me—every ounce of his concentration was on that portal. But I couldn't be sure where Riccu and Galta might be—or Taltho or Zanze, for that matter. I made it across without being killed, though, so I considered that a good sign.

Down the steps to the tower, through the decrepit halls of the garrison, I found the tale of Dogsjaw's rebellion painted on its walls. The Husks had already been rife with unstable magic and a battle between three hundred mages hadn't helped anything. Here, stray sparks of a lightning blast long cast still danced across the floor. There, the shadows of soldiers who had been disintegrated were forever stained across the stone floor, their arms raised in futile defense of the spell that had taken every last inch of them. Shattered shields and broken crossbows drifted lazily through the air, carried by unseen hands long severed.

I plucked one such floating weapon—the only sword I could find that looked like it might actually cut someone without breaking—out of the air as it drifted past me. The sword's hilt pulsed with a life not its own, an agonized life of a thing that shouldn't be.

I had no idea how well the sword would hold up after so many years and all the magic it had seen, but it was better than nothing.

The suffering suffused everything here: the stone, the steel, the very air. Occasionally, I could hear voices, final words torn from throats and forever preserved in the echoes of the dead. Some were angry, hurling curses and accusations at rebels or loyalists who hadn't survived. More were sorrowful, weeping in horror at the violence or begging for help that would never come. And a few were...

"No."

I froze. I knew that voice. And it was no ghost.

I reached for the Cacophony, eyes scanning the hallway, trying to remember where everything was before Taltho's hallucination swept over me and took me somewhere else. But nothing happened—no shadows stirring, no song of the Lady. Just the sound of the wind.

"Can't."

And his voice.

I crept through the hall, toward a room hidden at the corner of it. A storage room, strangely untouched but for a skin of dust, its crates of sundries and supplies forming an odd sort of mundane serenity among the suffering and chaos. I only barely noticed Taltho's bandaged form crouched at the center of it, his back to me, his clawed hands clutching his head.

"Stop."

His voice was so far gone that it was hard to discern emotion, yet whatever fear that lurked inside him was enough to give him an edge of panic as he spoke.

"*Unfair.*" He shook his head, as if to shake stray thoughts out of his ears. "*Not me.*" He hissed angrily at a conversation partner I couldn't see. "*Go away.*"

So...this was new.

Maybe living a lifetime on only three hours of sleep had finally caught up with him. Maybe the endless waking nightmare of existence had finally delivered him to a new plane between life and death, where ghosts walked as people and people were as shades drifting in and out of the night.

Or maybe he was just crazy. I don't know. I wasn't going to fucking ask him.

Whatever kept him too distracted to read my thoughts or notice me creeping past his little meditation chamber, I wasn't going to protest. I found my way through the halls, searching through the scenes of ruin and massacre left behind before I finally found it: the only door in the whole fortress that hadn't been blown to pieces.

Thick oak, solid and freshly installed—someone didn't want whatever was behind it getting out. A heavy lock hung off it—no sign of sigils on it. Lucky me—a wright's work took time and energy to get around. But a regular lock, I had solutions for.

Well, only one, really. Kicking it really hard. But it worked.

The door swung open to a staircase leading into a dark room. I drew my gun, crept down into the gloom. The light of an alchemical globe glowed dimly from the ceiling. I could barely see anything.

I didn't even notice them until one of the kids cried out.

I whirled, saw them quivering in the corner. Beneath the grit and exhaustion painting their faces, fear shone plainly through the twelve children huddling in the corner, clinging together. They let out whimpers, moans, sobs for mothers and fathers who would never answer them.

These kids had been through hell.

And I guessed a strange woman kicking down the door with a gun and a sword probably didn't help that at all.

"Okay," I said, holding up a hand. "I know this looks bad, but—"

I didn't get a chance to finish. What with someone breaking a stick over my back and all.

I snarled and whirled around, gun raised, expecting to find Galta or Riccu lurking in the darkness. What I saw, however, was a girl not more than fourteen, anger on her face and a broken stick in her hands. She immediately rushed around me, imposed herself between me and the other children, and raised to take another swing.

"Listen, I—" I began to say.

"Stay *back*!" she screamed, swinging it at me. "Don't you hurt them or I swear to fuck, I'll take your head off!"

"Okay, first of all, *language*." I snatched the stick out of her hand, tossed it away. "Second, I'm not here to hurt *anyone*." I held up a hand as she pulled herself up defensively. "I'm here to rescue you."

The anger and fear began to melt off her face. I was expecting to see gratitude and relief underneath. What I got, however, was confusion.

"Seriously?" she asked.

"What do you mean 'seriously'?"

"Are you with the Revolution?"

"No."

"The Imperium?"

"No. Is it that hard to believe I came here on my own to save you?"

"You just don't look like any hero I've ever heard of," she said.

"Yeah?" I growled. "You look too young to be asking to be punched in the mouth, but I guess we're all surprised today."

I wouldn't have it said that Sal the Cacophony did wrong by kids. But I wouldn't have it said she took any shit from them, either.

"What's your name?" I asked the girl. "You look like the oldest."

"And you look like an asshole," she said. "And I don't give my name to assholes who don't give me theirs first."

I decided I liked this girl.

"I'm Sal," I said, lowering my gun. "Sal the Cacophony."

She furrowed her brow. "A Vagrant?"

"Problem?"

"Since no one else is coming, I guess not. I'm Erel." She gestured to the rest of the children. "Their names are their own."

I nodded. "Tell me what happened."

Erel regarded me suspiciously, her hands clenched into fists. Those fists, that tension, was what had kept them all alive, I knew. She wouldn't release them easily.

"They came to our township long ago," she said. "They rented out a few rooms, never bothered anyone. We didn't know what was happening until..."

I caught a glimpse of her lip quivering, a wet, shuddering breath. But as soon as the kids behind her began to moan, she drew herself up again, becoming a wall once more. She reached back, laid a hand on someone's wrist, and squeezed it gently.

"Two of them grabbed us, pushed us through a glowing circle or something and then we were here. We've been here ever since. We don't know what happened back in Stark's Mutter."

The cut of her words told me that was a lie. She might not know the specifics, but she knew damn well her town wasn't there anymore. Not as she knew it. And the hardness of her stare told me that now wasn't the time to tell the truth. The thought of getting home was all that was going to keep these kids going.

Her name was Erel. She couldn't have been more than fourteen. And she had to carry everyone on her back already.

"Have they hurt you?" I glanced over at the children. "Anyone injured?"

"No." She shook her head. "I overheard them talking. They said they need all of us intact"—she swallowed hard—"in case one of us isn't a suitable host."

"What does that mean?" one of the kids whimpered.

"I don't want to die," another whined.

"No one's dying," I said. "I'm going to get you out of here."

Erel looked like she didn't believe me. But when I flipped the blade in my hand and offered her the hilt, her expression changed. Steel, she could believe in.

"You know how to use one of these?" I asked.

She nodded, taking the blade and giving it a heft. "My mother taught me."

"You keep an eye on that window." I pointed to the thin slit of a window at the top of the room, peering out into the courtyard. "Up these stairs, down the hall, toward the north battlements and into the northernmost tower, you'll find a portal." I shot her a look. "You know what a battlement is?"

She blinked at me. "I'm fourteen. I've read books, asshole."

I *really* liked this girl.

"If I don't die, I'll come back for you," I said. "If I do, or if it looks like I will, you start running. Stab anyone you see that isn't me. Get through the portal. It'll take you home."

We exchanged a brief nod, curt and professional. She was too young to know how to nod like that. Too young to hold a sword so easily, to stand in front of kids like that, to carry the fears and pains of everyone like that. And even if I got her out of here, she was going to carry that weight for the rest of her life.

But she didn't need to hear that now and I didn't have time to tell her. I placed a hand on the Cacophony's grip, turned away, and stalked back up the stairs. I had gotten halfway up when she called out.

"Sal."

I looked back at her.

"If he..." She paused, swallowed. "If you die and he comes after us..."

A silence hung between us. So vast that all her darkest fears filled it.

"Go for his eyes," I said. "If you lose the sword, use your fingers. Claw them out. If he grabs you, grab his fingers and twist them until you hear them snap."

Erel nodded at me. I nodded back. And I left to go kill a man who had to die.

FIFTY-THREE

FORT DOGSJAW

I'd run it through a thousand times in my head.

Sometimes, some parts of it were different. Sometimes, there was a great battle between us. Sometimes, it happened when I took him by surprise. But it always ended the same.

He would be on his knees, in the dirt before me. He would look up at me with those eyes, so bright with the Lady's light and so full of ambition and cruelty. He would say his last words—maybe he'd beg, maybe he wouldn't. Then I would put the Cacophony against him. Then I would pull the trigger.

Then I would watch the light in his eyes disappear. If there was anything left of him.

I even had the shell picked out. Hellfire. It would be slow, painful, poetic. Then I'd scatter his Dust to the wind and there would be nothing left of him. All his plans and ambitions would disappear on a strong breeze, and as years went by, there would be nothing left of the man who tried to bring down the Imperium but rumors and stories that people barely remembered.

And they would say that this was what happened when you made an enemy of Sal the Cacophony. They would say she left nothing of you. They would say she looked you in the eyes when she killed you.

The Cacophony seethed in my grip as I stared at him, the hollow man standing in the center of a circle of corpses beneath a halo of light.

From here, I could see Vraki's face illuminated. His hair was a disheveled mess of red and gray, hanging around eyes that had sunken into pits. His cheeks were gaunt and his lips moved in muted words I couldn't understand even if I heard them. Five nith hounds stood at attention around him, their faces locked upon the great light in the sky, the horrified expressions of the humans they'd stolen their visages from painted in the light.

He'd been at it for days, I realized, this summoning. He was leaving nothing to chance this time, perfecting the spell, holding his concentration absolute. Stark's Mutter had been an accident—the host was too unruly, the ritual had gone wrong, there wasn't enough magic in the air. I didn't know what had gone wrong.

But I knew why he took the children.

His Scrath might reject one of them, but it would adapt a little easier to each new vessel, each new host. And the ones that didn't make it...

I couldn't let myself think of that. Of anything except this moment.

Vraki the Gate, last of the Imperial Prodigies, had poured his entire life into this moment.

And now Sal the Cacophony, the girl who once flew like a bird, was about to ruin it all.

I hoped he appreciated that before I blew his head off.

I started to walk out. My legs felt cold with each step I took, all the blood rushing to my chest. I only held on to the Cacophony because he wouldn't let me drop him. We had both been waiting for this, this moment. We had seen this before, in those dark times he spoke to me.

This gun in my hand, burning.

This chill in my breath, anticipating.

The scream in the wind going silent, as though the entire world paused between breaths.

Long enough for one of them to hear me.

The nith hound's human ears twitched. It looked toward me, whirled about, and backed defensively toward Vraki. The others followed suit, their growls a burbling mishmash of human whimpering and bestial snarling.

When Vraki finally noticed their distress and looked at me, his eyes were wide with shock, his mouth hanging open.

"Salazanca," he whispered. "You're . . . you're . . ."

"Yup," I replied.

The Cacophony burned in my hand as I raised him. And somehow, through the brass of his barrel, I knew he was smiling when I pulled the trigger.

The shell flew. Vraki let out a cry. Quicker than I could blink, one of the nith hounds leapt up and took the impact full in its chest. Hellfire erupted in a spray of smoke and flame, black gore boiled away in wisps of foul-smelling smoke as the remains of the beast fell and lay smoking on the earth.

In the clouds above, the halo of light fluctuated, trembled like a timid child. From somewhere deep in wherever the hell it led, something groaned.

"No! *No!*" Vraki thrust his hands back out, his eyes erupting with a violet glow as he looked back toward the light with an imploring expression. "I'm sorry! I know that one was your favorite. Please don't be afraid." He stole a wild-eyed glance toward me. "Stop, Salazanca! You don't know what you're doing."

I knew exactly what I was doing. I was aiming my gun. I was drawing back the hammer. And I wasn't wasting a single word more on him.

"GALTA!"

His shriek was answered with a note of the Lady's song. I pulled the trigger. In the instant before Hellfire exploded into sheets of flame, I could see her, appearing out of the dust like a wraith. Her arms were crossed, her eyes were narrowed, and her face was twisted into a thorny snarl.

When the flames dissipated, she was still standing. Her clothes were singed and wisps of smoke trailed from the tips of her thorns, but considering I had been hoping for something a little more piles-of-ashes-esque, I was irritated.

She idly brushed ash from the luckscarf—*my* luckscarf—that had so generously saved her life. The Lady's Song filled the air as her Mendmage powers came to her and the few burn wounds that she bore began to heal, red flesh replaced by new, pale skin. The thorns bursting from her forehead clicked together as she knitted her brows in a scowl.

"Why the fuck am I not surprised," Galta the Thorn growled.

"I'd be insulted if you were," I replied, leveling the gun at her.

The nith hounds let out a mishmash of gibbering and screams, starting to edge toward me. At a gesture from Vraki, they fell back, huddling around him defensively.

"She can't stop us now, Galta," Vraki said, his voice shrill with panic. "Not while I'm so close." His eyes were locked on the portal, unblinking. "I can hear her so clearly, Galta. It's so beautiful."

Uncertainty flashed across her face. Vraki had always had the courtesy to at least mask his insanity with ambition, but his voice now was weak, the rasping breath of a madman. And Galta knew who she was working for.

I'd have told her to get out of the way, to let me finish this clean.

But she knew she was on my list.

And I wouldn't have it said that Sal the Cacophony didn't keep her word.

I drew the hammer back. She smiled. And in the second before I could pull the trigger, I heard the song. And she disappeared.

I searched the dust for her but a moment before I heard something land on the ground behind me. I didn't even have time to turn around before I felt something rake across my back, tearing open a great gash in me. I staggered away, whirled about with my gun up, and saw Galta there, smiling behind her fingers, my blood wet and glistening on the sword she carried.

My sword.

"Oh, don't look at me like that." She flicked my life off my blade, even as she drew her own black sword in her free hand. "An opera lover like you has to appreciate the poetry of being killed by your own blade."

Now was usually the time for banter, where we'd exchange a few barbs to prove which one of us was going to be the cleverest carcass rotting in the dirt. But I was out of words and I was out of patience and I was out of anything except this cold blood running through my veins and this burning brass in my hand and this little voice in my head that whispered:

They deserve it.

I drew the hammer back. She disappeared, simply vanishing into the dust and out of sight. The Lady's song filled my ears and I heard her land behind me. I twisted out of the way in time, her blade only grazing my side, drawing a red rivulet in my skin. She pouted, or at least she tried to.

"Figured it out, huh?"

She leapt backward, vanished. She reappeared at my side, lashed out. I darted away, watched her disappear and heard her reappear behind me. A blade caught my shoulder, drew a deep gouge, pulled a scream out of my throat. I tumbled forward, out of her grasp, whirled around, and saw nothing but dust.

Riccu was helping her. Hidden somewhere, he was teleporting her around, pulling her in and out of sight. Had to find him, had to stop her, had to kill Vraki, had to save the kids, had to, to...

Blood weeping out of my skin, clothes going red. Dust in my mouth, seeping into my lungs. Breathing too hard, not thinking. She had my luckscarf, my sword, more numbers, more magic, more—

Stop.

I forced my breath to slow, my blood to cool.

Listen.

And my ears to open.

The Lady's song, growing fainter. The screaming of the wind. A sudden rush of air and the clicking of thorns.

Above me.

I leapt out of the way as Galta came crashing down from above. When she landed, she found only dust beneath the blade. And when she looked up, she found only the butt of my gun coming down.

The Cacophony found her cheek in the crunch of bone and the spray of blood. Thorns snapped off where its grip struck, sending her body reeling to the earth to lie amid the shattered barbs. She roared, swung the sword up, angling for my belly. I stepped into the blow, catching her arm and pulling it against me. Her thorns sank into my skin, sent blood weeping out. It hurt.

But hopefully, not as much as what I was going to do.

I brought the Cacophony down, his burning brass like a gauntlet, and smashed him against her elbow. There was a loud, sickening crack as the bones snapped. The sword fell to the dirt, along with her, as she collapsed to her knees. I drove my boot into her side, sending her rolling across the earth.

I plucked the sword up, held it out as she found her way to a knee. She rolled her tongue around in her mouth, spat out a pair of teeth onto the red-stained earth. Slowly, she staggered to her feet, her right arm hanging shattered and useless at her side, and turned toward me with eyes glowing violet.

The Lady's Song rang out. The blood dripping from her mouth ebbed off. She winced at the sounds of bones realigning beneath her skin and raised her hand, thorned fingers twitching.

"I can't die," she growled. "Not here. Not while we're so close."

"I'll take that bet," I replied, raising the Cacophony at her.

"Vraki is right, Sal. This is the only way to save the Imperium. You never understood that." She raised her black sword in her newly repaired hand. "And you never will."

I clicked the hammer back.

"I can live with that."

Heavy limbs rushing awkwardly across the earth. The baying of a voice in perpetual agony. I heard the beast's charge a moment before

I heard it leave the earth. I whirled, gun aloft, just in time to see the nith hound's horrified man-face plummeting toward me.

It crashed upon me, driving me into the earth and pinning the gun against my chest. Through the frenzy of movement as its jaws gnashed at me, barely held back by my sword, I saw the horror locked in the face of the man whose face the monster wore. Fine-boned, clear blue eyes—an Imperial.

Hopefully he wouldn't mind.

I angled the Cacophony toward the beast's belly, pulled the trigger. Hoarfrost shot out, a jagged icicle punching through the creature's emaciated torso. It stiffened, a sheen of frost coating its rubbery black hide before it collapsed onto its side, human face still frozen in gaping terror.

I scrambled to my feet and whirled to see Galta already vanishing, carried off by Riccu's magic. Before I could even begin to guess where she'd gone, though, the sound of baying filled my ears once more.

And I started running.

The remaining three nith hounds closed in on me, jaws gnashing and ungainly limbs pawing and voices filled with human suffering. One, I could take. Three—along with who knew where the fuck Galta was—meant I couldn't stop.

I rushed through the courtyard, trying to ignore the wailing of their voices. Flashes of light and song assailed me from the corners of my eyes. When I darted left, Galta appeared out of nothingness to lash at me with her blade. When I pivoted right, the hounds leapt, jaws gnashing.

I almost didn't notice until I saw the wall looming before me.

I was being herded.

They were pushing me into a corner, where I wouldn't have room to escape, where they could finish me off. But through a sidelong glance, I could just barely see what they were trying to push me away from.

The stables, long abandoned, stood at the other edge of the courtyard. Its interior was shrouded in shadow. And through the darkness, I could just barely see the dim violet glow of two eyes staring at me.

Hello, Riccu.

I drew my gun up, aimed. I shut out their baying. I shut out the thunder of my heart and the panic in my breath. I shut out everything but the sound of the hammer clicking and the delighted sound of the Cacophony as I pulled the trigger.

And my very last Hellfire went shrieking out.

It disappeared into the stable, went dark for a single, heat-choked breath.

And then it exploded. The corral erupted into flame. Great gouts of fire burst out of the thatched roof. In an inferno bright enough to make Galta's little runes seem like sputtering candles, the stables went up. And if you squinted, you could just barely make out the man with the limp hauling his paralyzed body out with the strength of one arm, screaming through numb vocal cords and trying desperately to put the flames out with limbs that wouldn't work.

Galta reappeared above me, falling out of the sky in a flailing, shrieking heap. His magic had ended too soon. She hadn't expected to reappear there. She tumbled onto the dirt, rolling onto her back. The nith hounds turned, stared at her, instincts suddenly confused at her appearance.

And I was ready.

I turned, ran toward them, jammed my sword through one of their spines and left it lodged there. Its squeal of pain drew the attention of the other, who stared at me with terrified human eyes as I brought the Cacophony down upon its skull, sending it crashing to the ground with the sound like a bag of vegetables hitting the earth.

Galta had just gotten to her feet in time to see me tackle her back to the ground.

I ran, leapt atop her. I ignored the pain of her thorns punching into my leg as I straddled her. I ignored the curse she spat as she looked up at me. I ignored everything but the amused burning of the Cacophony in my grip as I brought him down.

In a spray of red. In a splinter of bone. In a steaming, seething snarl.

Over and over. I smashed the butt of the gun against her face, splintering thorns, breaking bones, painting bruises and blood across her skin. She struggled, flailing beneath me, thorns punching through my clothes, my skin, legs bleeding as she tried to claw me off her.

I didn't care. I couldn't feel pain. And I couldn't stop. The Lady's song was rising, Galta's wounds were closing almost as fast as I put them on her. The only way to stop her would be to beat her until she couldn't think anymore.

I couldn't feel her clawing at me. I couldn't feel the shock run down my arm or the blood splash against my face. I couldn't feel anything but the mechanical motion of my arm bringing the Cacophony up and down until she stopped struggling beneath me.

And Galta the Thorn lay still beneath me.

The feeling returned to me slowly—the blood weeping out of me from a dozen cuts, the exhausted agony of my limp arm, the weight of the gun in my hand—as I rose to my feet. With my free hand and one foot, I pulled the luckscarf—*my* luckscarf—off of her and put it on.

It was stained and bloody, but that would come out. It was torn from her thorns poking through it, but I could stitch it. All I needed from it now was the familiar crinkle of paper as I reached into the hidden pocket and pulled out a square of parchment and the little piece of charcoal.

I opened the list. I looked down it. I found her name and I put the charcoal against it.

~~Galta the Thorn.~~

I stalked through the dust, pulled Jeff out of the nith hound's corpse, and shouldered him. I sheathed the Cacophony and took a moment to survey the carnage.

I heard a groaning from across the courtyard, wandered over

toward the inferno that had been the stables. I found Riccu, his skin red and blackened, his clothes in charred tatters, clambering to one knee. It was all he could manage, the rest of his body completely paralyzed.

Lucky him. He wouldn't even feel this.

"Sal," he gasped through numb lips as he looked up at me. "Please. The others... I never meant... I didn't want..."

"Just answer me one thing, Riccu," I said. "If you had a chance to do it all again, would you?"

A coward. A cruel man. A Doormage. Riccu had never been a good liar.

And when he looked at me, his mouth was set into silence. And he didn't blink.

"Yeah." I jammed the blade through his back. "Same."

~~Riccu the Knock.~~

I stared at the name, a collection of faded ink smudges, and looked to the body, a still and unmoving carcass on the cold earth. In my head, it was more dramatic than this. He was still a pair of glimmering eyes in the shadows, a frightened whimper hidden in that dark place I went to sometimes. In my head, he was a monster, like they all were.

I couldn't tell you what I had expected to feel when I looked down at that sack of meat.

But I didn't feel it.

Not yet.

And, as if in response to that lack of feeling, something started burning at my hip. I could feel the Cacophony grinning through his sheath. And when I pulled him out, he burned in my hand, as if to say...

We aren't done.

I looked to that figure at the center of the courtyard, gaunt and weary features painted sickly by the light, his arms stretched to the sky and his lips twitching. I looked to that halo of light overhead, how big it had yawned open, how deep its groan was when it shuddered.

No. We weren't done.

I heard the rasp of my own breath, the drag of my feet across dirt as I limped across the courtyard. I flipped the chamber of the Cacophony open, reached into my satchel. Five shells greeted me— all that remained. One Sunflare. Three Discordance. One Hoarfrost.

Hoarfrost.

Not as poetic as Hellfire, was it? But killers can't be choosers.

I plucked three out, chambered them, flipped it shut.

I could just barely make out Vraki's face. His eyes opened wide, the light inside them beaming brightly. His face split open with his smile. And overhead, as if to return it, the halo of light began to shudder, twist, and writhe, a lover driven mad by the whispers of her suitor.

It glowed brighter, lighting up the sky like a violet sun. Its groan became a shrill, echoing song, overwhelming the sound of the wind screaming and my breath rasping. Behind the light, I could see a shadow blooming, something immense reaching down from somewhere far away, just as Vraki reached up to touch it.

I could just barely make out his lips twitch in a single word.

"Yes."

And then I went and ruined it.

Discordance shrieked out. There was a moment of silence. And then, the eruption.

He glanced up in time to see me pull the trigger, threw a hand up. The air shimmered, glowed as he tried to erect a shield in the half-second he had to react. Enough to save him a messy death, not enough to save him from the second shot.

Discordance struck him, exploded in a wail that rendered even the great song of the portal mute. Vraki shrieked, flying through the air to skid across the dirt.

He staggered to his knees. And when he looked up, a dying light painted despair across his face.

The halo of light overhead twitched and shuddered. Like a mirror, cracks began to appear across its surface, etched with great black scars. Its song became a bleating, warbling sound, as though it—whatever made it—was confused. A moment later, the song became a scream, something desperate and terrified. The light deepened from a bright violet to an angry crimson.

"No," he gasped. "*No, no!*" He found his feet, started stumbling toward it, hand outstretched like he could save it if he just reached far enough. "Wait! I'm coming! I can fix this! I can help you—"

I was almost insulted that he didn't notice me.

At least until I smashed the Cacophony against his nose.

He fell back to the ground with a cry. And when he looked up again, my gun was in his face.

"Sal," he whispered, staring past me. "What have you done?"

I had imagined what I'd feel when I finally killed him. Sometimes I thought I'd laugh and dance over his corpse. Sometimes I thought I'd spare just a morbid smile once the light left his eyes. And sometimes, I thought I'd just sit there, staring at him through numb eyes.

I don't know why I felt like crying at that moment.

"You can't be serious," I said. "All this time, all these years later, that's what you say to me?"

"I can still save this." He staggered to his feet, started limping toward the halo. "He's in pain, but I can still save him. It... I took every precaution to..."

I caught him by the shoulder, shoved him back to the earth. He didn't even put up a fight. He was so light in my hands, falling down to his rear like he was just a little kid. I put the gun in his face again and he didn't even notice. His eyes were on that portal, his face twisting at its shriek.

"Can't you hear him?" he whispered. "He was speaking to me. The last one was too rebellious, too angry. But this one, this one was going to work." His voice trembled, on the edge of tears himself. "We were going to save the Imperium."

Where was the monster I was supposed to kill?

Where were his gloating cackles? Where were his spewed curses?

Where was the begging, the regret, the defiance, the anything? I didn't recognize this disheveled creature, this whimpering voice, this desperate stare from the man in the dark place.

"She sent him herself," he said. "I spoke to her. It was going to be perfect. No Barter this time." He shook his head. "This one... this one was going to be a gift, her favorite son. He has to be welcomed..." He got to his feet again. "*I have to help him.*"

I stood in front of him. I put the gun up. I couldn't figure out why my hand was shaking, why my voice trembled in my throat.

"You stop right there," I growled. "And you look me in the eye before I kill you."

And for a moment, he did. He looked away from the portal. He looked directly into my eyes. And I looked into his.

And I saw that they were empty.

The final insult. The last scar he would ever give me. I was here, after all this time chasing him, ready to kill Vrakilaith, Vraki the Gate, the Imperium's last Prodigy, architect of the Crown Conspiracy and the man who took the sky from me...

And he was too insane to know it.

I hit him.

I don't even know how. I didn't even feel my arm do it. I just felt the shock run through my hand when I smashed the Cacophony against his face.

He recoiled, touched his face, and drew back blood. He looked at me with confusion on his features, unsure what had just happened.

And I hit him again.

And this time, I felt something. Not my arm, not my muscles moving, not even the gun in my hand. I felt something hot behind my eyes. I felt something hard between my teeth. I felt something reaching down into a cold place inside me and twisting.

And I just hit him again.

"I have to complete the spell." He staggered backward, then tried to push past me. "I have to finish it. I—"

I hit him. Bone crunched. He fell to his knee, tried to get back up.

"It took so much time, so much effort. She told me exactly what I needed to do and—"

I hit him. Blood blossomed. He groaned out of a mouthful of broken teeth.

"Please. *Please.* This is the only way. I have to do this for her. She *trusted* me to—"

And I just kept hitting him.

Until my arm went numb. Until the blood left my body. Until there was nothing left in me but to raise the gun and put the barrel of it against the ruin of a face that looked back up at me. And even then, through those empty eyes, Vraki just whispered.

"*No.*"

I followed his gaze to the portal overhead. Black veins mapped it, like cracks across a glass pane. Its light was bloodred and grotesque. Its song was weak and dying until it finally ebbed to a soft, pitiable moan.

"Sal," he gasped. "You ruined it. I can't... I can't save him now." He swallowed blood, held out shaking hands. "She was going to give him to me, to hold the door open so she could... she could..."

A tear slid from his eye, cut a clean path through the blood staining his cheek.

"Her song," he sputtered, "was so beautiful."

I could tell myself, at least, that I had taken that away from him.

I turned back to him. I closed my eyes. I pulled the hammer back.

"Sal..."

I heard a voice. It wasn't his.

"Don't."

I opened my eyes. Vraki wasn't there anymore. On her knees in front of me, smiling behind those big glasses of hers, was someone else. Without ever breaking that smile, Liette looked up at me, down the barrel of the gun I had pressed against her forehead and asked in that breathless whisper of hers:

"Are you really going to shoot me this time?"

I let out a sound—a cry, a curse, I didn't know. I staggered backward, almost dropping the Cacophony. Liette looked back at me with a grin growing too wide, a face stretching too long. Her body grew broad and dark, her limbs twisted into branches, her skin hardened into bark. When I blinked again, there was a tree there. She was gone.

And so was Vraki.

"NO!"

I rushed toward the tree, searched it. The bark was rough beneath my fingers, the decayed reek of its dead branches thick in my nose. I hammered it with a fist, hurled a scream against it when that didn't work.

"No, no, no!" My voice sounded pathetic as I clawed at the tree, but I didn't care. "I was so close! I was so . . ."

My voice trailed off as I became aware of a chill seeping into my bones and the reality of my situation sank in just as swiftly. I turned around and beheld the thousand dead trees sprawling out before me.

Taltho.

How the fuck did I forget him? Did I just assume the sound of a battle going on wouldn't stir him from his freaky little reverie? Had I gotten that stupid?

Easy, I cautioned myself. Getting mad wasn't going to help now.

I looked around me. The courtyard was gone. The scars of ice and fire had vanished. In all directions, a lonely forest of shadows and black trees stretched. The wailing of the wind had disappeared, leaving only the distant call of a crow somewhere far away.

My eyes swept about in a frenzied panic, but I saw nothing. No Liette. No Vraki. Nothing but dead trees and cold mist and whatever else the fuck Taltho wanted me to see. He was in my head now, tearing my thoughts apart and planting these black trees in their stead. Meanwhile, Vraki could be getting away, could be coming toward me with a knife, could be . . .

Stop, I told myself. *Stop, stop, fucking stop. Control your breathing. Listen.*

But all I heard was the lonely sound of trees aging, of a dying crow's song. I couldn't trust my senses. Everything smelled real, felt real, tasted real in my mouth. I didn't know how to break it, short of killing him. But he could be anywhere. Nowhere. He'd lurk in the shadows until I stumbled into a fire or he could creep up behind me with a knife or...or...

Couldn't think. Couldn't think of what to do, what to trust. Couldn't trust my eyes, my ears, anything. Couldn't see anything but dead trees and couldn't hear anything but ghosts and couldn't... couldn't...

I couldn't.

But someone could.

And I could feel him burning.

Almost by instinct, my fingers wrapped around his grip. And they burned. Patches of blood, fragments of bone sizzled on the metal as I raised him to my face, as he looked at me with those eyes of brass and powder.

And he smiled.

We made a deal, he and I.

Revenge for ruin, he said to me.

And I said to him...

"Show me."

And I closed my eyes. And I held my breath. And I started walking.

He seethed in my hand, his heat dim as we walked in one direction, warming up as I turned. I could smell the mist swirling around my feet, hear the crunch of dead leaves beneath me. And between the sounds of branches breaking and mist whispering, I could hear a voice.

"Sal."

Her voice.

"What are you going to do, Sal?" Liette's voice, so serious and heavy, in my ears. "Are you going to kill me, Sal? Are you going to kill everyone, Sal? Are you going to hold me in your arms when I die, Sal?"

I wanted to open my eyes. He told me not to. His heat grew bright in my hand, his grip hurt to hold.

"I'm sorry, Sal." Jindu's voice, whispering from all edges, crawling into my ear and curling around my brain like a cat. "I'm so sorry, Sal. Please forgive me, Sal. Please don't kill me, Sal. Please, let me help you, Sal."

I wanted to go back to the dark place. He wouldn't let me. He was burning in my hand.

"You'll never find me, Sal." Vraki, sharpening his cackle to a thin shiv and jamming it into my skull. "You'll never kill me, never hurt me, and I'll never even think of you before I—"

I stopped.

The smell of my own flesh cooking was in my nose. I could feel my blood seeping between my fingers, slippery on the trigger. The gun pressed against something firm.

I opened my eyes.

And I stared into Taltho's.

One bloodshot eye stared at me from either side of the barrel pressed against his forehead. Between a mass of bandages, his mouth hung open and rasped a single word.

"Inevitable."

A click of metal. A short burst of air. And Taltho the Scourge finally found his rest. He slumped to the ground, motionless, staring up at an empty sky through a pair of bloodshot eyes and an icicle protruding perfectly from the center of his forehead.

The forest melted away around me, trees becoming ash that were lost in the wind, the scent of cold and mist giving way to smoke and earth, the voices ebbing away and disappearing beneath the sound of my own long, slow breaths.

I looked at the Cacophony in my hand, at my blood sticking in burnt patches to his metal, at the steam rising out of my hands.

And I knew, somewhere in all that brass and blood, he was looking back at me. And smiling.

I knew, then, that I had made a mistake in asking him to show me. I knew that his was the kind of smile reserved for watching people fall down stairs and children being lied to. We made a deal, he and I. And whatever he had just given me, he would take something for someday.

I took my wrist with my other hand, forced him back into his holster and pried my fingers, one by one, off his grip. Feeling crept back into them, bloodied and trembling, and they splayed apart to reveal the skin torn from my palm.

He had taken my skin. My blood. And somehow, I knew, something else.

They call it an art and dress it up with fancy words and complex theories, but magic is as simple as love. It is just a price and a person willing to pay it.

I stared across the courtyard and saw them. They would be Dust soon, but for now, they were testaments. Lessons for anyone who thought they could do what they'd done to me.

Riccu the Knock, facedown in the earth as the fires behind him chuckled and danced at his misfortune. Galta the Thorn, a garden of briars and flesh forever watered by her own blood. Taltho the Scourge, asleep with three eyes open. And Vraki the Gate...

I knew he wasn't there. Even before I turned and saw the patch of earth he had just been in, empty but for a few bloodstains on the dirt. Taltho had simply been buying him time to escape.

That wasn't so bad, I told myself.

Three people who deserved death had found it—four, rather. I forgot about Kresh. The children were safe. Stark's Mutter had been avenged. And a plot to pull a monster into this world had been foiled, even if I hadn't gotten the monster behind it. That was enough.

That's what I told myself.

And I wished I were good enough at lying to believe it.

I sighed. I turned my back to the death and the ruin. And I started back toward Erel and the others. They would be safe at least. I would take them and all their scars to someone who could handle them.

And I would leave this place to the dead and the dust and the sound of the howling wind.

"*You.*"

A voice. A wail of the wind. A single note of a fractured melody sang from the bottom of a deep hole in a dark cavern.

I had no idea what to call it. I had no idea what had said it. And when I turned around and stared up at the sky, I had no idea what was looking back at me.

The halo of light was no longer a circle, but a wound, a jagged and lightless red tear opened across the clouds. And within it, something huge and impossibly dark stirred. Something with a head and endless arms and a great, gaping eye that leaned out of the portal, hauling itself out on black claws.

And stared right at me.

"*Where is our herald?*" I heard its voice in my bones as its head swung ponderously slow, looking this way and that. "*Where are our green trees and blue skies?*" It stared at me, with eyes I couldn't see, and peeled back my skin and my sinew and pried apart my bones and looked into that dark place inside me. "*He promised us.*"

I reached for my gun, completely oblivious to the stupidity of that. What the fuck was I going to do with it? I'd never even *seen* a Scrath like this.

Behind the wound, it raised a boneless arm, long as a tree was tall. It swung it down, smashing against the red light as though it were a pane of glass. And all the stones in the earth and wind in the sky shook with the impact.

"*He promised.*"

I started backing away. It let out a howl. The earth shook beneath me, knocked me from my feet. Black cracks appeared across the jagged rent in the sky, the portal threatening to fracture.

"*He promised.*"

It smashed its limbs against the portal. It shook. I staggered to my feet.

"HE."

It smashed against the wound. It groaned, cracked, weakened.

"PROMISED."

Broke.

The Scrath emerged with a shriek that cut through the wind, the stone, my skin. It pulled itself out of the portal, a writhing column of shadow and bone, of skin and light, of colors I didn't know and words I couldn't hear. It twitched and trembled as it erupted out and onto the ground, its skin writhing as though the very air were trying to tear it apart.

I clasped my hands over my ears as it screamed, but it did no good. I could feel its pain inside me, slithering in through my mouth and nose and trying to pull itself out again. It swept itself around, searching through the courtyard with eyes of darkness and light, for something to ease the pain.

And it found Galta.

In a coiling, shrieking column, it swept toward her. It dissipated like a mist, slithered in through her nose, her mouth, her many wounds. Instantly, her body shot upright, a scream tearing itself out of her mouth as her eyes grew wide, searching about with terrified confusion.

And I found myself screaming, too.

I hadn't killed her.

Fuck me, she was still alive to feel it.

But not for much longer. The Scrath flooded her body, bloated her as it tried to fit itself into her skin. One eye shot wide open, growing to the size of a melon. Her jaw snapped, teeth becoming jagged spikes of bone as it pulled itself impossibly wide. Her left arm burst, muscle the size of a tree trunk suddenly erupting from skin too small to hold it. Her flesh rippled like water, twitching and trembling and twisting and tearing as it tried and failed to hold the creature inside it.

"It hurts it hurts it hurts it hurts IT HURTS IT HURTS it hurts," it screamed, its voice a ragged bleat. It swept that gigantic eye toward me. "YOU DID THIS YOU YOU YOU YOU YOU—"

It had more to say, of course.

But fuck, I wasn't going to stick around to listen.

I was running, back through the courtyard, toward the fort. I could hear it hauling its great walking charnel heap of a body after me, screaming and wailing and begging for a peace neither I nor any living thing on this dark earth could give it.

I burst through the doors into the halls of the fort. Erel was there, the kids in tow behind her, quivering and crying and weeping. She stared at me with eyes wide and unthinking with fear.

"Sal," she gasped, "what is—"

"No." I held up a finger, pointed it down the hall. "*Go.*"

Whatever else, she had the presence of mind to nod. She pointed the kids down the hall and screamed a word. They followed that fear, along with her, as she ran down the hall toward the tower. I pursued, digging out whatever shells I had left and jamming them into the chamber of the Cacophony.

"hurtshurthurtshurtshurtsHURTSHURTSHURTSHURTS—"

The door exploded behind me in a spray of splinters. The Scrath pulled itself into the hall, stared at me with that single eye as I ran after the children. It let out a shriek, dragging its body after us as we ran through the twisting halls, trusting in Erel's fear and memory to guide us.

"Why does...not supposed to hurt..."

We found the north tower's stairwell; the children fled up it in a flood. Those who stumbled, they helped up. Those who wanted to weep, held it back. Fear was all that kept them going as we rushed up the tower's stairs and onto the battlements. At the bottom of the stairs, the Scrath stared up at us through that colossal eye.

"He...promised...promisedpromisedpromised...PROMISED...he said...he said...he said..."

I didn't listen. It didn't chase us. Fucking fine by me.

I could hear the children's breath run ragged as we rushed across the battlements. They didn't have anything left in them by the time we made it to the other side. Whether it was fear for each other or something else that kept them going, I didn't know. A hallway stretched out before us, the doorway leading to the portal at the other end.

"A little farther!" Erel screamed from the front. "Come on, you *have* to try!"

She rushed forward, leading them as they charged for the room. From below, I could hear stone shattering, timbers breaking. My heart caught in my throat, choked me as I shouted out.

"Erel, look out—"

I didn't get to finish it before the floor exploded.

Erel fell back against the screaming heap of children as a hole was rent through the floor. The Scrath hauled it open. The bones of its shattered jaw creaked and cracked as it opened its mouth in a scream.

"WE WERE GOING TO BE LIKE YOU."

Over them, around them, between them, I pushed my way to the front of the crowd. I threw my arm out, shoved Erel backward. I put the Cacophony's grin in the thing's face and pulled the trigger and prayed to gods I didn't believe in that it would help.

Sunflare hit it in the face and exploded in a bright burst of light. I had barely enough time to shield my eyes as it hit the Scrath's oversized eye. It tumbled, screaming, through the floor. I turned around, shouted into a world I could only half see.

"Erel!" I screamed. "Can you see?"

"Yeah," she replied. "You were in front of me, but the others..."

"Help them to the portal," I said. "I'll cover you."

She started barking orders, too young to do that but too scared not to. The kids who had seen the explosion were helped around the hole in the floor by those who hadn't. One by one, they made it across and disappeared into the room.

I nearly collapsed with the relief I felt from hearing the Lady's song coming from within. The portal was still active—Galta's runes were keeping it open and Galta...

"whywhywhywhywhywhy"

...was still alive.

I looked into the hole. Three floors down, in the darkness of the fort's basement, I could see the thing stirring back to life. With an overlarge arm that stretched to obscene lengths, it hauled itself onto the first floor.

"Hurry up!" I screamed at the kids, who screamed back in reply. "Come on, faster!"

Not helpful, maybe. But not false, either. The remaining children pulled themselves across the floor and into the room. Erel stood in the doorway, looking at me as the Scrath pulled itself up again.

"Sal!" she cried. "Come on, you're the last one!"

I edged around the hole. A great clawed hand reached up, seized the lip. I pushed Erel into the chamber, toward the portal in the wall. The Scrath's twisted shape appeared in the doorway, stared at me, straining to express a sadness its face couldn't manage.

"we were going to be..."

I shoved Erel through the portal.

"...like you."

I leapt afterward.

The sensation of being ripped apart and put back together on the other side was intense. I emerged into a dark tunnel to find kids weeping, some vomiting. But I didn't have time to tell them what they were feeling. And I sure as shit didn't have time to feel it myself.

"*Get back!*" I shouted as I turned to the portal. "*Cover your ears!*"

I didn't know if they did or didn't. I didn't have time. That mass of twisted flesh masquerading as an arm reached through the portal. I aimed the Cacophony at the runes surrounding it, pulled the trigger.

A wall of sound.

A burst of stone.

I was hurled backward, dashed against the wall, and fell limp onto the floor. The light vanished, casting the world into darkness. The arm was sucked back through a portal that winked out of existence.

And even as I breathed out a breath I had been holding for ages, the sound of its scream still lingered.

In my skin.

In my bones.

In my blood, weeping gently onto the floor.

FIFTY-FOUR

LASTLIGHT

The human body is a finite thing.

It's only so much skin and so much blood that can hold so many dreams, disappointments, and most importantly, fear. Get enough fear in you—or hate or anger or whatever, it doesn't matter— and you can push out things like pain and sense and futility and just fill yourself with all the terror you need to keep you going through just about anything.

It's not the worst way to go through life, but it's not great, either. Because fear, like any other part of you, is finite. Some of us have a lot, some of us have a *hell* of a lot, but eventually, it runs out. It seeps out of you in every breath and it gives way to all the pain and the blood and the regrets stirring around inside you.

I didn't have any fear to carry me out of that dark tunnel and into the starlight. But when I came limping out of the sewers of Lastlight, I had plenty of everything else.

My wounds nagged after me, the gashes left by Galta's claws and the bruises left from being hurled around and the skinless palm wrapped beneath a bandage all spoke to me in various mutters, pleas, and outright curses, begging me to stop walking. My exhaustion agreed with them, every bone in my body complaining and demanding I sit down. And, through it all, I couldn't ignore the little nagging voice wedged between my skull and the top of my spine.

You didn't kill him.

I had other things to worry about besides that, of course. I had children I had left in that hole, bidding them to wait as I checked things out. I had lost a lot of blood. My body felt like it was going to fall apart if I took another step. Another Scrath had been released into the world and I hadn't stopped it. I had *plenty* of more pressing matters than whether or not I had killed Vraki.

I wish I could tell you I was worried about them and not him.

I shambled out of the tunnel mouth into a city gone silent. The canal water lapped around me, its murmur broken only by the bump of a corpse bobbing gently against its wall. The lanterns overhead hissed as their light flickered, desperately trying to stay lit. The exhausted sigh of smoke carried itself in weary clouds over the shattered roofs of buildings.

From below, it looked like a city.

When I reached the bridge overhead, it looked like a graveyard.

Like headstones, the ruins of buildings marched silent, shattered, and smoking down the streets. Broken glass and abandoned belongings were left abandoned on stoops like flowers laid on graves. The silence was a dirge all its own, its chorus the hissing embers of fires dying and its verse the groan of a building as a great chunk of stone collapsed and splattered across the streets.

In the distance, I could hear the sounds of fighting. So faint, I could have pretended it was a bad dream if I was just a little bit more tired or a lot more drunk. But I could hear the crack of cannons and the roar of Revolutionary chants between the shrieks of Krikai birds and the sound of thunder.

They were still fighting, then. They hadn't bled each other dry, so perhaps reinforcements had arrived. Perhaps they would never stop, this conflict a bomb with a fuse so long it wouldn't stop until there was nothing left to blow up. Perhaps this was inevitable. Perhaps this wasn't my fault.

But I don't know if there was enough liquor in the world to convince me of that.

That didn't mean I wasn't going to try, though.

I limped down the ruined avenue, pointedly avoiding looking into the alleys where motionless limbs lay and shattered storefronts over which still bodies were draped. If I looked too long, my aching body might start to envy them and my weary mind might try to make me remember that they were dead because of me.

Right now, I needed something that would shut both my body and mind up.

And, as if in answer to that, my foot brushed against something and I heard the clink of glass.

Now, like I said, I don't believe in gods. But my faith isn't unshakable. If I looked down at my feet and found a bottle of whiskey there, I was more than prepared to admit the existence of a kind, forgiving deity who wanted me to be happy and pledge a life of atonement for my many, *many* sins.

I looked down.

A bottle of wine, rather than whiskey, looked back up at me.

So there was a god; he or she was just kind of an asshole.

Good enough.

I picked it up. I uncorked the bottle and stalked to the edge of the canal and sat down. A drop of my blood slipped off the toe of my boot and fell into the canal to stain a chunk of magical ice drifting lazily downriver. I put the bottle to my lips. I took a deep drink and tasted nothing.

And I simply stared at the great fucking mess I had made.

Minutes had gone by—or hours or days, I didn't know, the bottle still wasn't empty—when I heard the sound of footsteps. From the ruins, an old woman, bent and wrapped in a dingy shawl, emerged. She shambled toward me, politely stepping over a corpse and around a mass of rubble, before creakily taking a seat beside me.

I didn't bother looking at her.

When I heard the Lady's song and the sound of her skin shifting, I handed the bottle over to her.

Alothenes took it.

"You're alive," I noted.

"I'm afraid I can't say the same for you," he replied, taking a deep swig. "You look rather like a corpse that hasn't figured out how to sit still yet." He glanced over the ruin of the city. "But then, I suppose you'd be in good company."

I didn't say anything. I just waited for him to put the bottle back into my hand. Instead, he pointed out toward a shattered spire of a building.

"There was a detachment of Krikai riders outside the city. They came swooping in there." He pointed down to a stretch of street scorched black by flame and electricity. "They arrived there, driving off the Revolutionary detachment that had been firing at our mages. They were pursued into there"—he pointed to a nearby alley—"where three civilians were caught in the crossfire and . . ."

He simply gestured over the ruined avenues, no more explanation to offer. I took the bottle back, took a deep swig, waited to be drunk enough that I couldn't see straight. Maybe it'd look better, then.

"Did you help the civilians?" I asked.

Alothenes waited a long moment before speaking. "I tried."

"How many were saved?"

"Many."

"How many weren't?"

A longer pause. "Many."

I sniffed, took a longer swig. "There are some children down in the sewers. I told them to wait until I got help. About twelve of them. Including a tough girl. She's the one in charge."

"The battle has moved on," Alothenes said. "I can see to it they get out safely." I could feel his eyes settle on me. "I take it Vraki is . . ."

"Still alive," I replied, taking another drink. "Maybe, anyway. Taltho's dead. Riccu's dead. Galta is . . ." I fell silent, choked on something I forced back down. "Galta's . . . I don't fucking know."

"Three conspirators slain. You must feel proud."

I didn't say anything.

"I wouldn't linger for much longer, Salazanca," Alothenes said after a long moment. "Two Lonely Old Men has long vacated the city, but his forces remain and he's very certain of the parties he has to blame for the destruction of his freehold." He cast me a sidelong glare. "I imagine you running down the streets screaming your own name and firing a gun into the air left little to doubt."

Like I said, a human is a finite thing. And once you're too tired for fear and too drunk for pain, all that's left are the regrets. And I found mine in a breathless whisper as I put my face in my hand.

"Fuck."

"Language."

"Shut the fuck up."

"Now that's hardly—"

"Can you just let me fucking hate myself in peace?"

I whirled on him. His face was different than when I had seen him last. His features were less distinct, his skin a little paler, his whole face a little smoother. He had paid a tremendous Barter tonight, used too much power. To save civilians? Civilians who wouldn't have needed saving if I hadn't...I hadn't...

"They're dead," I said. "They're fucking dead. Everything's gone to shit because of me. Because I couldn't..." I screwed up my face. "I couldn't *not* kill him. And now everyone's dead because of it."

Alothenes looked back out over the ruin of the city. "Maybe."

"Maybe?" There wasn't enough room in my voice to sound hopeful.

"Maybe this was always going to happen," Alothenes said, sighing. "It's not as though we were bringing scholars to Lastlight. We wanted its wealth, its trade. We sent soldiers to it with the intention of them one day killing to take it. So did the Revolution."

"Yeah, but I started it," I said. "I fired the first shot."

"You did. Or maybe I started it when I drugged you." A long, pregnant pause lingered where an apology might otherwise have been. "Or maybe Vrakilaith started it when he did what he did to you. Or the Empress, when her child was born. Or the Great General, when he instigated the Revolution." He waved a hand. "And on and on, so through the ages until the first two people on this dark earth decided to kill each other."

"I'm not in the mood for fucking philosophy," I growled.

"Philosophy brings answer. And it should be clear that I have none." He rose to his feet, dusted his clothing off. "All I have, Salazanca, is my duty."

I heard the Lady's song. I heard the sickening sound of his skin rippling. When I looked up, a man in Revolutionary garb that looked disturbingly like Cavric looked back down at me.

"Whatever you have, I hope you find it," he said. "But you will not find it here."

And he walked down the stairs and into the sewers and he vanished. And I was left alone with the silent graveyard of a city and the corpses lying on the ground and in the water and the bottle of wine that wasn't enough for what I needed it to be.

And I picked myself up. And I stalked out of the gates. And into the Scar.

And I just kept going.

FIFTY-FIVE

THE SCAR

I can't even remember his name.

He was a soldier, a newly commissioned mage out to fight his first battle against the Revolution. It hadn't gone well. Both sides wiped out, only stragglers returned for a fight over some hill somewhere. He came back to the garrison, completely unbloodied. I was going to give him hell for cowardice, but then I looked into his eyes.

And there was just nothing there.

He walked past me. He walked out of the garrison and into the night. And he just kept on walking until we found him cold and facedown in the dirt three days later.

"Desertion" was the official cause, they said. They didn't know what else to call it. Neither did I. The idea that you could go to battle, suffer not a single wound that anyone could see, and somehow still die was completely foreign to me. I saw it a few more times, enough to tell myself that it would never happen to me.

It's the wounds.

And it wasn't going to happen to me.

You've just lost too much blood.

And it wasn't happening to me at that moment.

You're dying.

I only knew I was still alive because I was still moving. Even then,

I only knew because the dunes and hills and scrub continued to pass me. I couldn't feel my feet pulling my legs out of the dirt to take step after step. I couldn't feel the breath in my lungs or the blood in my limbs. Only the world moving around me and the voice muttering in my head.

Took too many hits, it said. *Galta cut deeper than you thought. You haven't rested, haven't recovered. You've lost too much blood and let too many wounds go untreated. You're dying.*

I'd taken worse hits, of course. I'd bled more, of course. And maybe it was just that I had taken so many over so many years of not resting and always hunting that I felt like I did now. Like all the blood was rushing out of my limbs and into my chest, like my heart was beating too much.

Too fast.

Too loud.

That could be it. That could be why I felt like I was going to die.

You're dying.

Or it could have been something else.

Just like Lastlight died.

Something that went so deep, no one could see it.

And you didn't even kill Vraki.

Long, slow breaths that didn't fill my lungs. Short, stuttering steps that didn't take me any farther. My head felt like it was too full of blood to keep up, even as I felt it weeping out of me and falling on the ground around me. And still not so full that it could keep that thought out.

You chased him that far, you made so much noise and did so much damage and so many people are dead, it said. *And you couldn't even kill him.*

The ground got closer to me and I realized my legs weren't working anymore. I saw my scarf fall off onto the dry, dusty ground and realized I was lying in the earth.

What was the point?

My breath slowed down.

You didn't stop Vraki. You didn't accomplish anything.

My vision dimmed.

What the fuck changed?

And I watched myself ebb out onto the earth.

——◆——

You see it all the time in opera.

The darkest moment, when everything's lost, the hero steps up and delivers this amazing speech about how important love and life and honor are. And everyone rallies and the villain dies and then you hope someone gets to have sex after the curtain falls.

It wasn't like that.

The hero never falls down like this. The hero never lies in the dirt like this. The hero is always cheated out of a fair contest, betrayed, or does something that says it's not his fault. The hero doesn't destroy a city and leave people dead to chase a monster he couldn't even kill.

And the hero doesn't get woken by the smell of birdshit. That's just not how it goes.

I opened an eye more out of reflex than desire. I saw the great scaly legs of a creature approaching me, heard its guttural croaking. A scavenger of some sort, here to feast—I wanted to call it poetic, but I wasn't quite sure how.

Then the bird looked down at me and I recognized Congeniality's surly glare.

Eaten by my own bird. That was certainly poetic.

She must have broken free when Lastlight went up, burst out of the stables. She always was clever like that.

The hero wasn't supposed to be eaten by a bird. The hero was supposed to be supported by someone, pulled out of the darkness by someone pretty with a musical voice.

"Sal?"

Yeah, kind of like that.

"Holy shit, Sal."

Except with less swearing.

I saw boots hit the earth as someone dropped off of Congeniality's back. I couldn't feel the hands on my shoulders, turning me over, nor the ground on my back. I could barely see Cavric's face, fraught with concern, as he looked over me.

"She's bleeding out! For fuck's sake, I..."

His voice came and went.

"...get her into the Boar. My supplies are in there and I can..."

Someone else's voice. Someone else's hands on me. Someone else's tears glistening behind big glasses as she looked down into my eyes and wept over me.

"...why did you...hang on, I'm going..."

That thought was suitably poetic so that when my eyes went dark, I didn't really mind.

Metal.

Rattling.

Moving.

Something was happening. I opened my eyes to a cold metal tomb. Something was rumbling around me, under me. Was something moving? Was I? There was the roar of something that felt familiar in my ears. I opened my eyes and looked.

The Iron Boar. Just like the one I had stolen. And its pilot, too, was just like the one I had stolen. Cavric sat in the chair of its helm, occasionally glancing back at me, lips moving in a language I couldn't understand. Liette, beside him, screaming soundlessly as she fidgeted with an inkwell and quill. Congeniality, curled up in the corner, spared a single, semi-interested eye, before closing it again and drifting back into sleep.

I looked back to Cavric before he turned his attentions back to steering. But his lips were still moving, still talking.

"Did it feel like this?"

That wasn't his voice.

"When he cut you?"

My eyes drifted toward the bench on the Iron Boar's walls. I didn't recognize the man I saw there, sitting in the shadows.

But I knew him.

His stately garb and fine bones marked him as Imperial, a finely polished edge of a man regarding me with the kind of dispassion with which a wealthy man watches a poor man die. But in the shifting darkness of the vehicle, I could make out flaws, imperfections that ruined the façade of aristocratic displeasure.

His eyes betrayed a flinty gleam, not so honed and not nearly so polished. There was far too much pleasure in them, no matter how hard he tried to hide them. And his grin...

His grin was bright brass.

"It doesn't seem so dissimilar, when I think about it," he said. "It's not the wound itself that hurts, is it? Sal the Cacophony cannot be stopped by mere wounds."

My eyes flitted toward Liette. She did not look up from her ink. Cavric did not look away from the controls. None of them saw the man, nor noticed his burning voice.

"It's the knowing, I think, that hurts," he continued. "After all, blood is so dreadfully common, isn't it? It's the one thing we have in abundance and part with so easily. Loss of blood kills common people. Loss of purpose... well, that kills people like us.

"The knowledge that you failed, that for all the suffering you inflicted, for all the blood you took, you couldn't kill him." He chuckled. Cinders fell from his mouth. "Why, that knowledge must cut as deep as the knowledge that Jindu always loved a dream more than he loved you."

"The others are dead." My voice sounded distant and dead in my ears, like an echo. "The children are safe."

"*What?*" Liette's voice sounded even farther away, even as she leaned over me. "*She's talking. Slow it down. I need to...*"

Maybe she said more. I didn't know. I looked right through her, to the man with the grin.

"Common people might be satisfied with such deeds," he said. "They might sleep well with dreams of grateful children and villains ended." His eyes turned toward me. "But that was always just a side benefit with you, wasn't it? Mere gilding on the true prize. Death. Blood. Revenge."

"No," I rasped.

"No?" He peered down at me. His mouth opened in a bright smile, alight with flame. "Then why are you so ready to die?"

"*Stop it! She's bleeding out!*" Liette called out. "*I'm going to try something. Hold on, Sal, just hold on so I can—*"

Her voice vanished. And so did I.

The smell of coffee.

Of blood.

Of birdshit.

I opened my eyes to find a quill scratching against my skin. My wounds, my flesh, so much of me was coated in ink as Liette's hands scrawled sigils around me. Congeniality, her beak full of dead rabbit, glanced toward me before going back to scarfing down the dead animal. A campfire burned in the shadow of the Iron Boar, a pot of coffee going over it.

Cavric's eyes were ringed with darkness—how long had we been driving? What day was it? He was pacing nervously, gesturing out into the darkness. Lights continued to flash on the horizon—cannon fire, spells blazing, the riotous joy of battle not far away. He spoke words I couldn't hear, hurling them desperately at Liette. She shouted something back at him, never looking away from me. I couldn't hear them.

"She's a touch clumsy, isn't she?"

But I heard that.

The man with the burning grin stood over her, hands folded neatly behind his back as he looked over Liette's shoulder, studying my wounds. His smile was seething with malice when he watched my blood drip onto her hands.

"But only around you. I suspect that's why you infuriate her and fascinate her in equal measure," he said. "No one else can make her act so hastily, so rashly. Everything else comes so effortlessly to her.

But not you. To have such power and to have someone who can simply snatch it away..."

He blinked. He laughed. Ashes fell from his mouth.

"Well, of course *you'd* know what that's like."

Liette did not so much as glance at him as he knelt down beside me. He stared at me, through me, that flint-hewn gaze of his jamming into my wounds and tearing them open, flaying me apart until he could see what lay beneath all the skin and scars and blood.

And he was not impressed.

"You've probably seen a thousand back-alley operas where masked villains cackle about some nebulous definition of power, no? Some magic, some weapon, some *thing* that will give them dominion. But you and I both know what power truly is, don't we?"

Smoke poured from his mouth as he spoke.

"*Power* is a single word," he whispered through ashes. "A word that makes a warrior live in fear of the day his weapon fails him, that makes a mage look at all she's accomplished and realize it is nothing. It warps the mind of the scholar and makes him fear his own knowledge. It makes the farmer leave his crops to rot for fear of going outside. It makes the gentle turn cruel and the cruel run screaming into the night."

He raised a hand, lay it down upon my face. Somewhere inside me, something screamed at the burning touch, but that part was smothered, buried under so much numbness and pain. He traced a finger past my jawbone and down to my collar, where his digit thoughtfully pressed against my scar.

"But again," he whispered, "you knew that, too."

He rose up, folded his hands behind his back, and walked beside Cavric. Together, they stared out over the horizon. The night sky was alight with stars of war—cannons erupting, guns blazing, lightning flashing, and fires burning. Cavric bounced uneasily from foot to foot, watching the stain of battle spill farther across the land.

The man simply stared, bored. He'd seen a thousand wars before and this one barely even topped it.

"The wisest Revolutionary turns into a gibbering fanatic when he hears the word *Imperium*. The most sagacious mage becomes a bleating, quivering sack of fear at the Lady's name. Just words. Names. Nothing more. But they change people." He glanced over his shoulder. "What is yours, I wonder?"

"Sal," I gasped. "Sal the Cacophony."

"Mmm." He turned and stared behind him, to the distant ruin of Lastlight. "And what, do you suppose, becomes of people who hear that name?"

Cavric turned and rushed toward Liette, grabbing her by the shoulder. She snarled, lashing out with her quill like it was a dagger.

"*DON'T TOUCH ME!*" she screamed. "*This is delicate. If I don't do this perfectly, she could—*"

"*The Revolution line broke,*" Cavric interrupted. "*They're in retreat. And they're coming this way. We have to go now or else—*"

"*I can't move her now! She's not ready! I need more time!*"

"*We don't have any!*"

They yelled. Shouted words I couldn't hear. Eventually, Liette bowed her head, sighed, and packed up her supplies. Together, they propped me up and began to carry me toward the Iron Boar. The man, with his flinty gaze, continued to watch the distant war. No one noticed him. I didn't call out.

And when the door to the Boar slammed shut as the engines roared to life, he vanished.

⸺◆⸺

"You're dying, you know."

I didn't know how long I'd been out. Nor did I know how he'd made it back onto the Boar. But when I opened my eyes, I saw his grin burning in the darkness. But the fire had dimmed. The glitter in his eyes was going dark. It was harder to tell him from the shadows he sat in.

"Her sigils are not working. Nor will the alchemics she tries. Nor the bleakbrew she keeps in her belt that she never told you about, since she knows it unnerves you."

I knew he was right. In the iron weight of my limbs, in the cold creeping into my skin. I had often wondered what it'd be like, to be called to the black table. Would my last moments be panicked and screaming? Or would I find the dark cold and comforting, like a thin blanket on a winter's night?

I hadn't ever thought that, as the darkness closed in, I just wouldn't care.

"Dreadfully passé, isn't it?" the man asked, as if in response to my thoughts. "Every opera has a verse about the poignancy of death, but I found it entirely boring. A few difficult breaths, a few final thoughts, and then"—he blew a wisp of smoke from his mouth—"you're simply gone. With too much left to do."

He was right. There was too much left to do and not enough left in me. I had taken too many hits, lost too much blood—

"Oh, it's not the blood," he said. "It's something else you've lost. Really, I know you're about to die and all, but that's no excuse for not listening."

He rose from the bench and walked over to me. The shadows clung to him, crawling across his face as he knelt over me.

"But it hardly seems the time to go rehashing it, doesn't it? You've got such precious little time left." His fingers traced across my scars. "I can feel your heart shutting down, going black inside you. I can hear the wailing of your lover when she stands over your warm corpse ten minutes from now. I can see the black earth they'll bury you in."

His eyes narrowed to thin slits. His smile twisted into a snarl of ash and soot. His face twisted into an ugly brass mess.

"All that we had planned," he whispered, "the future we'd bring, the ruin we'd cause, the deal we made...all for nothing. All because you couldn't kill when you had the chance."

Not my fault, I wanted to say, but I couldn't make my lips move. *Taltho interfered. Galta ambushed me. I had to save the—*

"And who will remember that?" he interrupted my thoughts. "We leave nothing behind when we go but our names. Mine built an

Imperium. Mine discovered the Scar. Mine sowed terror in the nuls for a hundred years. But yours?"

He shook his head. Dying embers fell from his mouth.

"You will vanish beneath the dirt. Your name will disappear to all but the people in this iron casket. And whatever schemes Vraki the Gate goes on to perform, whether he succeeds or fails, lives or dies, he will never again think of Sal the Cacophony as anything but a fleeting thought, a bad dream of a failed ambition."

I didn't think I had enough feeling left in me for that to hurt as much as it did. But that reality, to know that the people who did this to me would never live to regret this, to see themselves staring down the barrel of the Cacophony...

Dying suddenly seemed not such a bad thing.

"Your time here is at an end," he whispered, "nothing but a few pieces of steel and a scrap of paper. You will die and fade from this world, leaving behind not even Dust to remember you by. Your song has gone silent... unless..."

He leaned down close to me, so close I could smell the ash on his breath, so close I could hear the song in his voice. A dark and droning sound from somewhere deeper than flesh or ghosts.

"You find a reason to come back."

Through blackening vision, I stared at him, searching that burning smile for an answer.

Liette, I thought. *I have to survive. For her.*

"Her name wasn't enough to stop you from killing. Why would it stop you from dying?" The embers in his mouth faded a little more. "What else?"

I have to stop Vraki. I have to protect all the people he'll hurt.

"If other people concerned you, you wouldn't have the name you do." His mouth went black, wisps of smoke trailing away as the fire died. "Do you really have nothing left?"

I gritted my teeth. I shut my eyes. It couldn't end like this. I still had so much to do.

I still have to kill him. I have to kill them all.

And I felt a warm glow.

"Go on."

I opened my eyes. The embers in the man's mouth kindled themselves to burning life again. His lips twisted into a smile.

They took my magic.

"More."

The fire filled his mouth.

They took the sky from me.

"More."

It spread to his beard, his hair, his clothes, setting them ablaze and chasing them away.

They betrayed me, tried to kill me, took everything from me. They have to die. They have to suffer.

The flames engulfed him, engulfed Liette, engulfed me, until the inside of the Boar was awash with fire. They did not crackle, nor laugh as flame should. The fire sang, an ugly and dark song in a language no one knew. It poured out of his smile, that burning song, as he threw his head back and laughed.

"MORE!"

Eres va atali. Eres va atali!

"I USED TO FLY!"

I realized, as it tore itself free from my throat, that was my voice. That was blood returning to my limbs. That was warmth returning to my body. That was feeling in my hand as Liette took it in her own and stared into my eyes.

The man was gone. The smoke and embers had disappeared. I was left with nothing but the pain.

"*She's burning up,*" I barely heard Liette say. "*How far are we?*"

"*Not far. We'll have to rush once we reach Lowstaff, though.*"

"*Well, hurry the fuck up! I can't help her if you don't . . .*"

Her words faded. The warmth faded. Sight and sound and feeling faded as I slipped back into somewhere dark, somewhere cold, somewhere far away. But even as I did . . .

That song, his burning verse, followed me.

FIFTY-SIX

LOWSTAFF

My sleep was long, dark, and empty. In a void that closed in around me from all angles, I was buried so deep that I was deaf to the wailings of the dead and blind to their smiles of whatever horrors awaited me after my corpse was picked clean by the carrion birds and the Dust of my skeleton was cast adrift on the shrieking winds.

So things were looking up.

But all good things come to an end. And eventually, I woke up to a bed with nice sheets, a basin full of cold water, and not a drop of whiskey in sight. So, clearly not hell, but far from heaven.

Which meant I must be alive.

A quiet burbling sound filled my ears. I glanced to my side and saw a large black bird squatting on the sill of a window, its beak rapping thoughtfully against the glass. It canted its head to the side, white eyes studying me, disappointed I hadn't died.

Alive for less than a minute, I was already letting people down.

At least this one was content to simply turn and flap away, leaving me alone with my pain.

As my eyes adjusted to the light of a fading afternoon seeping through the shutters, I saw that I wasn't alone in the room. Every spare inch of space had been taken up by piles of books, pages marked with various scraps of cloth and paper. The mirror of the dresser was completely obscured by a stack of tomes as high as I was tall.

Liette's house. It felt like someone else's life, waking up here, a tomb of happier times and dreams that never could be.

My breath came easy, my heart beat slowly, and my body had gone from waiting for death to screaming in pain. I could feel her sigils scribed across my wounds, each one wrapped tightly beneath a bandage delicately applied. And as I rose out of the bed, body creaking and wounds protesting, the scent of pungent medicinal herbs assaulted my nose.

Her skills must not have been enough, then.

Liette resented medicine. The human body, she said, was a ridiculously simple machine that perpetually refused to do what it should, hence it was neither challenging nor satisfying to maintain. Plus, medicine kept a lot of people alive and she was of the opinion that additional humans in the world was something she could do without.

Yet I could feel the care with which she had treated the wounds and applied the bandages. The muscles that had been stiff, she had massaged out. The grime and dirt and blood, she had washed clean. She had even washed my hair while I had slept.

I guess you could call that creepy. But when it's someone you like, it's considered sentimental.

I found my clothes on a chair, washed and folded neatly. Less out of concern for me, I suspect, and more that Liette had probably found their smell offensive. She had been industrious while I had been out.

And, in the midst of pulling my shirt on, I paused.

How long *had* I been out?

"Are you certain you want coffee?"

Liette's voice lilted it from the other room. I heard the sound of a cup being set upon a table, someone picking it up and taking a long, slow sip. I could almost hear the frown in her voice.

"The way you look I think something stiffer would be more appropriate."

"I don't drink." Cavric sounded like he had gargled a glass full of gravel. "Thanks, though."

"Huh." I could hear her appraising stare gliding over him. "You should probably consider taking it up."

He chuckled. "And thanks for that, too. But there's still work to be done and it needs me alert."

"Then you probably shouldn't have driven across the Scar for two nights straight." A chair scraped as Liette sat down. There was a thoughtful pause, a hesitant word. "I'm...I'm glad that you did, though."

"*I'm* glad you came back with the Boar," Cavric replied.

"Yeah," she sighed. "Sorry about that whole...leaving you to die in the Husks...thing."

"It's fine," he said, then paused. "I mean, not *fine*, but...it's behind us, at any rate." He drained the last of his coffee, slid the cup back over. "Sorry to bother you for more, but I've got a report to file on this."

"Mmm." Liquid splashed against porcelain. "I trust you will be selective in what you opt to report. Don't misconstrue it as ingratitude, but as much as I value what you did, I..."

I could almost feel her eyes drawn inexorably toward me, as though she could see right through the walls to where I stood.

"I...I can understand that," Cavric said. "But my duties mean I have to be thorough."

Another pause. This one less thoughtful.

"I'm sorry to hear that," Liette said after a long moment.

Now, it's certainly not true of all women, but in my experience, one who says those five words is either about to go home or pull a knife out. And Liette was already home.

I was just about to intervene when I heard the exhaustion set into Cavric's voice.

"I have to tell them...tell them..." I could hear him slump in his chair. "Tell them what? That I let myself be abducted by a Vagrant? That I watched Lastlight go up in flames and abandoned the battle to go chase a bird on its way to a dying woman? That I drove a Boar to its breaking point just to get back here? If I tell any officer this, I'd be executed for desertion if I was lucky, treason if I wasn't."

"There's . . . there's a difference?" Liette asked.

"If you desert, they get it done in one day."

"Oh. *Oh.*" The tension ebbed from her voice, leaving behind something that hurt her to speak. "I . . . thank you, then. For what you did."

"For failing in my duty?" he asked, scoffing.

"If it means you brought her back," she replied, "then yes."

Cavric, like all men with thoughts too heavy for their head, had a noisy stare. You could hear the weight of it striking when it settled upon something. Just as I could hear him staring at his cup, the weight of his eyes threatening to pull his whole head crashing onto the table.

"The official report from the Cadre," he said, "is that the Imperium was secretly building forces in Lastlight with the intent of subverting its government and conscribing it to Imperial rule. Revolutionary forces were sent to ensure the freedom of the city and to protect its people from Imperial corruption."

"Do you believe that?" Liette asked.

"I believe they believed it," he said. "I believe that every soldier there thought they were doing good. I believe that the Revolution would have found a reason to occupy the city, regardless."

Silence fell and he clung to it like a drowning man clings to a rock. But eventually, he had to let go.

"What I believed didn't keep everyone from getting killed, though, did it?"

In operas, everyone dies loud. Villains get dying monologues, heroes lament about the futility of existence, or sometimes they just scream real loud if the writer can't think of anything. That's so you know their death meant something, that all the fighting and bloodshed was for some reason.

In life, though, people die quietly, meaninglessly. They're tiny lights that flicker for a moment and get extinguished, leaving behind something cold and empty. No meaning, no resolution, just a dark stain where a person used to be.

And I wondered, when Cavric looked at that big black stain where Lastlight once was, if he thought they had died meaninglessly.

Or because of me.

"You don't think..." Cavric's voice came timid, afraid. "Do you believe it could have turned out different? That they could have been saved?"

"No."

"Oh." Cavric coughed. "Well. Shit."

"By that, I mean..." Liette sighed. "Belief doesn't exist. Or it doesn't matter. Whichever. There is only what is known and what is unknown, a question and an answer. Belief is something that people use to excuse themselves when they give up finding it."

"You sound certain," Cavric said.

I could hear the glare in her voice. "I am a Freemaker. I am always certain."

"So..." His words drew out like a knife. "Is that why you came back for her?"

Liette's silence was strained, long and painful.

"It was necessary," she said softly, "to save the children."

"The children," Cavric muttered. "It was never about them, was it? For you or for her."

I expected her to deny it. I expected her to argue. I didn't expect her to whisper.

"I know..."

"If it was, you would have thought of something different. Something better."

"I know."

"And she wouldn't have—"

"*I KNOW!*" Liette's scream was accompanied by her fists smashing on the table. "Do you not think, in that tiny little grass-fed brain of yours, that I realize that? That every ounce of good she did was incidental? That it was all for . . . for those names on that list?"

"Then why?" he asked, voice rising. "Why did you come back?"

I heard her jaw set, her hands clench. "I don't know yet."

"Will you ever?"

"I don't know that, either," she said, sighing. "But I do know that, whatever her reasons for doing so, those kids are safe because of her. And the Scar is cleaner without those people she killed in it. Whatever else she does, she does good along with it."

Cavric's noisy stare settled on her. "And what happens when she doesn't do good? What will you do then?"

Liette's answer was a long, slow blade of silence. And it cut me deeper than I thought I could be cut.

"I don't know what I'll do," she whispered. "Only that I'll do it. For her."

That sharp silence persisted, stuck a little deeper into my skin with each passing second. When it was broken, it was done so by an exhausted sigh, a scrape of a chair, and the weight of Cavric's voice, falling onto the floor.

"I can leave you out of my report," Cavric said. "But I can't leave Lastlight out. Unless people know what happened there, we can't help anyone."

"And you really believe your Revolution will help them?" Liette asked, voice cold.

And Cavric was just as frigid. "It doesn't matter what I believe."

"Do what you have to, Low Sergeant," she replied. "And I will do the same."

Without realizing it, my hand had found my sword and my body stood rigid at the door. I recognized that coldness in their voices, the threat lurking beneath their words. I knew what they'd do if I didn't stop them.

And I couldn't let more people die because of me.

But all that came of it was a grunt and a muttered thanks for the coffee from Cavric before I heard him turn and leave down the stairs and out the door.

Part of me wanted to leap out and chase him, to apologize to him for all the trouble I'd caused, to try to tell him that I never should have done it and that, for all the bloodshed and carnage, it was worth it.

But I wouldn't have it said that Sal the Cacophony was a liar.

And so I did the kindest thing I could think of. I eased my hand off the sword. I sat back down and I let him disappear.

I sat there, staring at the door for a long time. Outside, I heard Liette settle back into her chair. I heard her pick up a book and thumb through it, pretending to read it. I heard her lose her patience and hurl it against the wall before she buried her head in her hands and began to cry.

I pulled the rest of my clothes on and reached for the doorknob. I knew just what to say when I came out, too.

I could be funny and say something like: "*Shit, if you cry this much over me while I'm wounded, what the fuck are you going to do when I'm dead?*" She'd glare at me angrily; then a smile would slowly creep over her face and she'd look away before she laughed.

Or I could be dramatic and burst out and say: "*Until this moment, I have never felt a pain so keen as yours and I would do anything that neither of us had to feel it again.*" And she'd cry harder and fall into my arms and we'd hold each other like we did before we knew what each other had done.

Or I could just say nothing, just step out there and take her hands and pull her into me. I could kiss her and let all the blood rush out of my limbs and into my head until we both collapsed to the floor and just lay there, not saying a word and not listening to anything but the need for each other.

Any of those would be good. Any of those would make her stop crying. Any of those would make this feel better.

And yet…I didn't open the door. I didn't come out. I didn't say anything.

Because I knew how it'd end. We'd make our vows—she to never leave me, me to never make her cry again. We'd pretend to be normal for a while and, for a while, it'd feel nice. And then one day I'd look in the mirror and see the scar across my chest and remember the people who had put it there and I'd pick up my gun and then...

And then I'd be staring at this same door again, with her crying on the other side as I tried to figure out what to say, over and over until I finally did her the kindness of dying.

I believed her when she said she'd come back for me, no matter what. I believed she'd do anything to keep me safe. I believed she would fight the Revolution, the Imperium, the Ashmouths, the Freemakers, every last human on the Scar if she thought it would fix me, fix us.

And that's why I knew I wasn't going to say anything.

I belted my sword and my gun around my waist. I pulled my luckscarf around my head. I walked to the window of her room and cast one final glance at the door before I pulled the shutters back, pushed the window open, and slipped out onto the roof.

She'd hurt, I knew as I shimmied down the eaves and onto the street. When she went into that room and saw me gone, she'd hurt worse than she ever had. But she'd only hurt once more, only until she realized what scum I was, only until she learned to curse my name, only until she forgot about me and wouldn't even notice if I ended up in a plot of earth somewhere.

If I stayed... then she'd keep hurting so long as we kept pretending I could ever stop.

Better this way, I told myself. Better to hurt just once. Because I knew what it was to hurt all the time.

I fingered the scar on my chest. It ached.

She would do anything to protect me. I would do the same for her. Turns out this was the only way.

I walked until I found the center of Lowstaff. The sun hung fading in the sky, bleeding orange as it continued to sink below the horizon of the Scar, far away. I stood in the center of the town, staring out over the walls. And then I looked down at my hip.

And the Cacophony looked back, as if to ask where we'd go next.

Somewhere out there were the rest of the names on my list. Maybe I'd go out there and find them. Or maybe I'd just go far away, find Congeniality and the whiskey in her saddlebags and get drunk as shit. Or maybe I'd just find the biggest, ugliest, most bloodthirsty thing in the Scar and fight it. Maybe I'd survive. Maybe I wouldn't.

But there was some small comfort.

I'd be far away from Liette. I'd be far away from Cavric. I'd leave them alone and they'd be safe because of it.

Whatever else they said about Sal the Cacophony, they'd say she didn't ruin the lives of *everyone* she cared about.

And that would be enough.

Yeah...

So, anyway, that was about the time the explosion hit.

FIFTY-SEVEN

LOWSTAFF

I found my feet upon a world of broken glass and laughing fire.

My head reeled—the blast had knocked my feet from beneath me and the sense from my head. Glass from shattered windows crunched under my feet, the only sound I could hear through the ringing in my skull.

The world returned in fragmented shrieks—the crackle of horror, the distant cries of people smothered beneath the wail of warning sirens. Sight followed sound, revealing the streets of Lowstaff.

And, as was the fashion these days, they were on fire.

I saw a smoldering black crater where something had struck, a black maw in the streets belching smoke. And, as if this were horribly funny, flames lapped at the various buildings, laughing through mouthfuls of wood and tinder as they devoured homes and shops and stray rubble.

I saw the people flooding out of their homes to join the stream of people rushing panicked through the streets. Their mouths were open and wailing, but I couldn't hear them over the sound of the siren, speaking a tinny language that only a few people could understand.

And those people came flooding out in a blue tide.

Revolutionaries came streaming out of their cadre in a solid formation of blue coats and gunpikes. Sergeants stood by, bellowing orders and firing hand cannons into the air to be heard over the siren that called them to battle. They pushed through or stomped over the civilians that got in their path as they rushed to set up battle formations, establishing sandbag barricades and setting up mortars.

I wagered they had about as much idea of what was happening as I did, yet they already had their answer. Whatever had happened, whatever had come, they were going to respond by shooting it.

This couldn't possibly go wrong.

Fuck if I had any better ideas what to do, though. I came rushing out onto the street, looking for some indication of what might have happened, how I could help or, failing that, to get the hell away from it.

What I wasn't looking for was a hand wrapping around my waist, but I got it anyway. Something grabbed me, pulled me into an alley between buildings, and pressed me ungently against a wall. I pulled the Cacophony out and pulled the trigger. A click greeted me.

Ah, right. I hadn't loaded the last of my ammo back in Dogsjaw.

Just as well, though—I would have hated to put a hole through Cavric's head. Though, with the wide-eyed terror that was etched across his face right now, it might have been an improvement.

"What's happening?" he asked, breathless.

"You don't grab a person and haul them bodily into an alley unless *you're* the one with answers, Cavric," I snarled, shoving him away. "It just isn't done."

"That's the assembly siren." He pointed up, as though I could see the screeching sound in the air. "Lowstaff is under attack."

That would *explain the big, smoldering crater in the street*, I thought to say. But I doubted that would be helpful right now. I held up a hand for calm.

"By what?" I asked.

"No idea." He shook his head. "I was just about to go into Cadre Command when I felt the explosion. Then the others came rushing out and there were guns and...I..." He stared at me. "I ran, Sal. I hid from my own people. I...I've never done that before."

I glanced out the alley to all the screaming people, the growing fires, and the many, *many* angry people holding big metal things designed to kill other people.

"Seems sensible to me," I said. Yet, weirdly enough, that didn't seem to soothe him. At seeing the panic etch itself onto his face, I sighed. "All right, we're not going to know what to do unless we know what's going on. Come on."

We hurried down the alley. I put my back against the wall, made a stirrup out of my hands, and bent low. He nodded, getting the idea, before he put his foot into my hands. I grunted, boosting him up to the roof. He scrambled over the ledge, reached down for me, and helped haul me up.

We kept low—Revolutionary snipers were already on the other rooftops. But their long guns were turned toward the northern gate of Lowstaff, and from up here, I could see that the other soldiers also had their sights turned that way. I had just begun to wonder why when the realization hit me like a brick to the face.

Lastlight was up north.

I turned my eyes upward and I saw them. Black wings against the blood orange of the fading sun, alight and flying.

Krikai.

"The Imperium," I whispered. "The Imperium is coming."

"What?" Cavric gasped. "Why?"

Because this is a war.

Because they're out for revenge.

Because who the fuck knows.

I didn't have an answer. None that Cavric would want to hear, none that would help. This was just more bloodshed, more violence that we'd never be able to explain until we sifted through the ashes left behind.

And I wish that had been true.

But you should know by now that there's no such thing as random violence. Follow a scar long enough, you'll trace it back to the knife that carved it, the hand that held it, the grudge that demanded it. I wanted, in my heart and my head, to believe that this was just war. And if I closed my eyes, I could have tricked myself into thinking exactly that.

But then I realized that the Imperium was still at least two miles away. Far too far away for that explosion to have come from them.

And then I looked down.

The soldiers didn't see him. A second ago, he hadn't been there. And when a portal opened in their midst and the thin man with a mop of unruly hair stepped out, barely anyone seemed to notice him, let alone stop him as he raised his arms, as his eyes glowed a bright violet.

I heard the Lady's song.

And then Vraki the Gate started killing.

It happened in three seconds. One second for the air to split apart, portals torn open. One more for a Revolutionary to look up and notice him and begin to shout a warning. And one last for his cry to be drowned under the sound of horrific baying as the nith hounds came leaping out.

And then the screaming started.

The Revolutionaries scattered, their formation broken as they emptied their weapons at the fiends that had appeared in their midst. The crack of gunpikes and the thunder of bullets ended in gory sputters as they struck the horrors rushing toward them. Some hounds fell. More didn't, leaping up to seize Revolutionaries in human hands and start tearing pieces off.

A halo of corpses fell in Vraki's wake. The Revolutionaries went down—screaming, stabbing, or simply silent in uncomprehending horror—yet he never so much as looked at them. Instead, he threw his head back and his scream shook the town to its foundations.

"CACOPHONY."

Me.

He's here for me.

That thought reached down from my head with little black fingers and seized my heart in a cold grip.

The portals. He had followed me through the portals, knew

where I had gone. He followed me here. And the Imperium had followed him. And now they were here, to fight him and the Revolution just like they had fought in Lastlight because I had started the war in Lastlight and there were going to be more deaths and more blood and more fire and more and more and more...

No.

A voice. Burning. Seething. The pain in my hand, that ugly little harp, plucked itself and drowned my thoughts beneath a wave of agony. I looked down to my hip. The Cacophony looked back to me.

And he smiled.

And I knew what I had to do.

"Cavric."

I looked to him. He was staring at the violence below, at his friends' corpses being mutilated as the nith hounds started grafting human pieces to their bodies, with empty eyes.

"*Cavric.*"

I seized him by the shoulders, forced him to look at me.

"Where's Congeniality?"

"Huh...who?" His voice came out on a breathless whisper.

"My bird, Cavric. Where's my bird?"

"I...the..." He shook his head, forced the ghosts from his eyes. "The stables. I took her to the stables. West end of town."

I nodded. "I need to get down there. I need you down there, too."

"Right...right." He bobbed his head back, numb. "I have to... We have to fight..."

"*I* have to fight," I snapped back. "*You* have to get the people out of here."

At that, the fear, the ghosts, everything fled from his eyes. He looked at me intently, his brow furrowed.

"The people?" he asked. "But the Revolution..."

"You think your fucking Great General is going to help them?"

I hadn't meant to snarl. It had just slipped out. But I had no more patience. No more time. And not much of a plan. Cavric drew in a deep breath, nodded.

"I'll get them all out," he said.

"As many as you can," I said.

"All of them," he replied.

I sighed, nodded. "All of them." I pointed to the west. "I'm going to get Vraki's attention, draw him to the west gate. Imperials are coming in from the north. Get people out through the south. Tell them to keep running."

I pulled Jeff out of his sheath—a beat-up, dingy sword wasn't ideal when going up against a mage, let alone a Prodigy. But what the fuck else was I going to do? Seduce him?

Probably not after I broke his face, no.

I reached the edge of the building. Cavric called after me.

"What are you going to do once you've got his attention?"

I glanced over my shoulder. A grin creased my face. I shot him a wink.

"The best I can," I replied.

Then I swung my legs over the edge.

"Or maybe die, I guess. We'll see how it goes."

FIFTY-EIGHT

LOWSTAFF

In the face of death, Sergeant Courageous was as defiant as his namesake.

Blood poured from a wound above his brow, sealing one eye shut beneath a layer of red. His body shook with every breath, life escaping out his mouth on hot, ragged gasps. His hand still clutched tightly about his officer's sword—which would have been a truly impressive sight, had his arm still been attached to his body. Regardless, he swallowed blood down a throat constricted by an iron grip and scowled up with one good eye.

"Against foe innumerable," he snarled through bloodied breath, "in the face of adversity implacable, beneath storm unceasing, the Glorious Revolution marches on." He tried to defiantly spit blood, only to find it dribbling out his chin and onto the hand wrapped around his throat. "Ten...ten thousand years."

Vraki the Gate did not seem particularly impressed.

"Were that the strength of your ideology matched the skill of your speech-writers," he replied, sneering. "I have heard the wail of pigs and the baying of nuls and found it beyond even my skill to tell the difference between the two."

He waved a hand. A portal opened above his fingers. A blade of jagged stone and bristling thorns descended into his waiting palm. He angled it an inch away from Courageous's quivering eye.

"And if you cannot feed a more worthy society, then you are but gristle to be hewn with a sharp edge and left for scavengers upon the earth," Vraki whispered harshly. "Die with the comfort that for all your noise, neither you nor your petty Revolution were enough to warrant the ire of Vraki the Gate this night."

You know, as much as I was loath to admit it, Vraki was pretty gifted in the art of making threats.

Almost made me hate to interrupt.

There's very little in this world that can scare a mage. A person who can hurl boulders, conjure hurricanes, or make things explode with their mind doesn't have a lot to be afraid of except the price they pay for doing so. And a person like Vraki doesn't even have to fear that.

To that end, maybe there's nothing I could do that could scare him.

But I like to think that, when he heard a screech pierce the smoke-filled sky and looked up to see a giant, angry bird charging toward him, me astride her with glistening sword in hand, he knew what was coming.

Congeniality, fearing no flame, blood, or magic, went rampaging toward him, eyes ablaze and beak open. He dropped Courageous, threw his hands out wide. His eyes glowed as the Lady's song rose. Portals opened, a forest of thorny vines weaving itself in front of him, doubtlessly impenetrable to any weapon I had.

But that was where the bird came in.

I kicked Congeniality's flanks and she responded, leaping into the air and coming down, talons-first, upon the wall. All five hundred pounds of feather and muscle crashed through the brambles in a spray of shards and thorns. I was treated to the spectacle of Vraki's offended face before a portal opened behind him and he fell through it, vanishing.

Some part of me had hoped that Congeniality would have just disemboweled him, but another, more bitter part knew it would never be that easy. And it knew that Vraki hadn't gone far.

And, sure enough, as I spurred Congeniality down the street, my ears were full of the Lady's song. At the corner of my eye, I saw another portal open. I jerked her reins away, narrowly avoiding the great brambled spike that burst out.

"Cacophony!"

I glanced over my shoulder and saw him. From a shimmering hole in creation behind him, a beast crawled. An amalgamation of spindly limbs—some human, some not—attached to a crooked spine and headed by a face that looked like a snarling hound had begun swallowing a sobbing man feetfirst and stopped at his neck, lurched to his side. It bowed its head, one eye flitting about in horror, as Vraki ascended it and stood upon its bent spine, staring down at me through eyes alight with magic.

He waved a hand. The creature answered, throwing back its head in a sound that was a dying man's wail and a starving beast's howl fighting to be heard over each other.

And, upon its horrific mass of limbs, it charged.

I kicked Congeniality's flanks, sent her running through the streets. Behind me, the beast bayed, though not loud enough to drown out Vraki's voice.

"Your bones will be a city, Salazanca!" he screamed. "A bedrock of misery upon which I'll erect a monument to your failure!"

See? How come I never say anything that badass?

"You made me break my word!" he howled. "You ruined everything! It will take years to earn their trust again!"

His words didn't make sense to me, but he spoke them with a clarity he hadn't before. The desperation that I had heard back in Dogsjaw was gone. His thoughts were as clear as the anger in his eyes.

He was lucid.

Good. I wanted him to know what was happening when I ended him.

Of course, I also wanted to not die horribly, so . . .

I pulled Congeniality's reins, kicked her flanks, sent her weaving as portals opened around us. We darted between pikes of thorns and stone that burst out from thin air. We leapt over walls of grasping hands and gnashing teeth erupting from the earth. Purple fire that whispered with human voices erupted in gouts around us.

But he couldn't touch us. Prodigies didn't pay Barters, but even the Lady Merchant couldn't teach him how to aim. I kept Congeniality running as we rounded a corner toward the north gate. Just so long as I kept this up, I could—

"Halt!"

Of course.

A line of blue coats and black barrels appeared before me. Revolutionaries, kneeling in a firing position, stood before me, their officer raising his sword.

"Get out of the way!" I screamed.

"In the name of the Great General and his Glorious Revolution, I hereby order you to cease all hostilities and submit to—"

I stopped listening about the time I heard a whistle behind me. I ducked, pulling Congeniality's head low, as a flurry of rock-hewn blades went spiraling over my head. They struck the Revolutionaries in a burst of crimson and a riot of screams, sending the officer flying through the air in chunks.

Maybe if he had shortened his speech, he would have heard it, too.

I spurred Congeniality forward, leaning over in the saddle to pluck up a gunpike as we rushed past. It wouldn't be much of an advantage against his magic, but it was all I had.

Aside from the scattered Revolutionaries I ran past—or over—I didn't see many people in the streets and what few I did were running south, away from where I was leading Vraki. Cavric had gotten word out; the people were getting clear of danger. They'd come home to ruins, but they'd come home. They could rebuild. They could endure.

Unless I died here, of course.

Then I guess they'd all be killed to summon another Scrath.

So I guess no plan is perfect. But this was the best one I had and every part of it required me to be alive.

And Vraki dead.

I jerked on Congeniality's reins. She squawked and pulled hard down a corner. The main thoroughfare of the freehold sprawled out before us, a long and empty stretch of street leading straight to the north gate. Less obstructions to hide, fewer corners to take—I'd be an easier target. But I had no choice.

I spurred Congeniality forward, heard the crash of ice behind me as Vraki caught up. I glanced over my shoulder, saw the blood and chunks of meat staining the hide of his beast, stray limbs shoveling chunks of flesh into its mouth as it loped. His hands were raised, his eyes were focused, but he held his spells. He was waiting to get closer, wanted a clear shot.

Me, I was fine just where I was.

It had been years since I used a gunpike, but I knew how to shoot. I twisted in the saddle, leveled it at Vraki, steadied my breath, and felt myself rising and falling with the bird's stride.

In. Out. Up. Down.

And then, at the moment where her feet left the ground and gave me a clear shot, I pulled the trigger.

Gunfire cracked. So loud I almost didn't hear the Lady's song.

Time seemed to slow down as the bullet flew. I know that's cliché as fuck to say and sounds like something out of a cheap opera, but here's the thing. The operas always say time slows down in moments of great passion—when the villain falls, when the heroes embrace, that sort of thing. Reality isn't romantic like that. In reality, time only ever slows down to give you time to appreciate how completely fucked you are.

Like I felt when the air in front of Vraki blurred. As if from shadows and smoke, a lithe form appeared, a blade flashing in its slender hand. It swung, a flurry of sparks where the sword struck away the bullet, keeping it from finding Vraki's chest. The figure seemed to hang there for a moment.

Just long enough for Jindu to look me dead in the eyes.

And then he vanished again.

I caught him moving as a blur, disappearing and reappearing, each time closer to me. He swept up the street, moving like a bad dream. He vanished and reappeared beneath the lampposts at the corner of my eye. Behind me. Beside me.

In front of me.

By the time I saw him appear in front of me, it was too late. His blade flashed, quicker than I could scream, let alone pull on Congeniality's reins. A bright arc of blood painted the sky. The bird reared beneath me, letting out a terrified squawk as a gash was torn in her breast.

I flew.

The wind was knocked from me as I struck the earth. I swallowed dust and cold, scrambling to my feet. Congeniality tore off running, terrified, leaving me with bloodstained earth, a sword, and a gate sprawling before me.

I made a break for it. But before I could even feel like I might have made it, a wall of thorns and stone rose out of the ground between me and the gate. I whirled, bringing the gun up. I saw Vraki's hand wave.

Then I saw the wall come to life.

Thorns pierced my flesh, stone groaned as they lashed out and coiled around my arms, my waist, my legs and lashed me to the wall behind me. A scream formed in my throat as I felt my blood weep down the briars, but I swallowed it back down.

I wouldn't give him the satisfaction.

The horrific beast came shambling forward, Vraki atop it. Without the adrenaline of the chase to fuel it, I could see how broken and tired it was, shambling on crooked and bent limbs, its sole human eye twitching in unthinking horror. It came to a shuddering halt, bowing its head low to allow Vraki off.

I expected to see a smile when I looked at him, an ugly grin as he commanded that beast to add my blood to the stains upon its glistening hide. What I didn't expect was to see him turn toward it, stroke the misshapen flesh of its face affectionately, and press his brow to it. Its eye closed. It let out a low moaning sound.

"You have done well. Thank you." He opened his eyes and light filled them. "Go back to her now."

Another portal opened beneath it and, like ice melting, the beast slid into it, its last sound an agonized moan that lingered long after the portal closed.

"To be in our world hurts them," he said. "The light, the sound, the emotion. It's too much for them. That's why they need hosts." He looked toward me, his jagged stone blade in hand. "You have no idea what trauma you caused that creature at Dogsjaw."

Too breathless to speak, too dizzy to focus, I found the energy to scowl at him as he approached me. Though the thorns denied me even the dignity of a futile struggle, constricting my body so tightly, it chased what little breath I had left.

I still had enough in me to scowl, though. Over Vraki's shoulder, I saw a shadow of a man who had once stood tall. Jindu met my eyes for but a moment. Before his frown became so deep that it pulled his eyes away.

"Don't watch, Jindu," Vraki muttered. "I will handle this."

I kept my stare on him, daring him to meet my eyes. I opened my mouth to curse him when he turned away from me. But what was left to say? He vanished from sight. I let him go. I turned my anger back to Vraki.

"Don't wait for me to beg," I rasped. "The only thing coming out of my mouth will be spittle and a request that you step closer and open your mouth. Not in that order."

"I don't want your dignity, Salazanca." Vraki shook his head slowly, regarding me through those burning eyes. "I merely desire understanding."

"You desired to kill hundreds to drag out a hellbeast from beyond the stars," I spat back. "What the hell about that sounds 'mere'?"

He shook his head. "After all this, you still don't understand them. Like all the others, you still think of them as monsters, your judgments rendered from stories told by grandmothers to frighten children into obedience."

"Yeah, fucker, it's *me* who doesn't understand." I tugged against the thorns, even as they tried to crush my wrist. "Not the guy who tried to murder children to make friends with inhuman *monsters*."

"Monsters, no," Vraki replied. The vague nostalgic sort of smile that you only ever see on mothers and murderers crept across his face. "Inhuman…only for the moment."

I narrowed my eyes. "If that's your big 'I've gone fucking crazy' speech, I have to admit I'm disappointed."

"I don't blame you."

I couldn't bear the sound of his whispers. Cursing, snarling, gloating, laughing—I could have handled anything but the soft, almost pitying voice he offered me.

"I was afraid of them, too, when they first spoke to me. They are afraid of themselves. And she is afraid for them." He shook his head. "I still thought of them as merchants, traders of power. I thought they could give us a new emperor. But they can give us so much more."

"I've seen what they desire," I growled. "And I've seen what you've given them. Whatever the fuck they desire isn't worth it."

"They desire what we desire," he snapped back. "Peace. Stability. A world bereft of war or hatred." His eyes drifted skyward. "They see everything. It hurts them to watch it. They would give us so much more if they could only set foot on this earth. And I can show them how. I can help them. As they helped us."

I'd have retorted but if I opened my mouth, I might have vomited at his saccharine opining. But in another second, his eyes were filled with anger as he turned back to me.

"But you *ruined* it," he hissed. "As you ruined the Imperium, as you ruined our ambitions, as you ruin *everything*. And though I was content to leave you to your devices so long as you could leave me to mine, your machinations drive me mad. I find my thoughts clouded, consumed by a single word."

In the blink of an eye, he swept toward me. His hand was around my throat. That sword of stone and thorns leapt into his other and he leveled it at my heart.

"*Why?*" he hissed. "Why do you destroy everything? Why do you seek to undo all our work?"

"Don't pretend to be dumb enough that you don't know why," I snarled through his hand. "You stole my magic. *You took the sky from me.*"

"It was never *your* magic," he roared back, yet his voice sounded almost petulant, wounded. "It was *hers*. It was always hers. No one knows why she gave it to you, but you didn't deserve it. I gave it back. I *had* to give it back to open the door."

I always wondered what my last thoughts would be before I died. I had hoped it would be faces of people I loved. Failing that, memories of times I was happy—or close to it, anyway. At the very least, I thought it'd be people that I killed, staring at me accusingly as I joined them in death.

I hadn't expected them to be the words that left my mouth.

"What did you give at Dogsjaw?"

They were just words. Yet Vraki recoiled, as though slapped. The ice spike withdrew. He stared at me, dumbstruck. And as a cold realization settled at the base of my head, I asked again.

"What were you going to give at Dogsjaw to summon the Scrath?" I asked. "You said you needed my power, down in the catacombs all those years ago. But you didn't have anything to offer at Dogsjaw."

"The...the sacrifices," he stammered. "They were..."

"Hosts," I replied. "For the Scrath. You weren't using them in the summoning." My eyes narrowed, my mouth hung open. "You're a Prodigy. You don't pay a Barter even for a summoning, do you?"

And suddenly, my breath left me. The petulant, whining tone of his words resonated in my head. And then I realized...

"You never needed my power to summon it," I whispered. "You never needed *anything*, did you? You could open the door whenever you wanted."

He released my throat. "At the time, I—"

"You what? You couldn't do it? You hadn't figured it out? You were too fucking stupid to open a door, even with all your knowledge and unlimited power, but you thought you were smart enough to fix the Imperium?"

He stepped back, shaking his head. "N-no, that's not it. Our cause was too important to—"

"Our cause? *Your* cause? Your cause to fix the Imperium? To fight its armies and its mages and all its resources? And you didn't think you might need me, another Prodigy? I was *Red Cloud*, fucker. The people would have rallied around me. With my power, I could have toppled the Imperium and all its—"

My voice died.

My eyes went wide.

The realization hit me, a bullet that punched through my skull and settled in my brain.

"It was my power," I whispered. "You wanted a way to get rid of my magic."

Vraki the Gate, whose lips had spoken spells that had ended worlds, hung his mouth open in a silent grab for words he couldn't find. Vraki the Gate, whose eyes burned with the Lady's favor, shot me a wounded look like a child who had been caught sneaking treats before supper. Vraki the Gate, whose schemes strove to bring the Imperium low, couldn't think of what to say.

He stepped back, seemed to fold in on himself—had he always been that skinny? He looked at his feet, licked his lips—had he always seemed that nervous? In my head, he was huge, imposing, a shadow looming large over me. This man before me, this scrawny, fidgety weakling who couldn't look me in the eye...I didn't recognize him. Or maybe I always did. Maybe *this* was the real him.

Vraki the Gate, last of the Prodigies...

Vraki the Gate, Scourge of the Scar...

Vraki the Gate, greatest weapon to ever be used by or against the Imperium...

As petty, as greedy, as spiteful and envious as any regular piece of shit you could pull out of the gutter.

I felt sick, like I'd throw up just looking at him. I felt angry, like I could tear my own limbs off to get to him. But more than anything, I felt a cold sliver of disgust.

"Fuck me, Vraki," I whispered, "were you always this clichéd?"

"Silence," he hissed back.

"It was all about power? All your lofty ideas? All your grand speeches? And you just didn't feel special enough? Like some kind of opera villain?"

"*Quiet!*" His hiss became a growl as he scowled at me.

"Not even a *good* opera. For all that power you had, you couldn't aspire to more than a two-knuckle, cheap piece of—"

"SHUT UP!"

He threw his hands over his head. More blades emerged from portals in the air. They came together, joining into a great spike of stone and thorns. His howl so loud that it drowned out the Lady's song. His scream so vast that it swallowed the sound of flame and carnage. His wail so loud that neither of us heard the hum of a bowstring.

Nor the whistle of the arrow.

Nor even the sound of a damp explosion as it punched through his side.

He paused, blinking. He looked down to see the red patch blossoming upon his clothes. And for the second time that day, he was speechless.

I've got to say, though, I liked this one a lot better.

I looked over his head, to a distant rooftop. She was faint, a shadow against the setting sun. But I saw the smoke trailing from the barrel of the *very* big crossbow she carried. I saw the glint of the dying light reflected off her glasses. And though I couldn't tell, I liked to think that, at that moment, Liette was smiling.

"Jindu..."

My attentions returned to Vraki. His ice spike fragmented, fell to pieces around him as he collapsed to his knees, clutching his side. I felt the chains around me go slack, vanish into dust. Vraki shut his eyes, screamed.

"JINDU."

I heard the Lady's song before I saw him. A blur of motion, Jindu rushing down the streets, leaping onto the eaves of buildings, his blade naked and his eyes on the distant rooftop.

In hindsight, I could have killed Vraki right there. He was wounded, distracted, bleeding. I had one shot left. I could have put one in his head and been done with everything.

But, at the moment, I wasn't thinking. I was only feeling.

My legs pumping under me as I ran.

My heart trying to claw its way out of my chest.

Her name, lodged in my head, like a knife.

Liette.

I seized another fallen gunpike from a nearby corpse, checked to find it loaded. But even as I ran toward her, I knew I couldn't get to her soon enough. Jindu was faster than me, faster than the human eye. Already, I saw Jindu leaping from the eaves of a building onto its roof, onto the next roof, until he was right next to the one Liette stood upon.

No time, no time, not fast enough, not fast enough, I can't, I can't...

Those words in my head faded into silence. And somehow, through the panicked screaming inside my skull, I heard four words, crystalline and cold.

He strikes from behind.

And then, I wasn't thinking anymore.

I skidded to a halt as close as I dared. I brought the gunpike up, steadied my aim as I pointed it at Liette. From atop the roof, I could see the confusion and fear on her face as she saw me aim my weapon at her. I drew in a deep breath, held it.

Blinked.

Opened my eyes.

Jindu appeared behind her, his blade naked and shining, his eyes cold and distant and fixed on her neck.

I fired.

He swung.

Blood stained the sky.

I could hear Jindu's scream as the bullet punched through his shoulder. I could hear Liette's cry as his blade missed her neck and carved a line through her back, sending her toppling over the edge of the roof. I could hear my feet crunching on the dirt as I rushed forward, as I leapt, arms extended to catch her. I could hear the sound of my body hitting the earth as I landed belly-first.

And while I couldn't hear the noises I made when she landed on top of me, I bet they weren't nice.

She clambered off of me, wincing. When I looked up, her hand was extended. She helped me to my feet with a grunt and held my hand in hers, her other on my arm. Her eyes were intent as she looked at me and, for a minute, I could almost forget what I'd done.

"You came back for me," I whispered.

"I did." She nodded. A smile fought with a wince for control of her face. "You saved me."

I glanced at the blood weeping out of the wound in her back. "Sort of?"

"I'll be fine." She glanced over my head toward the many flames and corpses decorating her city. "Possibly."

"You need to get out of here," I growled. "It's not safe."

"It's fine," she insisted. "I can handle it."

"You're not cut out for this."

She stared at me, unblinking. "I just *shot* a guy. Pretty good."

"With a giant crossbow, yes," I replied. "But that's not a guy. That's a Prodigy and—"

"And I *shot* him in his fucking liver." She swatted my hand away. "I can handle this, Sal. I need to help you. I need to—"

"You need to *leave.*"

"He almost killed you." An edge of panic crept into her voice. "You can't handle him alone. If he's not dead, then—"

"Then nothing changes," I said, taking her hands in mine. "I destroy everything I touch. I'm going to burn this town down, whether I live or die. But I can't let you burn with it." My voice came breathless. "You were right... You were always right. You..."

I pressed her fingers to my lips. I drew in the scent of oil and Dust and flowers I saw in my dreams. I closed my eyes and tried to ignore the way her breath shuddered when she held it.

In opera, this would be the point where I made a great overture. We'd confess our true feelings, I'd come out of this okay, and we'd ride off the stage together. And I always thought I'd have a great speech—or at least some good words—to say when this moment came.

But everything I wanted to say turned to ash in my mouth, choking me whenever I tried to say it. And when she looked at me, waiting for me to say something, I had nothing.

And then there was the sound of thunder. And suddenly, it didn't matter anymore.

I followed the sound up to the smoke-stained sky and saw the birds, their great wings beating back columns of soot and fanning flames. From atop their backs, arcs of lightning flashed as thunderbows fired upon the town below to strike through fortifications, barricades, and anything else that might have been close.

I heard the Lady's song. I saw flashes of violet light burst into being across the spattered streets. Portals carved themselves out of thin air, swirling halos wrought by Doormages flying overhead. In another instant, troops wearing Imperial violet, carrying weapons flashing with flame and frost, emerged from a dozen different points.

"Fan out!" one of them called. "Find the traitor Vrakilaith! Kill anyone who tries to—"

"TEN THOUSAND YEARS!"

The Revolutionary battlecry cut through the air as they came flooding out from beneath cover and behind barricades. The crack of gunpikes and cannons accompanied them, met the sound of roaring fire and hissing steam as they clashed with their foes across the city in bursts of blood and flashes of fire and the hail of bullets.

And my eyes were on Liette. And I found the only word I could.

"Go."

Her eyes trembled, her mouth hung open. But she said nothing. She simply reached into a pouch at her hip and produced a small box. She placed it in my hand, closed my fingers over it, then turned away.

"Stay alive," she said. "Or I'll kill you."

That didn't even make sense.

But I didn't say anything as she turned and vanished around a corner.

I looked down at the box. I opened the lid. And my face, warped in the reflection of circular metal and scarred by writing scratched upon it, looked back at me in fifteen different circles.

The Cacophony seethed with pleasure at the sight.

Shells.

She had made me more shells.

I inhaled sharply. I plucked three of them out. I pulled the gun from his holster, chambered them, and flipped it shut. His eagerness burned so brightly that I thought my hand might catch fire.

It hurt.

But it wasn't the worst pain I'd felt.

FIFTY-NINE

LOWSTAFF

I put my head down and tried to ignore the sound of the world ending around me.

My body ached—wounds hadn't healed, breath hadn't returned, bones shook in my body with each frantic step I took. But I kept running, I kept breathing, I kept my eyes on the dirt as I rushed down to the street, back to where I had left Vraki.

The sounds of war encircled me. Above, Krikai birds shrieked to accompany the crack of thunderbows raining electric arcs onto the town below. Behind me, the silence of the dead made an oppressive wall to block the screaming of the dying. And pretty much in any spot that wasn't filled by one of those two sounds, the staccato crack of gunfire provided a grotesque chorus.

The Lady's song filled my ears. I heard the whisper of smoke that preceded the roar of flame. I skidded to a halt. An eruption blew gouts of fire from the windows and doors of a nearby building, like a many-headed dragon from whose mouths the charred and burning bodies of Revolutionaries fell or fled, screaming as flame consumed them. An Imperial Embermage, hands ablaze, wandered nonchalantly out a moment later and dawdled off to find more enemies to incinerate.

I kept moving.

I leapt over the smoldering carcass of a Revolutionary who reached out for me with a blackened hand. Nothing I could do for him. Or anyone, really. Cavric would be the one to save the people. All I could do was find Vraki and finish him. However bad things were, they'd be worse with a Prodigy running around.

I returned to Lowstaff's north gate and found only a pool of blood remaining.

Perhaps he had tried to escape. Perhaps he had teleported away. But I knew he wasn't dead.

Because I hadn't killed him.

I closed my eyes. I opened my ears. I took in the sound of guns blazing and fires roaring, of birds shrieking and of machines whirring, of death and blood and weeping and homes collapsing. And everywhere, the sound of the Lady's song arose in perfect, harmonious chorus.

Save one spot.

I glanced down a nearby street. There, down a narrow path winding its way between the homes and buildings, I heard something faint. It was the Lady's voice, but... mournful. Still a song, but no longer the elegant choir I was used to. More like... a dirge.

I pulled the Cacophony out and followed it.

My suspicions grew with every step I took into the street. Its path was decorated with corpses. Revolutionaries were impaled and twitching on stony thorns bursting from the earth. Imperial mages and soldiers were hurled through walls and torn into pieces and scattered like shredded paper on the wind. Nith hounds lay broken and moaning in the dust. Guns—from small gunpikes to massive cannons—lay twisted and torn apart in the dust like the discarded toys of a bored child.

I know it's a little fucked-up, but the whole scene was oddly serene. The death and destruction was so absolute that it rendered the distant sounds of the battle muted. As though an entire war had to sit in quiet awe of the carnage.

A Prodigy didn't have to pay a Barter to use his magic, but that didn't mean his strength was infinite. For Vraki to use this would have taken immense concentration and power. He was panicked, worried.

Weak.

I followed the path of carnage through the city streets, listening for the ebbing song that led me across bloodstained earth and through forests of iron and ice, until I finally came to a halt before the doors of a shop.

Selmin's Sundries.

Just a humble shop, far away from the main street. Too small to be of help to anyone. You wouldn't ever know it was here unless you knew where to look.

And here was where Vraki the Gate came to make his last stand.

Ironic. Or poetic. Or just coincidence. I'd let someone else figure out which, long after he was dead.

The Cacophony in hand, I took a breath and kicked the door open.

I swept the gun's barrel across a scene of shelves packed with bags of rice and dried meat and barrels of pickles. Darkness greeted me as I entered, the owner long having fled and left everything behind. A trail of black stains across the floor led behind a counter to an opened trap door and a staircase leading down.

And from the dark below, the mournful music wafted.

I kept the Cacophony trained before me as I took each step, finger ready to pull and unload a torrent of fire and frost the second I saw Vraki's face. But I never did. By the time he came into view, his back was to me.

He sat in a dark puddle, yet didn't seem to notice. His attentions were on a swirling sphere of light before him, a tiny echo of the great portal he had ripped open over Dogsjaw. Its song, far from the shrieking echo back then, was a lonely murmur now. And its pitiful light was only enough to illuminate his pallid, sweaty face staring into it intently.

Like he could understand it.

"Strange how we never figured it out, isn't it?" he whispered. "We listened to her song for so long and yet we never once even suspected there might be a language, let alone try to understand it."

He reached out, as if to touch it, and the light trembled, fragile and weak.

"Even now, it's like listening to a child..." He stared at the light, winced. "I understand a few words, but they're out of order, more sounds than speech. But I know what they want. And they know what I want."

He closed his eyes. His breath made his body shake, every gasp an effort.

"They know what I'm afraid of."

He reached out for the light. A stray, glowing tendril separated itself from the sphere, as if attempting to reach back.

"In my heart, I know I wasn't lying when I said the Nul Emperor needed to be overthrown." He sucked in a hot breath. "I said a nul cannot lead the Imperium, and that was true. I said it dishonored the memory of we who built the Imperium, and that was also true. Many of those who entered the conspiracy with me believed them."

A sad smile creased his face. The light let out a soft, mournful whimper.

"Jindu, most of all,". he said. "He had seen too much death, lost too many friends to let the Imperium crumble under a nul's watch. I did not lie to him when I said we had to save it...but I didn't tell them the truth. Perhaps I didn't even know it until now.

"But on that night, when we...when I sacrificed your power, when I gazed into the portal and saw her looking back at me, they revealed what I had always feared. They showed me a world without magic at all. Where the nuls walked over roads under which our Dust had been buried and thought not once about the greatness that shaped this land."

He let out a sigh. The light flickered, a candlelight that threatened to snuff itself out.

"Perhaps it was that fear, that fear that I would disappear and someone else would be there to fill a void I thought only I could fill, that led me to…what happened with you. With your power. For that, I regret it. But I do not lament what I did."

He rose to a shaky knee, took a few deep breaths.

"It was for all mages. For this land we tamed. For the lives we built. For the worlds we have yet to create, that *they* could help us create. My fault was my passion. I see that now. And I am sorry."

He rose to his feet, his arms hanging heavy at his sides. He drew in deep, gasping breaths, his body shaking. Slowly, he turned to me, eyes dim and soft.

"So, if you still want to kill me after—"

Steel flashed. He stopped talking. He stared down at the blade in his chest like he wasn't sure how it had gotten there. He looked back up at me, staring into my eyes. He blinked, mouthed a word.

"But—"

And I stabbed him again.

He fell to one knee.

I stabbed again.

He fell onto his back.

And I just kept stabbing. His body twitched with every cut, every red blossom that burst across his skin. I stabbed him until he emptied out on the floor. I carved him until he was more meat than man.

Until his body was almost completely red. Until the light left him entirely. Until I took the hilt and found it stuck fast in his body.

I stepped back. I whispered a word.

"Sorry."

Not to Vraki. But to the weight burning on my hip. After all this time, the Cacophony hadn't even been the one to kill him. But he didn't seem to mind—perhaps he appreciated the poetry of a common piece of steel bringing down the scourge of the Imperium in a basement full of dried goods. Or maybe he just enjoyed being here to see it.

Through it all, the light remained.

The tiny glowing sphere trembled and shuddered but made no

other move. And though it lacked a face, or even eyes, I knew it was looking at me. It turned its attention back toward Vraki. It let out a single, crystalline note that slowly died as the light, too, dimmed.

Until they both stopped.

And I was left alone, in a dark place, cold and quiet.

SIXTY

LOWSTAFF

Maybe this was just my life now.

Maybe I would forever be going into dark places and coming back out to find everything destroyed.

Maybe someday I would look back on this and call myself clichéd.

But when I emerged into the ruins of Lowstaff after who knows how long I spent below, I couldn't yet feel anything but sorrow.

The freehold wore its wounds like jewelry—bullet-hole necklaces and crowns of corpses. Fires still burned from windows and doors, their laughter occasionally punctuated by the groan of a building collapsing under the weight of the flames. Spikes of never-melting ice punched through suits of Paladin armor; repeating gun nests lay abandoned and shattered.

The dead were an afterthought, corpses of Revolutionaries and Imperials lying still in the wake of the carnage. Another price paid, another Barter offered. I took some small, cold comfort that I saw only soldiers dead. No civilians.

However many people Cavric had gotten out, they'd still live.

"Thank goodness for Sal the Cacophony," they'd say. "Our homes are ruined, our livelihoods destroyed, our very memories wiped the fuck out, but thanks to her, we'll at least be alive to appreciate dying in crushing poverty."

Actually, they probably wouldn't say that. There'd be, like, a *lot* more cussing and crying and oaths of vengeance.

But I wouldn't blame them if they did.

A cry filled the air. I glanced up and saw a black bird with white eyes, the same from when I had woken up, sitting atop the crown of a smoldering building. It regarded me carefully for a moment, as if impressed that I had managed to destroy an entire city since it had seen me last.

There was something terribly familiar about that look.

It turned one way; I turned the other. And we both vanished into the smoke.

When I walked out of that still, silent ruin and onto a hill outside the gates, I looked back and saw the lights of the fires dying, swallowed by the night. Soon, it'd stand as still and silent as Stark's Mutter. Vraki had taken every soul from that town but left its houses standing. I had destroyed their homes, but the people were still alive to curse my name.

Fair trade, I figured.

But I hadn't done it alone.

The armies had retreated after the skirmish. There would be negotiations for the corpses later, bodies returned to each other. When the mages turned to Dust, their magic would fade—even Vraki's horrors would be forgotten. The Revolution would build more machines. More mages would be born. They'd find a new place to ruin and we'd do this all over again and maybe I'd be alive to see it and maybe I wouldn't.

Maybe Vraki was wrong. Maybe no one ever gets replaced because nothing ever changes. Not really.

But then again, maybe he was right. Because he sure as shit wouldn't be around to see what happened next.

I reached into my pocket. I pulled a sheet of parchment out and unfolded it, looked at the top of the list, and pressed a piece of charcoal against it.

~~Vraki the Gate.~~

I stared at that name for a good, long moment. And for another good, long moment, I didn't even recognize the name. It looked less like a collection of letters and more like... like a landmark. Like I could only see the shape of it and know what it was, where I stood in relation to it.

And now that it was gone... I didn't know what to feel when I looked at the space where it used to be.

But in the next second, I felt only a burning heat on my hip.

And I knew I wasn't alone.

The whisper of wind, the soft moan of steel filled my ears. I felt the cold tip of the blade leveled at the back of my neck. I turned around, felt the tip an inch from the hollow of my throat as I stared down a length of black steel into a pair of eyes I used to know.

Jindu just stared back at me.

It's funny. You only ever remember people in pieces: eyes, hands, smiles. Once you look at the whole of them, they look unfamiliar. In my head, Jindu had always been a perfect smile, shining eyes, a flashing sword, and nothing else. But standing before me, he was a man. A man with tense hands, messy hair, dirty skin, slumping shoulders. And every part of him was shaking.

I felt the chill of his sword, even felt it brush against my throat. But I didn't even blink. This wasn't the man I saw when I slept, the last thing I saw in that dark place.

This man, whoever he was, couldn't kill me.

"Vraki," he whispered, voice hoarse. "Is he..."

I nodded slowly. "He is."

His body shook. I could see his fingers tense, struggle to hold on to the blade that suddenly looked too big for him.

"Did he..." Jindu paused, swallowed. "Did he say anything?"

"He did," I replied.

Breathlessly, he asked, "What?" After a long moment, he stepped forward, tilted my chin back with the blade. "*What did he say?*"

I didn't move backward. I didn't blink. And when I answered him, I didn't whisper.

"It doesn't matter."

Those were shitty last words. I always thought I'd say something more epic. Something that would make undergarments tighter when people watched the opera of my life just before the curtain fell. But they felt right. And if they were what I said before I got a sword run through me, then that was just fine.

Liette was alive. Cavric was alive. Vraki was dead. That wasn't so bad. And it was fitting that it would end like it began.

With Jindu's blade. With my blood.

I closed my eyes. I waited.

And I heard the blade fall.

I looked down, saw it glimmering in the dirt. The man before me stepped back, hands shaking too hard to hold the weapon that had cut me. His eyes darted, as if he couldn't bear to lay eyes on me anymore. But everywhere he looked, he saw the bodies, the ruin, the blood that had been wrought by Vraki.

Vraki, whom he had followed.

Vraki, whom he had betrayed me for.

Vraki, who lay in a pile of dirt in a pauper's basement, all his plans come to nothing.

"How?" Jindu's eyes searched the distant ruin of Lowstaff, as though he could find an answer in the carnage for a question he didn't know. "He was supposed to save us... He was going to fix things... He told me..." His hands trembled, in need of a blade to hold, a weapon that would fix everything. They found only his skull, clutching his temples. "And I... I fought for him... I killed for him..."

I watched him there, collapsing to his knees and searching the dirt for an answer that, up until now, Vraki had provided for him. And now that he was dead, and left nothing more than Dust, Jindu didn't even know the question anymore. And I, standing and watching him silently, didn't have any answers for him.

But someone had an answer for me.

And he whispered it on a burning breath.

Almost unconsciously, I reached for him. And, as if he had been waiting for that, he leapt to my hand. The Cacophony seethed, giggling in anticipation as I walked toward Jindu, raised my weapon, and leveled it at his head.

"I ruined it..." Jindu whispered. "The Imperium, the mages, the... I betrayed...I fought...you..."

The broken babble of his voice became background noise, just another moaning wind and crackling fire. An empty collection of words shattered by the click of a hammer being drawn back.

"Salazanca."

Until he said my name.

I wasn't ready for the sight of his eyes, uncomfortably bright and clear and looking straight at me. I wasn't ready to wonder how, for all the times I had seen him in my dreams, he must have seen me. I wasn't ready for him to see me like he did.

What had I been in his dreams? An obstacle? A shadow? Just a collection of regrets put together in a human shape? I didn't know. But when he looked at me now, he looked at me like he used to, and I know what he saw.

A woman. White-haired. Covered in dust. Tattoos running down her arms. Her body decorated with scars.

That he had put there.

"I...I can't..."

And when I looked at him, down in the dirt and without a weapon, I saw something else, too. I'm not going to tell you it was anything as saccharine or satisfying as true love or shit like that. I just saw a man.

A man who had been there when I remembered still being happy. A man I had stood beside and fought with and yelled at and screamed at. A man who had been there when I still had the sky instead of the scars.

The last part of my life that had ever been normal.

My hand shook. The gun burned. My breath left me. And I kept staring at him until I didn't know what I was looking at anymore.

But when he vanished and only a bare patch of earth remained... I let him go.

And I was left alone with the dying fires and the cold night sky and the gun burning in my hand.

I felt a surge of agony rush through my hand, into my bones. The Cacophony roared soundlessly through my skin, carved through my sinew with burning knives. He was displeased, of course—this death was the whole reason we had made this deal and I had just let it go away. The pain of his anger hurt, I won't lie, but when I thought about pulling the trigger, when I thought about taking the very last time I felt normal and casting it to the wind...

Well, like I said, his wasn't the worst pain I had felt.

It wasn't even going to be the worst pain I felt that night.

"Why?"

That pain came when I heard Liette's voice. And when I turned around to see her—her face smudged with ash and dirt, strands of hair falling around her face, one lens of her glasses cracked so that she looked at me with those eyes, big and fractured—I thought I might die.

"You had him," she whispered like every word was a razor pulled out of her throat. "You had him right there... and you didn't kill him."

"You came back." I hadn't intended that to sound as accusatory as it did.

"Of course I came back." She hadn't intended that to sound as angry as it did. "How the fuck was I *not* going to come back? I always come back. Just like you do. And neither of us has the decency to die so the other will just *stop doing this*."

"Liette, I—"

"Why?" She stepped toward me, hesitant, like she was walking across profaned ground. Maybe she was. "Every morning I woke up next to you and saw you staring out the window. Every time you left me without a word. Everything we could have had and don't. All because of *him*. All of that, every last piece, could have been fixed if you'd just *killed* him... but you let it go."

It hurt to look at her, so I looked away. But it hurt more to have her look at me. And when she reached out, trembling like she was going to touch something so delicate, and laid those expert fingers on my cheeks and forced me to look back at her...

Something inside me broke.

"Why?" she asked again.

I couldn't speak. My throat was too tight. The wind was too loud. Everything was too much.

"Tell me," she whispered. "I came back, Sal. I'll keep coming back. No matter how much it hurts, no matter how many times I fail, I'll come back every time if you just *tell me*."

It felt like being punched. Like she knocked the wind out of me with her very first word and I couldn't find my breath anymore.

"Tell me how to make this work." Her voice was breathless in that way it was when machines don't work and nothing ever goes right. "Tell me what I have to do. Tell me what I have to say. There has to be something I can do, some way to fix this, some way to make you *normal*."

In hindsight, I had an answer for her.

In hindsight, I would have told her that it's like... I've got this knife in my chest. It hurts me when I walk, when I breathe, when my heart beats. But I can't take it out, I've lived with it so long. It's the only thing holding in my blood. And if it ever comes out, I don't know if there'll be anything left.

In hindsight, I would have told her that I don't think I know what normal is anymore. I don't know if I ever did.

"Sal."

In hindsight, I had an answer.

"Tell me."

But at that moment, when her eyes were big and fractured and full of tears...

"Please."

I said nothing.

I said nothing when she dropped her hands from my face.

I said nothing when she turned around and walked away.

I said nothing as I watched her disappear.

And when the wind died to a whisper, I looked back to Lowstaff. I sat down on that hill. And I watched the freehold crumble as its fires died out, one by one.

SIXTY-ONE

HIGHTOWER

A nd then?"

Sal's eyes were fixed on a scar upon the palm of her hand, her finger tracing its length, still old and sinewy even as tender flesh grew around it. She glanced up suddenly at Tretta.

"Huh?"

Tretta narrowed her eyes. "And then what?"

"Then what what?" Sal asked, oblivious.

"Then what happened?" Tretta had intended to sound significantly less incredulous and far more angry. "You killed Vraki, you let Jindu live, you watched Lowstaff be destroyed. What happened after that?"

"Oh." Sal shrugged her shoulders. "Nothing."

Tretta's jaw set. "Not nothing."

"Nothing." Sal leaned back, shrugged. "I sat there on that hill until I saw someone in a blue coat come out."

"A Revolutionary," Tretta noted. "And then what?"

"And then there were a bunch of guns in my face, chains on my wrist, a long drive, and"—she held out her hands, as demonstrative as her manacles would allow—"here we are."

"*Here we are?*" Tretta fell back to her seat, as though she had just been punched in the stomach. "You can't be fucking serious."

"Well, what were you expecting?" Sal asked.

"I...I don't..." Tretta leaned forward on the table, brows furrowed as though she could suss out some pattern in the sense of the wood. "What happened to the Freemaker? Where did she go? What of Jindu the Blade? What about the rest of the Crown Conspiracy? What about Zanze the Beast?"

She seized the table's edge as though she could simply snap it in two.

"What happened to *Cavric*?"

Sal shrugged. "Gone."

Tretta's mouth hung open. Her eyes forgot how to blink.

"Gone?"

"Vanished during the battle. Perhaps he fled. Or perhaps Vraki didn't leave enough of him to be found. Either way, he's gone."

"Gone?" Tretta wanted to scream, but found she couldn't find the breath for it. "It can't simply end like that. All that time, all that talk and you just...just..."

"Unsatisfying, isn't it?" Sal let out a black chuckle. "You always think it'll be like it is in opera. Heroes victorious, or at least satisfactorily dead, and someone presumably kisses someone else at the end." She looked up, glanced over Tretta appraisingly, and shrugged. "But that's not really how it goes, is it?"

She looked back down at her hands, scarred and grimy, flecks of blood and dirt under her fingernails. She stared at them like she expected them to stare back at her and tell the rest of the story.

"Operas are better, though. Whether they end happily or not, they end. You don't have to worry about what happened or what else might happen. No matter how many dead people are onstage, the curtain drops and you go back to living. But if you're on the other side of that curtain..."

She curled her hands into fists, set them upon the table, and closed her eyes.

"All you're left with are the bodies."

A silence hung over the table. The same silence that follows a blade drawn, a body found cold in bed, a word spoken that can never be taken back. For a moment, Tretta was tempted to leave it at that, leave this woman and her tale to this room and go drink until she couldn't hear the sound of a gun fired and a body hitting the floor.

"Birdshit."

But she still had a job to do.

"*Birdshit*," Tretta spat. "You expect me to believe that?"

"Well, *I* thought it was poignant."

"When I first laid eyes upon you, I thought you another Vagrant, nothing more than a killer," Tretta said. "But as we spoke, I thought there might be more to you, something deeper than the thousands of other killers roaming the Scar."

"And now?" Sal asked.

"And now I see you're both." She thrust a finger accusingly at Sal. "The sole difference between you and the other scum crawling across the earth is that your depths have no end. There's nothing you won't do, no honor you won't betray, no one you won't kill to get what you want. Your farce of a confession is proof enough of that, if any of it is even true."

"What, you think I made it all up for no reason?"

"I said you were scum, not stupid." Tretta narrowed her eyes to skewers, pinned Sal to her chair with them. "You, who destroyed two cities to kill a handful of people, who deals with thieves and assassins, who ruins lives simply by showing up..." She shook her head. "Nothing you do is without reason. Neither is this. You're plotting something."

"Like what?" Sal laid both her hands on the table and regarded Tretta through a serene stare. "Like perhaps I struck a bargain with Alothenes? With Jindu? Like one of them has been tailing me this whole way and I've simply been biding time for a rescue to come crashing through that door right about..."

The reflected light of the lantern flickered in Sal's eyes.

"Now?"

A breathless silence hung between them. And it took a moment for Tretta to realize she had grown tense. Some part of her—that small, niggling pain at the base of her neck that had kept her alive across a dozen battlefields—bade her to turn around, to draw her weapon and start firing on a door that was about to burst open, blazing with gunfire and magic. That pain spread down her spine, into her fingertips as she clutched the table, ready to leap out of her chair and start shooting.

Right up until Sal started smiling anyway.

"Yeah," she said. "That would have been pretty good, wouldn't it?"

Tretta felt like the correct answer was to snarl a curse or, even better, just shoot her. She was surprised to find that, as the tension leaked out of her in a tired sigh, all she could manage was a weary nod.

"It would have."

There should have been rage, she knew. Rage for the time wasted, for the lives lost, for Cavric gone, and for the senseless destruction and endless suffering that followed in this woman's wake. If it was true, if *any* of it was true, then the dead demanded that much of an answer.

And yet, Tretta could simply stare. And ask.

"Why did you tell me this, then?" She folded her arms over her chest. "Why any of it?"

Sal's smile was as long and as slow and as sad as the last broken string on an old harp.

"Like I said at the beginning." She looked down at her hands. "This is all I'm going to leave behind." She reached up, traced the scar over her eye with two fingers. "Even before this, before the gun, before the list, I didn't have much to my name but corpses. It's only gotten worse since then. This story, what I did, is all I have left to give."

She let her hands drop. She closed her eyes.

"Everything else is just dust and scars."

Rather annoying, Tretta thought, that Sal should wait until now to be interesting.

It galled her to even be interested in this killer. And yet, her voice, her words, hung over Tretta and settled upon her shoulders like snowfall. After all the carnage wrought by her namesake, Sal's final gift should be words.

But perhaps that was fitting.

After all, was it not the Great General's words that hung hallowed in the cadres across the Scar? Was it not the words of the great commanders of the Revolution that spurred the soldiers to battle? Were those words what gave Cavric Proud the strength to continue through his ordeal? Were words all that anyone ever really left behind?

A philosopher could give an answer. Or perhaps a poet.

Tretta was simply a soldier with a duty.

Wordlessly, she rose out of her chair. She drew her hand cannon and circled around to Sal's back. Without quite realizing that she had done it, let alone why, she reached down and placed a hand on Sal's shoulder.

And pressed the barrel of the gun against the back of her head.

"No."

There was the groan of wood against the floor. Sal rose out of her chair and turned around. Her smile was gone. Her eyes were hard as she looked into Tretta's.

"If you kill me," she said softly, "you look me in the eyes when you do it."

There was the urge to backhand her for her audacity. No one, let alone a filthy Vagrant, gave an order like that to a Governor-Militant of the Revolution. Protocol demanded she be executed from behind. Pride demanded she be shot through the heart instead of the head.

Yet, for the second time, Tretta surprised herself.

Without another word, she placed the pistol against Sal's head. She drew the hammer back and she looked into the eyes of a killer, a thug, a Vagrant.

Salazanca ki Ioril.

Red Cloud.

Sal the Cacophony.

And the woman looked back at Tretta.

And she did not blink.

Not until the explosion, anyway.

Tretta lowered the gun. The smell of smoke filled the air. The room seemed deathly silent for a moment.

And then the sirens started to wail.

She rushed to the cell's window, peered up to see boots thundering across the street. Revolutionary soldiers barked orders as they sprinted toward the sound of the explosion, even as civilians ran screaming in the opposite direction. Through the sound of carnage, she could make out words like *attack* and *eastern wall*. She started to call out to the soldiers.

No one could hear her over the sound of the second explosion.

From her vantage, she saw a great plume of flame rise over the houses of the city, smoke lifting into the air on black wings. The sirens blared louder to be heard over the sounds of more screams, more orders, more boots. Through the chaos, she only barely heard the voice behind her speak softly.

"Tretta?"

She turned around just in time to see a pair of heavy iron manacles smash into her face. She collapsed to the ground, stunned as a pair of hands rifled through her coat. Blood cloyed her nostrils, darkness ringed her vision. Her senses returned in time to see a pair of empty manacles thud to the floor, a key bouncing off of them.

And then she looked up into the barrel of her own hand cannon. And behind it, a pair of blue eyes shining brightly over a broad, scar-framed grin.

"Turns out," Sal the Cacophony said, "I actually *was* plotting something."

Fear fought pain for control of Tretta's body and both of them sent her scrambling across the floor, struggling to get away. Half blind from the pain, blood spilling down her face, she found the table completely by accident. Her hands groped around until she found the lid of a box, flipped it open, and wrapped her hands around a grip inside.

She didn't even know what she was holding until she felt it grow warm in her hands.

She whirled around, holding the Cacophony up against Sal. The Vagrant stared back at her, tense. She held up a hand, as if to ask for calm. And that's when Tretta pulled the trigger.

It wouldn't budge.

She tried again, pulling as hard as she could on it. But the trigger was frozen in place. She slammed the heel of her palm against it, as though she could simply beat it into working for her. And when the barrel stared back at her, grinning and empty, she let out a scream.

"Won't shoot for you?"

She looked up, expecting to see Sal smiling that insufferable smile. Instead, the Vagrant wore a look of concern as she stared down at the gun.

"For a second there, I thought he might," she said. "He wasn't happy about this plan. But I managed to convince him. We made a deal, after all."

Sal raised the gun. Tretta's body went tense as she felt her own metal pressed against her brow. And only then did Sal smile.

"You want to see how it ends, don't you?"

— ◄►◄ ─

Whatever he had done to earn the name, Clerk Inspire did not. Nor was he concerned with that, nor anything else but the distant wail of warning sirens through the city. Plumes of smoke wafted through the windows of the cadre, filling his lungs as the distant cries of soldiers filled his ears, each sending his flight through the cadre halls into a frenzy.

Somehow, a very long list of things had gone to shit in a very short amount of time.

And exactly how much time that left him to get the fuck out of here, he did not know and wasn't inclined to stick around to find out. He rushed down the halls of the cadre, past the offices of the commanders and down the stairs. The cadre quarters were empty of soldiers, all of them having gone to check on the explosions. Inspire sighed with relief and began to rush toward the exit when the only thing that had gone right also went wrong.

The doors of the cadre burst open, flinging him aside as a quartet of soldiers emerged from outside, gunpikes drawn. The one in the lead, a young fellow whose name he hadn't bothered to learn, looked at him with a mixture of shock and resentment.

"Inspire?" he asked. "Where the hell do you think you're going?"

"Getting out of here, obviously." Inspire paused before realizing that had sounded a little too confident. He coughed, made a show of cowering, and whimpered, "Th-the explosions are so frightening…"

"There's no enemy behind them," the soldier grunted. "We've searched the city and seen no invasion. They didn't even hit any occupied buildings. That's when we figured it might be a distraction for—"

"*Sergeant!*" one of the others soldiers barked.

The gunpikes clicked as they went up, drawn upon the doorway leading down to the cells. Inspire shrank away from his now-rather-inconveniently-blocked doorway—he could still slip out, he thought, once they were distracted by…

"Let's all settle down, shall we?"

And that's when things got worse.

Inspire glanced toward the doorway where the Governor-Militant emerged, her steps staggered and a furious glare painted across her face. The manacles securing her wrists behind her back clinked over the sound of her growling as one tattooed arm wrapped around her throat and the other raised a hand cannon to Tretta's temple. From behind, a single blue eye looked out and a single white eyebrow cocked.

"This situation doesn't look like it'll be helped by anyone getting excited." Sal the Cacophony's voice lilted as she hoisted Tretta forward. "Does it?"

"Do not do anything to aid this scum, soldier," Tretta snarled, struggling against her captor. "That is an *order*."

"Release the Governor-Militant, filth," the lead soldier growled.

"I'm hurt." Sal clicked her tongue. "You were so eager for us to spend time together and now you're pointing a gun at me. I'm so insulted, I might just have to leave." The pistol's hammer clicked. "Be so kind as to fetch my things, won't you?"

Inspire's heart hammered. His breath went short. He had hoped to escape before something like this happened. He had hoped not to be in this spot at all. How had he thought this was a good idea? *How?*

It was supposed to be so simple. Get in. Grab the gun. Get out. But when was anything with *her* ever simple?

He glanced toward the door. The soldiers were all focused on the Vagrant and her hostage, but were standing so packed together he didn't have a chance of pushing through them. They simply stood there, eyes locked, fingers pointedly off their triggers.

They weren't going to shoot.

"Those are your demands?" the lead soldier asked.

"More like a request," Sal replied. "Just return what's owed to me and I'll make sure only one person dies here." She glanced toward a nearby desk, gestured with her chin. "I believe they were put there when you first brought me here."

"Do not listen to her, soldier," Tretta snarled. "You take orders from *me*, not her, and I am commanding you to disregard her. Shoot through me, if you must, but do *not* let this filth escape."

The soldiers stood, hands shaking, eyes darting, as if they could find an answer somewhere in the room. Tretta snarled, tried to lunge forward as Sal held her back.

"That is an *order!*" she barked.

Inspire swallowed hard. No way out down here. He had to get to a window, had to find a new shape. A flyer, something light—that would do it. He edged back toward the stairs, trembling. He had to get out of here, had to get free and warn...

"Inspire."

The lead soldier gestured with his chin toward the desk.

"Do what she says."

"*SOLDIER!*" Tretta snarled.

Further protests were muffled as Sal clamped a gloved hand over her mouth. "Your hospitality knows no limits, kind soldiers of the

Revolution." She glanced toward Inspire. "If you'd kindly hurry, though? I suspect the fires must be growing. Every man is needed in the city, yes?"

Inspire gulped down the urge to run. The lead soldier had his gunpike trained on him. If he fled now, he'd be shot quicker than he could flee, quicker than he could change. He nodded weakly, shuffled to the desk—he knew where her effects were, already having rifled through them in his search for anything useful. Quietly, he collected them: a dirty scarf, a satchel rattling with bullets, and a bottle of whiskey.

"Take them to her," the lead soldier grunted.

Meekly, he toted the small burden toward Sal and began to set them at her feet.

"Ah, ah."

He looked up. Sal extended a hand from Tretta's mouth.

"Hand them to me, won't you?"

He held her effects in trembling hands, fighting back the urge to flee. Quietly, he reached out and she took her gear back in one hand. He tried to keep his eyes low, but in a moment of nervous instinct, he glanced up and saw her looking back at him. And that's when he realized...

She knows.

He had to get out of here. They had what they wanted now. He could run as soon as it was over. He could still escape. He could still...

"I know you guys don't have any good taste in opera," Sal said. "So, when your Great General asks you what happened here today, let me suggest a plausible explanation." Her voice went cold. "You tell them that you did your duty. You tell them that you made your choices. You tell them that you did your best, but you got in my fucking way."

Inspire started shuffling toward the stairs, heart hammering. Her eyes tracked him as he went, narrowing.

"And you tell them no one..."

His skin twitched. His body trembled.

"No one..."

He called his magic. He heard the Lady's song.

"No one gets away from Sal the Cacophony."

Gunfire cracked. A red blossom erupted from the lead soldier's thigh. He went down screaming. The other soldiers immediately turned toward him, away from Sal's smoking hand cannon and from the Governor-Militant, whom she had grabbed by the shoulder and shoved toward them.

With a cry, Tretta bowled into the pack of soldiers and went down in a tangled heap. A stray soldier lashed out, struck Inspire, and sent him sprawling to the ground. He glanced up, caught a glimpse of Sal reaching into her satchel, pulling out a shell, and drawing the Cacophony from the waist of her trousers. There was writing on the shell, writing he had seen before. A spell. What had it been?

He didn't remember until he saw her draw the Cacophony on him and stared down its grinning barrel as she pulled the trigger.

Ah, right.

The world exploded in a bright flash of light.

Sunflare.

The soldiers screamed as the bright light burst across their eyes, blinding them. From the sound of it, there was a lot of thrashing and struggling as well. He couldn't tell, of course. His vision pitched into an empty white light, he blindly groped about for the stairs, breathing hard. He reached a hand out, expecting to find a step.

And instead found another gloved hand.

His vision cleared just enough to look up into her grin.

"You didn't think I'd forget about you, did you?" Sal the Cacophony asked.

As she brought her namesake up over her head.

And then down upon his face.

And the empty whiteness turned black.

SIXTY-TWO

THE SCAR

From atop the ridge, Sal stared out over the city of Hightower in flames and wondered how many more times she was going to see this sight.

Even here, so high up on the city's outskirts, she could still see the fires. Great columns of flame rose twisting into the predawn sky, smoky, sated sighs escaping them as they glutted themselves on wood and mortar.

How many buildings had been lost to the flame? she wondered. How many homes? How many shops? Would these fires die out? Or would she just keep setting new ones until they devoured everything?

"They were empty."

His voice sounded more haggard than it used to, his breath sounded more tired, but she knew it all the same. And though the man standing behind her wore a dirty brown coat and days of stubble instead of the nice blue and clean shave he once he did, she recognized Cavric when he came up beside her.

"One's an armory." He pointed to one column of flame, then to another. "The other, a derelict prison. Once executions became the norm, it was abandoned." He lowered his hand, watched the fires eat. "I made sure no one was in them."

Sal sniffed. "Is that what took so long?"

"It was the last of the Righteous Fires. I had to be careful." Cavric regarded her through exhausted eyes. "I didn't have to do this, you know."

She nodded. It had been some small fortune that he had been the only blue coat to emerge from Lowstaff. Some small fortune that, after all that had happened, he would listen to her and agree to this plot.

It hadn't been particularly intelligent, after all, to be taken into Revolutionary custody intentionally. They could have shot her on the spot once she surrendered; Tretta could have lost her temper and shot her at any moment—really, there were a hundred things that could have gone wrong and at least eighty-two of them ended with her brains splattered on the floor.

Why Cavric had agreed to it at all, she still had a hard time understanding.

"Was anyone..." he began to ask before he seemed to realize he was afraid of the answer. "I mean, did you—"

"I had to shoot someone, yeah." She felt his eyes widen and sighed. "In the leg. No one got killed."

His sigh was a stale, wasted breath.

"So, do they know, then?"

When she looked at him, his eyes were intent on hers. The weariness burned away, revealing a spark of that fear, that anger, that passion that she had gotten to know during their time together.

"Do they know what happened to me?" he asked.

For the last time he ever would, he still looked like a Revolutionary.

Sal shook her head. "I told them you had vanished. Probably dead. I don't think they'll be looking for you anymore."

That spark died. The same fervor that had carried him through his military life vanished, buried beneath something hard. Not unfeeling, Sal noted—the same concern flashed in those eyes as ever, but gone was the Revolutionary zeal and the common man's doubt. All that remained was another dirty, tired soul in the Scar.

"Should I ask why?" she asked.

"You shouldn't." A moment of silence passed before he closed his eyes and sighed. "Are you going to anyway?"

"I mean, I was definitely thinking it."

"I was Revolutionary from birth," Cavric said. "I saw the same operas, I heard the same speeches, attended the same schools as everyone else. And for a long time, I thought the same thing: that we were there to help people, to make things better." His lips twisted into a frown. "Then Lastlight happened. Then Lowstaff happened. Then *you* happened."

Sal looked away from him, back over the flames.

"I'm not going to apologize for what I did."

"I didn't ask you to," Cavric said. "You just showed me that we could build the biggest guns to make the biggest mountain of corpses we could...and people would still suffer. Because there would still be people like you."

"You mean killers."

"I mean people who don't hear the same thing," he said. "People who see every rule of every city and act like it's just not there." He shook his head. "I don't think you're a killer, Sal. You kill people, but it's not the same. You're just a...a..." He sighed. "You can tear down the nasty shit in this world. But someone's going to have to build something better back up."

A long moment of silence passed before he glowered at her.

"I'm not going to thank you."

"I didn't ask you to," she said, though she had certainly been thinking he *should*. Instead, she simply glanced back at him. "Where are you going now?"

"Same place you are, I suppose," he said as he turned away from her. "Somewhere I need to be." He raised a hand in a weary wave. "See you around, Sal. Maybe."

There was a small part of her that wanted to stop him. A small part of her that wasn't willing to let go of what they'd had on the road, to let go of someone who had looked at her like she could do anything, even put down the gun. There was a small part of her, a savage little knife of her that lodged itself in her neck, that wanted to reach out and grab him and pull him close and...

And do what? she wondered.

Tell him it was all worth it, in the end? Or tell him the opposite, that trading all those lives for seven on a list wasn't a good trade? Or maybe just collapse and hope he caught her?

Maybe there was a good answer to that question. Maybe she could even think of one. But by the time she had thought of one, he had already disappeared over the ridge.

And so she sighed and laid a hand on the gun at her hip. Through her glove, she could feel him seething. And though he had no voice that she would ever want to hear, she could almost imagine the grin of his barrel whispering to her.

Let's finish it, then.

She turned and trudged down the other side of the ridge. Behind a pair of large rocks, she found her campsite. Congeniality glanced up from a rabbit carcass Cavric had so kindly left her when he brought her here for as long as it took her to realize she wasn't interested in what Sal had to do and returned to her feast. It wasn't a particularly big rabbit. She'd be done soon.

Just as well, Sal thought.

This wouldn't take long.

She found Clerk Inspire's unconscious body where she had left it, pressed up against the stone. He still drew breath, though he did not stir. And so she took Jeff out of his sheath, checked his edge, stared at the clerk...

And waited to hear the Lady's song.

His magic stirred before he did. The distant note of her song lit up Sal's ears as Inspire's skin trembled, rippled like water struck by a stone. His body twisted, changed, arms vanishing into his sides and body becoming elongated.

His eyes snapped open.

His jaws followed.

The great serpent that had been Inspire lunged at her, scales black as pitch and mouth gaping. As though this were just a brief nuisance—as, indeed, it was—her hand shot out and seized the beast by its throat.

"Oh, come *on*." She met its fanged maw with a sneer. "I take all the trouble to track you down and you give me a fucking snake?"

She brought up the hilt of her sword, smashed it against the animal's jaw, and sent it writhing to the ground. Its skin shimmered as the Lady's song rose once again, and in another second, a great black bird with wide white eyes scrambled to its feet and flapped its wings in a desperate frenzy.

"Why not a wolf?" Sal's hand shot out, seized the bird's tail as it clumsily tried to flap away. "Why not a rothac? A giant crab with a spiky shell or maybe a really big ape? I don't know, *something* better than this."

She jerked her hand back, slamming the beast back down to the ground. It tried to scramble for footing again when her foot came down on its wing. There was a loud snapping sound. The bird's beak craned open in a decidedly human scream.

"Did you think I wouldn't notice?" she asked. "The chicken in Stark's Mutter? The turkey in Vigil? The fucking *rat*? You tried to beat Sal the fucking Cacophony by turning into a *rat*?"

The bird's scream became a moan as she brought her boot down upon its neck, her heel digging into its throat. She aimed the sword at its neck.

"Come on, Zanze," she said. "Is this really the shape you want to die in?"

The bird lay still upon the earth, breast shuddering with labored breathing. Slowly, it closed its eyes. And the Lady's song rang out one more time.

When it opened its eyes, there was a human throat beneath the heel of her boot.

"Lucky guess," Zanze the Beast groaned.

Or, at least, he had once been a man. Years of magic had left the Maskmage almost without features. His nose was nothing more than a pair of nostrils. His eyes were wide and lidless. His skin was pallid, hairless, and pale. All that served to differentiate Zanze the Beast from a very large grub was the familiar groan in his voice.

"Aw, Zanze." Sal made a mocking pout. "You already made me spend this whole fucking time hunting you. Don't insult me on top of everything." She grinned at him. "I figured it out back in Lowstaff, once you showed up outside my window. You've been trailing me since Stark's Mutter, haven't you?"

"I was covering Vraki's trail," he grunted. "He thought someone would come looking for us."

"And you didn't think it'd be me? I'm hurt, Zanze." She shifted her weight, ground her heel into his neck, drawing a scream from him. "Truly."

"Yeah, fuck me, right?" he said through clenched teeth.

"Not even if you could turn into a bottle of whiskey with an ass," Sal replied. "But you didn't do that, did you? You turned into a Revolutionary. I saw you, back in Lowstaff."

"Left that part out of your story, didn't you?" he muttered. "I was listening."

"Like I'm going to tell a Governor-fucking-Militant I let myself get captured to kill a shape-shifting mage hiding in her midst." Sal leaned forward on her knee, driving her boot farther against him. "And somehow, that sentence isn't even the most fucked-up thing about this. I'd have thought you'd flee, Zanze. Vraki was dead. The Crown Conspiracy was over. You had to have known that, once I found you, I'd kill you. You had no reason to stick around in the cadre, unless..."

She leaned forward, her voice a harsh whisper.

"How long have you been keeping this up, Zanze?" she asked. "Working for Vraki, working for the Revolution, who else are you taking money from?"

"Now you're insulting me, Salazanca." Zanze's laugh was throaty and guttural. "You think they'd call me Zanze the Beast if I cared about money? They'd call me Zanze the Girl With a Nice Pair of

Tits and a Pretty Mouth and Give Me Your Fucking Inheritance, You Dick." His body deflated. "Nah. It was never about money. I'm the Beast. All I cared about was survival."

He craned his neck to look at her out the corner of one white, wide eye. And Sal, for reasons she couldn't quite explain, felt colder.

"You told Tretta a good story, but you left out a few parts." He chuckled, his voice black and rasping. "I thought I heard you slip up a few times, thought she'd catch on, but she never did. She thinks your gun is just a funny magic weapon."

His eye craned lower, toward the burning brass hanging at her hip.

"She doesn't realize that thing is alive, does she?"

His lip curled back in an ugly sneer.

"She doesn't know you've been feeding it."

That cold feeling crept over her, settling like a wispy cloak across her body. He knew, then. Of course he knew—he'd been following her the entire time; he had probably seen it happen.

The pang of dread she felt, she told herself, was ridiculous. What did she care for the judgment of a fiend like Zanze the Beast? What had she done that could possibly be worse than what he'd done to end up on her list?

And yet...

A sudden surge of heat brought her attention down to her hip. The Cacophony, she knew, was staring at her expectantly, reminding her.

No one could say that Sal the Cacophony was a liar. She had told Tretta Stern that she and the gun had made a deal. It wasn't her fault that Tretta Stern had falsely concluded what it was.

"That's why you wanted him," she whispered. "Thought you could save yourself from him."

"I thought I could save us all," Zanze grunted. "I deserve to die for what I did. To you. To a lot of people. I made peace with that. But what you did to Kresh, to Vraki..." Zanze sneered. "Even they didn't deserve it."

He sighed. His eye craned away, stared off toward the burning horizon.

"There's nothing I can say that would make you stop, is there?"

Sal said nothing. A long wind sighed across the sky.

Zanze nodded to himself. "Yeah," he said. "That's what I thought." His eyes closed. He laid his head upon the ground. "See you around, Sal."

Sal nodded slowly.

"Yeah."

Steel flashed. Flesh parted. His body twitched. The earth grew dark beneath him.

"See you around."

She stepped back, watched the damp, dark earth spread beneath him as he stared out over the great, endless sky. Quietly, she reached into her scarf and pulled a piece of paper and charcoal from it. She unfolded it, found a name upon it, and made a single stroke.

~~Zanze the Beast.~~

She stared at the name for a long moment, at that black mark, through it like one more scar.

That long moment stretched into eternity, broken only by the sudden sear of heat at her hip.

Ah, right.

She had almost forgotten.

She tossed the sword aside, pulled the Cacophony out of his sheath, and cradled him in her hands as though he were a child of brass and cinders. She approached Zanze's cooling corpse and held the weapon over him.

She always hated this part.

A song rose. Not the Lady Merchant's dulcet tones, ringing out from somewhere distant and growing impossibly closer. This song was low and dark, torn from the belly of a beast long buried. It sang a single, droning verse that carved its way into her skull and sat there, groaning, laughing.

Burning.

Zanze's corpse twitched suddenly, a puppet of flesh and bone on tangled, invisible strings. Violet light bloomed in his eyes. Then his mouth. Then every pore of his pallid flesh. The light engulfed him, his power coalescing into a glorious brightness that hurt her eyes.

And then the Cacophony fed.

The song burned brighter in her head, a great inhale in preparation for the next verse. And the light came flooding out of Zanze's corpse, twitching and writhing and screaming in a discordant harmony as it tried to flee into the sky before it was drawn, inexorably, toward the gun.

The light disappeared down his barrel, past his grinning jaws, and into the brass. Its wailing song faded. And slowly, the burning verse fell silent as well. And Sal stared at the gun.

And the gun stared back at her.

Blinked a pair of brass eyes.

And grinned a little broader.

"Ah," the Cacophony whispered. "Much better." On a voice of burning cinders, he chuckled. "Shall we?"

Sal stared at him wordlessly for a moment before nodding. She replaced him in his sheath. She pulled her scarf up over her face and pocketed the list.

She turned around and walked down the ridge, back to her bird, back to the list, the next name, the next scar.

And in the sky behind her, the smoke continued to rise.

ACKNOWLEDGMENTS

There are few feelings as good as the easy smile and beating heart that comes from crossing into new territory with old friends.

And *Seven Blades in Black* is as new a territory as I've ever ventured into. Guns, machines, more magic and worldbuilding than I've ever done in one sitting—this was an all-new undertaking, and I was pleased to have my old friends with me.

I thank Danny Baror, my agent, for selling it. I thank Will Hinton, my editor, for setting it up. And I thank my family for being there for me with each shaky step I took onto this new ground.

But for as valued as old friends are, the new friends are their own experience, and special thanks is owed to my new editor, Bradley Englert, who ably, swiftly, and nobly took up the reins of this piece when Will had to move on.

And above all of them, this book is thanks to you, readers. Whether you've traveled with me before or are just signing on to the journey for the first time, I hope we go far together for many years to come.